PRAISE FOR M. L. BUCHMAN

Buchman has catapulted his way to the top tier of my favorite authors.

— FRESH FICTION

One of our favorite authors.

— RT BOOK REVIEWS

Buchman has catapulted his way to the top tier of my favorite authors.

— FRESH FICTION

A favorite author of mine. I'll read anything that carries his name, no questions asked. Meet your new favorite author!

— THE SASSY BOOKSTER, FLASH OF FIRE

M.L. Buchman is guaranteed to get me lost in a good story.

— THE READING CAFE, WAY OF THE WARRIOR: NSDQ

I love Buchman's writing. His vivid descriptions bring everything to life in an unforgettable way.

— PURE JONEL, HOT POINT

Nonstop action that will keep readers on the edge of their seats.

— *TAKE OVER AT MIDNIGHT*, LIBRARY JOURNAL

M L. Buchman's ability to keep the reader right in the middle of the action is amazing.

— LONG AND SHORT REVIEWS

The only thing you'll ask yourself is, "When does the next one come out?"

— *WAIT UNTIL MIDNIGHT*, RT REVIEWS, 4 STARS

The first...of (a) stellar, long-running (military) romantic suspense series.

— *THE NIGHT IS MINE*, BOOKLIST, "THE 20 BEST ROMANTIC SUSPENSE NOVELS: MODERN MASTERPIECES"

I knew the books would be good, but I didn't realize how good.

— NIGHT STALKERS SERIES, KIRKUS REVIEWS

Buchman mixes adrenalin-spiking battles and brusque military jargon with a sensitive approach.

— PUBLISHERS WEEKLY

13 times "Top Pick of the Month"

— NIGHT OWL REVIEWS

Tom Clancy fans open to a strong female lead will clamor for more.

— DRONE, PUBLISHERS WEEKLY

(Miranda Chase is) one of the most compelling, addicting, fascinating characters in any genre since the *Monk* television series.

— DRONE, ERNEST DEMPSEY, AUTHOR OF THE
SEAN WYATT THRILLERS

(*Drone* is) the best military thriller I've read in a very long time. Love the female characters.

— SHELDON MCARTHUR, FOUNDER OF THE
MYSTERY BOOKSTORE, LA

Superb!

— DRONE, BOOKLIST, STARRED REVIEW

A fabulous soaring thriller.

— *TAKE OVER AT MIDNIGHT,* MIDWEST BOOK
REVIEW

Meticulously researched, hard-hitting, and suspenseful.

— *PURE HEAT,* PUBLISHERS WEEKLY, STARRED
REVIEW

Expert technical details abound, as do realistic military missions with superb imagery that will have readers feeling as if they are right there in the midst and on the edges of their seats.

— *LIGHT UP THE NIGHT,* RT REVIEWS, 4 1/2 STARS

THE COMPLETE NIGHT STALKERS WHITE HOUSE: BOOKS 1-6

M. L. BUCHMAN

Buchman Bookworks, Inc.

Cover images:
Helicopter over Baghdad © U.S. Army
Declaration of Independence on White House building © izanbar
Discover more by this author at: www.mlbuchman.com

Buchman Bookworks

Other works by M. L. Buchman: *(* - also in audio)*

Thrillers

Dead Chef
One Chef!
Two Chef!

Miranda Chase
*Drone**
*Thunderbolt**
*Condor**
*Ghostrider**

Romantic Suspense

Delta Force
*Target Engaged**
*Heart Strike**
*Wild Justice**
*Midnight Trust**

Firehawks
Main Flight
Pure Heat
Full Blaze
*Hot Point**
*Flash of Fire**
Wild Fire
Smokejumpers
*Wildfire at Dawn**
*Wildfire at Larch Creek**
*Wildfire on the Skagit**

The Night Stalkers
Main Flight
The Night Is Mine
I Own the Dawn
Wait Until Dark
Take Over at Midnight
Light Up the Night
Bring On the Dusk
By Break of Day

and the Navy
Christmas at Steel Beach
Christmas at Peleliu Cove
White House Holiday
*Daniel's Christmas**
*Frank's Independence Day**
*Peter's Christmas**
*Zachary's Christmas**
*Roy's Independence Day**
*Damien's Christmas**
5E
Target of the Heart
Target Lock on Love
Target of Mine
Target of One's Own

Shadow Force: Psi
*At the Slightest Sound**
*At the Quietest Word**

White House Protection Force
*Off the Leash**
*On Your Mark**
*In the Weeds**

Contemporary Romance

Eagle Cove
Return to Eagle Cove
Recipe for Eagle Cove
Longing for Eagle Cove
Keepsake for Eagle Cove

Henderson's Ranch
*Nathan's Big Sky**
*Big Sky, Loyal Heart**
*Big Sky Dog Whisperer**

Love Abroad
Heart of the Cotswolds: England
Path of Love: Cinque Terre, Italy

Other works by M. L. Buchman:

Contemporary Romance (cont)

Where Dreams
Where Dreams are Born
Where Dreams Reside
Where Dreams Are of Christmas
Where Dreams Unfold
Where Dreams Are Written

Science Fiction / Fantasy

Deities Anonymous
Cookbook from Hell: Reheated
Saviors 101

Single Titles
The Nara Reaction
Monk's Maze
the Me and Elsie Chronicles

Non-Fiction

Strategies for Success
Managing Your Inner Artist/Writer
Estate Planning for Authors
Character Voice

Short Story Series by M. L. Buchman:

Romantic Suspense

Delta Force
Delta Force

Firehawks
The Firehawks Lookouts
The Firehawks Hotshots
The Firebirds

The Night Stalkers
The Night Stalkers
The Night Stalkers 5E
The Night Stalkers CSAR
The Night Stalkers Wedding Stories

US Coast Guard
US Coast Guard

White House Protection Force
White House Protection Force

Contemporary Romance

Eagle Cove
Eagle Cove

Henderson's Ranch
Henderson's Ranch

Where Dreams
Where Dreams

Thrillers

Dead Chef
Dead Chef

Science Fiction / Fantasy

Deities Anonymous
Deities Anonymous

Other
The Future Night Stalkers
Single Titles

Come to the White House for the holidays!

See the halls decked with holly.

Travel to foreign and dangerous climes.

Journey forth and find true love, under the Christmas tree or lit by the warm glow of fireworks. It's time to read all your favorite holiday books in a single set!

Daniel's Christmas

The White House Chief of Staff finally meets the woman of his dreams. The only drawback? She's a CIA analyst who insists he fly a life-or-death mission into hostile territory.

Frank's Independence Day

The head of the President's Protection Detail never expected to fall for a woman he'd tried to carjack years before. Now her life is in danger and only their shared past can save her.

Peter's Christmas

As President, Peter Matthews can't afford the dangers of falling love. Especially as "the right woman" might be leading him to his death.

Zachary's Christmas

Vice President Zachary Thomas' political career thrives. However, his

Christmas wish to find the right woman to share it with hits a few icy patches along the way.

Roy's Independence Day

Secret Service sniper Roy Beaumont must descend from his favorite perch atop the White House roof. But nothing prepared his heart when he must protect the new National Security Advisor.

Damien's Christmas

The new White House Chief of Staff Sienna Miller understands her job. Or thought she did. Until a national crisis threatens Christmas in D.C. and a man steals her heart.

DANIEL'S CHRISTMAS

TWO BRILLIANT MINDS
AN ADVENT CALENDAR
ONE IMPOSSIBLE ASSIGNMENT

Top CIA Analyst Dr. Alice Thompson *discovers a covert strategy to create diplomacy with the most reclusive nation on the planet. She needs help from someone in power.*

White House Chief of Staff Daniel Drake Darlington III *has survived flying with the Night Stalkers before. Now he must survive Alice—and a mission into North Korea.*

Alice's discovery launches him once again into dark and dangerous skies. Will Daniel survive to see all 24 days of his Advent Calendar?

INTRODUCTION TO DANIEL'S CHRISTMAS

This whole series started because of a misunderstanding—a misunderstanding on my part regarding Daniel Drake Darlington III.

To unravel what happened we have to travel back before the very first Night Stalkers novel, The Night Is Mine. *It was my first attempt at writing a romantic thriller—at the time I didn't even know that the proper term within the publishing industry was romantic suspense.*

When my editor-to-be called to purchase the book, she held the first five pages and a one-page synopsis.

"Tell me about this book," she'd called on page three and hadn't even reached the synopsis. I don't have to tell you the good things that still does for my ego.

So I told her.

"That's a thriller," she pointed out.

"I suppose so."

"I only buy romances." I'd been sending the query to both types of houses, unsure of exactly what I'd written.

"Okay."

There was a long silence after my remark, then we spent an hour-and-a-half discussing romance structure and why what I'd written wasn't a romance.

"Let me take a run at it." I ripped out forty thousand words, wrote fifty

thousand to replace them, and sent it back. I retained the original story, but now skewed to the romance.

After she read it, we had our second phone call.

"You got really close," and we discussed romance some more. "The only thing you're still missing is that the reader must know very early on that the hero and heroine are fated. They're the only ones meant for each other."

That was a problem. I had a conflicted heroine. Emily Beale's heart was being torn in multiple directions throughout my manuscript and it was only at the very end of the book that she resolves who she loves.

Well, okay, that's still true of the book even in its final form. For her. The problem was that it can't be unclear for the reader.

And the real problem was that I had given her viable and valid options during the course of the book. The one she was most tempted by in the middle of the book wasn't her soulmate, pisses-her-off-all-the-time Major Mark Henderson. It was Daniel Drake Darlington III, the First Lady's chief assistant.

So, for that final draft, I cut ten thousand words of Daniel and added another ten thousand words tying her more tightly to Mark Henderson.

The book had a very successful launch, eventually being named "Top 10 Romance of the Year" by Booklist—a very prestigious review journal by the American Library Association.

However, there on the cutting floor lay poor Daniel's shot at true love.

In the sequel, I Own the Dawn (which went on to be named NPR "Top 5 Romance of the Year"), Daniel was promoted to the White House Chief of Staff, but he found that to be small consolation.

So I spent some time trying to figure out how to make it up to Daniel. Besides, I really liked the guy. But he wasn't a Night Stalker, he didn't belong in my main series. That was all about the warriors who fly beyond the safety of the front lines.

A new factor entered at this point. My wife has always been a huge fan of Christmas. She has a way of making it real and magical. Even the years we were dead broke, she found ways to make it a happy occasion.

"I've always wanted you to write a Christmas story."

So, there I was feeling loyal to Daniel on one hand, and on the other I had a request for a Christmas story.

One more element was needed and I didn't have to search far to find it.

My wife's birthday is very close to Christmas. So when she was little, she thought that Advent calendars—with their little windows for counting down the twenty-four days of December until Christmas—were actually a countdown to her birthday.

Daniel, Christmas at the White House, and an Advent calendar.

Literally, that's all I had when I started writing.

Alice Thompson created herself in the moment she walked into the Daniel's office shortly after midnight on December 1st, the moment when Daniel is about to open the first window of the calendar.

Emily Beale in The Night Is Mine *is powerful for her integrity.*

Kee Smith in I Own the Dawn *is powerful in her attitude.*

To be a proper match for Daniel, I wanted Alice Thompson to be powerful in her intellect.

I didn't give her the knock-out beauty that I had given my previous two warrior women. She was more cute than stunning physically. The other thing she had was a sense of humor. Neither Emily nor Kee were noted for their wit. Their dedication, yes. Their skills, absolutely. But these were two very serious women.

Alice? Not so much. Her first words to Daniel are teasing him about violation of the strict rules regarding Advent calendars.

Wanting to add depth to the story, I started thinking about two of my favorite television shows: The West Wing *and* Star Trek: The Next Generation. *In* The West Wing *the White House Chief of Staff never gets to have an adventure—even less than the President himself. Yet in* Next Gen *it is the second-in-command Riker who gets most of the adventures.*

So, as the President's right hand man, I wanted to send Daniel on an adventure with the Night Stalkers.

I wrote this story at an interesting moment in recent political history. After seventeen years under the harsh, dictatorial thumb of Kim Jong-il, North Korea had a new leader. Kim Jong-un was young, Western educated, and a huge fan of basketball and foreign luxury goods. There was hope that he would be a voice strong in reform and improved foreign relations.

I conjectured how that might begin and that became the core adventure of this book. Regrettably, those hopes were crushed only a few months after the release of Daniel's Christmas with Kim Jong-un's declaration of martial law throughout his country and his order for nuclear testing to proceed. But that is the real world and thankfully my characters live in a fictional one.

Before I close, there are two things to point out about this particular story.

The first is the technology. I always make my best effort to be accurate about technology and the role it plays in our military. I described the various helicopters' capabilities as accurately as I could, without fabrication. North Korea's defense system is also as accurate as I could make it.

However, I needed to transport the North Koreans a long distance very quickly and very secretly. To the best of my knowledge, no small business jet has ever landed on an aircraft carrier. However, the Gulfstream jet I chose—if it was structurally enhanced to make the landing—could land on one of America's super carriers. So this one fact is plausible, if unlikely.

The second is the estate on the Canadian island.

I spent a summer in my twenties sailing about the American San Juan and Canadian Gulf islands in the Pacific Northwest. On one sunny summer afternoon, I sailed past the tall island with its single beautiful house that is central to the book's climax. The exterior is exactly as I describe it. I have never visited there, so the interior is conjecture, but I'd love to someday. Looking fantastically romantic, it always struck me as the perfect place to celebrate a cozy Christmas. It just took me twenty years for this image to find the right story.

CHAPTER ONE

D_aniel Drake Darlington III_ pushed back further into the armchair and hung on for dear life. Without warning the seat did its best to eject him forcibly onto the floor. Only the heavy seatbelt, that was threatening to cut him in half he'd pulled it so tight, kept him in place.

"You never were the best flier."

Daniel glared at President Peter Matthews as Marine One jolted sharply left. They occupied the two facing armchairs in the narrow cargo bay of the VH-1N White Hawk helicopter. The small, three-person couch along the side was empty. The two Marine Corps crew chiefs and the two pilots sat in their seats at the front of the craft.

"I'm fine," Daniel managed through gritted teeth. "I just don't like helicopters."

President Peter Matthews sat back casually. Apparently all the turbulence that the early winter storm could hand out had not interfered with his boss' enjoyment of Daniel's discomfiture.

"And why would that be?"

The President knew damn well why his Chief of Staff hated these god-forsaken machines. Even if Marine One was probably the single safest and best maintained helicopter on the planet, he hated it from the depths of his soul along with all of its brethren of the rotorcraft category.

"My very first flight. I suffered—" a jaw rattling shake, "a bad concussion. Then we crashed."

"Yes," the President stared contemplatively at the ceiling less than foot over their heads.

Daniel kept his head ducked down so that he didn't bang it there as they flew through the next pocket of winter turbulence.

"That was one of Emily's finer flights."

And it had been. If the helicopter had been flown by anyone of lesser skill than Major Emily Beale of the Special Operations Aviation Regiment, Daniel knew he'd have been dead rather than merely bruised and battered. Thankfully the Army trained the pilots of the 160th SOAR exceptionally well, even better than the four Marines flying the President's personal craft. And Major Beale was the best among them, except for perhaps her husband.

The tape of that flight and the much more fateful flight a bare two weeks later had become mandatory training in the Army's Special Operations Forces helicopter regiment. To this day he knew his life would have ended if he'd been aboard for that second fiery crash. The crash that had taken the First Lady's life a year ago.

But that didn't make him like this machine one whit better.

"There's home." President Matthews nodded out the window just like any tourist. Any tourist who was allowed to fly over the intensely restricted airspace surrounding the White House.

Daniel managed to look toward the window as the helicopter banked sharply to the left. Please, just let them land safely and get out of this storm. The White House did look terribly cheery. November 30th, she wasn't sporting her Christmas décor yet, but she was a majestic building, brilliantly lit, perched in the middle of the most heavily guarded park on the planet. Another jolt and he squeezed his eyes shut.

He did manage to force his eyes open as they settled flawlessly onto the lawn with barely the slightest rocking on the shock absorbers.

In moments the door slid open and a pair of Marines stood at sharp attention in their dress uniforms as if the last day of November were a sunny summer day, and not blowing freezing rain at eleven o'clock at night.

Daniel stumbled out and managed to resist the urge to kneel and kiss the ground. For one thing, it would stain the knees of his suit. For another, the President would laugh at him. Okay, he'd laugh even more than he already was.

Both feet on the ground, Daniel found himself. Managed to pull on his Chief-of-Staff cloak so to speak. He grabbed his briefcase and kept his place beside the President as they headed toward the South Entrance. They each carried umbrellas of only marginal usefulness that the Marines had thoughtfully provided. Now that they were on the ground, Daniel didn't mind the cold rain in his face. It meant he was alive.

"I'd suggest turning in right away, sir. We have an early start tomorrow."

The President clapped him on the shoulder, "Yes, Mom."

"Your mother is over in Georgetown."

"Well, I'm not going to call you 'dear' so don't get your hopes up there."

Daniel had come to really like the President. Even at the end of a brutally long day, including a flight to Kansas City, then Chicago, and back, he remained upbeat with that indefatigable energy of his. He was easy to like. There'd now be no oil workers' strike in Kansas City and his Chicago dinner speech had benefited the new governor immensely.

"You go to bed too, Daniel."

"Just going to drop off this paperwork," he held up his briefcase.

The President headed for the Grand Staircase and Daniel turned down the white marble hall and headed over to the West Wing.

Somewhere behind them in the dark, the helicopter roared back to life and lifted into the night.

CHAPTER TWO

T_he phone hammered him_ awake. Daniel came to in his office chair with the phone already to his ear.

Someone was speaking rapidly. He caught perhaps one word in three. "CIA. Immediate briefing. North Korea."

He must have made some intelligible reply as moments later he was listening to a dial tone.

Daniel rubbed at his eyes, but the vista didn't change. Large cherry wood desk. Mounds of work in neatly stacked folders that he'd sat down to tackle after the long flight. His briefcase still unopened on the floor beside him. Definitely the Chief of Staff's office. His office. Nightmare or reality? Both. Definitely.

Phone. He'd been on the phone.

The words came back and, now fully awake, Daniel started swearing even as he grabbed the handset and began dialing.

Maybe he could blame all this on Emily Beale. In the three short weeks she'd been at the White House, Daniel had risen from being the First Lady's secretary to the White House Chief of Staff and it was partly Emily's fault. As if his life had been battered by a tornado. Still felt that way a year later.

Okay, call it mostly her fault.

As he listened to the phone ringing in his ear, it felt better to have someone to blame. He rubbed at his eyes. A year later and he still didn't know whether to curse Major Beale or thank her.

Maybe he could make it all her fault.

"Yagumph."

"Good morning, Mr. President."

"Is it morning?" The deep voice would have been incomprehensibly groggy without the familiarity of long practice.

Daniel checked his watch, barely morning. "Yes, sir!" he offered his most chipper voice.

"Crap! What? All of 12:03?"

"12:10, sir." They'd been on the ground just over an hour.

"Double crap!" The President was slowly gaining in clarity, maybe one in ten linguists would be able to understand him now.

"Seven more minutes of sleep than you guessed, sir."

"Daniel?"

"Yes, Mr. President?"

"Next time Major Beale comes to town, I'm sending you up on one of her training rides."

"Sounds like fun, sir." If he had a death wish. "Crashing in the Lincoln Memorial Reflecting Pool is definitely an experience I can't wait to relive." The Major was also the childhood friend of the President, so he had to walk with a little care, but not much. The two of them were that close.

"Time to get up, sir, the CIA is coming calling. They'll be here in twenty minutes."

"I'll be there in ten." A low groan sounded over the phone. "Make that fifteen." The handset rattled loudly as he missed the cradle. Daniel got the phone clear of his ear before the President's handset dropped on the floor.

Daniel hung up and considered sleeping for the another fifteen minutes. There was a nice sofa along the far wall sitting in a close group with a couple of armchairs, but he'd have to stand up to reach it. All in strong, dusky red leather, his secretary's doing after discovering Daniel had no taste. Janet had also ordered in a beautiful oriental rug and several large framed photographs. Even on the first day she'd known him well enough to choose images of wide-open spaces. He missed his family farm, but the photos helped him when D.C. was squeezing in too hard.

If he didn't stand and resisted the urge to seek more sleep, all that remained was to consider his desk. Its elegant cherry wood surface lost beneath a sea of reports and files.

Fifteen minutes. He could read the briefing paper on Chinese coal, review tomorrow's agenda which, if he were lucky, might stay on schedule for at least the first quarter hour of a planned fourteen-hour day. Or he could just order up a giant burn bag and be done with the whole mess.

He picked up whatever was on top of the nearest stack.

An Advent calendar.

Janet, had to be.

Well, the woman had taste. It was beautiful; encased in a soft, tooled-leather portfolio and tied closed with a narrow red ribbon done up in a neat bow. He pulled a loose end and opened the calendar. Inside were three spreads of stunning hand-painted pictures on deep-set pages. He took a moment to admire the first one.

It was a depiction of Santa and his reindeer. Except Santa might have been a particularly pudgy hamster and the reindeer might have been mice with improbable antlers. One might have had a red nose, or he might have had his eggnog spiked; the artist had left that open to interpretation. A couple of rabbits were helping to load the sleigh. Little numbered doors were set in the side of the sleigh, as well as in a nearby tree, and in the snow at the micedeer's paws. The page was thick enough that a small treat could be hidden behind each little door.

He shook the calendar lightly and heard things rattling. Probably little sweets and tidbits to hit his notorious sweet tooth.

The day Janet retired he'd be in so much trouble. Not only did she manage to keep his life organized, she also managed to make him smile, even when things were coming apart at the seams. Midnight calls from the CIA for immediate meetings didn't bode well, yet here he was dangerously close to enjoying the moment.

He started to open the little door with a tiny golden number "1" on the green ribbon pull tab. The door depicted a candy-cane colored present perched high on the sleigh.

"Don't do that."

He looked up.

A woman stood in the doorway, closely escorted by one of the service Marines. A short wave of russet hair curled partly over her face and trickled down just far enough to emphasize the line of her neck. Her bangs ruffled in a gentle wave covering one eye. The eye in the clear shone a striking hazel against pale skin. She wore a thick, woolen cardigan, a bit darker than her hair, open at the front over an electric blue turtleneck that appeared to say, "Joy to the World." At least based on the letters he could see.

"Don't do what?"

"Don't open it early," she nodded toward the calendar in his hands. "That's cheating."

He double-checked his watch. "It's twelve-eighteen on December first. That's not cheating."

"Not until nighttime, after sunset. That's what Mama always said."

"And your Mama is always right?"

"Damn straight." Though her expression momentarily belied her cheerful insistence.

He glanced at the Marine. "Kenneth. Does she have a purpose here?"

She sauntered into his office as if it were her own living room and an armed Marine was not following two paces behind her. More guts than most, or a complete unawareness of how close she was to being wrestled to the ground by a member of the U.S. Military.

"Remember what they say about the book and the cover?"

"Sure, don't judge." He inspected her wrinkled black corduroys and did his best not to appreciate the nice line they made of her legs.

She dropped into one of the leather chairs in front of his desk and propped a pair of alarmingly green sneakers with red laces on the cherry wood. At least they were clean. All she'd need to complete the image would be to pop a bright pink gum bubble at him. And maybe some of those foam slip-on reindeer antlers. He offered her a smile as she slouched lower in the chair. In turn, she offered him a clear view most of the way to her tonsils with a massive yawn.

She managed to cover it before it was completely done.

"Sorry, I've been up for three days researching this. Director Smith said I should bring it right over." She waved a slim portfolio at him that he hadn't previously noticed.

CIA Director Smith. Well, that explained who she was. Whatever lay in that portfolio was the reason he'd only had forty-five minutes of sleep so far tonight. And he'd spent that slumped in his chair. He did his best to surreptitiously straighten his jacket and tie.

"You've been researching." Maybe a prompt would get her to the point more quickly.

"Yes, Mr. Darlington. I'm Dr. Alice Thompson, with dual masters in Afghani and Mathematics at Columbia. Which makes me a dueling master. PhD in digital imaging at NYU and an analyst for the CIA. Which means something, but I have no idea what. The reason you're awake right now is to meet with me."

"No, the reason I'm awake right now is to meet with both you and the President."

"The President?" She jerked upright in her chair, her feet dropping to the floor. "No one said anything about that to me." She twisted right and left as if seeking a place to hide.

"And it's Dr. Darlington of Tennessee. Degrees in agriculture at University of Kentucky—"

"Go Wildcats," she mumbled automatically without losing her somewhat frantic expression.

Daniel wondered how a New York girl living in D.C. would know that, but didn't sidetrack to ask.

"Poli Sci at Yale, and socio-economics at Princeton where I had the great opportunity to study cooperative economic game theory with Dr. Nash." And why he felt the need to brag to this lady once again settling in his office chair like she was hanging out in a college dorm room remained a bit of a mystery. He didn't feel sleepy anymore watching her across the mess that he called a desk. Instead he found himself truly smiling.

"You didn't really wake the President for this meeting, did you?"

Her voice was little more than a whisper as she struggled to fight her body upright in the chair. She leaned forward far enough for the cardigan to fall open and reveal that the front of her turtleneck actually read "Oy to the World."

Daniel offered her his blandest smile and would have admired how snugly the material clung to her frame, but he couldn't look away from those hazel-green eyes.

"You did wake him?" her whisper more than a little panicked.

"I wish he hadn't." The President entered as she spoke. "Does this mean I can I go back to bed?"

———

Alice spun around to face the man who had come up beside her unnoticed. Tall, even more handsome than on TV. Stained sweat pants and a faded sweatshirt from Oxford didn't detract from the image in the least.

The President held out a hand. She offered her own in some ingrained social response mechanism, like a trained puppy, only to find her paw shaken and released before she had a chance to do more than allow her arm to be moved up and down.

He settled into the chair beside her before she belatedly remembered you were supposed to stand when the President arrived. He propped his sneakered feet on the edge of Dr. Darlington's beautiful cherry wood desk right where hers had been. What had she been thinking when she'd done that? Had she hoped to fluster the man and his immaculate three-piece suit behind the desk? Or had she felt so comfortable around him she hadn't cared? Must have been the first but it felt like the second.

Daniel leaned forward, "Don't worry. The complete intimidation wears off eventually. He's not all that important really; it only feels as if he is."

"Hey, I'm the one who they elected President. And I'm not a 'he.' I'm a POTUS to you."

"Right, and I'm just the guy who makes sure that the all-important

President of the United States doesn't screw up at 12:30 in the morning."

"True, true." The President nodded sagely and the guys traded smiles. The mutual respect and friendship was clear between them.

They made an interesting contrast. The President had all of the magnetism she'd seen on TV, and more again in person. Even sleepy-eyed and wearing sweats, dark hair ranging loose down to his collar, he looked as if he should be framed up on a wall. Most popular President in recent history, probably all the way back to JFK. The world's ulti-mate bachelor since his wife's tragic death in the helicopter crash.

Whereas Dr. Darlington was perhaps the most beautiful man she'd ever seen. Yale and Princeton; *Bulldogs and Lions. Along with the Wildcats* that made two cats and a dog, that part of her mind that collected useless garbage offered up. The White House Chief of Staff looked like a classic surfer bum with those sparkling blue eyes and gold-blond hair, despite the short cut of it and his sharp three-piece suit that he filled really, really nicely.

She'd always been a nerd, only comfortable with other analyst nerds, but even her few moments with Daniel had been easy.

Before she could stop herself, she caught herself glancing over at his hands.

No ring.

Some insane part of her brain said, "Goody."

If she could slap it, she would.

Way too classically Alice. "Oh look, an intriguing rabbit hole, I think I'll fall down it." Of course, she usually fell for useless pretty boys. She'd bet that phrase had never been used to describe the White House Chief of Staff. Beautiful and, by reputation at least, brilliant as well. He was so far out of her league that it almost hurt. Still, she did wish she'd worn something nicer than her Christmas turtleneck and the old cardigan she'd knit a couple years back. It was her comfort sweater, made in a dozen shades of autumn forest browns and dusky reds.

"So, Dr. Alice Thompson, what did you bring us?" The Chief of Staff was back, all smooth and businesslike. He glanced up and over her head. "We're good here, Kenneth. Thanks."

She tipped her head back on the chair far enough to see the upper part of the upside-down Marine, her shadow who she'd completely forgotten about, looming close behind her. He offered a precise nod, did a neat snap turn, and walked out of her range of view with the back of his perfect white hat being the last thing to disappear.

Her head spun a little as she brought it back upright. She really needed some sleep.

Then she remembered what she held in the thin portfolio. It had kept her awake for three days, it would keep her going a bit longer.

That and the fact that, no matter how casual and collected he'd sounded, Dr. Daniel Drake Darlington III's hands still hadn't moved from the pull tab on the Advent calendar.

———

Daniel couldn't help noticing the quirk of a smile across Dr. Thompson's lips. With the unruly mop of hair, it was hard to tell, but she appeared to be staring at his hands.

He looked down.

The Advent calendar still lay in his lap. His hand half an inch from grabbing the little number "1" ribbon. Still.

Her smile bloomed, but she'd shaken down a few more of those soft-flowing curls and her eyes were almost invisible, except as a bright glint. Damn, it was about the cutest thing he'd ever seen.

He slapped the calendar closed and dropped it atop the nearest stack of papers. It over-balanced the stack, which slid to the right. In his sleep deprived state, he was nowhere near fast enough to stop the falling dominos as Chinese manufacturing cascaded into Arctic ecology and on into the Baja oil spill. Daniel rescued the calendar, but the oil spill took out the most recent fisheries and timbers trade reports. The budget was almost big enough to stop the whole thing, would have been if it weren't sitting on top of the east Africa political report he'd been trying to review for the last three days.

The budget slammed to the floor with a crash loud enough that they all jumped a bit. A minor blizzard of paper followed it to the oriental carpet.

Kenneth stuck his head back in the door, but the President waved him off. All Daniel could do was watch the out-of-control disaster as file folders spilled open one after another to release a fresh splash of white and blue sheets of paper. Spreading like some cubist piece of floor performance art.

The President glanced at the pile of reports fluttering to a landing beside his chair.

"Janet is gonna be so pissed at you," his boss practically crowed at him.

"Janet?"

Daniel heard Alice's voice, tentative for a moment.

"His secretary. She's lethal about Daniel's methods of organization."

Alice stretched up to peer at the disaster beyond the President's chair.

Then she aimed that impossibly cute smile at Daniel. This time those twin, hazel-colored laser beams were exposed with an easy head shake that flopped her hair back.

"How soon does she get in? Can we watch? Where do we get popcorn?"

CHAPTER THREE

Daniel **read through the** CIA intelligence report for the third
time.

"If this is right, we'll need a very unique asset."

POTUS looked over at him, "I know just who to call. Even if it's
not a 'go' yet, we can start moving the asset into position."

Daniel nodded. "We can do it from the Game Room." He started
around his desk, but had to double-back around the other side to avoid
the paper disaster. His watch claimed barely one a.m.; there'd be plenty
of time to fix it before Janet arrived and sentenced him to death by
paper cuts.

He arrived by Alice's chair as she offered another jaw-cracking
yawn.

"Sorry. I— Sorry."

She'd slipped even lower in the chair, far enough that the only thing
keeping her from flowing down onto the floor were her knees bumping
into the front panel of his desk.

He offered a hand to help her to her feet.

She did her one-eyed inspection of him for a moment, then
accepted the offer. Her hand was deceptively strong for how fine-

fingered and delicate it appeared. She rose to her feet in a smooth, fluid motion that bespoke some form of training. He'd seen it before somewhere.

"Ballet?" He knew it was wrong even as he said it.

"Sad."

"Why are you calling me sad?" Daniel knew he was missing something.

She laughed, a bright, merry sound that he could only describe as elfin, though she wasn't but a few inches shy of his own five-eleven.

"S. A. D."

"You're S.A.D.?" he barely managed to choke out.

Even the President looked shocked by that one.

The Special Activities Division was the CIA's black ops squadron. They were better trained than even the Army Rangers and were deployed in far more questionable situations.

She grinned wickedly, "Now you're the one saying I'm sad? I'm half tempted to say, 'yes,' just to see you twitch. But no. They offered us senior analysts a month of S.A.D. training to better appreciate what could and couldn't be done in the field. Found I liked the physical part, though I'd never be crazy enough to go for field ops. There's an ongoing course at the gym. I don't do the weapons or field skills, but there's dance, yoga, strength training. I keep that up."

Daniel tried to get to the gym a little each day and do some weight training. He had the sudden feeling that, despite being a slip of a woman, she could probably beat the stuffing out of him. And senior analyst? If she was much past twenty-six or seven, he'd be shocked. Senior analysts usually sported decades of experience.

She freed her hand, which he didn't realize he'd still been holding until its soft, strong warmth had been removed. She turned to follow the President who waited by the door. Alice Thompson passed close enough for Daniel to smell the woman, past her soap or shampoo; a heady scent of springtime in winter washed over him. She left him wobbly on his feet, as if he were the one who hadn't slept in three days.

She and the President both stood at the door watching him.

"You coming?" Peter Matthews offered him a knowing smile over Dr. Thompson's shoulder.

And Dr. Alice Thompson merely offered that crazy, elfin laugh.

All Daniel knew was that he couldn't wait for next opportunity to get that close to her again.

CHAPTER FOUR

"**Y**ou said we were going to the Game Room. This is—" Alice nearly choked on her words as she watched Daniel press a palm against a glass plate reader. She'd been tired enough to not think much as they descended from the main level down a long flight of stairs.

She didn't need the two Marine Guards at perfect attention to indicate what lay behind these heavy doors. She'd seen enough movies to know they stood at the entry to the Situation Room. A place that in many ways served as the political center of the planet. Decisions made here affected global politics, started and ended wars.

"Game Room. Definitely." Mr. Smooth-Chief-of-Staff Daniel Darlington was back in place. "Most administrations call it the Woodshed, but President Matthews is Washington D.C. born and bred. Didn't seem appropriate."

Alice still couldn't believe that she'd flustered the White House Chief of Staff. She. Alice. It was pretty flattering. Well, maybe it was lack of sleep that warped her perceptions, though she felt alarmingly awake at the moment, even if her body didn't.

"There are refreshments," the President spoke in such a friendly, normal fashion that it was proving difficult to remain gobsmacked by being in the President's presence. "An amazing video system attended by the finest Marine Corps technicians. Global politics is more like chess than say, Chutes and Ladders, but there are pieces always in motion and we try to keep track of them in here. So, the Game Room fits."

The Marines pulled back the double doors and Alice felt herself sucked inward as if by a vacuum.

Without preamble, President Matthews called out to what appeared to be an empty room, "I need to speak with Majors Beale and Henderson. They're probably still at that little SOAR base in Pakistan."

A disembodied voice spoke in soft, clearly articulated tones, "A few minutes, Mr. President."

"Pakistan?" she whispered to Daniel. With relations the way they were in Pakistan, it was hard to imagine that there was a U.S. airbase still there. Though with SOAR. Maybe. The Army's Special Operations Aviation Regiment often showed up in the damnedest places on her reports. The Night Stalkers, as they called themselves, were even called on by the CIA's S.A.D. because no one could deliver a crew by helicopter the way SOAR could. Or get them back out as consistently. Though CIA pilots would never agree, Alice had seen the reports and it was true.

"Pakistan," the President confirmed. "A special deal. Bati airbase is a small desert location that gives our folks close access to the Hindu Kush passes between Pakistan and Afghanistan. Their primary mission there is to curtail the massive arms flow that Pakistan is sponsoring. However, in exchange for the airbase and certain other considerations, the Pakistan government also receives, shall we say, stabilization assistance along their contested border with India."

That was just about the craziest arrangement she'd ever heard. But it also explained the oddities of the mission to take down Osama bin Laden. SOAR helicopters had penetrated deep into Pakistan as if coming out of nowhere, no reports ever emerged of where the flight had begun. One leak said northern Afghanistan, but that made even less sense. But perhaps from the secret, Pakistan-sanctioned airbase at the foot of the Hindu Kush mountains. That would explain the infiltration issues she'd been unable to puzzle out.

After they'd raided bin Laden's compound, they fled the country while being chased across the border by Pakistani jets. They must have been very slow jets to allow the helicopters fly from so far in-country, get clear of Pakistan airspace, and fly out over international waters. Or they had a secret pact with the government. Therefore, the Pakistani jets had chased the American helicopters for form's sake, but not been allowed to interfere because of special on-going military agreements. That made the whole bin-Laden operational logistics make sense, finally.

Alice appreciated that. There was a back-burner portion of her thought processes that worried and chipped away at unexplained problems. That one had been there for a year or more, and now she could tell by the sudden mental silence that enough of the pieces were in place and she could let it go.

It also illustrated different aspects of the notorious southwest Asian schizophrenia. It was the reason her job never grew dull. It was like they thought with both sides of their brain, separately. Iran, a paranoid, extreme Islamic nation that cast aside all things Western, was now one of the few space powers on the planet. Afghanistan, desperate to shed the mantel of the Taliban, reviled the U.S. presence to suppress the brutally violent fanatics. The dichotomy of thought and action remained endlessly fascinating.

Daniel offered her some coffee and a doughnut. But her nervous system was so scrambled with exhaustion that she settled for hot chocolate and a croissant to avoid the bizarre effects caffeine would perpetrate.

As they sat at the table, the giant screen at the end of the room lit up. A beautiful blond glared balefully out at them.

"What the hell do you want at this hour, Sneaker Boy?"

Sneaker Boy? Alice looked around to see who she was addressing. The President was smiling at the screen.

"Morning, Squirt. What are you so surly about?" There was a tease in his voice.

Daniel leaned over to whisper in her ear, "Childhood friends."

Alice turned to glance at him which brought them nearly nose-to-nose. Just the slightest bit of lean and they'd be kissing. She looked away quickly and took a large bite of her croissant to cover just how stupid her brain could be when she was tired. Her cat would be laughing at her for being such a goofball. If she had a cat.

The woman on the screen covered her face with both her hands as if impossibly weary. "Peter, you idiot!"

Alice choked, coughed, and spewed a small cloud of flaky croissant crust all over the polished Sit Room conference table.

"What time is it?" clearly meant as a rhetorical question. Rhetorical with an acid bite.

"One a.m. our time," the President responded pleasantly. "Makes it midday for you."

The woman uncovered one eye and just scowled at the President.

"Oh, right." He didn't sound very chagrined.

Alice finally got it, too. The Night Stalkers were called that for a reason. They lived in a flipped clock world, flying missions at night, sleeping during the day. The President had just rousted them after two or maybe three hours of sleep. And by the look of it, last night had included an exhausting mission.

She idly wondered if a report of it might be crossing her desk at the CIA even now. No, she'd left the southwest Asia desk six months ago. For half a year she'd been specializing in the craziest, most isolationist country on the planet.

And when she'd pulled her latest report on North Korea together, the Director had sent her scampering to the White House to report.

The Night Stalkers. The President had asked for Majors Beale and Henderson. That meant this was Major Emily Beale. Alice inspected the sleepy woman more closely. She'd shown up in enough of Alice's reports over the years for her to know about the legend the woman had become. She out flew everyone, with the possible exception of her even more famous husband. Well, famous to the very small world of those who knew about black ops helicopter pilots.

All Alice saw was a sleepy looking woman in a sand-colored t-shirt.

"At least I didn't wake Mark."

A square chin in need of a shave appeared over Beale's shoulder, "I wish, Mr. President."

A hand reached out and filled the screen for a moment as it

realigned the camera a bit higher. The two most successful pilots in SOAR history now looked out at them. Their most captivating features were Henderson's gray eyes and Beale's brilliant blues, almost as bright as Daniel's. Even rumpled, tired, and grumpy, they made a beautiful couple.

Alice had always wondered how she'd look as part of a couple. Her sporadic relationships typically burned out long before her imagination had time to really take hold. And any efforts to make a portrait-type image, even in her head, had never gelled. Even in her naïve teenage years she hadn't been able to imagine herself a couple with her massive crush, Leonardo di Caprio. And by the time *Firefly's* Nathan Fillion came along, she'd lost the dreamy-eyed teenager completely.

She glanced again at the profile of the man seated beside her in his three-piece suit in the depths of a Washington D.C. night. Daniel was concentrating on the screen at the moment, revealing only his profile.

Him she could picture easily.

CHAPTER FIVE

*A**lice was positively weaving** by the time they left the Situation Room and passed by the Marine guards.

Daniel offered his arm.

She slipped her hand through the crook of his elbow, as if they were a couple promenading through a formal garden rather than striding along the West Wing basement hallway. Alice took a deep breath, trying not to acknowledge how much she enjoyed the feeling.

"Set her up in one of the spare rooms." The President nodded to her.

Stay in the White House? She stumbled on the carpeted steps, would have tumbled to the ground if not for Daniel's support. Yet another proof to her mother that she lacked any of the grace that ten years of childhood ballet should have taught her.

"I'll get her settled and be right back down, Mr. President."

Not that she'd stay awake long enough to get back to her apartment. Once she'd handed off the information that had kept her awake for three days, she felt limp.

"No, we're done. We needed to get Emily in motion. Next steps tomorrow. I'm just going to swing through the office for a minute and then go back to bed."

At the head of the stairs, Daniel turned her to the right, resting his left hand over her own where it curled about his right forearm. The sudden warmth felt both startling and comforting as her fingers were freezing cold by contrast. She'd pushed through enough M-LOS projects, as she called the ones causing massive lack of sleep, to know her body would go through chills and dizziness until she had at least a half dozen hours under her belt.

The chill only deepened as they walked the West Colonnade, passing the Marines standing stock still in heavy winter coats, rifles at the ready.

"They do that all winter?"

"I know. Pretty wild, hunh?" He pretended a shiver that she could feel through his arm, even as one of the Marines opened the door for them to enter the Residence.

In moments they were inside the Palm Room, Daniel acting the genial tour guide. His words blurred beneath the grandeur of everything. The room, little more than a pass-through with a bench, a marble table, and some potted palms, was alive with lacy woodwork and watched over by clearly historic paintings of Lady Liberty. The double doors beyond led to a wide, red-carpeted hallway, marble archways, chandeliers.

"Where's the Christmas decorations?" she'd never actually been to the White House before and was sad that she'd be missing them.

"Not here yet."

She bit back her disappointment. Of course, for an analyst to sit in the Situation Room and watch the first piece in the next game move across the board, that was a pretty good treat as well.

"Now you've done it, Alice."

"What was that?" Daniel turned to face her.

"Fallen down the rabbit hole."

Daniel's laugh was easy, comfortable, and helped bring the whole place back into a little perspective.

"I thought Alice had long blond curls on her trip to Wonderland." He led her into a mahogany-lined elevator.

"Mama hoped, but I ended up with this." Or maybe it was walnut.

Daniel was quiet long enough for her to look up at him as they rode smoothly upward to the number three he had punched.

He was looking down at her. She'd need serious heels to be eye-to-eye with him. She'd never been good at heels.

"No, blond isn't you. Russet suits you perfectly."

"Always thought of it more as mouse-brown."

"No. Russet. A beautiful russet red."

She glanced back up at him as he led her out of the elevator to see if he was making fun of her. He studied the top of her head with a look of intense concentration. As if he were ascertaining an initial assessment of a situation rather than the bit of a flirt she'd expected. He was the perfect straight man.

"Like a russet potato?" she was never able to resist prodding a straight man.

"No. I meant the color of roses at sunset." She tried to catch her breath, but hadn't succeeded by the time he led her to a spacious bedroom. Even if she'd wanted to continue the conversation, all her body saw was somewhere to stretch out.

"Kitchen over that way if you get hungry."

Hungry? The word didn't anchor to anything in particular. It was still consumed by bed and sleep.

"President lives on the Second Floor, so don't be concerned about disturbing him."

Some saving grace there.

"I'm the First Chief of Staff to live here in decades. It was a little strange at first, but I'm getting used to it."

"Hungry." Her lagging brain finally found a use for the word. Hungry for a beautiful man who said her hair was the color of roses at sunset.

"I'm just across the hall if you need anything."

Needed anything.

She went up on her tiptoes, rested a hand on that nice, broad chest of his to steady herself, and kissed him.

He didn't respond at first. She could feel the shock and surprise warring in him. All the propriety you'd expect from a gentleman.

Too much, Alice. Too forward. But the warmth of his lips, the strength of his muscles beneath her palm held her in place a moment longer.

A moment just long enough for Daniel to return the kiss.

A gentle, tentative gesture that in moments heated to melting. Specifically, her melting against him as his hands wrapped around and supported her. As his mouth explored hers.

Alice heard a small moan. She'd never in her twenty-seven years moaned when she kissed a man. But the sound was too high to come from Daniel, so it must have been hers.

She wallowed in being cradled in his arms, in being held as if she was someone desirable, even precious.

The change came suddenly. A freeze. A breath of space. A whispered, "sorry."

"I'm not." She opened her eyes, she didn't recall closing them, and looked up at the summer-sky blue ones inspecting her.

Okay, this was awfully forward for her. She'd be more likely to go a half-dozen dates and barely hold hands, than to kiss a stranger.

But she wasn't sorry. Especially not with a man who could kiss like that.

"You're an amazing kisser."

Daniel blinked at her. Sliding his hands down her arms until he held her hands. His were big, warm hands. Strong. Not what you'd expect from a paper-pusher.

"I'd best say goodnight."

"Sure you don't want to tuck me in?" She slapped her hand over her mouth. She'd never said such a Mae West line in her entire life. Next she'd be asking him if he knew how to whistle.

He slid a hand up to cradle her cheek.

"I'd love to, which is exactly why I'm not going to." He kissed the back of her hand where it still covered her mouth.

"Now go."

With gentle hands, he turned her to face the bedroom, and pushed lightly against her shoulders to send her forward.

A soft click indicated the door had closed behind her.

The hand that yet covered her mouth was no longer cold. Instead it was warm with the heat of the kiss she could still feel against the back of it.

CHAPTER SIX

D$aniel$ **had spent most** of his lunch hour in the workout room. Now, he was reading through the overnight reports, ones that he'd been trying to get to since breakfast, over a quick lunch of a BLT sandwich and a Coke when she came into the kitchen.

She entered the kitchen from behind him, but he didn't doubt that it was Dr. Alice Thompson for a single second. The President would have arrived with his normal bravado and be already in the middle of a sentence before the door was even open. A trait he shared with his deceased wife, a comparison Daniel kept to himself as the man would not have appreciated it. If it had been the Secret Service entering the room, as they would have done if the President was in tow, there'd be at least two sets of very business-like footsteps.

But there weren't.

The kitchen door opened part way, paused for a long moment, and then swung a bit farther. No soft slap of the rubber soles the agents wore for traction, but instead the almost silent step of a pair of sneakers on a woman who weighed half as much your average Secret Service agent.

"Good afternoon, did you sleep well?"

He didn't turn to look at her, but remained instead perched on his stool, his reports spread out across the light and dark stripes of the maple-and-cherry wood island. Didn't want to acknowledge the advantage he'd taken of an exhausted woman. He'd wanted to take that advantage though. For the first time in a long time, he really wanted to. Daniel tried not to cringe and simply hoped that she wouldn't recall how he had kissed her.

She wasn't drunk, you idiot. Just tired.

"I guess. Not really awake yet. Did you get any sleep?" She drifted into his peripheral vision over by the refrigerator.

"Not much." Not at all really. First he'd gone back down to his office to clean up the mess. Then the phone rang and he'd clarified the instructions the President had set in motion half-a-world away. That was the problem when he and the President classified something "need to know" only, all the little questions shot straight to the top.

Then he saw the report newly placed in the middle of the teetering stacks on top of his desk. The upcoming G-8 summit had just had another bomb threat which led to a meeting with the Secret Service detail in charge of arranging that. One thing led to the next as he caught up with e-mail, fired off instructions to his staff for the morning. The overnighters discovered he was awake and began routing their questions to him.

Around three-thirty a.m. the President had drifted in from the Oval Office, "just to see if Daniel was available." They'd spent the next hour reviewing and revising the new South African trade agreement, which had involved rousting the policy analysts from bed to straighten out an addition that someone had slipped in about Japanese whaling rights around Cape Horn. All of which had to be in place by five a.m. local-time before the eleven o'clock African-time round of talks restarted in Johannesburg.

When Janet arrived at six-thirty, Daniel had managed to clean up exactly three papers from the foot-deep stack that spread all the way under the couch beside his desk. With the rough edge of her contempt for how he let his desk become so out of control in first place, all communicated articulately by her not uttering a single word, she had it completely reorganized in less than twenty minutes.

Daniel hadn't even tried to go to bed, especially not just across the hall from Dr. Alice Thompson. He'd been too aware of her from all the way over in the West Wing. Here in the residence, way too close.

The only reason he'd come over now was for a workout and late lunch. The break helped recenter him before the typical afternoon mêlée.

Some part of him had thought Dr. Alice Thompson would have long since been awake and gone. And some part of him had known she still slept across the hall.

He waved a hand toward the refrigerator, "Help yourself." Then he tried to recall the notation he'd been intending to write in the report's margin which lay open before him. Completely vanished.

Tossing down the pen, he sighed in frustration. He didn't even know what the report was about at the moment. All he could think about was how much he wanted to taste her kiss again. *You aren't a sixteen-year old dying of hormones,* he instructed himself; which had no affect at all on the path of his thoughts.

"Sorry to interrupt you, maybe I should just go." She turned for the door. Daniel ran a hand through his hair. "No, this is a never-ending quest here at the White House. The elusive Completed Task."

"Maybe if you hunted it with ..."

"A butterfly net?"

She laughed. It was a light, merry sound. One quickly muffled by the hand she raised to cover her mouth.

In that moment Daniel discovered just how much he enjoyed making her laugh.

"Please," he waved at the refrigerator again. "I can make you coffee or tea."

A quick glance checking once more for permission, she finally opened the door and peeked inside the stainless steel monster. "Juice is fine." She took a bottle. And a container of Greek yogurt.

"Or the chefs could make you a proper lunch." He pointed toward the silverware drawer for a spoon.

"I think breakfast will be fine. And this is good, honestly."

She went to sit across the island from him and peeked into the open box in the middle of the counter. "Ooo, Christmas cookies!"

"Help yourself."

"I couldn't. They're so beautiful."

Daniel looked in. They were. "Old family tradition. We make cookie boxes for anyone, family or close friends, who can't be around for the holiday baking. My big sister probably made most of these." He poked around until he found a gingerbread man sticking out its tongue at him. He held it up for Alice to see. "Definitely Melanie Anne."

She took a reindeer that had one leg lifted to relieve itself against an elf. "You sure I'm not interrupting?"

"No need to be so tentative. Please, join me. It has to be better than," he had to flip to the cover of the report to remember what it addressed, "Pacific Northwest Reforestation."

It wasn't that she was just hesitant. He watched as she settled onto the bar stool opposite him. He'd shared several meals here with Emily Beale when she'd been posing as the First Lady's chef. Major Beale cooked like a magician and looked like a modern-day warrior goddess. And while it was hard not to be stunned by that, combined with her military achievements, it was also exhausting. The woman was driven in a way that left even the President breathless.

It was an interesting contrast to Dr. Alice Thompson, sitting exactly where Emily Beale had sat across from him just a year before. The steel backbone, the warrior's reflexes, and the black-and-white razor of the Captain's mind contrasting with the quiet thoughtfulness of Dr. Thompson.

Alice was, Daniel had to cast about his mind until he found it, she was shy. An odd and unusual feature in the world of political extroverts who constituted the bulk of the White House Staff. Perhaps last night had been an aberration, her relaxed attitude and quick ripostes a result of guards lowered by exhaustion.

He knew that having missed last night's sleep, he'd be in a similar state by late afternoon. But at the moment, he'd rather put her at her ease.

"About last night, I'm—"

"Not the least bit sorry." She cut him off. Her head popped up just enough from where it had been concentrating on her yogurt for him to see that one eye peeking out from under her bangs.

Well, no question remained regarding her memory.

"You're luscious."

Daniel found himself dangerously close to a blush. Clearing his throat didn't seem appropriate, something his father would do.

He had to say, something. "Uh, so are you."

That earned him the head toss that cleared both of her eyes and revealed that smile that had lit up his imagination last night.

"Good thing we'll never see each other again then, hunh?"

Daniel could feel himself blanch. Never see her again? No. That couldn't be... "You're teasing?"

"Oooo," Alice clapped her hands and rubbed them together as if preparing for evil deeds. "A gudgeon! This is going to be fun."

"A what?"

"A small fish."

Daniel did his best to glare at her, but she didn't appear daunted in the slightest.

"It's also military slang for someone who will take a straight line, hook and sinker. Straight man. Gudgeon. Dr. Drake Darlington. All one and the same."

Then she slapped a hand over her mouth again and her eyes grew quite wide and very distressed, looking as comic as she had last night right after he'd kissed her. And she'd kissed him back. Nothing wrong with his memory either.

He couldn't stop the laugh.

"Sorry," she mumbled through her fingers. "I promise I'll cut my tongue out later."

"I'll help." *Gudgeon indeed.* He could keep up just fine.

CHAPTER SEVEN

"**I** **can find the** front door on my own." Alice wished she had on much more sophisticated clothes. What had been comfortable at one in the morning looked very out of place at one in the afternoon in the corridors of the White House.

"How?" Daniel guided her down a second flight of stairs that opened into a grand foyer. She'd seen this staircase, or a good replica, in far too many movies. The Grand Staircase was just that. A sweeping majesty trod by Annette Bening in a killer blue gown and great shoes. And now the real set of stairs bore Dr. Alice Thompson in garishly green sneakers and dirty corduroys.

Though she did have a killer handsome guy by her side, so it wasn't a complete loss. At least until she turned the corner of the stair. A long marble hall spread before them. A sea of gold-trimmed red carpet flowed down the marbled length as if it would never end. It was staggering, sunlight pouring in from tall windows made the room glow.

The room itself so dazzled the mind that it took her a moment to focus on the horde of people at the far end of the hallway. Dozens and dozens of people, with a watchful phalanx of security guards, were stringing garlands, erecting and decorating trees, hanging dazzlingly intricate paper snowflakes several feet across from the ceiling using a high-lift platform.

"Christmas is here." Her voice had a sense of breathy wonder as if she were witnessing a modern miracle.

Daniel paused and looked out with her. "Four hundred volunteers. It will take them the better part of a day even at the rate they're moving. By this evening there will be musicians in the lobby, the whole bit."

He led her around the turn in the staircase as she rubbernecked like any tourist trying to take it all in. Right until she came face-to-face with Franklin D. Roosevelt, seated ever so grandly in a painted portrait almost as tall as she was.

It took her a moment to recover. Daniel almost had her turned toward the next set of descending stairs when her head cleared enough to spot the towering double doors. At the midpoint of the marbled foyer sufficiently spacious to hold a ballroom dance, the decorators hadn't reached them yet.

"Those are doors," she pointed. "And it is bright and sunny on the other side of them. They lead outside. Those," she paused for emphasis, "are doors."

"They are." He continued to coax her toward the set of descending stairs, ignoring her discovery.

"Well, I found them." She emphasized the "I" strongly and imagined herself discovering the North Pole.

"You did." He started down the next flight of steps and she was half tempted to call his bluff and leave through the lately-discovered doors. She'd need to think up what to name them if she were going to publish her findings.

"Do you know what's on the other side of those doors?" Daniel asked from where he'd paused three steps below her.

Alice wasn't really sure. Other than the now-famous Doors of Alice discovered by one Dr. Thompson while journeying through new and definitely strange lands, White House cartography wasn't exactly her thing. She could name the leaders of the hundred-and-ninety-three U.N. member nations and the three that weren't, draw a to-scale map of southwest Asia including every city with a population over twenty thousand and most of the clandestine weapon supply routes, on-or-off road. But what lay beyond those doors, not so much.

"What?" she demanded in a voice that echoed surprisingly in the long stairwell and attracted the attention of some of the closer decorators.

"Half of the capital's press corps is through those doors. We've had the new Egyptian President visiting this morning and he and President Matthews are finishing a photo op out on the North Portico at the moment. That's why we held back the decorating until after his visit."

"Oh. Right, he's a leader in the Muslim Brotherhood. Wouldn't be right." Alice tried to think of a good comeback, but it failed aborning. Maybe for the moment she'd leave herself in Daniel's hands and not explore the Famous Alice Doors. She followed him down the stairs and through the vaulted underground corridor they'd now entered, not one bit less grand than the main hallway upstairs, if not quite so flashy. No decorations here. At least not yet.

"Where did you get such nice hands?" *Where did she get such a stupid question?* But it was out there and now she'd have to live with it.

He held one up as if to inspect it as they once again passed through the Palm Room and along the West Colonnade. The decorators had definitely been here. Garlands of green pine spiraled up each of the columns, broad red ribbons wrapped between.

"My dad. I think I can blame my hands on him."

"Daniel Drake Darlington II?"

"What? No, that was Dad's idea of a joke, he's Johnny by the way. He thought it was funny. He'd found two Daniel Drakes in the family tree. One, an authentic Brit turned pioneer, who stumbled into the Tennessee wilderness in the early 1700s and never left. The second, a lieutenant in the Civil War, fought for the South. Died young and stupid, but left behind a pregnant farmer's wife who ran the place with an iron fist. Dad felt one a century was a good mark and realized that he'd better use the name in a hurry if he wanted to get it done in the 1900s. He added the 'third' just to be funny, I guess."

"So, you're a slaver."

"Born and bred."

Alice followed him past another set of Marines who opened yet another set of doors for them before they could get there.

"Should I worry?"

"Nah. You're not my type." His voice was pure tease.

"You're not mine either." She shot back. But it was wrong, on both sides. An awkward silence fell for a moment. She glanced sideways at him as they stepped past a pair of Marines and through a door. Then she faced forward and she squeaked.

It was all Alice could do.

She tried to speak, but all she could emit was another, equally ridiculous, high-pitched squeak.

A quick turn to retreat back out the door she'd just come in proved fruitless. The Marines had already closed it behind her. She turned reluctantly back to face the room. It was huge. Magnificently furnished. Washington, Lincoln, and JFK stared down at her from the wall. She couldn't say walls, because there was only one wall.

The room was oval.

CHAPTER EIGHT

T*he President entered and* shook Alice's hand a hearty good morning.

"Good afternoon, Dr. Thompson. You slept well I trust?"

Wholly unable to speak, she again managed little more than another puppy-dog limp handshake in response. The man must think her totally witless. He waved her toward the inevitable cluster of seating.

"Oval!" still rattled around in her brain like a ship lost at sea. Presidential portraits glowered down at her. The bloody Resolute desk, built from the timbers of the HMS *Resolute* anchored one end of the space and a large fireplace anchored the other. Nothing on television prepared her for the impact, for the sheer power of the room. It towered two stories tall, the Presidential Seal built into the center of the ceiling, mirrored by the one in the vast rug.

She dropped onto a couch. Far more comfortable than it looked. It would be a good slouching couch for watching a sappy movie, she resisted the urge to test that theory. As she'd half expected, the President and his Chief of Staff took the two armchairs. A small rosewood table separated her from Daniel. From its surface, a rather stumpy

Christmas gnome considered her carefully. His open satchel sported a selection of cheerfully wrapped chocolates.

"I wanted a chance to speak with you before you left."

"Me?" She blinked hard, but remained clearly wide awake. The President didn't fade leaving a Cheshire Cat smile, and they were definitely still seated in the Oval Office. Or maybe Daniel was the Cheshire Cat for he too was smiling at her, though in apparent empathy, as if reading her complete discomfiture at finding herself on the wrong side of the looking glass.

"Yes, I'd like to ask for your professional assessment of the situation."

Her assessment? The situation? She checked her hands, but they looked normal-sized and clutched no little glass bottles or bits of half-nibbled mushroom. She really was here, in this room, with these two men.

"I'll try to help, Mr. President." She glanced over at Daniel, "It's not wearing off."

He shrugged and offered her a slightly crooked smile. "Don't tell him," he nodded towards President Matthews. "It will just make his ego even more unbearable knowing he has that effect on you."

The President ignored the comment. "Your Director at the CIA feels that the S.A.D. is the proper operational asset to deploy into this situation. He states that the Special Activities Division can extract and reinsert personnel with the lowest statistical probability of detection. Quite adamant on that point in fact."

She would bet Director Smith was adamant. To have end-to-end control of such a high profile situation would be a distinct feather in the agency's cap.

"I also spoke with the Chairman of the Joint Chiefs. Brett was former commander of the U.S. Special Operations Command. As former head of SOCOM, he has an equally adamant predisposition favoring the SOAR assets. I'd like an analyst's opinion. Director Smith speaks very highly of your acumen in these situations."

"Something he is careful not to voice in my presence."

"A bit taciturn, but an exceptional man for the role."

Alice couldn't argue.

" 'She possesses," the President intoned in a fair imitation of Director Smith's voice, "the finest operational instinct the agency has seen in a dozen years.' I'd like to hear what your instinct says on this one."

Those were certainly words she'd never heard from the Director. In point of fact, over the six years since she'd first met the Director, that might be as many words as she'd ever heard from him, total. But that didn't help her much in the Oval Office.

Maybe if she could find a flagon of something that could make her shrink enough to completely disappear, then she'd feel much, much better.

Shape up, Alice. You've been studying for this moment since you first played the Take Off! *board game at age six, and then stayed up all night to memorize the country data on every single playing card.*

"Fact," good place to start. "We have a tentative contact requesting an extraction and subsequent reinsertion of a single individual out of and back into North Korea. Fact, as odd as this request appears on the outside, if certain recent changes following Kim Jong-il's death are considered, a certain logic may be conjectured." She wished she had a white board. She always did her best thinking with a white board.

She closed her eyes for a moment to let the patterns of the last three days of research reintegrate in her thinking. Then opened them again. They both still waited quietly. Well, she couldn't ask for a more attentive audience.

"Straight-line conclusions—"

"What does that mean in analyst-speak?"

"It means, Mr. President, that the only reasonable conclusions I can draw from the existing data lead straight to a single set of conclusions. Each change of factors decreases the scenario likelihood, significant decreases in this case. In other words, no matter what other geopolitical influences I consider, I can only see one conclusion that makes any sense without stretching into impossible realms. And as my buddy, Sherlock says..."

"Sherlock?"

"Holmes, sir," Daniel completed for her. " 'Once you have eliminated the obvious, whatever remains, no matter how improbable, must be the truth.' "

It was like they'd been thinking together for years, the thoughts just flowed. Daniel just kept getting sexier. To get some distance, she stood and walked toward the far end of the room.

"My dear Daniel Watson is quite correct." She winced at her insertion of the word "dear" but forged ahead. The fireplace mantel had been adorned with a splendid collection of homey items, though she'd bet this was the White House staff's doing, not some volunteers. Maybe even the President's; this one little group of decorations looked age-worn and personal.

Red-and-white candy-cane-twist candles. A little set of brass angels poised to ring tiny brass bells. A heavy iron strap sporting three very old bells the size of the palm of her hand. She picked it up and gave it a shake. Sleigh bells! Real ones. They clanged merrily and echoed loudly about the room reminding her of the auspicious place where she stood.

She put the bells down hastily and turned back to the room. She couldn't approach the problem head on, she always had to come at problems a bit sideways. So, she followed the wall past a grandfather clock and a curved door, the same shape as the wall.

"The only thing that fits the data is that a high-ranking official of the North Korean government wishes to have an unofficial conversation with an equal member of the United States government. The trip must be a secret, hence the unofficial channels of the request and the request of non-North Korean transport." She moseyed past the doors with a hazed view of the backs of the Marine guards, the glass so thick that it blurred the light. People shot bullets at this room. She shivered and hurried by only to be faced with Lincoln glaring at her from the ever-present oval wall. To his left stood a Christmas tree so perfect that it belonged in a catalog, not in real life. No family ornaments, no little kid decorations. A bachelor's Christmas tree set up by others.

"It must be a high-ranking official, one with sufficient profile to be recognized if traveling via normal transport. Hence, the request for clandestine transport. Perhaps even to be missed if gone overlong." She whistled. She'd missed that. "Top six, at least that's how I think of them. One of four leaders of the major political organizations: Central

Committee, the Presidium, Worker's Assembly, or National Defense. Or perhaps one of the two people who make up the ruling triumvirate with Kim Jong-un: Sung-il or Pak."

She ducked under Lincoln's gaze and returned to the fireplace and its Christmas-bedecked marble mantelpiece. The room wasn't actually that big, about the size of her whole apartment. Looking up she saw that a very solemn George Washington inspected her closely. This place was crazy. The first President's steady gaze finally drove her back to face the current President's thoughtful expression.

"A three-day extraction, which means they'd be missed if they were gone longer. And they don't want to be missed. They don't want to be noticed as having anything to do with the Wicked West.

"They aren't stupid. They know it will take three days. Two days in transit, out and back in, and one day on the ground. The request mandates neutral territory. Neither China, Russia, Japan, nor the United States. We have three weeks to arrange a location, set and rehearse the extraction, and execute. And it must be flawless or the whole thing comes apart."

She sat back down, her throat dry from talking. Daniel had poured her a cup of tea in a delicate, holly-painted cup, and rested it on the small table between them. She'd never even seen him go to the sideboard. She took the lemon, careful not to spray the table or sofa arm, but didn't add any sugar.

"Special Activities Division?" The President reminded her.

She considered the pieces. Knew the profiles of Saul and his crew, the best the CIA had in helicraft. Nothing else could perform this operation but a helicopter. There was no way to fly a comfy passenger or military-jet into North Korea, twice, yet remain undetected. Saul had certainly done some nasty missions and come out with his crew and his cargo intact.

"It must be one of the Top Six." She whispered it aloud, even capitalizing it in her mind though there was no so-named group, to test the sound of the hypothesis. Unless it was... No, that theory didn't quite work. Still, the factors didn't block it. No! It was too ludicrous to consider. Certainly too unlikely to voice in this room or to this company.

"Top Six," she said it definitively and knew it was right. Most likely. Now she focused back on her audience.

"Beyond secrecy, this mission will require finesse. The S.A.D. assets could do it. But if a North Korean Top Six asset caught the least little whiff of CIA involvement, or the attitude those fliers tend to carry with them, they'll be gone. Never come aboard. No, you need a SOAR operative. One with the kind of finesse I've seen on Beale and Henderson's reports. I'd trust your first instinct when you called them in last night." And with that simple assessment, she'd probably just cancelled out every nice thing the CIA Director had ever thought about her.

CHAPTER NINE

D*aniel escorted Alice along* the underground corridor to where her car had been moved and parked beneath the Treasury Building. A valet had it rolled up to the door, heater already running against the December chill.

"Thank you, Daniel. It would have been just too weird walking through all of that security alone." She glanced back through the glass doors at the last of three security desks they'd passed. Designed to keep people from getting in, it also made sure that she retained nothing important on her way out.

"Always glad to serve as your Dear Daniel Watson."

Damn! She really hadn't meant for it to come out that way, though of course he'd caught it. So, she did her best to smile in response.

He held her car door for her, shooing the valet off with a five-dollar bill. By the boy's expression, Alice could see that tips weren't really called for, but he was being so overeager and helpful Daniel properly assessed it was the only way he could have a final private moment with her.

Alice found herself not minding a private moment in the least.

"I have a meeting tonight, but do you have plans for tomorrow evening?"

She found herself shaking her head even before she could think as to whether or not she really did.

"Good. I'll come get you at 7pm. Casual."

Her first thought, as she tried to tug her cardigan more tightly around her, was there was no way she'd ever again risk wearing casual around Daniel Drake Darlington III. Her second thought was that she couldn't wait.

He clicked the door closed behind her, the closed window cutting off any chance of a response.

It was only after she was driving away, and she spotted him still watching her departure, that she felt the warmth where his hand had brushed down her cheek before he'd closed her door.

CHAPTER TEN

By *midnight Alice had* convinced herself that she'd imagined the whole thing, especially the line of warmth she could still feel on her cheek.

By one o'clock she was pretty sure she hadn't, and around two a.m. she decided she'd better be ready in case he actually came for her.

Sometime around three she'd finally passed out for four hours of shuteye.

By ten the next morning she'd dropped a significant portion of her next paycheck on a killer dress and new shoes. That had required a new winter coat to avoid looking totally ridiculous; can't wear a killer dress with a worn blue parka. She'd had her hair cut just last week, the only reason she didn't go in and have something drastic done to "fix" herself. Even in the salon, her hair had never behaved, though how she wished it would just for one night.

To get over herself, she swung by the office and dove into her own analysis. Her premise, try to prove it wrong. If she couldn't, well, then she had even more thinking to do. She reviewed the last six months of news from the incredibly spotlight-shy communist nation and its equally elusive leadership. Nothing revealed a softening to their strict isolationist attitudes. No comment reported by any of North Korea's

Top Six gave the least hint of who was coming out or what they'd want to talk about. The new supreme leader, Kim Jong-un, now named Wonsu, the highest active military rank, provided no indication of any change to his deceased father's paranoid policies.

When Betsy asked if she was coming to S.A.D. training or not, Alice observed the time in shock. Six o'clock. She locked down her work and was out of the building before Betsy could repeat the question. Thankfully no cops waited along the two-mile drive to her apartment.

A shower and fast change.

The dress was nearly impossible to zip up by herself, but she managed, thankful for the flexibility gained in the S.A.D. gymnasium.

Her nose shone, despite powder. Her cheeks didn't, despite a bit of blush.

Disgusted with the whole effort, she washed it all off her face and accidentally dribbled water down her cleavage. The dress hadn't seemed so revealing in the store. She had just managed her shoes, a mid-heels compromise, as a knock sounded on the door. A quick glance proved that there was no way she was letting Daniel into her apartment in its current state.

The couch had a rumpled afghan she'd knit years ago to snuggle under while watching movies, a fair pile of which she hadn't filed away. A stack of books covered much of the armchair she didn't use. Her home computer and a friendly disarray of paper, projects, and empty teacups were scattered about the surface of the dining table. With a quick kick, at least the clothes she'd stripped and dumped on arriving home would be out of sight.

Coat. That was it. Be completely ready to leave. She snagged the knee-length wrap-around black cashmere coat. She overlapped it and tugged the wide belt tight around her waist. She liked that it had made her look like a modern secret agent in the store mirror.

She opened the door just as the knock repeated.

It wasn't Daniel.

She didn't manage to suppress either her surprise or her disappointment.

"Dr. Thompson?" The man was big, crew cut, mid-forties. The

kind of square features you wouldn't want to mess with. The incongruous black suit looked distinctly out of place on his fighter's frame despite the good fit. The small coiled wire leading to an earpiece marked him for what he was, an agent of the U.S. Secret Service.

"Uh, I'm she." Lame! "I'm Alice, er, Doctor, uh. Oh crap! Yea, that's me."

"Frank Adams, ma'am." He didn't even blink at her being a total idiot. "Sorry that I'm a disappointment, but Dr. Darlington was unable to get away. He didn't want to be late, so he asked if I could come and provide you with transportation."

"Oh, okay." Alice had hoped to wow Daniel with her new look, and instead she was suddenly facing one of the President's personal bodyguards. The shift was jarring.

"May I say ma'am, that if I weren't married, I'd be even more sorry that I'm a disappointment. You look great."

"Uh, thanks." That gave Alice some hope of not appearing like a total frump.

"Though, if I may?"

She shrugged her permission.

With a move that she barely registered despite her S.A.D. training, the massive man suddenly held a short, but nasty looking knife to her wrist. Before she could protest, he gave it a practiced flick and then it disappeared again from view.

With his other hand he offered her the price tag that had been dangling from the coat sleeve.

CHAPTER ELEVEN

aniel met her at the garlanded North Portico, the very entrance Alice had discovered the day before. Now she knew what lay on both sides of the Doors of Alice. Daniel opened the car door himself and handed her out.

"I thought you said, 'casual'." She admired the charcoal gray suit that revealed a breadth of shoulder unusual for an office worker. Of course she knew why. Yesterday, wow, was it just yesterday, she'd woken earlier than Daniel thought and had gone out in hunt of food on the top floor of the White House Residence.

Instead of the kitchen, Alice had stumbled on the small gym where Daniel, clad in only shorts and sneakers, had laid on a bench pumping iron while watching CNN. And she'd thought he was gorgeous clothed.

She'd headed back to her room and waited for her nerves to settle before returning, by which time he was showered, dressed, and eating lunch. She'd had a terrible time meetings his eyes as she ate her yogurt for fear he'd see the truth in her face. The truth of what even being in the same room with Daniel made her feel.

"I had different plans, more casual plans," Daniel apologized as he led her inside. "There's a quiet little fish house I was going to take you to, but South Africa happened and we've only just wrapped it up. We'll just have a quiet dinner in the Residence."

Alice slowed to a halt as the door shushed closed behind her. The broad marble hall of yesterday morning had been transformed into a winter fairyland. Giant paper snowflakes of impossible intricacy dangled down the entire length of the Entrance and Cross Halls on the first floor of the Residence. A spray of glitter and subtle lighting had made them glow; the sole source of light in the hall. Columns of ice, she tapped one, plastic, flowed from floor to ceiling as if they held up the snowflake sky.

In sparkling contrast, a massive Christmas tree shone through the open double-doors ahead of her.

Daniel took her arm and coaxed her forward, "The Blue Room Christmas Tree. The room is just a little bigger than the Oval Office. This is only the second year since Jackie Kennedy that there hasn't been a First Lady to decorate it." Last year and this year. Following the death of First Lady Katherine Matthews.

Alice could only stare. It soared magnificently. A thousand ornaments must dangle from its limbs. Industry. It took her a moment, but that was clearly the theme. All of the ornaments had been made from a warm, dusky metal; pewter and bronze. Tiny airplanes, trains, automobiles, ships, and hundreds of other familiar objects had been created with a perfection and grace.

Each ornament lit by a pair of tiny Christmas lights in a vast rainbow of colors. She'd always favored using only white lights, but this tree could convert her to the many-hued camp.

The deep blue walls had been lit like the night sky, tiny sparkles making the room appear boundless. It was breathtaking.

Daniel allowed her to look to her heart's content before leading her up the Grand Staircase.

She kept her secret agent coat firmly wrapped around her as he led her up to the second story and down the massive central hallway. The decorators had been here as well. A couple of cheery Christmas trees made the long hall homey. Wreaths bedecked the doors and someone with an immense amount of patience had woven overlapping red-and-green ribbons in a spiral about each column. Everything here was designed to make her feel small, but tonight she was simply going to refuse. Somehow.

"This is the President's personal living room," he turned for an open doorway.

"I thought you said a quiet dinner in the residence?" Somehow, she'd pictured the two of them back in the cozy brass and cherry wood kitchen on the third floor. Just the two of them.

"Just the President."

"Do I look like the President?" A female voice sounded from past Daniel's shoulder where he'd half-turned to speak to her.

Alice didn't need the reminder of the midnight video conference to identify the first female pilot of SOAR. Major Emily Beale was dressed casually in ACUs, but made it look formal. The Army Combat Uniform had golden oak leaves that shone on the collar points of her blouse. That's all that was needed to dress her formally. The long, slender, perfectly-formed blonde was so stunning she could probably make rags appear elegant.

Alice, as the queen of frump, didn't need to be reminded of the fact by having to be in the same room with this woman. Sure thing no one would be paying her any attention tonight. Which normally was fine with her, but tonight it bothered her.

"Major Mark Henderson." Beale's husband came into view as Alice fully entered the room. His handshake was solid and friendly. He'd have stood out in any room that didn't contain his wife. Or Daniel.

"Dr. Alice Thompson," she managed a decent handshake this time.

"CIA analyst Dr. Alice Thompson?" Major Beale who hadn't even bothered to shake her hand now inspected her carefully with a full attention so complete that Alice almost stumbled backward.

"You did the report last year on that new arms route they were developing southeast of Asadabad?"

Alice nodded. That had been three months of her life.

"You'll be glad to know that your information let us wipe the hell out of it. If they even think about trying it again, we'll own their asses. Well done."

Major Beale's simple nod may have been the highest praise Alice had ever received in her life. The woman was clearly a primal force. If she'd thought it was a load of crap, Alice would bet she'd have said as much.

"That is good to know. Thank you."

"Yep!" Major Henderson wrapped an arm around his wife's waist and pulled her tight against him. "We cruised up there just last week or so; all part of our full inspection and on-going maintenance service. Whole sections of that pass don't even exist anymore. Seems that some significant chunks of the road disappeared off the cliff face and wound up in the valley a few thousand feet below. Can't imagine how that happened."

Alice could tell just by the immensely self-satisfied tone in Henderson's voice. A dozen Hellfire missiles here. Call into the Air Force for a bunker-buster bomb there. No more Kunar-Bajaur Link Road. The Taliban had moved a million or more dollars of ammunition across that pass last year alone, wholesale. Nice to know that had stopped.

———

Daniel took Alice's coat and turned to hang it up in the closet.

"Holy shit!" he heard the President's deep voice.

Daniel spun to see what had caused a President, who didn't even swear at midnight wakeup calls, to curse.

His eyes quickly passed over the occupants of the room and almost made it to where the President stood stock still at the door to his private bedroom. But Daniel didn't quite get there. A sight dragged his attention back to the woman whose coat even now slipped from his numb fingers and cascaded about his feet.

Cream skin and russet curls had been offset by a sleeveless green sheath dress so dark and rich that it made one understand what Mother Nature had been striving for when she'd designed the leaves of a holly tree. It draped left over right in a cascade that appeared to flow from one of Alice's shoulders, the other exquisitely uncovered. Not a curve of her body missed or hidden, but neither overemphasized. It was perhaps the most elegant dress he had ever seen.

Then Alice turned those hazel eyes on him and, though her skin had flushed red, that amazing smile lit her face.

"You appear to have dropped my coat, Dr. Darlington."

He looked at his feet indeed lost in a puddle of black cashmere, but he couldn't think of what to do about it. All he could do was look back at the woman.

The President came up and thumped him hard in the center of his back driving what little air remained out of his lungs. "Breathe, man. Breathe before you pass out."

Daniel gasped and suddenly felt quite lightheaded as his body dragged in desperately needed air.

The President retrieved the coat from about Daniel's feet. As he rose, he leaned in and offered in a loud whisper that anyone could here. "Speak, man. At least tell her how nice she looks."

He tried, he really did.

Then he cursed, spun, and strode from the room.

———

Alice stood frozen by his abrupt and apparently furious departure. Had he been upset that she'd dressed nicely when he said casual? She fought against tears when Emily hissed in her ear.

"If he's what you want, go! Move, damn it!"

Alice was out of the room and down the hall before she had time to chicken out.

Alice caught up with Daniel at the far end of the Central Hall where he'd come to a stop against a grand piano. He clutched the edge of the case like a man drowning.

"Do you play?" she did her best to ask, to make it light and funny, but she couldn't be sure that the words actually escaped past the tension that throttled her throat.

He nodded. Didn't speak. Didn't turn. Just a nod.

Alice couldn't do it. Whatever momentum had carried her this far was gone. She felt drained. Once again she'd proven her mother's words right, no one would ever want her. No one ever had, except for maybe a quick tumble and an equally quick goodbye. She was always too smart or not pretty enough or who the hell knew. By twenty-seven you think she'd be smart enough to know that men like the White

House Chief of Staff would never want her to be anything other than meek and mild. A neatly classifiable object.

Well, she was better than that. She hadn't spoken to her mother for the last five years the woman had been alive for a reason. Self-preservation. Well, that too was a hard won lesson. Her best option was to go. Now.

Her eyes hot and stinging, she turned to leave. Maybe she could find that Secret Service agent who'd brought her and go home. Or maybe not. The building was as hard to get out of as it was to get into.

"Wait." His voice, barely a whisper, drifted down the hall.

"Why?" She stood with her back to him, no more than a half dozen steps between them.

"Please?"

So she stood. Stood and started counting to thirty. At thirty, to hell with what he wanted, she would leave anyway.

At twenty-two, she felt a fingertip brush ever so slightly across the bare shoulder. Rather than a shiver, a ring of warmth radiated from that brief contact.

Paralyzed, she couldn't turn to face him.

Another brush of fingers and he caught some of her tears where they'd run unnoticed down her cheek.

"This is going to sound wrong."

"It's got to be better than silence."

She could half see him nod in her peripheral vision, but she refused to turn. The silence was killing her.

"I don't want it to be about the physical."

"It?" she asked. "You're so good with words, use them now when it matters."

Again the peripheral nod.

Alice's eyes focused down the hall. A pair of Secret Service agents stood outside the room where she could hear the others talking. Twenty paces away, they were clearly trying to not pay attention to the drama unfolding over by the piano.

"Will you sit, please?"

At her nod, he led her a little farther down the hall from the agents to a pair of armchairs placed close in friendly companionship. A small metallic tree dangling with dozens of tiny ball ornaments graced the small table.

She sat carefully, remembering she was wearing a gown and not corduroy slacks. Alice inspected her own hands. Could just see Daniel's where they were folded together. There was a similarity that she could now identify, why his hands had looked particularly nice to her. They both had pianist's muscles, a strength that came from the constant practice.

Again that crazy-making silence.

"You were going to define the 'it' you were talking about."

"Right." He took a deep breath and puffed it back out. "Right."

She considered pointing out that he was repeating himself rather than making any headway, but she was afraid that would just earn her another "right" and she'd probably scream if he did that.

"I have all of these stupid ideas."

"What kind of ideas? And don't say stupid ones. I've heard that bit already."

"Right—"

"Or 'Right.' I've had enough of that word too."

Daniel reached out and took her hands. Somehow that forced her to look up into his brilliant blue eyes.

"You, in that dress, are the most beautiful thing I've ever seen."

"Thing?" she managed to give her brain a moment to shift gears, but it wasn't enough. She knew she could pass for cute, but "most beautiful?" Not likely.

"Yes. Yes, for crying out loud! 'Most beautiful woman,' while nonetheless true, is far too small a category."

"Oh." Her voice was small, even she could barely hear it.

"I always believed that attraction should be built on a mutual respect, two minds that find similar interests. On the rare occasions when I have dated—"

"How rare?" The question popped out of the cataloging side of her mind.

"Rare enough. On those occasions, I've always grown to know the woman well before I, before we, before..." He huffed out a breath in exasperation, glanced over toward the two agents down the hall and then lowered his voice and leaned a little closer until she could truly see the amazing purity of blue in his eyes, no hints of brown at all.

"I'm so sorry I kissed you."

"Why? Why are you sorry, Daniel?" She'd liked it so much.

"Because it was inappropriate. I did it just because I wanted you so much I couldn't stop myself. It's a lousy excuse and it won't happen again, but I have no better—"

She leaned the last few inches and stopped his words with her lips. She ran her fingers up into the soft blond hair and dug them in so that he couldn't pull back without taking her with him.

Daniel held off for the longest moment, then groaned and leaned in. His hands slipped along her cheeks and gentle thumbs rubbed along her ears. He kissed her so long and deep that she practically felt ravaged. She'd had sex that was less meaningful. Actually, Alice would wager that she'd never had sex that was anywhere near as meaningful as this kiss.

When at last he released her lips, he didn't move away, but remained forehead-to-forehead, nose tip-to-nose tip.

"If you say you're sorry, I'm going to smack you."

"Then," his whisper matched hers, "I won't. I've dreamed of nothing else but kissing you again since when I kissed you goodnight the first time. And maybe before that."

"Well, if you behave, maybe I'll let you kiss me goodnight tonight, too." If her heart could stand it.

He rose from the chair and helped her to her feet, which was good because her knees were distinctly watery and the mid-height heels were proving more precarious than planned. She and Daniel headed back to join the others, the pair of agents studiously inspecting the wall across the hall from the doorway they guarded. It was only as they reentered the room that she realized that Daniel had not released her hand from when he'd helped her to her feet.

Just the moment before anyone noticed their return, she leaned close and whispered quietly in Daniel's ear.

"I've been thinking about a lot more than just kissing you."

CHAPTER TWELVE

D_aniel sat at his_ desk the next morning and ignored the piles of paper that had grown significantly overnight.

He couldn't help smiling at the memory of that moment last night in the President's living room. For the second time in a dozen minutes, President Matthews had been required to slap Daniel's back and remind him to breathe. Over cocktails, they divided pretty typically along gender lines, but for atypical reasons.

The men often stopped to join in on the women's conversation. They appeared to have become instant long lost friends and the energy of it was electrifying. They were long lost friends who were both fascinated with the ebb and flow of global military tactics as they swept back and forth across the planet. Emily and Mark had amazing insights into the variations of localized conflict and the shifting tactics in the actual theater of operations.

Daniel offered country-level insights, and the President posited some fascinating cultural-level aspects in understanding some of the conflicts and their global ramifications that Daniel hadn't previously considered.

Again, it was Dr. Alice who startled and amazed. She backed up her beauty with a very serious mind. She followed Mark and Emily into actual battlefield tactics that completely eluded Daniel even when they tried to explain them. At the same time, she was able to expand his and the President's thinking on several subjects. When questioned, she backed up her comments with facts.

As their small party shifted and regrouped into different conversations, first in the living room and later around the dining table, he never managed to remove her from his awareness. That this breathtaking woman had been thinking about a lot more than kissing him had now rooted his thoughts there as well. He tried to imagine helping her out of that dress.

It was a thought he definitely enjoyed. But he couldn't quite picture it. Whereas making love to her dressed only in that well-worn cardigan sweater, that he could picture just fine. As if that were the real Alice, and last night's stunning and brilliant beauty in the perfect evening gown who had radiated as the center of the evening, she was someone he'd never deserve.

Suddenly his desk phone rang from somewhere under the latest Mexico currency crisis. The drug cartels had hinted that they were going to wholly abandon the peso in favor of the more stable U.S. dollar. The news had crashed the peso's valuation badly. Again.

"Daniel."

"You aren't opening today's Advent calendar window are you?"

"Good morning, Dr. Thompson." He pulled the calendar into his lap and opened to the first picture.

"Did you? No cheating or mama would know."

"No cheating. As a matter of fact, thoughts of you so distracted me last night that I haven't even opened December 2nd's window and today is the third. You distract me, Dr. Thompson."

"Bad luck."

"Your distracting me?"

"Not opening the window. Do it now, I'll wait."

He pulled on the "2" ribbon, attached to a little flap door in the snow at the base of a tree. He pulled out the butterscotch drop and admired a pair of squirrels sleeping curled up inside. The sides of the little space had been painted with tiny cupboards. One open cabinet revealed a bountiful stock of acorns.

He described it to her.

"Hmm," she hummed in his ear. "Butterscotch. I'll bet you taste good with butterscotch."

"I really didn't need that image stuck in my head all day."

"Tough," her laugh sparkled even over the phone line.

"When can I see you again? I have to see if you taste as luscious in normal clothes as you did in that amazing dress." Their full-body good-night kiss had almost led him to throw her over his shoulder and drag her upstairs to his bedroom.

"Hmm," she hummed at him again. "I'll pick you up this time. Eight o'clock. Eat first, dress warm."

"Hmm," he hummed back at her. Sounded stupid when he did it. He glanced up to see Janet standing across his desk holding a couple of files.

Clearly she made a similar assessment about the inefficacy his hmm-ing ability.

"Tonight at eight." He tried to sound business-like.

"Janet just walked in, didn't she?" That merry giggle sounded in his ear. "Tell her I said hi."

"Will do." Not a chance. He hung up the phone.

"**I** **considered sending an** agent to pick you up, but came myself instead."

Alice always seemed to start conversations without any preamble. Daniel didn't even have both feet inside her fire-engine red Prius yet. It had flames painted on the front like a 1960s GTO muscle car instead of a mundane hybrid. A cheery little garland of tiny red-and-green lights glowed softly around the rear view mirror.

She headed them back out the White House gates.

Maybe it was his Tennessee background, but conversations had a normal flow, a way they were supposed to work. A greeting, a checking in, those pleasant little inanities that served no purpose he could put his finger on at the moment, but he liked them nonetheless. It wasn't as if she was in a hurry, she was simply always in forward motion and he always lagged a step behind.

"I did apologize for sending an agent to pick you up."

"Sent me home with one, too."

"I..." He had. Hadn't even thought about it. He was so used to the building, it seemed that he never left it except for meetings up on the Hill.

He'd moved into the White House Residence when Peter

Matthews had made him the Chief of Staff. "Every time you leave for your apartment, you're going to lose another half-hour of sleep between walking to your car, driving, parking." So, he'd kept the apartment for a while, but finally moved fully into the third floor of the Residence. With Katherine Matthews dead in the helicopter crash, that had left President Matthews living alone in the entire Residence. Daniel had felt sorry for him and did really appreciate the man's company when they could stop moving long enough to enjoy a gathering like last night.

Daniel had never given a thought to delivering her home himself. In hindsight, it would have been a very dangerous choice, vastly increasing the likelihood of his ending up in her bed. But last night, he'd been too dazed by her goodnight kiss to form any coherent thoughts.

"What did Janet put in the calendar for tonight?"

Apparently his silence had lasted too long. She cleared the gate and turned south.

"I don't know. I didn't look."

"Don't you get the rules at all, Dr. Darlington? It's after dark. There are rules to these things."

"Rules like not pulling over so that I can drag you into the tall grass and neck wildly like two teenagers?"

The car actually wavered on the road and he reached out a steadying hand to the wheel for a moment.

"Well," she cleared her throat and tried again. "Well, being early December, the tall grass has long since been mown by the Parks Department and died back for the winter. Otherwise that sounds like a great idea."

Now it was his turn to try and speak. It took him several tries.

"I'm new to Advent calendar rules, but I'm learning. I brought it with me."

"Well, that's better. So open it already!" She turned onto the Frederick Douglass bridge and crossed south over the river. Still no word where she was taking him and he wasn't going to ask.

He pulled the calendar out of his bag that also included a hat and mittens. By the light of the street lights strobing by overhead, he found the "3" ribbon, a small, gift-wrapped present that an owl had dropped in the snow and was in the process of retrieving.

"Black licorice. A Scotty dog."

"Ooo. They're the best."

He plucked it out and another lay behind it. Two Scotty dogs. Had Janet originally given him two? Or had she somehow discerned he had a date and slipped in the second one while the calendar lay on his desk? He'd rather think the former, but suspected the latter.

"Here, there's two." He held one out so she could take it with her teeth. She did so, nibbling on the ends of his fingers in the process. He was suddenly glad he wasn't driving or they'd be weaving all over the road.

He popped in his own and started chewing.

"That's so good," she mumbled. "I need to stop and see how you taste." And she did. Turned into a side road, parked, and leaned over.

He met her halfway. Winter and summer and sweet licorice. Unable to stop himself, he reached for her, and to the limits of the seatbelts, pulled their bodies together, one hand running down over her coat, tracing the many-layered curve of her breast making Alice moan against his teeth.

A sharp knock on the window made him open his eyes. A Marine in full uniform was leaning down to inspect them through the driver's window. Where had he come from?

CHAPTER FOURTEEN

"*A nacostia?" Daniel had waited* until the Marine cleared them through the gate. Obviously they'd been expected. "What the hell are we doing at Anacostia? The only thing here are Marine helicopters used to transport the President."

"Not the only thing." Alice was clearly enjoying whatever little secret she had. What else could possibly be here?

"Hey, who are these guys who keep following us?" Alice was checking the rearview mirror.

Daniel didn't even bother to glance back. "Secret Service. They're my protection detail."

"Since when?"

"Since the day Katherine Matthews' helicopter was shot down and I became Chief of Staff."

"No, I mean when tonight? It was shot down?"

"Yes." Daniel had heard enough to know gunfire had been involved in the final, fatal crash. He still wondered what had truly happened on that final flight. No one was telling him and he'd decided that discretion was the better part of curiosity and never tried to pull the file for study. If there even was a file. It had been a very strange three weeks while Emily Beale was working undercover in the White House.

"Emily Beale," he finally connected the pieces. "She's here at Anacostia. With her helicopter." He groaned. "Please tell me we're not going flying."

"Absolutely! She called to invite me this morning and I can't wait. It's gonna be great!" Her excitement was contagious, or would be under other circumstances. He'd seen Emily fly only five or six times in those three weeks and she'd crashed during two of them. Not odds that he liked even if he knew the reasons for the first one. He'd been there and survived only because of her amazing skills. But still, they'd crashed.

"So how long have they been following us tonight?"

Funny, Alice might start in the middle of conversations, but she never lost their thread once begun.

"Since the White House gates."

She went silent at that as she pulled up into the parking spot by a hangar door.

"You live like that?"

"Part of the job."

She went quiet again.

Daniel had to acknowledge, it could be a shocking price to pay. The loss of personal privacy in trade for a measure of security against being murdered by some nutcase.

If this attraction between them built into something more, would it be a price Alice could stand to pay?

CHAPTER FIFTEEN

"*We have two flights* tonight." Major Beale indicated the two helicopters parked inside the hangar. Alice tried to get her clothes to settle properly. They'd given her a flight suit that covered her from collar to boots. The vest added another layer. Daniel wore a similar rig and managed to make it look enticing; like you'd want to strip it off to see what lay beneath. She felt like a balloon animal.

The black-painted Black Hawk bristled with armament and radar domes. It had to be the DAP version. She'd never actually seen one of SOAR's notorious Direct Action Penetrator modifications. No one else flew these. There were perhaps twenty of them in existence and it was the nastiest and most effective piece of airborne weaponry ever launched into the night sky.

It looked modern, cruel, and impossibly deadly.

The other helicopter was almost a joke beside it. She'd seen a thousand pictures of the Mil's Mi-4 "Hound." The first true workhorse Russian helicopter by Mikhail Mil. Over three thousand had been built. So ubiquitous and stubbornly tough that a number of countries still flew them, though the last new one had come off the line in 1964. Based on the American 1950s-era Sikorsky S-55, it looked completely out of place besides its cousin, the Sikorsky Black Hawk MH-60M.

Alice didn't have to ask what it was doing here; the idea had a brilliance in its simplicity. Emily nodded to her, acknowledging Alice's quick understanding.

Beale and Henderson could enter North Korea in one of two different ways. On board the DAP Hawk they would have speed, night-vision, and nap-of-earth flying capabilities making them as nearly invisible as any weapon of war could become.

If they flew into the country with the Mi-4, they'd also be near enough invisible for a different reason. North Korea still used them as military trainers and agricultural birds. One of the last dozen countries to do so. No one would think twice about seeing one. But the mission would give up speed, maneuverability, and any chance of taking drastic action if called for.

"A tough choice," Alice acknowledged.

"Mark and I have been back and forth on it." Emily scowled at the two birds as if it were their fault. "We're doing simulated missions in each tonight, hoping that will help answer the question. They're the same weight, but the Hawk has half again the speed, twice the range, and four times the power. Should be interesting."

Alice had already learned that in Emily Beale's world, "interesting" was a word indicating a complete and all-consuming fascination. The mistress of understatement, nothing was more important to the Major than helicopters and especially the task at hand.

"Let's start with the Hawk," Alice suggested. "That's your familiar ground, your baseline. Set your calibration point and then reference variations from there."

Emily nodded agreement and waved a hand toward the Black Hawk.

Several things happened from that simple gesture. A couple of men Alice hadn't previously noticed back in the shadows moved forward and began working over the DAP Hawk. These would be her crew chiefs, a mismatched pair.

One no taller than Alice but exceptionally broad-shouldered and slim-waisted, a six-pack ab kind of guy. The other was a huge man. Not an ounce that wasn't muscle, but tall and wide. If he played a hockey goalie, no one would ever see the net past his bulk. They moved over the bird with the ease of long practice and the silence of long familiarity. A good team.

"We dropped in a couple of observer seats for you." Emily indicated the back of the cargo bay. Two seats had been added, just like the ones for the gunners, low because of the four-foot height of the cargo bay. A circle of red-and-green Christmas lights had been arranged around the back of the pilots' seats lending a cheery glow to the cabin.

"That's great. I love it. Thanks." Alice wondered if she could tease the woman, always worth a try. "Daniel says you like to crash a lot."

Emily offered the slightest smile. "Well, we'll see if we can keep tonight's mishaps limited to just the simulated ones."

Alice nodded, just as upright and forthright as she'd expected.

Then Emily offered her a beatific smile. "But don't tell Daniel it's only practice."

Alice laughed.

CHAPTER SIXTEEN

The Black Hawk ride had been everything Alice had imagined. They took off low and fast and roared down the Potomac as if they were racing over the Sea of Japan. A winter storm on the Atlantic had kicked up wind and whitecaps on the Chesapeake Bay. The helicopter bumped and dropped in the wind while they flew so low it looked as if the waves were going to claw them from out of the sky.

With a hard slam, they tilted nearly sideways and turned overland. They flew so low that they actually had to bounce upward to clear fences. The silence on the radio was absolute. The heavy helmets they wore offering only the slightest hiss over the built-in headphones to indicate they were latched into the radio and intercom system at all.

Alice could see the infrared projection of the FLIR across the inside of her visor, passed to her by the nose-mounted forward-looking-infrared camera. It revealed trees with alarming suddenness as they traveled over the Virginia countryside at just under two hundred miles an hour.

"Pending engine failure," Mark Henderson announced from the left seat with a calmness that was startling, even in a practice scenario.

"Oh no!" Daniel's whisper. "Not again."

Alice had heard Emily tell the rest of the crew that they wouldn't say the word "simulated" on this flight. Everyone was in the know but Daniel.

He convulsively clutched Alice's hand.

"Silence on the intercom," Beale snapped out. "Roger failure on one and two. Restart check."

"Restart failure on one and two."

"Roger. Initiating auto-rotate emergency landing."

Alice's could feel the adrenaline pounding her heart against her rib cage as the bird backed hard in a nose-high position to shed their forward speed. The ground was so close.

Alice bit the inside of her cheek hard enough that for a moment she'd thought she'd drawn blood. If she felt this stressed, even knowing it was a test, she now felt awful for pulling the trick on Daniel. But she didn't dare speak while the pilots were so busy "saving" them. So instead she did her best to calmly pat his arm.

At the last moment, with the ground barely a dozen feet away, but still moving forward quickly, Emily did something and the rotor blades dropped into silence. The helicopter fell, causing Alice to float out of her seat, her body only held in place by the safety harness. They hit tail first. Then the front wheels slammed down hard enough that twenty-thousand pounds of helicopter actually bounced back up by several feet, then they hit again and remained earthbound this time. The helicopter rolled forward neatly across a handy ballpark's outfield.

"End simulation." Henderson remarked dryly.

"Roger end simulation." Emily acknowledged and in moments the rotors were biting air and they were once again aloft.

"Simulation?" Daniel shouted into the headset.

Emily Beale actually laughed. "Didn't want you to be able to say you'd ever flown with me without crashing."

"Crap!" was all Daniel offered.

Alice could feel him shaking with the post-adrenal fear-reaction. Okay, not one of her better jokes.

———

Daniel tried to beg off the repeat flight on the Mil Hound, but somehow Alice talked him into it. He'd been angry when he found out she was in on the joke, but Dr. Thompson proved to be a very difficult person to remain angry at.

Being angry was a skill Daniel had never developed. On purpose. He was often called unflappable and had always been proud that the petty sniping so traditional in D.C. politics didn't get to him. Not when clerking in the Senate, not when serving as the First Lady's personal secretary, and not when the Congressional Leadership was fighting him just for the sake of being pigheaded.

Alice managed to make it all her fault, though he knew Major Beale had played a significant role. But Alice was so upset that he'd agreed to make the second flight with minimal protest. He managed to keep his mouth shut and not say that he could think of little he'd like less while still on this side of the Apocalypse.

The Mi-4 Hound sounded completely different. The high whine of the Black Hawk's turbine engines was replaced by the buzz of the massive radial engine in the nose. The beat of the helo's blades wasn't all that different once they were underway. But despite the bigger cargo bay, Daniel felt quite claustrophobic.

On the Black Hawk, he'd been side-by-side with Alice. The open cargo doors had offered a wide view to the Virginian night and he hadn't felt any fear that he might fall, except for those few heart-stopping seconds of the emergency landing. He could observe the crew chiefs Big John and Crazy Tim sitting right in front of them and by looking up the middle, he'd been able to at least partly watch what the two pilots were doing.

On the Hound, he and Alice were seated across from each other on little fold-down metal seats amidships with only small, round porthole windows to offer any view. John and Tim actually lounged back on a pair of seats that were built into the rear doors that swung outward. With no miniguns and only one gauge on helicopter status, they had nothing to do during the flight. The cockpit was up a ladder and through a small hole, making the pilots almost unobservable.

And the front of his helmet didn't have an infrared view painted across the visor. It had clear plastic, so all he could see was the inside of the cabin.

The pilots weren't quiet on this ride.

"Let's run her an extra twenty feet high until we're sure of her," Henderson showing some caution.

His wife gave a running commentary, "Night vision has a lousy field of view low and forward. I don't dare try to terrain follow. Climbing an additional twenty."

Hard turns side-to-side threw Daniel back and forth between harness and hard metal hull of the helicopter.

"She's tough, but she sure doesn't dance."

One of the crew chiefs chimed in with, "Don't ask us to shoot anything; we'd have to kick a hole in the side of the helicopter and stick out a FN SCAR."

The Special Forces Combat Assault Rifle was very useful hand-to-hand, and each of the crew wore one across their chest as a matter of practice. Daniel felt far safer with the two mini-guns of the Black Hawk. Instead of the little rifle magazines that could fit in his hand, the miniguns fired thousands of rounds a minute from large boxes. He liked that.

Yes, it might be more clandestine to visit North Korea in a Mil Hound, but he'd take firepower when entering the most hostile country on the planet outside of Somalia.

This time they called "simulation" on the emergency landing test, but he didn't like it one bit more this time than the last.

They landed more slowly, but the helicopter complained much more loudly. Sheet metal banged as it flexed. The sharp ringing sound of the shock absorber right under his seat that sent him leaping against his harness made his ears hurt.

"Bottomed out the shocks there," one of the pilots remarked drily. "Not as forgiving as you'd expect."

Daniel was so wound up he couldn't even tell if it was Mark or Emily's voice. His leap was the only thing that had avoided a seriously bruised butt.

Moments after they were airborne, while they were still clawing for the altitude to clear the bleachers behind the baseball field, Beale shouted over the intercom.

"Incoming! Portside." An alarm sounded. "Cracked cylinder head, ten percent loss of power." Sure enough, the sound of the rotor blades slowed, faded ever so slightly.

The helicopter veered to the right, away from the attack, but even Daniel could tell that it was sluggish.

Despite the deck heeling sharply, the two crew chiefs were on their feet. Their vests had a large D-ring on the front. Long tethers were snapped to them which let the chiefs move about the cabin. The other ends were clipped to metal loops in the ceiling.

Some visual signal passed between the two men. The giant one heaved open a side hatch close beside Daniel. The metal door slammed open so hard that the helicopter rang loudly enough to hurt Daniel's ears despite the protection of his helmet.

The shorter one, Tim Maloney, unslung his FN SCAR rifle and was aiming it out the door. Sergeant Big John Wallace held him in place with one fist wrapped around a handhold and the other grasping the back of Tim's flight vest.

There was no rattle of gunfire. No flash of— Tim's suit sounded an ear-piercing squeal!

"Shit!" Tim dropped to the floor still blocking part of the doorway.

Alice screamed and Daniel nearly did the same.

Big John crouched behind Tim and brought his own rifle to bear. Tim remained in place, apparently too wounded to move.

Without hesitation, Daniel reached across the middle of the helicopter's narrow cabin and pulled Alice's head down, as far toward his knees as the harness allowed, to reduce her exposure to incoming fire.

Daniel glanced back at the wounded crew chief even as he crouched over her. Tim's raised hand still grabbed the doorframe. He was wounded past being able to fight, but he was staying in place to act as a human shield for his fellow crew chief. Buying him precious moments to fend off the attackers. It was the bravest thing Daniel had ever seen.

That was when Daniel noticed the bright red flashes on the bulkhead right where Alice's head had been moments before.

Lasers. It was a training flight and they were being shot with lasers. Tim's suit must have registered him as hit in the firefight. That's why it had squealed, a hit. And why his rifle, and now John's, sounded with no rattle of gunfire.

It was only a mock battle.

Despite that, Daniel was still impressed that Tim had shielded his friend with his own body. He couldn't imagine doing such a thing. To want to protect someone so much that your instinct put you in front of the bullets.

Once they were in the clear, Daniel realized that he still had Alice trapped down across his knees. Even if he couldn't imagine throwing himself in front of the bullet, his instincts apparently had other ideas about who he wanted to protect.

CHAPTER SEVENTEEN

"*You have the strangest* idea of what constitutes a date." Daniel's smile was soft and his voice teasing. He'd walked Alice to her apartment door and now they huddled under the narrow porch roof to escape from the light snow that started falling as Daniel drove her home.

Alice admitted she'd bit off more than she'd intended. Her nerves were still freaking out. The attack had seemed so real, her death so imminent. Nothing in the CIA's S.A.D. training had prepared her for the reality of SOAR training. Of course, all they'd gotten from S.A.D. as non-combatants was a helicopter ride and a quick thirty-minute flight in a jet that could flip and roll better than any amusement park ride.

What she hadn't been prepared for was the realism. Or that Daniel had thrown himself between Alice and the attackers, simulated or not. She'd always stood up for herself, known she was on her own.

He ran a gentle thumb over her lower lip, his fingertips brushing her cheek, cradling it with a tenderness that brought tears to her eyes and a pounding to her heart that she'd only read of and scoffed at in books.

She wanted to run inside and weep at the wonder of a man who would willingly sacrifice his life for hers, even in simulation. She wanted a cup of hot cocoa with a very large shot of brandy in it to calm the jitters. And Alice also wanted to drag Daniel into bed and lose herself in the throes of the passion that was raging for release. A passion she'd kept safely under wraps her whole life because no one had ever called it forth.

Alice slid her hand up Daniel's chest and around his neck. She pulled him down to her, their breath steamy in the cold night air mingling, merging, and gone when their lips met.

A warmth spread through her as he tipped her back the last few inches until she lay back against her own closed front door. The soft porch light shone down over Daniel, lighting him like an angel. Her own personal angel.

She couldn't stop the smile crossing her lips.

Daniel smiled back in response and pulled back just far enough to speak. "What?"

"Sounds stupid." And it did.

"Say it anyway."

She looked up into his eyes and over his shoulder saw a Secret Service agent standing just a few paces back.

"I'm sorry, sir, but you've been called back to the White House." He held out a cell phone.

In moments, with barely a word beyond "South Africa conference again," a few choice moments of silence when any less tactful man would curse a blue streak, and a final light brush of fingertips down her cheek in apology, Alice lay alone against her front door and Daniel was giving rapid instructions over the phone as they hustled him back to the escort car.

She unlocked the doors and turned on the hallway light. As usual, the mess that was her apartment had not magically rectified itself during her absence.

"Is that the kind of life you want?" Alice asked the empty room. The lack of privacy. The inability to complete something you hadn't even started yet.

She didn't know which was more shocking, that she even considered asking the question or that the answer was yes. For this man, it
just might be worth it.

79

CHAPTER EIGHTEEN

D_aniel listened to the_ phone ring in his ear while ignoring the pile on his desk. It had actually lowered over the last week, just not as much as it needed to.

All week Daniel had fought against two conflicting agendas: the tide on his desk and finding a moment to actually see Alice. To discover what might lay past those kisses of hers that were so much richer than the best apple cider fresh off the press. Through the calendar's nightly treats of a candy on an elastic bracelet to a tiny chocolate bar and a half dozen other variations, he'd only managed to spend time with Dr. Alice Thompson on the phone.

He'd seen Henderson twice and Beale three times as they continued testing the possible scenarios for infiltrating a heavily militarized, paranoid country not once but twice two days apart.

But not Alice.

It was really quite unsatisfying in so many ways. But she'd made it clear that no matter what time he called, she'd gladly answer the phone. It might take a few minutes before her words were actually comprehensible, but once she was awake, they talked easily and often long.

Still no answer. Usually she'd answer by now.

Yet it didn't feel real or satisfying. Maybe the whole thing was in his head. Maybe she was merely being nice on the phone. He could feel a distance building. A couple of premature kisses and a pair of heart-stopping helicopter flights didn't make up for a week apart.

And when they talked, he felt... They talked far more about him than her. She was the one he wanted to know about. Instead, they talked about the family farm in Tennessee.

How he'd come to Washington to promote the Slow Food movement in the southeast. She didn't know about that and they'd spent whole conversations discussing seasonal and local rather than unsustainable farming and having to ship food immense distances. To eat the flour that was made from the wheat just down the road, Daniel's research had shown that the nearest flour mill was five hundred miles away. His local wheat had to travel a thousand miles just to become flour, never mind be baked.

He reluctantly reached out to cut the connection. He hung onto the receiver, considering calling her cell phone. But it was nearly midnight. Maybe he should just leave her be. He didn't want to speak to her on the phone anyway. He wanted to hold her close. He wanted his world to stop the way it did when she rested her head on his shoulder. He wanted to know about her.

When he did manage to turn the conversation to being about her, it was her professional life they explored. Her work was truly fascinating to him.

He'd always been a people person, almost as good a negotiator and peacemaker as the President. The President excelled on the larger issues: averting national strikes, international relations, and so on. Daniel's specialty was becoming the fine art of convincing the swing vote on a key bill. They'd recently passed a very controversial education financing package and Daniel had stood at the center of it. It had been his victory.

And once again, Dr. Alice Thompson would somehow not be the topic of conversation. Maybe if he had the FBI pull a file on her he'd find out something. Surely the FBI would have a file on a senior CIA analyst. Wouldn't they?

Daniel set the phone back in the cradle and stared out his office window. The ledge was the perfect height to prop his feet and stare past the tips of his polished shoes. Something he'd never done until Alice had propped her green and red sneakers on his desk almost two weeks ago. Beyond the heavy glass, the White House grounds spread before him, brightly lit as always. That was one thing that the movies got wrong, it was never dark inside the White House without closing heavy curtains.

He knew he shouldn't turn around, his desk would just be there waiting for him. He had to get focused on the North Korea problem, but the ever-shifting files and crises kept it off the top of his list.

A clandestine visit could be anything from a defection to personal bribery in exchange for vague promises to stop their next space launch. That the latest launch had shredded itself shortly after liftoff and scattered debris over the Yellow Sea hadn't mitigated the serious international furor.

Alice had said something in their conversation yesterday. She didn't speak much during their phone calls and Daniel often lost the thread of their conversations when she did speak. Her voice was calm and soothing, and he had to admit sometimes he simply enjoyed listening to the lilt and flow.

He couldn't pin down her accent at all. A D.C. resident who didn't have that soft touch of the South. But neither did she have the New York rhythms, though she did admit to being raised there in addition to schooling there.

It was a voice he could listen to for hours... But she didn't speak on the phone.

That was it. So much of Daniel's life was done by phone. Calls to the Hill, overseas with the assistants of other world leaders, that was his comfort zone. Alice, so open and cheerful in person, was, at best, reticent on the phone.

He dropped his feet to the floor and stared out at the white oak tree beyond his window. Bare of leaves it spread its arms in reaching majesty. It had been too long since he'd been out in the country. Camp David a couple of times, but he hadn't been down to visit his dad or sister on the farm in at least six months, maybe closer to a year. If they hadn't come to D.C. every month or so for a visit he'd have gone crazy from missing them.

That's what he had to do. He had to get out of the White House and go see Dr. Alice Thompson. See if there was more behind those few kisses that turned his well-ordered mind into a cloud of confetti. She didn't mind whatever hour he called, maybe she'd be okay if he just showed up instead.

Without turning from the window, he reached back for his phone. He punched for the Secret Service office.

"Hi, I'd like a car." He told the on-duty officer who answered. "Destination is Woodmont, the home of Dr. Thompson."

He hung up the phone, nodded to himself in the window. Good decision. Do something for Daniel rather than the country. He liked the way that felt. It felt right.

A gift. He should bring her a gift. Especially since he'd be rousting her out of bed.

There was a thought to stop him. Daniel found it very easy to imagine how Dr. Thompson would look tousled with sleep, blinking up at him through a partially open front door.

He spun back to his desk seeking something better than a White House-logoed mug and there she was. Sitting in his chair as if she'd been there a while.

Daniel searched for words. Found none.

He blinked twice. Still there. A third time. No change.

Her smile grew, "You might want to raise your jaw. It looks funny all open like that."

He managed to close it.

"You're here?" It came out as little more than a croak.

She reached out with one of those beautiful, slim-fingered hands and poked a single finger against her thigh as if testing.

"Yes, I appear to actually be here."

"That's why you didn't answer your phone."

She nodded.

"You were here when I called you."

"I could hear the ring. Something like fourteen times. How deaf do you think I am?"

Daniel didn't know what to do with that one and decided the wisest course might be to just let it go.

"I did like that you'd memorized my number rather than just setting me up on speed dial."

Then he'd avoid mentioning that he barely knew how to work the new phone system. And hers was the only number he'd called during his year in this office that wasn't routed through Janet.

"You are going to say something substantive eventually, aren't you?"

He nodded but still couldn't find the clutch to engage his brain.

Her laugh rippled out and up, rising a quick octave.

That finally shook him loose. He rose and circled the desk, or started to.

His jacket caught the stack of files on the desk and only a quick dive saved a repeat performance of the earlier night. By the time he had the mess stabilized and dared once more turn his attention on Alice, she too had risen to her feet.

"I—"

She raised a hand, palm out. "Nothing mundane."

That threw out the half dozen sentences that tumbled into his mind. "I'm so glad to see you. Why are you here? How..." Nope. Chuck them all.

Daniel could converse with world leaders, charm their children, placate their wives. Why couldn't he be coherent around Dr. Alice Thompson.

He considered, then edged slightly away from the desk and its teetering paperwork.

Alice tilted her head sideways as if listening to the late night silence of the West Wing.

No sound. More importantly no light from the open door leading to the Oval Office. If Daniel could take time to do one thing, it would be what had been in the forefront of his thoughts since the last time he'd been with her.

He leaned in to kiss those smiling lips. Raised a hand to brush back her hair so that he'd be able to watch both of her eyes close on a sigh. And—his phone buzzed.

He cursed. "No!" He growled at Alice from a mere inch away. "Let the world run on its own for one blasted moment."

"The car." Alice told him as the phone buzzed again.

"What car?"

"The one you ordered."

"I ordered a car?" All he could concentrate on at the moment was that Alice was here. So close he could feel the warmth of her skin on his cheeks. The phone's shrill buzz was not helping the moment.

"To come see me. There was some reason you wanted to see me. What was that?"

The phone interrupted his response. He answered it with what he could only describe as a snarl.

"Your car is ready, sir."

"Why would I want a car?"

The agent sputtered for a moment.

Alice rested a hand on the center of his chest, toying a little with his tie where it stuck up out of the vest. She tugged him down by it until her lips were by his open ear.

"So that we can neck like teenagers in the backseat." Her breathy whisper tickled.

"Uh," he managed. That was almost exactly why he'd wanted a car. He'd had some idea of talking with Dr. Alice Thompson face to face, perhaps over a glass of wine and getting to know her. But he'd also had a clear idea of that slumberous look he'd imagined.

"I," he cleared his throat twice before he could continue, "uh, won't be needing it after all. Thanks." He did his best to get the phone back in the cradle but knew he fumbled it badly.

He turned back to kiss her. But it was too much, too fast. No matter how much he wanted her, it was a lousy way to run a relationship. An even worse way to start one.

"I," was all he managed.

Her smile had shifted, subtly, from amused to soft. "It seems you missed me."

He nodded. Not trusting to words yet.

She glanced up at him through those bangs.

This time, his hand rose more naturally to brush her curls aside. He cupped her cheek and leaned into a kiss.

They moaned in unison.

Daniel couldn't pull her close enough.

He didn't have the strength to take her home.

He didn't have the patience to take Alice upstairs.

Daniel broke the kiss and walked away.

CHAPTER NINETEEN

A*lice stumbled a half* step forward as Daniel strode away from her across his office.

This couldn't be happening.

For a week his voice had filled her ears, her thoughts, and was now invading her dreams. His stories of his life had wrapped around her until she could taste them more clearly than his first kiss.

It had taken all of her bravery to come to him, to find her way back to the office of the White House Chief of Staff. To expose herself to whatever Daniel's reaction might be.

She watched him close a door to his secretary's office.

Yet Daniel had never explained his reactions during the conversation at the piano in any of those late night phone calls. He'd never said why he had turned from her and practically run from the room at that dinner with President. The man radiated such light, but some darkness tore at him. It tore at her too, like a knife.

He closed the door to the hallway.

Alice steadied herself with a hand on the edge of Daniel's desk. She'd come to the White House because there was no one else she could trust to test an idea she'd had about North Korea. An idea too impossible to trust, yet it ate at her until it reaching the tipping point between skepticism and possibility.

His reaction to her had been electric. Listening to his frustration of trying to call her had been funny and absolutely charming.

Daniel closed the door to the Oval Office. Then he leaned his forehead against it. As if wrestling with something. How to tell her they were done? That couldn't be it.

Maybe she'd ruined it by coming here. On the phone, fine, but not in person. No one who knew her wanted her. All too intimidated that they weren't the smartest in the room. All those men who couldn't handle how easily she saw through their games and stratagems.

Daniel was the first man she couldn't read. She'd thought there was something there, but she'd been wrong.

She pulled up her shields and turned to run from the room.

Daniel hadn't moved. He still leaned against the door. Then actually turned a key, an old brass key, in the door to the Oval Office.

Alice could hear the bolt click home in the echoing silence of the room. Then Daniel turned to look at her, his back against the door he'd just bolted.

She'd misjudged? Could his need for her possibly match her own for him? Her mother's voice was asking how could she use this to her own gain, and Alice did her best to shove that aside.

Alice's own question dragged her across the dark green oriental carpet that covered most of the dark wood floor.

He watched her without moving. His eyes a dark blue so intense that no shield could stop his gaze. She'd worn a knit red sweater, intricate with clockwork cables that she'd had to tear out a half-dozen times in order to make them right.

Not once as she approached did he look down at her sweater. Not at her chest. Not at her jean-wrapped hips. Not at her sneakers, red with green laces this time. All he did was watch her eyes, and she couldn't look away. If there'd been a chair or table between them, she'd have walked square into it.

Only when she came to a halt did he react.

He reached a hand as if to tentatively stroke her from shoulder to elbow, but let it brush air instead, then drop to his side.

Alice watched him a moment longer. Trying desperately to read his face.

For half a moment she considered calling his bluff. Perhaps toss off some funny line.

It was a half moment too long.

Daniel swept her into his arms. He'd have knocked the wind from her lungs if his mouth had not already covered hers. She wrapped her arms around his neck so that there was no possibility of him walking away from her this time.

The fire of need wrapped around them despite the chill December night beyond the window. She'd never been the forward one in sex, but she had his tie pulled loose and his vest and shirt undone so that she could curl against his chest. It was as beautiful as when he'd been pumping iron over in the residence. That she'd been prepared for.

What took her totally unawares was the softness of his skin and the heat of it. This was a place dreams were born.

With a near shoulder-dislocating wrench, he shed his coat vest and shirt into a pile on the floor. She wrapped herself next to his warmth like a good winter blanket. It was only half a surprise that they were skin to skin. She hadn't noticed the loss of her sweater and ever-present turtleneck.

"Wow! Dr. Thompson." He was holding her out at half arm's length and looking down at her torso.

She went to cover herself with her arms. "What?"

"First, you need to know that I have an excellent imagination."

"So?" She got one arm free and across her chest.

With the gentlest motion he took her wrist and moved her arm out of the way.

She'd never felt so naked in her life.

"I never imagined how good you could look. Not even in that knock-out evening gown. You're beautiful."

The heat flashed to her face. Cute? Sure, she'd been called that. But beautiful? Not that she could recall. Not ever.

He was smiling down at her.

"What!?" It came out with more force than she'd intended.

"Your blush starts lower than I expected."

She glanced down at the fair skin atop her breasts, the capillaries now flushed with blood attempting to release the heat coursing through her.

Some rebellious part of her self-defense mechanisms rose to the fore. "Well, what are you going to do about it?"

His smile grew. Grew until it lit his eyes. Damn! She could almost swear they twinkled. Why not? Christmas was coming after all.

"I'll revel!" And with that he leaned down and did just that.

CHAPTER TWENTY

lice stretched comfortably back to consciousness.

No surprise revelation of where they'd landed. Daniel's bedroom. Daniel's bed. A sturdy four-poster that had belonged to an 1800s President. He'd said he liked the bed. So had she. It was a beautiful piece of furniture, and if she'd had a couple of bathrobe belts handy, she might have tied him to it. She'd have blushed at the thought, if he hadn't suggested doing the same to her.

In Daniel's office, with no protection handy, they'd still done more on his office carpet than two kids ever did in any backseat. At some point they'd dressed, traversed the corridors, and used the elevator to the third floor so that they wouldn't disturb the President on the second floor.

Alice did her best to not look at the Secret Service agents they'd passed in the lower halls. Even if the agents didn't reveal knowing looks, she knew they were there, carefully masked by neutral expressions.

Some of them did smile at her as she gawked at the decorations. Even the lower level passage of the Center Hall had been strewn.

"Last year was pretty somber, so recently after the First Lady's death," Daniel had told her. "I think we're overcompensating this year, but it is terribly cheerful."

She couldn't argue on either point. The length of half a football field, it had been done as a Christmas in miniature. Walls had been lined with multi-tiered villages, as if the Swiss Alps had been shrunk down to fit into the White House. You could spend a week and never see it all.

She smiled to herself, remembering they'd spent less than five minutes in their desperate need to get upstairs.

Here Daniel did have protection and they'd made use of it until they were so exhausted and sweaty that they'd scampered down the hall wearing only a couple of his dress shirts, through the Music Room, and up the half-flight of stairs to stand on the wintery Promenade. They'd had to dance foot-to-foot because the deck glittered with a dusting of frozen dew. They'd held each other so close that they were almost warm enough despite the freezing temperature as they watched the chill moonlight battle the nighttime lights of D.C.

They'd scrambled back inside, plunged into a hot shower and fallen back into bed.

Yes, she knew exactly where she'd woken. No surprise there.

Where she'd woken alone. Also not a real shocker. It was mid-morning by the discreet bedside clock and Daniel would have plunged into meetings long since.

The surprise instead was how she felt.

Her body was languid and supple after such an incredible bout. Sore in more than a few spots, but Daniel was a gentle lover, even at his most energetic. Despite her fair skin, she didn't see a single mark. Alice wasn't sure if her body had ever felt this good.

But that bone-deep made-of-liquid feeling didn't surprise her either. It was the guilt. She felt no guilt about the sex, they'd both enjoyed it far too much for that.

No, Alice felt bothered by her own silence. Daniel had again probed into her past. Ever so gently, in that immensely tactful way she'd learned was the trademark of a very successful man. But she could feel his disappointment as she again evaded describing a past she'd much rather disown. He no longer fell for her redirection and razzle-dazzle subject changes. He wanted to know about her past. Didn't he understand how little it had to do with her present?

She dragged her lazy bones out of bed. There was a probably a maid waiting somewhere, but she did her best to reorganize the royal blue flannel sheets and the Irish Double-Chain quilt done in rich cheery golds and Kelly greens. She rubbed her fingers over it. Hand-stitched and a really fine job of it. Maybe from his family farm. She liked to think of that being his touch of home.

The rest of the room radiated maleness, with rich walnut wainscoting and white-on-white patterned wallpaper. A massive dresser stood staunchly in the corner, matched in style to the sturdy bed. The top was decorated with just two photos. She eased over and inspected them.

First, clearly a family photo. They were an impressive group. Daniel stood out for his beauty, but his sister could do very well in a pageant herself. The photo had captured Mom, Dad, gold retriever, and a big blue tractor the same color Daniel's eyes had been last night. They had shone with a brilliance the moment before he jumped her. Or had she jumped him first?

Second, was a close-up of the sister. Her look was wicked. Just her shoulders and head showing above water that must be in a flowing stream. It was apparent that she had no swimsuit and was not in the least amused by her brother's camera. The look promised a painful retribution. Alice could feel herself smiling at recognizing the shared moment, even if she didn't know the whole story.

She'd have to ask.

Which brought her back to the guilt that kept tickling up her spine. Daniel would tell her anything, and she'd tell him nothing. It was an unfair bargain and she didn't know what to do about it. Alice didn't want to destroy what they had.

She turned for the shower, going past the red leather armchair that held her neatly folded clothes, including the sweater she'd lost somewhere in the hallway. Maybe it had been during their brief stop at the grand piano. No, they'd made love beneath that shortly before getting a late night snack in the kitchen. Early morning snack. The sweater had been long since gone by then.

She stood under the hot shower spray, appreciating the pressure that could deliver a needling massage even here at the top of the building.

The problem was during those moments they'd curled together to briefly recover. Her head on his shoulder, her hand tracing the fine outlines of his chest. Or when he'd curled against her, one ear resting in the center of her breastbone as he listened to her heart.

He'd left her silences to speak into, and she hadn't. She'd felt them grow and expand, take on shape in the dark of the heavily curtained bedroom.

Alice notched up the heat in the shower a bit more, she'd always favored a searing hot shower.

She knew what he wanted. He'd made it clear in the last few phone calls as well. No matter how intimate they were, she was terrified of destroying it by bringing up her past. To someone like Daniel, the past was everything. Filled with family and life and joy. Poster boy for a good upbringing.

While her past hadn't had the terror that some of her friends had, it was just not something that existed anymore. She'd discarded it all and rebuilt herself in her own image. She even had an imagined past; one she shared only reluctantly so that people didn't probe. But with Daniel, each time she tried to pull out the granny who'd raised her after her dad had left and her mother died... It was just wrong. She hadn't been able to lie to him.

What did it matter that she didn't have a past? She was Dr. Alice Thompson, self-made woman.

She rinsed her hair and did her best to pretend that all of the water running down her cheeks came out of the shower head.

CHAPTER TWENTY-ONE

"You dog."

Daniel just laughed which only increased the President's smile. They sat across from each other in the West Wing presidential dining room. The European Union's latest Greece-bailout plan covered the parts of the table that weren't already covered with sausage, pepper, and onion sandwiches, macaroni salad, and potato chips. Tall glasses of iced tea perched on cork coasters.

"You finally saw her."

Daniel nodded. Did way more than see her. He did his best to hide his smile in a large bite of crunchy hoagie roll. Knew he'd been too slow by Peter Matthews' smile.

"Good?"

There were a dozen layers to the question.

"Really good. The sandwich that is," he spoke around a partially chewed bite, but wasn't fooling Peter in the slightest.

"Good." This time the statement was definitive. The President's approval a tangible thing of great importance.

"I think we did way better than 'Really good.'" A woman's voice sounded from the doorway. "'Great!' would at least get you in the right ballpark."

Daniel stumbled to his feet and attempted to swallow nearly choking himself. Alice stood in the doorway to the dining room. She radiated. There was no other word for it. She slouched lightly against a doorframe and looked at perfect ease. Her hair, still slightly damp in spots she'd missed with the blow dryer, a shining cloud about her face. Her eyes were wicked.

The President rose much more elegantly and crossed to her. He took her hand, and shook it with that perfect, real sincerity that Peter Matthews brought to everything he did.

"Good afternoon, Dr. Thompson. Care to join us for lunch?"

She nodded her assent and crossed to the table.

Daniel shoved some of the Greece plan toward the other end of the table, and one of the ushers had a place set even before the President had tucked her chair in beneath her.

"If you don't kiss her good morning, I will."

Daniel finished his swallow, wiped his mouth with a napkin, and did just that. Reveled for just a moment in how soft her lips were. Knew enough about her now to feel both the bright smile and the nervousness beneath. He squeezed her hand in encouragement, a gesture quickly returned, before he returned to his seat.

"We were just taking a quick look at the EU bailout plan for Greece. They dropped twenty billion Euro, twenty-five billion dollars, and it appears to finally be working six months later."

"Now if only the same thing could work in a U.S. market, Mr. President." Alice offered brightly as someone set a plate and sandwich down in front of her.

The President sighed. "The previous administration dropped half a trillion dollars, and mostly it shuffled the balance of problems around. Mitigated the worst of the disasters, but we're still a long way from a solution."

Daniel offered the President a nod. The President had known that Alice would be nervous and chosen a neutral topic to allow her a moment to land. Walking in on the middle of being the subject of conversation... Not good. Really not good.

And the President continued until Daniel found himself able to enter the conversation as well. For twenty minutes or more, they explored general topics while simultaneously working their way through the lunch spread before them.

After they'd set plates aside, and the ushers had swept them away, he could see Alice clearly had something on her mind.

He nodded to her and she smiled back at the encouragement.

"I actually came to see you last night for a, ah, another reason."

———

Alice took a deep breath, thankful that at least the President showed a steady hand. No wry glance at Daniel. No roll of his eyes.

Daniel, on the other hand, should never get near a poker table. He had progressed through a dozen shades of red and twice as many stages of awkwardness since she had invited herself to lunch.

"Good." Somehow, there'd been a whole conversation between them, all wrapped up in one, single word. Guy speak was so strange. Maybe that's why her father had never spoken. Could never even get his one word in edgewise past his wife.

Clear your head, Alice. Back to business.

"I have a theory. And it's a little on the completely whacked-out side of possibility."

The two men nodded in unison, sharing a neat sense of accord. The President waved the ushers out, and the door behind Alice closed with a discreet click.

"I presume we're discussing North Korea."

She nodded to the President. Right. These two could talk about twenty different countries a day. She, however, was only paid to care about one at the moment.

"Who are you planning to send to the meeting?" She'd decided to cast aside any lingering doubts about whether or not there would actually be a meeting. It had been someone else's task to determine the efficacy of that original request. Her task was to decide what to do about it if it was real.

The problem was the back check to verify the situation, however in the world that was done. The response hadn't come through the same channel. The first had been a simply encrypted message, just sufficient to stop prying eyes, but not requiring the NSA to crack it either. The message had passed off to an NGO. Some Non-Governmental Organization that had been granted a three-day pass into North Korea to test for mercury in the coastal waters. They'd come out with a message in hand.

"Daniel has suggested Vincent, the deputy ambassador to the U.N. I was more inclined to Elisa, the Assistant Secretary of State. We never got much past that. Why?"

Alice sipped at her iced tea to buy a moment to collate factors, but they didn't change. The back check had come from the conductor of the Sea of Blood Opera Company at a carefully staged performance in Paris. An abruptly scheduled event, very reminiscent of the 1972 North Korean circus ensemble who had stormed Paris the week before Nixon went to China.

"We could send somebody military, that is if you think that's more appropriate." Daniel's idea.

"I believe," Alice rolled her mental dice and came up double-sixes. A good backgammon roll; the same one that had landed her in Daniel's bed last night. Which had been amazingly worth it. What the hell! Play the game! Double or nothing.

"I believe that we're thinking too small. I think that the Vice President is the minimum you should send, but that you Mr. President should be prepared to follow immediately if not attend yourself."

The President started to shake his head, then noticed Daniel's silence.

Alice studied Daniel as well. In the last few seconds he'd done that mercurial shift; this time from slightly fumbling lover to most astute advisor to the most powerful man on the planet.

She could see the cogs turning. Shifting the pieces to include what he knew of the situation, and what he knew of her.

"What don't I know?" his question came after a full thirty seconds of echoing silence.

"Methods of communication of the two messages. Personalities of the individuals who I termed the Top Six, the highest advisors and leaders in the North Korean regime."

"The personalities I know; which is why I had difficulty accepting your initial report. Two messages?"

"Original channel and back check."

"Which were?"

She shook her head. Alice wasn't even supposed to know, but Director Smith had released the data to her when she'd insisted it was necessary to assess the request's authenticity. Names and exact movements had been expunged from the reports she read, but there was no questioning them. However, she also wasn't at any liberty to reveal them, not even to the President.

Again that silence. Daniel stood and walked slowly to the window and back. God! The man even moved beautifully. She could spend a day simply watching him walk about, with or without clothes.

And in addition to beauty, she realized his other blazingly attractive quality to her; Daniel Drake Darlington would have made an amazing analyst. She could she him working through the possibilities. Interpreting and discarding them far faster than she had. Of course she'd had to build up from a blank slate. He'd had a head start built by her reports and information. Still he—

A low whistle indicated that he'd reached the same conclusion she had. He shook his head in clear rejection of his own conclusions being too preposterous. Definitely the same result she'd synthesized in eight days of hard work.

But finally he turned to her and softly voiced a question, "Really?"

She nodded, which appeared to cut his knees out from under him and dropped him back into his chair.

The President turned from one to the other and finally said, "No. That's not possible." But drew it out in a tone revealing he too would have made a fine analyst.

CHAPTER TWENTY-TWO

"*I can't believe that* you talked me into this!" Daniel had to shout above the roar of the C-17's jet engines and the air being plowed aside at five hundred miles an hour. The Black Hawk helicopter crew were up at the front of the plane. He and Alice sat about halfway down the side of the immense cargo plane.

Alice didn't deign to answer. If her conclusion was right, and the Supreme Leader of North Korea was the one requesting the conference with the American government, then the President had to be ready to appear on a moment's notice.

Daniel's afternoon had been immediately hijacked from all other considerations. Added to that, a second sleepless night in a row, planning and coordinating this time, left him feeling lightheaded and hazy.

Now he was flying West to verify a portion of the preparation personally.

"What did Janet give you in the calendar tonight?" Alice sat on the next fold-down seat mounted along the side of the plane. They were hard and his butt hurt.

The woman was going to make him crazy. He checked his watch. Three in the afternoon. Fourteen hours ago he'd been having a nice sit down lunch with the President, now he was freezing his behind at thirty-thousand feet. How had this happened?

"The sun hasn't even come up yet." Especially not the mid-winter D.C. sun. "And we're flying West through the time zones. We won't even land until sunrise never mind sunset. Now you want to break your own rules?"

They sat in heavy parkas on barely padded seats. They should have pulled on the flightsuits when they were offered, but he'd thought a ski parka would be sufficient. They kept the air inside the plane heated, but the metal skin of the hull sucked the heat right out of his bones.

Two Black Hawk helicopters were aboard. Their rotors had been folded over their tails and they'd been slid in tail-to-tail. The Mil Hound was nowhere to be seen and the two Black Hawks looked absolutely vicious. These were attack craft, weapons hanging to either side from stub wings. Missiles, machine guns, something they'd told him was a cannon able to fire rounds wider than his thumb at a rate over eighty times per second. He'd assumed Major Henderson was kidding, but maybe not. He didn't seem the type to joke about weaponry.

Alice grabbed his arm and rolled his wrist toward her so that she could see the watch upside down.

"Looks like nine-thirty to me. You know, you should get a watch that has those little numbers instead of just hashy marks. It would help you read time better."

"Another of your mother's rules? Adjust everything around you to suit yourself?"

Some of the light went out of Alice's eyes and she released his wrist. She drifted off to a silent place. A place he suddenly feared because maybe he couldn't reach her when she went there.

He did the only thing he could think of and pulled the Advent Calendar book out of his flight bag.

"Now let's see." He turned it so that she could look at it with him. Her face aimed down and her bangs flopped over her eyes, he hoped she was looking with him.

He did his best to make it a cozy moment, despite the need to shout to be heard above the engines.

"I seem of have eaten the first page out of house and home." He made a show of inspecting inside each of the eight pull tab windows on the first page. Sure enough, all empty. He'd described each to her on the phone, but now she could see them one by one. And they were lovely art work.

He turned to the middle page.

This image was a grand sweep of delicate art. A sleigh piled with gifts and a dozen tiny micedeer perched on a roof peak as if they did it every day. Daniel had already eaten the caramel behind the door showing where Santa's hat had caught on a brick inside the chimney.

Around the Christmas tree, a balding but undeniably jolly Saint Hamster, in a red and white jumpsuit that barely contained his furry girth, was scattering presents from his bag.

Daniel opened day ten; a tiny drawing of milk and cookies half eaten, the nibble distinctly two-toothed. Day eleven; inside, a naughty kitten trying to peek through a child-gate pulled across the head of the stairs. Day twelve, behind a picture of great uncle Rex; the good kitten asleep in bed. Day thirteen, Daniel could finally feel Alice's smile though he couldn't see it, a tiny mouse behind a tiny mouse hole curled up and fast asleep in a nest of red-and-green wrapping paper.

Day fourteen; the fourteenth of December, was a tall door running right up the length of the tree's trunk. Inside were a pair of tiny candy canes, shorter than his pinky. Somehow Janet once again knew there would be two of them together. And once again, he'd missed the addition to the calendar's pages.

Two weeks. He'd only known Alice two weeks. It was unimaginable. Partly because he'd had sex with her, he'd never done that so soon, and also because he couldn't imagine a day when he couldn't at least speak with her. How had she become so important so quickly?

Daniel handed one of the candy canes to Alice and took the other himself. As they peeled off the plastic, they looked inside the calendar window to see a different version of the tree. Smaller, standing still in the woods with its companion trees. Somehow it looked to be asleep wearing a little nightcap of snow, and it had a dream bubble reaching up into a starry sky of being a real Christmas tree someday when it grew up.

"So, do you taste like a candy cane?" When Daniel brushed her cheek, she looked up at him with a slow reluctance. He didn't say anything. Didn't ask anything. He simply kissed her. Long and slow and deep, reveling in the taste of her. The feel of her.

He pulled back just a little and nodded. "Yep! Alice and candy cane. Knew that was a winner combination without even guessing."

Her smile thanked him for not pushing. The eyes, those amazing hazeled eyes, he wished he could borrow a bit of elf magic and wipe them clear of whatever bad memory still lurked there. She held his hand tightly in hers, and leaned her head on his shoulder.

Daniel leaned back against the hull of the aircraft, feeling the vibration become a part of his body. With the Advent Calendar across his lap in one hand, and Alice's fingers wrapped warmly in his other hand, Daniel could feel content. As if he were in the right place at the right time.

He rested his cheek on Alice's impossibly soft hair, closed his eyes, and let the exhaustion of a pair of sleepless nights take him under.

CHAPTER TWENTY-THREE

Daniel *tried to assess* him, but the man was so totally nondescript that Daniel never would have noticed him on the street. Now they sat in a small restaurant at Skagit County airport, which sat in a far corner of Washington State.

"Captain Smith," the man they'd flown across the country to meet smiled with a bit of chagrin, "My real name, I promise."

Captain Smith of the Canadian Special Operations Aviation Squadron. SOAS was one of those spec ops groups that almost no one had heard of. They weren't Delta or SEAL or SAS, but they were impressively effective in their own quiet way. Daniel had read the reports carefully when Beale had recommended he contact them.

He and Alice, Majors Beale and Henderson, and Captain Smith sat upstairs in the restaurant looking out over parked private planes and the sleepy runways. At the far end of the room, a half dozen vacant tables scattered across the space between them, sat the two Black Hawk crew chiefs, Tim and John.

No one else. The waitress had returned downstairs to fill their various breakfast orders.

Almost lost in the rainy haze, dull gray against the gray-green of the moss-covered fir trees, the C-17 transport lurked on an unused taxiway at the back of the airport. The flight crew had remained there as a standing guard. The flight engineer was downstairs getting some breakfasts to go for them.

No scheduled flights bounced through Skagit, not until the tulip season. The waitress, recognizing them as obvious out-of-towners, had regaled them with stories about the local farms which supplied ninety percent of the nation's tulips. The wall was hung with dozens of colorful photos offering mute testament to her statements about the number of sight-seeing flights in the high season. Each incongruously draped with red-and-green Christmas garlands that had seen a few too many seasons.

The two crew chiefs were sitting nonchalantly by the head of the stairs at the opposite end of their otherwise vacant dining area. Big John, the giant of the pair, was riffling a deck of cards. Tim, "Crazy Tim" Daniel had been informed, had tossed some coins on the table. Daniel had learned enough about them to know that no matter how casual they appeared, they were intently watching the parking lot out the window, listening for stray noises from the main restaurant below, and guarding each other's back. They moved with that perfect harmony of good friends and immense training.

"Skagit County airport in mid-December," Captain Smith observed. "Stone quiet and perhaps a twenty-minute flight for the U.S.-Canadian border. I find those are interesting aspects of your curious locale for a meeting."

"Captain Nathaniel Smith?" Alice asked with surprise, emphasizing the first name.

He nodded easily.

"You flew the Sudanese mission in 2006?"

The man didn't move. He'd shifted from a pleasant man with a light British accent to cold steel in a single heartbeat.

The crew chiefs sensing the change visibly tensed at the far end of the room. The Majors set down their coffee cups ever so nonchalantly, probably to empty their hands in case sudden action was required.

Daniel braced to interpose himself between the man and Alice. Captain Smith would be easy to remember now. The captain, so common-looking a moment ago, now radiated the chill of death.

"That was well done, sir." Alice held out her hand. "I'd be honored to shake your hand."

Captain Smith gingerly shook her hand as if she were a grenade about to go off in his grasp.

Daniel recognized the look, as if the Captain's brain had just been sideswiped by a speeding locomotive. Daniel often felt that way around Alice.

The two Majors inspected the Captain more carefully, but Daniel could see by their quick exchange of looks that neither knew what Alice was referring to. He didn't either.

"How?" the Captain's voice was rough.

"That was approximately the same time that I was performing a departmental assessment of flight abilities of various allied Special Operations Forces operators. Your career has been, I believe 'distinguished' would be a fitting word. Naturally when I learned that the asset of a close U.S. ally had flown the mission, there was at least an eighty-five percent probability you had been on that flight."

"Uh, I was commander of the mission."

"Seventy-two percent probability. Yes!" Alice raised her hand palm out and the Captain high-fived her before he could stop himself.

Captain Smith glanced around the table, eyed each of them warily before returning his attention to Alice. He rubbed his fingers together as if the high-five had somehow changed their texture.

"What are you?"

Daniel leaned forward, ready to jump to her defense, but she simply offered one of those disarming smiles.

"I'm a specialist in logistics. There are perhaps a dozen people in the world who could recognize your trademark actions, if they bothered to look, maybe only a half dozen. I'm one of them."

Once again he assessed the circle about the table, then offered a soft laugh.

"My job is to be invisible. I find it, ah, less than reassuring that I am not."

Alice patted his arm. "If I were allowed, I could tell you some stories about these two that would alarm them no end." She nodded toward the Majors. "Several of them with well over ninety percent probability."

Henderson positively blanched, but Beale nodded. "That would not surprise me. Alice can be remarkably astute, Captain."

"So I see."

He stood and took his coffee cup over to the glass pot the waitress had left on a warmer plate when she'd taken breakfast order.

Daniel could see that his hands were not rock steady. Apparently the captain made the same observation of himself. He stopped pouring for a moment, took a deep breath, then finished the task with rock-steady hands. Captain Smith returned to the table and took his seat with a calm that almost belied the moment he'd needed to recover.

"And what remarkably astute observation has caused me to cross into U.S. territory for such an eclectic conference?"

Daniel had thought about sliding up to the subject carefully, to test the man out. But if Alice approved of Captain Smith, and he in turn was apparently coming 'round to appreciating Alice, perhaps he would forego that step.

"We need a meeting location."

The Captain did not state the obvious, that U.S. soil had thousands of locations just as obscure as the present one. He knew that he wouldn't have been contacted if that were the issue. He nodded for Daniel to continue.

"As I'm sure you just surmised, it cannot be on U.S. soil. Yet we want it to be very near. It must have immense security that can be implemented by a minimal force."

"As the White House Chief of Staff is seated across the table from me, I can assume some measure of the care required. Though your lack of Secret Service escort must be truly irritating someone back in Washington, D.C. Does that also speak to the scale of your ultimate operational requirements?" The Captain waited with that amazing stillness Daniel had witnessed in so many of the Spec Ops best operators.

Highest security was required for this mission. And with each person they added, that needed secrecy became less reliable. Daniel nodded toward the flight crew presently in the room.

"This is it. Full team. Maximum protection. Maximum." He let the last word hang.

The Captain whistled quietly.

Achieving a truly high-level protection force with only four people was a contradiction of terms. A simple bodyguard detail even for Daniel would normally be two or three. The President's public visits, between advance site prep, security, press, and so on, often exceeded five hundred people not counting local law enforcement for crowd control. President Clinton had once planned to visit the African nation of Burkina Faso. They'd had to cancel when the advance team determined that there were insufficient hotel rooms in existence in the entire capital city of Ouagadougou to accommodate the President's full entourage.

"We're the site approval and inspection team. I doubt there will be many more for the meeting itself." Daniel tried not to think about that. "A day of site prep. Probably two nights and one day on site."

"Don't suppose you're going to tell me who will be visiting?"

Daniel glanced at Alice for a moment.

After a hesitation, she nodded her head.

Daniel could feel his shoulders ache as if he'd just done fifty reps with too much weight. Every single thing Alice had said so far had played out. From the arms smugglers in Pakistan, to Captain Nathaniel Smith, to the back check that North Korea actually would be sending someone.

Except for the absolute impossibility of the situation, he had no reason to doubt her next conclusion either. North Korea's Supreme Leader Kim Jong-un was leaving the safety of his country to meet privately with the President of the United States.

Alice reaffirmed the nod more certainly. Brushing her hair aside to glare at him without even the partial screen of her bangs.

Daniel resisted the urge to sigh. This grew trickier by the minute.

"We're unsure," he had to decide how completely to trust the Captain. He hadn't even told Majors Beale and Henderson yet about Alice's conclusions. Need to know. Well, to keep the President safe, they now needed to know. All three of them. He took a deep breath and forged on, keeping his voice low.

"I wouldn't be shocked if we were hosting two heads of state."

That caused enough reaction at the table for the two crew chiefs seated at the far end of the room to spring to their feet and slip hands onto their sidearms.

Beale recovered first and waved for them to stand down.

Tim and Big John returned to their seats very slowly. But not until they performed a careful scan of the room, out the window to the sparsely used parking lot, and down the stairs to where the lone morning waitress was waiting for the breakfast order to be cooked. They finally settled back into their chairs.

Daniel turned back to face Captain Smith and the Majors. Daniel offered a slow nod as confirmation that he too believed the assessment.

The Captain didn't need to know which other country was involved. The fact that the U.S. President would likely be holding a secret meeting on Canadian soil with a tiny security detail was already too much information.

The Majors had obviously reached other conclusions based on their deeper knowledge of the situation. They looked even more sober than usual. They'd been ready to fly into North Korea. That hadn't fazed them for a moment. That they might well be transporting Kim Jong-un, the country's Supreme Leader, was a different matter entirely.

The chill remained only half a moment longer.

By the stairs, one of the crew chiefs scraped his chair back loudly sending a clear signal. The cheery waitress climbed the stairs wielding a large tray piled with dishes. The smells of a hot breakfast reminded Daniel that all he'd had in the last twenty-four hours was a quick sandwich at his desk and a finger-sized candy cane.

Everyone slipped into casual-mode so easily that Daniel had trouble crediting the room's tension from a moment before.

"Did you ever sail among the San Juan Islands, Alice?" Captain Smith asked it as if they had been discussing nothing but sailing for the last half hour.

Right in character, she shook her head, rested her elbow on the table, and propped her chin on her hand. So attentive she appeared to be flirting. Daniel was a little surprised at the hot trickle of jealousy up his spine despite his mind knowing the reaction to be ridiculous.

"I really prefer the Canadian Gulf Islands myself," Smith waved a negligent hand out the window and toward the northwest using the excuse to slouch a little closer to Alice. "Quiet up there. Fewer folk, on and off the water. There's this little bakery in Pender Harbor, fresh baked sourdough every morning. Whenever I sail in there, I buy a loaf and a stick of butter. That bread alone is as fine a meal as they set in any landside restaurant. No offense, ma'am," he nodded to the waitress.

"None taken. I've had that bread when we've gone up gunkholing on our little boat." She turned to Alice. "Fine eating if you get the chance, Miss."

"Gunkholing?"

"Definitely not from 'round about here. Gunkholing is, well, it's just puttering around for the hell of it. Pardon my language."

Daniel took a deep inhale and let it out slowly as he received his two eggs over easy on English muffins with hash browns and bacon.

When the waitress finally left, after regaling them the best way to cook fresh Dungeness crab on the boat barbecue, Smith returned them to the main topic.

"There is a little island that should interest you. A tad bit over eighty kilometers to the northwest. Privately-owned island. A single building. Non-resident owner. Only access is by air, unless you have the control code for the dock crane. That will better explain itself when viewed in person. High cliffs, large front lawn. Trees and, at this time of year, a truly deep sense of privacy. Not many fools sailing the channels in mid-December."

"How well known?" Major Beale asked.

"Not very," Smith dug a fork into his tall stack with bacon and sausage. "When the joker who built the crazy place was looking for an on-call helicopter service, he wanted the very best. Ended up calling a buddy of mine, retired SAS pilot who had moved from Glasgow to open a small Vancouver helicopter service. Flies for him, and still does the odd flight for me to keep his hand in."

He turned to the Majors, "Either of you ever flown with James McKee?"

Emily Beale burst out laughing. "Tried to pick me up in the midst of a deep-ocean search and rescue operation back when I was a first lieutenant and he was a charming son-of-a-bitch freshly done with wife number four."

"Yes," Smith smiled. "That would be James. You're his type, doesn't surprise me."

"What?" Beale asked. "Female?"

Smith laughed. "Exactly. Also he's very partial to a woman who flies. Regrettably he's on vacation to see his second or maybe it's his third set of kids. They're in London."

"Do we need him?" Major Henderson's voice was little more than a growl. His protectiveness of his wife, even for events long before they met, made Daniel feel less bad about his own reaction of jealousy about Alice.

"Don't need him for a second," Smith offered. "All you need is the ten numbers of the security code, which I happen to know."

CHAPTER TWENTY-FOUR

They unpacked one of the Black Hawks from the C-17.

Alice watched from inside the cavernous cargo bay of the transport jet as the crew chiefs hauled one of the helicopters down the rear ramp and out into the chill rain. It required the better part of thirty minutes for Tim and John to unfold the rotor blades and prepare for flight. The Majors had spent about ten minutes circling the bird doing the external preflight checks before moving into the cockpit. Captain Smith had tagged along and now squatted just behind the pilots' seats, clearly talking shop.

They were all acting as if it were a normal day. Perhaps it was for them. Alice was ready to find the nearest walk-in freezer to warm up. It was merely freezing in Washington, D.C. The Pacific Northwest weather had supplied a slanting rain that was several degrees warmer and felt twice as cold. Even though she'd been sitting dry inside the belly of the C-17, she could feel the cold wind as it tested and probed the entire length of the cargo bay through the open rear ramp.

Daniel stood outside too, the hood of his parka up. Not quite in the way, but not out of it either. Clearly enjoying being a guy around other guys doing guy things. He'd watched as they pinned the rotor blades in place. Once they showed him how, he'd tossed a line over the ends of the long rotor blades that had been tucked over the tail. He towed each one so that Tim and John who were perched atop the Black Hawk could pin them into place. Then as the crew chiefs worked their way around the bird undoing covers, checking door latches, and a hundred other little details, Daniel asked questions.

Alice would bet that he didn't forget a single detail either. Every item finding its cubbyhole in his neatly ordered mind. Her own mind felt more like a filing system crossed with a smallish hurricane. Her ability to retrieve and relate facts remained a constant mystery whenever she tried to explore her own process. Daniel didn't appear to go there. His mind, while at least as exceptional as his body, appeared to be something he simply used. Didn't analyze. Didn't deconstruct. He just used it.

Sounded like a nice, gentle place to be. She wished she could try it someday.

They finally waved her over and she scampered through the rain. Only Daniel's quick hand atop her head spared her cracking it on the cargo bay doorframe. The Black Hawk's deck was a high step up, but the bay itself measured barely over four feet from deck to roof of the cabin. A couple of small seats had been attached there, three across the back facing forward and two at the front facing backward.

She and Daniel took two of the seats in the back. He patted the middle seat and she slid in gratefully, as far as possible from the freezing outside world and able to rub shoulders with Daniel.

Captain Smith sat across from them.

The two crew chiefs went forward and took their own positions after sliding the cargo bay door shut. They rode sideways, each facing out a small window. The windows actually only appeared small. Each was mostly filled with a steerable minigun capable of firing six thousand rounds a minute, a buzz saw of death.

A shiver having nothing to do with the temperature shook Alice so hard it almost hurt. Never had it been so personal, seeing the danger she was placing people in. She rarely left her cubicle at CIA headquarters. She'd make an analysis, and people would act on it. These people, ones she now knew, would fly into harm's way because of what she'd learned. They were sitting in a craft of war. And this time her analysis would be sending them into North Korea.

The Majors closed their own doors and within moments the twin turbines had spun up until they were a high background whine, a sound she knew would be in her sleep for days to come. The heavy thud of the rotors began to beat the air hard enough that it felt like a body blow.

With a deepening of the rotor's roar and a slight forward tip, they were airborne. Within moments they were over water, barely, but above it. She knew that Puget Sound was close to the south end of the runway, but she knew they were supposed to heading northwest. Maybe they were circling around to make sure no one had their trail. At twenty-feet above the curling winter whitecaps of Bellingham Bay, no radar would be following them.

Daniel slid an arm over her shoulder, but there was no way to talk. She leaned in for the warmth and comfort, and watched the world flash by out the large windows in the closed cargo doors. Steep islands appeared abruptly, stabbing their conifer-covered heads briefly toward the sky before sweeping back toward the roiled ocean waters. They slalomed between the islands as smoothly as any ice skater, at least one dumb enough to be gliding a half second above instant death. If they caught a wave at this speed they'd be dead before even the best pilots could react.

Somehow the impossibility of the situation didn't worry her. Whatever the fates had in store, they were in control at the moment. Not Alice Thompson. Not even a little.

With Daniel's arm warm about her, she felt safe. She felt for the first time as if she belonged.

The brilliant outsider, the analyst that no one could feel comfortable around, faded away. The one that everyone assumed could see right through them. But she couldn't. She didn't understand individuals, herself least of all. Politics, sure. Socio-economic dynamics of battle, no problem. What the guy next to her was thinking, never. At least not until Daniel.

She lay her head against his shoulder and soon fell asleep in the safest place she'd ever known.

CHAPTER TWENTY-FIVE

D*aniel didn't hear any* change to the helicopter's rotors, but Captain Smith signaled they were nearing their destination.

He wanted to tell Beale and Henderson to just keep flying. To never stop. Alice asleep inside the curl of his arm, her hair soft, brushing his cheek.

The Canadian Gulf Islands out the window looked wilder than the American San Juans. The forests had fewer breaks for houses. Roads were narrow lanes rather than stretches of well-paved-and-striped two-ways. Fifty miles northwest of the airport and they'd also illegally crossed an international border.

He shook Alice gently awake. There was no way over the rotor noise, but he'd swear he could hear a hum of contentment from Alice as she turned her face into his shoulder.

Daniel hesitated because Captain Smith sat there facing them from two feet away.

Screw it.

He brushed Alice's chin upward with a soft caress and then kissed her awake.

Half awake, she leaned in; soft, warm, slow, luscious.

Daniel's seatbelt was abruptly too tight across his lap in exactly the wrong place.

When fully awake, there was no sudden hesitancy. As if she knew even in her sleep exactly who she was kissing. Sitting here, in a roaring helicopter, might well be the sexiest moment of his life. Not for any of his body's happy imaginings about sex, but for the familiar sensuality in Alice Thompson's kiss.

The helicopter banked and Daniel glanced up to see a daunting cliff wall very close outside the window.

"Holy wow!" Alice's observation was just audible.

Thirty or forty feet high, the cliffs soared straight out of the pounding waves. The water must be deep because no pile of boulders huddled around the base. Anything that broke free here was headed for deep water. A steady turn lasted them through a full 360-degree circuit around the island. All cliff.

Then the Majors flew the helicopter upward on a second circuit around the perimeter. Tall stands of dark, dark evergreen trees capped the rugged island that couldn't be much over a quarter-mile across. As they returned to the south side, an opening appeared in the forest.

A green lawn notched back into the trees. Near the cliff edge perched a massive metal-lattice crane. At the end of the crane dangled a floating dock, presently placed on the high meadow. Clearly, you could show up in your boat, engage the remote control, and swing the dock down to the water forty feet below for moorage. A long walkway dangled from the lower side of the crane boom, creating a bridge from ship to shore when it was in position.

Of course, right now, you'd have to be suicidal to brave the roiled winter waters.

Upslope, beyond the crane, a helipad had been leveled out in the middle of the yard. Even a bright orange windsock, which stood pointing like an angry finger to the north indicating a strong southerly wind despite the shielding trees.

At the head of the slope stood a very traditional stone house. The kind of house that would stand out even in an affluent neighborhood. Not for its size, though it wasn't small, but rather for an English elegance. Ivy had climbed up the lower third of the front, creating a sunshield over a deep porch facing the view.

Daniel lost the view as the helicopter spun to face the wind and the wheels touched down on the helipad.

With the rotors still cranking, the crew chiefs piled out and tied the helicopter down to the large iron rings sunk into the helipad's surface.

As the rotors finally wound down, and Daniel's ears popped in relief, they all piled out into the roaring wind beneath a sky of crystalline, winter-blue and just stood there staring at the house. It was impossible, unlikely, and absolutely perfect.

The house looked pleasant, stood on neutral soil, and could be secured by a minimal team.

"Damn! That's sweet." Alice's comment, barely louder than the wind, set them in motion across the lawn toward the house.

CHAPTER TWENTY-SIX

O*ne of the things* Daniel had learned during his year as the White House Chief-of-Staff was that any concept of what he'd thought it meant to be busy was impossibly naïve. And in the week following the visit to the island house, it only got crazier. Seven days since his one-day trip across the country and back. He must have slept and eaten at some point, but right now he was far too tired to recall.

He slumped in his office chair.

Janet had somehow made room for a tiny Christmas tree, more of a Christmas bush, at the corner of this desk. A pine bough trim had been woven around the edges of the "Death Board"; a whiteboard covered with the strategy to defeat a couple of exceptionally short-sighted bills put forth by the opposition party. A small tintype print of a dollhouse that he'd grown rather fond of had been replaced by a triptych of original Currier and Ives lithographs on loan from the Smithsonian.

Daniel closed his eyes and tried to catch up with the last week's events.

The island house had been toured, reviewed, and approved in under ten minutes. They'd ducked back across the border, thanked Captain Smith, and parted ways.

The Black Hawk crew departed to place their equipment and practice for the upcoming assignment. Daniel and Alice had found a small charter to take them to SeaTac airport. At D.C. they'd gone their separate ways and found even less time to be together over this week than the prior one, if that was even possible.

The inner circle on this operation was impossibly small which meant that practically everything had to be done by Daniel himself. That was above and beyond all of the work that came from the tail end of the pre-Holiday session in Congress.

In the last forty-eight hours he'd brokered peace and an acceptable approval margin on bills in education and farming. He'd failed on border and immigration controls, but the President had wrangled that one to the ground by a three-vote squeak in the House and two in the Senate. A win was a win, no matter how close, but it had left both of them strung out and exhausted.

Meanwhile, preparation for the upcoming North Korean operation continued. Beale and Henderson had moved their two Black Hawks into position.

Alice managed to push a message back up the chain to let their mystery guest know the plan once the Majors had finished formulating and rehearsing it.

The head of the PPD, the Secret Service's Presidential Protection Detail, Agent Frank Adams, had been brought into the inner circle.

Frank had headed the detail since the President had first polled in the double digits, long before he was nominated. Frank had ridden herd on three Presidents and dozens of VIPs in his twenty-plus years in the service.

He had protested vehemently when not allowed to add another agent, or preferably an entire division. And when the head of the PPD protested, in that gravelly deep voice of his, and all six-two of him looming over Daniel, instant death in an immaculate black business suit, he paid attention.

Daniel had thought Adams would lock the President in the Oval Office. And maybe just shoot Daniel for good measure. Then the President had mentioned that Major Emily Beale was involved. In that instant the tone of the meeting changed entirely and Frank Adams was on board.

Daniel was left to puzzle over that abrupt change. As far as he knew the only time they'd met was when the First Lady had been killed and the animosity between them at the time had been unmistakable. Daniel tried to get Frank aside on the subject, but he was as mute as the Secret Service always was about security matters.

The one person Daniel never saw outside of strategy meetings was Dr. Alice Thompson. And that was killing him. She'd taken to texting him after the third time he'd fallen asleep with the phone to his ear, while they were talking.

"What's in the calendar tonight?" she asked one night.

"Cinnamon Bears. Spicy!"

"Drink milk."

And milk had worked to soothe the burning heat that had been boring a hole through his tongue.

"Spice drops tonight."

"Christmas wish," she'd texted whatever that night was. "I want to be there to kiss you."

"Sour ones."

"I take back my Christmas wish. Well, not really."

Back and forth by phone and text as the entire middle page of the Advent calendar was emptied door by tiny door.

December 17th. Daniel slumped in his chair, ragged with exhaustion. It took concerted effort to reach out his arm and pull the Advent Calendar off the top of a mountain of vetting folders for a new Supreme Court justice. Arnold Johnson had let them know he'd be announcing his retirement on the first of the year and the scramble was on to choose President Matthews' first replacement on the high court.

Daniel's phone buzzed as he pulled the calendar into his lap. He dragged it out and had to blink several times before his eyes would focus on the message.

"What's the third picture?"

Of course Alice would notice and keep track. Three page spreads, twenty-four days, hence eight days per page. December 17th, the start of page three of the Advent calendar.

He untied the red ribbon and carefully unfolded the book to inspect the interior.

Page one, loading the sleigh.

Page two, the Christmas Hamster leaving the gifts under the tree in such bounty they spilled across the floor.

Page three. He had to stop a moment and catch his breath. It was simply that beautiful.

"What is it?" Alice's text buzzed his phone again.

"It's us." Daniel hit send before he quite realized what he'd done. He looked desperately for an "untext" option, but there wasn't one. Besides, it was true. It was an image that had been forming slowly in his head. Building in quiet layers without his noticing until he saw the image of it spread before him. An image of his life as he couldn't quite see it yet. Or rather hadn't until he opened the page. It was how "home" was meant to be.

"Show me."

"Wish I could," he sent back. But he had hours of work before he'd have a chance of going to bed, never mind time to see Alice.

"Show me."

Daniel hit reply on the phone, but something didn't look right. That's when it registered that he'd heard the last comment, not read it.

He looked up and there she sat across from him, slouched in his chair, red-and-green checked sneakers propped on the edge of his desk. A bountifully soft-looking sweater in palest gold wrapped her like a warm embrace.

When he looked into her eyes, her soft, hazeled, smiling eyes, his phone buzzed sharply.

Habit, he couldn't help himself, he glanced down.

"Show me."

When he looked back up, she raised her hand from below his line of sight and revealed her phone.

He handed across the calendar.

She took it and set it across her lap without sitting up.

Daniel slumped back in his chair and watched Alice as she viewed the final picture on the calendar.

Her bangs had slid down over her eyes but he could see the softness enter her body in the rounding of the shoulders, the cool hand placed against a cheek perhaps suddenly too warm, and finally the palm of her hand rested over her heart.

She looked at it for a long, long time. Then she closed it slowly, as if it were delicate and precious and held it to her chest wrapped in both arms for a moment. She stood and placed it on top of the most stable stack on his desk and circled around to him.

Alice didn't speak. She didn't kiss him. She simply held out a hand. When he took it, she pulled him inexorably to his feet.

In silence, she led him through the twisting passages of the West Wing and the White House. Only when they arrived in his bedroom on the third floor of the Residence, did she speak.

"Show me."

CHAPTER TWENTY-SEVEN

lice woke alone. Knew she was alone in Daniel's four-poster bed without even opening her eyes.

She knew she shouldn't be surprised, but it hurt anyway.

Toughen up, Thompson. You're used to this.

She was. Most men she'd ever dated left before daybreak. Left her alone in her bed or even stranger, alone in theirs. Over time she'd gone out on fewer and fewer dates. And become more and more selective on who passed through the first date successfully, never mind through her door.

Somehow Daniel strode through her barricades from the moment she saw him in that three-piece suit befuddled by an Advent calendar.

Last night had been another voyage into amazing, mind-bending sex. Yet now she woke alone.

She opened one eye to inspect the dent in the navy blue flannel-covered pillow beside her.

No note.

No flower.

Nothing.

She rubbed at her eyes with the heels of her hands and let out a frustrated growl. When the hell was she going to learn?

Time to get moving.

She sat up, the sheets sliding into her lap and one bare leg stretched out to snag her underwear from the floor, when she heard the door open.

"Holy shit!" Daniel's voice was low and hoarse.

He stood barefoot, his shirt partially buttoned, wrong by two buttonholes, and a pair of pants with the belt undone and riding low on those delicious hips. He held a large tray that he was dangerously close to bobbling onto the hardwood floor.

It had a single flower in a slender-necked crystal vase. A red rose. And a breakfast spread that could kill her. The man had cooked for her. It smelled glorious.

"Hold it." Alice thought back through their various conversations. "You never swear."

"I also don't often see the Goddess Venus rising naked from my bed. And I do, too, swear."

"Never heard it." Alice pulled the sheet back up to her neck, and slid her leg back under the covers fighting a blush as hard as she could. At least Daniel had regained control of the tray.

"I don't swear around you."

"Why?"

"You're a lady."

Alice laughed. "No, I'm not!"

Daniel straightened in ire, clearly ready to leap to her defense. His control-of-tray skills once again drifted dangerously toward loss. Not with her flower on it. She scooted forward, trying to trap the sheet across her body with her chin as she rescued the tray. It sort of worked, only one breast was exposed by the time she'd maneuvered the tray to the bed and had the vase safely cradled in her hands.

"Who says you aren't a lady?" He was truly indignant on her behalf.

She let the sheet drop and held her arms out to the sides, careful to keep the rose upright. "Hello, naked in your bed. For the second time. We met less than two weeks ago."

"More than. Sixteen days, five hours, and thirty-eight minutes." He barely hesitated to check the bedside clock.

Alice reached for the sheet again. "What am I going to do with you?" She also knew it to the minute, but that was simply how her mind worked. She certainly hadn't expected him to as well. He kept charming her, even when she didn't want to be.

"Well, I could make a few suggestions, but your breakfast would be cold."

It was long gone cold when they finally got around to eating it.

CHAPTER TWENTY-EIGHT

Alice was tying his tie as he buttoned her blouse. Such a damn gentleman he didn't even feel up the woman he'd just spent most of the night ravaging, and not so many minutes ago slathering with a soapy washcloth in the shower.

"There actually was a reason I came by last night."

He leaned in and kissed her so slowly and gently, as if he had all day rather than a mere six minutes to get to his first meeting of the day.

"Nice, Dr. Darlington. Really, really nice." Alice tried not to sigh like a schoolgirl. "But that wasn't it."

"Oh, well, worth a try."

"Try again..."

He leaned back in eager as a teenager.

"Later." She managed to complete her sentence and place a hand on his chest in time to stop his forward motion. If he kissed her like that again she'd be dragging him back to bed whether or not the Minority Whip was waiting for him.

"They've decided to take the Black Hawks?"

Daniel was sharp enough that he didn't even blink at the topic change. "Yes. The Majors believe they can fly a lower profile with the

Hawks than in the Hound. And the Mil Hound simply didn't have the necessary reactive ability if the situation became sticky."

"Picture it. The new leader of North Korea, a clandestine meeting, and a military helicopter."

"It's probably expected."

"Filled with military personnel..." Alice let her words drag out.

Daniel only hesitated a moment longer before offering a low whistle.

"I didn't see that." He straightened her sweater and her blouse, fussing with the collar, but clearly his mind was somewhere else.

"A civilian needs to be there for the ride." Alice did her best to make it a perfectly neutral statement.

"And that someone is?"

Alice didn't like her answer. Didn't like the image of that helicopter risking its way into North Korea, opening a door into unknown danger, and the man stepping out was...

"Me." Daniel's face went white as he answered his own question. "Oh man. Now I really wish I did swear."

CHAPTER TWENTY-NINE

"**Y**ou promise you aren't going to kill me?" Daniel had to shout to be heard over the noise on the deck of the aircraft carrier.

"Nuh-uh! No such promises." Major Beale was practically laughing at him and Daniel had no recourse.

He was only so much baggage. Had been for the last twenty hours.

Civilian transport had moved him from Dulles to Tokyo over the pole. Then a quick transport had shuffled him down to Kadena Air Base on Okinawa. Thirty minutes later, a Marine Corps V-22 Osprey, only recently authorized to operate over Japanese soil, lifted him into international waters and dropped him on the deck of the aircraft carrier U.S.S. *Harry S. Truman* at close to midnight.

Beale and Henderson had awaited him there. The Sea of Japan was in a very bad mood tonight. Waves strong enough to roll the carrier's deck by several feet rushed by unseen in the darkness below. The wind cast nasty ice particles at his face; cast the same way a machine gun cast bullets, continuous and painful.

The group of them as much blew into as climbed aboard the waiting Black Hawk.

"Is this safe flying weather?" he listened to the rattle of the ice against the cargo bay door windows once they were closed and he could hear himself think.

Big John, one of the crew chiefs, flashed a grin at him from where he somehow had mashed into the tiny seat set up for the crew chiefs.

"When the post office gives it up as a bad job, we do their deliveries."

Great.

Tim handed him a helmet and suggested he buckle in as the turbine engines began whining to life. Outside he could see the organized scurry of the deck crew preparing to receive an incoming jet and launch their helicopter. All their vests color-coded by their tasks. The deck was not awash in a blaze of light as he'd expected. For night operations, they didn't want to blind the pilots, so lights were low and carefully positioned.

Inside the helicopter there was actually very little to see. Daniel sat in one of the three seats across the back of the cabin. Cabin, a glorious word for a space four feet high and perhaps eight-by-eight feet inside. He tried to imagine it crammed with a dozen troops and all their gear and couldn't imagine it. Of course, the Major's helicopter was an attack version, so carrying crew would be less of a priority.

At the very front of the cabin the two crew chiefs sat back-to-back. Immediately in front of them were closed windows. Daniel knew they could swing those windows aside in moments and grasp the controls of the mini-guns rigged there. For now, they were just passive travelers, any information they might need projected on the inside of their visors.

Daniel's visor was clear. A "dummies helmet" he'd been informed. They didn't want to be revealing any more than they had to for their North Korean guest. Henderson figured it would be more politic if Daniel wore the same thing they had. Clear plastic, audio hookup only. And an emergency locator beacon if they had to ditch in the ocean.

What in the world had he gotten himself into?

Straight ahead, between the two armor-wrapped seats, Daniel could see only the dimmest of console lights. They were rigged to be used with the pilots' night-vision goggles; no extra light. There was little variation inside the cabin whether Daniel opened or closed his eyes.

The rotor blades were at full speed now, pounding the night air with the ferocity of a rabid dog.

Daniel contemplated his chances for survival. Storms, aircraft carriers, helicopters at night, North Korea. And he knew that if he lived there were things he'd have to do. One especially. He sent a quick message from his cell phone to set them in motion.

He managed to hit "send" as they jolted rather than lifted into the night sky. Once they crossed over the edge of the carrier's windswept deck, the helicopter plunged abruptly down toward the black of the deep ocean.

Daniel's yelp was going to be the last sound of his life before the waves swallowed him. He wished he'd told Alice. He wasn't sure what, he just wished he had.

He should have sent the text to her instead.

Too late!

With a twist and jerk that elicited another cry he couldn't quite contain, the helicopter's nose tipped forward and they raced ahead.

Daniel leaned over to glance backward out the side window. The aircraft carrier rapidly disappearing astern. Before it wholly disappeared from view, he was able to guess that they were skimming ten or twenty feet above the waves.

"Damn. It. Emily!" It took him two gasping breathes and a dozen racing beats of his heart to get out the three words.

"Sorry, Daniel." Her voice didn't sound in the least contrite. "We didn't want any radar image to show a flight departing westbound. Rather than circling around, we decided to lose ourselves in the clutter cast up by waves and spray."

"You're making me feel so much better."

Daniel decided his best bet was to ignore her. And her husband. He could feel Mark's grin even though he faced forward in the left-hand pilot's seat.

"Left seat? I thought pilot flew right seat on military helicopters." Mark was the senior commanding officer.

"Yep!" Mark replied in a terrible Texas drawl. "My little lady likes to drive and who am I to complain?"

Future note for self, Daniel thought, *this helmet mike picked up even an idle whisper.* Henderson had to be one brave man to call Major Emily Beale, "my little lady." Daniel would bet that even her father didn't take such risks. He knew the President, her closest childhood friend, certainly didn't take such liberties.

"Okay, now it gets interesting. Entering Russian airspace."

"Russian?" Daniel tried looking out the window, but only darkness met his gaze. Away from the carrier, the only light glimmered from the dim console instruments. Unseen waves below, solid overcast above, nasty storm in between. All pitch black.

Henderson continued his commentary as his wife flew the helicopter. "Even in bad weather, North Korea watches their waters pretty closely. There's a risk crossing over a land border, but perhaps less of a risk."

"How much longer is the flight because of the detour?"

"Just a few minutes. Thirty minutes each way total if all goes well."

Daniel wished he'd started a timer on his watch, though it was buried under parka and heavy gloves that barely cut the December cold.

The carrier had been steaming south through the Sea of Japan. That would also draw most of the region's attention with it. It wasn't often that a full carrier group cruised this particular stretch of the world's oceans.

"Feet dry," Beale announced.

At least they were over land now and clear of any rogue wave that might be reaching out to grab them.

Then the helicopter banked hard left, jerked up and dropped back down. Daniel floated for a moment in the chair's safety harness, then slapped back down into his seat.

"Sometimes it gets a little rough," Big John observed in a laconic voice suitable for a summer picnic, "but this storm's mostly out to sea, so it should be a quiet flight."

The helicopter threw him sideways against his harness as it tipped right then left.

"Just got to watch out for trees and things."

"Cows," was Emily Beale's sole offering to the conversation.

Daniel thought about the implications and then just closed his eyes against the darkness.

They were flying so low that she had to maneuver to avoid the cows.

CHAPTER THIRTY

The *helicopter pulled sharply* nose up and felt that forward motion had ceased.

At some point in the flight, he had dropped into a meditative fog, letting the helicopter simply fling his body back-and-forth as it deemed fit. He'd stopped thinking of the long flight since D.C., of the travesty he'd be faced with for having been several days away from his desk. He didn't even think of Alice much. Not as some separate thought. She simply nestled there in the corner of his mind. Giving him a reason to come out of this alive.

It took him a moment to tune into the report that Major Henderson was giving.

"Small building, perhaps five or six rooms. Two outbuildings. Only one vehicle. Coordinates and conditions match. Drone shows no other heat signatures within three miles, though it is not a good night for observing."

Drone. A remote-controlled drone must be patrolling the area, forty pounds of plane flitting through the overhead clouds taking quick peeks below with its infrared camera.

Daniel managed to pull off his gloves and slide up his sleeve enough to see his watch. They were ten seconds from the time that Beale had insisted they'd be arriving. How she nailed ten seconds after a half hour flight across unknown terrain was a good trick indeed.

"Rolling in slow," Emily announced.

The crew chiefs opened their side windows and leaned out. Neither actively grasping the handles of the mounted guns, but he could see them poised to do so.

Daniel unclipped his belt and moved forward between the crew chiefs until he crouched between the pilots' seats. Through the front windshield, he could see very little. A small house, a porch light.

The porch door opened and Emily brought the helicopter to a halt once again, now hovering barely a hundred feet from the building.

One figure stood on the stoop and scanned the night. Clearly hearing the Black Hawk, but having trouble seeing it, a blacked-out bird on a foul night.

A second figure joined the first, a machine gun held across his chest, pointed toward the sky. The second figure took only a moment to pinpoint them in the dark and swing his rifle to bear on their position.

That the second man held a small rifle and Daniel sat behind a bullet-proof windshield in one of the toughest weaponized vehicles ever sent to war, did little to calm his nerves.

"I thought you said just one." Beale's question was clearly meant for him.

Daniel considered Alice's final conclusion during the briefing she'd given him in the back of the car as he'd been driven to the airport.

"If the first man is who we think it is, the guy with the gun is probably his version of Frank Adams."

"You better be right about this." Beale began easing the helicopter forward. "Be real quiet about it boys, but be ready for steel."

Daniel wanted to protest. He knew what that meant. They were in a DAP Hawk, a Direct Action Penetrator Black Hawk, the nastiest weapons platform ever launched into the night sky. The DAP's motto was "We Deal in Steel." A call for "Steel" meant the unleashing of a nearly unimaginable amount of firepower.

But it wasn't his flight. He was only there for the meet-and-greet moment, not for the danger of fifty million dollars' worth of highly classified weapon invading the planet's single most paranoid nation.

Beale eased forward until the rotor was mere feet from the eaves of the house and settled to the manicured lawn. Daniel could feel that she was barely letting the wheels touch, still technically flying and ready to maneuver at a moment's notice.

She left the helicopter's nose pointed directly at the two men on the porch. All weapons to bear.

"You're on, Ace." Henderson leaned into the space between the pilots' seats and nodded his helmet in Daniel's direction.

Right. He moved toward the cargo bay door being opened by one of the crew chiefs, Tim Maloney. Tim snapped a line to the large ring on the front of the vest they'd made Daniel put on.

"In case we have to bug out quickly. Wouldn't want to be leaving you behind."

Daniel stepped down onto the hard-frozen ground and tried not to picture himself dangling beneath a speeding helicopter, then accidentally being smashed into the side of a stray cow.

He stopped at half the distance to the two men, at the limit of his tether, doing his best to ignore the rotors spinning just three feet over his head. They'd told him not to raise his hand above his head if he chose to wave.

He and the two men held the tableau for the better part of thirty seconds. Daniel seriously considered giving the bug-out signal that they'd taught him.

Then the man without the machine gun came forward. He was silhouetted by the porch light behind him. Not until he stopped just a pace away was Daniel able to see his face.

Alice had been absolutely right.

Daniel reached out his right hand to greet North Korea's Supreme Leader, the Supreme Commander of her Army and the First Secretary of the Communist Party, Kim Jong-un.

CHAPTER THIRTY-ONE

The guard had come up close behind the leader.

Kim spoke in rapid Korean. His bodyguard translated, "With who do we meet? You do not look military." By the way he eyed the helicopter, Daniel decided it was a good thing he had come along. In the dim glow of the porch light, with her rotors spinning just an arm's reach overhead, the Black Hawk looked lethal and ready to pounce at the slightest provocation; a mad dog barely chained.

"Daniel Drake Darlington, White House Chief of Staff. At your service."

Another back and forth.

It might have been his imagination, but both men appeared to relax even before the translation began. How good was the leader's English? His file said educated in Switzerland. That meant German and probably French.

"And with who do we meet? And where?"

Daniel wanted to glance back at the helicopter for support, but he knew they were the ones waiting for him.

"I come bearing an invitation from President of the United States Peter Matthews to meet with him on a quiet and secure island in British Columbia, Canada. Other than myself and the four aboard the helicopter behind me, there will only be two others. Only two other people on the planet know about this." Captain Smith was one. And the Vice President had been briefed in the event of foul play.

After waiting for the translation, the two men looked at each other. Daniel could feel his heart beat once, twice, three times. Then, with no signal that Daniel could discern, the one with the machine gun returned to the house, turned off the porch light plunging them into near-total darkness, and closed the door. When he returned, they indicated that Daniel should lead the way.

In sixty seconds the three of them were helmeted and strapped in side-by-side. In ten seconds more they were airborne. The flight then proceeded in perfect silence, not even any comments about the cow and tree dodging.

Not until twelve minutes away from the house.

CHAPTER THIRTY-TWO

"**W**e have a fast-sweep radar ahead." Henderson's comment was calm, uninflected.

"That's a problem. They weren't there when we were inbound." Beale had jerked them to a standstill.

Without asking, the crew chiefs had shoved open their access doors and had their hands on their miniguns.

"Did they hear us on our inbound leg?"

"We entered five clicks to the west. Unless they've lit up the whole border."

Daniel and the two Koreans leaned over to look out the cabin windows. Some vague glimmer of light revealed that they were hovering only a few feet above an open meadow. Trees ahead and to the side were visible as dark blotches in front of the stars.

"We have to climb to get out of here. Twenty-five feet at least. That will put us right in their eyes. All we're hearing now is the spillover and reflections. They won't have any signal on us yet."

The Koreans conversed briefly over the intercom and the guard spoke for the first time since boarding.

"Tests. Last five minutes, no more minutes. We conserve power, no continuous radar." He tried to speak proudly.

But Daniel could hear the bluff, read between the lines. Either they were unsophisticated enough to think that leaving them off most of the time meant they weren't known and mapped; unlikely. Or, more likely, they didn't have sufficient fuel to justify constant operation of the power draining equipment. North Korea had many problems, food and fuel shortages nearing the top of those lists.

Daniel started the lapse timer on his watch.

They knew Pyongyang was surrounded by more anti-aircraft guns than all other cities in the world combined. Over six hundred known sites surrounded the city. Hence their remote country meeting at one of Kim Jong-un's vacation retreats.

But the border was also guarded.

If the radar sweep spotted their helicopter, they might still get out, but they'd never manage to get the Supreme Leader back in with the whole country on alert for an invasion.

The guard started to speak and Daniel could see him waved to silence. He tried again, but finally relented at the sharpness of his leader's gesture.

So, they sat and waited.

Daniel stared at his watch through three minutes. Then four. Then five. He closed his eyes and did his best to not count in his head. To not think about the sheer mass of weaponry planted about them. North Korea's weaponry was old, but current estimates stated that they were so heavily armed they could throw over sixty-thousand tons of highly explosive shells into the air in the first minute.

"It has been seven minutes," Beale stated.

Daniel could feel the sweat soaking this palms, his forehead, his thoughts—murky, confused. His breath was short. Ragged.

"There we go." Henderson sounded cheerful enough that Daniel's thoughts of imminent death eased slightly.

"Sky reads clear. We'll give them another minute."

Daniel spent the very long sixty seconds blessing the people who had trained this flight crew and designed the equipment they used to keep him alive.

CHAPTER THIRTY-THREE

Twenty-five minutes after they set off again, the Black Hawk again flew over the water. By forty minutes they sighted the aircraft carrier.

That's when Daniel told Henderson to send the prearranged signal. The signal that would confirm the previously arranged tour of airbases by the President. The Commander-in-Chief had hastily arranged to offer a personal delivery of pre-Christmas wishes to many of America's fliers.

A tour that conveniently started with Joint Base Lewis-McChord in Tacoma Washington. There, he could land to meet with the Air Force at McChord very publicly, and then quietly cross over to Fort Lewis on the other side of the street; the home of the 4th and 5th battalions of the SOAR 160th, the U.S. Army's Special Operations Aviation Regiment.

When they swooped up from the wave tops to land on the carrier's flight deck with the softest kiss despite the heavy winds the two Koreans came to life.

Daniel couldn't help but enjoy the excitement with which the leader of a country so heavily invested in military strength plastered himself to the rain-streaked window to watch a jet catapult into the night sky. The fighter jet shot aloft with a roar that shook the helicopter. Kim Jong-un's bodyguard was no less interested, for the first time forgetting his absolute vigilance to protect his Supreme Leader.

Even as they watched it disappear into the low cloud cover off to the left, a large battleship-gray jet came from the right, slammed into the deck, and trapped on one of the wires. Its wingspan dwarfed the fighter that had just launched upward, but it lacked the lethal look. It was long, sleek, and had curled tips on the ends of the wings. A Gulfstream passenger jet. Right on schedule.

It was the only idea they had come up with to mobilize their group. The U.S. didn't have any supersonic passenger jets. And with Kim Jong-un's insistence on not setting foot in most countries within a couple thousand mile radius, it had been the only solution to move them all together.

They had discussed putting each individual of the party into the backseat of a Hornet FA-18 two-seat supersonic trainer, but decided against it at the last minute. It would mean increasing the circle of people who knew about the operation and who was aboard. Not the Air Boss, nor the carrier's commander knew who was crossing their deck. They didn't know where the helicopter had gone, it had been flying even below the sophisticated systems of the carrier once it was more than a few miles out.

As soon as the passenger jet came to rest, she was swarmed by a crew. Tail hook restowed, the plane was dragged immediately to the catapult position. After their helicopter was tied down, no one had approached them. No one opened the Black Hawk's door.

Suddenly the carrier's deck was conspicuously clear.

"That's our cue." Henderson climbed down and slid open the cargo bay door. He offered the two Koreans rain slicks with large, overhanging hoods that hid their faces. It only took moments to escort their guests from the helicopter to the steps on the Gulfstream jet.

A fresh flight crew would already be in place in the cockpit with specific instructions not to enter the main cabin short of an emergency. They even had the door itself closed off while boarding so they couldn't see who entered.

The crew chiefs, Tim and John, settled in the forward crew cabin right behind the entry door as if seeking privacy from the rear cabin, but actually guarding against any curiosity by the flight crew.

As Daniel followed the group last up the fold-down steps, a gust of freezing rain found its way down his neck.

Beale hit the door-close switch and Daniel walked through the short crew cabin and entered the main area. There were two groups of four arm chairs set in facing pairs on either side of a central aisle. Half had their backs to him, half facing him. At the far end a couch ran alongside one wall of the cabin facing across the plane to a fair-sized television. The entire cabin was dressed with white leather chairs and wall coverings. The trim and carpeting were charcoal gray.

Daniel scanned the cabin quickly. Per instructions, there was no sign of Christmas. In 2011, North Korea had threatened to shell a hundred-foot tall steel Christmas tree that shown over the border from South Korea. The President and Daniel had both recalled the escalating tension and decided to avoid it as much as possible. The aircraft carrier, involved in night operations, had no visible Christmas lights anyway.

Henderson was directing the Supreme Leader and his guard to take seats facing forward for the take-off. Right. Catapult-assisted takeoff. Sit on the couch and you'd end up spilled off the end and into the rear galley and probably right on into the small lavatory.

Beale and Henderson sat down in a forward pair of facing seats, leaving Daniel the last forward-facing armchair for the takeoff. He dropped into it with deep appreciation, closing his eyes in relief as he settled into the soft leather. He'd been traveling for almost twenty hours so far, and there was eight more to go to get back to Canada.

And the adrenal crash from hovering for nine long minutes in the midst of anti-aircraft radar systems had taken what little reserves he'd had.

Had he really served a purpose? He'd have to assume that the Supreme Leader of North Korea would not be seated right behind him at the moment if he hadn't gone. So, it had been a good decision, even if he was too tired to appreciate it.

The twin jets of the Gulfstream wound to life with a pleasantly muffled, high whine of a well-insulated passenger jet, rather than the mind-numbing roar of most military aircraft.

The engine's whine built and the pilot warned them to buckle up. Daniel groped around, clipped himself in and sank further into the seat. Exhaustion rolled over him like a wave.

He had done well. He'd survived a flight with Emily Beale, perhaps too busy worrying to actually be concerned with whatever near death experiences she'd been handing out in flight. Against all odds, they'd pulled off an impossible assignment, or at least the first half. Alice's guiding hand of knowledge and risk assessment had been flawless from the moment she'd walked into Daniel's office just three weeks before.

Three weeks. How did a world get so turned over in three weeks?

His world had become divided: before and after Advent calendar. Before and after meeting Alice. He'd thought the big change was his journey to Washington D.C. three years ago. Starting as champion of the Slow Food movement and the farming community of Tennessee. Becoming assistant to the First Lady and ultimately the White House Chief of Staff. How could any change in his life have surpassed that crazy set of circumstances? He'd thought that anything past serving President Matthews was bound to be a letdown.

The engine's roar increased until finally it was a palpable pressure in the cabin.

He'd been wrong though, the before and after moment that mattered was December first and a tiny door bearing the golden number "1" in finest filigree. That and a russet-haired beauty who'd turned his life upside down.

Someone patted him on the knee and he heard a soft, "Good job!" over the peaking roar of the engines.

The pilot warned over the intercom, "Launch in three."

Not takeoff. Launch.

He opened his eyes and there, like a miracle, sat Alice.

He opened his mouth to exclaim his shock just as the catapult fired ramming him hard back into the seat and driving out what little air had survived in his lungs.

CHAPTER THIRTY-FOUR

"*I thought I might* be useful." Alice had pulled off the conveniently padded strap that had slipped down over her forehead to anchor her in place during the catapult takeoff. As her seat faced backwards, there would have been no support for her head during the immense acceleration.

Daniel wondered just how much had been done to this particular aircraft to make it aircraft-carrier capable. Trap hook, head straps, structural reinforcements. All he knew was it was the only small business jet that could get them across the northern Pacific Ocean in a single pass without landing for refueling, and that could travel at nearly the speed of sound while doing it.

"Useful," Daniel managed. He'd learned a dozen words in Korean, which thankfully he hadn't needed. He'd actually been banking on his French or German being sufficient as Kim Jong-un had been educated in Switzerland. Alice had picked up the language for the fun of it, one of the reasons for her transfer to the North Korean desk at the CIA. She did know more about the Supreme Leader than most Americans, maybe more than most people on the planet.

"Do you know anything about basketball?"

Daniel just shook his head. He knew there was a team based in

D.C., but that was about all he really knew. He hadn't attended but one or two games in college.

"Major Henderson," Alice leaned across the aisle toward him.

Daniel became dreamily mesmerized by her long, elegant neck and thinking of the way she moaned quietly when he kissed her there. He slid his feet forward and they hugged ankle to ankle.

"Are you a basketball fan?"

"Sure. Don't have much time to catch games, but I follow it."

She aimed one of those radiant Alice smiles at the Major.

Daniel felt drifty as he considered the possible uselessness of being jealous of a happily married man who could probably beat the crap out of him using only one pinky. Daniel tried to imagine their battle, himself in heavy armor with an array of lethal weaponry and Major Mark Henderson, the most decorated pilot in SOAR with his pinky. Daniel made a couple bets with himself on how many seconds it might or might not last. Under ten seconds before Daniel was down and done? Fifty-fifty. Under twenty seconds? No contest at all. He'd be a little smear on this amazingly comfortable seat that was rapidly sucking the willpower out of his bones.

"Did you know," Alice continued in her sweetest voice to Mark, "that Kim Jong-un became a crazy basketball fan while going to school in Switzerland? And that channel 56 is running the UCLA versus USC game right now?"

Long before any seatbelt sign turned off, Mark had the two guests on the rear sofa and they were all noisily involved in the game on the large-screen TV.

Emily leaned into the aisle toward Alice and whispered, not that the other guys would have heard anything, "That was very well done."

Daniel's sleepy brain wondered if his virility was in question because he didn't troop back to watch the game as well.

Probably.

CHAPTER THIRTY-FIVE

Daniel *slammed awake and* wondered if he really had fought Major Henderson, or even more dangerous, his wife.

Other sensations started penetrating his consciousness.

The engines began winding down.

They weren't moving except for a rock and sway as if a giant rubber band had just grabbed their tail.

There was a strap across his forehead.

The carrier.

He was still in the forward facing seat, which means he'd had to be braced against the sudden deceleration of landing on an aircraft carrier. Someone had strapped his forehead so that the sudden vicious grab of a wire trap wouldn't injure his neck.

He'd slept all of the way across the Pacific, his first decent sleep in several days. Now they were on the U.S.S. *John C. Stennis* which had just finished unloading most of its jets to the Whidbey Naval Air Station in Washington state's Puget Sound. This was a common practice when coming into port; done in order to avoid flight deck operations inside civilian air space. Of course, their carrier would now sit for a little more than a day with nothing on its deck but a passenger jet. It would cause no interference with flight operations because all of the other planes would be gone.

This had been his idea, based on something Beale had said. One thing he'd contributed to the strategy rather just being baggage.

Alice no longer sat across from him.

He struggled out of the seat belt to see her chatting with one of the most feared leaders on the planet as if they were old friends. A moment longer, his brain now fully awake, he realized they spoke in English.

Kim Jong-un's voice came out heavy, deeper than when he'd spoken in his native tongue. He made awkward but clear use of a distinctly British accent. And they were chatting about the best restaurants in Grenoble.

If there was any way Daniel could be more gone on this woman, he didn't know what it might be. Alice had not only just charmed the leader of North Korea to relax enough to reveal that he spoke English. She had also just paved the way to make President Matthews have a much more productive meeting.

They filed off the jet into the late evening light, once again wrapped in coats with hoods up. Their entire end of the flight deck was vacant of service personnel. They crossed to the helicopter tied down along the side of the deck. It was the Majors' other Black Hawk.

Normally they flew them in tandem. For this mission, they'd each left behind their copilots and two of their crew chiefs. This was the "A" team, the very best that SOAR had.

They had separated the helicopters by five thousand miles. One helicopter was still parked on the U.S.S. *Harry S. Truman* in the Sea of Japan. The other now sat on the U.S.S. *John C. Stennis* a few dozen miles off Cape Flattery, the northwestern most point of the continental U.S. Also conveniently close to the Canadian islands.

After staggering about for a minute on a deck far more wind-torn than the *Truman's* deck, Daniel climbed aboard an indistinguishably lethal copy of the helicopter he'd ridden into the heart of North Korea. Accommodations were a little more crowded with Alice aboard, but they were far from the half-dozen troops plus field gear that could squeeze into even a heavily weaponized Black Hawk like the Direct Action Penetrator.

An odd silence settled over them as the helicopter performed the mirror of the movement it had made in North Korea, plunging them down to skim the wave tops before roaring landward. Daniel glanced out the window and what little he could see revealed storm-torn waves.

This time he felt both more and less panic; less for himself, more for any potential danger to Alice. A glance revealed that Alice was enjoying the ride immensely and he did his level best to switch off his over-protective instincts.

Kim Jong-un and his interpreter appeared completely relaxed and at ease with helicopter flight. Any novelty they found aboard a U.S. military helicopter clearly sated in the first flight, they now settled into patient waiting. Daniel had observed that more and more in non-Western countries. Most other world citizens consistently exhibited a patient self-reliance that Americans somehow lacked.

These reflections carried him through the first half of the thirty-minute flight up the storm-torn Strait of San Juan de Fuca and around the southern tip of Vancouver Island. The second half was spent white-knuckling as the helicopter dodged between the ten thousand rocks that were the southern end of the Canadian Gulf Islands. The only radar that was going to spot them would be would be some psychotic fisherman out fishing at night among craggy rocks during a nasty northerly storm.

And he'd also be the only person who would find them if the Majors screwed up. If they slammed into a cliff face even a psychotic fisherman would be of little use.

With an abrupt jolt the helicopter slammed him down into his seat. He clenched his hand over Alice's and held on tight as they climbed into the night. With a sharp tilt toward the stern, he lost all sense of motion.

They hovered.

Outside the window he could see that the lights were on up at the big stone house. Warm, inviting, stable lights that didn't bob or weave in the dark of the night.

CHAPTER THIRTY-SIX

"**D**inner's in an hour." Emily Beale announced as they managed to close the heavy weathered-pine front door against the roaring night.

"I'll help." Alice felt disoriented as she looked about the house and needed something familiar to anchor her in place.

"Make that forty-five," Beale called out then dropped her voice. "Let's go see what we can rustle up."

Daniel, back on his feet after sleeping like a baby throughout the flight, was making sure that their guests were guided toward their rooms. She left him to it.

The fact that he had never doubted her strategic assessment still floored her. That she'd actually been right, shocked her. That he'd slept with his ankles wrapped around hers for the whole flight on the Gulfstream jet had touched her heart and she'd rather not think about that.

Alice moved to follow Emily to the kitchen. She'd toured the house during their initial daytime survey with Captain Smith, but it looked far different at night. During the day, the light and the outdoor world had dominated. A grand vista of the islands and the waves far below. Wide windows invited those inside to notice the surrounding conifers and lawn.

Now, under the warm glow of tastefully recessed lighting, dark tile and lush wood floors invited her to linger in the nearly opulent warmth. The heavy furniture proffered a welcome, an invitation to settle in with a good book and never move again. The walls between the windows wrapped cozily about the room. They were covered with a mix of Native American art with its shocking red and black and white contrasts, and tall bookcases almost spilling over with a wide variety of novels and histories revealing the owners' eclectic tastes.

The kitchen continued the theme. The cookbooks on a nicely recessed shelf covered a half dozen cuisines. Yet the size and efficient layout of the kitchen revealed that the family cooked here, rather than some servants.

Emily had already pulled out a big tray of steaks.

"You had this place stocked." Alice couldn't believe she hadn't thought of it.

Emily nodded, "I was the First Lady's chef for three weeks after all."

Alice slapped her forehead eliciting Emily's rare laugh, then reached for an apron. Beale's flying had made national news and her cooking shone front and center in the country's gossip pages. It had all been while the Major performed some secret security assignment that Alice had never uncovered. Alice typically felt disjointed around women like Emily Beale. Alice knew how to handle men. Well, men other than Daniel. But women often eluded her.

Emily Beale felt like the sister she'd never had.

"So what am I making?"

"Steaks for entrée. Can you tackle a garlic pasta for a side? I premade cookie dough, so we can hack some off and make a batch of chocolate chip while everything else cooks."

Alice dug out a large pot and set water to heat on the stove. She scrounged around and came up with garlic, sun-dried tomatoes, a small bundle of basil, and some broccoli. They worked together in companionable silence for a while. Emily rubbed a pepper and sage combination into the meat. Alice floreted the broccoli and started to sliver the basil.

"He's quite in love with you."

Alice would have cut off her finger if she'd been using anything more dangerous than a garlic press at the moment. Instead, it merely slipped from her nerveless fingers to clatter down on the counter spreading tiny splatters of garlic across the broad granite surface.

Gripping the counter edge she managed to turn herself enough to face Beale. Emily was leaning comfortably back against the opposite counter and holding out a large glass of red wine. Alice rarely drank. She grabbed the glass and knocked half of it back, leaving her hard pressed to catch her breath.

"What," she tried to ignore the amount of effort entailed to speak the word. "Whatever gave you that idea?"

Emily smiled. That slow, calm, self-assured smile of a woman who has faced down, well, the President and her husband among others.

"It isn't an idea. It's a fact. I'd have to be blind to not see it. Why don't you?"

Alice took another deep swallow of the wine that did nothing to slake a throat long gone dry.

The door to Alice's right opened, but she couldn't turn away from Emily Beale's brilliant blue gaze.

"Go away," Beale said without looking around.

"Uh..." Alice heard Daniel and did her best not to cringe.

"Come, my friend." Major Henderson cut him off with a fake Texas accent thick enough to deep-fry in hot oil. "We'all better be walkin' in places safe for mere men to tread. Which does not include our continued existence if we should remain in this here kitchen."

The door swung closed and silence once again reigned in the kitchen other than the soft sizzle of steaks on iron and the bubbling of the pasta water nearing a boil.

"Just asking." Emily turned back to preparing a bowl of salad with wild greens, hazelnuts, and dried cranberries.

Even as she struggled against the idea of love in her life, Alice's analyst mode kicked in.

Emily Beale, she knew, ranked as an exceptionally acute observer, just one of many areas in which her file stated she ranked far above the norm. She had known Daniel when they were both working for the

First Lady. Beale had a frame of reference that spanned the year following as well.

Alice had… What? Her own clear sense that she was not capable of falling in love. And the certainty that no one could ever love her. Not the firmest logic. It was like saying, if A equals B and X is not equal to forty-two, then L must be false. Logic simply didn't work that way.

She tried flipping her thoughts to a more intuitive framework, one that served her well enough to identify Kim Jong-un's desire to speak with the President in private. One that observed Daniel grabbing her hand when panicked in flight, or protecting her during the simulated helicopter attack, of his hand frozen above the first small door of an exquisite Advent calendar. Three weeks and she still hadn't been able to forget that moment.

Never in her life had she imagined that Dr. Alice Thompson had the ability to freeze a man in his place. Her parents had made it clear that her place in the world would never include a relationship. That love was a façade.

Every one of her friends loved Alice's parents. They were perfect hosts. Intelligent, funny, friendly. Everyone always told her that she was lucky to have such parents. For a father who retreated into impenetrable silence the instant the guest left. Or the harpy with a martini in one hand and a list of Alice's on-going faults in the other.

Not for her. Never that trap.

Once again Emily was facing her. A glass of wine in her own hand.

"I don't like where my thoughts are going."

Emily nodded, "Probably means they are on the right track at last."

"How do I know?" Alice turned the question about. "How did you know?"

Emily's face shifted, a gentle smile revealing a softness difficult to equate with the SOAR Major; a smile that shifted her eyes from bright blue to misty summer sky.

"I didn't. I had to beat the shit out of Mark before he convinced me."

If that was a dreamy memory, Alice wasn't sure if she wanted to know the rest of the story. But she couldn't help but be cheered by Emily's obvious good mood.

"So, that's how Majors choose a mate?"

"A lifemate. Oh yeah. Absolutely. How about brilliant and beautiful CIA analysts? How do they do it?"

"Carefully." Alice replied even as she fought against the echo of Beale's correction. "A lifemate," she tried the word out. A strange and foreign word. Her parents were married for life, that had become clear years before, but it was more of a life-inmate arrangement, locked in a mutual prison that neither knew how to break.

Emily moved around her to drop the pasta into the rolling water.

Alice finished the garlic, set it beside the diced tomatoes and basil. She grated a couple cups of Parmesan cheese. She felt better, more stable. This time she was able to sip her wine. Which was a good thing, as she could definitely feel that initial slug loosening her brain.

"I don't want to be in love with him."

"Why not?" Beale flipped the steaks.

"You're bloody relentless, aren't you?"

"Special Operations Forces pilot. Who knew I'd be like that?"

Emily left Alice with the relentless silence of her own thoughts. Really unfair.

She knew she wasn't in love. She knew she couldn't be.

She also couldn't shake the sneaking suspicion that she was wrong on both counts.

CHAPTER THIRTY-SEVEN

It was an early night for everyone. Late evening in the Canadian Gulf Islands, late afternoon in North Korea at the end of a long day, and little or no sleep the prior night.

North Korea's leader hadn't been rude at dinner, but he'd made it clear that if it wasn't about basketball, he wouldn't be talking to anyone other than President Matthews.

Daniel offered Alice a separate room. The gentlemanly thing to do, and there were just enough beds. Big John and Tim, the two crew chiefs, had bedded down in bunk beds, generous enough for John's tall frame. Beale and Henderson in one suite, Kim Jong-un in one of similar comfort and style. Daniel and the Korean bodyguard, who had still remained nameless, were to share another bunk room.

The crew chiefs and the Korean guard had found some degree of trust and set up a schedule so that two could sleep and one patrol.

He gave Alice the last bedroom, which sported a frilly set of curtains and a double bed with pink and pale blue pillows. Clearly a girl's room, the nicest in his estimation. He set out a glass of water and a small collection of fine chocolates as he'd done for the others. Sometimes it was the little touches that counted.

He debated at length about just setting a chocolate and glass for himself on the other side, but it felt presumptuous.

She'd been strangely silent during dinner and it had been left to himself and Henderson to carry the conversation. Tim and John had chipped in with stories of their more famous escapades as the self-declared pranksters of SOAR's fifth battalion. Something about painting a general's Humvee bright pink, every single part right down to the insides of the panels and the under the armor. They'd fully disassembled it to make sure no piece was missed.

"He had a bad habit of calling SOAR pilots 'pansy girls' compared with the 101st airborne." Tim had clearly been deeply insulted.

"Along the way, we may have happened to rebuild the steering system so that the steering wheel worked in reverse. But maybe that wasn't us." John ended wistfully. Tim had cut his steak in a thoughtful silence that spoke volumes.

No one had anything to say, and no one had the energy to fill the lagging gaps in the conversation.

All in all, everyone was relieved when it was bedtime.

Daniel had helped Mark with the dishes. By the time they were done, everyone had retired.

Mark slipped into his and Beale's suite, the lights already out.

Daniel took a quick turn of the house. Lights were out under all the doors, except one.

Alice's door stood open just an inch. A thin beam of light slid out into the hallway.

He peeked in through the crack.

Alice was under the covers, already asleep.

The light that shone through the crack came from the other side of the bed. There, beneath the soft light stood a half-empty glass of water and half of the chocolates he'd left for Alice. The cover was folded back and his travel bag rested on a chair by the window.

He closed the door and slipped into bed beside her as gently as he could.

She mumbled something as he clicked off the light. It took him a moment to unravel that she'd said, "I'm awake."

"Sure you are." He whispered back, gently patting the pleasing round of her hip where it shaped the quilt beside him.

With a soft sigh she settled into a truly deep sleep.

Daniel, perhaps due to sleeping on the jet plane, lay wide awake long into the night.

CHAPTER THIRTY-EIGHT

D*aniel woke briefly and* thought he heard the sound of fading helicopter rotors, but the night was dark and the howl of the wind a low moan that whipped sounds out of their normal shape, spattering them across the night sky.

It was light when he awoke alone. This time he did hear rotors. Distinct, the heavy thud of a Black Hawk pounding the air. An arriving helicopter.

He whipped out of bed, checked his watch, and decided he'd be much better off if he caught a shower later. Dressed in two minutes, teeth and hair brushed by three, he met President Matthews and Secret Service agent Frank Adams at the front door.

"Good morning, Daniel."

"Good morning, Mr. President." Daniel could see the Majors and their crew chiefs tying down the helicopter under a heavy sky, which was now shedding snow flurries among the morning's icy rain.

The President looked comfortable and easy in the long blue parka more fit for a polar expedition than crossing the front lawn. He'd have slept aboard Air Force One while at McChord Air Force Base. A training ride with his childhood friend Major Emily Beale would not look out of the ordinary when she arrived unexpectedly at the co-located Fort Lewis; unexpectedly and right on schedule.

Frank Adams entered the house before he allowed the President across the threshold. After careful inspection of the entryway and hall closet, he nodded that the President could come this far and no farther. He moved on to inspect the living room.

Daniel heard Alice's bright voice answered by the much deeper voice of the Supreme Leader of North Korea as they entered from the kitchen.

Ignoring Frank's protest, the President breezed over to meet his guest.

Daniel offered the agent a sympathetic look.

Before the President led his guest into the study, Frank did manage to check it out. Daniel watched his rapid and intense inspection. A leather and cherry wood theme decorated the office, that had been painted in a surprising pastel that offset the substantial furniture quite nicely. A woman's touch.

Alice's hand rested on his arm as the door closed.

"Are they settled?"

"I suppose."

"Ten people know."

Daniel nodded. Then paused. "Eleven people know. Beale's crew of four, two leaders, two bodyguards, the two of us, and the CIA Director."

Alice tipped her head down, letting those bangs swirl forward, but he stooped to keep a clear view of her face.

"You never told your boss."

She shrugged. "Seemed appropriate."

He kissed her on the forehead. "You done great, Dr. Thompson."

"You too, Dr. Darlington."

They both glanced at the door, where Frank Adams had stationed himself solidly before the threshold. The Secret Service agent, despite being in his forties, was immensely fit and towered like a temple guardian statue. The inner sanctum was not to be disturbed.

Kim Jong-un's bodyguard was not nearly so vigilant.

A poker game quickly formed in the kitchen. Apparently Seo-yun, having relaxed sufficiently to speak his name, was eager to learn how to fleece his fellow countrymen upon his return. Henderson and the crew chiefs appeared more than happy to oblige him with a few lessons. Daniel just hoped the man had been fortunate enough to bring no money to America. The fact that no bank in the country could exchange North Korean Won notes wouldn't have stopped them from taking every one they could.

In moments a noisy game ensued and was in full swing along with glasses of soda and mugs of hot tea, a large pile of American candy bars close by Seo-yun.

Daniel landed on the living room couch for lack of anything else to do. He had a thousand memos, phone calls, e-mails... all begging for his attention. And with what might be occurring behind the closed study doors, Daniel couldn't think straight long enough to deal with a single one.

When he gave up and shut off his computer he became aware of Alice sitting on the other end of the sofa chatting quietly with Emily Beale. They too were constantly casting sidelong glances at the door.

Daniel went over to the fireplace that someone else had lit and fed it a log it didn't really need.

That was how their day went. Reading, chatting, sitting blankly. When Daniel, Emily, and Alice made lunch for everyone, the game broke up. After delivering two trays into the study, someone raided the extensive DVD collection. But no one could really focus.

The tension built inside throughout the day as the storm built outside. The rising howl of the storm sheeted freezing rain against the windows. The waves, only a few hundred feet away and fifty feet below, were rarely visible through the blurred glass. High winds sent the rain across the lawn in mesmerizing waves that held others as rapt as it held Daniel.

Daniel just wanted to curl up on a couch somewhere with Alice. This was why animals hibernated, to avoid storms like this one.

The weather peaked mid-afternoon with a final blast that shook the house and would have cut the power had it been provided by power lines rather than a sturdy diesel generator.

As the day's light faded toward evening, the indistinct murmur of voices from the study stopped. When at last the door opened, everyone had gathered in the living room.

Daniel noticed that the President, despite his usual ability to appear totally unflappable, was sagging beneath his upbeat attitude. Kim Jong-un, still weeks from his thirtieth birthday also appeared exhausted as if the two of them had wrestled desperately with matters of great importance and only together beat them into submission.

The two of them stopped just past the door, Frank Adams now standing close behind, the rest of them forming a loose arc around the living room.

"Well," the President glanced at the Supreme Leader and they traded a silent nod. "There is much work to be done. And perhaps now less to fear. Time is needed. Time and common sense. You have all done a great job."

"Yes." Kim Jong-un clearly didn't want to leave the stage solely to the President. "Progress. Perhaps the beginning of partnership. Much work yet from what you might call friendship. But progress. Yes, fine work. You have good people, Mr. President."

"Thank you, Supreme Leader."

They shook hands once more. Daniel wondered if there could be a more important political moment in recent history, and yet there was not a camera to be seen.

"Now!" the President clapped his hands together. "We need to get off this island. How do we do that?"

CHAPTER THIRTY-NINE

Earlier *this morning, Emily's* SOAR team had flown the President and Frank Adams back to McChord, just over an hour round trip and no one the wiser. Officially President Peter Matthews had spent the day aboard Air Force One with a head cold.

With the President gone, Kim Jong-un had collapsed into a deep armchair, making no more pretense of how exhausting the meeting had been. Whatever work they'd done, it had been hard on both men. Good work often was. Alice could only hope that it was.

The Majors had fought their way back through the storm as if it were a quiet summer's day and merely a routine flight.

On their return, Emily had handed Daniel a FedEx package.

Alice saw that it had been addressed to Daniel, in care of Major Beale at McChord. Beale had looked at Daniel strangely as he tucked it under his arm. Alice barely saw that the return address was Tennessee before it was out of sight.

When she'd looked up, she came under the penetrating inspection of Major Emily Beale, and she'd be damned if she knew why. Alice felt like a bug facing a windshield.

Then, a moment later, Alice stood at the door of the island house, waving politely to Supreme Leader Kim Jong-un's back. He merely huddled against the sleet, the umbrella she'd provided to his bodyguard remained useless in the chaotic winds shooting over the sea cliff to swirl wildly between the house and trees.

He had thanked her most politely upon learning she was the analyst who had made this all happen. But now that he was out the door, he clearly just wanted to be out of the weather, into the Black Hawk, and homeward bound.

Which was fine with her.

She closed the front door and leaned back against it with a gasp of relief.

Despite the horrid weather, the crew was departing to head out to the carrier parked off the coast. There they'd board the Gulfstream jet back to the Sea of Japan and deliver the North Koreans home. They'd left in the middle of one night and would be returning in the middle of another two days later.

Daniel had offered to accompany them on the return flight into Korea, but Emily had vetoed it. The weather was bad enough that they didn't want to risk the extra weight of Daniel and Alice aboard the helicopter. That had meant only two passengers to McChord for the return trip to D.C. and only two out to the aircraft carrier where a passenger jet waited on the flight deck for the return trip to Korea.

Finding some reservoir of energy Alice couldn't tap to save her life, Daniel had swept through the house stripping beds, turning off lights, tossing dirty dishes into the dishwasher.

Alone.

They were alone in the house.

She and Daniel.

And would be for at least one day and more likely two until the Majors returned from their second flight into the Korean night or the storm broke enough for Captain Nathaniel Smith to fly out from Vancouver and fetch them.

Marooned on a Canadian island with Daniel.

She could think of many things that she did and didn't want to do with Daniel. She wanted to curl up against that beautiful chest and just weep with exhaustion. Ever since she'd seen that first message out of North Korea that had sent her scrambling to the White House, she'd barely slept. And assuming that the Majors flew as safely as they always did, it had all worked.

Another part of her wanted to make love to Daniel until she was too exhausted to either weep or laugh.

And there was the problem.

"Make love to."

She'd never "made love to" anyone. Sex. Sure. Amend that. With Daniel? Mind-bogglingly good sex. Who knew her body could even feel that good?

Alice reached deep and tried to wake her analyst's mind, but wasn't having a lot of luck with that. Instead, she leaned against the closed front door, and did her best not to think.

Finally at a stop, her body took over and noticed the smell that had come slowly wafting out into the living room. Burgers. Food. Her stomach loudly reminded her of its empty state; none of them had done more than nibble at their lunches during the meeting. And everyone else had left before dinner.

She trailed her way into the kitchen. In some ways not so different from the kitchen in the third-floor Residence of the White House. A little more country kitchen than elegant interior decor, but both were small enough to create a cozy, intimate feel.

Daniel had set two plates on the counter. Full service with folded napkins, silverware, water and wine glasses. He'd even scared up a few Christmas decorations now that the North Koreans were gone. A small family of elves and reindeer sat at the far end of the island. Daniel had set them up with tiny plates and their own six-inch tall Christmas tree.

For the humans at the table, he'd made a delicate salad in wooden bowls. And on the plate rested toasted burger buns and a pile of golden-brown French fries.

"Will you—" Alice clamped her teeth down on her tongue in a hurry. She'd almost jokingly asked if he'd marry her. It would be funny in any other situation when a man cooked something that smelled this good. She would have said it if Emily Beale hadn't stood right where Daniel now flipped burgers and asked Alice what she was going to do about Daniel being in love with her.

What was she going to do?

She didn't want her mother's past. Or her father's. Trapped in a life neither of them understood. They'd started out happy. She'd seen the photos. The video of the wedding. Listened to them laugh, actually laugh together, as they filmed their only daughter's first steps. A joy between them that had long since passed into the realm of impossible. So far gone that it was now unimaginable despite the evidence caught on tape.

Whatever they'd had was long dead.

Alice had sworn she'd never make that mistake.

But would she?

Was she capable of making that mistake, of letting love die?

Would Daniel even let her screw it up that badly? This was a man who loved family. A grown man who had his family's and his big sister's photos on his dresser. He'd probably find some way to make her happier with each passing year. It poured out of him, straight from his heart. The question was, could she do the same for him?

Hadn't she answered her own question last night when she'd left the light on and the door open? His mere presence had unnerved her since Beale's question, but Alice was a better person, far better and far happier with Daniel beside her than when they were apart. And Daniel had chosen to accept the invitation and sleep beside her. She wished she'd had hours to just lie there and watch him sleep.

Daniel served up the burgers, drowned them in sautéed mushrooms, and sat down across the chopping block island from her. He lit two candles and turned off the lights.

Damn, he was turning even a simple dinner into an occasion. A very romantic occasion. Marooned together on a wild but homey island. He looked exhausted, and absolutely, positively stunning. Not just the handsome man who sat across from her. She also saw the man who both helped a President rule and made her feel as if she had a home she'd never imagined. And he made both look effortless.

Comfort food. Daniel had made them comfort food.

"What's for dessert?"

He tapped the Advent calendar that was sitting on the corner of the island counter.

"We missed last night, too."

"Gimme!"

Daniel laughed that rolling chuckle of his that made her think of hillsides in the sun.

"Don't you want to eat first?"

"Gimme now!" she pushed aside her plate, folded her arms across her chest, and did her best to pout.

Daniel considered her for a long moment. That smile hiding something. Shifting for just a moment into the White House Chief of Staff mode, despite wearing a turtleneck shirt rather than a suit and tie. But then he shifted back to merely being amused. As if he'd had to adjust some thinking, tweak some master plan. She had to remember that for every molecule of her being that was a supreme analyst, he was a master strategist.

"Here's last night's." He opened a little door at the base of the pictured tree, down among the unwrapped presents. And extracted a pair of dark chocolates. So dark that they looked black under the candlelight.

She didn't raise her hands, but rather leaned forward and took one directly with her teeth, leaving a small nibble on his fingertips in her wake. The chocolate flowed warm, lush, creamy, rich. "That may be the best chocolate I've ever had." She felt as if her body melted into a gentler version of herself along with the chocolate.

He nodded, looking a little dazed himself.

"You," his voice caught. "You can open the last window."

She pulled over the Advent calendar.

Once again she looked at the magnificent final image.

"It's us," Daniel had texted when he saw it. The two young kittens were peeking out from the wrapping paper under the tree, deep in a game of hide-and-pounce. Crinkly balls, feather toys, catnip mice, and more spread far and wide from the tree and across the living room floor.

On a deep, embroidered pillow, before the crackling fire, the mama and papa cat curled together. It was impossible to tell quite where one began and the other ended. Painted so finely that she wanted to stroke their fur.

That Daniel saw the two of them that way had actually made her heart hurt. She had to cover it again with her hand to keep it in place.

She checked the number on the door that had hidden the dark chocolate. Twenty-three. The next one opened into the side of the pillow on which the two cats curled together.

"The last one. Twenty-four," her voice such a soft whisper even she could barely hear it.

"Christmas eve," Daniel answered little louder.

Alice looked up at Daniel. But his eyes were hidden in candlelit shadows. She wished she could see what was going on in those deep blue eyes of his, but his thoughts remained hidden.

It was always her most important holiday of the year. She'd always loved Christmas, even though she'd usually celebrated alone. But the last weeks had become so frantic that she'd lost all track of time. She hadn't even finished the snowflake mittens she'd been knitting as a surprise for Daniel.

She'd barely started her special project. She'd missed her favorite season of the year. A small price, she supposed, for making the world a safer place.

"Tomorrow we'll be spending Christmas together." Alice realized. "Just us." There was a bright side. She could think of no one else she'd rather spend it with.

He nodded toward the calendar with a "go ahead" gesture.

Taking a deep breath, she pulled open the last door.

"It was my grandmother's. I had my sister send it. I texted her right before we went into North Korea."

The FedEx package from Tennessee. From Daniel's home.

She pulled the circle of gold from the recess. A trio of small diamonds in a simple band. Not posh. Not gaudy. Absolutely elegant. Absolutely Daniel.

Alice looked at it sparkle in the candlelight.

Daniel was anchored in the past. Family. Tradition. Honor. Love.

Her past... Well, she wouldn't be anchored by it. Not any longer. She would cut that cable.

"Here," she handed the ring to Daniel.

He took it tentatively. His brief look of worry cleared as she held out her left hand.

She had cut the cable and was now flying free.

Daniel slid the warm gold over her ring finger and anchored it in place with a kiss.

Alice and Daniel.

They'd soar straight up into the night sky.

"Tomorrow," she told the man still holding her hand so tightly, "we'll be spending our first of many Christmases together."

FRANK'S INDEPENDENCE DAY

US Secret Service Agent "Beat" Belfour *comes under fire when a coup erupts in the West African country of Guinea-Bissau. A routine diplomatic assignment goes wrong, and the Ambassador's life now is slipping through her fingers.*

Head of the President's Secret Service detail Frank Adams' *only weapons to save her are: the President's strategic skills, the dedication of the U.S. Army Night Stalkers helicopter regiment, and a past history with "Beat" that changed his life and his heart.*

INTRODUCTION TO FRANK'S INDEPENDENCE DAY

With the success of Daniel's Christmas *(and how incredibly fun it had been to write), I wanted to write another White House Holiday romance right away.*

I had the character—Frank Adams received a great deal of fan mail for his confrontations with Emily Beale in The Night Is Mine. *The problem was, in that book, Frank was already married. I wasn't sure to who, but the fact was undeniable because I'd written it in the book.*

That gave me a new kind of puzzle, which as a writer is something I'm always looking for. I love the challenge of not simply writing a new romance, but also of trying something I've never done before.

So, how to write a romance for a man already married?

Writing it in the past wasn't the solution. I wanted it to occur in my Night Stalkers' world which is very present tense. But the love story had been in the past...

That's when I conceived of writing the story in two, overlapping timelines. By bringing the past and the present together, I could perhaps tell both stories: how they fell in love, and have a current-day military adventure.

I actually knew only a few facts about Frank. He was big, stubborn, and loyal as all hell—hard to get on his good side, but once there, a person was all the way in.

I had two other facts.

One, he was black. Having friends of African-American heritage didn't mean that I'd presume to be able to write the issues they face with any authenticity, barring an immense amount of study. So, I opted to not presume. He is a skilled man, the head of the Secret Service's Presidential Protection Detail, who just happens to have dark skin.

Two, he was from the street, a fact he does his best to hide. That told me he had a past, and it probably wasn't a pretty one.

During the 1960s, when New York City was a disaster beyond imagining, I frequently traveled with my parents to visit my maternal grandmother. Dad always had this thing about driving the absolute shortest route from upstate New York, even when it led us through battle-torn sections of the city. (I wish this was an exaggeration.) Out my backseat car window I witnessed: fire-bombings, robbery, massive lines of burned-out buildings that had filled the television news screens, and even the first moments of a car jacking from just feet away.

It was that last image that gave me the opening scene for Frank's Independence Day.

There had been a violence to the real-life scene that I didn't think was fitting for my hero, so I wrote it in a different form...and to this day I think it is one of the best scenes I have ever written.

I knew nothing about Beatrice Ann Belfour until the moment she rolls down the window in the midst of the carjacking. Our hero's first view of his true love is:

Then he was facing the rolled down window, just as he'd planned. He could taste the new-car fine-leather smell as it wafted out.

What he hadn't planned was to be staring right down the barrel of a .357.

I think I fell in love with "Beat" from that very moment. This was a woman who took no shit from anyone, not even the guy trying to steal her car.

Now I had my first historic timeline. Or at least the first moment of it.

For the other timeline, I took a piece right out of the news. The same month I was starting the research on this title, a former admiral of the failing African state of Guinea-Bissau was captured by the DEA for running a drugs-and-arms-trafficking scheme between South America and Africa.

Further research revealed that Guinea-Bissau had suffered from a coup every few years for decades.

And there was my current timeline.

Of course getting Beat to Africa took a little finagling. She was a specialist in the Secret Service. That sent me off on a road of discovery about America's diplomatic corps...and that was where I found the anchor for her story.

The Foreign Service Diplomats are immensely brave people in their own right. There is no US embassy in Guinea-Bissau, because it is considered to be too dangerous. Instead, the US ambassador to nearby Senegal travels frequently to Guinea-Bissau despite its incredible instabilities.

There was the rest of my current plot. An ambassador and his aide, with Beat as their protection detail, land in the middle of a coup and become a target.

From that point on, my greatest challenge was one of balance and interconnection. I had to keep the two timelines of equal interest to avoid a reader simply skipping ahead to read the events occurring in only one or the other timeline. But I also had to keep the tension of each timeline connected.

Technically, this is perhaps the most complex book I've ever attempted. However, if I did it right, it should simply read as one smooth continuous ride.

Even with all of those challenges and background aside, the first scene is still my favorite opening, and one of my very favorite scenes ever.

CHAPTER ONE

FRANK: JULY 4, 1988

Frank *Adams had his* boys slide up around the metallic-blue late-model BMW at the stop light on Amsterdam Ave. One stood by the passenger door, one ahead, one behind, and he took the driver's window himself as usual.

It was only the third time they'd done this, but Frank saw, without really watching, that they made it look smooth. They'd split the thousand that the chop shop had just paid for the Ford they'd jacked and two grand for the Camry. But a new Beemer? That was a serious score. What they were doing so far uptown this late on a hot, New York night was the driver's own damn fault.

He started it like any standard windshield scam. Spray the windshield to blind the driver, then shake them down for five bucks to clean it so they can see to drive away. The bright bite of ammonia almost reassuring to New Yorkers who had come to expect the scam. He'd long since learned to flick the windshield wiper up so that the driver couldn't just clean their own damn window. It was when the driver's window rolled down, and the person at the wheel started griping, that the real action would begin.

A glance to the sides showed not much traffic. Lot of folks gone down by the water to watch the fireworks, or off with family for July 4th picnics at the park, or on their fire escapes in the sweltering summer heat. The acrid sting of burnt cordite hung like a haze over the city from a million firecrackers, bottle rockets, M-80s, cherry bombs, and everything else legal or not. Hell, Chinatown would be sounding like they were tossing around sticks of dynamite.

Night had settled on the roads out of Columbia University and into his end of Manhattan, and as much darkness as could ever be happening beneath the New York City lights had done gone and happened.

Frank's boys were doing good. At the front and back, they'd leaned casually on the hood and trunk of the car not facing the prize, but instead watching lookout up and down the length of Amsterdam Ave. They'd shout if any cops surfaced.

And no self-respecting BMW driver would run over someone they didn't know just to get away, especially ones who weren't even looking at them threateningly.

Other drivers were accelerating sharply and running the red light just so they weren't a part of whatever was going down at the corner of Amsterdam and midnight.

Three minutes. That meant they had about three minutes until someone nerved down enough to find a pay phone and call the cops and he and his boys had to be gone.

They'd only need about one.

The Beemer jerked back about two feet with little more than a hiss and a throb from that smooth, cool engine.

His boys were on the pavement before Frank could even blink.

Japs had been sitting on the trunk but was now sprawled on his face and Hale sat abruptly on his butt when the car's hood pulled out from underneath him. It was almost funny, the two of them looked so damn surprised.

Then he was facing the rolled down window, just as he'd planned. He could taste the new-car fine-leather smell as it wafted out.

What he hadn't planned was to be staring right down the barrel of a .357. Abruptly, all he could taste was the metal sting of adrenaline and the stink of his own sweat.

He'd seen enough guns to know that the Smith & Wesson 66 was not some normal bad-ass revolver.

He was facing death right between the eyes.

His body froze so hard he didn't even drop the knife nestled out of sight in his palm.

The woman who looked at him, right hand aiming the gun across her body, left hand still on the wheel, had the blackest eyes he'd ever seen. So dark that no light came back from them, like looking down twin barrels of death even more dangerous than the gun's.

A cop siren sounded in the distance, but his boys were already on the move out of there.

"They're leaving you behind."

Her voice was as smooth as her weapon. Calm, not all nervy like someone surprised by a carjacking or unfamiliar with the weapon she held rock steady.

"What I told 'em to do."

"Don't risk the whole team?"

He shrugged a yes.

That siren was getting louder and it was starting to worry him. But even doing a drop and run, well... He was fast, but not faster than a .357. He stayed put. Classy lady in a Beemer and a dead carjacker, she wasn't risking any real trouble if she gunned him down where he stood.

"Decision point. Go down for it. Spend some time in juvie—"

"I'm twenty, twenty-one next week." Why'd he been dumb enough to say that? Not that the cops wouldn't find out, but they didn't have his prints anywhere in their system... yet. He didn't carry any ID either, but there was only so long you could play that card.

"Okay, do some time or get in the car."

He looked into the deep well of those dark eyes, allowing himself three heartbeats to decide what the hell she was up to. The sharp squeal of cop tires swerving around some other car too few blocks away won the argument.

Frank moved around the front of the car fast, flicking down the wiper blade as he went, and slid into her passenger seat.

While he circled, she'd shifted the big gun into her left hand. Could shoot with either hand, that took training. Some off duty cop in a Beemer, just his luck.

He was barely in the car when the fuzz rounded the corner, their lights going.

"Buckle up."

It was only after he buckled in that another thought struck him. A bad one. She just might drive him somewhere, gun him down, and dump his body. Never knew with cops in this town. Then she wouldn't even have to fill out any damn paperwork. *Little bit late to think of that shit, Adams. Dumbass!* Once around the passenger side, he should have just kept running, not climbed into the lady's damn car like a whatever it was that went to the slaughter. Sheep? Calves? Something. Frank Adamses.

She slid the gun under the flap of her leather vest so that it was out of sight, but still aimed at him across her body. She ran the windshield wiper and together they watched the blue-and-white roll up fast. The cops pulled up driver to driver, facing the wrong way on the street to do so.

"Everything okay, ma'am?"

Frank had the distinct impression that even though the woman was reassuring the cop, if Frank so much as flinched, there'd be a big, bad hole in his chest and that the thing that would really tick her off was the damage to her German-engineered car door where the bullet would punch a good-sized hole after making a real mess of his body on its way through. It took her long enough to talk the cop down that Frank had time to register how the car's seat fit to his body. It was way more comfortable than any chair or sofa he'd ever slouched in. Damn seat alone probably cost more than everything he owned.

Finally satisfied, only after blinding Frank with a big flashlight a couple of times, the cops rolled away real slow. He'd purposely dressed okay in his best jeans and a loose button-down shirt he'd worn to Levon's courtroom wedding. That way he wasn't too scary for the windshield-washing scam to work. It paid off now, he didn't look too out of place in this classy car. He eyed the woman carefully, as classy looking as her vehicle. Or even more.

She pulled her hand out from under her vest of dark leather even finer than the seat upholstery, leaving the gun behind, and rolled up the window. Shoulder holster. He'd tried to carjack a woman who wore a .357 in a shoulder holster. What were the chances of that kind of bad luck? Well, one in three. Third carjacking ever, woman with large gun. Not exactly high-level math.

Though he'd never heard of anything like it on the street. He'd been told to watch for crazies, diving for glove compartments and purses, so full of nerves that they were more danger to themselves than anyone else. Best advice on those had been to run. Toward the back of the car. Make yourself a hard shot when they're all buckled in and facing forward. They'd be undertrained, have lousy aim, and probably wouldn't shoot if they thought they'd won. That's if they could find the damn safety.

Not this lady. Cool and calm.

He'd bet she could execute his ass without havin' a bad night's sleep.

"Let's go somewhere and talk." With the window up, the air-con dropped the temperature about twenty degrees from the July heat blast going on out in the real world which was sweet, but left a chill up his spine that started right where his butt was planted in the fine leather seat.

She punched the gas and popped the clutch, in seconds they were hurtling downtown on Amsterdam and Frank knew he better hang on for dear life.

·····································

CHAPTER TWO

·····································

T*hat's how I met* Beat, Agent Beatrice Ann Belfour of the United States Secret Service." Frank Adams hung tight onto the fold-down arms of his seat aboard the Marine One helicopter. He'd recently learned to despise helicopters.

President of the United States Peter Matthews burst out laughing and Frank, now the head of his Presidential Protection Detail, did his best not to feel foolish. It wasn't even his usual, engaging, buddy-buddy laugh. The man thought he was being downright hilarious.

"You got into the Secret Service by trying to carjack a Secret Service Agent?" He managed to gasp it out between guffaws like the American public never got to hear on TV.

"It's not like she had a sign on her damn Beemer saying, 'Federal Agent, Don't Screw with Me'." Frank had to speak up to be heard over the pounding rotors of the helicopter and the President's laughter.

He'd learned that while this President didn't swear, he liked the chummy feeling of occasional curse words from others, as long as it didn't go too far.

The last President had been the opposite, cursing a blue streak in private but expecting no one else to say so much as "darn." And then only if they'd been very recently shot.

The Presidential White Hawk had better sound insulation than your standard Sikorsky Black Hawk, but it still wasn't quiet. It also had about two tons more armor than any other helicopter flying, which Frank appreciated since it was his job to keep the man riding in it alive. But he'd rather be in anything than a helicopter, especially a Black Hawk. Frank had barfed his guts out on a simulated-combat flight with the Special Operations Aviation Regiment, the 160th of the U.S. Army's Special Operations Forces, and hoped he'd never have to fly with the Night Stalkers again. He'd take the Marines in the White Hawk any day.

Out of well-trained habit, he scanned the blue skies outside the helicopter. The New Jersey shoreline lay below, and not much else except the morning sunshine sparkling off the rolling Atlantic. The window was hazy due to the thickness of the bulletproof glass. It would stop anything up to fifty caliber and it would do its best to stop that, too.

They were in transit from D.C. for a meeting at the United Nations. This flight was also way more secure than that training mission had been six months ago. Not only had they been simulating combat, who knew helicopters could roll over and dive upside down, but they'd been far away from the usual bubble that surrounded the Commander-in-Chief. Sure, they'd been traveling with two of the most heavily-armed helicopters on the planet and with Henderson and Beale, the two best pilots the U.S. Army Special Operations Forces had ever created, but still... No one except those on the flight had even technically known the President was aboard and they'd crossed half the country with only Frank beside him.

For this trip, Frank felt much more comfortable. They were Number Two of two in a flight of identical VH-60N White Hawks. The other bird was there to confuse any potential attacker as to which craft the President actually flew in. The pilots had switched the lead several times to deceive anyone trying to track them. A trio of well-armed Cobras flew escort on the White Hawks.

On top of that, air traffic controllers were keeping the skies clear of any other flights for a box that extended five miles behind them and to either side, and ten miles ahead. Any aircraft that entered that box would rapidly receive attention from the Cobras. In seconds more, intruders would also be facing the pair of F/A-18 Super Hornet fighter jets and the F/A-18 Growler, an electronic-warfare version of the Hornet, all flying out of Langley Air Force Base and presently lurking another twenty-thousand feet above the helicopters.

Unlike that training mission, this flight was also unlikely to include any aerobatics maneuvers. Yet another thing to be deeply grateful for the Marines flying this machine.

He was seated backwards in the White Hawk, sitting opposite the forward-facing President. No one else was in the aircraft's cabin other than the two pilots seated in the cockpit over Frank's shoulder. Frank glanced behind him, but they both appeared alert and focused forward. President Matthews sat at ease in the narrow, brown leather armchair just like Frank's own. His hair, the longest of any occupant of the Oval Office in a couple hundred years, clearly marked the youngest President in history. His dark hair flowed to his collar and his deep brown eyes radiated both intelligence and humor. The television cameras just loved this man.

Frank's wide shoulders didn't fit the narrower helicopter seats nearly as well as the President's. And at six-foot-two, the low ceiling of the White Hawk's cabin was disconcertingly close. He kept his seat-belt cinched tightly for the entire hour flight so that he wouldn't bang his head if they hit an air pocket.

"So, how did you enjoy being taken, uh, into custody?"

"Well," Frank scanned out the window again. "I managed to not crap my pants on her nice leather, but it was a close thing. You remember how Tommy Lee recruited Will Smith in *Men in Black?* The secret world, the bench, the change-your-whole-life lecture, and all that?"

The President nodded.

"It was just like that. When that movie hit after I'd been in the Service for about a decade, it was like a bad drug flashback without ever having done any drugs to earn it."

CHAPTER THREE

BEATRICE: 1988

U*nited States Secret Service* Agent Beatrice Ann Belfour looked over at the kid sitting in her BMW's passenger seat. She was only three years older than he was, but she couldn't help thinking of him as a kid. A young street punk. But not just a young street punk. If he had been, he'd be locked in the back of the blue-and-white cruiser of the NYPD at this very moment.

Beatrice had only been an agent of the Secret Service for a year. And only authorized to enter the field and carry a weapon since last week. Good timing. She rubbed her palm against the steering wheel, thankful for the absorbent leopard-spotted steering wheel cover that her little niece had insisted she purchase. Beatrice's hands were not steady, but she certainly couldn't show that to this kid.

She should have just turned him over, but there'd been indicators that intrigued her. And a significant portion of her training had been learning to trust her instincts. Her problem, she was often told, was that her instincts were also crazy stupid, but that wasn't any news to her.

He hadn't flinched when she'd pulled her weapon, hadn't even dropped the knife he thought was so carefully tucked out of sight. That showed a steadiness of nerves. He'd worked up a carjacking scam with the guys sitting on the hood and trunk acting as both spotters and deterrents. That was a scenario that she hadn't been briefed on in training. Similar yes, but not the same. It was a good twist. He'd even trained them to run at trouble to minimize losses, which made him a team player as well as a good leader. Clearly all of this was his idea. Even the attention to detail as he dropped the wiper blade back into place, despite the distraction of the muzzle of her S&W 66 staring him between the eyes, spoke to his ability to remain focused under stress.

Even most junior agents didn't do as well in practice scenarios and for this guy, it had been live.

"If you can make your hands work," she'd bet they were shaking like Gene Wilder in *Blazing Saddles* when he was needing a drink. "You can put that knife and any other hardware you're carrying into the glove compartment. They won't like you carrying where we're going."

"Only have the knife." His voice was deep and resonant as befit someone with a chest his size. She guessed six-two, two-ten or two-hundred-and-twenty pounds, and none of it fat.

No gun. Maybe he couldn't afford it, which seemed unlikely in the neighborhood she'd found him in. You'd think a woman would be safe driving down a New York street six lanes wide, bright under the lights. He probably didn't carry because he knew penalties went way up if something went wrong and he was picked up packing a firearm.

He held the knife up for her to see, his hand didn't shake much at all, less than hers would be if she took them off the wheel. Not a switchblade, nor a spring-load, but it had a heavy blade she'd bet he could flick open one-handed. Again, legal. Not by a lot, but it would pass for a standard pocket knife under the New York criminal code. She'd bet no one else on his crew was carrying even that. He ran his team as clean and legally deniable as possible.

He popped the glove box with the back of his thumb and wiped the knife on his pants before dropping it in and knocking the little door closed with his knee. No gloves, which would have stood out on the mid-summer night, so he was limiting where he left fingerprints. She made a bet with herself that he'd use a shirttail to wipe the seat-belt buckle and the door handle as he exited the car.

This kid was careful. Which reaffirmed her first instincts.

At this time of night she made it all the way downtown in under twenty minutes and the guy didn't say a word. Halfway there, she'd asked his name.

"Frank."

No last name offered. He didn't look nervy, again just being careful.

She flew down to 7 World Trade Center and whipped into the downward-spiraling ramp of the underground parking garage with a bright squeal of tires. Her parents had given her the car as a make-up present when she'd been named a field agent last week. She'd retired the very old gray Honda, probably only days before its final collapse. She'd named it Witherspoon, for what she thought Michael Caine might have called his Aston Martin in *The Italian Job*. She was thinking of naming her new BMW Jean Claude, after Van Damme's kicking performance in *Bloodsport*. But that had only been released a few months ago and didn't have the classic feel of the 1969 heist movie. She'd find its name eventually.

Her parents felt that a federal job was beneath their only daughter. They'd worked hard to get out of the same poor-ass neighborhood where she'd just found Frank. That their daughter hadn't taken her Columbia University education to become a doctor or lawyer, or at least marry one, had made them more than a little bit crazy. After a year of simultaneously completing her Secret Service training and managing to finish her degree in criminal law, they'd felt contrite and given her the Beemer. She wasn't any less pissed at them for all the hassle they'd dished out over the last year, but she did love this car.

It practically stood on its nose when she hammered the brakes at the control booth of the restricted section of the underground parking. She lowered the window.

"Hi Beatrice," Harry popped the button inside his booth to raise the steel gate and lower the tire punchers into the pavement surface. "Knew it was you when I heard the wheels hit the upper ramp."

She flashed her ID at him for form's sake. Added a grin of thanks and goosed the gas, spinning down two more layers to her assigned spot.

Beatrice kept an eye out as the kid climbed out of the car. Sure enough, Frank applied his shirttail to belt buckle and both the inside and outside door handles.

———

"Any record?"

Frank didn't "huh" this lady as he tucked his shirt back in as smoothly as he could. Didn't pretend to not understand. He looked at her over the top of her car, kinda surprised at how far down he had to look. She'd seemed so damn big with the fancy car, the shiny damn gun, and the total lack of fear. She couldn't stand more than five-seven or eight, but there was no question which of them was holding the power at the moment.

And he didn't like that it was her. Not one lousy little bit.

He shook his head. No record, no time, no juvie.

"Not even detention, much."

He'd been top twenty at the high school, which only said he wasn't as out-and-out lazy as everyone else there. College hadn't been all that high on anyone's to-do list in his class. He'd had some idea that the chop shops might eventually pay him enough to hit Columbia or City University, but he'd never figured that as real likely.

The "no detention" line got a laugh he hadn't expected, and he had to reassess her again. Bright white teeth, and hair as dark and shining as those eyes. The smile also made her look younger than the thirty he'd originally tagged her with. Low twenties. He moseyed around the rear of the car and tried to make no big deal out of checking her up and down.

Red Converse sneakers and faded jeans that showed hard use and good quality. Certainly not Goodwill or Woolworths. High-necked yellow blouse. Black leather vest, dressy kind that wasn't for warmth, but instead for looks... and hiding damn big guns. The combo promised a slender waist and a serious enough chest that the gun in the shoulder holster didn't show much under the soft leather. If he didn't know it was there, he might not have thought anything out of place. And a whole lot of things were in the right place on this woman.

"Do I pass?"

He went for a safe shrug. Okay, so he hadn't pulled off much in the way of smooth, but she was a woman who deserved a long look.

"Turn around." She didn't make it a request.

He narrowed his eyes at her and she twirled a finger. Well, he knew that his looks didn't leave him nothing to worry about in that department. He and his boys worked out together every day 'cause there sure wasn't shit else to do in the projects, and he'd received more than his fair share of fine benefits from the ladies to keep him working the iron.

"Describe what I'm wearing."

Some kinda test. So, he stared at the row of cars parked across the way, lined up neat as bowling pins. They were all driven by skilled drivers like her, each car slid into its spot sweet and straight. This wasn't no office-bozo kinda parking. The garage was all pretty quiet on this side of that security gate up there. Not much in the way of traffic. 'Course it was one in the morning on July Fourth. The place smelled of garage, oil, fuel, and rubber. Where the hell was he?

So, he described her. Got into it. She'd left a damn clear impression. She didn't stop him after her clothing, so he got into her high cheekbones and full lips, her black hair, long, straight but threatening to curl madly, and the thin gold chain around her neck with no ornament dangling on it. And she didn't need anything more to look seriously fine. No rings or bracelets and...

He spotted a reflected motion on the flat rear glass of a Ford Bronco parked across the way.

Her reflection pulling out that damn big gun.

He dove for the ground and rolled between a couple of cars.

Sweat poured off him even as he regained his feet in a low squat and began thinking on the best direction to run. Blown away in a parking gara—

That laugh again. It stopped him cold.

She wandered around the car until she was facing him, hands empty. Out where he could see them plainly. Did nothin' to calm his nerves.

"You recall what you see accurately, are exceptionally aware of your surroundings, and have good reaction time."

"Which means what?" He managed to make it come out more as an angry shout he meant than the choked squeak he was feeling. He stood slowly, his heart still pounding against his ears.

"Which means I was right. Let's go."

She walked off toward the steel-faced garage elevator set in an unadorned concrete wall. He glared at the low pipes wandering along the garage ceiling, but finding no kinda clue up there, he followed her.

———

Beatrice pressed the button that brought the elevator down, but didn't say a word. She stayed quiet to let Frank stew in his own juices. He stalked into the elevator like a grizzly bear who'd just crawled out of its den and found no food anywhere. Seriously grumpy. She keyed in the lock code to take them up to the seventh floor.

"You like being right." Frank didn't make it a question and he didn't waste time asking her where they were going.

Beatrice had to grant that the kid had the patience to figure out that he'd find that out soon enough. And also enough smarts to know that she wasn't likely to tell him before then.

"Damn straight!" She loved the feeling. "Being right is fun. It's one of my favorite things. And if I were blond and could sing, I'd be Julie Andrews."

His look told her that his education in movies needed some serious fixing up.

For the life of her she couldn't figure out why she so enjoyed messing with this kid.

Kid. He was seven inches taller than she was with a workout chest big enough that he made the elevator feel small. Nor had she missed how fine a form he had when he'd turned away from her. That she'd even noticed was interesting in itself, but she absolutely wasn't going to think about that.

The door opened and they stepped into the inner building's lower entrance foyer, the one which lay seven stories above the front-entrance street-level signs for brokerages and banks that filled the bulk of 7 World Trade Center, New York, New York.

Frank grunted when he saw the sign above the desk. But no more than that. Steel letters on dark wood: United States Secret Service. She remembered the feeling the first time she'd seen this sign, as if the world had just become a great deal more serious. Of course that had been on her new recruit tour, she'd known what building she was in. She gauged Frank's reaction. "Adapts rapidly to changing situations," was added to her initial assessment.

He eyed her sideways for a moment, then nodded to himself as if she finally made sense in his world. Of course a Secret Service agent would outsmart a simple carjacking scheme.

She'd spent the last year training in driving, weapons, investigations, research, and a dozen other skills. She'd also been trained in unarmed combat and wanted to see how Frank Adams did. It was stupid to take on an unknown street fighter twice her size, which made it just her style.

She signed in at the desk and signaled one of the guys to come out and pat Frank down, which he submitted to but clearly didn't like.

"Escort him through. Find him some sweats." She glanced down. His feet were as big as the rest of him and there probably weren't any loaners that size. "Barefoot is fine."

She turned and headed into the women's locker room to change. She considered handing him to someone else for testing, which is exactly why she didn't. Her instructors were always telling her she was much too impulsive, too quick to leap into the fray. But one of the old-timers, one who actually used to ride on President Ford's protection detail, the only PPD agent she'd met so far, told her never to stop doing that. From then on she ignored all instructions to back off and had graduated top of her class. Maybe it was part of some test to see if she'd comply. She hadn't.

She wandered into the gym. They told her it was nothing as nice as the one in D.C., but it worked fine for her. A row of weight machines down one side and a gray foam mat that covered the rest of the floor. She knew from experience that it wasn't as soft as it looked.

When Frank arrived, he looked amazing. The black t-shirt with large white U.S.S.S. stretched tight across his chest and showed actual six-pack abs. Black gym shorts revealed legs that rippled with muscle. She could feel the heat rising through her body, so she turned away and led him onto an open corner of the mat.

He tried to turn so that it was his back facing the wall, rather than hers, but she didn't let him. It left him watching the other agents over his shoulder, keeping an eye on them. There were only a couple working out. Things were quiet on July Fourth night, these few were probably just killing time before their shift started. She knew one of them well enough to wave, but that was all.

She herself was glad of the reason to be missing the party at her parents. That was the main reason she'd been cruising up to Columbia to check on a posted summer class schedule she could have just as easily called on tomorrow.

"Hit me."

Frank goggled at her so she repeated herself.

"Ladies first," he replied.

She shot a rabbit punch at his sternum without hesitating. She'd thought to drop him as a lesson, but her fist mostly bounced off a tight gut, though the breath did whoosh out of him. He'd also managed to twist enough to make it a partially glancing blow.

Beatrice went for another punch and Frank, predictably, went for the block.

But she didn't land the punch, instead she went low and swept his leg.

On his way down, he was fast enough to snag a hand behind her leg and take her down as well. She landed on top of him and almost got the nerve pinch on his hand, but he was strong enough to wrench free, despite the pain that must have caused.

They pushed off each other and rolled to their feet.

"Damn," Frank shifted lightly on his feet circling.

Now he was going to be predictable and gripe about surprise attacks.

"You smell wonderful."

It flustered her enough that when he went for the takedown, she landed hard on her back before she could recover.

Frank knocked the air right out of her.

CHAPTER FOUR

I *can't begin to tell* you how good that lady was," Frank massaged his chin where Beatrice's elbow had surprised him twenty-five years before, after he'd slammed her to the mat. Even now, he could remember the scent of her as clearly today as if no time had passed at all. Like midnight and roses. Dark, mysterious, and lush.

And then she'd clipped his chin with her elbow and planted his face in that stone-hard mat of the Secret Service gym.

The White Hawk was circling down to the Manhattan Downtown Heliport. Nine a.m., exactly on schedule. Frank looked down to check the dock.

They'd cleared the pier of other flights. A quick scan below showed that the police boats had cordoned off the part of the East River that flowed by the heliport.

The heliport itself was a pier and a barge near the south tip of Manhattan. The tiny parking lot off South Street that could hold about a dozen cars was presently blocked by half-a-dozen black Secret Service SUVs. They'd closed a short section of the street, and the rest of the Presidential motorcade waited for them including a pair of

Humvees with turret guns and an ambulance, surrounded by a phalanx of New York's finest mostly on motorcycles.

A long pier stuck out from the shore separated from the land by the terminal building. His earpiece confirmed what his eyes could see. The "all secure" mirrored by the agents in dark gray suits standing watch outside the terminal's doors. The long pier stretched out into the East River. Brooklyn rose on the far shore, bridges soaring above the boat traffic on the bright water. The four helipads were empty, and a pair of Beasts, the Presidential limousines, were parked there. Then the big barge, that looked little different from the pier, floated to the north. About a third of the ten helicopter parking spots on the barge were taken, but the only guys near them were agents.

"Merlin inbound," Frank announced over the radio.

President Matthews grinned at him as he did every time he heard his Secret Service codename. If the main man got a kick out of being dubbed a wizard, that was fine with Frank. And it fit. Youngest President in history, he'd fostered more peace accords than anyone had pulled off in a whole lot of terms. Halfway through his first term and he'd already visited the United Nations more times than any other prior President in their entire incumbency.

And being there on July second, right before the July Fourth holiday would look good in the press. He knew that wasn't what motivated the Man, but neither was he going to be stupid and miss the chance to leverage the opportunity a bit.

They circled as they descended toward the pier, providing Frank one last look in all directions. Nothing caught his eye, nothing pulled his attention. The only thing he noticed was that the ambulance was behind the rearmost Humvee. It was supposed to be in front so that the Humvee's gunner would have a clear field of fire and the ambulance would be inside the bubble with the President if they had to crash down a defensive perimeter. He called down and they started shuffling it as the Marine One helicopter settled at the outmost spot on the main pier, the most defensible spot.

"Check the drivers, ambulance and Humvee. They should both know better."

As the wheels kissed the pier, the answer came back into his earpiece. "Ambulance broke down, they had to send their second team. Rolled in late, but they're on my cleared list." Then after a brief pause. "He won't forget next time." He could hear the laugh in Hank Henson's voice. Hank took deep pleasure in making rookies suffer. Probably been hell on new pledges at whatever Ivy League fraternity he'd belonged to. Frank had done night school at NYU.

Even before the helicopter's rotors stopped, Beast Two was backing up close to the door. They alternated which was the decoy car. Once the rotors halted, a Marine opened the side door which rolled toward the back. Frank stepped out first, scanned once more, receiving nods from the key agents.

Second day of July in New York City. The heat rolled across him like an old friend, hot, thick with flavor, the smell of home. No other city smelled like it. He tugged at the jacket of his custom-tailored suit to make sure it both hid his weapon and offered easy access. Damn suits cost a fortune, but he didn't look armed in them, so it was worth it. No need to remind the President more than necessary that he was surrounded by armed men every minute of the day.

He let Merlin down, making sure he was between the President and the bulk of the Manhattan buildings. Two more agents to either side flanked him for the thirty-foot walk to the car. Human shield in place.

In moments, he and Merlin were locked in and the motorcade was moving. That was one of the secrets of Presidential security, never stay still, a moving target was much harder to hit.

Frank hated this next stretch. For the next four-point-one miles there was no question about where the Presidential motorcade would be. There were alternate routes through the city. However, up the FDR was the safest and fastest, but it meant being predictable.

"You said meeting Beatrice Belfour was like *Men in Black?*" President Peter Matthews was ignoring whatever crises he carried in his briefcase. He'd snapped it shut halfway through the flight and asked Frank about how he'd ended up head of the PPD. Boss' prerogative.

Main Man wanted to talk? Then Frank would. Wanted to play Scrabble? He'd play Scrabble, and lose horribly no matter how hard he tried. It was the President's secret vice, he loved strategy, he played online in competitions and often finished in the money at tournaments. He was always harassing Frank about finding some way for him to compete in the National Scrabble Championship, but you had to show up in person for that.

Frank had almost crapped his pants laughing when Beale had told him the origin of his preferred anonymous player identity, Sneaker Boy. Had to do with Beale chucking the President, back when he was much younger, into the Reflecting Pool in D.C. while wearing brand new sneakers. He'd have paid good money to see that.

And now the President wanted to talk.

Frank let his guard down, as much as he ever did when riding with the Man. Locked inside the Beast with the President, security was someone else's issue. Mostly. There was only so long that you could stay on alert, so he relaxed as much as he could when he wasn't front and center.

"Well, yeah. She showed me this whole weird world behind the magic curtain, training gym, high-rise offices, high-tech communication war rooms that could span the globe. Then we sat right over there." He pointed out the right-hand window across to where a small park wrapped around the Brooklyn side of the Brooklyn Bridge.

He took a cold bottle of water from the small cooler and knocked it back. July first and it was high-nineties in the city. What was August going to be like? At least it hadn't stunk of garbage. When he'd met Beat it had been so damn hot that the city didn't need a garbage strike in order to reek of it.

CHAPTER FIVE

They filmed **Moonstruck** here last year." Beatrice told him as they sat side by side on the park bench and looked out at the East River and Manhattan shimmering in the nighttime heat steaming off the water's surface. Once again in their street clothes, he couldn't help remembering her in her workout gear. Her chest gave the big, white U.S.S.S. logo a whole new meaning. No vest hiding curves that really needed to be seen and appreciated. And legs, damn but the woman had amazingly serious legs.

"Moonstruck." Frank had no idea what she was talking about. He just knew his chin still hurt like hell, it was two a.m., and he was sweating like a pig because the temperature hadn't broken in almost two weeks. And he knew that Beatrice was limping bad on the right and trying not to show it. Damn but she was tough. No whining at all though they were both sore. "What's that?"

"Boy, we've got to do something about your movie education. It is seriously lacking."

Movie? He looked around the dock. It didn't look like much. It stuck out a little ways into the East River, Manhattan and the

Brooklyn Bridge made for an amazing skyline, from the Twin Towers right up to Roosevelt Island. Here there was just water, warped old wood on the dock, and a couple of steel benches so clean that tourists must come here. Sure weren't no benches this clean in his neighborhood. To the south was a small park. To the north, a fancy restaurant all closed and dark inside, though the perimeter lights were on so it would be hard to sneak around. He spotted a couple of security cameras up high, but they didn't have cables to them. Fakes. Dumb fakes. He knew some boys into smash-and-grab, maybe he should tip them off.

"So what movies did you see?"

What was it with this woman and movies? *"Platoon* kicked ass."

"Okay, it did. I'll give you that one."

"Uh, Stallone was good."

"Rambo III. Like two weren't enough. Sequels are a waste of celluloid. We really gotta do something about this. You're a walking disaster."

"What? First, you're dissing my man Sly. And now you're gonna make another weak-ass attempt to kick my ass or something?"

That got a smile out of her. He seriously liked that smile. And he'd bet if he tried to do anything about trying to kiss it, he'd end up with a faceful of dock splinters.

"That will be up to you."

Whether or not he got to kiss her? No. He shook his head. Whether or not she tried to kick his ass.

Beatrice looked out over the water. Tide was coming in so it smelled of salt and the Atlantic rather than old diesel fuel and other crap that floated down the river when the tide was running.

"I think you've got what it takes. The United States Secret Service is not for the weak of heart. We've got two mandates. Money laundering, counterfeiting, and fraud is the first. Then there's head-of-state protection. All dangerous as can be. That's if they let you in. First they'll do so much investigating on you that an alien crawling out of your chest would be a relief. They'll know so much about you that you won't know what hit you."

While he had a weak spot for Sigourney in too little clothes packing a serious damn gun, the thought of what an investigation would dig up about him sent a chill up his back. He'd just twice committed grand theft auto by carjacking. That wouldn't go down good at all if they found out.

"I, uh, don't think that's gonna be happening."

"I know I wasn't your first carjack. You were too sure of yourself."

"Until you stuck that damn gun in my face."

"Until I stuck my gun in your face. But what you've got going for you is rarer than you think. It's also a way out of your present mess. I've been an agent for a year and it's awesome. I learned enough to stop you."

Frank considered that while a tugboat worked its way against the tide, a long barge of gravel piled in tall mounds trailing far behind. She had stopped him, stopped him cold. If there was ever a good advertisement for what she was sellin', she was it. The woman looked and smelled amazing, and had almost beat his ass on the wrestling mat. He sure wasn't going to think about how good she'd felt in his arms even as she'd planted a knee in his gut and he'd had to partly sprain her ankle to get her off him.

"So why did you join?"

"I'm going to be on the Presidential Protection Detail some day."

"Why there?" He tried to picture that. Riding with the Main Man. Sure, and catching a bullet so that he didn't. Frank had seen enough gunshot wounds and deaths to last him a hundred times his twenty years. Wouldn't find him steppin' in front of no bullets on purpose.

"Because the PPD are the very best on the planet."

"And you're just that damn good."

"Damn straight."

He gave her a knowing smirk. But the thing was, he believed her.

CHAPTER SIX

Then she left it up to me whether or not I showed up the next day to start filling out the paperwork."

The President smiled. "But you're the one heading up my Protection Detail."

"Yeah," Frank returned the smile. He'd gotten the assignment when Peter Matthews announced he was running. They didn't start guarding the candidates that soon, but they started studying and planning and he'd pulled the duty detail on that. By the time the D.C. native became a Presidential contender, Frank was on him. When he was elected, President-elect Matthews had asked to have him stay on.

"Yeah, heading your detail... Kinda pisses her off." He grinned. When they were alone, he knew the casual helped the President relax, as if he were with a friend rather than his bodyguard. But now they were rolling up the semi-circular drive in front of the main building of the U.N. He threw the mental switch... back into agent mode.

A voice in his ear reminded him, "Entering Turtle Bay." Turtle Bay, which probably hadn't seen a turtle since it was named back in the 17th century, was the Manhattan neighborhood that included the United Nations Headquarters and often referred to just the U.N. section of it.

"You're a brave man, Frank Adams." The President didn't even glance out at the phalanx of agents ensuring the front entrance was secure for their arrival. "I don't think that Agent Beatrice Ann Belfour is someone I'd want to 'piss off' even a little bit."

"Well, I'll admit, she has her more dangerous moments. The woman knows no fear."

"Nor do you," the President checked his tie and jacket. Today it was a sharp gray with a garish red-and-white Washington Nationals tie. He was known for his ties and his love of the D.C. baseball team. Frank had accompanied him to more than one game and watched him eat ballpark hotdogs until any normal man would be sick. It always struck him as funny that the Harvard and Oxford graduate, leader of the country, always so calm and collected, could scream and rant about bad calls against his home team.

"You wear that tie around New York, Mr. President, there's nothing I can do to protect you from a Yankees fan. Just so you know."

"Good thing we aren't technically in New York then."

The U.N. grounds were extraterritorial, subject only to the laws of the U.N., rather than the U.S. and the city of New York. They'd just left the country, right in the middle of Manhattan, which had always cracked him up.

Frank nodded for him when the President had the gray suit straightened-around just right, like a human mirror.

"I've never seen you show a moment of fear," the President grabbed his briefcase and glanced around to make sure he'd left no papers behind.

"Well, sir, you didn't see the color of my pants after we climbed off Major Emily Beale's Black Hawk helicopter on that flight. Fear may only be a seven-point word, but I sure felt it that day."

A last laugh for the President before he entered the fray of international politics.

A voice in his ear called the, "All clear." Frank could see the agent outside ready to open the Beast's door, over a hundred pounds of armor and bullet-proof glass.

"You ready, sir?"

"Ready for an entire day and evening of arguing with China and Russia over the latest North Korean fiasco, and trying to calm down Myanmar about the Thai raids into their poppy fields, and... Sure. Can't wait."

"Do it." Frank announced into the wrist microphone of his radio.

The agent standing beside the car swung open the door.

CHAPTER SEVEN

FRANK: 1988

The car door caught Frank sharply on the knees and he tumbled back. It was a ratty 1967 Ford Fairlane, peeling white paint, Alabama plate number four-three-seven-five-something, hard to see in the moonlit semi-darkness.

It hadn't looked like any trouble. Just a driver. Another Secret Service trainee, Jake Hellman, had him covered.

Frank had gone to the back door of the beater car and someone lying on the floor had kicked the door open, hard, just as he'd looked in. He'd fallen on his ass just like Hale at the carjacking. He fell on the red Georgia dirt of the Federal Law Enforcement Training Center.

Then his shins stung like hell as the lower edge of the door scraped across them.

He shot out a palm strike and rammed it full force against the car door before its edge could scrape off his kneecaps. That at least stopped the excruciating progress of the swinging steel along his shins. With his other hand he managed to shove off the ground, into a roll, and slam his shoulder against the door, snapping it shut.

Whoever was playing the perpetrator in the car hadn't expected that. A woman's squeak sounded through the front window that the driver had rolled down when Frank and Jake stopped the Fairlane for inspection.

Agent Beatrice Ann Belfour. Had to be.

Hadn't seen her in weeks, different agents rotated through the FLETC training scenarios. But she was always causing him pain when she was down here.

He yanked out his gun and rolled up to kneel on the hard-packed, deeply rutted earth. That was a big, damn mistake, his shins screamed.

No live ammo in the gun, he couldn't shoot out the window.

Instead, he rapped the glass sharply with the butt of his gun, right where he'd glued on a bit of shattered spark-plug ceramic.

The safety glass practically dissolved, now instead of hard glass, the ceramic had triggered the safety glass into shattering. It was now a loose, wavering sheet, opaque with tiny crack lines and barely holding together. Old car-thief trick.

He shifted to his feet, swallowing the hiss of pain, and slapped the friable glass with his elbow.

The window disappeared in a shower of tiny pieces.

Even as he aimed his weapon into the car, Beatrice kicked the door again.

This time he had his hip against it and all her violent kick did was force her to slide the other way and smack her head on the far door. He couldn't see her clearly in the shadows, but there was no question in his mind.

"You, Agent Belfour, are under arrest for bloodying an agent of the United States Secret Service." He could feel the hot blood trickling down his shins. The long scrapes were already stinging with the sharp salt he'd been sweating from every pore since the moment he'd landed in Georgia three months before.

In answer she popped open the far door she'd just banged her head on and tumbled out the other side of the car and into the dark.

He dove over the trunk and managed to snag her by the ankle before she could sprint into the night. She was clearly the target of interest, the driver probably just a driver. And not his concern at the moment. There were big-picture moments, and stay-focused moments. Stopping Beatrice was definitely in the second category.

Already moving forward fast, his grip around her ankle and her forward momentum slammed her to the ground.

"Ow! Crap! That hurt."

"Welcome to my world, Beat—" That's when she flipped around to get him in a headlock between her knees.

It took three tries, but he managed to find the pressure point on her thigh that had her writhing away before she'd quite choked all the air out of him.

He managed to stand and lean forward to grab her just as she shot to her feet to run again.

The top of her head and his nose intersected.

It was mostly luck that he snagged an arm around her waist and dragged her to the ground with him.

"Damn it!" He groaned and wondered if she'd broken his nose. "Why you got a need to beat on me so goddamn hard?"

She struggled to get free.

He just kept an arm clamped around her waist, let her struggle all she wanted. He'd dropped his weapon when she'd rammed her head into his face, not a good thing for his training score, but when he'd fallen with her, he landed on the gun, a hard lump under his butt causing yet more pain he could blame on her. At least while he was sitting on it, she couldn't steal it.

With his other hand he tested his nose. He managed not to scream in pain, so he figured it wasn't broken. Not even bloody. Just hurting like hell.

"That's your new name," he told the woman who aimed an elbow at the charley-horse point on his thigh, the same move he'd just used on her to get free of the headlock.

She missed, thank God. Woman had sharp elbows he knew from experience.

"Agent Beat Belfour."

Finally realizing that he had her and her only way out would be to shoot him, she relaxed.

Once again he was captivated by the feel and smell of this woman. So much strength and power, but so soft and warm in his arms.

He'd thought of little else since the last time she'd beat the crap out of him up close and personal like this.

With a twist of his arm, he hauled her into his lap and kissed her.

For a long perfect moment, she leaned into the kiss. Hard and strong, just like the rest of her, and soft and warm as well. What was a heady scent on her skin, was a mule kick of flavor on his tongue.

He'd been wrong before. His nightly imagination, for those few moments he'd been awake before crashing into hammered-down sleep each night, had remembered her smelling of midnight and roses. True, her lips tasted of that, but beyond that her mouth was pure fire, lit up inside him so hot he burned.

Then she got him.

Finally landed that right hook square into his solar plexus. Then Beat Belfour was gone into the night.

CHAPTER EIGHT

Gone! *What the hell* do you mean she's gone?"

"Keep your voice down." Hank Henson had pulled him aside the moment that the President had entered his first conference with the U.N. Secretary-General. They stood fifteen feet from the Sec-Gen's door, thirty-eight stories up in the Secretariat Tower.

"We don't know much yet. You know where she was stationed?"

"Sure," and Frank felt sick. Beat had pulled escort duty on the ambassador to Senegal right at the westernmost bulge of Africa. The U.S. ambassador had been receiving death threats and the Secret Service had sent her to investigate the degree of danger. She was an expert on both West Africa and personal security, so the Secret Service had loaned her to the Office of Foreign Missions for a couple of weeks. That in itself was pretty normal, but—

"Agent Belfour..." Henson kept his hands up as if to fend off Frank's anger. Not a bad idea. Right at this moment Frank could understand the desire to kill the messenger.

"... was accompanying Ambassador Sam Green and three assistants, left Dakar yesterday, July first, at seven a.m. local time. They were headed to a series of meetings at Bissau in Guinea-Bissau. There's no ambassador there because we have no permanent diplomatic mission there."

"Because the place is such a goddamn hellhole they can't keep a government in place."

"Granted." Hank rolled right on with his whispered report that several of the closer secretaries were trying desperately to overhear. "It's only a one-hour flight. The locally-staffed liaison office called at five p.m. to ask if they'd left Dakar yet, they were eight hours overdue at that time. Then the locals went home because it was the end of the work day. When the Senegalese operator tried to confirm with Guinea-Bissau this morning, July second, they couldn't get a response at all, so they finally reported them late. The G-B liaison office is still not answering."

Frank needed to hit something and hit it hard.

The fine wood paneling smelled faintly of a recent lemon-oiling. The Sec-Gen's secretaries sat in a row of neatly aligned desks. Several elegant comfortable chairs were clustered in front of the thirty-eighth floor window, with its spectacular view of the Manhattan shoreline, to accommodate waiting dignitaries. Not a single Senegalese or Guinea-Bissau office worker to punch anywhere. Not even a padded wall in a sparring gym to pound on.

"Twenty-four hours?" was all he could grind out of his tight throat. They'd been missing for twenty-four hours before word had gotten back.

"No, Guinea-Bissau is ahead of us. In local time they are thirty hours overdue now."

"Someone just kill me now."

"You wouldn't like it." Hank's sense of humor never lurked far beneath the surface and gave Frank a tempting new target. "If I killed you, you wouldn't have a chance to pummel whoever screwed this up."

"Great. You're a big help." He paced to the Sec-Gen's office door and back. He allowed himself up to a max of twenty feet away before he considered himself off post. Typically a nation's guards waited in the comfortable chairs over fifty feet away, and watched the view of the

Manhattan skyline. He was the United States Secret Service, Frank stayed close and watched the area around the door.

"We're having a hard time getting any communication in or out. We think they may be having another coup. It has been over a year since the last one, and we did just capture that rear admiral of theirs in the drug-and-arms-trafficking ring."

Frank couldn't shake the need to do something, anything, and he had only one option on that score.

"Keep me posted." Then he turned until he once again stood two steps to the right of the office door, behind which the President of the United States was in a meeting, and shifted into parade rest.

He scanned the room, everything and everyone where it had been two minutes before. Everything in place.

Except his world, which had now been turned upside down.

CHAPTER NINE

BEATRICE: 1988

Beatrice sat in the dark of the Georgia night, a hundred yards from the battered Ford Fairlane and the bleeding Frank Adams. She hadn't meant to bloody him, but that happened during training. Still, she hadn't meant to.

The heat scorching the Federal Law Enforcement Training Center had been at the front of her mind while she'd waited hidden in the back of the car.

Now she had a different heat to consider. And it wasn't one she liked. She didn't want to feel this way about anyone. Especially not some piece of crap off the street who had tried to carjack her. Except Frank Adams wasn't that. She knew more about him than she was supposed to, had managed to talk her way onto the background investigation team.

He lived with three other guys in a third-floor walk up. A Morningside Heights project at the far upper-west end of Manhattan. One so bad that it should never have been built to begin with, never mind torn down. When the investigating team went in, she was glad there were four agents together, the neighborhood was that rough.

They'd done round-robin interviews of all three of his roommates, each team member conducting their own individual interview. That way the Secret Service team could compare stories and answers afterward.

Big guy named Hale might have been the one to sit on her car hood. The build was right, but she'd only seen him from the back, and only briefly at that before Frank had blinded her windshield with his window-cleaning spray. She'd bet that the three roommates had all been around her car that night.

She didn't worry about that. Without Frank, they weren't likely to be more than petty criminals. What was interesting was that none of them would give up the least thing about Frank despite, she knew, Frank telling them it was okay. Their various stories about him were somewhat inconsistent, just as always happened in real life unless you practiced the stories, but they were totally loyal to him. She'd pushed hard on the carjacking, without mentioning that to the other agents or in her reports.

She hit a stone wall, even after saying she'd been the woman in the car and recognized each of them. These guys would lie their way right into jail to protect Frank. He'd earned absolute loyalty in a world that didn't trade in it.

Only child of a coke whore who'd been dead half a decade. Apparently she'd tried to be a good mother despite that. Father, no one had a clue. Even Frank had simply put a question mark on his background form. Hospital records had no other information. No one in his Morningside Heights project recalled a steady boyfriend for her, especially not from twenty years ago. Memories were short in the projects. But they'd remembered his mother as a lost soul, though pleasant and seriously pretty, right up to the overdose. Those were never pretty.

School teachers were deeply frustrated by him. Intelligent. Good grades. Didn't talk much, but had shown up consistently, a rarity in itself, and was never found without a thoughtful answer when questioned. The only telling remark she found was from a junior year science teacher. "Boy has no real focus on what to do with himself."

Beatrice sat with her back against one of the concrete barriers of the Georgia training grounds. Despite the night's heat, she pulled a dark hood over her head until it hung just above her eyes, masked to near invisibility like a Jawa. She wondered if Frank had ever seen *Star Wars*.

She wondered entirely too much about Frank for her own comfort. She'd discovered and shepherded him through application and recruiting, then dumped him into the training system. It should have ended there.

But her world hadn't returned to center. If it had, then what was she doing squatting in the cicada-throbbing darkness of FLETC with a knot on her head where she'd been shoved against the car door? Who knew the guy was so damn strong that he could stop a two-footed kick against the door with the palm of his hand. Her thigh still twinged where he'd dug his fingers into the nerve cluster to break a perfectly good headlock. And her lips still burned with the heat of his kiss.

She needed to put some real distance been them.

Then why are you sitting in the dark watching Frank Adams continue the exercise, Beatrice? You are so not going to be caught mooning over some man. You got away. You've got a role to play. Move your ass.

That the last order to herself sounded more like something Frank would say than herself, well, that only added to the problem. She kept an eye on his dark silhouette against the white Fairlane as she started moving sideways into the night.

Frank prowled the perimeter, his empty weapon drawn, aimed low, and swinging slowly before him exactly per training so that it was already in motion if he had to aim. It was faster to change direction of an active motion, than break muscle lock of a position held still for too long.

He hadn't sprinted after her.

Again, team player. It was a two-man exercise, and he didn't leave his partner with the unknown variable of the driver in the car. Any trainee that did was marked instantly dead by the trainers.

Actually, he wasn't moving quite per training. He was spending the bulk of his time on the side of the test zone that she'd exited from. Still looking for her.

He froze, his massive frame silhouetted by the flashlight his partner was using to inspect the vehicle. Frank was looking straight at her, or at least it felt like that. There was no way he could see her. No way he could know she'd begun to circle around and hadn't simply kept going.

But still he stood facing her, as if he could sense her even if he couldn't see where she stood a hundred feet into the brush.

Then he put one hand to his lips and ran it across his mouth. As if his lips also burned.

———

"Frank."

"Yo," he didn't turn at Jake Hellman's call. He could feel her out there. Over by the concrete barriers, that's where he'd bet Beat would go. At least to start, but then she'd move... that way... left. She'd be nothing but a shadow of a shadow, but he knew she was there. That kiss wouldn't have let her just run. There'd been more than heat, more than his need... or hers. It was as if they understood each other.

"Frank. She's gone."

"Right, sorry." He turned and blinked against the ghoulish brightness of Jake's red-lensed flashlight. They said that red didn't mess with your night vision. It did, just not as much. He'd felt, against all reason, that another thirty seconds and he'd have been able to see Beat, nickname definitely worked, out there in the darkness.

The Ford Fairlane sat on the empty dirt road. All of the doors wide open, and the dome light now definitely shot his night vision all to hell.

He ran the scenario through his head again. They'd stopped the car with a log dragged across the road, improvised road block. Driver had pretended to not understand what was going on, only speaking in something that might have been Czech or maybe just gibberish. The person-of-interest role played by Agent Belfour hiding on the floor of the back seat.

But she hadn't acted like a victim. No, she'd acted like a bodyguard. The hidden asset.

"Jake, where's the driver?"

"I've got him tied up on the other side. All nerves."

"It's a switch-out. He's the target, she's the guard."

"You sure?" But even as Jake asked, he raced around the hood of the car while Frank circled behind the trunk.

The driver was gone.

No. He wasn't. He'd rolled into a roadside ditch, hidden himself. Given away by his white shirt and light-colored khakis.

Wait. Not hidden. He'd gotten himself low.

Frank dove at Jake and tackled him down into the ditch on top of the driver just as a flashbang went off under the car, simulating an explosion that would have blinded them for several minutes as well as labeling them both as severely wounded if they were outside a fifteen foot radius, dead if they were inside it.

Simulated car bomb.

The Fairlane still rested in the middle of the lane instead of being blown into a thousand bits of shrapnel.

Before the light of the flashbang had fully faded, Frank had the driver up on his knees beside the ditch, and placed the barrel of his empty sidearm up against the man's temple. He held the man around the chest, pulling him close like a shield.

He put his back to the car to ensure he made the smallest target possible.

"You okay, Jake?"

"Mostly." Jake's head and sidearm popped up out of the ditch for a second, then ducked back. "You ever play football?"

"Nose tackle."

"Uh, I can tell." Jake's head popped up where he'd crawled fifteen feet farther down the ditch and he scanned the trees.

Closest Frank had ever gotten to football was the big screen at Slade's Bar. But the Hispanic gangs of the Upper East Side were nasty in a street fight and Frank had learned that the best defense was indeed a good offense. Hammer them to the ground before they could respond.

But he'd more recently learned to keep that part of his past hidden. People didn't want to know about his street background. Most agents in the various training scenarios wanted to think their partners could've gone All-American, rather than gone lifetime sentence for manslaughter.

The driver, still wrapped in Frank's grip, flinched hard and looked down at his chest. Then he spoke his first clear words of the evening, "Oh shit!"

Three splotches of red oozed down his chest. He'd been shot from somewhere in the dark woods on the far side of the ditch. Three shots so fast, that he'd never stood a chance.

"Hate it when I'm sacrificed."

"Shut up, you're dead." The smell of fresh paint stung Frank's nose, almost making him sneeze.

"Don't I just know it." The paintball pellets must have stung through the driver-agent's light cotton shirt. Frank could feel the man shrug, then fall limp in his arms.

That's when Frank made the mistake of letting him slide to the ground.

Knowing instantly that he'd screwed up, Frank dove to the right, but was too late.

A line of paintball shots stitched across his own chest.

He lay on the ground, technically bleeding out, as Agent Beatrice Ann Belfour slid out of the trees.

"Bang! You're dead."

Can we at least confirm if she's dead or not?" Frank trusted to his instincts to watch the Secretary-General's outer office and yet allow his mind concentrate on the information coming in.

"Maybe the ambassador too?" He knew Hank was teasing him over the encrypted two-way radio link, but he couldn't organize his thoughts enough to care about Ambassador Sam Green at the moment.

"Sure," Frank conceded begrudgingly. "But I can guarantee that if Beat is alive, then so is the ambassador." No question that she'd be down before whoever she was protecting.

Hank had radioed on a private frequency that went straight to Frank rather than the open channel to the whole PPD team. Hank was in the U.S. security office down in the U.N. basement.

"Only thing I can confirm is that another coup is going on. The French Embassy has told us that everyone is shut down and waiting for the next government to be installed."

"There's a joke for you."

"Yeah," Hank agreed. No trace of humor in him this time.

There'd been no need to explain the joke. "Government" was not something Guinea-Bissau had experienced much of lately. For a decade, G-B had been a narco-state. Coups were frequent and bloody. In 2009, the on-again, off-again President, the only one considered even close to decent, was gunned down in revenge for assassinating the head of his joint chiefs of staff. Of course, he'd had the supreme military commander killed for attempting a coup. And so it went on. In 2012, the latest military ruler had disbanded parliament as a "cost savings measure." The country had the lowest standard of living in the world, which was really saying something. Something awful.

Now it sounded as if the Acting President would be next under the gun, after having his two opponents arrested when he'd lost an election against them. Cocaine shifted across the G-B borders in multi-ton quantities, enroute to Europe or the U.S. Just a few months ago, the former head of their navy had been caught transshipping eleven hundred kilograms of cocaine and enough surface-to-air missiles to make a real mess of the DEA helicopters flying in Colombia.

"Any idea who is ousting who?"

"No. The last three coups have all been military factions in-fighting for control of the drug trade, so your guess is as good as mine. They always kill off a few top politicians along the way."

"When can the French Embassy get someone on the ground?"

"Their best estimate is five to seven days based on prior upheavals, though they said the worst coup required two weeks. Until then, they're keeping their people locked down. Russia was able to evacuate their people last night, along with Belgium and Germany. Assets in the country are real thin."

"Shit!" Frank let go of the frequency and glared at the secretaries who had turned to look at him. They saw his hot glare and abruptly found work to do on their desks.

The door beside Frank opened and the President strode out of the Secretary-General's office.

"Everything okay here, Frank?"

"Yes sir, Mr. President." There'd be a briefing ready within the hour, but there was no point in distracting the President with incomplete information before that time.

CHAPTER ELEVEN

BEATRICE: 1988

T*he key, people,*" ***Beat*** stood at the front of the training center lecture room. "The key is learning to act accurately and quickly on incomplete information." Two dozen agent-wannabes slumped in their seats, well past exhaustion. The room was a double-wide trailer, shabby from a hundred training classes and thousands of post-action analyses. The Georgia heat was so concentrated in here that she was surprised the plastic carpet didn't melt.

"Most of you pre-judged the roles. Make no assumptions. Ever!" She put a slide up on the screen. "Lynette Alice 'Squeaky' Fromme assassination attempt on President Ford during which no shots were fired." Click-clack of the advancing slide. "Sarah Jane Moore repeated the attempt seventeen days later, actually firing her weapon and wounding a nearby taxi driver." Click-clack. "Mark David Chapman who had John Lennon sign an album, then gunned him down six hours later." Click-clack. "Two months after that John Hinckley, Jr. succeeded in seriously wounding President Reagan in an effort to impress Jodi Foster who he was stalking. She was eighteen at the time."

Beatrice click-clacked through another dozen slides, all types of would-be and successful assassins operating on U.S. soil, and not a one looked demented or stereotypically terrorist. The slide projector clicking and the hum of the air conditioner that failed to fight back the heat or the body odor of the twenty men and four women struggling to stay awake in their chairs, were the only other sounds in the room.

"Only one of you recognized the driver was the target of the scenario." There was no need to point out who, the three paintball stains across Frank's chest had dried dark red on his shirt and were there for all to see.

"However," Beatrice pointed out before he could start to be too pleased with himself. "He made the false assumption that the companions of the person-of-interest would think him important enough to keep alive. Instead, they decided to sacrifice him to keep him from being questioned, which was the stated top criteria of the exercise. Most of you were killed by the simulated car bomb, he was killed by three bullets to the chest, and critical information on a terrorist plot was lost with the driver's death in all cases. Never assume."

She waited in silence, staring at the room in general and carefully not looking at Frank's hurt expression. That he'd gotten the highest score from observers by a factor of two was beside the point, and one she wouldn't be mentioning. She'd also be keeping silent about Frank being the only trainee to take her down, even briefly.

She didn't invite questions, that wasn't the point. She wanted to drive, to "beat" the point home. Damn him. That nickname had already begun to run through the other trainers. It was better than her childhood nickname of Beebee, for Beatrice Belfour, but not much. She'd had to pound that one into the ground throughout grade school, but the more she attempted to bury "Beat" the more often it cropped up. She had a nasty feeling this one was going to run through the agency.

"Dismissed. Get clean and get some sleep." After three months of FLETC they knew that they wouldn't have time to catch up on sleep. Drills at odd hours, functioning on high alert for days in crisis situations, learning to fight through the time when hallucinations from lack of sleep set in.

She waited until they were all gone, then shut down the projector and the lights.

He was waiting for her in the midnight shadows, leaning back against one of the trees of the low forest cultured for use in these scenarios.

Of course, he was. As she'd known he'd be.

She stood under the small yellow porch light of the double-wide, four steel steps to the ground.

He didn't move, leaving the choice to her.

Her boyfriend in college had not understood her sophomore-year turn from art, originally chosen to piss off her parents, to criminology, chosen to please herself.

Once she'd signed up for agent training, she only seemed to attract the men who were interested in proving they could out-wrestle a Secret Service agent. None of their egos had taken kindly to her definitive proof that none of them could.

Frank Adams was the first man in a long time who hadn't seen her as a target, something to conquer. Instead he waited and watched as her blood burned in the hot Georgia night and her pulse raced.

She was barely conscious of the steps she descended or the rough ground she crossed until they stood just inches apart under the trees. The night air scented by the tiny white flowers of the glorybower tree, punch strong but with a sweetness as soft as a truly fine gelato on a hot summer night. The blooms looked like stars lost from the sky and scattered over the dark green leaves, the only light in the darkness.

"Last time you socked me in the gut," his voice was a gentle rumble in the shadows.

She had.

"Good punch by the way." He slid his hands around her waist.

"Thanks," she wrapped her own around his neck.

He nuzzled her hair, "Even hot and sweaty you smell amazing."

She let herself lean her cheek against his chest and breathe him in. "So do you."

He scooped her up into his arms as if she were a feather. "Now's the time to say it if you're going to."

She kept her mouth shut, her arms around his neck, and her cheek on his chest.

He waited three heartbeats that she could feel and hear in his chest, then he strode into the woods until she wondered how he navigated at all. Even the tiny five-petal flowers faded away, though not their glorious scent that wrapped about them like a protective shawl.

He didn't set her down to kiss her, but simply kept her cradled against him. His mouth impossibly soft, his arms incredibly strong.

Beatrice had fought against everything in her life: her nicknames, her parents, the system, even the training rules. In Frank's arms, there was no need to fight at all. His kiss was everything she hadn't expected from the man she'd swept off the street three months ago. It was soft, playful, and included a smile when they finally moaned in unison.

He set her on her feet and leaned her back against a tree. He pinned her there with his lips, with the gentle brushstrokes of those big hands. He knelt before her and feasted on her body, and all she could do was hold on. When at last he had her naked against the tree, she guided him over her. A willing lover, one who made her feel things she hadn't felt before.

Not just the amazing rocketing sensations firing through her body in unprecedented waves of heat and pleasure. Not simply desired either. He made her feel needed. Important. As if being here with her was the only thing he cared about in the world.

When he had shed his own clothes and leaned naked upon her, skin-to-skin, she didn't go wild as she'd thought she'd might, ravenous for his touch and smell. Instead a peace settled over her as she traced her hands over his beautiful chest, invisible in the darkness, but still beautiful.

"Been thinking about this, haven't you?" she whispered when he reached down to his pants and pulled out some protection with a soft crackle of foil.

"Since the moment you pulled that damn gun on me."

"A gun turns you on?" She teased his pecs with her tongue.

"No." His groan rippled against her lips. "A gun makes my balls shrivel in fear."

She laughed and rested her forehead against his sternum as he stroked his hands up and down her back.

"But the woman who was wielding it turned me on since before I even heard her name."

"Damn you," her soft curse was lost against his lips as he lifted her by cupping his strong hands into a seat as she wrapped her legs about his hips.

He leaned her back against the tree and took her, one of the most incredible experiences of her twenty-three years.

"You feel even better than my car."

His chuckle was deep and rippled along her chest.

"Damn high praise that."

CHAPTER TWELVE

FRANK: NOW

S *he's the best."*

Frank knew better than to feel offended. First, the President was trying to make him feel better in a potentially ugly situation. Second, he was absolutely right. Even he wasn't as good as Agent Beatrice Belfour.

He needed to remember that.

If anyone could get out of this alive, it was Beat.

"So, what's the situation?"

Hank had radioed Frank that they were ready to brief the President on the G-B situation. Frank had informed the President as he came out of a quick meeting with the European Central Bank representative to the U.N., checking in on the latest banking crisis to hit the European Union. All of the aftershocks of the American recession were still having brutal ripple effects around the world. The recovery ripples just now crossing America were still a year or more in the future for Europe and Asia.

When Frank told the President about the problem in Guinea-Bissau, he'd immediately rescheduled a coffee chat with India and they'd taken the elevator down to the Secret Service's security office in the basement.

"I don't know the situation yet, Mr. President." Frank stuck his head out of the elevator and looked carefully both ways despite being inside the U.N. security perimeter. Two of his agents at either end of the hall signaled clear.

Frank led the President across the hall and down two doors. "I just know that she and the ambassador have been missing for thirty-one hours now. I'm hoping we've found out more than that." And if they hadn't, he just might steal a plane and fly over there himself to see what he could find out.

He went through the first door and inspected the small outer room. Six feet square, it had an American flag, a steel door, and a camera.

Once the outer door had latched behind them, two sharp buzzes filled the room. The first, driving bolts into the door behind them. The second, releasing the bolts on the door ahead. They moved into the war room.

A line of agents sat at terminals along the right-hand wall. They were responsible for the security of the room, coordinating all U.S. agent activities within the U.N. complex, and controlling outside security. Along the left wall a series of stations faced inward, about a third of these were staffed. They were responsible for communications, research, and anything needed by the active teams on site, including the U.S. Ambassador to the U.N., presently in London.

In the center, a table that could seat ten faced a trio of large flat screens on the far wall.

The room wasn't as secure and flexible as the White House Situation Room, but it was close. Close enough to observe and address world crises. Frank glared at the G-B map presently filling the central screen. Especially in unstable little ratholes like Guinea-Bissau.

The President joined Hank at the table, Frank stood behind a swivel chair and held on until his fingers ached where they dug into the leather. But he couldn't let go.

It was Hank's briefing. Frank had retasked him to prepare this briefing because, despite his constant joking and deep joy in hazing rookies, he was a top agent. No military commander could get to New York, cleared into the U.N.'s extraterritorial zone, and be sufficiently briefed in time, so Frank had loaned Hank to them as a liaison. If the situation escalated, they could call the Joint Chiefs into the Situation Room and link down to them.

At least with Hank on the case, Frank could stay focused on the President's security.

Mostly.

"We've been able to confirm that the ambassador's plane landed in Bissau at Osvaldo Vieira International. Thankfully we had the Nimitz-class aircraft carrier *Harry S. Truman* in the vicinity. They flew a Raptor drone overhead twenty minutes ago and were able to identify the plane."

A slide came up of the one-strip airport. A white circle around a tiny white cross on gray tarmac. The next slide a close-up so good he could almost count the rivets of the embassy's Beech King Air.

There was a dark blotch on the tarmac at the foot of the steps. A blotch that didn't look like spilled oil. Hank didn't comment on it, so neither did Frank. They'd both seen the spray and bleed-out pattern of a single headshot before. It wasn't important to the tactical situation, other than to confirm it sucked. They already knew that, without the confirmation. No body in evidence, no way to tell anything about who it had been.

The President's skin, gone abruptly gray, told that he'd reached the same conclusion.

Hank put up the next slide. It showed a small building, or rather the remains of one.

The walls had been blown out sideways, the roof was gone. Inside were the remains of a pair of SUVs. A close-up revealed a leg and an arm, the first stuck out from beneath a section of the roof, the other wasn't attached to anything.

The silence in the room was so thick that it pressed in on Frank from every side. Everyone was waiting for his reaction and he wasn't ready to have one yet.

"Do we have a higher resolution image?"

Hank said something to one of the left-wall techs and the image jumped inward until the two body parts were nearly life-size projected against the wall. So close you could smell the red dust, the black char from the fire, and the deep-in-the-throat bite of copper that was spilled blood.

The arm wore a golden bracelet, not something Beat would ever wear in the field.

The leg had a men's shoe.

He swallowed hard and managed to keep his voice steady.

"What else do we know?"

———

"What we know," Beat turned to face Ambassador Green. "Is that we need to remain calm and quiet."

"But..."

She held up a hand to silence him.

Okay, she hadn't killed the man, yet. Though she was certainly going to reserve that option. He still survived mostly because it was bad form to kill the man you were sworn to protect. And a little bit because he was such a fish out of water that she had to pity him. He'd been a political appointee by the prior administration rather than a career diplomat. And that he'd been assigned to the Senegalese embassy only said how low he was on the totem pole. He should have contributed more to the last President's campaign, or to a different party and stayed in Kansas or wherever he hailed from.

Three years he'd been in Senegal and he had the common sense of a hamster. For one thing, after seeing what he'd signed up for, he'd stayed. Bad choice right out of the gate. This would be a hard posting even for a career Foreign Service diplomat. At least he appeared to be trying to do the right thing, but he really needed to learn to listen to direction.

Of course his *chief attaché* was currently lying in little pieces along with the remains of the embassy's two SUVs and airport garage. Up until the explosion, those vehicles and a small liaison office downtown had been the sole assets of the U.S. government in Guinea-Bissau. Now only the office remained.

When the explosion occurred, she and the ambassador had been waiting halfway to the garage while his assistant trotted back to the plane on her mid-heel pumps for his forgotten briefcase. The *chief attaché* and the *chargé d'affaires* hadn't been so fortunate. They'd gone ahead to the garage, a fancy word for a concrete block with two metal roll-up doors she could have unlocked in less than a minute without keys or explosives.

After much hiding, and three miles of sneaking through the suburbs of a city at war, the airport now lay thirty hours behind them. In their weaving track, they'd covered perhaps a quarter of that distance from the airport as the crow flies.

They huddled now in a hut of cracked, sun-baked brick walls and a rotting tin roof. The red dirt floor bore little in the way of debris or belongings, indicating that it was, perhaps, if their luck was changing even a little please, vacant. She'd erased their footprints for a hundred paces back, but they had to stay quiet and out of sight.

The ambassador and Charlotte his personal secretary, clearly with side benefits, huddled hip to hip against the back wall. Whatever they did on the side wasn't her business, neither wore a ring anyway. They were swathed as she was, in clothing snagged from clotheslines.

Sam Green's black pants with a simple white *dashiki* hanging to mid-calf over them worked well. She had him scuff up his black dress shoes. If anything had driven home the reality of their situation for him, even more than witnessing the explosion that had killed his two top-ranked staffers, it was when she'd grabbed the shoe from his hands as he gently patted it with red dirt. Beatrice had scrubbed it against some broken concrete until it was deeply scarred, then shoved it into the soil and handed it back to him.

Charlotte actually looked quite fetching in the traditional golden yellow-and-brown print *buba* and wrap-around sarong skirt. Beatrice had snagged a traditional head wrap for her, but Charlotte couldn't keep it on her long, smooth hair. Even the head scarf kept slipping down around her shoulders.

Beatrice herself had found a bright blue *pagne* blouse and matching skirt. It would have been garish or at least stand-out in any environ other than West Africa, but here it blended in.

Charlotte's feet weren't up to running barefoot, so she'd retained the bright blue pumps that didn't fit in at all. Of course, neither did her or Green's blond hair, blue eyes, and New England-fair skin. They'd be a beautiful couple in a Boston townhouse, but they sure didn't belong on the streets of an African country on the verge of collapse.

And neither of them knew how to move. She'd tried to show them the lazy, ambling walk of sub-Saharan equatorial Africa. That had been a fiasco. It was as if they'd traveled direct from prep school to an alien planet and learned nothing during their time in Africa. Charlotte was doing better than the ambassador, but not much. No matter how nice they might be as people or how good they might be at diplomacy, they were lost causes when it came to hiding out and blending in.

The three of them had been barely a dozen yards from the garage when it went up. She'd seen the fizzle of a failed explosive device and thrown the ambassador and Charlotte behind the next garage over just as the backup device blew the world to shit.

She'd turned to sprint them back to the plane, hoping she could find some way to fly it out of there before someone shot it down. Then she'd spotted the army jeep roaring up beside it just in time to duck back out of sight. A ragtag trio climbed aboard the Beech King Air, their Soviet-era Kalashnikov machine guns leading the way. They hauled the Senegalese pilot out of the plane. Only Beat's hand over Charlotte's mouth had stopped the scream when they'd executed him on the tarmac beside the embassy plane.

Beatrice had dragged them to their feet and actually hit and slapped them until they started running.

Now, thirty hours later, they huddled in the midday heat. Her throat aching with the dry dust and blazing equatorial heat.

Their assets included her handgun, four spare magazines, one briefcase full of paperwork and a few pens that the ambassador had refused to abandon, but she'd gotten him to stuff it into a stolen burlap sack he'd then carried over his shoulder, and a pair of blue pumps. No cell phone signals, and the neighborhoods they'd passed through had no overhead lines, so no electricity or landline phones.

The shocking number of tacticals, white Toyota pickups with .50

caliber machine guns turreted in their beds, did not point to finding much help in the city.

Still, she'd listened initially to Ambassador Green's insistence on reaching the American Liaison Office or the Presidential Palace in the heart of the city. But the black smoke now rising from that direction indicated that this time, if it was again a coup, it had not gone as smoothly as the prior executions of a few key leaders. Thirty hours of hard work and they'd covered less than two of the six kilometers to the city center. And the chances of survival decreased with every meter in that direction.

After dark, she'd see if the people around here had any food to steal.

And maybe someone had a pair of sandals for Charlotte.

———

"Is the Guinea-Bissau ambassador to the U.N. here today? Ambassador Anselmo?"

Frank looked at the President in shock. Why the hell hadn't he thought of that? And how had the President remembered the guy's name? He was always doing that, as if his brain operated on a whole different level.

Frank hadn't thought of it because they barely have a government was his answer. But anything was worth a shot.

One of the techs rattled her keyboard, "Yes."

"Extension?" Hank called out and dialed it on the central table's speaker phone even as she dictated it.

In minutes they had an appointment.

Frank could definitely appreciate traveling with the President. The man got things done.

CHAPTER THIRTEEN

FRANK: 1988

No *way in hell* that this is done." Three months they'd been sleeping together on the sly. Three months and the heat, smell, taste of Beatrice Ann Belfour was burned right into Frank's nerve endings.

They sat on the bench where they'd perched a lifetime and six months ago. This time it was late morning rather than two a.m. And it was frickin' January-butt-clench cold. But everything else was much the same.

The Brooklyn Bridge soared above them, the restaurant and its lousy fake security cameras was doing a lively business despite the frigid winter morning. The East River Ferry slid into DUMBO dock. He kept meaning to look up why they called it that, but never had. A glance over his shoulder and he could see by the giant clock atop the Watchtower building that the boat was running ten minutes late as usual.

They were sitting right where the old man had howled at the moon along with his dogs in *Moonstruck*. He almost smiled at the memory of the frantic love they'd made after watching it, right down to the full moonlight streaming into his Brooklyn studio apartment window. Still a third-floor walkup, but the tiny apartment in the brownstone owned by a couple of artists was a hell of a lot better than the Morningside Heights projects.

He finally forced himself to look down at Agent Beatrice Ann Belfour sitting beside him on the cold metal. Her dark hair was tucked under a knit hat of blue and green stripes. Her red parka was zipped so far up her neck that her face almost disappeared into it. It made her appear about twice her true size. He could appreciate that, as his sweatshirt and jacket were not up to the task of keeping him warm even with the hoodie up. But her words had sent a much greater chill coursing down his spine.

"We have to be done. We're fraternizing."

"I'm not the goddamn enemy." He knew his anger wasn't helping, but he was way past being able to control that.

"I'm a full agent, you're a trainee. I can't keep putting that at risk for me and I can't put that at risk for you."

"Like I could give a rat's ass." Though he actually did, which was kinda weird. He wanted this to work, a whole life beyond the projects that he'd never imagined. But he wanted her more.

She wasn't looking at him.

That's what was killing him. Those dark, fathomless eyes were glazed over and facing off somewhere in the direction of Manhattan, not at him. Not making him feel warm inside. Instead, they froze him out.

"My next assignment arrived this morning."

"And you didn't tell me?" His shout was loud enough that some of the passengers debarking from the East River ferry stumbled on the gangplank in the hurry to look in his direction and just as quickly away.

"I'm telling you now."

She was. Damn it! He bit his tongue.

"I'm telling you first."

Double damn! For six months he'd kept his temper in check. Once the trainers had learned he could control that, they'd pounded on him, trying to get a rise, trying to find out just how deep his control ran. It had gotten so deep that some of the other trainees had gotten mad on his behalf and stepped in the way of the obvious hazing. He'd kept his cool, except around Beat.

He couldn't do it now when he needed it. Not with Beatrice telling him they were done. He closed his eyes, took a deep breath.

"Okay." Another. "What is it?"

"I'm going to be working Africa for the next six months. Traveling station to station, verifying and standardizing Secret Service security operations and interface with local agencies. It's a great oppor—"

"And now you're telling me that you're going to take it no matter what I say." Frank had been prepared to ride out whatever she'd be doing. But not this. Not six months of it. That he couldn't figure how to swallow.

She didn't look at him, not even after the ferry reloaded and moved on across the shining water.

Finally she nodded, then hung her head.

Beatrice Belfour never hung her head.

Think, Frank. You've always let her do the thinking. Time you tried some of that. She's the one who pulled you out of the shit projects and the hard-time future. She risked her career and shared her body. She was the one he was totally gone on. What have you risked?

Nothing!

And she never mentioned her family. He'd only met them once, totally by accident when they spotted her car and flagged her down. New York was weird like that. You could be way out of your normal 'hood and you'd run into a friend on the street you hadn't seen in six months, despite knowin' you lived just three blocks apart.

Family wasn't a place he bothered to think of much. But it had been real damn clear that her folks weren't expecting no Frank Adams.

That must hurt like hell too. She'd given everything and he'd just been cruisin' along for the ride, not giving it any thought.

Well, it was time to start doing that.

"Okay," he breathed deep until the cold air pierced his insides like frozen needles. "Okay." He turned to face her.

She didn't look up.

Thinking it better not to cup her chin and turn her face, he pressed a finger against her hunched shoulder, slowly turning her toward him and forcing her shoulder back until she looked up.

"I'll wait."

"But—"

"I'll wait!" He cut her off harshly. Knew he was being a jerk, not letting her finish her thoughts. But he had to make the point so she heard it.

She stared at him for a long time, those dark eyes boring into him, seeking some truth he'd never find.

Finally, that single nod.

What the hell was that anyway? Frank Adams didn't wait for any woman.

Beatrice got up and walked back toward her car to head into the New York office of the United States freaking Secret Service.

Frank stayed and blinked against the cold sunlight burning his eyes.

For Beatrice Ann Belfour, he'd damn sure wait.

CHAPTER FOURTEEN

No, *we need answers* right now, Ambassador Anselmo." The President was not in one of his patient moods. "What is happening in your country, in Guinea-Bissau, right now?"

"Nothing is bad happening in my country. Can assure your nation of that, President Matthews."

Frank wanted to pound his fist into the man's dark face and then his ever so bright diplomat's smile wouldn't look so pretty. And by the time he was done, the man's Brooks Brothers' pinstripe would also be seriously mussed.

They sat in the Guinea-Bissau ambassador's office in the U.N. Secretariat Tower. It had none of the grandeur of the U.N. Secretary-General's. A lone receptionist, a pretty woman in a traditional red blouse, sarong, and sandaled feet, had greeted them kindly. Clearly one of the highlights of her day, not just meeting the American President, but meeting anyone in this quiet corner of the floor where the West African nations were clustered together. Her desk had been clearly devoid of any work, despite the ambassador's presence.

Anselmo's office bore little of the traditional African décor. Instead he had drawn deeply on the designs, colors, and motifs of his country's heritage as a former Portuguese colony. Frank felt like he'd been trapped in an Iberian version of a Pottery Barn store. Nothing felt authentic.

"Then perhaps you can explain the attack on my embassy aircraft," the President's voice was calm. Matter of fact.

Hank Henson set down the photo of the massive bloodstain by the airplane's exit stairs as the President spoke.

Frank had heard the President angry before, but this wasn't angry. This was something new. He'd gone very quiet, so soft-spoken that Frank could barely hear him though he stood only two steps behind his chair. This was dangerous. In two years of serving with him, and six months on the campaign trail before that, he'd never heard that tone from Peter Matthews.

"After that would you care to explain the deaths of my embassy personnel?"

The photo of the exploded garage landed on the ambassador's broad and empty desk, next to a gruesome close-up of the body parts, still there thirty-two hours later.

"The torching of my liaison office."

A photo of the smoke still smoldering around the remains of the U.S. Liaison office building in downtown Bissau.

"These are acts of war, Mr. Ambassador. You have one hour to produce answers. After that, I will make any decisions I deem appropriate to determine the security of my remaining personnel on the ground."

The President stood and moved from the room so quickly that Frank was hard pressed to stay in front of him. Hank brought up the rear.

As soon as they were in the elevator, the President began speaking quickly.

"You saw his face. He doesn't know anything is wrong. Completely out of the loop, he's playing the game with a tray full of vowels. I'll wager he can't even communicate with anyone in G-B at this time, though I'm sure he is only at this very instant discovering that."

Frank blinked, it took him only that long to catch up with the President's thoughts.

"Then why did you give him an hour?" Frank wouldn't have given him thirty seconds.

The President didn't answer, instead he turned to Hank as the elevator continued downward.

"Hank, what's our closest asset? The *Harry S. Truman* where they launched the Raptor drone?"

"Good memory, yes sir. Operation Sure Seas off Nigeria. Nigeria's trying to outdo Somalia on being the terror of ocean-shipping channels. The *Truman*'s leading a task group to fight them back."

"Find out how fast they can have assets into Guinea-Bissau. Get the Joint Chiefs involved. We aren't waiting an hour, we aren't waiting a minute, I just wanted to give their ambassador some motivation. I do wish I hadn't mentioned surviving U.S. citizens on the ground."

In retrospect, Frank agreed. If the ambassador could get through to whatever was the government of the moment, he would tell them there was someone they needed to find. The question was whether it would be to find and save, or find and silence.

At the basement floor Hank got off the elevator, but the President remained, so Frank stayed with him. The President held the door as he finished passing instructions to Hank.

"I have a luncheon with Russia, a meeting with Pakistan that isn't going to be any fun at all, and a dinner with Great Britain and France. After dinner there's an informal but essential meeting with Laos, Cambodia, and Vietnam about a combined trade agreement. I can't delay any of those, but I'll run things through Frank. Keep him posted. Call Daniel at the White House. Tell my Chief of Staff to get his wife on this and to get everyone in the Sit Room. I'll deal with the attacks on U.S. property and personnel later. I want our people in Guinea-Bissau found and found now."

He let the elevator door close without completing the statement to Hank, which Frank appreciated. He didn't need to hear the President of the United States say about Beatrice Belfour, "if there is anyone still alive to be found."

Once again, he was stuck with waiting.

"What we need at the moment is patience. You have to stay here."

Ambassador Sam Green and Charlotte looked at Beatrice as if she'd gone mad. Well, that wouldn't surprise her much at the moment. Trapped with the two of them in a narco-state undergoing a coup wasn't exactly a rational experience. Guinea-Bissau didn't have a large number of motor vehicles, and most of those were ancient motor scooters.

Yet, through the cracks in the wall of the hut they were hiding in, the roads were far from empty. They were hiding in a warren of ramshackle huts southeast of the airport, but one that afforded her a narrow view of the one main street in the whole city. In the last few hours squatting here, she'd seen a dozen tacticals, the white Toyota pickups just bristling with armed and angry militia, and two tanks that looked to be left over from when the place had gained independence in the '70s. She knew they had about thirty tanks, but intelligence had been unsure how many actually worked and how many of those had shells for their main cannon. She could hear something pounding away in the city center, clearly someone had some ammunition. The place was really coming apart. Again. She even spotted one of their two known helicopters.

"You have to stay put here," she pointed emphatically at the hut's dirt floor.

"Not alone. We can't."

Beatrice was never prepared for this stage of working protection jobs. The moment when the protectee turned into, what the department carefully didn't call, "the sniveling child" phase. Young children never dared circulate far from their parents. Protectees would latch onto their bodyguard's metaphorical skirts and become a real pain.

Technically, it was called a stage-two trauma response.

Beatrice sighed. At least they were finally out of the stage-one denial. Now the ambassador had apparently opted for fear and confusion in stage two. She could do with the help from anger, but he hadn't gone there. The Secret Service had trained her how to shift in mere seconds from precipitating event to stage three, new equilibrium. Only from equilibrium could the decision-making process accurately resume.

If she could do a Vulcan mind-meld and shift Sam Green forward through the stages, she would. Though she seriously doubted she'd like what else she learned about him during the meld.

Charlotte had moved on to anger. Apparently she and the now dead *chargé d'affaires* had been shopping buddies. That would be helpful, so she addressed Charlotte.

"Look, if you want to get out of this alive so you can work on fixing this place so this never happens again..." Fat chance of that. Guinea-Bissau would be cycling through hell for decades to come just as it had for the last half century. These kinds of places always did. "... Then I need you to stay here and stay quiet. I'm going to get food and water. I'm also going to try and scout our way out of here."

Charlotte's sharp nod of agreement confirmed that the woman's brain had kicked back in. And that she was really looking forward to kicking some serious butt to revenge the *chargé d'affaire's* death.

Beatrice momentarily considered handing over her gun, but decided against it. The last thing she needed was for Sam Green to suddenly take it from his more rational assistant and decide he was G.I. Joe. Or, more likely, to go out and think that he could talk sense to these people at gunpoint.

Instead, she told Charlotte. "Don't let him leave. There's half a million people here. If I lose you, you're going to be dead."

"And if we stay with you?" She saw in his eyes that Ambassador Green was at least part way back.

Beatrice shrugged. "Then I'll see what I can do to improve our chances."

For three hours Beatrice prowled the streets of Bissau. Starting her scouting in late evening, blending smoothly among what people there were along the street, darkness descended with that sudden slice-of-a-knife abruptness typical of tropical countries. The moonlight, and the warm glow of cooking fires lit her way. But between each calm cluster of families going about their dinner-time life, explosions racketed from the direction of the city center.

Bissau was turbulent. It was a city at war. Which was odd. As she understood the political structure, it was the military and the politicians who were constantly struggling for control of the drug trade. And no one else cared. For some reason, this time the entire city had erupted into violence.

It reminded her of the World Trade Organization riots she'd ridden out during the 1999 Battle of Seattle. America had managed to set a new low for international standards of supposedly peaceful protest. To quell the "peaceful" rioting and looting had required the activation of two units of the National Guard and the entire police force. Massive vandalism, tear gas, stun grenades, rubber bullets, and over five hundred arrests. Seattle had exported their new brand of peaceful-protest-gone-violent to every subsequent meeting of the WTO, the G-8, or anyone else trying to improve international relations. This had the same feel. The place had simply gone nuts.

Out here on the periphery, near the airport but not too near, the houses had mostly emptied. Everyone had either run to join the fray at either end of the main road, or run to the countryside to get out of it.

She slouched against a wall along the avenue between the airport and city center, the only four-lane road in the whole country. She heard it called the *Fera di Bandim*. She thought that *Fera* translated as "Beast" in Portuguese, but that didn't make much sense. *Bandim* was the central market, the anchor for the center of the city. Beast in the Market. Nope. Probably meant "road" in the local Kriol language, "road to market" worked. Or maybe it meant "market." Market in Bandim? She preferred her translation. A street-corner sign, rusted and tipped badly, declared it as, Avenida Combatentes de Liberdade da Pátria. Avenue of the Patriotic Combatants of the Liberation? Avenue of the fighters to liberate some guy named Pátria?

She was losing it. She knew from training and real-world experiences that her exhaustion was going to make her useless, beginning sometime within the next twenty-four hours. So, she set that as her timer and felt better for the focus. They had to get out within twenty-four hours or they were going to die here, and that wasn't on her list of things to do in Guinea-Bissau.

Beat was tempted to try the walk into town to see what was happening, perhaps she could make an international call.

"Hello. Pentagon please. Could you please send a battalion to clean this place up?" Not likely. On an open line, sure to be monitored if it even worked, she'd be dead before she hung up the phone. Stupid idea. After just forty-two hours of being awake, she already wasn't thinking straight.

Here on the "Beast" the traffic remained light. In an hour she counted seven more tacticals, though three may have been repeats roaring from town to airport and back. That she wasn't sure was another bad clue to her state of mind. She'd been awake too long already, twenty-four more might be a bad stretch, but she couldn't think of how to rescue them sooner. Actually, she couldn't think of how to rescue them at all, that's what she was really out here looking for, wasn't it? Though she couldn't tell the ambassador that, he wouldn't make it if she told him that.

Three more tanks rolled through and one of the country's six MiG-21MF fighter jets actually roared by close overhead in a display of... she had no idea what. No one had thought that any of the six were still flying.

The MiG hadn't had any bombs tucked under its wings, but it did have a very effective built-in 23mm cannon, if it was working and they had rounds. What was certain was that someone still controlled the tiny Guinea-Bissau air force and was making a statement. A statement which told her that even if she managed to sneak back to the airport, steal the embassy plane and figure out how to fly it, they'd be gunned out of the sky.

That was it.

Right there.

Beat felt as if she'd been electro-shocked awake.

They knew that there were Americans still alive on their soil. No one in the outside world would know, but someone in Guinea-Bissau did. Someone who'd counted bodies at the garage compared with the number they had called in to the custom's office before they landed.

And the Bissau-Guineans, at least whoever presently controlled their air force, didn't want them leaving. She, Ambassador Green, and Charlotte were now being hunted.

No one else in the country had access to airplanes, the airport had been empty except for the daily passenger jet out of Dakar, and even it wouldn't come in while a coup was in progress. Only the Americans, unable to fit their schedule to the one daily commercial flight, had brought their own craft. The MiG clearly said, "We will kill you if we find you."

Time to get back to work.

Beatrice found that sandals were commonly available, so she let herself drift several blocks before stealing any. That way the theft wouldn't localize their whereabouts for any militia or angry locals that came prowling. By some miracle, they'd gotten away from the airport clean, and she didn't want to risk that little sliver of security.

Food and water didn't prove hard either. Everyone was out and about with the city at war.

She went back to their hideaway by a long, circuitous route, dragging the tail of her skirt the last few hundred feet to erase her footprints.

The hut was so silent when she returned that she feared they'd actually been stupid enough to leave, or worse, been captured. She stood motionless. Staging a one-woman rescue across the landscape of Bissau wasn't her idea of a movie that had any chance of a happy ending. Rambo she wasn't.

She hadn't seen any footprints outside, but in the soft moonlight, she might have missed them.

Then she heard it.

The ambassador and his assistant were trying to be quiet. They clearly hadn't heard her return as they moaned softly together.

Beatrice moved back outside the hut and sat in the dirt, resting her back against the doorframe. It was in moonshadow, she would be close enough to invisible resting here. She could afford to wait a little while.

Sometimes people in fear for their lives needed a little privacy.

CHAPTER FIFTEEN

BEAT: 1989

Beat **really didn't need** any more alone time.

Six months she'd been traveling in Africa and, she really hated to admit it, she missed Frank. She'd decided after her parents had been such total pains about Frank, that she didn't need any family. They'd hounded her so badly about "that boy not being good enough" that she'd cut them off. Had even taken to screening her calls with the answering machine. Finally, she'd decided that no one, including Frank, would have that hold over her and she wouldn't let herself need anybody at all.

But, she hated to admit it, she'd missed him.

She'd returned from the Africa security assignment to Brooklyn both exhausted and turbo-charged. She'd showered in every barracks, hotel, and Secret Service office that had one, from Johannesburg to Cairo to Ramstein to JFK airport, trying to wash off the last six months.

She'd missed the premieres of *Field of Dreams* and *Dead Poet Society*. And she'd wager that without her guidance, or "hounding his ass" as he called it, Frank had probably gone to see nothing except *Batman* and the unpredicted hit *Bill and Ted's Excellent Adventure*. She'd been stuck with that on the commercial flight from Germany and could have shot herself. She'd fix his movie habits straight off.

After spending six months overseas, she thought maybe they could get together. At least for movies. There was no real question in her mind that Frank was the kind of man who would wait for her, simply because he said he would. He was just that much a man of his word.

The rest of it, well, she'd have to wait and see. Some great no-strings sex, that she'd definitely be up for. He'd be up for that. Wouldn't he? She certainly wasn't going to have with-strings sex, so it had better be good enough.

When she'd left, he hadn't laid any guilt trip on her about staying single or anything, but there hadn't been even one man on the road who'd measured up to the Frank Adams' standard. More than once she'd cursed the damn street punk for ruining her for casual sex with other men. Whoever she hooked up with, they had a whole new level of fine they'd have to rate. And none had.

After her third shower, a meal, and sixteen hours of sleep, just to prove she didn't need him that badly, she dialed his phone.

She had to get the Chinese grocer three times before she checked the number. She dialed it a fourth time to be sure.

Where the hell was he?

It might be six a.m. Friday morning here, but her body was still on Africa time and she'd been up for hours. Thought she was being nice by not calling him when she'd woken up at two a.m.

Well, she was supposed to have the next five days off, but it was clearly high time to head into the office. Someone would know where he'd gone.

———

Frank sat in the Secret Service liaison office at Fort Sam Houston. The U.S. Southern Command in San Antonio, Texas had given them one tiny room for the four of them to cram into.

He looked at his watch. Beat'd be home by now, probably still sleeping off the flight. Back from six months of silence in Africa.

He'd kept a track on her schedule, but had decided it would be better if that remained very quiet. She'd made it damn clear before she left, and by her utter lack of communication while gone, that the next move was up to her.

Focus, he ordered himself for about the four-thousandth time in the last forty-eight hours. Knowing she was on her way home, his focus had seriously sucked. Not enough for others on the Fort Sam team to comment on it, but pretty bad.

She'd missed some interesting times.

Earlier in June the Ayatollah Khomeini had died and the next day halfway around the globe had been the Tiananmen Square massacre. Two days later, back in Iran, the Ayatollah's body had almost been dumped to the ground during a hastily aborted funeral as thousands of grief-ridden mourners had tried to snag a piece of his death shroud to remember him by.

Emergency Secret Service teams had been formed to assess dangers to both U.S. diplomatic security in China and possible terrorism threats from an Islamic right wing seeking opportunities among an entire people gone mad with grief.

Frank got pulled into active service two months ago. He'd gotten his orders about two hours after he graduated training and been declared an agent. He'd made it through as head of his class, a distinction he shared with Agent Beatrice Ann Belfour. He closed his eyes for a moment, ignoring the pain that had grown as she hadn't called throughout that day. He'd known she was at the Nairobi Embassy all that week. It would have been so easy for her to find out how he was doing. Easy to have called or sent a god damn telegram. Would faxing an inter-office memo saying, "Congratulations!" have frickin' killed the woman? Apparently.

She hadn't done any of it, and that had been a bitter pill.

Focus.

He looked at the cork board he and the four other agents had been covering with information over the last two months. His first assignment had landed him on a Panama diplomatic security planning team in San Antonio. As if the back-to-back messes in Iran and China weren't enough, bloody Noriega had to add this drug-gang-boss shit on. The world was really cracking at the seams this year.

Manuel Noriega had run completely out of control. Originally nurtured to power by American support, things started to go bad in the 1970s. By 1986 it became clear that it was bad, and President Reagan had tried to force him to step down. By 1988, the Pentagon was pushing for an invasion but Reagan had refused. Presidential-hopeful Bush had ties to Noriega from his years as Director of the CIA and heading the Task Force on Drugs, and President Reagan hadn't wanted to damage his Vice-President's chances of election, so he'd held off.

It looked as if it would finally fall to President Bush to deal with his former colleague. It now appeared that Bush had carefully ignored numerous reports regarding Noriega's activities in money-laundering and drug-trafficking.

Noriega had just lost an election and then declared the results invalid. Two thousand U.S. troops had been sent in to secure American interests in the Canal Zone. And Frank's team was building scenarios on how to protect and, if necessary, cleanly extract American diplomatic personnel if it all went to hell.

The phone on the table rang and Frank answered it for something to do, because he sure hadn't been following the latest conversation on the on-going Operations Sand Flea and Purple Storm. The idea was to stage numerous military exercises in Panama that showed U.S. might, to prove "Freedom of Movement" rights throughout the Canal Zone and into surrounding countryside, as well as to utterly overwhelm and confuse Panamanian observers with the sheer volume of the exercises.

Nine different military operations, most grouped under Operation Prayer Book, formed a dazzling confusion that kept the Secret Service almost as bewildered as the Panamanians about what the American military was up to. Like an old razzle-dazzle move in a street fight. "Don't look over here, because if you do, we gone kick your sorry ass from over there."

"Adams here."

"What the hell are you doing in Texas?" Beatrice Ann Belfour sounded pissed.

And he was so damn glad to hear her voice, that his knees folded right out from under him, and he dropped into a chair. The other three guys startled and turned to see what was up. What was up was a huge grin that he couldn't stop from spreading across his face.

"Workin' is what I'm doin'."

"But in Texas?"

He loved that she was pissed that he wasn't in Brooklyn. It felt so damn good, he could really get to enjoy this. Did she even realize how upset she sounded? Man, this was the kind of ego stroke he'd been needing and needing bad.

"You missed some good movies."

She growled, actually growled at the change of topic. It also clearly told him what she'd expected him to go see. So, he didn't mention *Cyborg* with his man Van Damme kickin' ass.

"*Indiana Jones III* came out, funny as hell. Had Sean Connery as his dad, I know you're all hot for him." One of the guys in the room laughed loud enough that Frank knew the phone had picked it up and shot it straight to Beat's earpiece. Beat would know he was sitting in a room full of guys while teasing her. That should make her crazy. And worse, it really had been her kind of movie. He'd sort of gone to it so it would feel like they were connected. All it had gone and done was make him sad.

"The new *Star Trek* sort of sucked. All about Spock's brother or some kinda crap." She had a weak spot for Nimoy, too. She'd gotten him hooked on the series so he'd have gone to that one on his own anyway.

He could feel her fuming all the way down the phone line.

"Texas?" With a single snapped word, she refocused the conversation where she wanted it.

"It be where de action at, man." Again, the other agents were eyeing him strangely. They were used to his cleaned-up NYU use of language. To tease Beat, he'd slid right down into Morningside Heights street.

"What kind of action?"

"You cleared for this?" God, this was just way too much fun.

"I damn well will be." And she hung up on him.

He couldn't suppress his smile. He wasn't sure what her response would be, but he couldn't wait to find out.

FRANK: NOW

Frank **ground his teeth** as the President's Southeast Asia trade meeting ran for an extra half hour. It was all he could do to retain his position at the end of the Woodrow Wilson Reading Room, the center of the Dag Hammarskjöld Library.

Down the left wall, a long line of built-in card catalogs filled the entire long wall. And the U.N. people were using them. He wasn't sure the last time he'd seen a card catalog in use. Of course, this catalog was everything from the League of Nations, which predated the U.N. A lot of what existed in this catalog were still the foundations of international law. His head hurt just thinking of the automation nightmare to catch that up.

The room was twenty-plus feet wide and about eighty long. Several low bookcases against the right-hand glass wall partially blocked his view, so he kept a very careful eye on who went to those. Frank had checked the glass and the view of the central fountain. The glass was thick enough to stop low-caliber fire. A double-tap with a big sniper rifle like a Barrett would get through and a Steyr probably wouldn't even deflect. That Steyr had designed a hand-carried rifle that could punch holes in an armored personnel carrier creeped him out.

What would it do to the "Beast" if targeted while the President was inside. It might resist it. He ran some foot-pound force comparisons in his head, Steyr vs. armor. They might be okay. The "Beast" was a tough car. But maybe not.

Deep breath. Focus.

Lesson number eight-ninety-three, worry only about what you can control. But so damn much was out of his control. Any of a half-dozen apartment buildings that he could see out the window could have a shooter on the balcony. There were a pair of Secret Service counter-snipers tasked with watching for that, but that was a whole lotta apartments to cover. And if the shooter was standing back in the shadows of an open window…

His mood had gotten way too dark.

The G-B ambassador had at least called back promptly on the hour and made it thoroughly clear, by how much he'd said without saying anything at all, that he couldn't reach anyone in his government.

The President already had U.S. armed forces moving some heavy assets down onto the Cape Verde Islands which lay just five hundred miles offshore to the northwest. The Air Force was planning to put the assets in place after dark fell there, with hopes they could be done and gone before daybreak.

There was a Carrier Strike Group within six hundred miles of Guinea-Bissau that was already shifting position. They could halve that distance in the next eight hours which would shift possible operation scenarios. The President had made it clear that he'd be moving them anyway because of the coup, but that was his careful political side talking. The comforting hand he'd rested on Frank's forearm told him that was definitely not the only reason he was moving so fast.

And Frank had no proof Agent Belfour was dead.

He needed to remember that.

The last report, between dinner and this meeting, had placed two C-135 Stratotankers, used for mid-air refueling, ready on the runway at Cape Verde. A trio of C-17 transports were also enroute from Ramstein Air Force Base in Germany with fully manned APCs in their cargo bays, just in case they found a use for Armored Personnel Carriers during the rescue. Also, one more transport with a bellyful of 75th Regiment U.S. Ranger paratroopers armed for some serious trouble, in case they needed to jump in and take the airport by force. But all that was a level of international involvement that no one on either side wanted to get into.

Except him. Right now it was a good thing he wasn't the one holding the go button.

He scanned the room again. They were in the peaceful center of the U.N.'s library. The ceiling rose in gentle, wood-sheathed waves rising from the card catalog to the outer window, which washed the room with soft northern light. At a small table near the west end of the room, President Matthews sat casually with the ambassadors of Laos and Cambodia. Also at the table were the Vietnamese ambassador and one of their Deputy Prime Ministers.

And there was a woman who was the cause of all Frank's pain.

It had started as a trade meeting, and the woman had been seated quietly between the Laos and Cambodia ambassadors. But then she'd started talking.

And the President had listened, started drawing her out, much to the consternation of the men who had thought it was their meeting.

Frank could see why she'd so grabbed the President's attention. She reminded Frank of Carole Bouquet, the Bond girl from *For Your Eyes Only*. He'd been thirteen and madly in lust with her enough to slide into the theater an extra couple times. All long dark hair, that actually billowed, light eyes, and a serious body. The best part was that she didn't hang around going, "Oh James," with a sigh. She brought a crossbow and kicked ass.

This woman looked like that, but with almond-shaped eyes and the dusky skin of a Vietnamese Eurasian. France and Vietnam twisted together into one fine-looking woman. Fine enough to turn even the President's head which was saying something. Since his own wife had died in that helicopter crash during his first year in office, he hadn't looked at a single woman. Well, except his childhood friend Emily Beale, who'd already fallen for Major Mark Henderson, even if it took her a bit to figure it out.

As the trade meeting stretched long past any reasonable ending time, she took over the conversation, gently at first, so smoothly Frank thought she'd make a good agent. There was no ripple as she took full control. Watching her political savvy, Frank moved past irritation and began to wonder more about who she really was.

"Hank," he triggered his mike and whispered into it. "I know we cleared this Kim-Ly Beauchamp. What have you got on her?"

"Chief of Unit, Southeast Asia for the World Heritage Center of UNESCO. As far as I can tell, that's a pretty serious role."

He clicked his mike once to acknowledge receipt.

"We've got scenarios for the President when he's done."

Another click and a deep-rooted effort not to scream with impatience.

The lady wasn't making her points with her beauty, she was making it with her brains. He could hear bits and pieces about at-risk heritage sites and how their protection should be an essential requirement before the settling of any trade agreement, because they needed large levers to enforce protection of fragile environments.

Frank could get to like her, she had the Laotian and Cambodian ambassadors squirming about something, though he couldn't quite tell what. Seventeen billion dollars of yearly trade on the table compared with a couple of old temples and she was taking it on as if it made sense. He wished her luck.

The thing was, she was having some as she talked about tourism dollars. She'd sure caught the President's ear. More than his ear, she'd caught his attention.

"Hank, read me the longer version."

It all appeared very friendly, but he wasn't paid to trust to appearances. As the woman's background sounded in his ear, thankfully read by one of the techs without Hank's twisted sense of humor, he kept his eyes and his attention on the room.

Frank and the other three bodyguards lined the west wall like statues, except for their roving eyes. They each stood a little over an arm's-length apart. It provided each of them with a maximum field of vision and range of action. Frank had to admit, these guys were acting like a cut above. He'd met Kim Jong-un, the North Korean ruler's bodyguard last Christmas. He'd been less than impressed. These three guys were either trying to show off for him, the head of the U.S. Presidential Protection Detail, or they were just that damned serious about their jobs.

Probably a bit of both.

Now he just had to wait.

———

As they sat in darkness on the hut's dirt floor and ate the stolen spicy peanut *fufu* with their hands, the starchy cassava sticking to their fingers, Beatrice filled in the ambassador and Charlotte on the situation. Despite the food being cold, it burned the tongue and forced them all to drink a lot of water, which was good. Beat could tell by the sharp stench of their urine, despite the hole they'd dug in the corner of the hut and reburied, that they were all badly dehydrated. She was no exception, not daring to go out in the daytime to get water.

"We're being actively hunted." Beat kept her voice soft and slightly breathy. That would make it harder to distinguish directionally. "They appear to know that we survived the attack on the airport."

"But that makes no sense, why would they hunt us?" Charlotte handed her blue pumps over to Sam Green who slid them into his burlap bag with his briefcase. The sandals fit just fine and would be far more comfortable. That should help their speed.

"Regrettably, it does."

Beatrice tried to see the ambassador's face in the darkness of the hut, but couldn't make it out.

"How? I haven't been able to make sense of it."

"Last April…"

She whispered, "softly," to him and he tried, but didn't succeed much.

"… we captured their former Chief of the Navy in a drug-running and arms-trade bust at sea. He had thirty million dollars of cocaine and two dozen MANPADS." Sam Green's whisper became more assured. They were getting back into his territory.

"MANPADS?" Charlotte hadn't heard that one yet.

"Man-Portable Air-Defense Systems. Shoulder-mounted anti-aircraft missiles. They were headed to the Colombian drug lords for shooting down the U.S.'s D.E.A. helicopters. We're close to tying him back to the acting President of Guinea-Bissau and, with time, about a third of the power elite. If we can prove that, we can perhaps convince the U.N. Coalition Forces that it's time to clean this place up."

"But that didn't work in Somalia." The U.S. had tried to do exactly that about twenty years ago and the country still wasn't working.

"But Somalia," Green pointed out, "had no functioning government at that time. G-B still does, mostly. If we can get control of that back into the voters' hands, where their constitution says it belongs, this country might stand a chance."

"And that's what's in your briefcase."

"Right," he rested a protective hand on his burlap bag. "I'm carrying a proposal to the people we were unable to connect to the drug-running, and if they agree, we'll land heavily on their side. If we can even get U.N. peacekeepers and international election monitors in the door, maybe we can start working on free elections and shifting their economy off the drug trade. Then, eventually, we can end this disaster that started the day they claimed independence in 1973. But these documents also include their names, a death sentence to these people who might be our friends, and the death of all our hopes if it falls into the wrong hands. My notes and appointments would become a kill-list of every potentially reliable politician and leader."

Maybe he wasn't quite the lost cause Beatrice had thought him to be. Terrified out of his skull, definitely, but he'd hung onto that stupid briefcase for a reason. And maybe something about making love to Charlotte in a darkened West African hut, or being hunted like a criminal, had given him a focus.

"But why would they want to kill you?"

He shrugged. His white *dashiki* just catching the light from the one window to reveal the gesture.

"Different factions. One faction sees a chance to lash out at the U.S. by killing me, not realizing the world of hurt that will land down upon them should they succeed in doing so. The more rational factions think my death would send a clear message to stay out of G-B politics, not that it would work any better. Others would perchance prefer me alive as a bargaining chip. They'd use me to save their own skins with transport to a country they can disappear in, the Congo and Senegal don't have an extradition treaty with us. Perhaps a few people think they can gain a favor from the U.S. government if they save my life, maybe the politicians and military leaders on my list, but maybe not. How can I tell them from the others until we've had a chance to meet and talk?"

Beatrice let it all process. It fit. Not all of it, but enough that she knew what was going on and what had to come next.

"Okay, this is going to get harder, starting right now. Are you two up for it?"

By their too-bright hair, she could see them turning toward one another. Sam reached out and took Charlotte's hand, then brought it to his lips.

They turned back to Beat.

"Okay, we're ready."

Beatrice moved to the door, checked both directions, listening to the silence of the streets, and moved them out. They had four, perhaps five more hours of darkness and a lot of ground to cover.

CHAPTER SEVENTEEN

Half a step before storming into the conference room at Fort Sam Houston, in San Antonio, Texas, Beat stopped herself.

Secret Service liaison office to U.S. Southern Command regarding the Panama situation.

This was Frank's first assignment, a huge feather in his cap to be assigned the project straight out of training. She'd gotten some of the history on it. The whole thing was tiny when it started, so they sent down a senior agent and three rookies, one of which was Frank. Two months in, the senior guy got offered a cherry assignment. He'd insisted that one of the rookies had it in hand, so rather than send a new lead, they'd sent the new leader a mid-level guy to help.

So what had she done?

She'd gone from six months in Africa to being assigned to the Panama mission in under seventy-two hours.

By being so angry at Frank Adams that she hadn't been thinking, was how she'd done it. Beatrice had blown through the Secret Service command hierarchy so fast that she'd bet her section commander had shipped her out just to be rid of her demands to be assigned to the Panama project.

Panama? What the heck was up with that?

She'd landed from Africa Wednesday night, slept most of Thursday, tracked Frank down on Friday morning, and was supposed to have the week off but instead been on the road by that night. She'd driven twenty-four of the last forty-eight hours, crashing into a Motel 6 in Chattanooga, Tennessee for fourteen hours in the middle of it. Now it was Monday morning, July third at eight a.m. She was in San Antonio, Texas and through the Fort Sam security.

And Panama?

If she went storming into the Secret Service liaison office, Frank would just laugh his head off and she'd be forced to kill him. And she sure didn't like the idea of being one of the peons like he was, but she didn't want to start a battle for control either. Her section commander had made it clear that some new agent was shaping up well and they were going to let him run with it and see how he did. He'd told her that they were only letting her jump on because she'd done so well in Africa, but it wasn't her team.

So, one, she didn't want to tromp on his toes.

Two, the fact that she'd showed up at all... well, he'd know he'd won. She hadn't thought of that. She'd just been so damn angry she hadn't been thinking right up to this moment. He'd made her angrier than the day he'd tried to carjack her new car. And she was angry now for his not being where she'd left him.

That in itself was pretty damn stupid. Of course he'd take a great opportunity like this one.

She didn't like these feelings one bit for a whole lot of reasons.

She turned and walked back to the white porcelain water fountain hanging from a gray tile wall between the bathrooms. She wasn't thirsty, though her throat was dry. She just needed a moment to think.

Beat knew that if she were rational, she'd go and climb back into her car and head right back to Brooklyn, to beg for a new assignment.

No strings. No ties. Her parents had always been trying to tie her in knots to fit their plans for her. It had sure worked on her sister.

Hannah had a degree in literature, a pediatrician husband she'd met at Vassar and helped support through Columbia, two cute kids, and she was barely twenty five. They'd just bought their first place barely ten blocks from her parents' place, serious parent heaven. Hannah's life was all neat and set. And it probably was, her husband was a great guy. Good for her.

Not for Beat.

Over the last six months she'd finally decided that she liked her new nickname, even if Frank Adams had been the one to give it to her. Beat was a tougher, stronger woman than Beatrice Ann. Beat wouldn't be shying away from facing Frank Adams. She'd just sweep into that conference room and take over.

She turned, made sure her vest hung straight and headed for the office door. Just as she hit the door she realized that, without thinking, she was wearing the exact clothes she'd been wearing when she first met him.

Well, he better not get all smug, or he'd be going down.

Going down hard.

———

Frank heard the door slam open, rocketing into Malcolm's desk with a sharp thwack. He didn't even bother to turn, he knew exactly who stood now in the doorway behind him.

The other three guys, so used to the banging door they didn't jump, did turn to look. Frank could see by their total shift of concentration just how much they appreciated the vision standing there.

He turned his chair slowly from where he'd been studying the latest information regarding the thirty-five thousand Americans living and working in the Canal Zone.

Beatrice Ann Belfour looked incredible. The first time he'd seen her in these clothes, it had been in the darkness of a New York City hot-summer night. Now she was lit by the Texas sunlight streaming in through the window. The damn woman shimmered.

He made a point of inspecting her exactly as he had so long ago in the underground garage at the Secret Service building. Her red sneakers had been replaced by blood-red cowboy boots, but the jeans were still tight, the lemon-yellow blouse brought her glowing skin to life, and the leather vest that he now knew was almost as soft as her skin had just enough bulge to show that she was packing her revolver in its normal shoulder holster. Her hair was about six inches longer, she hadn't cut it since they'd met, and it now fell in a glorious thick wave well past her shoulder.

And those dark eyes were boring holes right into him.

"Hey, Beat." He made it sound as casual as he could. It took effort 'cause he was so damn glad to see her.

"Hey, Adams." She didn't move, just stood there letting him drink his fill of her.

He'd never get enough. He knew he'd missed her, but had no idea how much until she stood there in front of him.

Gone, Adams. You're twenty-one and you're completely and totally gone. That wasn't supposed to happen until he'd played the field much wider and longer. It was something he'd never expected. Find a woman some-day, sure. A main squeeze. But in the six months she'd been gone, he hadn't even noticed another woman. Oh, he'd had offers, but there was not a one for him other than Beat Belfour.

Then she glanced over his head at the other three guys, "So, who's in charge here?"

Frank let the silence stretch a bit before drawling out an answer.

"It's gonna really suck for you..."

Her eyes came back to his. She glared at him with that splendid mix of arrogance and pride, of a woman who knew she was just that damn good. Then a bit of smile that she did her best to hide with a scowl.

"You."

"Me."

———

Frank had sort of forgotten how good she was. By lunchtime he had

Beat up to speed with what it had taken his team three months to gather together, by mid-afternoon she was adding ideas to his scenario planning. And he was loving it. It was like there was some kinda hyperactive feedback loop between them and the ideas just circulated back and forth between them. The other guys had gone, but he'd stuck around to show her what they knew and they'd taken off from there.

"So they're mobilizing everything?"

"Rangers, Delta, Air Force, Special Operations Forces helicopters, everything. All running as exercises now, but everyone knows they're gearing up for a big hit. We're doing a razzle-dazzle down there, moving troops in and out so fast that no Panamanians can count 'em and make a counter-plan."

"Helicopters, huh?"

Frank glanced down at the paperwork. "Some outfit called the 160th Special Operations Group. What are you thinking?"

Beat just smiled at him. He could see that something had just clicked in her brain and she wasn't going to share it yet. So, he looked for a change of topic.

"It's July 3rd, you know."

"Yeah," she said it like it was nothing important and that pissed him off some.

The other agents had left after lunch. They had families in the area. Only he and Beat had stayed. The heat in the office had gone up several degrees since lunch even though the sun had moved around the other side of the building. It forced Frank to loosen his collar. The four white walls covered with maps pressed in around the four desks and table, all crammed into a space that had probably been one man's office prior to the Secret Service's arrival. Gearing up for a potential invasion of Panama had made space a premium at Fort Sam.

"What I'm thinking... " she drew out the words in a way that definitely made him think some very nice things.

God, she was muddling his brain. All he knew was that he wanted to get his hands on Beatrice Ann Belfour and he didn't care how, as long as it was soon.

It was a trap. Had to be.

"I'm thinking that I saw a place on the drive in that's still running *Ghostbusters II*. Want to go?"

"You hate sequels."

"You love Sigourney Weaver."

Yep. A complete and total trap.

CHAPTER EIGHTEEN

FRANK: NOW

W*hat do we know* about her?"

"Who?" Frank knew exactly who the President was talking about, but he wasn't going to let him off that easy. They were effectively alone, walking through the underground corridor that connected the Dag Hammarskjöld Library with the Secretariat Tower. Two agents cleared the corridor ahead and two followed behind.

"Don't give me a hard time here, Frank."

"Or what, sir?"

"Or I'll name Beat the head of my detail when she gets back and put you somewhere you can be of use like an Alaskan sewage treatment plant."

Damn he liked working for this man. He took a joke and built in a ray of hope and confidence that Frank sure wasn't feeling.

"Kim-Ly Geneviève Beauchamp, mixed French and Vietnamese descent, French side came to Vietnam in the 1930s. Traditional plantation owners. Had to leave to avoid the War and the Reeducation Camps, but the ties were too deep and they came back almost right away. She was born there. Educated John Hopkins and Cambridge, the one in England."

"A Cambrian?"

"Cambrian, sir?"

"If it weren't a proper noun it would be a good Scrabble word, with the C, M, and B it's worth thirteen points and is eight letters long, a good length. If you can find just one letter to play off, you can score an extra fifty point Bingo for clearing your tray. Cambrian is from an old story at Oxford. We always said Cambridge was founded by some Oxfordians who couldn't cut it. So they were banished to the fens, the marshes, and founded a silly little school named Cambridge. Cambrian is an ancient geologic age, out of date, slow. Worse, she's probably a Cavendisher, one of the all-women colleges at the University."

Frank had no idea what he was talking about, but he seemed pretty pleased by it all. Frank turned back to his report. "Straight to UNESCO, now Chief of Unit for World Heritage of Southeast Asia. Very determined lady. Cavendisher by the way is a also proper noun, so you don't get to use that one either."

President Matthews nodded his head and kept his silence as they continued down the corridor. At the stairs they went down one flight to get to the United States Security Center.

The President was thinking some pretty serious thoughts when he didn't even smile at a Scrabble-based tease.

Frank knew that silence. Knew it from deep inside when he'd waited in Texas wondering when he'd get to see Beatrice Belfour again.

He offered the President the next layer.

"Thirty-two years old, married once, didn't stick. Broke off with last boyfriend two weeks after being named Chief of Unit last year. Word is he didn't like that her career was dusting his, a German named Klaus of all things."

That actually got the President to stop right before they went through the outer security door. That caused the other agents up and down the hall some consternation, but Frank flickered an "all okay" sign and just waited.

Nothing.

President Matthews' face was normally intensely expressive, man couldn't play poker to save his life as his friend Mark Henderson kept proving to him time and again. And right now it was very carefully showing nothing.

Frank whistled quietly to himself. How long had the President been in conference with her? An hour, a little more.

He thought back to the day he'd met Beat. Once around the nose of her BMW, he could easily have run. Cops might have laid chase, but he'd have a pretty good chance of making it clean. She probably had expected him to. But something about her made it so that he got in the car. He'd stood there for three heartbeats, then trusted her with his life. It had been that fast. At least for him. He'd seen that lady with the dark, dark eyes and just had to know more.

"I bet, Mr. President, that she'd be glad of a chance to do a lecture series at George Washington University or something like that."

"Are you trying to matchmake me, Frank?"

"No sir, Mr. President. Just thinking out loud, sir."

They walked through the outer door of the basement security offices together, Frank flashed a hand signal clearing the other agents in the hall to close the distance from either end of the hall and to take up station on the door.

While the outer and inner door bolts were shifting with their sharp metallic buzzes, the President spoke without looking up at him.

"So, maybe I'll keep you around after all. Now let's go see about getting Agent Belfour in from whatever limb she's stuck out on."

Frank followed him in with the first feeling of hope he'd had all day.

"By the way, Frank, 'cavendish' is a sweet tobacco cake. So I can use it. Seventeen points."

———

"The problem we have, Mr. President, is that we have no way to contact any assets on the ground, or even determine if they're still alive to do so." Chairman of the Joint Chiefs of Staff Brett Rogers stared at them out of their screen which linked to the White House Situation Room.

So much for hope. Frank resisted the urge to lay his head down on the table.

Once again, the President sat at the head of the table. Frank and Hank sat to either side. Frank had sat, 'cause otherwise he'd pace and that wouldn't help anything.

In the hour since they'd been gone to the U.N. meeting with Southeast Asia, the staff in the room had been sharply upgraded. The left-hand seats along the wall were now filled with Army, Navy, Air Force, and Special Operations Forces reps, all officer ranks. They each had direct links to their superiors sitting to either side of General Rogers in the Situation Room as well as to whatever other points of contact they needed.

The screens which had held a few photos of the plane, garage, and burning liaison office in Guinea-Bissau were now filled with images of the center of downtown Bissau. Dozens of buildings were on fire. Two dozen tanks were scattered about the town like dropped toys, except several of them were burning as well.

"Intramural. The Army is fighting itself," the President observed.

"That and probably worse. Only the core of the town has ever had cell phone service, but Guinetel pulled the plug on that, or someone pulled it for them, about six hours ago. Phones aren't exactly common either, especially not outside the core. There aren't more than a couple dozen Internet lines for public use in the whole city, fastest thing they've got wouldn't run my four-year-old grandkid's MathWiz game. But they pulled the plug on those too. So not even Twitter to give us ground intel as there would be in any other disaster of a nation. The only people with satellite phones are the drug lords, and they're all lying low or engaged in the battle. We've kicked a Global Hawk drone into the air and it should be on site shortly. We're hoping we can grab some radio chatter. The Raptor we sent earlier was an imaging bird, doesn't have the heavy intel-gathering package."

It was all still a jumble.

Frank looked about the room and tried to spot why. Everyone was doing their thing. The screens to either side of the Chairman of the Joint Chiefs were alive with data. But it didn't feel right.

He'd ridden out enough of these with the President now to know that when they were on the track of a solution, even if it wasn't there yet, you could taste the crackle of it in the air.

This air tasted of nothing but air conditioning and worry.

He looked at the satellite photo of Bissau taken on the last pass before darkness had fallen.

It was midnight there now.

It was time to be on the move.

But each time she moved, Beat would become harder to find. Clearly, going back to the airport hadn't been her first choice. Couldn't blame her since she'd already lost two people there. By now Beat would know that downtown wasn't worth risking either. Not even on the chance of finding a working cell tower.

"Cell phones."

"What?" The buzz of conversation dropped. The others had been talking about something else. Mapping patterns of unexpected thermal movement. Like that would work in a city of a couple hundred thousand people with a coup going on.

"They've shut off the cell towers, Frank." General Rogers and he had become friends over their last few years serving together at the White House.

"Right," Frank could see the idea forming in his head. "But maybe Agent Belfour hasn't shut off her own phone. Do the Raptor or Global Hawk have cell phone scanners? Can we piggyback it onto a radio and talk to them?"

One of the techs on the left-side of the U.N. security office must have put up a request to join the conference. The Marine Corps intelligence officer who was running the conference popped an image of the tech's face into the lower corner of the main screen. Navy Lieutenant, cute Asian woman, sitting third down the left-wall row.

"Sir, the Global Hawk drone as rigged can only receive calls for monitoring purposes. But the Raptor bird already on site for imaging had been previously tasked for alert broadcast to all cell phones in an area. That hardware is still aboard. It will take some time to set up, but we should be able to transmit with one bird and receive with the other."

"Get it built. You've got twenty minutes until everything is on site."

Twenty minutes. Frank closed his eyes and tried to do one of those telepathy things like in the movies. He'd be the first one ever to successfully send a telepathic message and save a life.

"Stay low, be careful," he thought as loudly as he could.

———

"Why can't we just steal the plane?" Ambassador Green whispered from close beside Beat. At least he'd learned to keep his voice down.

They squatted close beside the wreckage of the garage. Still no one had come to clean it up. The flesh of the pieces of the two embassy personnel killed in the explosion had started to go putrid in the tropical heat. There was a slight land breeze headed out to sea, so she moved them to the upwind, east side of the garage to cut the smell.

When Charlotte and Sam had asked what that stench was, she hadn't answered. Thankfully they already knew to never ask her something a second time. They'd learned that she always heard them and when she didn't respond it was because they didn't want to know. Not the screaming of a burn victim, nor the wailing of half the family as they were told the other half was now dead.

"Can you fly a plane?"

"Always meant to learn, but no. Can't you?"

Like she was some sort of miracle girl. Actually, she'd be willing to try if it weren't for the two tacticals parked at the other end of the main terminal. Their crews might be asleep and/or drunk, but they'd snap to the moment she tried cranking over the plane's engines. Two turret-mounted machine guns would make a real mess of the plane and any passengers long before they reached takeoff speed.

No, she had a different plan.

"Wait here." While she'd been out prowling earlier, she'd traded her blue *pagne* and skirt for a dark *dashiki* and loose pants that would allow her move well.

She slid up to the bottom of the plane's fold-down steps and waited. She'd found a cooking knife during her prowl and held it hidden in her hand, the blade held flat against her wrist. While it was no K-bar survival blade, it would be quieter than her Sig Sauer. Though she made sure that too was close to hand.

The pilot's large blood stain at the base of the steps had dried, not even the flies could find anything more there. She spotted his body shoved under one of the wings.

The lights were out over the whole airport, only the moonlight had revealed the tacticals. The steps were still hanging down and the inside of the plane was pitch dark. The third of the four steps creaked and the plane rocked ever so slightly on its shocks as she climbed aboard. Up the narrow aisle between the facing pairs of armchairs with the little tables between them to either side. Not even the smell of stale peanuts remained.

The cockpit was quiet and the moonlight through the windshield let her see enough to find the switch for the panel lights.

She turned them on with a flick and saw that she was screwed.

The pilot must have been trying to radio for help after the garage blew up, before being dragged from the plane. Whoever took him had shot the radios. Five neat shots right through the faces of each radio and transponder. No calling for help from here. She shut off the panel lights.

She knew the King Air had an ELT in the tail, but she wasn't exactly sure where. Emergency Locator Transmitters triggered for crashes. They must have manual switches. If not, she would beat it with a length of steel pipe until it decided to cry for help.

It would be a messy call, ELTs were designed to scream long and loud on common radio frequencies, but at least it would tell someone to come looking for them.

She was halfway back through the plane when an alarm burst out in the cabin.

Not an alarm!

Her cell phone.

It rang again so loudly in the plane she almost wanted to cover her ears. It vibrated harshly against her rib cage, under the *dashiki* in the pocket of the shirt she'd kept on beneath her native clothes.

She bent over to dig for it under the layers of cloth.

As she did so, a roar and flash slapped at her, knocking her sideways into a seat with the sheer force of the concussion.

Another burst and she saw the origin.

Bending over had saved her life.

Someone had been asleep in the back of the plane, probably after raiding the tiny galley. Someone with a rifle.

Woken by the cell phone, he'd fired wildly at her inside the plane. Her ears still rang, the only thing she could hear, though the cell phone buzzed once more against her rib cage.

Blinded by his own rifle fire, the man stumbled forward down the aisle.

Go just one more step, she coaxed him forward.

He fired at the cockpit again, shattering the windshield. The spent cartridge casing ejected right past her head, fast, and pinged off one of the windows. Had to be a Czech VZ with that kind of ejection. Amazing that the thing still worked, it should be in a museum.

In the light of the muzzle flash, he saw his mistake. She was lying mostly in one of the seats, now right beside him.

As he turned, she struck.

She'd kept the blade despite the shock and with a single stroke she dragged it across his jugular vein and throat.

Hot blood splashed her face and arm. She was moving before he hit the floor. He was still trying to gasp his final breath when she dove out the door and hit the tarmac. With a fast roll she regained her feet and sprinted back to the protection of the garage.

Sweeping up Sam and Charlotte, she raced into the night.

Behind them the tacticals opened up on the plane even as their drivers raced the Toyotas to redline, sprinting down the field.

There was a low cough, like the world catching its breath, and Beat dragged her two charges to the ground.

The plane blew with a deafening roar that lit the night sky like a torch a dozen stories high.

One of the tacticals, its driver still too drunk or hung over or asleep to compensate, twisted the wheels on his truck sharply while traveling too fast. The vehicle rolled into the burning airplane taking its driver and gun crew with it.

Their screams didn't last long.

While the other tactical was distracted by the mayhem, the three of them slipped further into the night.

———

"What the hell happened?" Frank's roar filled the room. It wasn't his place, but he couldn't help himself. One moment they'd had a clear ring tone on Beat's cell phone and the next it looked like the airport had blown up.

"Someone get me a clear shot of the airport," General Brett Rogers snarled out. Frank had never heard that tone from the Chairman of the Joint Chiefs before and decided he'd better shut up.

A tech sent the command to some obscure bunker, probably in Utah, and the remote pilot sent his command over satellite to turn the Raptor's camera. Moments later it centered on the flame. One tactical had rolled in and also burned, they could see the bright sparkles of the ammunition firing off in the intense heat at the heart of the fire.

The other truck was backing off slowly, being beaten away by the heat.

"Someone roll back the footage."

Moments later they were staring at the long view with the airport off in the corner of the picture. It was a ghostly image of greens and blacks that came from infrared cameras for night vision. Cooking fires flared bright in some of the surrounding neighborhood. No streetlights or houselights. Power was out in the largest city in the country.

"Zoom and enhance," Rogers ordered. "C'mon people. Think ahead. Work the problem."

The resolution was lousy, but in moments the little embassy plane filled the screen, a dull green cross a couple-dozen image pixels square against the cooler black of the airport parking area.

"There!" Frank pointed. A lone figure, about ten pixels big but large enough to see how carefully they were moving, sidled up to the plane.

"That's got to be Beat. No one moves like that but a trained agent." She was alive. Frank had never been so glad to see a heat trace. Or she'd been alive three minutes ago.

The silence in the room echoed as the video spooled in real time.

The three pixels at the nose of a plane brightened.

The Navy tech whose face had remained in the corner of screen reported, "Brightness change approximately equal to control panel lights."

Before he could wonder if Beat was going for flight or radios, the brightness disappeared. She'd made it to the cockpit and either found what she'd wanted, or what she'd hoped to find wasn't there. He knew the pilot was dead. He also knew she didn't know how to fly.

"Radios. She went after the radios. They must not have been usable. That's why—"

"Here's where her phone rang," the tech cut him off.

Nothing.

"Agai—"

Before the tech could finish, a flash of light, and another. The brightness shone out all of the side windows on the side facing the Raptor's camera flying far overhead.

"Brightness change indicates gunfire. Single rounds."

One more.

Their phone call had gotten her shot. Someone asleep on the plane, and they'd woken him with a goddamn phone call. His idea had gotten her killed.

"Phone signal lost."

Then a figure dove out of the door, did a hit-roll-run combo that every aching inch of his body knew by heart. And she'd just done it out an airplane door opening five feet above hard tarmac. That had to hurt.

But Beat was alive. It was all he needed to know. She was alive. Relief flooded through him like a salve to his soul. The world just wouldn't be a worthwhile place without her in it.

The tech followed her. She swept up two other dim figures of only a few pixels each some distance from the plane and disappeared back into the city right off the edge of the Raptor's field of view.

She'd kept the ambassador and one of his assistants alive.

Damn she was good.

CHAPTER NINETEEN

1989: FRANK

Beat *wasn't the only* one with tricks up her sleeve. After the *Ghostbusters II* matinee at the East San Antonio six-plex, which was only okay, though Sigourney had been damn hot, Frank got Beat into her car. But he managed to snag the keys and settle her in the passenger seat. Still exhausted from her cross-country drive, she'd obviously been feeling weak and pliable. And he wanted to keep her that way.

He took the northern route across town from Fort Sam, telling her he had a special spot for dinner. Which he did. It was Monday, July 3rd. Because most folks didn't have to work tomorrow, San Antonio was having the big city party tonight. They'd met one year ago tomorrow.

He merged into the late afternoon mayhem, got as close to Wood-lawn Lake Park as he could in the thick traffic and parked it. The temp was 90s-ugly falling toward 70s-not-quite-so-ugly. It was a little cooler by the lake, but about a hundred thousand people were showing up. Here, instead of July Fourth smelling like hot dogs and sauerkraut in Manhattan, it smelled of roasted chilies and fresh salsa. Temperature, though, was about equally brutal.

The food vendors were doing an awesome business, and he and Beat snagged some fish tacos and lemonade and chose their spot by the lake. It wasn't packed solid with people yet, still an hour or so until the fireworks. The all-dayers were there with kids and float rafts and picnic baskets and blankets and sunburns and all that noise.

He and Beat just took an empty spot and sat back on the grass. The lake was a couple hundred yards across and folks were still out in those little paddle wheelers for two. The cops actually had a couple of power boats on the water ready to chase away anyone who tried to get too close to the fireworks setup.

Frank would start mellow, pick a safe topic.

They talked about Africa. Security standards. Communication. They wandered through the best summer street food in New York. As the evening light settled toward fireworks dark, he went back to her comment from the afternoon. The crowds were pretty serious now. Everyone jabbering excitedly on too much sugar and anticipation. They could have shouted the combination to the Fort Knox bullion repository and no one would have noticed.

"You said something about helicopters."

"Yeah."

Frank liked how they could pick up a conversation hours later and stay on the same page. She was so easy to be with.

"Panama City is going to be a mess."

Frank pictured the maps and reconnaissance photos that were covering their office walls. A mess was an understatement. The Panama Defense Force was everywhere. Multiple airports, not counting the one at the far end of the canal. Taking them all out while trying not to kill the thirty-five thousand Americans living there would be a good trick. Taking out radio and television stations another one. And on top of all that, bag the Pineapple himself. Dictator Manuel Noriega had an acne-pocked face, and some brilliant Army guy had dubbed him the 'Pineapple.' Did they hire people to be that stupid on purpose? Worse, the name had stuck.

"You said they're banking hard on these helicopter pilots."

"SOAG, Special Operations Aviation Group. These guys apparently kicked some serious ass in Grenada and the Persian Gulf on some piracy gig. It looks like the powers that be are having them play front and center."

"Where are they stationed?"

"Fort Campbell, Kentucky."

"Good. I have to go visit those guys."

Frank rubbed a hand across his eyes. She'd just gotten here about eight hours ago and she was already planning on leaving.

He sat up.

Would have gotten to his feet to leave if she hadn't stopped him with a hand on his shoulder.

"Not right away."

He kept his back to her, just sat there and stared at all the happy families. The ones where the women could sit still for thirty damn seconds without picking the next battle and rushing off to it. How was he supposed to survive this?

She shifted until she was kneeling in front of him.

"Hey."

She inspected his face and he managed not to look away. He watched the rapid shift of emotions. He'd been trained to see it. He could see it at the macro level where hate, anger, or fear rippled so fast that the people in a crowd didn't have time to register the sudden change, they simply felt it. He'd also learned to see it in an individual face. And he knew no face better than the one looking at him from less than a foot away.

It started coy, playful, with that wonderful hint of sex that always seemed to dance around the corners of her mouth. Then it shifted. First uncertainty, the tightness in brows, the smile sliding off the lips. The widening of the eyes and slackening of the jaw as surprise rippled through on its way to...

It had been a single year since he'd met Beatrice Belfour and signed up for training. They had beaten, chased, challenged, and strained him past anything he'd imagined possible. They made living in the projects look easy by comparison.

None of that had prepared him for the final expression hardening on her features. The narrowing of eyes, clenching of jaw, the head pulling back as if trying to retreat before the body could get the message to move away.

"No, Frank. This wasn't the goddamn deal."

He hadn't meant for it show, how much he wanted her. How much he needed her. He could feel the pain shifting to anger but couldn't stop it. Could feel his teeth ache with the pressure and the forward lean. His head shifting forward "like a goddamn pug dog," he really wished the instructor had given him a different image for that emotion.

Then it blew out of him. Beat Belfour brought cold, but Frank's anger brought heat.

"No, it's not your goddamn deal, Be-a-trice, but it is mine." He gritted his teeth to keep his voice low. Of course it was this conversation that the fat ladies on the next blanket over suddenly decided to listen to.

"I found the woman I want, but she doesn't want me. So go fly off and see the flyboys."

He struggled to his feet and dropped her car keys in front of her.

"Happy anniversary, Agent Belfour." He had to space his words around the opening salvo of fireworks bursting overhead like a howitzer. "Pleasure seeing you again."

He turned and walked away. It was the hardest damn thing he'd ever done.

———

Beat didn't show up at Fort Sam Houston on Tuesday. No one did except Frank. It was a national holiday, everyone else was busy celebrating or relaxing somewhere.

He received her first report Wednesday morning. She'd somehow managed to embed herself as the Secret Service liaison to the Army's immensely secretive 160th aviation group.

It was hard to credit the tactical capabilities she was reporting. These guys were as crazy as the Secret Service in their training habits. Night vision was still so new that Frank hadn't even been trained on it yet, and these guys had been flying helicopters at night for two years using that technology.

They redesigned their helicopters just as thoroughly as the Secret Service redesigned Presidential planes, helicopters, and cars. He'd tried to get on the 747 team, but that was a seriously huge step that not even a top-of-class rookie could hope for. Developing the next Air Force One was a cherry assignment and only cool guys with tons of experience got it. He hadn't even gotten a letter, his application had simply been returned with a small, red tick mark in the "Not accepted" box.

At first he always had the other guys process her reports.

As time passed, he started reading her reports rather than his team's summaries. She sent them to the team from stranger and stranger places. One came from D.C., though he knew she was in Miami at Hurlburt Field watching scenario practice. Then one routed through the New York office that talked about a simulation flight in Panama. It was like she'd somehow become disconnected from him and from wherever she was in world at the same time.

Sometimes he held a report and wondered if she still truly existed.

Each one he opened was fascinating, and ripped out his gut all over again. There was nothing personal in them, not a single thing. But he could still hear her voice in the writing.

As specialists in head-of-state protection, the Secret Service was getting pulled in on planning for Operation Nifty Package, pulled in by the point guard of Beatrice Ann Belfour.

Inside the overarching Operation Just Cause, intended to depose Noriega and neutralize the brutal Panama Defense Force, the combined military and secret police force, lay a smaller, trickier task.

Noriega had been convicted as a drug trafficker by a U.S. Federal Court. The U.S. government didn't want a dictator-martyr on their hands. It could destabilize a half-dozen other countries. They wanted him alive. That was Operation Nifty Package.

They tracked down his personal jet and a damn serious little gunboat. They pinpointed a dozen villas, uncovered several mistresses, and a thousand little habits. This was all fed into the overall Nifty Package plan through the conduit of Beat and Frank.

The game was escalating. He no longer had time to be pissed at her.

Hell, he didn't even have time to sleep. It was mid-December and soon, very soon, the game would be on.

CHAPTER TWENTY

BEAT: NOW

What happened?”

Charlotte had collapsed, Green had grabbed Beat's arm, and they'd all swerved and tumbled together behind a stone wall that was probably a goat pen. It sure stank like one. Her side ached as if they'd run a hundred miles, not less than one. Her right knee was screaming, must have twisted it when she dove out of the plane. The moon had set and the world had gone pitch dark, the last fifteen minutes were more about stumbling into things than running.

About three a.m. local would be her best guess.

“What happened?” Green shook her arm and it hurt.

“They shot the radios.”

“While you were in the plane?”

“Before. When they killed the pilot, they shot the radios.”

“Then what was all the shooting when you were in there?”

“What, Green, is this twenty questions?”

“Yes, it's our lives too. Now what happened?”

Beat lay her head back against the stone wall, glad of the darkness. Glad that Ambassador Green couldn't see the blood sprayed all over her face. She'd tried to wipe it off her face as they ran. Even if she'd succeeded, it didn't matter, she could still feel it. Imprinted there. All that training just hadn't prepared her for the first time she'd killed a man. She'd been in the Service for, gods, two-and-a-half decades, and this had been her first one.

In the past she'd always managed to take them down, captured for questioning. She'd been with agents who'd taken down a shooter, but she'd never had to do it herself. All she wanted to do was curl up and shake for a while.

Charlotte wasn't even doing that. She was simply collapsed across their feet, too exhausted and strained to even weep. She just lay there until the time when they'd make her get up and run again.

Beat couldn't afford to do that no matter how envious she was. And Green was right, his life was on the line as much as hers.

"My phone rang."

"I thought you said there was no cell service here."

"There isn't."

"Then how."

"I'm not sure." But she had an idea. She looked up at the sky. Was someone up there watching them? Forty hours. They'd been missing for forty hours, someone had to be looking for them. Other than the Guinea-Bissau militia. She liked the idea of Frank up in the sky watching over her. Assuming he even knew. G-B wasn't exactly his area of concern, his job was the President. Still, she liked the idea that it had been him calling.

She dug for the phone, wincing at the sharp pain all along her ribs. She wasn't winded, well, not only winded. Her ribs felt as if they were cracked. She'd hit something hard.

Pulling out the phone, she scanned around to see if anyone was in sight on the streets. She couldn't see anyone or much of anything in the darkness other than the dull red light of a dying cooking fire in a hut a couple dozen yards down the road, so there was no way to tell. The smell of burning cow dung from the fire added to the goat pen in a most unpleasant way.

She and Green huddled over the phone to shield as much of the light as possible. She stroked a finger over the glass to wake up the phone. It was rough, jagged. She'd dropped enough smartphones in her day to know that was a bad sign. Though sometimes they still worked even if cracked.

The light came on and revealed a shattered screen.

She rubbed at her ribs again under the stolen *dashiki*. Her skin over the ribs was especially tender exactly in the shape of the phone.

But what had she hit? Casting her mind back, she reviewed the events of the last thirty minutes. Was that all it had been? Her mind assured her that was the case.

She'd been fine entering the plane, then the fight. Next time she'd go in with her gun drawn and cocked. And check the rear of the plane before going to the front.

There'd been the fall into the chair and hitting the table, but that had been her other side. She could feel that bruise, but it was no worse than an average training blow.

The butt of the rifle. He'd rammed it into her side even as she'd killed him. If not for the phone taking the blow, he'd probably have busted her ribs right into her lung and she'd have burned to death gasping for her own last breath right alongside him.

Almost killed by the ringing of the bell, she'd also been saved by it.

"No way to see who called. No way to call them back. Where's your phone?"

Green hesitated long enough for the answer to be clear.

"You left it on the plane because you knew the service here is so bad?"

"Not worth carrying around," his whisper was deeply chagrined. "It's so useless here. I think I successfully have made three calls in three years, and Guinetel can't link you to international, or won't. The SUVs have, had, satellite phones. That doesn't help us much now. Wish I'd tossed the phone in my briefcase this time."

"Me too." Beat started to laugh at the friendly moment, but decided against it when she felt the pull on her battered ribs.

She powered the phone off. She almost threw it away, but instead shoved it back in her pocket. It had saved her life once already. It deserved being laid to rest in some trash heap better than this place.

After considering for a few seconds, she revised the clock in her head. Their chances of making it through another day were not good. Her target of "rescued by tomorrow evening" wasn't going to cut it.

They'd have to be rescued by sunrise or they'd be goners.

———

"Signal lost."

Frank was going to kill the technician. They'd only just cracked into Beat's "lost my phone" automatic locator application.

"It appears she turned off her phone. Or perhaps the battery died."

"I'll kill her. I'm going to kill her if she lives through this."

The President had delayed the return flight to D.C. The situation was either going to resolve in the next three hours or not until tomorrow night. If the latter, they could fly back to D.C. while Beatrice laid low for one more day. But based on the firefight they'd just witnessed, he didn't like the chances if they had to delay through another Guinea-Bissau day. Didn't like them at all.

In the meantime, the next shift of agents had escorted the President off to meetings with the U.N. ambassadors for Senegal, The Gambia, and Guinea, the three bordering nations. The President had insisted that Frank stay as long as it took to recover Agent Belfour and her charges. Frank had managed not to kiss the man in thanks.

Word was, France and the Secretary-General were in on the meeting. Coups were rarely an improvement on regional stability. And while the French embassy hadn't been touched, several of the others had been shelled, predominantly with duds. These guys couldn't even put a decent coup together, which was a good thing for Beatrice.

"Actually, that action of shutting down her phone may have just saved her." The Navy tech appeared to be wholly unflappable.

"What do you mean?"

She remained at her station and started drawing on her screen with a lightpen. It showed up on the big screen and was automatically repeated in the Situation Room.

"We know they're in this general area, here." She drew far too big a circle. There were thousands of human body heat signatures in that circle.

"I've been following this vehicle." She circled it. "And this one." She circled another. "Here are their prior tracks." She turned on long white lines that snaked back and forth along the streets. He looked at the time stamps along the way. They weren't moving fast like the prior tacticals.

They were quartering the area. They'd picked up on her cell phone's signal as it tried to find a cell tower to hook up to, and they'd been triangulating in on it. They were close, less than a quarter mile to the east and south. Another few minutes and they'd have had her pinned down.

He rested his forehead on the table. He was the one who wasn't going to survive this.

CHAPTER TWENTY-ONE

BEAT: H-HOUR, DECEMBER 19TH, 1989, 11:45P.M.

The information started fast, then got faster. Navy divers had been attacked in Panama Harbor. To get beneath the range of grenades dropped into the water, they'd dived well below the limits of their breathing gear, then come up directly under Noriega's gunboat to attach the scuttling charges.

A SEAL team had taken out Noriega's private jet, cutting off that line of escape, but at a terrible loss of life. The Pineapple wasn't there, nor in his palace.

Beatrice had been allowed a corner of the 160th's control center. When the first helicopter was shot down over the marshes near the mouth of the Canal, the shock wave had rippled once around the room and been gone. She'd had lunch with "Sonny" Owen and John Hunter just last week. The guys in this room had trained with them for years. Now they were dead.

The 160th's air mission commanders were in active combat, too busy to grieve now. That would have to come later. But with little to do until the hunt for the Pineapple became a primary focus, all she could do was sit and think how Frank would feel if she died. Snuffed out in seconds, shot out of the sky. Especially with how they'd left things back on July 3rd.

It had been weeks before she'd discovered the pendant. Her key ring always had too many keys. Her place, her parent's, her sister's, the car, Frank's old place... they were always accumulating faster than she could shed them.

At some point, on that single San Antonio day, while he'd had her keys, he'd slipped a small pendant onto the ring. It was a tiny, silvered firework explosion, no bigger than her thumbnail. He'd purchased and given her an anniversary present. A thoughtful, funny one. The anniversary of his final carjacking attempt. And she hadn't even remembered the date.

She listened to the next report coming in. They'd rescued an American from nine months' solitary confinement in a maximum-security prison. It had taken four small helicopters transporting a lot of Delta Force operators and a couple more attack versions of the Little Birds flying as armed guards. On the way out, the commanding officer had taken a round that shattered his arm and lodged deep inside his right lung. She knew him best of all. She saw them land right outside the command and control center.

One of the Delta Operators jumped off his narrow bench where he'd ridden on the outside of the helicopter. They all bristled with weapons: pistols, rifles, knives, bolt cutters, explosive packs. The D-boy had slapped the commander on the arm in celebration of the mission. The commander screamed and cursed. The medics finally realized what had happened and rushed forward.

Beat wasn't in harm's way. She was a back-of-the-line consultant. But what if she weren't.

She took the little firework pendant off her key ring and hung it from the thin gold chain her sister had given her the day she'd become a Secret Service agent. The only jewelry she ever wore, until now. Now if she were killed and they found her personal effects, Frank would know she'd accepted the gift.

The rest of it she'd have to think about after they took down the Noriega.

CHAPTER TWENTY-TWO

FRANK: NOW

I have an idea."

General Rogers returned to his chair in the Situation Room so that Frank could see his face. He had a fresh cup of coffee and red-rimmed eyes.

Frank expected he looked far worse. Even the unflappable tech was drooping in her chair. Fourteen hours since the first report that something was wrong, now barely two hours remained until daybreak in Guinea-Bissau. The fighting in the city center had peaked an hour ago and was tapering off.

Still no word from inside the country. The Guinea-Bissau ambassador had holed up in his office and refused to answer his locked door, though they knew he was in there. It was hard to blame him. He had family there who might not survive the night. And if things went the wrong way, it was possible that he could never even go home to be sure.

Based on the pattern of destruction of selected high-value homes, it appeared that the faction presently winning was not friendly to the U.S. in general. If they finished their task before darkness fell tomorrow night, they'd go hunting three Americans lost in a strange city with no resources but Beatrice Belfour's brains and stamina.

That meant they needed a solution within the remaining two hours of darkness.

How many movies had Beat dragged him to over the years where all they needed was two hours? The end of the world, *just give me two hours and I can save humanity*. Can't find true love, *in two hours I'll make her see what true love really is*. Need to save some woman's ass from the center of an African coup...

"Go ahead, Frank. What's the idea?"

"How close is the carrier group?"

"Two hundred miles. About eight minutes with an F-18 Hornet."

"They won't do me any good. Anything that lands at that airport is going to get itself shot up. Anyone around from SOAR?"

"Two DAP Hawks and three Little Birds," the Special Operations Forces captain along the left wall chimed in. "They've been assisting on the anti-Nigerian piracy force, Operation Sure Seas. We have another company of them off Somali on the same Operation."

Two DAP Hawks? The Direct Action Penetrators were exceptionally rare birds, the nastiest Black Hawk helicopters ever put into the night sky. There were barely a dozen of them flying anywhere in the world, all flown by the Night Stalkers. What were the chances?

"Henderson and Beale?"

"It's them." General Rogers knew them well also, he'd once threatened Beale's father with fisticuffs, only half-jokingly, for the right to give away the bride at her wedding. Beale was the sort of person you'd do that for.

Frank smiled. It was the first good news he'd had since finding out Beat was alive. Her life expectancy had just jumped by a significant factor.

"Get them airborne. And one of those Stratotankers you have parked out at Cape Verde. They'll need refueling."

"Roger that. They can be on site in about an hour."

"Have them burn it hard. We're running out of darkness."

Frank thought quickly about how to make this work. Since the helicopters wouldn't know Beat's location, he needed a way for Beat to come to the helicopters.

"And General, there's one thing we need to make sure the DAP Hawks are fitted with before they start out."

———

Beat still lay against the stones of the goat pen wall. She was tapped. For an hour since the plane exploded she'd tried to come up some alternate plan. Charlotte had recovered enough to sit up and lean her head against Sam's chest and weep quietly.

The ambassador had the decency to assure her they were going to get married as soon as they got back stateside, even if he had to roust a judge out of bed. Beat and Sam Green both knew their chances were not good and diminishing with every passing minute.

She'd try hiding them again. Would find the energy in another few minutes to give it one last effort, but she'd now been awake for two days, running, hiding, and battered. Her ears were still ringing, in fact ringing was all her left ear was giving her. Her directional hearing didn't exist at the moment.

Hearing.

There was a sound in the night. It was an odd sound. Like an over-sized washing machine or a...

"Sam, where's that sound coming from?"

"What sound?" But he was turning his head one way and another hunting for it, so she kept quiet. He glanced up more than once, but couldn't seem to locate it.

Then she knew.

"Okay, everyone this is it. Get ready for one last effort."

"This is what?"

Beat blessed her association with the 160th SOAR that had started all the way back in Panama in 1989. She'd kept up with them, made sure she was a contact point when they needed a liaison for a diplomatic security mission. She hadn't ridden with them but once, and that hadn't been combat, real or simulated. Damn but she'd been envious when Frank got that training ride last winter. Well, maybe this was her chance.

Please let it be her chance.

"That's a stealth U.S. Special Operations Forces Black Hawk helicopter. The same kind that went into Osama bin Laden's compound. That's why you hear them, but you can't tell where the sound is coming from. Now all we have to do is figure out where they're expecting to find us and get there."

"Where's that?"

"Damned if I know."

Then she heard the sound, blaring out of the sky. She watched which way Sam and Charlotte's heads turned, the helicopters were to the south of them, deeper into the city than she'd dared go. It was music. Unlike the odd sound of the stealth helicopters rotors, that often sounded as if they were flying away when they were actually coming right at you, the music would be intensely directional. It would blast from a loudspeaker attached to the helicopter and tell bad guys exactly where to aim.

It was music she knew well. It informed her that Frank Adams was involved and looking out for her. The sudden relief so sharp she wanted to cry.

He'd absolutely known what to play. It was the only movie series where she'd dragged him to the opening night of every sequel. She had a weak spot for Tom Cruise. And the *Mission Impossible* theme echoing through the pre-dawn darkness of Bissau city, told her that the message was for her and she'd better listen and listen hard.

"But that doesn't make any sense." The President was back in the U.S. Security Center in the U.N.'s basement. Hank was still at the table and General Rogers was still on the screen. The President was looking at the script John had just recorded and sent to the helicopters for playback.

"Trust me, Mr. President, it makes perfect sense. It's at least a triple letter score, and I'm prayin' plenty hard that it's a triple word score." Frank knew it would work. It just had to. If Beat Belfour was still alive in the city, she'd get there.

He just hoped to god she was still mobile. Because they had no way to go find her, she had to find them.

"Major Beale?"

"Here Frank." The right-hand screen was now showing a four-segment feed from the DAP Hawk helicopter as she now circled over the city. The screen was cut up into quarters and showed what Beale saw as she turned her helmet, the ghostly gray images of the ADAS cameras they'd installed six months earlier that showed the nighttime city in the stark imagery of a black-and-white movie as bright as daylight. The other three segments on the screen were views from the belly of the helicopter, ahead, and to either side. Bissau was laid out before them.

"I think we've played the music long enough to get her attention. I need you to circle slowly enough that she can hear a full set of instructions."

"Just reminding you that these people have surface-to-air missiles. Slow wouldn't be my first choice."

"Okay, uh," Frank thought quickly. Thought about how Beat had attacked him at the Federal Law Enforcement Training Center—fast repeated attack of his body.

"How about multiple faster passes? Let her pick up the segments as she needs them."

"Roger that."

Typical Major Beale and typical SOAR. A two word acknowledge before flying into a hot battle zone.

"Switch over to message broadcast."

"Switching."

Frank heard his own voice, picked up faintly through Beale's microphone.

"Beat your ass. Start where..."

———

Beatrice laughed and had to muffle her mouth in her *dashiki* to hide it. She almost missed the first instruction.

"Beat, your ass." Was one of the compliments that Frank had paid her the very first time they'd made love in the woods on that Georgia night at FLETC. It had been in an awed, breathy whisper, the memory of which could heat her blood even now. He'd made a real thing about cupping her behind in those powerful hands of his to pull her against him. No question about the authenticity of this message.

And he'd also told her to that they had to "beat their asses" if this was going to work. Time to move fast.

Start where Bruce fought the second time, the time after the tower.

Sam Green started to ask her what that meant, but she shushed him so that she could listen. She started to translate to him in whispers as she waited for that message to repeat several times.

"Bruce Willis, *Die Hard 2*, the second movie. The first time he fought in a tower, a skyscraper, the Nakatomi Plaza. Otherwise it might have been Bruce Lee, who fought in a temple. The second time Bruce Willis fought, it was in an airport. That's our starting frame of reference." It was perfect. No one, who didn't have their common ground of going to so many movies, would be able to follow these directions.

Go the direction Cary and Eva Marie didn't go.

"They're fading away," Charlotte's whisper was panicked.

It was true. The helicopter circling out toward the airport, too far away to hear the next instruction.

"It doesn't matter, they'll be back."

"But what did it mean?" Sam helped Charlotte to her feet as Beatrice rose. Her side had stiffened badly and she had definitely sprained her right knee when she dove out of the plane. She just hoped she hadn't torn anything. She ran a quick hand over her leg down the outside of the *dashiki*. Definitely swollen. Swollen badly, but it still took her weight.

"It means that we're in the wrong neighborhood." She led them off into the night. Cary Grant and Eva Marie Saint had been chased all over the landscape of Mount Rushmore in *North by Northwest*. "Go the way they didn't go." She needed to be south-southeast of the airport.

One hour to first light. She ignored her knee and got them moving. They had to hurry.

———

"We're starting to pick up some fire," Major Mark Henderson's voice remained absolutely calm. "Request permission to engage." It even sounded as if he was looking forward to it. As pilot of the second DAP Hawk, he'd be flying as backup wingman to his wife commanding the primary rescue bird.

The President and Frank looked at each other. The situation was escalating. G-B military forces had finally noticed that there were helicopters circling overhead. Hard to miss, even if they would have trouble locating them. The airport's radar should be useless against the stealth modifications. They would appear as flickers no bigger than a large bird, and never quite in the location where they actually were.

The problem was that most of the anti-electronic warfare defenses they carried, the ones that scrambled sophisticated tracking-and-homing equipment, were useless. The G-B army didn't have the high-end detection gear or automated aim and fire anti-aircraft. They had fifty-year-old Russian cannons that were aimed by hand and fired one inch shells. Rifles, rocket-propelled-grenade launchers produced in Brazil and left behind by the Portuguese when they left in the 1970s, five-inch howitzers. The weapons were so unsophisticated that they actually posed a considerable threat.

"Major Henderson. This is President Matthews."

"Hello, sir. How's the poker coming along?"

"Smart enough to not play you the next time you're in town."

That got a laugh. They all knew that the President would play anyway and didn't really care that he rarely won. It had also given him the moment to make sure his thoughts were clear.

"Yes. You are hereby authorized to use limited force, only as necessary, to ensure the security of this operation. Discretion is yours."

"Roger that, sir."

Even as Henderson spoke, a sharp hiss sounded in the background. Frank recognized it as one of the FFAR rockets mounted in pods on the sides of the DAP Hawk. Through Major Beale's view, they could see the rocket streak downward from her husband's otherwise invisible helicopter.

It impacted an armored vehicle with a multi-rocket launcher mounted on its roof. It was visible for just an instant before it disappeared in a massive fireball when all of the unfired rockets exploded simultaneously sending a huge ball of fire skyward.

"I guess they know we're here now." Mark didn't sound the least contrite.

They went back to their circling, Major Beale continued her broadcast.

CHAPTER TWENTY-THREE

B*eat flew with SOAR.* They had her in the back of one of the big twin-rotor Chinook helicopters. It was filled with the roar of the massive twin turbines and the sharp, stinging scent of kerosene from the Jet A fuel. Other than the red, night-time lights in the long cargo bay, there was little to see. Even pressing her face to the glass of the small round windows only revealed the stars.

She spent most of the trip sitting on a giant rubber bladder filled with fuel. Cases of rockets and ammunition were stacked at the front of the cargo bay.

She was sitting in a flying bomb.

All of this was part of a FARP, a Forward Arming and Refueling Point. Their destination was too far away for the Little Birds and Black Hawks to make the round trip. They were flying from Panama City down to the Colombian border as part of the Hunt for Elvis. That's what the Special Operations Forces operators, showing a little more imagination, had renamed the hunt for the Pineapple. Noriega had remained elusive right into day three of the taking of Panama, three days without a single sighting, as rare as Elvis.

They'd gotten a report of a jungle hideaway he often used down near the Colombian border. It was expected to be a dry hole, no one home, or they probably wouldn't have let her come along. But they'd wanted her expertise on hidden security systems and possible hideaways.

"Engaging now," the pilot announced over the intercom. There was nothing to see or hear, their helicopter was five miles behind the others. They were here for resupply, not part of the battle. Though the crew didn't act that way. In addition to the four crew chiefs ready to reload and refuel any helicopter, there were the two pilots up front, a pair of chiefs manning M60 machine guns mounted in side-opening windows. The big rear tail ramp had been lowered and a chief wearing a harness, in case he fell during radical maneuvers, stood at the end of the ramp manning another large gun.

The announcements by the pilot occurred on about a thirty-second pulse revealing again how practiced these guys were.

"First team in."

"Security guards down."

She fingered her fireworks pendant and wondered what had led her to run from Brooklyn to Fort Sam Houston, and from there to the Panamanian jungle.

"Perimeter secure."

In some odd way, unable to witness what was occurring in the nearby jungle, she was finally able to see her own actions from a distance.

"Inside cleared. Appears to be a dry hole."

That was her cue. The Chinook nosed down and roared forward. They'd search the place for any intelligence and possible hiding places, but he wasn't here.

Neither Elvis nor Frank Adams.

BEAT: NOW

Three times the length of Kate and Leo's boat.

And what part of Frank's thick head thought she'd remember the length of the *Titanic?*

The three of them were sprinting from shadow to shadow just one block west of the Beast in Bandim road. It was almost perfectly south-southeast of the main airport terminal. But tanks and tacticals were roaring up and down the main road.

At each intersection she'd wait and listen. Listen for the roaring of diesel engines, the high-whine and grinding gears of the pickups. When there was a break, they'd jump the gap and move farther from the airport.

And the idiot assumed that she knew exactly where they were from the airport. Like she'd be carrying a tape measure with her.

Wait, he'd know that. He'd know that she could only approximate. The *Titanic* was way longer than five-hundred feet and definitely less than a thousand. Times three. Call it a third to a half mile. That she could manage and kept heading south by southeast. They still had a ways to go.

Follow Witherspoon and get Blonde.

She froze and Sam and Charlotte actually ran into her.

She leaned against a wall, first light couldn't be more than fifteen minutes off. In the tropics that meant daybreak within half an hour.

And they'd be dead an hour after that.

At the most.

"Idiot." She hissed out.

"What?" Sam and Charlotte did their best to shrink into the shadow with her.

A helicopter flew overhead heading north fast. Gunfire followed it. Handguns, rifles, and the sharp bark of a tactical's big machine gun spewing out ten rounds a second.

"I don't know that reference."

"Which?"

"*Legally Blonde.* I had the flu and never much liked Reese Witherspoon anyway. He went by himself."

"*Legally Blonde.* Cute movie," Charlotte gasped, desperately trying to catch her breath and speak at the same time. "She's all blonde. And empty-headed. Or so everyone thinks. Including crappy. Ex-boyfriend."

All of the clues had been about places. "What's the setting?"

"Harvard Law School."

Sam pointed down the road. "There's a University about a dozen blocks that way." His breathing wasn't much better than his lover's, or Beat's own.

"Big empty lot across the street from the school. I think. I was taken there once, tour of the country's progress. It wasn't much, but it was a university."

"That's it. Last stretch." She got them running again. Had never reached so deep, hadn't even known she had reserves that went that far, but she did it. And this had better be it, because it was the last stretch for all three of them.

———

"That's them. Has to be." The tech called out.

Major Emily Beale flew fast over something which was such a blur on the screen that Frank hadn't registered anything unusual.

The tech had seen it though. She pulled up the image on the central screen and revealed three figures ducking from house to house, cautiously moving south. So close, but there was no way for the helicopter to get in among the huts and houses to fetch them. Everything was too tightly packed. They needed the open field of at least sixty-feet across for the Black Hawk's rotors.

"This doesn't look good." Major Henderson announced and the tech picked up his helmet camera's view and set it over General Rogers' image on the feed from the Situation Room.

The battle for the center of the city had run its course. Tanks and APCs, armored personnel carriers, were moving onto the Fera di Bandim road. They'd be hurrying out to the airport to secure the most significant asset of the country other than the downtown and the port. Indeed some of the traffic turned and raced to reinforce the port, but the bulk of it was heading their way.

And at the rate Beat and the others were moving, they'd reach the empty lot at about the same time as the bulk of the Guinea-Bissau army. There was no way to tell which faction had won and they couldn't risk waiting to find out.

"Beale!" Frank shouted. "Put me direct to the speakers."

He yelled out a command.

———

Beat heard Frank's voice roar out of the sky.

It was so loud, the helicopter flew low and fast directly overhead, that it took her a moment to unravel the words from the sheer blast of volume.

Neo! Take the red pill! Now!

The Matrix. Take the pill of the harsh reality.

"Run!" she yelled at Sam and Charlotte.

She pulled out her pistol and shoved them so hard they almost landed on their faces.

A local looked out their hut door to see what was going on and she fired a shot into the top of the door frame.

They ducked back inside.

As they sprinted, Beat heard the helicopter swing over them again. It slowed enough to hover just behind them.

A blast of downdraft shoved at their backs.

She glanced back and saw that a cloud of dust boiled upward beneath the rotor blades. Anyone attempting to follow them would be blinded and choked by the brownout.

A glance up and she could see the bright sparks of small weapon's fire pinging off the hull.

With a brap like a dragon's roar, the hovering helicopter opened up with their mini-guns. These weren't the big machine guns on the tacticals firing five hundred rounds-a-minute. The M134 six-barrel Gatling guns rained down lead at eighty rounds-a-second.

They looked like a dark-red whip of God, right on the very edge of vision, but bright in the night-vision gear the helicopter crew would be wearing. Twin streams of hell swirled and slashed down from the heavens and across the street behind them and to either side. Anyone stupid enough to fire at the helicopter wouldn't last long under such an onslaught.

Something exploded. A car. A truck. She didn't wait to see.

With a shove against their backs, she got Sam and Charlotte moving even faster. Another local in a doorway to her right, this time with a rifle.

Her first shot drilled him in the forehead, the second in the heart before he even knew he was dead. They were past him before he even had time to collapse.

A second helicopter swooped low, passing through the raking gunfire from the ground and dropping down to street level a hundred feet ahead of them.

They'd reached the empty lot.

The two crewmen on the miniguns were pouring lead back over Beat's head so hard and close she could feel the heat of their passage.

She clapped a hand on Sam's and Charlotte's heads to keep them below the swing of the rotors and the slash of the gunfire.

They dove through the wide-open door of the Black Hawk's cargo bay in unison, almost tumbling out the far side with their momentum.

Charlotte screamed, and the helicopter roared as it clawed back into the sky.

Several FFAR rockets sizzled from the other helicopter in rapid formation and then a Hellfire missile roared down into the road. The nasty war cry of its rocket motor like nothing else in the sky.

The shockwave knocked their own helicopter aside as they scrambled for distance. A hand on her back was all that kept her from tumbling out the door as the helicopter struggled through the turbulence, and then, as suddenly as a light switch being thrown, they were above it.

A glance down at the fast receding ground showed a massive crater in the middle of the main road. Parts of a tank burned in the center of the crater even as another tank drove right in on top of it. People began pouring out of the hatches even as it too began to burn.

The hand on her back that had saved her belonged to one of the crew chiefs.

"Just the three of you?" A woman. The gunner was a woman. How cool was that?

Beat nodded, it was all she had the breath for.

The helicopters climbed into the lightening sky. Within moments they cleared the city. Before Beat could even think clearly that she'd survived, they were passing over wide mangrove swamps and finally off the coast.

As they climbed toward a refueling tanker, Guinea-Bissau was certainly a place she was glad to be leaving behind.

"You know that you're bleeding?"

She knew that her knee hurt like hell. Twisted, maybe torn. And her ribs, she'd escalated her assessment from sore to cracked.

It was only when the woman took her arm that Beat hissed with pain. The crew chief pulled out a long knife and carefully slit the bloody *dashiki* then folded it back from Beat's arm. A long scrape from shoulder to elbow, a graze that had removed a narrow line of skin before continuing on its way.

Beat turned to look at the others. Sam was sitting on the deck, still had his burlap sack tied across his back. Charlotte lay with her head in his lap as the other crew chief was binding her leg. Charlotte had pressed her lips white, but she was being brave about having a hole shot in her thigh.

Charlotte gave them both a thumb's up which were returned with thankful nods.

The crew woman who'd just finished bandaging her arm tapped her on the good shoulder.

"Welcome aboard. I'm Connie Davis. That's Kee Smith helping your friends. There's someone who wants to speak to you." Connie was holding out a headset.

Beat pulled it on.

"Beatrice Belfour here."

"So," she knew that rumbling voice better than she knew her own. "So," she could hear the smile and the relief as Frank Adams repeated himself.

"So, you've got skills."

Six Days and Seven Nights. She'd escaped the pirates alive because both she and Frank had skills.

"I've got skills." She closed her eyes against the brightness of the rising sun and listened to his gentle laugh.

"You'll be at the airport?" She had to know.

"I'll be there."

And he would be.

"I didn't get you a present."

It would be their anniversary. This was July third, she'd probably be landing back at Dulles or Andrews Air Force on the fourth.

"You never remember."

And she didn't. But she still wore the little silver firework around her neck as her only jewelry after twenty-five years together.

"But I'll be there."

And he always had been. After every single mission she'd returned from since Panama, he'd been waiting for her at the airport gate.

She'd radioed him from Panama City after they'd taken Noriega. He'd given himself up at the gates of the Vatican embassy and they'd shipped him to the U.S. for trial and incarceration.

Beatrice had asked Frank to be there in San Antonio and he had been. She'd asked him to marry her as she stepped off the jetway and into his arms. He hadn't even let her leave the airport. He'd bundled her on a plane for Reno and married her later that day because he didn't want her to get away. It had been plenty romantic. Though after the hunt for Noriega, she'd turned down his repeated offer to have Elvis be best man.

"I'll be there for you," his voice the sweetest sound Beatrice Ann Belfour had ever heard.

"And I for you." The words she'd promised that day from a country in flames to the man she loved.

A promise they'd both kept ever since.

PETER'S CHRISTMAS

They met at the United Nations, two people from different worlds.

US President Peter Matthews, *D.C. born and bred. Since the tragic death of his wife two years before, he ranks as the most eligible bachelor on the planet.*

Kim-Ly Geneviève Beauchamp, *a French-Vietnamese beauty, wields an intelligence that dazzles Peter. But in her job as UNESCO World Heritage Chief of Unit for Southeast Asia, she may be more than he can handle.*

Little do they know that both their hearts and their very lives will be at risk this Christmas season.

INTRODUCTION TO PETER'S CHRISTMAS

President Peter Matthews was starting to have major issues with me.

In The Night Is Mine *I not only killed his horrid wife, I denied him romantic love with his childhood friend, Emily Beale.*

Now, his White House Chief of Staff and the head of his Presidential Protection Detail had both found true love. Granted, Frank Adams had discovered his true love years before, but his story had only just been told. The President had to watch from the sidelines as the Night Stalkers Connie and Lola each found the one person they couldn't live without in Wait Until Dark *and* Take Over at Midnight.

Having the President of the United States of America ticked off with me (even if he was a fictional President), did not sit comfortably.

But a year had passed since Daniel's Christmas *and I was looking for another Christmas story idea. Peter issued an executive order that this book was going to be his.*

Okay, fine.

But how was I going to have the most carefully protected person on the planet have a dangerous adventure? And who was going to be worthy of the President of the United States? What woman would be strong enough to stand up to him and to help him become an even more unique person?

There is a curious thing that happens when writing fiction. A character will

*pop into a story for no apparent reason—at least none apparent to the author—
and then will refuse to go away.*

Dilya had done this to me in I Own the Dawn. *She started as a rescued
man (no, that wasn't working)...a rescued boy (still not right)...a rescued girl
(there we go) to make the horror of a moment in the story a little more real.*

*Then I couldn't get rid of her. There is a whole series of scenes in which Kee
and Archie attempt to shed themselves of the orphaned child that are actually
my own efforts to write her out of the story. With each attempt, Dilya became
more and more tightly wound about Kee and Archie's own story until she
became the common thread that bound everything together and provided some
of the most dramatic scenes in the book. Her gentle commentaries to other characters in later books would also have been sorely missed if I'd been able to cut her
role short.*

*Accidental characters may make a writer crazy at times, but we also love
them.*

In preparation for writing Peter's Christmas *(I was under an executive
order to do so, after all), I reread* Frank's Independence Day. *Much to my
surprise, there she was already created: Kim-ly Geneviève Beauchamp, the
UNESCO World Heritage Centre's Chief of Unit for Southeast Asia. This President would appreciate a woman of intelligence and sophistication...what he
isn't prepared for was her spine of steel.*

However, when Genny came onstage in Frank, *she was from Vietnam. Why
Vietnam?*

*This actually stems back to a solo bicycle trip I took around the world in
1993-1994. Vietnam was just opening to travel by Americans at that time, but it
was a very slim opening as this was before President Clinton "normalized" relations in 1995. Before I set off on the trip, a friend who had served in the Vietnam
War told me about his experiences there.*

*"I loved the country and the people so much. The war sucked so bad that I
would go AWOL (away without leave—a fairly serious military crime) sometimes and just hitchhike up and down the coast. I'd stay with locals, surf, eat
with them, help in their gardens. Those are some of the best memories of my life."*

*The plan was that he would meet me for the fourth month of my trip. We
would meet at the Swiss embassy in Bangkok, the only place an American could
get a Vietnamese travel permit at that time, and we would bicycle from Ho Chi
Minh city to Hanoi together. I was in southern Japan and it was less than two*

weeks before we were supposed to do this...when he cancelled on me. I didn't have the nerve to make the journey myself, so I skipped Vietnam. That is my single greatest regret of that entire trip as I've heard nothing but wonderful stories of Vietnam ever since.

I still haven't been there, though my friend's stories have stuck with me over the years.

But how could I set up an American President to fall in love with a woman of Vietnam?

One of the things that I try to do with my writing is to create awareness and create change. I write about issues that concern me. It's my version of: Think Globally, Act Locally. That is why I write about strong women—it is what I wish for my step-daughter to become. (Actually she'd grown now and incredibly strong without being tough. I couldn't be more proud, so I'll just leave that subject there before I get started and bore everyone to death.)

As in Daniel when I wrote of hope for a more rational North Korea, I wrote Geneviève in hopes of showing that America and Vietnam could have a future together. President Obama's visit to Vietnam in the spring of 2016 pleased me no end, especially considering that I wrote this moment in 2013.

I now had the hero and the heroine. I had an exotic setting of Vietnam, which is always a bonus.

But I was still missing a crisis.

I didn't want to set that in Vietnam. It was going to have to be an attack on the President to make the crisis worthy of Peter Matthews and I felt that wouldn't respect my "we need to rethink our image of Vietnam" theme.

Then, as she so often does in my manuscripts, my research-librarian wife tracked down a problem befitting both the President and Geneviève in her role as a Chief of Unit for the UNESCO World Heritage Centre. It was only as we dug into the history of the UNESCO site that we understood she had uncovered a place with an incredible depth of history. It goes back before the Vikings arrived in America and is still vibrantly significant today.

Sometimes I wish I could visit every single place I write about. But some are too dangerous, and some... Well, I'd be too busy traveling to do any writing.

And the President was already impatient enough with me already.

CHAPTER ONE

I*t was December first* and Kim-Ly Geneviève Beauchamp of Vietnam stood not twenty paces from the base of the American National Christmas Tree on Washington, D.C.'s Ellipse. The slight fluttering of snow was captured in the streetlights of the park, enchanting for the news cameras, making the scene glitter like a fairyland. Her breath made small white clouds that softened the night even more.

She had come to the lighting of the tree every year that her UNESCO job placed her in D.C. or even New York at the right time of year. Something about this moment—the colors, the children filled with wonder, the spectacular music, the President's message—had always filled her with a hope and a joy. It reminded her of so many good things in the world. She also attended the lighting of the New York tree in Rockefeller Center whenever she could. Though her tropical blood was never thick enough to convince her to join in ice skating with the holiday crowds who made it look so fun.

"*Tu es un* Christmas sap *absolu*, Genny," her mother often accused her with a gentle smile; their family language a crazy mix of French heritage and Vietnamese homeland, overlaid with the ubiquitous English. And her mother was absolutely correct. She was.

But this year was different. Genny wasn't shoulder to shoulder with mothers and children and small business owners and twenty thousand others who had braved the cold and dark of a D.C. winter night. She wasn't blocked from a clear view of the tree by the fifty reporters, their cameras, and their lights.

This year she stood close beside cabinet members, White House staffers, and soon, the United States President and his phalanx of Secret Service guards who would be arriving at the podium for the lighting of the tree.

"What am I doing here?"

"At the President's personal invitation," a Secret Service agent standing beside her whispered back in response.

"Oh sorry," she turned to face the female agent who looked neat and dangerous in her suit and long overcoat, with the telltale coil of wire leading up to her ear mostly hidden by dark hair. "I was actually speaking to myself. I do that."

"No worries, ma'am," the agent didn't look the least put out or the least worried that she might have offended. "Always takes a bit of getting used to, your first trip to the White House."

Of course, the Secret Service would know that about her. She wondered what else the agent knew about her life now that Genny was the President's personal guest to the tree lighting ceremony. Did the woman know that five months earlier Genny had practically hijacked a meeting at the U.N. to convince the President to pay more attention to the UNESCO World Heritage Sites in Southeast Asia? That had been one of her most audacious acts, irritating the Vietnamese, Laotian, and Cambodian U.N. ambassadors in the process. Or that she'd since dodged three invitations to the White House prior to this one?

The towering tree was still unlit. A U.S. Marine Corps Band was playing *Good King Wenceslas*. And who would follow in this good President's steps through the winter that seemed to chill the news headlines? She shook off the thought as being unworthy of a Christmas moment.

Most of the White House staffers were talking to each other as earnestly as if they were still inside their warm offices. A few of them had joined in singing carols with the crowd. She tried to sing along as she normally would, knowing she had a passable, if French-accented soprano, but she couldn't even seem to mouth the words in a throat gone dry.

Some delay in the proceedings left her too much opportunity to wonder quite why she had avoided the invitations before, though two out of three times she'd been legitimately flying out of the country the next day.

So, why had she accepted this one? Because she'd be in Washington anyway for the tree lighting, though the President had no way to know that. And she'd been surprised. The call hadn't come from some staffer as before, it had come from President of the United States Peter Matthews himself. She'd recognized his voice immediately despite only meeting him the one time. Though she'd certainly watched enough of his speeches since then, far more than could be justified by her passing interest in American politics. He'd charmed her into coming, made her deny that she'd been avoiding him, even though she had. And she wasn't sure why she'd been doing that either.

She liked the President the one time they'd met. Enjoyed his sharp mind and insightful questions. Through the U.S. Ambassador to the U.N., she'd begun receiving an uncharacteristic degree of cooperation. The United States had assisted her several times now with information and gentle political pressure. So, she'd decided her efforts had been successful and left it at that. She'd soon moved on to other avenues, to leverage her goals to protect Heritage Sites from desperate governments teetering on the edge of open conflict.

America's relationship with the U.N., and by extension UNESCO, had always been a little dicey anyway and she didn't see it as her mission to fix that. That would be far above her mandate, though the outstanding billion-plus dollars in arrears would have helped so much. Geneviève didn't expect more than had already been given. The Americans' interest in Southeast Asia had always been tinged with a combination of benign neglect for the present and deep-seated uneasiness based on the collective memories of the Vietnam War and what they'd perpetrated both in Vietnam and in the surrounding countries.

She had turned down the car that the White House had offered and taken the train down as usual. Then spent the three hours in transit worrying instead of enjoying the ride as she usually did. Agent Beatrice Ann Belfour had attached herself to Genny at the front gate, her guide and guard. That perhaps was partly to protect Genny, and partly to protect against her, regarding the President.

"Heads up, incoming," Agent Belfour whispered to her privately.

She was about to ask what she meant, then realized she already knew, and steeled herself. Sure enough. At the end of the tale of the good king trudging through the snow to feed a poor but worthy man, the President of the United States strode down the lawn from the White House.

The Marine Corps Band broke into *Hail to the Chief.*

President Matthews, still immensely popular despite this being near the end of his second year in office, practically leapt onto the platform and called into the microphone for them to hush. He did it with a laugh and a smile that was easy for the crowd and even the band members to join in.

She found that she too was laughing despite herself. He exuded energy and hope with that simple gesture. Was it natural or calculated? She'd butted heads with enough politicians over the years to assume the latter, but it didn't feel that way. It felt as if he meant everything he did.

He was tall and trim. His hair drifted down to his collar, befitting for the youngest President in history. His brown eyes sought hers, a smile lit his face as he spotted her among the crowd. He was also terribly handsome and clearly knew it. Before she could even think to respond in kind, he had turned away and then shouted to the crowd, "Merry Christmas, America!"

The crowd, obviously enamored of their leader, shouted back in near unison, "Merry Christmas, Mr. President!"

"Is he always like this?" Geneviève whispered to the agent.

"No, sometimes he's worse. At least according to my husband." She nodded to the massive agent who hovered close beside the President without appearing to. If Agent Belfour looked dangerous, the head of the Presidential Protection Detail looked lethal.

"What do you do when you're not riding herd on some guest?"

"Oh, odd jobs." Belfour's simple evasion spoke volumes to Genny.

She rarely needed security herself, did her best to avoid it even if she really should have it in tow. She'd found that negotiations were much easier at World Heritage Sites if you weren't totting along a personal militia. Even when the local warlords were, perhaps especially then. Still, she'd worked with security escorts enough to know that the really good ones played down their roles.

———

"So, Kim-Ly, did you enjoy the speech?" Peter knew it was a lame opening, but he didn't know how else to start off. The tree was lit, the crowd had cheered, and America had been given both a colorful display and a happy Christmas message. Now, clear of the reporters and their cameras, his nerves had set in.

He'd managed to time his placement in the crowd for the five-minute walk back to the White House so that he'd be beside her through the Presidential Park. It would have been too much to have her walk with him down to the tree lighting, so he'd come up with them meeting at the tree itself as a comfortable place to begin. But now he didn't know where to start.

"Geneviève. Only my Vietnamese grandmother calls me Kim-Ly as I was named for her."

Okay, so she went by her middle name. He'd missed that somewhere.

He'd refused to let the Secret Service tell him anything more about her after that first meeting at the U.N. He didn't want to take any advantage of his Presidential powers in this. Let the Secret Service do what was necessary to approve her for security, but keep it to themselves. It actually placed him at a disadvantage, as his own life was so public. But entering politics had been his choice, or maybe his first wife's choice, but that didn't mean it was Geneviève's choice. Her name was a bit of a mouthful but it had a long elegance, much as she did.

After they crossed over the closed 'E' Street, they entered the Presidential Park by the Southwest Gate. They were in the lead, a dozen agents ranged about them, and the rest of the staff followed behind chattering among themselves. The waist-high concrete wall could stop a large truck and the spike iron fence mounted atop it kept all but the most suicidal out of the grounds. They crossed the lawn past the tennis and basketball courts, presently covered with a light sheen of snow.

She looked at him, as if she were peering around the corner made by the thick fall of mahogany hair beside her cheek. Hair that reached to the middle of her back. Her features were poised and aristocratic. Her skin reflected her mixed French and Vietnamese heritage—European aristocratic features, almond-shaped eyes, and golden skin. She looked splendid and exotic. But he recalled that it had been her passion in her beliefs that had captivated him at the United Nations building in New York last July. Though her stunning looks hadn't hurt.

"As for your speech, it has its purpose served."

"Ha. Well, that puts me in my place, doesn't it?" Peter tried not to feel put out, but he did, no matter how childish the thought. "The speechwriters wanted a meatier speech, but I wanted to—"

"Keep it short, upbeat, and make people focus less on worry and more on good cheer." Her voice was like a fifth player in a string quintet. Once you were used to the sound of four instruments, then a second viola begins to play, offering new and unique insights into the music the four others had been creating.

"Uh, yes. That's exactly what I was trying for." Not a single thing was missed by his guest's sharp mind. Those had been his own guide-words for himself as he wrote it.

"Then, it has its purpose served."

"Is that Ms. Geneviève Beauchamp's form of high praise?" Was he so desperate for approval? For that, he could have talked to any of the dozen or more staffers and that many again service agents who accompanied him along the walkways back to the White House. No, it was *her* approval he seemed to be begging for. He'd convinced himself that it merely reflected a desire to engage and welcome her, but he did want her to like him.

"Staying and singing *O Christmas Tree* was a nice touch. I'm sure it played well to the public."

"Do I detect a note of Christmas cynicism in my guest?"

She stopped in place, halfway to the White House, as if her feet had just frozen to the ground. Geneviève, lit warmly by the soft lights, stood amid the fluttering snow that graced her hair like momentary stars.

The Secret Service flowed smoothly around them. Within moments they were as good as standing alone. The agents circled about them, facing outward. The rest of the staffers continued on their way to warmer climes and hot coffee indoors.

"No," she looked directly at him for the first time since last July.

Somehow, Peter had forgotten her eyes. Golden skin, elegant features, and rich brown hair that flowed down gloriously, practically to her elbows, were what drew your attention if you had even a hint of a Y-chromosome. But it was her green eyes that appeared to hide nothing that were her most startling feature.

"You misinterpret. I'm never a cynic about Christmas. You detect a note of caution because I don't know what you want from me, Mr. President. I am the UNESCO Chief of Unit for Southeast Asia World Heritage Sites. I am not political, I am *specifically* not political. So, therefore I am cautious, as I do not understand why I am here."

He smiled. He'd asked himself that exact same question. What had he been hoping for when he invited her. The fragment of an answer he'd come up with had influenced how he'd altered tonight's speech.

"You are here because I truly enjoyed meeting you and I wanted to see you again. I'm only sorry it didn't happen sooner."

She studied him for several long moments, her expression unreadable. He remembered that from their meeting at the U.N. This was a woman in absolute control of her own emotions. Not to mention her facial expressions.

"And that is all that you are intending?" She didn't radiate the doubt she must be feeling. She made it sound as if it were a simple question.

Peter nodded, "That's all. That encompasses the vast extent of my nefarious hidden agenda."

"Ah. I understand now, Mr. President," her soft smile appeared for the first time since he'd lit the tree.

Peter always loved watching the crowd in that brilliant moment when he lit the National Christmas Tree. That shared held breath when the decorations were lit and the year's design was revealed to the nation. He had worked with the designer and they'd created a red-and-white spiral of thirteen wide bands that swooped upward to a star-studded blue top, with a traditional golden star at the pinnacle. They'd overlapped the red and white strings between each stripe, wiring them into something called a "chase" unit, which caused the lines to shift slightly about the tree. The tree looked like a flag unfurling in the breeze.

No ornaments other than the fifty "stars" in the field of blue, each a shining image of the fifty states' official mammals. If the news agencies didn't catch onto that bit of whimsy in a day or so, the designer would tip someone off. His personal favorite was the Maine Moose with the Washington State Orca coming a close second.

But tonight Peter had watched only Kim-Ly Geneviève Beauchamp of Vietnam as he pressed the button that lit the tree. She had become glorious in that moment. Her smile radiating as brightly as the kajillion Christmas lights.

"If that is indeed the entire scope of your plan, Mr. President, what you should do is offer me a gentleman's escort. Then perhaps we can start this conversation once again." She made it sound as simple as that.

So he took her at her word and held out his arm for her. She slipped a hand about his elbow. He could feel her touch as if her thin red leather glove and his thick wool coat didn't exist.

She turned with him and they and their circle of protectors progressed once more along the frosty roadway toward the main entrance to the Residence.

"Where did I begin our conversation?" Peter was distracted by her simple touch.

"With the speech."

"Ah," he tried to think of a better opening, but had little luck finding one. "That was a lame beginning."

"It was, but the speech served its purpose."

He did his best to suppress a groan, but didn't succeed well. This was an improvement? Frank, the head of his Presidential Protection Detail turned to check that he was okay. Geneviève must have heard it, but she didn't react. Rather, she continued talking as if he had made no interruption.

"It served its purpose in that it has made me glad that I accepted your invitation."

It was a high compliment indeed. Peter had no response to it. He had again totally misread her meaning, which was very unusual for him. His gift was reading what people wanted, both as individuals and in groups. He'd then address everyone in their own worldview semantics in order to build agreement and accord. Yet, he'd misread her twice in under a minute. How had she done that to him?

"Now," she pointed across the South Lawn. "Tell me how you make this fountain work when any water with the least common sense would be now frozen." Her French juxtaposition of the verb made her sound even more charming.

He watched the central jet splash merrily despite their frosty breath and the snowflakes swirling gently down out of the winter's night sky.

"Maybe it thinks warm thoughts? I have no idea."

―――――

Genny had always wanted to see the inside of the White House, especially at Christmas. From the outside there were no great displays, no grand dressing of decorations. Perhaps, it was the woman's role to decorate the White House. But the First Lady had died in that tragic helicopter accident two years ago, not even spending an entire year in the White House. Katherine Matthews had never had a chance to decorate a single Christmas. That was a great sadness, on top of all the others.

Still, Genny would be terribly disappointed if she found it wasn't decorated on her first, and probably only, visit here.

It had been sweet of the President to invite her. But even if she were to trust that he had no ulterior motive, what possible reason could she have to be involved in any way with such a man? The American-proclaimed "Leader of the Free World" had much to answer for in many places. Though she had been pleasantly surprised that this one did not believe that a sound foreign policy was in direct conflict with a sound domestic one. So many of his predecessors had done just that.

They walked along the driveway that circled the South Lawn. Clearly uncomfortable, she let him play guide by pointing out the Putting Green, which he never used, the Swimming Pool, which he often used, though he noted that he did that only in warmer weather, and several trees which even she knew he named completely wrong, but the effort was rather cute.

The first glimmer of Christmas decoration hope came when she saw the two sweeping stairways leading up to the broad porch of the South Portico. White twinkle lights adorned the stair's handrails and the porch's stone balustrade. It was a delicate statement on such a massive structure but it cheered her nonetheless.

His attempts to play guide wholly collapsed as they climbed the steps. He clearly knew less about the building's history than the grounds. He huffed out a great cloud of frustrated breath, then spoke quickly, waving an arm to encompass the entire structure.

"It was designed by aliens. The whole place. George and Martha Washington were pod people. Probably Dolly Madison too, though not James. At least according to the super-secret Area 51 files that the FBI did *not* give to me the day I was elected."

"And what *did* they give you?" The frustrated rant had been the most human thing she'd heard from the man. It was the first time Genny wondered if perhaps he had spoken truth, and really had no political motive for inviting her.

"Frankly, they gave me a headache. It was a very disillusioning day. Do you know how many identified troublespots there are on this planet and how many of those are right in our country?"

"This is not my country, Mr. President."

"Right, sorry. Of course it isn't. Sorry. I really must learn to keep my mouth shut."

They climbed up the Portico's stairs in awkward silence for several moments. She finally could take it no longer and attempted to rescue him.

"The snow is so pretty. It was good of you to arrange that." It would give him a chance to say, "Did it just for you." Then she could dismiss the easy flattery and the man along with it. It was touching that he had been thinking of her when he'd altered his speech. Against expectation, he slowed and stared up at the fluttering flakes until a few began to accumulate on his cheeks and forehead for a brief moment before melting.

"Snow? I'd guessed that they were tiny crystalline alien spaceships, still cold from the depths of outer space, come to take back the White House that George built."

Genny looked away to face the building so that he wouldn't see her expression. She didn't want him to know that he had confused her.

Most men had one of two reactions to her, three actually.

One, they assumed she'd made her career with her beauty and discounted her mind totally. A view they rarely maintained after even a single meeting in which they did not agree with her.

Two, they saw her as a target for the bastioning of their male egos, because of course they could easily conquer her. All of the men with this type of response, she had gladly disillusioned. Only two had required a brief personal demonstration of her self-defense training to permanently convince them.

The third type simply became tongue-tied around her which she never really understood, she had a mirror after all and knew she wasn't nearly that level of extraordinary. But she had learned early on how to read and use all three reactions to her advantage. Genny occasionally felt guilty for doing this but, as she only used it to save precious Heritage Sites and not on her own behalf, she didn't feel too guilty.

With President of the United States Peter Matthews, she had apparently found a fourth response. Her presence did not stun him to silence nor fill him with avarice nor knot up his tongue, but it certainly did fluster him. Again the word "cute" came to mind, but she rather doubted that he'd appreciate the observation, so she kept it to herself.

He also provided a wit and humor that he didn't reveal to the nation. Charm? Yes. Quirky humor? Not that she had observed. He had more dimensions than Genny had anticipated.

He led her up to the center of the Portico. They paused at the balcony rail. The South Lawn was spread before them, and off in the distance, the patriotic swirl of flag-colored lights climbed the glowing three-story tall tree. Beyond it, the brilliant needle of the Washington Monument soared into the night sky, clearly stating, "Here lies the source of America's power. Here is rooted her mighty spear."

"Terribly phallic, no?" She teased.

"Maybe the Founding Fathers had an inferiority complex."

He made it easy for her to laugh. "They did but you do not?"

"Not until I met you." In the soft light of the Portico, Genny could see that he actually blushed. "Did I really just say that out loud?"

"Indeed you did." Nor was she likely to forget it. While he wasn't the first man she'd smitten, he was the first who was so honest about it.

"Come," he cleared his throat. "There is something I think you will enjoy before we go up to the Residence for a small gathering."

As he turned her by her hand still in the crook of his arm, she spotted the Secret Service agents, hers, his, and two others standing by the wall. The President did not appear flustered by their presence, so she did her best to not be as well. She'd felt alone with him for a moment, and been enjoying that feeling. Her attempts to hold onto that failed under the four agents' roving gazes. Though they didn't look at her, it was clear they were completely aware of her every move.

He led her to what appeared to be a large window in the center of the rounded wall behind the Portico that was the great signature bay of the White House. At some signal she didn't see, two of the agents raised up the window sash until it was higher than her head. Then reaching down, they opened a pair of waist-high double doors. It was like a secret passage through a window and into an unknown world. She and the President were able to walk through the door or window or whatever it was and into...

Her breath caught in her throat. A stunning tree of massive proportions filled the center of the room. The room was oval, but she was pretty sure the Oval Office wasn't located in the Residence, but rather over in the West Wing. And the Oval Office was decorated in white whereas this room was all decorated in blue. Then she remembered a broadcast on shelters for the needy that the President had given three months earlier. It had been from this room, the Blue

Room. That was it. While the room was gorgeous, it was the tree that dominated.

"It must be six meters tall."

"Eighteen feet this year. They delivered it by a horse-drawn wagon, can you believe that in this day and age? And, no, the decorations this year are not on your behalf. I didn't even think about that until today."

Genny focused on the ornaments, through the dazzle of the beautiful lighting. The lights themselves were flags, national flags. Made of Tiffany glass.

"The flags of the U.N.?" This was becoming a little creepy. Genny almost felt as if the President were stalking her.

"No. The League of Nations. I have been doing so much work with the U.N. this last year that it seemed appropriate to honor the first attempt to form a world government for peace. And it humbles me to remember that this nation, that worked so hard to create the League, was even then too divided to join it."

"Do you remember the name of the room where we first met?"

"Not really. Wait, maybe I do. The Woodrow Wilson Reading Room."

"Which is filled with the card catalog for the League of Nations."

"Really? I guess this looks pretty bad?"

"It doesn't look good, Mr. President."

He turned back to inspect the tree. "I just meant it to honor the League."

Genny studied the profile of the man studying the tree. Here stood a thoughtful man, but perhaps also a humble one. He had little of the arrogance she expected from the senior official of the United States of America. He had used his own tree to remind himself that he could do better if he just kept trying. How rare such men were.

She could feel this moment, this place somehow shifting around her. Genny always felt her way up to decision points, had learned to trust her instincts.

Many of her instincts said that the proper action was to remove her grip from his elbow and ask the nice Secret Service lady to get her out of this room, this building, and off these premises. Quickly.

There was no way in which she could keep her life, which she loved, and yet even consider staying in the room with this man due to the merest possibility of where it might lead.

And then the oddest thing happened.

Rather than letting go and allowing her to run, her gloved hand squeezed his arm. She leaned in and whispered, against all better judgment, "It is a beautiful tree."

She assessed her reaction for having acted so irrationally. And was intrigued to discover that it settled as lightly as the tiny spaceships, disguised as snow, fluttering down outside the bay window of the White House.

CHAPTER TWO

*T**he President's idea of** a "small reception" in the Residence was much in keeping with Genny's idea of what it turned out to be. She had been to enough political receptions throughout her career not to be surprised by this one.

Thirty or so guests, a half dozen waiters, and a trio of Secret Service agents milled about the Central Hall of the second floor of the Residence. Actually the Secret Service didn't so much mill about as stand unobtrusively, looking like black-suited structural pillars in a room otherwise done in white, pale yellow, and abounding with Christmas décor.

Small trees, not much taller than she was, were placed in three corners of the spacious room. A grand piano and harp stood in the fourth corner. The instruments did not intrude even halfway into the width of the space and had no impact at all upon its length. The musicians played Christmas carols, but softly enough that conversation was possible without raising your voice. Evergreen garlands draped above portraits of past Presidents and scenes of rural America.

Tables laden with canapés, crudités, spiced nuts, and other hors d'oeuvres were scattered down the length of the hall. Each table sported a centerpiece of a Christmas scene done in elegant gingerbread complete with lights and sugared walkways. She was absolutely and completely charmed.

Genny was also pleased to see that she had judged the attire appropriately. The President had said casual, and the White House Social Secretary had been able to translate that for her as, "The men will all be in suits. Though several will shed their ties after they get clear of the news cameras, the President will not. The women will not be in evening gowns, but most will wear designer slacks, tailored blouse, and a warm but attractive jacket for protection against the cold." She'd opted for Weizmann boots, Dior pants, a dark silk blouse, and a silver satin Asian jacket with black dragon brocade. Her only jewelry, a thin silver chain about her neck bearing a small pendant of the Chinese ideogram for "Serenity" that no one had yet recognized nor asked the meaning.

She was chatting pleasantly enough with the Chairman of the Joint Chiefs of Staff. He might be the highest ranking officer in the U.S. military, but General Brett Rogers had also been an Army Private forty years earlier, while serving at the end of the Vietnam War.

"By the time I arrived, Saigon was about as far north as a grunt could go. I was there less than a year before it was all over, spent most of it out on the Mekong Delta."

"I imagine that was not the most pleasant of assignments." Genny was reminding herself to be civil. This man had been fighting in the Vietnamese swamps, while her family had retreated to the safety of their ancestral village in the Languedoc region of southern France. They had escaped in the early 1960s and had not returned to Vietnam until the mid-1970s after the war was over.

"It wasn't," General Rogers agreed. "But I did love the countryside. I come from Fargo, North Dakota, one of our Great Plains states, and had never seen anything else like it. Amazing places and people, at least the ones not trying to kill a nineteen-year-old punk kid who wet his pants in his first battle."

People in the Matthews' White House kept not being what she expected. She'd expected a grizzled warrior who despised her country, yet he didn't. And the highest-rank soldier in their country had just confessed to being afraid.

"Are you monopolizing the second prettiest woman in the room, Brett?" Daniel Drake Darlington, the White House Chief of Staff, joined them. Speaking of beautiful men, he was quite the most beautiful one in the room. He looked like the magazine ad for blond surfers rather than the most powerful non-elected person in the country. Her little sister would go crazy if she ever met him, he was exactly her type.

"Second?" Genny hadn't meant it to sound borderline petty. There were a number of astonishingly well-maintained women here.

"Well, my apologies, but I do have a bias for my wife. Alice is here somewhere."

Brett harrumphed, "Damn woman knows more about my troop movements than I do."

"She's an analyst for the CIA," Daniel explained to Genny, a point that clearly gave him great pride.

"Good one too," the General agreed. Then he spotted someone over Genny's shoulder. "Oh no! Well, there goes the neighborhood." But the General's smile, the first she'd seen on his face, appeared quite genuine. "Emily, over here."

She turned in time to see a stunning blond walking beside President Matthews. They were similar in height. The woman's posture was impeccable, her walk so perfectly balanced that Genny knew she was exceptionally trained even without the green dress-uniform she wore. And she and the President moved with an easy familiarity that went far beyond mere friendship.

If he had a woman like this at his side, what in all the world was she doing here? Was that a stab of jealousy she felt? It was like meeting Lauren Bacall, who she had, or Meryl Streep, who she hadn't, and finding them on the arm of the man she had thought... Where those thoughts had arisen, she didn't know. Genny focused on kicking them back beneath the metaphoric jungle foliage of her mind. Even as she did so, she knew one thing for certain, she'd just been totally outclassed.

The President had invited her to Washington, D.C. for a tree-lighting ceremony and a drink. No more. *Remets-t'en!* She had surely been put in her place. She waited a heartbeat or two and checked in with herself. Nope, she wasn't over it yet.

The woman saluted the General.

"None of that here," Brett Rogers grumbled, but returned the salute so sharply that there was no mistaking how much he liked the woman.

"Major Emily Beale, Geneviève Beauchamp of UNESCO." The President introduced them. "Emily is presently on leave. She's the best friend from my childhood and perhaps of my present. And..." He turned to apply an introductory label to Genny and found—nothing.

Genny refused to be embarrassed, but found that choice very difficult to uphold. The swirl of her constantly shifting emotions over the last hour was making her head hurt.

Emily watched the President for a merciless second before extending her hand. "Well, you have totally flustered him, which is actually hard to do. He must be very attracted to you. Therefore, you and I had better start right off with first names. Call me Emily."

"Genny." The woman's handshake was warm and genuine and went a long way to easing Genny's nerves.

"Genny?" the President protested. "You're making me call you Geneviève."

"And that requirement, it remains not changed."

Emily laughed while the President sputtered. "I like you, Genny Beauchamp. I think we're going to become good friends. Keep him on his toes, it's good for him."

Genny nodded her agreement uncertainly. Emily was close to the President, but perhaps not with him? She needed a guidebook.

"Where did a UNESCO senior manager acquire those calluses?"

"How do you know I am a senior manager?" Genny clenched her hands, feeling the comfort of the hard-won calluses. Had this woman, this friend of the President been briefed on Genny's background along with who knew how many others?

"The way you carry yourself. Poise and calm in this setting," Emily's circling finger indicated the present company of the President, his Chief of Staff, and the Chairman of the Joint Chiefs. Then a nod toward the dozen or more Washington elite scattered about the room.

Genny nodded, feeling only a little foolish. It made sense. Emily Beale was simply a trained, perceptive woman. So, seeing no reason to evade, Genny held out her hand and turned it palm up. The President leaned forward in surprise to inspect it.

"Vovinam Việt Võ Đạo," Genny pointed to the primary calluses that Emily had noticed in a simple handshake. "Vietnamese martial arts. Those calluses are mostly from staff. I like staff."

"What degree?"

"Yellow, third Dan."

Emily faced Peter and then laughed right in the President's face. It seemed disrespectful, but his friend was clearly enjoying the President's perplexity. She took his shoulder and shook him easily. None of the Secret Service reacted, so this wasn't anything unusual between them. A part of Genny still wondered what was usual.

"What's so funny?" A big, broad-shouldered man arrived beside Emily Beale and slipped a hand around her waist. He also wore Dress Greens, saluted the General in a friendly fashion far less formal than Emily's had been, then clapped the White House Chief of Staff solidly on the shoulder in greeting. His eyes were as strikingly gray as Emily's were blue.

Emily kissed him on the cheek, which made Genny feel actively stupid for thinking there had been something between her and the President beyond friendship. Emily was exactly as the President had introduced her. An old friend.

"Peter has found a very pleasant UNESCO official who is a Việt Võ Đạo third Dan."

The newcomer laughed as well, then turned to inspect her. His eyes did a quick flicker down her length, but she didn't feel offended. It wasn't as if he were a male admiring her attributes. Instead, she felt as if she'd just been very carefully assessed for weapons and any other potential surprises.

"Mr. President," he had a deep voice obviously used to command. He also clearly didn't share Emily's "Peter" privileges with his Commander in Chief, or perhaps he did, but chose not to exercise them.

"Third Dan means she's a third-level Instructor just an edge below being a Master. Can see it in her posture and balance." He stuck out a large hand which she shook gladly. "Major Mark Henderson at your service. Do you find much occasion for using your martial arts in the Council Chamber at the U.N.?"

"My specialty is World Heritage Sites in Southeast Asia. I frequently must work with tribal leaders, military factions, warlords, and the like. I have not yet had to use those skills, Major Henderson, but I do appreciate having them."

"Perhaps you haven't needed to use them because they can see you already have them. Do you play poker?"

"No poker. But my two sisters and I play a mean Scrabble game though."

"You do?" The President brightened significantly while the other four in the circle groaned. "Ignore these heathens. Let me go find a board."

He turned as if to start the search immediately, but Emily hooked a wrist and with a simple twist, that Genny knew would cause sharp pain if ignored, brought the President back to the circle.

Genny wasn't sure, but she thought she caught the flicker of a smile on the big Secret Service agent standing at the wall.

"You have a room full of guests, Peter. You two can play games later." Emily's smile showed that she knew perfectly well the double-entendre she'd just offered.

Genny inspected the circle of friends that surrounded the President. For there was no question that while these people served at the pleasure of the President, they also truly enjoyed his company. It was a high recommendation of the man indeed.

For the second time that night, Genny did something that felt right though it ran counter to her better judgment. She tucked a hand around his elbow, no glove and heavy wool coat to separate them this time. His light jacket and linen shirt was all that kept them from touching. She could feel the difference in closeness.

"Do not worry, Mr. President Matthews." She made her voice as sexy as possible, playing up her French accent, knowing its affect on Americans. "We can play games in, perhaps, a later time."

He blushed bright red and the rest of them laughed.

Only Genny felt the slight pressure on her fingers as he squeezed her hand with a bend of his elbow. It was a very welcoming gesture.

———

Peter was wholly bemused.

It was past midnight. He'd shed his jacket and his tie and sat in the middle of the Central Hall on a low sofa.

Across the coffee table, Geneviève Beauchamp was the only remaining guest. Frank and Beatrice had retired to the far end of the Hall to guard unobtrusively while the woman massacred him on the Scrabble board. Maybe he should retreat back to playing on-line, as there he pretty much dominated. Too bad he couldn't play in the National Championships without actually attending.

Her silvered jacket was unbuttoned, but still draped upon her shoulders. Her hair, pulled forward over one shoulder, flowed in a lush dark wave. She leaned forward to study the Scrabble board, so that a small Chinese medallion she wore spun and sparkled with each movement. She was absolutely breathtaking.

"Enfilade, Mr. President." She'd spent six out of seven letters in her tray around the "AD" already on the board. The four-point "F," he was chagrined to notice, had landed on a triple-letter score. They had sat down hours before to play a single game to two hundred points. He'd foolishly given her the first move and she'd emptied her entire tray on the first play with "Debacle" gaining a quick eighty points including the bonus for playing all seven letters. They hadn't stopped at two-hundred points, they'd stopped when the tiles ran out.

Now they were on their third game and she was close to her second win. He thanked god that her final letter hadn't been playable or the point bonus for emptying her entire tray yet again would have locked up the game.

Frank, the head of his Presidential Protection Detail, would play with him when Peter was at loose ends, but they rarely finished those games. Peter did some of his best thinking while playing Scrabble with Frank as it left his subconscious free to nibble away at a political problem. The head of his PPD didn't appear to mind losing, or mind having the game interrupted once Peter had solved the problem.

With Geneviève, he had to completely concentrate and still it was a hard fight.

"Enfilade. Most appropriate, as you have just shot up my two best plays. And you still aren't calling me Peter."

"You are correct again, Mr. President." She drew four letters then shook the bag. Empty. The end was imminent and he needed a brilliant play to salvage his position.

"Why is that? And why am I calling you Geneviève, despite the 'Genny' liberties you offer to everyone else?"

"First, Mr. President, you are a head of state, I am not."

He grinned. Sparring with her was so much fun. "And second?"

"Your play."

"And second?" He sat back on the couch and crossed his arms over his chest making it clear that he wasn't going to play until she answered.

Now she looked up at him from her intent study of the board. He had expected her look of deep concentration, or perhaps the funny tease that had made him so enjoy her company, but instead it was a soft and somewhat bewildered expression that she presented.

"Perhaps it would be best if I go."

Peter came to his feet and extended a hand to help her to her feet. A lady said it was time to go, then it was time. No questions asked. At least not on that front.

"And second?"

But she didn't answer him. They walked side by side down the Grand Staircase, sweeping the two Secret Service agents before them. At the North Portico entrance, there was already a car waiting. Wishing he'd thought to put his jacket back on before stepping out into the freezing air, they stopped together for a moment on the outside steps.

"No clichés now," he warned her.

"I was not planning on one, Mr. President." Then she took both of his hands in hers.

He still couldn't feel the calluses, though he could feel the startling strength in those fine fingers.

"And second," she acknowledged his earlier question. "I will ask that you continue to call me Geneviève. For I do so enjoy how it sounds when you say it." She lifted up lightly on her toes and offered him a kiss on each cheek in the French style, and then a chaste, but not overly hasty one on his lips.

He held the car door for her as she climbed in. Then she spoke once more just before he could close it.

"If you play 'Redacted' on the 'E' I left open in 'Enfilade,' it will be your game, Mr. President."

Then she was gone, and he was left rocking on his heels. She'd counted each of the tiled letters that had been played, knowing that the bag was empty and what she had on her own tray.

"Wave, Mr. President," Frank Adams, the head of his protection detail, whispered at him softly.

So he did.

"She's got you, Sir."

He watched the taillights as Agent Belfour drove Geneviève Beauchamp off the White House grounds.

"Got you real bad," Frank was practically chortling.

There was certainly no chance of him redacting that bit of truth before everyone around him knew it.

CHAPTER THREE

*G**enny received a nasty** surprise over her room-service breakfast, but it took her a while before she found out about it. The White House had reserved Genny a room at The Hay-Adams Hotel. She'd had to close the curtains quickly on entering the room, for it had offered a clear view of the White House Residence directly across Lafayette Square Park and that had been just too much to think about.

She'd held herself together for the short ride to the Hay. It probably would have been faster to walk the two blocks, but her knees weren't really up to it, so she was quite appreciative of Agent Belfour's escort.

Once she was alone, then the nerves set in. President Peter Matthews, the leader of the American people, consumed her thoughts. Throughout the evening he had been charming, thoughtful, funny, and most importantly, real. Throughout the reception and then the Scrabble game he had simply been himself; laughing, casual, self-deprecating. He had granted her a thoroughly enjoyable evening. She knew better than to trust it. Gérard and she had any number of wonderful evenings, right until they'd become married.

Genny had married straight out of Cambridge University. Gérard had been beautiful, wealthy, and wholly incompatible. In so many ways: political views, disposition, temper. His desire to travel beyond Europe had been non-existent and she had missed home too much. The lush warmth and easy friendships of Vietnam had beckoned her too strongly. She and Gérard hadn't lasted six months.

In the years since, her career had broken even more relationships than it had made. She had climbed quickly at UNESCO. Her ability to obtain needed permissions from governments and locals alike to preserve culturally important sites had quickly catapulted her up the ladder. She was the Head of Section for Southeast Asia, which meant that she was more frequently in Paris at the World Heritage Center than in her own homeland.

And now, she was finding that shifting her attention to New York had allowed her unprecedented access to U.N. Ambassadors and hence the ear of their countries' leaderships.

Her work had led her to live much of the year in America, but her life was not here. It no longer resided in any one place. It was scattered across the globe. She rarely came to rest, but it was a lifestyle that worked for her. Genny could imagine no other way of being.

Yet, sitting last night with the President, just the two of them, had been comfortable. Despite the surreal setting and the unexpected company, she had felt oddly relaxed. As if it were a perfectly normal evening to be sitting in the Central Hall with the President and enjoying a game and friendly conversation as the house quieted. As the White House quieted. And that thought had only wound her nerves back up once more.

But Peter, it was comfortable to think of him that way, though surprisingly difficult to speak so, hadn't offered up some heirloom, valuable first edition, or ornate Scrabble board. Instead, it was old and worn—maroon cardboard, a cracking seam down the center, and well-worn letters in a brown paper lunch sack. And a heavily thumbed dictionary. An American one, so all of the handy Scottish words that had a "Q" without a "U" hadn't been allowed.

It was when she ordered room service that she received her nasty surprise. Along with a Lemon Ricotta Pancake with berries and American maple syrup, one of America's great contributions to international cuisine, came the morning's *Washington Post*.

The front page of *Post* had a grainy photo, obviously taken with a long telephoto lens at night. It was her chaste kiss with the President last night. But it didn't look chaste. "Mystery Woman Necking President" was the headline over the photo. Obviously late to press, it referred to page A14 for the rest of the story.

Page A14 had another photo of them walking arm in arm away from the Christmas Tree, identifiable only because of her long hair and his bodyguards. That was all they had, not even her name. But last night's guest list would provide that soon enough.

Her first instinct was to call the President and apologize.

Her second instinct was to scream in rage. It had been so pleasant and now it was tainted, made lurid by the American so-called journalists.

Thankfully, rational thought quashed that so quickly that it barely had an opportunity to raise its ugly head. The Americans were so very uptight about such matters. It didn't really affect her after all. Let them have their games.

Then her phone rang and her forkful of pancake flipped from her fingers and fell to the carpet. She swept it up quickly hoping that it didn't leave much of a stain on the immaculate white surface. What sort of a crazy hotel used white carpet?

With three phones in the room, she only had to reach for the one at her window-side dining table. When she answered, perhaps a little tentatively, she was asked to please hold for the President.

"I'm so sorry about this," Peter launched right in when he came on the line. His complete lack of morning niceties was so American that it made her smile. "I suppose we should have been somewhat more discreet."

"Mr. President, it is not my problem, but rather it is yours."

"Ah," he paused for a long moment. She could almost see him looking for a piece of paper or a pen to fool around with while he considered his response. "Clearly you've only seen the paper this morning, and not the television news."

"Ah, yourself." She fought against the irritation she felt as she understood what he was saying. "So, if it is now my problem, that would imply that your American media must be already camped in front of my hotel. They probably also watch the rear exits. I have heard of such foolishness. You really must fix those laws. Your so-cherished American Freedom of the Press has been taken past reason. What of Right to Privacy, I ask you?" The photo in the paper glared, garish in poor color. She flipped it face down.

"The Fourth Amendment promises security against unreasonable search and seizure. It states nothing regarding privacy."

"Therefore I am thinking that your country does not think. In my home country, we have far fewer laws and far more respect."

"We think very hard. However, that does not imply that what we have evolved over time necessarily makes any sense."

Genny considered what it must mean to be President of such a place. And how much she was enjoying this discussion, despite the topic. She had slept little last night for several reasons, but the main one had been that she'd felt vitalized by his attention. As if he brought some part of her to life with which she was unfamiliar.

"If you are thinking so hard, Mr. President, what are you thinking?"

"I'm thinking," his voice was suddenly warmer and softer, as if he were whispering into the phone. "That I don't care about any picture as long as I get the chance to kiss you again."

She laughed. Genny couldn't help herself. It was like a release of something deep inside. A part of her that a succession of arrogant men had frozen, she'd feared permanently.

"I think, Mr. President, that will cause no end of trouble for both of us, but," she had to be honest, "it is something I too should like to try."

"Excellent! So when can I see you again?"

"I was planning to return to New York this evening after my annual visit to the museum."

"Which museum?"

"Air and Space."

Again his laugh was warm in her ear, "Not Art, or Natural History?"

"Smithsonian Air and Space, the Udvar-Hazy Center, in Virginia."

She had to raise her voice over his laughter. "What do you find so amusing about me, Mr. President?"

"About you? That's perfect. That is what I find so amusing. That you are never what I expect."

Genny had no good answer to that and fooled around with the cooling pancake on her plate. Her ex-husband, past lovers, and even casual dates had always formed a neatly structured *casier* in their minds for her to belong inside of. It had made her very angry. This man, the first in her experience, was filled with joy so that it burst out of him, precisely because she didn't fit into a neat pigeon's hole.

"Hold on a minute, if you would."

He was back in under thirty seconds.

"It seems that my evening is free. Perhaps we could meet at the museum at six o'clock. I'm booked solid starting five minutes ago, but Daniel can handle the two meetings after six."

"It closes at five-thirty, Mr. President."

"Yes, it does."

Genny's position had more than once afforded her entry into a cultural site when it was technically closed. On such visits there was a sense of peace and you could feel the air prickling with anticipation and possibility, just as they must have felt when they were first formed. Yet she had never entered a major museum after hours. She could catch an early train tomorrow and still be in time for her first meeting.

"That is something I will be looking forward to, Mr. President."

"You never said why this particular museum, Geneviève." Peter looked about the massive hangar of the Smithsonian National Air and Space Museum's Udvar-Hazy Center at the south end of Dulles International Airport. He'd never actually been to this one, or known it was so close. Just twenty minutes outside of D.C., the two massive hangars had hundreds of aircraft. It was a kaleidoscopic whirl, so many wings, fuselages, and markings that his eyes had trouble separating one from the next.

The first hangar had been dominated by four massive planes: the Enola Gay that dropped the Hiroshima bomb and the Boeing Dash-80 that proved the viability of passenger jets. Close beside her was her extreme offspring, the Concorde and at the far end of the hangar stood an SR-71 Blackbird Mach 3 spy plane that could fly twenty miles high.

In one corner of the hangar, Geneviève led him on a tour of the various aircraft that had shaped Vietnam's history. The MiG-15 and the F-14 Tomcat jet fighters loomed above them, but it was the helicopters that had intrigued him. He knew that Emily had started out in a Huey UH-1 Iroquois.

"We captured one of these on our plantation. Gram used it for transporting a new roasting oven for the coffee before turning it over to the government. Then she let the pilot loose in the woods with a map and a compass, it was the best she could do for him. She received a thank you letter many years later from Alabama."

Peter had flown in both the White Hawk and bigger Sea King versions of Marine One and Emily's Black Hawk. Modern thoroughbreds compared to the Huey and the even more ungainly Seahorse parked close beside it. These machines were primitive by comparison.

Geneviève had let him look his fill, and now they were headed into the other hangar. A museum manager had made himself discreetly available, though it hadn't taken him long to fade back in with the Secret Service agents. He and Frank appeared to hit it off well, and he clearly liked Beat, which left Peter feeling as if he had Geneviève to himself.

Their footsteps echoed as they turned between a Messerschmitt and the American version of Hitler's V-1 Buzz Bomb. The whole museum was so quiet, he could practically hear the planes sleeping.

"This passage always gives me hope, Mr. President. So much of the Boeing Aviation Hangar is filled with machines of war. This hangar is much different."

They stepped through the brightly lit tunnel into the vast dimness of the next hangar. The vista slowly opened before them. At first he couldn't make sense of the black, bulbous nose that confronted him. A little farther down the tunnel the vista opened before him and he stumbled to a halt. He'd known it was here somewhere, but that hadn't prepared him for the impact.

The space shuttle *Discovery* dominated the space before him. It looked as if it had just now landed, surprisingly world-worn. All of the other craft had been so clean that they might have been manufactured just for the museum. Not the shuttle. Its tiles were discolored. It showed the wear and tear of dozens of missions, scorch marks on her white paint, yet still she stood proudly.

"This especially I wanted to see, Mr. President."

"Why is that?"

She clucked her tongue at him causing him to focus on her. "Clearly you forget my history."

"Your history? Now you're going to give me more lessons," he complained. He made it funny, fully acknowledging that the President of the United States was indeed whining. The amount she knew about this museum had staggered him.

"Yes, Mr. President your history is lacking and you need a lesson."

He tried a sulking pout and she laughed.

"That makes you look like angry two-year old."

"So, give me your lesson, Section Chief Beauchamp," he pouted harder.

She managed to keep a straight face, but it was clearly a struggle. She finally had to turn away and release a set of girlish giggles that echoed back to them off the high, curved metal ceiling. Catching her breath, she turned back to him.

"A very good friend of my grandfather flew on a Soyuz in 1980, they were in the VPAF together. What you would call the North Vietnamese Air Force, they both flew in that MiG-15 we just saw. He was made a Hero of the Soviet Union for shooting down one of your B-52 bombers, though your country continues to deny the incident a half century later. I also have an uncle, from the French side of the family, who flew on your space shuttle in 1992. Flew for the 'other side' if you will. Just because we are Vietnamese does not mean that we are not modern."

"Well," he gazed at her for a moment. "We Americans are innately arrogant."

"I was thinking it is acquired later in life."

"No, it's genetic. We're born that way. So, is this the shuttle he flew on?"

"The *Columbia*. But now she too is a casualty of war, though the battle was with space."

Thoughts of that shuttle disintegrating during reentry and killing the crew sobered them. They circled the craft in silence, gazing at the exhibits off to either side, but ultimately returning to the *Discovery*. When they had fully circled the craft, Peter noticed a long ladder leading up to a small circular hatch in the side. It was open and the light from within shone out into the hangar like a beacon in the night.

Geneviève looked longingly at the ladder, and Peter had to admit that... He waved over the hangar manager.

"Mr. Emerson, I don't suppose that we could," he pointed up the ladder, feeling stupid for even asking. It was clearly not designed for public usage.

"The exhibit curator suggested that you might wish to look inside. I admit, I took the opportunity to sit aboard her myself before she went on display. It was quite the experience."

———

Genny was in shock that she was climbing the ladder into the actual space shuttle. She'd never dreamed that she'd get to do such a thing. Ducking in through the small lock, she stood, and was immediately disappointed.

A couple of blue chairs with massive seatbelts filled much of the small space, little bigger than the bedroom of her Paris apartment; which was not saying much, especially at Parisian prices. No windows, no views. The walls were all covered in near-identical cabinet drawers. Most bore some incomprehensible label, equipment to fix things. She understood a few: tile repair kit, avionics spares, food stuffs. She tried to pull open that one, but it wouldn't move. The curator, who had come in behind her and Peter, showed them how to release the catch to either side. Of course it couldn't just pull open, not in space. Sadly, the drawer was empty.

A small corridor led forward, but a quick peek revealed more cabinets and storage lockers. Aft was a big round hatch, that must lead out to the Payload Bay beneath the giant doors on the back of the ship.

"It is all so tiny."

"Normally three to five crew members are in this space, along with their space suits," the curator pointed out. "They did not send much empty space into space." It was clearly one of his pat lines, so she laughed dutifully.

Then he indicated for her to climb the ladder that she'd missed on her first scan of the room. It climbed upward steeply.

"The proportions are all wrong," Peter observed. And he was right.

Her hands, holding onto the two verticals, were too far apart and the steps impossibly steep.

"Spacesuits and weightlessness," she and the curator said in near unison.

Then she finished the climb to the Flight Deck. This was spectacular. Smaller than the area below, it felt huge. Peter actually had to nudge her aside as she gawked. Banks of switches and controls covered almost every surface. There were three seats. One faced rearward, placed before the controls and window that looked out into the Payload Bay. The other two seats faced forward, looking out over the entrance from the Boeing Hangar. She glanced for permission, then slipped into the left hand seat. Peter into the right.

A large joystick fit her hand, though clearly it could also be used while wearing a spacesuit's heavy gloves.

"You, Ms. Beauchamp," the curator was still being obsequiously polite in the President's presence, "have chosen the Shuttle Commander's seat. That makes the President your pilot."

"Good, that is where you should be, Mr. President. At the command of the woman." Out of the corner of her eye, she could see him smiling at her in a strange way. So she carefully didn't look over, but instead inspected the controls before them. A half dozen screens, as big as the ones on her laptop, were arranged in front of her. From them, in every direction, ranged banks of switches, readouts, and rotary knobs. Some in bright red with special covers. One even needed a key, marked incomprehensibly as "RJDA 18." She pointed it out to Peter.

"So, is that the one to make your seat like an ejector seat? What if we get into space and I forget to bring the key?"

"Did you always want to go to space, Commander Beauchamp?"

"No, I would have liked to fly, but I fell in love with old temples and beautiful scenery. Did you always want to be President, Mr. Pilot?"

At his silence, Genny looked over at him. That's when she also noticed that the curator had tactfully withdrawn, leaving them to their momentary dreams of space.

Peter smiled slowly, but looked forward out the windows. She wondered what he saw other than the high ceilings of the hangar in which they sat.

"No. What I always wanted to do was help people to reach a better understanding. Never thought about politics until my wife came up with it." He said "wife" as if even that brief mention hurt him, and she was sorry she had caused such a bad memory to return. "Becoming President was simply a way to do that on a scale I hadn't previously imagined."

Genny needed a subject change, as that had all become much too solemn.

"Weren't you like other little boys, Mr. President? Didn't you want to go flying into space?"

"No. Flying was Em's dream, not mine." His smile became soft and wistful.

"How is it that you did not end up married to Emily?" Genny still couldn't make sense of that, they appeared so close. Even closer, or at least more familiar, than she was with her husband.

Peter turned to face her now, turning away from whatever visions lay beyond the shuttle's windows. His unblinking gaze riveted her to her chair. She couldn't look away if the shuttle were crashing and it was up to her to save it.

"I thought that at one time. But Emily was smarter than I was and ran, and I mean that literally, ran in the other direction." Then he turned back to the window and gazed out into the lights.

Genny left him to his thoughts for a long time.

Then he blinked as if coming abruptly back to the present. His smile wiped away any of the gloom that had hovered over his features.

"Besides, the one time I kissed her, it was like kissing my sister, if I had one. It just didn't work at all."

CHAPTER FOUR

Genny leaned back in the luxury of The Beast. The Presidential Limousine might be a heavily armored rolling fortress, but it was also very, very comfortable. The leather bucket seat wrapped around her. Though if not for the wide, shared armrest, she'd be rubbing shoulders with the President.

"I thought your car would be wider. It feels very narrow."

The President rapped his knuckles on the side panel of the car door as they zipped from the museum back to the White House with a full police escort. "Five inches of bullet-proof protection on all sides has to go somewhere."

They turned in at the gates to the White House.

"I am not returning to my hotel?"

"I was hoping that you would join me for a late dinner. You don't mind, do you?"

Genny began considering the various implications and then stopped. She didn't want their evening to be over, and that was enough for her. At least for now.

"My family may still be too French, we rarely dine before this time. Can you cook?"

"Not even a little bit. I can barbecue, but not cook. You?"

"I do not even do that." Genny had always loved food, just not enough to learn to prepare it for herself. And living so much on the road made any effort to maintain a kitchen utterly pointless. She didn't even have a place to stay other than her family's house on the plantation and her own a small apartment in Paris close by the World Heritage offices. Everything else was hotel rooms.

She noted that they pulled up to the South Portico, rather than the North. And that a canopy like a hotel's shielded the path from the car door to the White House doors.

"You are afraid to be photographed with me?" The journey to the museum had included an elaborate shell game in which Agent Belfour had led her through the Hay-Adams basement to the church on the other side of the street, and she had been driven separately from the President.

"No," Peter hesitated, then confirmed his initial response as if making it more true for himself. "No. I don't mind. I had thought to shield you from too much media attention for your own sake."

Usually Genny found men to be so easy to read, but with the President she had such difficulty that it was hard to be sure. Was he making it up on her behalf or did he not want the negative press? Like that movie, this President had absurdly high approval from the American people. But unlike the movie, he was not facing an election for two more years. Could he afford a girlfriend? Was that something she wanted to be? Too many questions.

"How is it that you know so little about me? Didn't your Secret Service investigate me? Even more now that I am seeing you a second time?" She remained seated in the car, so he made no move to open the door. She could just see his bodyguard waiting beside the car door, partially hidden by the thick glass as well as by the shadows beneath the canopy.

"I'm sure they did." The President turned on the light inside the passenger compartment.

Now she could see him more clearly, but she understood him no better.

"I asked for information about you after our first meeting in July," he continued. "They told me three things about you: your name, your job title, and that you had avoided any chance at having a decent education by attending Cambridge. I have asked them to tell me nothing else about you."

"You must have attended that second-rate place in the Midlands."

They shared a smile over the centuries-old rivalry between their schools of Cambridge and Oxford.

"They told you nothing?" Genny had assumed that she was operating at an immense disadvantage in this relationship. That her life was an open book to a man who she only knew through his public image.

"Nothing. I ordered them not to."

She'd have to think about that. Assuming he was telling the truth, it meant that he was being decent and fair far past any man she had ever met. And she could think of no reason for him to lie.

"So you asked me to come to the White House because I caught your eye?" If he said yes, he might become the third man she tried her martial arts on.

"While you are shockingly beautiful, no."

Even if she didn't tie her ego to her looks, the compliment washed over her and added to the warmth she was beginning to feel for the man. A warmth that was spreading far past her thoughts.

"It was that you, as a woman, talked three Southeast Asian U.N. Ambassadors to a standstill without even breaking a sweat."

"Breaking a sweat?" She knew a great deal of American idiom, but not that piece.

"You made it look effortless."

"Ah."

"And I thought that this was a woman worth knowing. I see your beauty as a mere bonus." His smile turned slightly wicked.

"And now you are baiting me. Well, I shall rise above it and you will now take me to dinner in your house."

The President knocked twice on the window with the back of his knuckles. After he helped her out of the car, he did not release her hand while escorting her inside.

———

They sat together in the Second Floor Kitchen. The staff had tried to place them in the formal dining room, but Geneviève had asked if they could simply dine at the island in the kitchen.

Peter had liked the sound of that.

Once dinner had been delivered from the main kitchen in the basement, he'd dismissed both the staff and the Secret Service. He knew the latter had merely retired to wait on the floor below until relieved by the next shift or Geneviève was ready to go home. Which he hoped wasn't anytime soon. Not only was he enjoying her company, but she was also a joy to watch. Not merely the sleek red dress with ornate golden needlework that wrapped so splendidly about her body.

When she spoke, her hands came to life. She would fold them quietly when being an attentive listener, and then, as she attempted to draw some mental image, her hands rose and sculpted the air about her until it vibrated with her energy. It was as if she pulled threads of Peter himself and made them glow in the air before her.

He kept wishing he had looked at her Secret Service file, then he might not feel as if he was constantly in over his head. But that boat had long since sailed. She simply overwhelmed him every moment they were together. Like now, they didn't even need to be speaking. They simply sat quietly and enjoyed their dessert of coconut ice cream with dark chocolate sauce.

They sat on barstools across the maple-wood island from each other in his private kitchen, a room he rarely used for more than a late-night scrambled eggs and toast. It was unfamiliar in many ways, but she made him feel as if he had sat here many times. With her. It was as if the room had been waiting only for her to place the final, proper accent upon it. She brought it too to life. The walnut cabinets picked up the highlights in her dark hair. Her eyes shone brighter than the brass fittings in the soft glow of the candles he had discovered in a corner cabinet.

He did his best not to compare her to his first wife, but it was inevitable. Katherine Matthews had been the center of attention in any room she entered. A red-headed whirlwind with a siren's body who had bowled him off his feet before he knew what hit him. Yet by the time they arrived at the White House they were barely on speaking terms.

She had lived on the third floor of the Residence, he'd lived on the second. To this day, he couldn't stand to go up there. Being a lone bachelor in the entire Residence had felt too foolish. When he made Daniel his Chief of Staff, he'd also given him the third floor to live in. Now he and his wife Alice resided there, and best of luck to them. It made the perfect excuse for him not to go up there. When the three of them dined together, which was several times a week when their schedule at the White House or Alice's at the CIA didn't interfere, they met on the second floor or over in the West Wing dining room.

Katherine had staked out her territory with her vivacity, her immense popularity, her slap-you-in-the-face sexual power, and a conniving streak a mile wide that had been her ultimate undoing.

Geneviève carried an air of quiet sophistication about her. Her temper was as placid as a mountain lake. Granted, one of unknown depths, but she was a center of calm. He felt better just for sitting with her. Even the first time Peter had met Katherine, she'd left him feeling drained.

He had to give his dead wife some credit, he wouldn't be President without her. She'd pushed and driven, arranged and maneuvered until he'd met all of the right people and been in all of the right places. Her sense of politics had far exceeded his own. In that one way, they had been a good team. She navigated the political landscape as if she had her own personal, private, executive roadmap.

His interests had lain elsewhere. What drove him to the Presidency was the opportunity to make a difference. He'd been a key player in dozens of corporate rescues, eventually including the restructuring of NASA and recovering whole sections of the auto industry that had teetered on the brink of bankruptcy. It's where he'd made his name and where he'd found his joy.

And it had nothing to do with Katherine. That part of his life, at least, was clean from the blemishes she had laid upon so much of his life.

But he didn't want to think about her. He wanted to know more about the passions of the woman sharing his dinner table.

"Tell me more about your Heritage Sites, Geneviève."

———

Over the long-finished meal, a very passable Thai curry on red rice and magnificent coconut ice cream, Genny told the President of a few of the dozens of wonders she'd toured, both in Southeast Asia and other places around the world. From the Phong Nha-Ke Bang Park of Vietnam, the largest karst limestone cave system on the planet, where the largest cave in the world had only been discovered in 2009, large enough to hold a New York City block, including its forty-story high skyscrapers. To the Buddhist Temple of Borobudur in Indonesia, lost for six hundred years in the jungle and second only to Angkor Wat. She'd also entered the Caves of Lascaux, not the replica that had been set up for tourists, but the original, now so carefully protected against further degradation due to moisture.

"I had to wear a rebreathing apparatus simply to keep the moisture from my breath from touching the paintings."

"And I'll bet you looked fetching in it."

Genny was beginning to trust her perception of the President's thoughts. By his smile, he clearly was thinking of how she must have looked in some sexy James Bond movie heroine fashion. It was hard to complain that he saw her in such a way. Though eventually reality would disappoint. But in the favor of his more practical side, his constant questions and interruptions proved he was also paying attention to her words.

Not only did he appear interested in her, he had made her interested in him. They had talked around a dozen topics and she could think of a hundred more that she would enjoy exploring with him. Never had she so appreciated a man's company.

"Do you have a music player in this White House home of yours?"

"Uh, sort of. I have a speaker system in the other room that I can drop my iPod into. But it's loaded with lectures on governance, international law, documents I don't have time to read unless I'm exer-cising or something. That sort of thing."

"Show me." She stood and waited for him to gain his feet. He sounded as compulsive as she was. Her own playlist included the complete recordings of the latest World Heritage Conservation Conference with a special focus on overly-rapid urban development and its effect on the present sites. She'd only heard the sessions at which she'd spoken or been on a panel, now she was trying to catch up with all of the other tracks.

But she did have one other thing stored there.

He led her across the Central Hall. Their Scrabble set had been cleaned up, though the board still remained on the low table from the prior night, as if awaiting another game. Another time perhaps. Directly opposite the kitchen was a small living room. Well, small in comparison to the vast expanse of the hall. Two sofas, several armchairs, a pair of low tables scattered with magazines and file fold-ers. A space shoved clear where he was obviously used to dining when eating alone. It had been decorated in dark greens with a tasteful eye.

"The previous First Lady," he remarked, noticing her attention. "Not my wife. Not my former wife, er, deceased wife. She decorated this room for her husband. I liked it and made Katherine leave it alone when she was doing the rest of the Residence."

"It looks comfortable, and very masculine."

"If that's an ego stroke, I'll take it. If patronizing, I'll ignore it. There's the player, but it doesn't even have radio."

She'd retrieved her purse as they passed through the hall and she fished out her iPod. Plugging it in, she found what she was looking for and pressed Play.

Genny set aside her purse and moved to stand before the Presi-dent. "It is not the best music for a first dance together, but perhaps it is good nonetheless."

A Christmas carol came out of the speakers.

———

Geneviève moved into his arms. Peter didn't know what to do with the surge of energy that coursed through his body. Other than when he'd taken her hand to help her out of The Beast and the briefest of kisses last night, they had barely touched. He didn't count her hand tucked in the crook of his elbow.

Well, okay, he had counted it, until he suddenly had his arms full of luscious woman.

Her idea of dancing was not some stand-offish American form of dance. It wasn't even a waltz distance. She simply filled his arms.

She placed a hand around his back and her cheek on his shoulder. With no other choice, he tentatively slid his hands around her waist. Never had he felt such a thing. "Thing," there was a good word. Mr. Scrabble King had just lost all his words.

Geneviève began a slow shuffle to some song he couldn't make heads or tails of. Not because it was unfamiliar, but because he didn't have sufficient attention span to identify what he was hearing.

The scent of her filled him as much as her warmth. She wasn't that much shorter than he was, so her head on his shoulder nestled up against his neck.

"Hmm, you are smelling very good."

He couldn't have said it better. "I took a shower."

Her laugh was soft and welcoming.

Then he lay his cheek on her hair. It was even softer and thicker than it looked. It was impossible to tell when he first came in contact with it. He brushed a hand over its length, and down onto her back. He stroked it again, pulling some of it aside so that her face would not be lost in it.

"I know, I need to cut it off. I just never get around to it."

"If you ever do that, I will immediately cancel your visa to our country."

"Hmm," it was practically a purr of satisfaction.

He could feel the sound ripple from her chest to his.

"You certainly know how to make a girl feel welcome."

All he could think about was his need to kiss this woman. And then it struck him that if she weren't willing, anticipating just that, she'd not be in his arms.

Sometimes he was a little stupid, but that didn't mean he was slow once he figured out what was going on.

———

Genny sighed with pleasure as he kissed her. She'd wanted it to be his choice. She'd wanted it to be his choice during dinner, and before that in the museum. Truth be told, she'd wanted it to be his choice since that very first chance meeting at the U.N. in the Dag Hammarskjöld Library six months before. Though she'd have laughed at anyone who had told her so at the time.

She didn't need a man. Her life was too full. Her last lover had been Klaus. He had been a good lover, right until she was named Chief of Unit for Southeast Asia World Heritage and he was passed over as Assistant Chief of Northern Africa. Then he had been not so good.

Perhaps the President would be her next lover. The way he kissed her made that a definite possibility. He might be a world leader, but he also smelled and felt wonderful. He held her with a gentleness of wonder. Did he also possess an animal side hiding down behind all of those defenses that were ever so polite and ever so careful?

For she could see his defenses as clearly as she could feel his lips searing against hers. That had been clear to her from the first moment of their meeting. He hid behind layers of hurt, of Scrabble games and ex-wives, of his past and most definitely of his job. Well, she might as well start there before his kiss melted her into an absolute puddle.

She broke the kiss and snuggled back against him as they moved softly to a slow rendition of *Have Yourself a Merry Little Christmas.*

"So, Mr. President, do you have a bedroom nearby as well?"

He laughed, a delightful sound that rumbled against her ear. "How can you ask that question and still not call me by my Christian name?"

Genny pulled back as if in surprise and looked up at him from the circle of his arms. "Oh, Mr. President, this isn't about you. This is about the most powerful leader in the world."

"So, if I lose my next election in two years, it will be over between us?"

"*Absolument!*" With a sly smile, she crossed her fingers and spit over them, a child's promise. "It is only the President I want to be making love to."

He scooped her up in his arms and moved toward a side door. "I'd better win the next goddamn election, that's all I have to say."

In the darkened bedroom, he began to undress her to Handel's *Hallelujah Chorus*.

CHAPTER FIVE

Genny *was going to* miss her luncheon meeting at the U.N. and she didn't care in the slightest. *Merde!* The way she felt, she didn't care if she never moved again.

The room was dark, but the man beside her was moving. "Where are you going?"

"Good morning. I was trying to leave without waking you."

"Oh, you are the love them and leave their bed in the middle of the night sort of President."

"No. First, you're in my bed, not the other way around. Second, I have a job."

"As do I. So, you are saying that you would leave your bed without even kissing the woman in it?"

"I can't even see where you are."

"Turn on the light." While he fumbled for a moment to do so, she pushed down the covers she'd been so comfortably ensconced in a moment before.

"There. I—" He turned to face her even as she blinked hard against the brightness. "Holy shit!"

"What is 'Holy shit!'?"

"You are!"

Genny had meant to tease him, but his reply was so emphatic. She squeezed open one eye enough to see that he was sitting up, his feet off the other side of the bed, and gaping at her over his shoulder. Though they had made love in the shadows of what little light washed in from the living room, she had known he had a good body. He had proved it many times throughout the night. But now that the light was on, she could see that the definition of it wasn't merely tactile. He really looked wonderful.

She especially liked the look of total shock on his face as he inspected her body. Inspected? Not the right verb. Perhaps 'devoured with his eyes' was better. She felt last night's heat slowly rekindling deep within her, a heat that he had stoked far past any level she had ever known.

"Why aren't you a model or something?" His voice was breathless.

"Because then I would not have ended up in your bed and we would not have had last night."

"Okay, you win that one." He reached out a hand, so tentatively it almost hurt to watch.

She finally took his wrist to pull his hand towards her.

Rather than reaching for her body, he stroked her cheek and down her arm.

"Did she hurt you so much? This dead wife of yours? That you are afraid to touch me."

Peter startled and his gaze jumped to hers.

"It is written on you, my lover. You think that you have secrets from a woman who has done what we did last night? *Non!* You do not, so you may let that go, Mr. President."

He opened his mouth to speak, once, twice, three times. Then he burst out. "I have never met a woman like you, Kim-Ly Geneviève Beauchamp." Then his kiss stopped any reply she might have made. A kiss that he didn't release until he had once more driven them both up and over heights that she had never imagined possible.

He collapsed back into sleep, his exhaustion overcoming the four a.m. time on his clock. Her leg across his hips and her head cradled on his shoulder were not enough to keep him awake.

A job where the man must work so hard was not a good thing. But what he did at his job was a good thing. It was a strange contrast.

Genny slowly traced a hand over his chest, feeling the even rise and fall of his breathing. His heartbeat, a soft song in her ear.

She knew she was in trouble as she lay upon him and sleep eluded her. She closed her eyes and relished once more the warmth and strength of him. As if he could conquer the world. As if she could too for simply being with him.

Then she spoke words that she knew she would wish to take back some day. Words that left a mark upon her that she swore no man ever would again.

"I have never met anyone like you, Mr. President."

———

The phone blasted Peter awake. He grabbed it out of an instinct of self-preservation. At that volume, another ring might kill him. He was a very heavy sleeper and it took a very loud sound to awaken him. But it made the second ring hell.

"Uh," was all he managed. The clock read five a.m. Normal call. No need to panic.

"Good morning, Mr. President." Daniel. "Time to get up. Also, I was going to drop off some papers on my way to the office, some things I think we could review over breakfast."

"Uh, sure, I..." He trailed off as a vision walked around from the other side of his bed. Clothed in nothing but a tiny silver medallion at her neck, she looked like a goddess walking upon the newborn world. Geneviève strode across his bedroom carpet long, lean, and golden with a confidence most women couldn't muster in a thousand-dollar power suit. Her hair even billowed as she moved. She disappeared into his bathroom. He hoped to god he wasn't hallucinating.

"Sir?" Daniel's question buzzed in Peter's ear.

"Sorry. Let's, uh, not do that today."

"Absolutely, sir. I'll see you in the office."

"Wait! Daniel?"

"Sir?"

"Could you have someone fetch Ms. Beauchamp's clothes and other belongings from the Hay-Adams?"

"I'll, uh, see to it, sir. And may I say, about time, Mr. President. I've only been hearing about her for six months."

"Go to hell, Daniel."

"After you, sir."

Peter may or may not have hung up the phone. His next clear thought was leaning against the door jamb and watching Geneviève stepping into his shower. A simple, ordinary movement that might occur a thousand times in a couple's life. It fired both his body and his imagination.

It had been but a single night, but she made him want ten thousand more.

———

"I swear that I'm not stalking you. I simply forgot today's schedule."

"There are many coincidences in your life, Mr. President."

"And still it's 'Mr. President!'" Peter faced a highly skeptical Geneviève across the island in the kitchen where he'd had dinner removed and breakfast delivered while they showered. On finding that her suitcase was soon to arrive, she had wrapped herself in his terrycloth bathrobe and nothing else. Katherine would have had on a nightgown, underwear, slippers, makeup, and who knew what else.

Geneviève wore only his bathrobe; her hair still hung wet down her back. He couldn't tell if she was angry or suspicious or quite what she was feeling. Like last night, she was several steps ahead of him and he trailed far behind.

"I have a luncheon speech at the Eastern Governors Association Conference in New York. Then several meetings on Wall Street this afternoon. So, I'd be glad to give you a ride to Manhattan."

"And what will your press think when I come out of the White House with my suitcase and climb aboard your Marine One helicopter? What then, Mr. President?" She crossed her arms over her chest.

"They'd think I was just about the luckiest man on the planet."

He could see her gathering for the next round of protest. Couldn't the woman just take a compliment and be happy about it? No. She was as tenacious as he was. Though he did seriously like the image of them as a couple.

"Yes, Geneviève, I know all of the arguments. Trust me on that. The President's private life is anything but private. So, I must live at least part of my private life in public. If you don't choose to, I understand *absolument*. I am glad to have you escorted out through the Treasury Building garage and delivered wherever you would like to go. We can try to keep it as quiet and private as we can. Frankly, I wouldn't blame you for running in the other direction entirely, though I truly hope that you won't."

She was listening. She wasn't raging or interrupting or jumping ahead. She was actually allowing him to speak his piece. And he'd wager a fifty-point head start for their next Scrabble game that it wasn't because he was President. This was simply how she would be in a relationship, a startling concept in itself. Her simply treating him as if his thoughts had value evoked an answer that was surprising even to him. He didn't speak from what he thought, but rather what he felt.

"I want to be with you. I want to see where this can go. We can keep that as private as possible, or we can be ourselves in public and damn the press. I assure you that little of my own life remains private, but I'm willing to try if you want."

"You want to see me again?" Her voice was suddenly soft. Her arms remained folded across her chest and she sat still as a marble statue on the kitchen stool ignoring her half-eaten waffle and the coffee she had declared as "too weak except for small children."

Peter looked at the ceiling, but found no guidance there to understanding this woman. One moment she was worried about the appearances of his presidency and the next moment she was shocked that this wasn't a one-night stand.

When he looked back at her, it was as if she'd changed, though she hadn't moved a muscle. He could now see that her arms weren't crossed in anger, but rather wrapped about herself for protection. Her caution wasn't just for his presidency, but for herself as well. A vulnerable Geneviève Beauchamp was something he hadn't expected.

He didn't know what to say to her, how to reassure her when he was sure of so little himself.

So, instead, he stepped around the island and simply enfolded her into his arms.

She didn't unclench her own arms. She just leaned her face into his chest and let herself be held. Geneviève wasn't crying, but he could feel her dragging in deep breaths.

It took a while, but she slowly relaxed until she lay against him, rather than just being held, and her shoulders softened beneath his gentle strokes. Finally she sighed deeply and appeared to fully let go.

"As Christ is my witness," her voice was rough, almost harsh. "You had better be worth it, Mr. President. You are making my heart in danger."

CHAPTER SIX

*G*enny *had spent the* morning alone in the Residence. Being alone, the first thing she'd did was her daily workout of stretches, techniques, and *kata*. Because she'd missed yesterday, she pushed for over an hour until she'd needed another shower. Then she'd worked on catching up on e-mails and trying not to feel self conscious about being in Peter's home when he wasn't. She'd started in his Living Room, but moved to the Central Hall. Even that was too personal, but she was unsure where else to go. He was taking a series of morning meetings in the West Wing before their flight.

Their flight.

Just minutes from now they'd be declaring to the world that they were seeing each other. Dating. Sleeping together. That didn't bother her overly much. What other people thought about them being a couple was not her concern, what they thought was their problem.

What was different about this public declaration was the impact on herself. It wasn't that she'd taken a new lover, they came and they went, not often, but it was part of the cycle of a healthy life. But to be dating the President, that was a more definitive statement, made more real by his office and his importance to the world at large. Such a thing meant that more thought and consideration had been given to the matter than someone you met at a conference and liked.

Peter Matthews had topped the most-eligible bachelor list for the two years since his wife's death. Of course, Prince William had been married by then. Young Harry, now fourth in line to the British throne, had only placed a distant second.

Even that was not the matter. It was how she felt around Peter. She had never been so comfortable except in her own home. She'd had lovers who were casual about nudity in the home, but she had never so enjoyed walking in front of a powerful and erudite man and striking him speechless. And how could such a man know her so perfectly that he spoke not a word when the nerves overwhelmed her, but simply cradled her until she could want to be nowhere else.

He was maddening, frustrating, beautiful, and kind. He was also almost as afraid of intimacy as she was. Not physical intimacy. That was clearly not a problem between them They had found such joy in each other's bodies that it was hard to credit. Even thinking of him caused her pulse to rise and bring a flush to her cheeks, despite the e-mail she was writing to her Assistant Unit Chief regarding how to gracefully accept a keynote speaker position for a major conference that she had already said she wouldn't be attending as a participant.

She and Peter hadn't been like two teenagers gone wild with hormones, nor had they been like two adults enjoying a good round of casual sex. They had made love as if each moment were a new discovery to be cherished and remembered. It overshadowed all her past experiences.

That was the intimacy that he brought to their relationship, unexpectedly and not entirely welcome. She knew this man. Not his past, there had been so little time for that. But she knew him nonetheless. As if he had slipped a piece of her heart into clearer view than it had ever been.

He did that to her. President Peter Matthews overshadowed all her experiences of men, and he had done it in only two days. How could she account for this to herself? It was impossible for a relationship to be built on such a narrow pedestal, and yet it felt as stable as the Borobudur Temple which had survived fifteen-hundred years despite jungle growth, being buried in volcanic ash, ever-chaotic Indonesian politics, and even extremists' bombs.

"Are you ready?"

Genny startled and looked up to see the same Secret Service agent standing nearby. She hadn't heard the woman's approach. She packed away her laptop and turned to make a quick survey, nothing left behind her. Just her suitcase and cross-shoulder bag that held her purse and computer.

The agent led her toward the elevator. "Sorry about not offering to carry your bags, ma'am. But I need to keep my hands free."

"It was not expected that you would do so. So, are you assigned to me?"

They traveled together down the long hall on the White House Ground Floor. Here the Christmas décor was more subdued than elsewhere. This corridor was only traversed by servants and by those from the West Wing with business in the Residence. There were no public tours here, and it felt more normal.

"I am, ma'am. For as..." She ended awkwardly.

"For as long as I am dating your President. I understand. Then you should call me Genny."

"That wouldn't be proper, Ms. Beauchamp." She held open a door and guided Genny through the Palm Room and outside along the Colonnade that led toward the West Wing.

"And why do we women care about such things as being proper? That is for the men to care about."

The agent stopped for a moment, just feet from a Marine guard at a glass door. At a glass door in a wall that curved.

Genny took a deep breath. The Oval Office was through that door. She had best make herself ready. It gave her more nerves than the first time she'd entered the U.N. Security Council Chamber to address the council.

The agent held out a hand. "Beatrice, most call me Beat."

"Beat, that is your agent name. Beatrice, that is what I shall call you. Me you shall call Genny." They shook hands and Genny took a deep breath and held it before nodding for Beatrice to lead the way.

The agent held open the door, let her through, and then let it close remaining outside. Leaving Genny to face the Oval Office on her own.

———

Peter was just finishing up with Daniel on the latest budget proposal from the National Science Foundation for next year's Arctic and Antarctic research when the door opened off to his right.

By the time he was able to glance over, Genny's face was turning bright red.

"Breathe, Geneviève! Breathe!" he called out as he went to her.

She blew out a breath, gulped in another, then managed little more than a squeak, "I can't, Mr. President. I just can't!"

He placed an arm around her shoulders and pulled her into the room. "I know. I know. I had the same problem. Sometimes I still do, so many great Presidents have walked here before me."

"Me too, Genny," Daniel offered cheerily as he gathered up the paperwork from the Resolute Desk. "First time I was actually in the room was for the interview that led to me being Chief of Staff. So scared you could hear my knees knocking clear back to Tennessee."

She blew out a breath again, loudly, and slowly her normal color began coming back.

"We should make love here, Mr. President."

"Whoops! I'm gone." Daniel practically sprinted for the door. Traitor.

"Uh, I don't think that even I have the nerve to do that, Geneviève."

"I'm not suggesting one of Jack Kennedy's naked coed pool parties, or that you smuggle me into your room like FDR did. I merely suggest that you and I should make love here."

"You're serious?"

"Well, I think it would be good for you. This is the center of your power, this oval room. And...," she abruptly blew out a final breath and laughed a little shakily. "But I think I agree with you. I would not have the nerve to make love in such a place."

A secretary breezed in through one of the doors. "Here's your speech and your coat, Mr. President." She held it open for him to slip on.

"Thanks, Jasmine," he turned his attention back to Geneviève. "Besides, there's a couple problems. For one thing, the doors don't lock."

Jasmine's sudden backward glance told him that he should have waited a moment longer before speaking. He almost called her back in to explain that they were joking, like that sounded believable. He let her go.

"That is why you have guards," Geneviève was studying the several doors that the room boasted.

"Well," he turned her by the shoulders to look at the bay window facing the broad South Lawn. "The guards also stand outside the glass on this side."

"So, tell them not to peek. We will turn out the lights. I will promise not to cry out too loud no matter how much you make me want to." Now she was clearly teasing him, her hand patting his cheek, placing a small kiss on his cheek.

"I am not having this conversation. I am not standing in the Oval Office and having this conversation." He checked the portfolio Jasmine had handed him to make sure she'd also included his schedule and the notes for the other meetings.

"What? You think that others have not been here and made love to their women in this place? If so, you are a big fool, Mr. President."

Peter glanced up at the portraits of Washington, Lincoln, and Kennedy hanging from the office walls. Kennedy definitely. Grant maybe. And...

"I am not having this conversation."

"How do you feel about kissing a woman in the Oval Office? Because I feel as if I am about to fly apart."

"I think I can accede to that demand at least." And before she could respond and make him even crazier, he swept her into his arms. She grabbed onto his coat's lapels and hung on.

Then he guided her toward the door she had just entered.

Great. Just great.

The image of her languishing naked and sweaty upon the Oval Office rug was now firmly lodged in his brain, and he knew it would remain there for as long as he served as President.

CHAPTER SEVEN

G**enny wasn't quite sure** how it happened.

Perhaps it was because the President was a sneaky, manipulative, tricky man. Perhaps it was because she was a wanton, lustful wench utterly beguiled by America's leader. Or perhaps it was just because he had asked so nicely and she couldn't resist him.

She was climbing out of the Beatrice's car and once again entering the White House just five days after she'd left it on the Marine One helicopter. Genny couldn't have come sooner, as she'd just had three days of meetings in Paris before returning to New York. She hadn't even slept, merely spent three hours in the office before hopping the train down to D.C.

"It's cookie night," Peter had said. "You can't miss cookie night. We'll wait until Friday night for you, but not longer."

So, here she was for cookie night, whatever that was. It was five o'clock local time, making it eleven at night in Paris. But she hadn't really had time to adapt, so she figured her body time was probably somewhere around the mid-Atlantic Oceanic Ridge. Lost in deep water far from any shore.

A butler appeared and collected her suitcase and coat, saying that he would place them in the Residence for when she needed them.

"The President and Dr. Darlington are still in the Oval Office. Would you care to join them there or wait in the Residence?"

She opted for the Oval Office and Beatrice led her away. Partly, she wanted to see if she had adapted to the room at all, but mostly she wanted to see Peter.

Even when married to Gérard, she thought nothing of traveling weeks at a time away from home. Perhaps she laid too much of the failure of their marriage at his feet. Yes, he was an arrogant Frenchman with such an insular view of the civilized world that he was practically American about it. But neither had she been the easiest person to live with.

Peter Matthews however, was making her want to be with him. Two evenings and one night together and she missed the man after only five days. Damn him! Even worse, she'd missed him the minute they'd driven in opposite directions from the Manhattan Downtown Heliport.

The Oval Office had not decreased its impact in the slightest. Peter waved her in and continued listening to whatever phone conversation he was having. She passed by his chair and planted a kiss on top of his head. It was only as she stepped by, that the gesture struck her. How many times had she seen her mother do that same thing on her father's head when he would come home and dropped with relief into his big armchair, glad to be among his family once again.

This was a little different in that the next moment Peter clearly cut off the other speaker. "Mr. Prime Minister, I'm telling you very simply, that if Israel takes such an action it will be without the support of the U.S. Not militarily, financially, or politically. If the U.N. court wants to take you down for that, they will have a hundred percent support of the United States Government. Do I make myself clear?"

Okay, maybe it was a lot different. But it had felt the same, a casual, easy acknowledgement that she was glad to see him. She did her best not to pay attention to the abruptly altered tone of the conversation as Israel tried to placate its primary ally. Instead, she turned to inspect the room.

Perhaps she was adapting to the room. This time she could see more detail. A Christmas tree, the three-meter baby brother of the ten-meter monster on the Ellipse, it had also been lit in a cheerful and bright imitation of the American flag. A few presents were scattered about the base, she glanced down, from the President to his staff by the labels.

"I don't let them buy presents for me," Peter slid up behind her and wrapped his arms around her waist. He nuzzled her neck in greeting. "I don't want them to be uncomfortable trying to decide what to give me."

"What do you give to them?"

"Oh, illegal land grants, major tax concessions. Have you met Felicia, cute little African woman who is also a fabulous speech writer? She asked for a bomb strike for Christmas, something to do with an exhusband. Things like that."

"I like the way she thinks."

"Maybe I should get one for all the women of America. Really tie up the women's vote for the next election."

"Yes, and it would also drop the population of your country by about a half."

"I'd win the women by a landslide that way. Of course, just to be fair, I'd have to offer the services of the Special Operations Forces to the men. No, the whole thing could get too messy and depopulate my constituency entirely, then there'd be no one to vote for me. I talked her into accepting a small Caribbean island just as soon as the Caribbeans are done with it."

Genny stepped away from him, waved to Mr. Lincoln, who didn't glower one bit less despite the gesture, and continued her tour of the room. It was startling in its simplicity. The three grand portraits were each framed by a pair of holly wreaths bearing large red ribbons. A fire crackled happily in a marble fireplace at the far end of the Oval Office. On the mantle above it were obviously the family heirloom decorations. Old sleigh bells, nicked candy cane candles, a slightly battered set of reindeer in a smoke-stained candelabra, and a small knit Santa who slouched against the wall. She straightened the Santa who was in danger of tipping over onto an alarmed looking ceramic gnome.

At the small tables among the seating in the center of the room, more gnomes cheerfully offered ceramic bags overflowing with choco-lates. She took one and bit into it.

"Oh my god, that's so good," dark chocolate with a Grand Marnier truffle interior. "That's as good as sex."

"I hope not, or I've been doing something wrong." Peter had remained by the tree and watched her inspection, hands slid comfort-ably into the pockets of his navy-blue slacks. His tie, something in Christmasy colors, hung slightly loosened about his neck. The white linen shirt made him look clean, no, pure. As if he were the purest version of himself while standing there watching her.

She moved back to him. And could now see his tie, sporting a team of Santas facing off in a hockey game against some very determined looking elves. Genny rested her palm on the center of his ridiculous tie and his wonderful chest.

"You, my lover Mr. President, are doing absolutely nothing wrong in that area. Someone trained you so very well on how to please a woman in your bed."

"You did."

"*Moi?*"

"*Tu*. I simply imagined everything I could do to make you happy and did that. You inspire me. In many ways." He said the last on a drifting voice, half to himself.

"You must stop this, Mr. President." Genny was having difficulty breathing. Each time he said something like that to her, he shifted her self-image.

"Stop what?"

"Your flattery." It made her feel as if she was more than she knew she was.

"It's working, is it? Cool!"

"Ugh. You are such a man. Now kiss me like you have been imag-ining since I arrived."

"You mean since the moment you left?"

Genny dragged his face to hers and kissed him before he could say more. He was going to kill her yet. Or slay her heart which, for the first time, she thought might be even worse.

———

"So, what is this cookie night?" Genny and the President waited in the Dining Hall of the Second Floor of the Residence. It was so formal, like everything else here. White wainscoting, elegantly tasteful wallpaper the color of a soft sunrise, and an elaborate crystal chandelier dangling over a circular table of dark mahogany that could seat ten. And the seam down the middle suggested that it could be expanded for even more. A spread of hors d'oeuvres had been spread upon the table. She took a few on a small plate. Peter, refusing to cave to the formality of his surroundings, grazed, taking an olive here, a deviled egg there, and eating them with little regard if they were to scatter crumbs.

Per instruction, she had changed into casual clothes, at least the most casual she had with her, black slacks and turtleneck. Peter wore jeans and a flannel shirt open at the collar with the sleeves rolled up. He looked comfortable, at home in this crazy house of the American President.

"You'll just have to wait and see. Besides, it's Daniel's thing, so we have to wait for him and a couple of others to join us. Oh, I should mention— Oh, here's Em."

Emily Beale stepped into the room. "Mark bagged out on us," she said by way of introduction. Not even a hello, as if Genny were simply a member of the family, expected rather than merely welcome. It was a nice gesture. She hoped that's all it was because otherwise she'd start to overthink how it felt to be here.

"Mark does that whenever I mention anything about a kitchen other than eating in one. I swear, the only place he'll cook is if we have a campfire and he just caught the trout. He made some lousy excuse just because we are shipping out on a training exercise tomorrow, as if that were something new."

"What you should do," Genny glanced sidelong at Peter to make sure he was listening. She decided to see just how much she could tease him, "is exactly what I plan to do with this Mr. President. Our first house," the President suddenly had a strangled look on his face as if he were choking on his own breath. Perfect. That would teach him to have secrets from her.

"It will have no kitchen. I will install an enormous American barbecue and make him always do the cooking for me."

Emily idly thudded Peter on the back with one hand to restart his breathing, hard enough to nearly drive him onto the table, while considering Genny.

"You're smart. I should have known you would be, since Peter picked you out of the crowd. I just might do that." Her smile lit her eyes more brightly than laughter ever could.

Before Peter had fully recovered, Daniel and his wife Alice arrived from the floor above. He carried a small sheaf of papers and index cards. These looked worn and tattered, oddly out of place in the White House. Something so simple brought to the eye the museum-like perfection of every adornment here, making the whole of it suddenly appear false.

Another couple arrived close behind them, an older couple that she didn't recognize. The attractive woman wore a short bob of graying hair that might have once been blond, a cashmere sweater and perfectly tailored jeans. The man was balding, dressed casually, and looked like an older version of—

"There they are. Hey Mom! Dad!"

Peter traded quick hugs with them as Genny felt all of the blood drain out of her body. It was a setup and she was the pretty woman suddenly on display.

"Please allow me to introduce you. Geneviève, this is Randolph, former Senate Majority leader, retired, so thank God I don't have to deal with him. And Gloria. She's still a U.S. Court of Appeals Circuit Judge. Mom, Dad, this is—"

"We know who she is, you idiot."

Gloria held onto Genny's hand which was good, for it was about the only thing that kept her from flattening Peter onto the hardwood floor. And she was going to make sure it hurt on the way down, because the Secret Service was probably going to shoot her before she'd have a chance to finish him off.

"I can't believe he didn't tell you we were invited," Gloria rested her other hand over Genny's, as if she knew she were enhancing the longevity of her son's existence by doing so. "There are some things about which he is remarkably stupid. I, for one, am pleased to meet you. After I saw the pictures in the news, because of course he doesn't even think to call his mother, I googled you. You are a very impressive young woman, perhaps you can keep him in line."

"Perhaps I can practice my martial arts sparring techniques upon him. Hard." Genny finally managed to shift her gaze over to Peter. He looked as if he understood that this was not a good surprise.

Randolph cuffed his son smartly on the back of the head, which made Genny feel a little better.

———

"It's an old family tradition," Daniel was spreading out his precious recipes on the table.

Peter had tried to get to Geneviève a couple of times, but she was clearly avoiding him. Every time he turned, she was on the opposite side of his mother or father. Even Alice and Em were putting up subtle barricades around her. He couldn't seem to get to her.

"We've always made cookie boxes for any family who couldn't be home for Christmas. I first thought, for this year, we could make some for our own families."

Peter tried to catch Geneviève's attention so that he could signal her to retire with him for a moment to the hallway to explain, but she wouldn't even look at him.

"But that would only be for me and Mark. Plus some extras for Emily to take to her parents here in town. Genny, I don't know if you have family."

"I do. In Vietnam."

"Good," Daniel continued as if there were no problem at all. Usually his Chief of Staff helped him muddle through situations, just as he'd helped some with Daniel's courtship of Alice. Right at the moment he was being completely useless.

"So that would make three boxes of cookies, not very ambitious. But I thought we should spread it wider. I think we should make as many boxes as we can, and send them out to the kids in shelters in D.C. Cookies not made by the White House chefs, but us personally."

"What a wonderful idea," everyone was agreeing and turning to inspect the recipes.

Peter tried to move in beside Geneviève and received a sharp elbow to the gut that hurt and forced him to back off.

"Okay! I screwed up! I'm sorry!" At his outburst, everybody turned to stare at him. Everybody except Geneviève.

He took her elbow and turned her gently until she faced him.

Her glare and the hurt was not a pretty expression on her face and he was sorry he'd put it there.

"I'm sorry. I didn't know if Mom and Dad could make it when I invited you."

"When you found out, you could have called me." Her voice was neither hot nor tear-choked as he'd expected. It sounded cold, and dangerous.

"I could have, if you'd given me your goddamned phone number." He knew he should be the one keeping his temper. He always did, in every situation. But his need for her, to be with her, was driving him near to madness.

Geneviève remained perfectly steady, not even needing to cross her arms in front of her to fend him off. "And your Secret Service doesn't have my number?"

"Of course they do, at least I assume so. But I didn't want to ask them. I have already made it so that your life is smeared across the front pages of the news, I wanted to leave you some privacy."

Was her look softening? He couldn't tell.

"And why didn't you tell me when I arrived?" Her demand sounded no softer. "I have been here over thirty minutes. Long enough for you to kiss me in the Oval Office. Long enough to try to drag me into your bed when we changed clothes though you said we would be late if you did."

Okay, now he was the one who didn't want to meet her eyes. Even less though, did he want to see the eyes of anyone else in the room. No one, not even his own parents, had the decency to make even the least gesture toward leaving, they all were too fascinated by the goings-on here.

So, this too would be public.

He took her hands in his. They didn't grasp, but neither did she pull them away.

"Kim-Ly Geneviève Beauchamp, you consume me. You make me think of nothing but you, every moment you are with me. I forgot that I hadn't told you my parents would be here, because I was too busy being happy." Then he waited. Waited while the woman with the greenest eyes he'd ever seen inspected him and decided her verdict.

Then, when he thought he might pass out from holding his breath, she stepped forward and kissed him on each cheek. He half feared that she was saying goodbye, until she kissed him lightly on the mouth, as lightly as that first kiss. Pulling him close against her by the strong grasp of their hands, she laid her cheek on his and whispered in his ear.

"I was right, you are making my heart in such danger."

Peter freed his hands, wrapped his arms around her, and simply tried to hold on.

His mother and Alice were crying, not even attempting to mop their cheeks. Even Em was looking pretty sniffly which was hard to imagine. His Dad thumped him on the back, though not hard enough to disturb the woman nestled in his arms.

Daniel just gave him a sharp nod of approval, as if he'd known all along it would be okay. Then he spoke loudly.

"So, about these cookies."

Everyone laughed and turned back to the task at hand.

He stayed close by Geneviève. If he was putting her heart "in such danger," what in the world was she doing to his? Making it pound until he couldn't hear a single thing anyone said. It pounded so hard that it set up echoes that would never stop, not until they were buried deep in his soul.

"There are no French-style cookies here," Genny inspected Daniel's recipe collection. "No dessert from Vietnam. I cannot send a Christmas box to my family without these ingredients."

"I have this," Daniel offered her a recipe for Sienese *Pan Forte.*

"That is Italian."

"I know how to make a decent custard," Emily offered.

"Oh, and that will ship well in a cookie box."

Emily looked chagrined, "Oh, right."

"I will need some ingredients." She did her best to maintain the appearance of calm. The pressure had eased in the room. And it had eased in her heart, in one way.

"We can dial down to the main White House kitchen for almost anything we need. They'll send it up on the elevator." Daniel pointed to a tall, but narrow steel door in the corner that Genny hadn't noticed.

She began making a list.

"Hey, I thought you said you didn't know how to cook?"

"This is not cooking, Mr. President. This is baking. Even more important, this is Christmas baking. That I know how to do." She focused on finishing her list so that she appeared busy.

For the pressure on her heart had not eased. In less than a week, she had fallen in love with a man, and she had only come to understand that in the last minute or two. It was not something she did easily. Or at all, in her memory. She had thought she loved Gérard, or she wouldn't have married him. But it had felt nothing like this. Nothing like when Peter had faced her and told her that she consumed his thoughts.

From another man, that would be lust. But this was not a normal man. This was one of the most powerful thinkers on the planet. And she knew by what he'd achieved already in his Presidency, a very smart and determined man. That her mere presence could distract him into indiscretions and poor communication spoke of far more than it would have in any other man. He had just laid his heart out on the table in front of his friends and parents for all to see. And he had offered it to her.

Whether or not he understood what he had done, she did. And how could she not be swept away by such a revelation?

"There," she finished her list. Her throat was tight and she was glad to find Emily close beside her. The woman leaned in to look at the list, and ever so casually draped an arm across Genny's shoulders. With no one the wiser, the woman hugged her. Clearly she too had seen what Peter, her childhood friend, did not yet realize.

"Interesting looking ingredients, what do they make?"

"This," Genny indicated the first column. "Will make a *Nougat Noir au Miel.* It is a dark, what would you call, caramel of lavender honey with almonds. It goes between wafer paper if they have it, or dusted confectioners sugar if they do not. And this a *Nougat Blanc,* a white sugar and pistachio nut candy. Both very traditional French. They are the black and the white, the bad boy and the good girl of Santa's Christmas list, or so my mother always called them."

"That definitely works for me," Emily looked up at the President. "Bad Boy, Peter. Bad Boy! Coal in your stocking."

"Could I get that dark caramel thing instead? Sounds good."

"Only," Genny looked up at him, the first time she had dared to face him since his confession. "If you promise me one thing."

"Anything." His statement was so emphatic that it set her back for a moment more. He might truly mean that in more ways than he knew. She needed something light and funny. Something to stop the fluttering he was causing in her chest.

"You must promise me, Mr. President. That the next time you have personal news, you will call your parents."

Everyone laughed. Gloria actually applauded and Randolph slapped his son on the back.

But Peter looked at her as if she'd said something else entirely. His gaze spoke of just what reason he might have for calling his parents in the near future.

It was not possible that she had just spoken of becoming engaged to the President.

———

They had baked and laughed and drunk wine and eaten cookies and relaxed more that evening than Peter had done in a long time. The kitchen was comfortably sized, but with seven cooks, there had been a constant friendly jostling for prime counter space.

Sheets and sheets of cookies had gone through the oven, over-spilling the kitchen counters and even the big Dining Room table. More coffee tables had been recruited from the Central Hall, dragged in and covered with paper boxes. They'd lined each box, the size to hold a ream of paper, with red tissue paper, then filled them with a wide variety of cookies, and tied them closed with red and green ribbons.

Some monster chocolate chip that Daniel called a Paul Bunyan Molasses cookie. Narrow slices of Em's decadent *Pan Forte* and her chocolate-dipped macaroons. His mom's Cinnamon-Raisin Biscotti. As a group they tackled several of Daniel's recipes. They'd made Ginger-Squared Squares, which included both fresh-grated and candied ginger in square oatmeal bars. Alice had contributed a Cream Cheese Cran-berry Curl that she called C-to-the-fourth. In addition to the nougats, Geneviève had made something she called Ginger Jam. Starting with three kilos of ginger root, she had peeled and sliced and boiled and mixed like a madwoman, ultimately creating a Vietnamese ginger candy similar to flattened jellybeans that no one could stop eating. And everyone had worked on the mounds of cut-out sugar cookies in the shapes of Santas, reindeers, and Christmas trees all decorated with colored royal icing.

They trashed the kitchen. Their hands were stained with food dye. Their clothes powdered with flour and sugar despite the aprons his mother had handed out. The entire residence had smelled heavenly.

And each time Peter found himself working shoulder-to-shoulder with Geneviève it was as if his world went quiet. It was simply where they belonged—close, comfortable, easy together. He knew he was being stupid, but there was no doubt what they had said to each other across the Dining Room without a word spoken. He knew as well as she did that they had each said the impossible.

They could both imagine being married some day.

The logistics of how they could even live together was beyond imagining; their lives, their worlds were different. But for this woman, he could easily imagine spending the rest of his years finding ways of making her happy.

It was well past midnight when they stumbled into his bedroom. She mumbled something about her body being on Paris time and he suddenly felt guilty. It was seven or eight a.m. her time. By the time he'd brushed his teeth, she was crashed down atop the covers.

She barely woke as he undressed her and tucked her beneath the covers, smoothing back the hair off her face. He sat on the edge of the bed and simply watched her sleep for the longest time.

Geneviève had not only won the sincere friendship of his parents, but she had also drawn Em's clear stamp of approval. Of all the people in Peter's life, no one knew him better. Though she'd been six years younger, they had still been best friends growing up, the impossibly precocious little girl next door. Their lives had gone separate directions, more his fault than hers, until two years ago when she'd stepped back into the President's world as a Captain of the U.S. Army Special Operations Forces. Now she was the very grown up, utterly daunting first female pilot of the secretive Special Operations Aviation Regiment (airborne), flying the 160th's most lethal helicopter and earning some of the country's highest medals.

Em had stepped in and saved his life. He could think of no person he respected more. Nor any person who was a better judge of character, not even himself or Daniel. He had also never seen Em, who so rarely laughed, so light and easy as she was around Geneviève. They had chatted, teased, and joked like long-lost sisters, the shining blond and the dark French-Vietnamese beauty.

At the end of the evening, Em had pulled him aside. "We took a vote, oh pal of mine. She's great. So if you mess this up, we're all going to drop you and hang out with her. Don't blow it or you'll be answering to me. We clear?"

He was clear. He'd never been threatened by Beale over a woman before. Well, there was Mitsy in tenth grade, but that was a threat to hurt him if he didn't get rid of her.

Geneviève... He now so enjoyed saying her name and letting it roll off his tongue that he couldn't imagine using her nickname. Geneviève had changed the White House for him. He had loved the work, the challenges, the successes, even the failures. But living here had brought no joy. The first nine months, knowing that Katherine was sleeping just on the floor above scheming, had been something he'd done his best to ignore, but it had definitely not brightened his days. The two years since her death, he'd done little more in the Residence than sleep or attend state functions.

In a single night, Geneviève had filled the Residence with joy and laughter. Friends and family had come together and they had all enjoyed being together. It was only the second week of December, and it was already his best Christmas in recent memory, perhaps ever. Christmas at his parents had been quiet affairs, this had been noisy, ridiculous, fun, and filled with cookies. What more could a sane man ask for?

The dark beauty sleeping before him had won over more than the approval of his parents and friends. She had won his heart as well. It was not a familiar feeling, but it felt as if it should be. As if now for the first time, his own feelings were finally in the right place. Even though it was somewhere they had never been before.

He rose and undressed. Before he slipped into bed beside her, he spotted a cookie resting on the middle of his pillow. He groaned. Sugar still permeated the very air he was breathing and here was yet more. She must have slipped across the hall during the cookie making without his noticing and placed it here.

But it wasn't a Santa or any other shape they had made that night. It was a sugar-cookie heart, half white dough and half chocolate, baked almost as golden as Geneviève's skin. The two-colored dough had been merged not with a straight line, but in a swirl, as if they were inseparably wound together. Delicately decorated with a skilled hand that had outshone all of the rest of them as they iced their cookies. Geneviève had piped a simple outline in Christmas red.

Inside the perimeter of the heart, she had piped a simple message in green script: GB+PM.

Oh God.

She felt the same way about him as he did about her.

What were they going to do about that?

CHAPTER EIGHT

"*A**s you may or*** may not know, and again this is not some secret stalking thing, I'm going to be in Southeast Asia for several days right before Christmas."

Genny focused on her luncheon omelet trying to decide if she was really awake yet. She'd slept right up to midday. By the time she had done her workout, showered, and entered the kitchen, it had been cleaned by the magical elves of the White House staff. Last night everyone had pitched in to clear and wash up the worst of the mess, but now it sparkled.

The mountainous stacks of cookie boxes were gone to the shelters, all down the tiny elevator in the corner of the kitchen that connected the kitchens on the Second and Third Floors of the Residence, with the big kitchen on the Ground Floor and the Butler's Pantry on the First Floor used to organize and deliver state dinners. Even the boxes prepared for FedEx to go to Daniel's, Mark's, and Genny's families were gone. Emily had left with a plateful for Mark and her parents consisting of broken cookies and design disasters, because she insisted none of them would care. And if they did, she didn't. They could just come and cook next year if they didn't like it.

Genny so admired the woman's strength, Emily's absolute

centeredness in who she was. Genny wished she could do the same, but all she could manage was to study her omelet and not shudder at the huge changes rippling out of control across her life.

Peter had joined her for lunch. He'd left a note asking her to dial an extension when she was awake and ready to eat. When she called, she'd been connected, not to one of the President's secretaries as she'd expected, but rather directly to Peter in the Oval Office. She'd wager that few had such a privilege.

Lunching with the American President, sharing his bed, enjoying his friends. This was not a life she understood. Meetings with reluctant U.N. Ambassadors, fighting for proper patrols against poachers from understaffed park rangers who were probably on the take to look the other way, who had to be on the take to afford to feed their families. Those she understood.

"Who are you meeting with?"

"The Association of Southeast Asia Nations." He picked up his BLT sandwich and took a bite.

"Yes. Of course. I forgot all about the ASEAN meeting. The meeting is in Hanoi this year. Kicked out of Indonesia by yet another typhoon and disastrous flooding." Genny rubbed her eyes. She really wasn't awake yet.

That was a total fib, even to herself. She was wide awake and trying to figure out how to deny to herself what was happening between her and this man. She knew almost nothing about him, other than she was happy almost every minute they were together. For her, the existence of love at all was in question. At "first sight" was *très ridicule.* A myth. It had to be. But then why did she feel this way?

Okay, perhaps it wasn't at first sight. For six months she had watched every speech he'd made. And a pair of biographies were on her e-reader as well, ones that she'd actually gotten around to reading, unlike the latest Annie Ernaux novel, never mind all of the reports and studies she was inundated with daily.

She knew an immense amount about this man, even items that weren't in his biography, his passion for Scrabble among others. And that his best friend Emily Beale had merely been identified as a neighbor of his childhood in both biographies. Portions of his life were private.

So, even if it wasn't love at first sight, it was still going too fast.

"Yes. So, we'll be in Hanoi together." Genny ate some of the salmon omelet with English muffins that the main kitchen had sent up for her. The coffee was good, stronger than the last she'd had at the White House, even if it was served in monstrous American-sized cups. Not as good as home, but it helped.

"I'd like to see you when I'm there."

"No, Mr. President, you'd like to sleep with me while we are there and I would like that very much also."

Peter grinned, "Okay, caught me. That too. But I'd also like to meet your family while I'm there."

Genny went very still. She became aware of the weight of the fork in her hand, the scent of fresh basil still rising from her luncheon, and her heart stopped absolutely still in her chest.

"Why?"

He didn't even bother to answer. Instead, he left a silence as if to say, "This is so obvious we don't need to talk about it, but it is also still too new and uncomfortable for us to actually talk about it."

"Why?" She knew the answer. Why was she insisting on the words?

He set down his sandwich and sipped some ice tea as he considered his words.

"As President, I must often make fast decisions based on too little information. And I have to be right every time or the newspapers will shred me, publicly, before I have a chance to correct it. My job is interpreting a thousand different factors, okay, maybe only hundreds, definitely dozens," his smile was easy. "As fast as I possibly can."

She nodded for him to continue, her head was the only part of her she was able to move. Her hand still suspended her fork halfway through slicing off the next bite of omelet.

"By contrast, in my personal life, I have with only one exception, always moved slowly and carefully. And that one exception led me to a dreadfully unhappy marriage."

There was another item not in the biographies. The country had worshipped and mourned Katherine Matthews. It was a topic of many articles and television shows right now because the President was seeing a foreign-national hussy who worked for the United Nations, who could never live up to the standards set by the amazing Katherine Matthews.

"I too do not want to be moving too fast. I do not want to do what I did to poor Gérard or suffer the many petty cruelties he did to me. You will need to be explaining about your wife to me."

Peter didn't look happy about that. He set down his sandwich as if it had lost all flavor for him.

"There are issues of national security here."

"There are issues of personal trust if we are to be in a relationship here." She managed to release her fork and folded her hands on the table before her.

Peter dragged a hand through his hair. "Can we just table this for later?"

"Mr. President," she didn't use the slight teasing tone that had become a part of her refusal to use his Christian name. She used the tone she might use addressing the U.N. General Secretary or any other head of state.

"Even if your relationship with your wife was a matter of national security, though I do not see how that is possible, there is a mutual trust that will be required or we will not be moving forward from this moment. We will not be sleeping together in Hanoi and you will not be meeting my family just as a contingency plan in case you happen to decide you want to propose to me at some later date. I trusted Gérard to be who he said he was, rather than who he turned out to be. I will not be making that mistake again."

Genny steeled herself to state the next line, but it must be said.

"Now," she kept her voice rock steady though her heart wanted to shatter inside her chest. "Do I stand up and go back to New York and you can tell your press briefing room that it was fun but didn't work out, which I will not gainsay? Or, do you explain why you are considering marriage with me when your first marriage was a public lie? Would ours be a lie as well?"

That she feared she might die inside if his answer was for her to leave, she did her best to ignore.

———

Peter rested his elbows on the kitchen island and buried his face in his hands just so he wouldn't have to look at Geneviève.

How could she appear so calm, waiting as patiently as Jonah crouched inside his whale?

His head was whirling so fast he couldn't begin to sort out the pieces. *Think, Peter. Just think!* It was an instruction he often shouted at himself when everything was spinning out of control in a political crisis situation. If he just thought his way through it, he could eventually find the starting point. The center that had caused the problem and escalated until the resulting problem was almost unrecognizable.

But he wasn't finding the starting point here. He knew she waited patiently, but that probably wouldn't last for long. She was an immensely practical woman and he was a damned mess. All he knew was that his world would crumble, that it would be far less happy, less bright, if she were to leave.

He looked up and faced her across their forgotten meal. This was not how he'd pictured their quiet luncheon together. A glance at the clock on the stove behind Geneviève told him he had about ten minutes to straighten this out before he was due back in the Oval Office. Ten minutes to figure out how to keep his love life heading wherever it was heading. Like that was going to happen. At least he could start. He knew one thing for sure.

"I don't want you to leave."

She sagged, "Thank God!"

He laughed aloud. He couldn't help himself. "You mean that you were sitting there so calm, beautiful, and perfect and scaring me half to death, and you were only doing it to make me crazy?"

"No, I am sitting here so worried, afraid, and such a mess, praying that you want to be with me."

"Christ, Geneviève. I didn't ask to meet your parents so that I could keep having sex with you."

She nodded, then nodded again as if registering that somewhere deep inside, and then went quiet again. She still wanted her answers.

Okay. So, she wasn't running away from him, as long as he didn't screw this up. He had a choice. While he might not trust a Vietnamese national, their relationship with the United States was still not the most comfortable, could he choose to trust this special woman? Trust that she would keep confidential that which had been so carefully kept secret.

Not trusting Geneviève felt like not trusting himself.

"Do you remember the video of that last flight? It was on all of the world media."

"Yes," she nodded. "A mechanical failure in the First Lady's helicopter, and the pilot was not good enough to save her life."

"I will offer you a different perspective. One that would not go well in the news."

Her look informed him he was being an idiot to doubt her discretion, which was probably true.

"What you may not recall is that Emily Beale was the pilot and only one person besides myself knows that her husband Mark was aboard as well."

"Well, that certainly takes pilot failure out of the picture. Wait!" Geneviève sat bolt upright as if she'd just been electrocuted. "You had them kill your wife?"

"No! No!" Now there was a conclusion he hadn't expected her to jump to. "Are Americans truly perceived as so cavalier by other countries? No, don't answer that, I don't want to get sidetracked. And besides, can you see Emily doing such a thing?"

"No," Geneviève shook her head and resettled. "No. Sorry. Tell your story."

"There are under ten people on the planet who know this next fact. Not even Daniel knows, though he suspects. Captain, now Major Emily Beale was shot during that flight."

He could see her mind working swiftly. It was only moments for her to absorb those facts and restructure the story herself before she spoke. By the look of sudden compassion and understanding in her eyes, he could see that she had realized that the only other person on that flight was Katherine Matthews. And that if someone had shot Major Beale, it had to be the First Lady who had pulled the trigger.

"Ah! I can't be sure of the timing, Mr. President, but it seems to me that approximately a month later you had a new White House Chief of Staff in Dr. Daniel Darlington. After your own Chief of Staff retired for health reasons?" She turned that into a question at the last moment. Then, "Your Chief of Staff didn't retire for health reasons. He was a part of it somehow."

Damn! He kept forgetting just how smart Geneviève was. Even Daniel couldn't put together apparently unrelated events as quickly. Yet another reason she swept Peter's feet out from under him.

"That's as long as we could delay the news. Ray Stevens did retire for 'health reasons,' so that he wouldn't be tried for treason as an unwitting pawn in the First Lady's plot. She planned to frame him for the murder of the President, and then to take over the country by marrying the bachelor Vice President, who she thought she was well on the way to controlling. Zach Taylor is a better man than that, though."

Peter wondered where she would go next, how many leaps would she make beyond the expected.

"Your taste in women apparently leaves something to be desired, Mr. President." She took up her fork and resumed eating as if the conversation were suddenly concluded.

"Until now."

"You're sweet." Her smile said much more.

"No, just enamored."

"Just enamored?"

"Deeply enamored?"

"You are so very male, Mr. President. But I will agree to that phrase. I too am deeply enamored. It is a good word."

"Only eleven points."

"Yes, but it uses all seven letters if played across a single letter, Mr. President. A nice bonus."

"A nice one indeed."

"So, how do we get you to my family plantation? It is not in Hanoi, but you will want to see it. And Gram, our matriarch, does not enjoy to travel often anymore. You should also get to see at least one World Heritage Site if you are to visit Southeast Asia."

CHAPTER NINE

"**And by what method** do you justify this to your American taxpayers?" Genny waved a hand to indicate herself seated aboard Air Force One, in the corner of the President's in-flight office. There had been only a few high-level meetings where she had retired to one of the equally comfortable seats in the corridor to afford him privacy. For the most part they both had sat quietly and worked. Now they were ten hours into the seventeen-hour flight and sharing a meal.

She was surprised to learn that dining on the President's airplane was nothing special. They served airplane fare, high quality and tasty, but she'd eaten far fancier menus when flying first class on Air France or SAS. Corned Beef on Rye along with potato salad, a fruit bowl, and a bag of chips. She drank a very nice wine and he a beer.

She didn't doubt that Peter would have a perfectly valid explanation of how he was not bilking the taxpayer in the slightest. She liked hearing such explanations from him, poking holes in them where she could. Which was always difficult because he was such an ethical man. Twice this week, he had brought a tricky problem from his workday to their bed and used her as a sounding board until he found a tenable solution.

Their bed. The President's bed. The lines were already blurring and she honestly didn't know how to feel about it. She decided that she wouldn't think about it until her family had a chance to meet Peter and she could ask Gram's advice. Genny knew she was in over her head, but her Vietnamese grandmother was wise in many ways.

In the week between the cookie night and the flight to Hanoi, she had actually been able to work mostly from the White House, only spending two days in New York. Peter had set her up with an office in the Residence. She didn't need much; her laptop, phone, and a fax/copier on loan from the IT department had filled most of her needs.

Air Force One had actually afforded her some peace. By refusing to use the aircraft's telephone system, she'd been able to get a fair amount of work done, though she did appreciate her guest access to the on-board wireless network so that she could continue the never-ending battle with her e-mail.

"I just tell them," Peter saluted taxpayers everywhere with a tipping of his beer. "That I'm not going anywhere without my main squeeze along."

"Main squeeze?"

"Sorry, American slang. Old slang from my parents' youth, maybe even earlier. It means my main girl."

"And you have so many others that you are not telling me about? I maybe am part French which makes me understanding, but I am also part Vietnamese and that makes me possessive and dangerous."

Peter didn't even have the decency to squirm. "You're the main one for me."

"*Tu es impossible!*"

"And proud to be."

———

Despite Peter's hints about his private cabin and an opportunity to join the Mile-High Club, Genny had decided that wouldn't be a good idea with his staff so close by.

She had defused part of it by making him explain just what kind of club it was, as if she didn't know. He was far from the first man to proposition her in flight, though he might eventually be the first to succeed. So, she questioned him to evade the request, for now.

Did one only have to claim to have had sex over a mile in the air or was some form of proof required? And where did one register for this club of his? Did it count to have sex a hundred feet in the air over Denver, the Mile-High city? Were there extra points for higher altitudes? What about over each different country?

At least she had sent him to his rest with a laugh on his face and a kiss on his lips. But it had also left her at loose ends. She had worked some more, then watched part of a movie, but she was too *agité* from being on Air Force One to sleep. And, though she was reluctant to admit it, terribly nervous to be introducing Peter to her family.

Even one of the comfortable chairs reserved for senior staff didn't enable her to settle for more than a few pages into her latest novel. So she took herself on a tour of the plane. After all, if things went poorly in Vietnam, this might be her only chance.

The communications room in the 747's upper level was clearly off limits, the armed Air Force guard watching her expressionlessly from the top of the steps was an unnecessary emphasis on this point. Her interest in the galleys and storage on the lower deck was also minimal, and she had boarded through the forward galley, so she skipped the downward stairs just as she had the upward ones. Most people entered through the lower level, staff to the front and press to the rear.

Only the President and the occasional special guest entered the plane from the long rolling ramp to the middle deck hatch. He had wanted her to join him for the long climb up those stairs in front of all the cameras. She was tempted, but her nerves had won out. If this didn't work out between them, and she couldn't imagine how it possibly could in the long term, then she would forever be "That Girl" in the photo, boarding Air Force One to sleep with the President in flight.

Just outside the President's on-board office, Frank and Beatrice of the Secret Service sat together in the two reserved seats. Agent Belfour stood as soon as she spotted Genny.

"Everything okay, ma'am?"

"That's Genny to you, Beatrice. Or I will not answer when you speak to me."

"Right, sorry. That habit is going to die hard." She offered one of her bright smiles. "Anything I can do for you?"

"No. I am just touring the plane a bit. I'm tired of sitting and needed to move about."

"Yeah, these long flights are tough."

"I haven't been causing you trouble, have I?"

"Genny, you are a seriously easy charge. Besides, gives me a chance to travel with my husband which hasn't happened much over the years." Frank looked up at her. She hadn't had much to do with him, though he'd always been pleasant enough. For some reason it took Genny until this moment to realize that these were the two people from whom Peter was specifically not asking for background information about her.

Agents Frank Adams and Beatrice Belfour would know everything about her. From Genny's first boyfriend, a lovely young lad named Huang who would carry her books as he walked her home from secondary school, to her politics, pretty much didn't have those, couldn't afford them in her job. Well, if someone had to know all about her, she couldn't feel much more secure than these two. The Head of the Presidential Protection Detail and his wife were a force to be reckoned with.

Frank had a file open in his lap. She could see the photographs of the Preah Vihear temple, one of the possible World Cultural Heritage Site visits Genny had suggested. She'd specifically suggested that temple as it was in Cambodia, offering him a high profile visit that might help the U.N. with the site's preservation. It would also assist him with cultural relations with Cambodia by showing interest in their problems with their Thai neighbors. It was an area with some border issues that were still unresolved despite a hundred years of efforts at all levels, from the 1962 International Court of Justice ruling to her own minor efforts at the meeting where she had met the President last July.

Genny waved Beatrice back to her chair. "Well, you clearly have a lot of planning to do. I think that I will continue my tour. I suppose I can't get in too much trouble on an airplane."

"As long as don't try climbing the stairs, you're cleared for the entire plane." Beatrice tapped the badge with the letter "Q" dangling about Genny's neck.

She looked down at the badge in surprise. She hadn't really thought about it, though she hadn't seen another like it. A foreign national at liberty aboard Air Force One. Sitting in the President's on-board office as his assistants rushed in and out. It had felt normal, expected, not deeply unusual as it must be.

Beatrice nodded as if reading Genny's thoughts.

"Not only did the President insist, but you also checked out as alarmingly apolitical, discreet, and trustworthy among many other unseemly habits. That badge gets you anywhere in the Residence or on the grounds unescorted, into the West Wing with minimal escort, namely me, and Air Force One, except up those stairs."

"Oh, all right. Thanks." Beatrice returned to her seat and Genny took several steps away to peer into the next room. It was the medical room which included a doctor, a nurse, and a fold-down operating table that they were proud to tell her had never been used. Next, in their own small conference area, she nodded to three senior staff who she was beginning to recognize. Too bad Daniel wasn't along, though he'd probably be even busier than the President.

Again she looked down at the piece of plastic dangling about her neck. The red, white, and blue pattern and the letter "Q" which could have any number of meanings. Though, as the badges changed with each President, perhaps the "Q" badge was Peter's handiwork. Did it mean she had James Bond-style clearance all the way to "Q" the exotic weapons specialist? Or...

Then she had it. "Q" was a ten-point letter in Scrabble. It denoted that she was the highest value of visitor who still needed a badge. If Peter was involved there would be some meaning beyond the colors of the flag. Red for Residence, White for West Wing, and Blue for the color of Air Force One seemed likely. "RWB" would be worth eight points. With the Red being the color for Triple Word Score and Blue denoting Triple Letter Score, it would be worth, she calculated for a moment, forty-two points.

Genny decided that someone should put her out of her misery now.

If she stayed with Peter much longer, she would become a complete mental case. Then she wondered. The badge had several layers of those shifting-background-image hologram effects, so that it would be very hard to duplicate. She held it up to a light and twisted it around for a moment. Sure enough, the deepest layer was a large "42." That did it. They should never be together. Two such nerds couldn't be allowed to exist in the same space.

With a sigh, she dropped the badge back to dangle about her neck and continue her tour. She really did like that man.

Genny wandered past the big conference and dining room without finding a soul to talk to. Most of the people in the staff and secretarial area were sleeping in their chairs, though one or two kept their eyes on the status of messaging to and from the aircraft. It was the dead of night in the middle of a seventeen-hour flight presently over the central Pacific, not much was going on.

She had half hoped to chat with the U.S. representative to ASEAN, but both he and his assistant were asleep in their guest seats. She was beginning to feel like the *Flying Dutchman,* forever haunting her ghostly ship. She had to reach the end of this aircraft at some point. It was only a little over two-hundred feet long, even if it felt like two-hundred meters.

Genny stepped through a doorway and discovered she had indeed reached the rear of the aircraft, and made a crucial mistake. Here at the rear were fourteen seats for the Press Corps. Most of the reporters were asleep, a few were eating a snack and watching a movie.

One woman, who Genny recognized as being from one of the networks, glanced up. For a moment her eyes spread so wide that it was hard to credit, then she recovered.

"Ms. Beauchamp." The woman's words galvanized the entire cabin into action. Fourteen people scrambled for cameras, recorders, even paper pads. They slapped seat neighbors to wake them up, pointing frantically toward Genny when they looked up in bewilderment.

She had avoided the press, carefully not saying a word whenever they mobbed her at the train station or airports. She had watched Peter on national television state, "Yes, we are seeing each other. But, no, I will not be reporting to you on any of the details beyond that.

Ms. Beauchamp is my guest and I shall respect her privacy. She may speak for herself if she so chooses, but I have promised not to invade her privacy any more than I already have."

Well, perhaps now was her moment.

Looking out at the rows of faces, Genny nodded to the woman who had spotted her, granting her the first question. Knowing full well that all she had to do was take a step backward beyond the door if she wanted to get away.

———

When Peter had woken after a couple hours, more of a nap than he usually managed on these flights, he had to ask and wait while Geneviève was tracked down as being with the reporters who rode in the rear of the plane.

He'd hustled down the length of the plane, Frank and Beat sweeping in behind him, but unable to overtake him. What had she been thinking?

"How long?" he barked back over his shoulder.

"Half an hour maybe," Beat replied. "I didn't think she'd go into the Press Corps area."

"Shit!"

Frank and Beat had the good sense not to correct his language. Each area went electric as he hurried through and he didn't give a damn. He ignored all questions, well aware of the consternation he was causing, and again couldn't care less. Frank reassured the other agents as they moved along.

Ten feet from the Press area, just at the head of the rear stairway, he stopped so abruptly that Frank actually ran into him, and had to grab his shoulders to keep from toppling him to the ground.

"Sorry, Mr. President."

He nodded, not trusting his voice. Taking a deep breath, he moved up to the cracked open edge of the doorway...and heard laughter. Geneviève's laughter, it was a sound he could pick out, even in the middle of a busy construction site. What had she... He listened without revealing himself.

"Yes," Geneviève was saying. "The French actually have this meal with three tablecloths and three white candles for the Father, Son, and the Holy Ghost. Seven dishes without meat for the seven sorrows of the Mother Mary, and thirteen desserts for the Apostles and Jesus. No matter what you believe, if eating thirteen desserts does not make you want to celebrate the life of such a man, then there must be something broken in you. Though my family is from Languedoc region, we are very smart and we take this Provençal tradition with us when we return to Vietnam. That is a proper holiday feast. Where you get this Roast Beef and Yorkshire Pudding, this I do not understand at all. Where is tradition in such a thing?"

"It tastes good," some reporter piped up.

"Okay," Geneviève replied merrily. "Yes, this I will grant. It tastes wonderful, but for Christmas in France or among the eight percent of Vietnam peoples who are Christians, it is not."

Peter moved through the door. The space was narrow, the rear of the plane had been cut into two sections. On the port side, it was an area for Secret Service and other flight security personnel. On the starboard side, were fourteen comfortable seats in pairs to either side of a narrow aisle. A lavatory on his right was the limit to how far the Press Corps were allowed to wander from their seats.

In the midst of the room, perched comfortably on the arm of a chair, sat Geneviève, looking as if she were entertaining casually in her own living room. Her thick hair pulled forward over one shoulder. The green turtleneck, just the shade of her eyes, hugged her amazing figure. Again that tiny silver Chinese character medallion was her only adornment. He couldn't imagine a more photogenic woman, and apparently neither could the Press Corps who appeared totally captivated.

Those nearest the entrance to the Press Cabin had their backs turned toward him, facing their guest. Those to the rear didn't notice his arrival.

She did though, the very second he entered. Just the briefest sidelong glance from those almond eyes, and a slight brightening of her smile.

"Well, it has been a pleasure to meet you all."

The sounds of disappointment that washed around the room sounded deeply genuine.

Then her smile turned wicked and she carefully didn't look at him. "I did tell you that I would answer no questions about the President and me. That was because, how would you like to have your fellow reporters and their news cameras in your bedroom?"

One of them actually shuddered theatrically eliciting a laugh from the others, as relaxed as Peter had ever seen the White House Press Corps.

"But perhaps I could tell you something, how do you say, off your record?"

They were so enamored of Geneviève, that they didn't even bother to correct her.

"You must promise."

They raised hands. Some as if swearing in on a Bible, a couple of Boy Scout and Girl Scout salutes, a Vulcan hand sign, and two traditionalists with a hand over their heart. He knew as President of the United States never to trust the Press Corps, but he'd half wager they'd keep a secret for foreign national Ms. Geneviève Beauchamp.

"Good. I will tell you one thing that I have learned. Your President Matthews has never made love to a woman in the Oval Office of the White House. He is afraid, as if he would be first in your history to do so."

Then she looked right at him. The reporters followed her gaze and then startled to find the President standing in their company.

"I think," Geneviève's eyes were positively sparkling as she spoke loudly enough to be heard over the bustle of everyone turning to face him. "I think we need to convince him it could be fun." Her smile, now for him alone as all of the reporters were turned in his direction, acknowledged that it would scare the daylights out of both of them to make love right in the center of that bloody carpet with the portraits of the past Presidents looking on.

Peter did his damnedest not to blush as they all looked at him with knowing smiles.

He was sure he didn't succeed.

CHAPTER TEN

"**A**re we really sure** this is the best option?" Peter looked at the itinerary Frank had worked up. They sat at Noi Bai Airport in his office aboard Air Force One after the second long day of ASEAN meetings. He had slept aboard, as it had offered him the best secure communications as well as being highly defensible. Geneviève had stayed in the city until now, far busier than even he was, and he had missed her terribly.

"There are two ways to approach this, sir. We can let everyone know the President is arriving at an old French plantation in the Northern Highlands of Vietnam far too close to the Laotian border for my taste. We can do this after taking three to six months to plan, then insert heavy U.S. and Vietnamese forces to lock down the entire area."

Peter looked at Geneviève who merely shrugged. Clearly the woman had enough sense to know when she was out of her depth, but so was he.

"The second option," Frank continued, "is to mimic the flight you made last year to Nevada with Majors Beale and Henderson. Simply don't let anyone know you're there and move with a minimal force. To this end, we have taken advantage of an offer from Vietnam's Prime

Minister. He is quite pleased that Ms. Beauchamp, a Vietnamese national, is 'your guide' for this trip to visit one of their most successful farming collectives and only regrets that he will be unable to join you himself."

Frank glanced at Geneviève, but his expression was unreadable. Perhaps he worried that the Prime Minister's careful word choice would offend her. Then Frank continued.

"The moment you authorize this, a body double will climb aboard the Marine One helicopter we brought from the States and will fly him to a quiet evening at the Prime Minister's personal residence. Ten minutes later, you will climb aboard Major Beale's helicopter, presently in the country on a training and goodwill exercise, and we will proceed to the Beauchamp plantation with a minimal guard force."

Peter knew he was unqualified to make the final decision on this one, he was far too biased in favor of going.

"What do you think, Frank?"

———

It took twenty minutes, rather than ten, before Peter was clambering aboard a Black Hawk helicopter of the 160th SOAR. He wore a standard flightsuit and survival vest as did Geneviève and their two Secret Service agents. They blended in easily among the busy goings-on at the area of Noi Bai airport that had been reserved for the use of the visiting Americans.

The two Black Hawks were transport versions, but still had the two mini-guns manned. A half-dozen Secret Service agents piled into one. Frank guided Peter to the second one. Four seats had been arranged in the low-ceilinged cargo bay. His and Geneviève's facing forward, Frank and Beat sitting backward to face them. The two crew chiefs made sure they were buckled in. They were small, even for Special Operations Forces. They had their helmets on and visors down, but he'd bet these were Sergeants Connie Davis and Kee Smith. This was Beale's elite crew. He felt safer already.

They were barely buckled in before they were aloft. They had left the large cargo bay doors open, which was good. Even though evening was approaching, it was ninety degrees and about a thousand percent humidity. He'd been assured that even locals were wilting beneath the unusually warm weather for this time of year.

"Welcome aboard Army One, sir." Mark Henderson greeted him as soon as he pulled on a headset. It was the proper call sign for an Army helicopter carrying the President. Though it certainly wouldn't be announced to any Vietnamese flight controllers. "This evening we will be simulating a training flight to the mountains west of Vinh, Vietnam. We anticipate a quiet flight with the cooperation of General Chu Huang who created a no-fly corridor for this exercise. He did ask us to provide a special greeting to Ms. Beauchamp."

Peter glanced over at Geneviève, who merely smiled at him. A glance at Frank and Beat revealed they recognized the name.

"Okay, give."

Geneviève shrugged, "He was a cute boy. He used to carry my books in secondary school. But then he left me before third year for another woman. I was heartbroken."

"Why would any sane man ever leave you?"

"You have never met Lê Mei, Mr. President. I must make sure you do not. She was so very beautiful. They are married and have a boy and girl, I believe."

He tried to imagine someone more beautiful than the woman beside him, but could think of no examples. Then he caught the wistful tone of Geneviève's voice as she spoke of the children. He didn't know how he felt about that. With he and Katherine there had never been any question. Even when they were still sharing the same bed and he had thought they were happy, it was clear that she would never slow down enough to have children.

With Geneviève... It was not something they had spoken of, but he could imagine her with children. How would she continue her work, though? How would she do that if she stayed with him? The topic was becoming much too complicated, so he kept his mouth shut and put the thoughts aside to admire the view out the open cargo bay door. It was really too hot and humid to close it.

They climbed out of Hanoi, circling to the west. Vietnam was a sunrise country. All of its coastline, except a small area far to the south, faced the Pacific Ocean to the east. The sun rose from the water and set beyond high mountains. They were out of the city quickly. Even the suburbs surrounding a city of six million faded away soon into lush farmlands.

"I didn't realize there was so much wetlands."

"We are over the Red River Delta, a vast and very fertile region, Mr. President," Geneviève pointed toward the ocean. "The coast is eighty kilometers away, yet Hanoi is only twenty-one meters above sea level, seventy feet. You really must do something about that. Do you know that only your country, Liberia, and Myanmar still use those English units? Even England has mostly changed over to metric."

"I'll make a note of that." He admitted that it was ridiculous, but knew it was a battle not worth fighting. Perhaps in his second term when tilting at impossible windmills was considered eccentrically permissible for the Commander in Chief. He looked down upon miles of lakes, rivers, and streams and fields. "There must be tens of thousands of bridges."

"More, I am sure, though I have never counted."

As the farmland decreased, the lush vegetation increased, soon the jungle was underlain by sharp ridges like none he had ever seen. As if the countryside was an entire mountain range, the valleys of which had been filled in by millions of years of silt. That, he speculated, was exactly what had happened. It made for a strange mix in his head. *Homo sapiens* had arrived here half-a-million years before crossing over to the Americas fifteen-thousand years ago. Yet, in sharp contrast, the land had a vitality, a life that sprang forth and covered the country.

The contrast of old and new should not have been surprising, but it was to him. Europe felt old and well contained, all so carefully groomed. Africa was ancient and weary, lost in arid wastelands and wild jungles. Here there was the vitality of a country constantly rediscovering itself, building itself anew, undaunted by past wars or more history than he could imagine.

The helicopter climbed up river valleys and over ridges.

"My family lives very close to Pu Mat National Park, which is the edge of the Highlands. We are at a hundred meters, though parts of the park are over a thousand. It was a rubber plantation that my ancestors started in the 1920s. When we returned after the Vietnam War, we converted it to coffee. It was a very large holding. One of the few that the North Vietnamese government was glad to preserve intact because of how well my family had managed it. We were welcomed back most kindly. We now own it as a cooperative in partnership with the state and the workers, and it is functioning very well. For example, Vietnam has a ninety percent literacy rate, better in the city, worse in the country. We pay for all of our workers' schooling. My family has always done that, so now we have close to one hundred percent literacy among even our oldest workers."

Peter looked down at the terrain. A wide river meandered through the low mountains. As they descended toward a large villa surrounded by tall trees, Peter could see the coffee. Hundreds of acres, perhaps thousands were covered in long rows of man-high bushes. A wide diversity of shade trees to decrease erosion dotted the hillsides like punctuation marks. Unlike the vineyards of France that climbed vertically up the slope, these swooped around the terrain like a living topographic map, vast level fields suddenly bursting upward as hills bedecked in horizontal wreaths of deep-green plants over red soil. He breathed in, half expecting a rich coffee aroma, instead tasting the thickness of the air so full of growing plants.

It was so beautiful, foreign yet familiar in some way, as if Geneviève had already biased him toward her country. She had biased him toward many things he had not expected even a few weeks before.

———

Peter stepped off the second helicopter into another world. They had landed in the front yard of the main plantation house. Tall, proud trees, that bore no resemblance to anything he was familiar with in the states, shaded the old plantation house. Even in the last light of day, he could see the mix of Western sturdiness in its two-story façade, squared windows and clapboard sides, enhanced with Asian details of ornate railings on the full-length porch, curlicues of the archway above the main entrance, and swooping lines to the roof. The siding shone a cheerful yellow. The roof was of dark, weather-worn wood shingle. What must have been a magnificent building a hundred years before had aged and grown stately rather than decayed.

He also couldn't help but notice the immense quiet as he dragged off his vest and flight suit. At first he'd thought it was merely because his ears had become conditioned to the helicopter's penetrating noise, despite the heavy headset. But as he listened, it was truly quiet. There were no cars, no busy Washington streets. Even Camp David, with its heavy patrols of Secret Service agents, was never so quiet.

"What are you listening to?" Geneviève came up beside him, but didn't take his hand.

"The sounds of your home." A late-nesting bird called in the evening light. Some distance off, he might have heard a horse whinny. "I'm not used to the quiet."

"It is something I forget about. I only miss it when I come home."

Despite their noisy arrival, and the sweep of Frank's team, no one came from the house to greet them.

"Maybe we scared off your family. I am a pretty scary guy after all."

"Nothing could scare off my family, Mr. President. They wait for you to enter as family, rather than to wait at the threshold as they would for a guest. Come, we keep them waiting and I'm sure they are shaking with excitement."

Peter was trying his best not to shake with nerves. It was ridiculous, but meeting Geneviève's family was turning into a far bigger fear than he had anticipated. Now he could appreciate some of her anger when his parents had simply dropped in. Though, he could almost wish for a similar experience himself, in over your head and then done with it. He'd had over a week for this to build in importance in his mind until it was a near to overwhelming tidal wave.

Beale and Mark and the others would be staying with the helicopters to help provide security, so no help there. He was on his own this time. Mostly on his own. He had told the dozen agents and the SOAR assets that they could secure the outside, but that he would trust to the residents of the house himself.

He took Geneviève's hand in his. Her slight resistance told him that would not be appropriate, but she would hold his hand if he needed her to. He placed her hand in the crook of his elbow, just as he had that first night at the National Christmas Tree, took up the gift he had brought, and they turned for the house.

As they walked to the house and climbed the dozen front steps, she told him some of her family's history so that he would have something to think about while he was panicking.

"My mother, Adele, was five when my family was driven out of the country at the end of the French War and they returned to France. She grew up there with her father who could not remain in the North Vietnam of 1960, as he was pure French blood and they were killing all of the French at that time. He did return at the height of the American War. My mother was eighteen and gone to college. He spent five more years with my grandmother, but did not survive the purges that came after the war. So I never met him."

She stopped two steps from the top to give him a moment and kept telling her story. He could kiss her for her thoughtfulness. He really had to remember how to breathe.

"My mother returned at twenty-five with my father, Henri, on her arm. They had me when they were thirty. She and Dad are very French, though they have been in Vietnam for almost forty years. Gram stayed here through the war. Even though she is a hundred percent Viet, we do not know how she survived the purges, but she did."

They set off again and reached the top step. The wide porch sported many chairs from a variety of lineages, clearly a common gathering space. A waist-high stone Buddha greeted him at the head of the stairs.

"I thought your family was French Catholic?"

Geneviève shrugged. "Just because we are Catholic does not mean we can't also revere Buddha."

Peter was just taking a breath preparatory to knocking, when Genny threw open the door, leading him inside and called out, "We're home."

She was, but he was totally lost.

———

"These are my parents, Henri and Adele." They traded cheek-to-cheek kisses and then quick hugs with her. They then each greeted Peter similarly, though without the hugs.

Geneviève had her mother's hair and fine features, and her father's length, that was easy to see.

"These are my sisters. They are both pills." A pair of brunettes came forward. They showed none of their Vietnamese heritage. Both would have been taken as French natives, fair-skinned and round-eyed.

"I'm Helaine. That is Dr. Ngô Helaine, M.D." Her English was American and reflected little of her native languages. "UCLA and University of Washington. And she only hates us because we are better than her. I work at the main hospital in Vinh. A hundred kilometers toward the coast. My husband, a doctor too, is in surgery. He sends greetings as he is unable to attend." Her handshake was Western as well.

The second sister subtly hip-checked Helaine out of the way. "I'm Jacqueline and Helly is wrong." Her voice was higher, making her sound like a Valley Girl with a pronounced French accent. She was also the most curved of the three sisters and had cheerfully curly hair and a tight blouse that revealed a fair expanse of cleavage.

"Gen-Gen hates Helly because when she arrived, it ruined Gen-Gen's chance at being an only daughter. Gen-Gen hates me cause I got all the curves and she didn't. You're cute." She made a show of actually kissing Peter much to his surprise.

Then she winked to show she was just teasing her big sister.

"You should stay. I'm a doctor too you know. Business economics from the Sorbonne and Vietnam National University." Well, that belied the airhead image she projected. "We need another man here so that daddy can retire. How would you like to marry into the family business?"

She started to move in again, but thankfully Geneviève just shoved her aside with little ceremony. In revenge, Jacqueline stuck her tongue out at her big sister. Henri trapped his youngest daughter in a friendly headlock to forestall further rounds between the siblings.

Peter didn't know what to expect of Gram Kim-Ly Beauchamp, but it was certainly not the woman who strode up as if parting the Red Sea that was her family. Geneviève had said she would be eighty soon but she certainly didn't walk that way. The trim woman barely came up to his shoulder, but it wasn't because she was stooped. She appeared strong, almost athletic, apparently just arriving back home from a day in the fields managing the coffee crop.

A black dog stood at her side, stout, strong, and not friendly looking. That must be Dais, which meant Bear in the Hmong language. Geneviève had described him as sweet, gentle, and a stone-cold killer when needed, though primarily of unwanted rodents. Wonderful. That made him feel so much better.

The woman who clearly ruled the dog wore sturdy boots that were well used, gray khakis, and a white men's dress shirt with long sleeves rolled up to her elbows. Her gray hair hung straight and long. Here was Geneviève's stunning face and amazing green eyes aged, mellowed, and grown wise with time. Beauty, while it had touched on the other three women in the family, had mostly skipped a generation to land squarely on this woman's eldest granddaughter. If not for the decades between them, Gram and Geneviève could be twins in all but height and the brush stroke of Adele's finer features.

"So, this is your President boyfriend." She folded her arms and bowed her head slightly to him. Her English was lightly French-accented.

"I am Ms. Beauchamp. I'm pleased to meet you." He did the same obeisance in return.

She stared up at him for a long moment. The room went silent. Even the dog stood still.

Peter half wondered if Geneviève was holding her breath. He would wager that she was. That's when he realized he was as well. Then he huffed it out and laughed before he turned to Geneviève.

"You're right. Your grandmother is deeply scary."

The others in the room laughed as well in understanding ways, though Gram's expression changed not even a little.

"And it is a trait," he turned to address the matriarch again in a more serious tone, "that you have very successfully passed on to your namesake."

Still the woman looked at him. Then she spoke to the dog, "Dais. Zaum."

The dog, who had been standing at alert and worrying Peter some fair amount, dropped to his haunches and his tongue had lolled out. He shifted from looking like a knee-high, angry, and dangerous bear, to a knee-high, not angry but could attack in a second, working dog.

"I think, young man, that you should call me Kim-Ly."

Geneviève's hand, somehow once again in the crook of his elbow, which had been clamping down painfully hard, abruptly relaxed, then squeezed again for a moment in reassurance.

"In that case, Kim-Ly, you must call me Peter. Especially as your granddaughter will not."

———

The meal had been long, and wholly untraditional. Mother had set the formal dining room, but Gram had vetoed that, declaring Peter as family, and they had moved to the big rough table in the kitchen. Genny had to fight back the tears. That Gram would so approve of him on first meeting meant that Genny was not going crazy. Of course, it meant... She really was not going to survive this day. She'd been able to feel Peter's nerves, but been able to do little to help him as she'd been in an absolute state of panic since the instant he had suggested coming here. Throughout the evening, Genny had been on the edge of cheering, laughing, or weeping. Or perhaps all three at once.

It had taken mere minutes from their arrival until it was as if Peter had sat a thousand times at the family table. And Genny's emotions were all over the map about that as well throughout the meal.

At least the order of the dishes made sense for a change. Normally at the Beauchamp table, there was no predicting what would be done and served first. They began with Jacqui's Vietnamese spring rolls, wrapped in nearly translucent rice dough. They had beef *Pho* followed by Gram's notorious Chicken Curry on Rice Noodles. It had left Peter so bright red and sweating so profusely that she hoped he didn't have a heart attack from the spicing.

It was perhaps the best meal Genny had ever barely tasted, all the familiar flavors of home. Every joke that came even close to her relationship with the President made her twitch. She couldn't remember from the beginning of one sentence to the end of it, what the subject might be.

Some remote part of her observed, *So, this is what an American means when they say they are totally freaked out. How interesting. I am indeed totally freaked out.* And that simple statement of fact about her emotions, well, it was freaking her out.

Jacqi swore that she'd made *Bánh phu thê.* Genny had searched the kitchen high and low for the South Vietnamese traditional "Husband and Wife" cakes so that she could throw them down the back steps. Instead, Jacqi had actually made Genny's favorite, *Bánh rán,* deep-fried sesame rice balls. They should have been an awful combination when served beside Peter's gift of American maple syrup-flavored fudge. But somehow, when combined with enough laughter and a fresh pot of decaffeinated coffee, they had tasted wonderful together.

Peter couldn't say enough praise for the coffee. At first everyone had assumed he was just being nice, but she knew better. She could tell when he was being disingenuous, and this was not one of those times. His sincerity became unmistakable when he began taking a real interest in their issues with exporting to the Americas. He begged them for at least a periodic care package that he would hoard in his own kitchen.

As the evening progressed, Genny wondered how to get her grandmother aside. Even after the meal, no one wanted to leave the table. There was a warmth, a friendliness that pervaded the room.

Genny passed through desperate and panicked on her way to resigned. She would just have to let go. Perhaps a phone call would be best, later in the week, or maybe next year. No, that was only two weeks away. Maybe the year after that. Though she had wanted to feel her grandmother's touch and see her as they spoke, but there was clearly no time for that to happen tonight.

So, Genny listened as Peter told the story of their first attempt to cook together which set off the smoke alarm in the Residence kitchen. He'd burned the French toast and she in turn had scorched the hot chocolate so badly they'd had to throw out the pot.

"Now," Gram announced as she rose to her feet at the end of Peter's story. "I must talk with my granddaughter. And then you, Mr. Peter President, must return to your plane before you are missed. Come, Genny." Gram turned for the door and, that simply, it was accomplished. Genny shuffled after her, feeling as if she were about twelve and was soon to be scolded.

———

Genny caught up with her grandmother exactly where she'd expected. Gram stood before the Weeping Wall in what had originally been the plantation's front parlor. Though connected to the family living room by a curved arch, it was wholly different in character. Favorite chairs and stacks of books and board games gave way here to a state-of-the-art office. The cooperative was managed from here, workers and their families welcomed right into the main house if they needed anything.

Now, in the light of a single lamp, all of that was but shadows. Desks, phones, copiers, computers, none of that mattered. What mattered was the powerful woman and the wall covered with hundreds of photos, each memory preserved in a small wooden frame.

Genny came up beside the Beauchamp matriarch, wrapped her arm around the old woman's waist, and rested her cheek upon the gray hair. For a long time they stood and looked at the pictures. Generations of images adorned the wall.

She and her sisters growing up in pink pinafores and in traditional *áo dài* white dresses with circular *nón lá* leaf hats. Working on the farm together. Three pre-teen girls going off to school together, each two years apart. Even at that age, she had been the tall, gawky one, Jacqi rounder and smiling mischievously, and Helaine the serious one constantly trapped between them. There were dozens of photos of the three of them together through the years.

There were also photos of her sisters graduating, Helly working in a hospital operating room, Jacqi at her first computer. Helly with her half-Viet, half-Lao husband. Jacqi with many different boys.

And photos of Genny. Some she knew, some she didn't. A series of her wearing her blue *vophuc* fighting uniform and a progression of belt colors. As the colors changed, so did she, from a young girl to a woman grown. But there were also photos of her at World Heritage Sites talking to reporters, and even one of her arguing a case to the U.N. Security Council just a few weeks ago, a grainy shot that must have been captured from an Internet news site.

Her mother and father were there as well. Henri typically in the office with Jacqi looking over his shoulder, or more recently working beside him. Adele dressed like Gram, the two of them working the cooperative and a succession of Hmong dock-tail dogs accompanying them into the fields.

Uncles who had died during the purges were here, as well as aunts who had died while fighting in the American War. And in the French War before that. And even her great, great granddad who had fought the guerilla war against the Japanese.

Gram and Grand were there too, mostly working the plantation before the war. There were pictures of them at their two weddings: one Catholic, one traditional Vietnamese.

"You looked so beautiful, Gram." The photo was black and white, but that did nothing to hide the rich splendor of her robe or the perfect shape of the circular *khan dong* rising from her hair like a crown of gold.

"As you will at your wedding, my dear," Gram spoke in Viet.

Genny looked at the Weeping Wall. At the wall that could make you weep for the pain of what was lost and at the same time for the wonder of what was gained. The wall always made her feel so full inside. As if, knowing where she came from, she could do anything.

"Right there," Gram pointed at a blank section of wall. "That's where I will put the photo of the day you marry the man you love."

Genny turned to look at her, as much as their arms around each others' waists allowed.

"But, how will I know, grandmother? I don't understand that."

"It's simple, child. You already know. It will just take you a little more time to find out that you know. But you will get there. And soon I will put up the photo."

Genny once more rested her cheek against her grandmother's hair and breathed in her rich smell of the farm life she still led. Of coffee and fan-palm, of jungle and river. Of home.

She studied the blank spot on the wall that Gram had chosen for her. Genny did not need to close her eyes to see the image that would hang there.

Her grandmother was right.

Genny already knew.

———

They spoke little on the flight back. The night and the helicopter were dark. Peter sat with his arm around Geneviève, holding her as close as he could without crushing her to him. And, as well as the headset allowed, she rested her head on his shoulder.

"Your family is wonderful," Peter had set them to have a private intercom but they had been mostly content with the silence. "Though I feel a touch of pity for whatever man Jacqi finally decides on."

"We all do. But for all that, she is an alarmingly sensible woman. The cooperative will continue very well under her management for many years. She loves the business, even more than mother. Maybe as much as Gram, if that were possible. I often think it is the only thing that grounds Jacqi on this planet."

More miles passed in silence. Peter was trying to assimilate Geneviève's family, to see them for who they were, rather than for the whirlwind that had just filled the last few hours of his life. Like digesting the gigantic meal they had prepared that still left his appetite feeling deeply content, he knew it was not something that could happen quickly.

"Your grandmother is everything you said and more."

Geneviève nodded her head against his shoulder.

"What did she say to you?"

Geneviève shook her head this time. She had been very quiet after her talk with her grandmother. Deep in thought. Not remote, just quiet.

"You are so like her."

"I am?" That brought her jolting upright so abruptly that her headset caught his chin and he bit his tongue hard.

"Ow! Yes."

"No, Jacqi is—"

"Like your father mixed with a California surfer girl right out of a Beach Boys song. Helaine has your mother's serious streak, those are two very formidable women. I still can't believe your mother came back while the re-education camps and long marches from the cities back to the country were still going on."

"But I'm not like Gram. She's—"

"Exactly like you. There is a peace and a centeredness to your strengths that runs so deep and so wide that you two are the great rivers others flow into. How's that for an appropriate metaphor while flying over the Red River Delta?"

They were approaching southern Hanoi now. By the city lights that washed into the night sky, he could see Geneviève staring at him. But not at him. It was as if she were staring at a reflection of herself in his face that she had never seen before. He found it so obvious that he wondered how she could not have known.

They swung around the western edge of the city on the last leg of their flight back to Noi Bai airport. The broad river was a dark anchor to the bright lights of the scattered skyscrapers and the busy city at their feet.

These were his last moments of being Peter. He could feel the Presidency lurking on the ground below him, waiting there like a crouched beast. Or like a mantle that, once pulled back over his shoulders, would change him. Change who he had been these last few hours with Geneviève and her family.

"There's something I need to say, Geneviève. Something while we are still in the air and I am not back to being the Commander in Chief."

She looked at him. Her focus changing from the reflection of herself back to that peaceful waiting she created so effortlessly for him.

This shouldn't be said over headsets and an intercom. But neither did he want to take them off and have to shout to her either, only to have her cup an ear and shout back, "What?"

But they were on final descent, and he had to speak while he still felt like Peter. He kissed her lightly on the lips, her widening eyes catching the airport lights and revealing their rich green as she guessed.

Did she hope, or fear? Well, there was only one way to find out.

"I love you, Geneviève."

Her kiss and the taste of her tears were the only answer he needed.

CHAPTER ELEVEN

Preah **Vihear Temple was** located at the northernmost edge of Cambodia, close to Thailand. It was over an hour-long helicopter flight from where Air Force One was parked at Phnom Penh International. They could have parked much closer, Siem Reap airport by Angkor Wat was within thirty minutes flight. The shorter runway would limit the take-off weight of the plane, but that could be compensated for with partial fueling. However, Peter had deemed it more politically appropriate for them to land in the capital city.

There he'd had lunch with both the King and the Prime Minister as well as key members of the Cambodian Parliament. Then, with their U.N. Ambassador and Deputy Prime Minister aboard, they had flown north on Marine One.

This trip was vastly different from the flight to Geneviève's, this was a full-on Marine Corps operation. Two VH-60N White Hawks, heavily armored versions of the Sikorsky Black Hawks, were the main flight. They jostled about, exchanging places in a shell game until no one except the pilots and their passengers knew which craft was which.

The Royal Cambodian Air Force provided a pair of their Aero L-39 Albatross ground attack jets to fly escort, and flight controllers had cleared a corridor twenty kilometers wide. Frank's briefing had selected this site, from the several Geneviève had suggested, as being the lowest-risk and most defensible for a Presidential visit. It had also been Geneviève's preferred location for cultural and political reasons.

"So, Ms. Beauchamp," Peter thought it best to keep it formal in front of the other officials, though any idiot would be able to see they were hopelessly crazy about each other. "Could you bring us up to speed on this site and UNESCO's involvement in it?"

Peter sat as he usually did in the White Hawk, in the sole, forward-facing armchair. Directly across from him, the Cambodian Deputy Prime Minister sat in the other armchair facing the back of the helicopter. The small couch running along the other side of the cabin included the Cambodian Ambassador to the U.N., the U.S. Assistant Representative to ASEAN, and Geneviève, as the Southeast Asia Chief of Unit for UNESCO World Heritage Convention.

He had to keep reminding himself of that. She was so close, her knees practically brushing the side of his seat. She wore a skirt that came to just her knees. It was snug, but elegant. So easy to rest his hand on her knee, which would be unfair to her position of status among the others.

Frank sat in his typical spot, in the jump seat directly behind Peter's armchair. This helicopter, unlike Emily's SOAR craft, was well enough sound insulated for them to talk without headsets.

"Well," Geneviève leaned forward, exposing the line of her neck.

Peter considered slapping himself, but knew it wouldn't help. There hadn't been a moment for them to discuss how she could possibly continue her career and be with the President of the United States. But it didn't matter. That she wanted to was all the answer that mattered at the moment. They had agreed not to tell anyone, neither staff nor family, until this trip was over. That would be only three more days. By then they should have figured out what to say to everyone.

"The temple is over a thousand years old, a masterpiece of the Khmer Empire, as is Angkor Wat, their capital city." She spoke easily, her voice engaging. "It is perched on a narrow promontory of the Dângrêk Mountains. This has caused both Cambodia and Thailand severe problems over the last century. The escarpment that separates the mountains from the Cambodian plains over five hundred meters below, was to be the line of the border. More correctly, the line of the watershed was to be the border. There were maps drawn in 1907, placing the temple and one of the approaches to it in Cambodia and another approach in Thailand. But the watershed line, had it been followed, would have placed all of the approaches in Thailand and only the temple itself in Cambodia. In 1962 the International Court of Justice became involved and ruled that because Thailand had not protested the border as drawn for almost sixty years, the 1907 map was valid and would stand."

Deputy Prime Minister Pok made an emphatic nod.

Peter had to force himself to remain focused on his guests. Geneviève had warned him that they would be entering a murky and emotional area when they discussed the border. But a fresh coup in two different African countries had cost him most of last night between the dinner with Geneviève's family and this flight. He'd crashed into his cabin for only two hours, pleased to see Geneviève asleep on one of the twin beds when he did so. She hadn't woken when he kissed her on the forehead, and she'd been awake and gone by the time he crawled back into his office.

"Yes," Pok insisted, nodding again as if it would make his statement more real. "It is the property of the Kingdom of Cambodia, just as is Angkor Wat. The Khmer Empire became Cambodia and it is rightfully ours."

The Cambodian Ambassador to the U.N., Moul, or was he Muy, looked apologetic. He thought it was Moul, but Peter would just have to be careful not to say his name until someone else did.

"I would not contradict the esteemed Minister Pok." Meaning the man had his facts totally wrong. "Suffice to say, the temple is on Cambodian soil, despite being atop the escarpment. Despite numerous international mandates and agreements, the Thai government places border stations and police barricades on these roads. They often close the road that is our only access to a piece of our own country. At other times, we have free passage."

"Yes," Geneviève stepped in before Pok, who was clearly getting ready to build a righteous national-pride argument, could begin. "Preah

Vihear, a UNESCO World Heritage Site since 2008, represents both significant cultural pride as well as substantial tourist dollars. And the argument over this balance is beyond the purview of today's discussions, Mr. President." But she addressed the last to Pok, clearly a reminder of exactly who was important in today's visit.

"UNESCO is attempting to work with both governments to set up a free economic zone that is shared by both countries. The International Court has required both Thailand and Cambodia to withdraw their troops from the area. The two governments agree only that they can't withdraw unless the other does so first."

"It is Cambodian land, why should we move first?" Pok felt that completed his argument.

"We're flying into the heart of a military stand-off?" Peter glanced back at Frank not giving a damn if the officials heard. Better if they did, it would emphasize that the President of America felt they needed to get their act together.

Frank's deep voice carried forward easily. "Last shots were fired in February 2011. Forces remain in the area, but there have been no more hostilities since that time. Both Cambodian and Thai commanders have assured us that we will have a peaceful visit. They each separately stated that it was to our advantage to have so much military security in such an unusually remote locale."

"It is further suggested," Geneviève picked up without missing a beat "By the UNESCO Director, ASEAN Director, and concurred with by the U.S. State Department, that a site visit will demonstrate international commitment to a peaceful solution."

It was almost as if she and Frank had rehearsed the handoff from security to veiled threat of U.S. and U.N. military involvement. Peter glanced at Geneviève's carefully neutral expression. He'd learned to read that face over these last weeks. Yes, she had clearly planned that last speech which had Minister Pok squirming in his seat. He had to remember not to mess with her.

"We're approaching the site. We have been cleared to land at the end of the temple grounds, as the most readily securable location," the Marine Corps pilot announced.

Peter looked out the window. He tapped the intercom. "Could you circle once please?"

The pilot swung wide, keeping Peter's window toward the view. The flat plains of Cambodia which had climbed just a few hundred feet in the three hundred miles from the coast were chopped off by the Dângrêk Mountain escarpment. The Preah Vihear Temple itself was perched on a narrow promontory that reached half a mile into the plains compared with the rest of the rise.

"How—" He cut himself off before he could continue. It made no sense. The temple was atop the escarpment, the rest of which was Thailand. How this little piece had been snipped off and given to Cambodia must have a background story. But it would be very impolitic of him to call the Cambodian claim illogical, especially sitting with the country's Deputy Prime Minister and U.N. Ambassador.

But Geneviève had read his question anyway. "The original agreed border was the watershed. If it drained north, it was Thai. The temple grounds drain south. Then a line was drawn on a map a hundred years ago by people who had never been here and much of the north-draining land, including the crucial access road, were given to Cambodia. Now, it is a part of the area's history. Would you, Mr. President, be willing to give up Point Roberts?"

"Point Roberts?"

"In your Washington State. It is a tiny piece of British Columbia land that sticks into the middle of the Straits of Georgia. This piece of Canadian peninsula is technically United States soil because a line of the forty-ninth parallel was drawn as a border between your country and Canada in 1846. Would you be willing to give that up?"

"You make your point, Chief of Unit Beauchamp." How carefully had she prepared for this meeting? What was just a one-hour stop-and-admire visit for him had been intense preparation by how many skilled people?

Together they turned back to the window. The temple was a long line of exotic stone buildings stretching half a mile along the crest of the promontory. "They really do look as if they belong to the land."

"Yes, sir, you have a good eye. This is not only an exceptional sample of Khmer Empire architecture, blending to both the stone and the site. It is also a very pure site, culturally. Due to its remote location, it was abandoned for hundreds of years after the fall of the Khmer Empire in the 1400s, preserving the design from future depredation. It has suffered more in the last fifty years than in the five hundred before that."

"What happened fifty years ago?" The helicopter circled over the Thai jungle, and he could see what he assumed were Thai Army vehicles stationed along the highway. A dug-in camp lurked farther back in the trees. A glance back revealed that Frank Adams was also observing them very closely.

"The Khmer Rouge, Mr. President." Pok and Moul both looked grim at even the mention of the name of that brutal piece of their country's history. Two million or more had died on the Killing Fields of Pol Pat, a quarter of Cambodia's population. Only Vietnam had stood against him, for which they had been internationally reviled. It was moments like this that made his heart hurt. How could he work to help improve a planet which was capable of such events?

———

Genny stayed close by the President as they toured the temple. The helicopters had gone back aloft to provide additional protection. A line of Secret Service agents had secured the entry. Other than a half dozen agents, the two Cambodians, and the dozen news people who had been authorized to join them after an arduous land journey of several hours duration, they were alone.

"You are beautiful. You belong in such places." The President's whisper was barely enough to reach her ears though they stood but a pace apart. Frank was next closest, and appeared to be listening to his radio.

"You are 'deeply enamored' and therefore also deeply biased. It is this place that is so beautiful, Mr. President. It is a sad horror, the things that occur here. This was the last place of resistance against the Khmer Rouge, the last holdout before Pol Pot destroyed this country.

It was also the last place the Khmer Rouge held, when Vietnam finally defeated them."

"Well, it is very defensible."

"It is also very steep. It is where in 1979 the Thai government drove forty thousand Cambodian refugees from the Khmer Rouge off the cliff to 'send them home.' Ten thousand died on the descent, or in the mine fields below. This is not a happy place, Mr. President. But it is an important one."

She led him to *Gropura IV*. "There is no building like this one left in the world. It is unique, and now it has been damaged by the gunfire between Cambodia and Thailand."

They stood side-by-side in the knee-high grass and looked up at the temple before them. The gray base rose person-tall in broad horizontal layers of curved and lined stone. It stretched ten meters wide and over fifty long. The roof was long gone, but square columns a meter through reached several stories into the air, holding an equally massive lintel of stone as easily now as it had for a thousand years. At either end of the *gropura* stood a massive crown of carved stone another half-dozen meters tall.

"That such a thing, older than Angkor Wat, should still be standing is a miracle."

"What does it mean?" Peter took her hand.

"You shouldn't do that, Mr. President, we are being watched." But he kept his hand in hers. He had decided they were a couple, and apparently no longer cared what anyone thought. Did she? Not enough to withdraw her hand.

"What does it mean?" he kept his voice even.

She looked around. Pok and Moul were enthralled to have such access to American news services and were making the most of it back at the Second *Gropura*. Only Frank and Beatrice were close to them. Several other Secret Service agents were ranged between them and the rest of their party.

"Preah Vihear was a temple built to Shiva, the Hindu God of Transformation, of Beginnings and Endings. It was a place of worship and meditation. We have also identified those two buildings," she pointed back the structures to either side of *Gropura III,* "as libraries. This was also a place of learning."

"Transformation, you say?"

"Yes." Once again she attempted to recover her hand. "You really should not do this in front of the reporters. It is not seemly for the President to be seen so with a woman to whom he isn't married." She lifted their joined hands and began peeling back his index finger.

"I plan to marry you, Kim-Ly Geneviève Beauchamp, if you'll have me. So, I think the American press will simply have to get used to it."

Genny struggled for a moment longer until his words sunk in.

"You...What?" Her ears were ringing. The vast silence that was Preah Vihear had suddenly been filled with a roar louder than a typhoon upon the ocean that lay five hundred kilometers away. She was suddenly glad for Peter's hand holding hers so that she didn't simply collapse to the ground.

"This is a place of transformation, is it not?"

Genny found a nod somewhere, but her voice was gone.

Peter turned to look at her with those soft warm eyes of his. He took her other hand. Her only anchors in the whirling storm about her, his two strong hands. Then he dropped to one knee before her.

She might have heard Frank Adams in the background say, "Oh shit!" But it was hard to tell.

"Will you have me, Geneviève? I don't know how we will live together, but I know that I cannot stand to live apart."

She made her living with words, with being able to handle and manage any situation. In this moment she had lost any words and could only nod her head and see Peter's answering smile.

Frank Adams shouted something in the background.

Then he tackled her from behind and drove them all to the ground.

CHAPTER TWELVE

 enny lay dazed for a moment. Had she just agreed to marry
the President of the United States? She had. Peter had asked
and she'd said yes. Okay, she'd nodded her agreement, but that didn't
make it any less true.

Then someone had tackled her.

Frank.

He'd slammed her to the ground.

He rolled off her and now lay on top of Peter. Then Beatrice
slammed down onto Genny.

"I wasn't trying to kill your President. I was only saying I marry
him. Would marry him," she corrected her English.

She struggled to sit up, shoving at Beatrice, who didn't give way.

"Damn it! Lie still, Ms. Beauchamp!" Beatrice's voice was clipped,
hard.

"That's supposed to be Genny..." But she didn't get much energy
behind it as she became aware of what else was happening at Temple
Preah Vihear.

Gunfire above them.

And, she looked skyward, a green-and-white Marine helicopter
spiraling down out of the sky.

CHAPTER THIRTEEN

Peter **had at least** seen Frank barreling toward him a moment before he crashed into them, but it hadn't soften the blow. Geneviève had flailed into him and Frank had driven them both into the grass.

He knew of only one reason Frank would do such a thing.

Sure enough. Gunfire. Up in the air. All the scenarios, all the lectures about domestic crazies and international terrorists did nothing to prepare him for the shock.

Someone was trying to kill him. He didn't know which was worse, the cold fear that swamped him, or the terror that they might kill Geneviève instead.

Even as Frank rolled over to cover him and Beatrice moved in to cover Geneviève, Peter could see at least some of what was happening. One of the escort planes had shot down one of the Marine One helicopters. Flames coming out of her engines, the helicopter was spiraling down toward the ground, the pilot clearly fighting to perform an autorotate landing.

Even as he watched, the second helicopter was struck. The crew chiefs were fighting back with rifles, but were no match for the fighter jet. They were close enough to the ground, that though they pretty much fell out of sky, they didn't have far to fall. Still they rolled and tumbled until they fetched up hard on part of the temple. A huge stone block high atop a column teetered, wobbled, and then settled without falling.

"I've got to move you, now!" Frank grabbed his shoulder and dragged him to his feet.

Geneviève was still struggling to free herself from beneath Beatrice.

"She's coming with us."

"No time, Mr. President." Frank pulled at him again but he resisted.

"My fiancée is coming with us!"

"Fiancée?" Frank stared at him nose-to-nose for two heartbeats as he digested the information, his fist still clamped in the shoulder of Peter's suit jacket. "Got it. Beat, up! We're on the move!"

In moments, Peter had Geneviève's hand clamped in his. The two of them stayed low and sprinted behind Frank.

The plane, having finished the helicopters, now strafed the people on the plateau, scattering them like chaff.

Frank dove behind a low temple wall. Peter dragged Geneviève down with him as he did the same.

The scattered Secret Service agents returned fire, but handguns and small rifles against a jet served as little more than a distraction to the pilot.

Then the agents grouped together and moved away.

"Hey, shouldn't they be coming to help protect us?"

"Mr. President," Frank had his gun out and was scanning the sky and ground for other attackers. "Per training, they're pretending they already have you with them to draw the aggressor's fire. Now shut up, I'm busy trying to save you."

Sure enough, the plane took another run at the cluster of agents moving toward the entrance of the temple complex.

Frank was calling into his radio. "Merlin unharmed. Continue to distract."

The plane fired a rocket that impacted a low stone wall a hundred feet away, close to the clustered agents. There was a roar that pounded against Peter's ears and a ball of fire. Fragments of rock whistled through the air, he saw two agents drop to the ground.

Then a second plane dove in.

It attacked the first.

"He's a renegade!" Peter shouted to Frank. It would fit. One plane doing his job, but the other one hijacked for the attack. Target of opportunity.

Frank nodded, "But why would they want to kill you?"

"They don't." Geneviève crawled up to face Frank. "Injure, perhaps. The pilot could easily have placed that rocket in the center of those agents. I think that the President is wanted alive, as a bargaining chip. The question is by who?"

Peter looked at her. Her hair was a mess, her lip was bleeding, and her hands scraped raw, but she didn't seem to care about that. Instead, she looked pissed, and calculating.

"Cambodians?" Frank was watching the two planes dogfight above, but he was clearly paying attention to what Geneviève had to say.

"No. The President is a guest of their country. You saw how offended Minister Pok was by Thailand's claims to the temple. Nationalist pride. He'd never want to harm the President while he was a guest of Cambodia. Thailand?"

Peter finally saw it.

"Yes, Thailand. And not some random terrorist. This is government sponsored, or at least a faction of it. They hijacked a Cambodian fighter jet to attack us. If he survives the Cambodian jet's attempt to protect us—"

An explosion shattered the air above. A ball of fire exploded just past the edge of the escarpment. A shattered jet spun downward in flames. No pilot ejected.

"Which was that?"

"The Cambodian, sir. One Thai fighter is still aloft."

"Then, if Geneviève is right," Peter kept an eye on the plane. "He will make one or two more runs at us for show, wounding but not killing. After that, he'll be shot down by the Thai Army forces we saw stationed beyond the entrance. But they'll shoot him down over Thai soil so that he has a chance to parachute to safety."

"Then," Geneviève picked up the story. "Then they will come to capture you, killing all of the Cambodians. They will claim that they saved you and use it as an excuse to attack Cambodia, if not in war, then in the international courts."

"Which means," Frank glanced at his watch. "We have about three minutes to get you off this plateau, Mr. President."

"I know the way!" Genny spoke as if she too were one of his trained agents. "But I need a *couteau*. A knife."

Frank looked at her in confusion as she held out a palm. With a shrug, Frank produced one from somewhere.

Geneviève used it to slit the side of her skirt well up her thigh. She handed the knife back to Frank.

"You own me a new skirt, Mr. President."

"I'll buy you a wedding dress, Geneviève."

She flashed him a smile, then was off and running.

Peter made to follow, but Frank stopped him with a hand against the center of his chest.

Frank stared him straight in the eye. "You trust her?"

"A hundred percent. And she's Southeast Asia Chief of Unit for UNESCO World Heritage. She knows this site better than anyone here."

Frank processed for an eyeblink, then nodded.

Then Peter, Frank, and Beatrice sprinted after Geneviève.

CHAPTER FOURTEEN

*"**T**his is crazy!" Beatrice* shouted in Genny's ear.

The agent had caught up, but let Genny lead as they dodged through the temple grounds. Now, they were holed up by the water cistern below *Gropura II*. They were twenty meters below the main temple level. She'd worn low-heeled shoes knowing they'd be walking around the site, but wished she'd worn sneakers. She tore the slit in her skirt a little higher, she should have slit both sides.

"The Thai Army is about to storm the entrance," Frank arrived with Peter close beside him. Then he pointed to the north. "And the Cambodian reinforcements are going to be coming up the road to the west. That's where we have to get, but you are leading us down to the east. Why?"

"Because we aren't using either road."

Genny focused on Frank, knowing it was him she had to convince.

"There are a few dozen Cambodian fighters near the entrance gate. They hold the high ground above the entrance stairs. These are veterans, if the Khmer people know anything, it is war. The Thais may be a better equipped, more modern army, but the Khmer will hold their ground for a long time despite being vastly outnumbered."

Frank nodded as he acknowledged her assessment.

"And the nearest reinforcements are probably in Angkor Wat. That's an hour away, even under the very best of conditions, which these roads do not ever have. The nearest air assets are in Phnom Penh, an hour away, if they even are aware of the attack."

"They know. If Beale tells them. I reached her and she's enroute overland."

Genny felt better for that. But overland meant Emily was still in Vietnam and would be at least an hour away.

"We need to keep the President safe from the Thai Army for at least an hour and I know only one way to do that."

She could see Frank weighing factors.

As if on cue, the hijacked Cambodian fighter plane made one more strafing run, this time clearly firing hard on the Cambodian positions at the *Gropura I* entrance. Then, the Cambodian return fire must have scored a hit, as the Thai forces would probably be missing the hijacked plane on purpose, just firing for show. The jet wobbled in the sky as if it had stumbled and tripped, then it caught on fire. Moments later, well into Thailand, the pilot ejected and a white chute opened up almost immediately.

"Bastard!" Beatrice cursed beside her.

"You need to decide now!" Genny ordered Frank and gritted her teeth. She did know what was best.

Frank looked at the President.

"Hell of a woman you chose, Mr. President. Congratulations."

"Thanks, I know."

CHAPTER FIFTEEN

Peter *followed his "hell* of a woman" as she led his Secret Service detail to the northeast through the trees. They struck down-slope whenever they could, avoiding both the cliff edge and any sight lines to the Thai forces above.

Frank reported that most of his Secret Service squad was joining with the Cambodians in defense of the temple. Only one of the six Marines from the two helicopters was uninjured and two were dead.

"You know that the Thais will simply claim it was one renegade Lieutenant or something, gone crazy and acting on his own. When we insist on having the pilot, they will conveniently claim that he was killed trying to escape." Frank's voice was grim.

"Doesn't change where the U.S. will be placing their voice on the international scene. But first, you've got to get me out of this alive."

"Not me. It's up to your girlfriend there."

Genny broke for the next group of trees, sprinting like a gazelle. Her legs, impossibly long, flashing from her skirt, her hair flying behind her like a banner.

"Well, if I'm going to go running after something Frank, it would be hard to find something better than that."

Frank clapped him on the shoulder and they sprinted off together.

CHAPTER SIXTEEN

"**There is a stairway** there," Geneviève was pointing at a spot another hundred yards along the escarpment. "Two thousand steps down the cliff face and we will be in Cambodia, far out of the reach of the Thai. Even a parking lot with room for Emily to make her landing."

Peter looked out over the edge of the escarpment. "That's like a two-hundred story building, right?"

"You have better idea on how to save your life?" Suddenly Geneviève displayed a new side to him. This was a woman out at her limits of confidence, terrified that a single mistake could kill them all.

"Anywhere you lead, I'll follow. That's a promise."

She took a deep breath, huffed it out, and nodded once, blinking hard. Geneviève turned to survey the next stretch. "But you should have instead a guarantee made," she added without turning.

"Why?" What was she talking about?

"Guarantee is worth more points." Then she was gone to peek around the next tree. "Bad news as I expect."

"Promise" versus "Guarantee." No. "Promise" was more Scrabble points. Except "Guarantee" would most likely be played off an "an" so it would use all seven tiles. Their lives were at risk and the woman was browbeating him with Scrabble.

He started to sidle up beside her, but Frank shoved him to the ground.

"Two Thai soldiers guard head of stairs." Her syntax was slipping even more than usual under the stress.

"Can't shoot them," Frank observed. "Too long a shot at this distance with a handgun. But, more importantly, we can't have anyone else coming to investigate."

"You three stay here, but be ready in case this doesn't work." Genny pulled off her shoes and took off running in just her stocking feet over the grass and rock.

"What the hell?" Frank moved up to Genny's former position behind the tree, which let Peter move up close beside him.

"Should I?" Beat asked her boss.

"No," Frank shook his head. "She's gotten it right so far."

"Help! Help me!" Genny cried out to the soldiers.

Peter could see her sprinting toward the two guards who had raised their rifles.

She tumbled and fell to the ground.

Peter surged to his feet and it took both Frank and Beat to keep him in place.

Geneviève scrambled back up and kept running toward the guards as if panicked, though now she was weaving and limping.

The guards had lowered their weapons and were moving toward her, perhaps thinking this was one of the hostages they wanted. Little did they know how true that was. But she was now much closer to them. There was no way to help her. What was she thinking?

"Please! Help!" Her cries were softer with distance, but she sounded winded as well. What if she'd broken a rib in her fall or...

Twenty feet from the first guard, she shifted into a clean sprint. At ten feet, she leapt into the air. Even later Peter was never able to fully credit what he saw.

Genny lifted into the air as if jerked aloft by a steel cable from the sky rather than just a leap with strong legs. A heel struck the first soldier's chin so hard that his head snapped back cruelly. She used the gained momentum to wrap her legs around the second soldier's throat in some sort of a scissored headlock flipping him over backwards and smashing him to the ground.

Frank, Beat, and Peter began sprinting to the scene in unison.

Even as they did so, he could see her force her knee up and the soldier went limp.

The first soldier was just sitting up, looking dazedly for his rifle when Frank tackled him from behind.

Peter saw the man's neck twist, then break as he rushed by.

Geneviève still lay with her knees wrapped around the second soldier's throat.

"He's done, honey. You can let go." The man's eyes were open but there was no one left to look out through them.

"No, I can't." Her voice was tight. Thin.

"Are you hurt?" Peter knelt down to check her over.

"No. Not much. But I can't." Tears were starting from her eyes and he didn't know what to do about it.

Frank came up to them, and slowly unwound her legs from around the dead man's neck, pulled her skirt into some semblance of order. Beat dragged the corpse clear then began stripping the two soldiers of their weapons.

Frank squatted down until he was looking right at Geneviève. He wasn't saying anything, just looking at her. In such a rush since the moment that the first helicopter had been hit, he'd suddenly gone quiet.

"What was that, anyway?" Peter had never seen anything like it.

"Việt Võ Đạo," Frank said softly not looking up from the silently crying Geneviève. "Flying scissor kick." Then he held a hand out and helped her to her feet.

When she was standing, he nodded once.

"Are you okay to continue?"

She nodded, but clearly couldn't speak.

Peter wrapped an arm around her, she was stiff. So stiff. As if she were made of steel not flesh and blood.

Frank addressed her once more, "Let's all hope you never have to do that outside of the dojo again, but you did it when it counted. And you did it perfectly."

Then he turned to face Peter.

"She just killed a man to save your life. Not many can do that. Even fewer can stand back up afterwards. I can only hope to God that you never have to try it yourself. You take good care of this one, Mr. President, or I'm going to have to hurt you. We clear?"

Peter looked into those dark eyes, and didn't doubt for a second that Frank meant exactly what he said.

"**Y**ou've got to save me!"

Daniel pretended to hide behind Peter while looking back over the crowd of guests filling the White House State Dining Room. Men in suits, women in elegant gowns. Daniel, as his best man, wore a very smart dark-gray tux which complimented his own black one. Even among the crowd, Peter could easily spot First Lady Kim-Ly Geneviève Matthews, a shining light in the swirl of the people gathered about her.

"What's the problem?" he asked without taking his eyes off the vision before him.

"Genny's sister Jacqi won't leave me alone. Keeps talking about dragging me back to her woman-cave, whatever that is."

Peter dragged his eyes away from his wife to inspect Daniel and squinted at him for a moment.

"You'd make a cute couple."

"You're not helping," Daniel snagged two flutes of champagne from a passing waiter and handed one over.

"She knows you're married, right?"

"Sure, even introduced her to Alice."

"And..."

Daniel took a deep swallow from the narrow flute. "Alice and Jacqi are negotiating using me on a time-share basis."

"Tell Jacqi that three months is my best offer. Can't spare you more than that."

"I'm not a damned condo."

"Sorry, buddy, best I can do. I have to go and be Presidential."

"Meaning you have to go ogle the woman you just married."

"Hard not to."

"Especially in that dress."

Peter didn't bother to reply as he headed into the crowd.

———

"Okay if I interrupt?"

Genny couldn't take her eyes off Peter as he approached where she stood with Emily and Gram.

Mrs. Genny Matthews. The sound of it was both intensely foreign and equally perfect. It was a statement of who she had become and where she wanted to be. His black tux and white tie gave him an old world elegance.

"No," Em shook her head. "She's ours. She'll be yours the rest of your lives. We get her a while longer."

Peter slid a hand around Genny's waist, pulling her tight beside him. He kissed her on the temple and whispered in her ear, "I love you."

She melted every time he said that.

"Easy there," Emily teased Genny's husband. "The night's still young and she looks too perfect. No mussing her up yet, Sneaker Boy."

"Sneaker Boy?" It was like a galvanic shock coursing through her body.

"Sure," Emily nodded toward the man even now threatening to undo Genny's hair from the elegant coif atop her head. "Tossed him in the Reflecting Pool out on the Washington Mall ages ago. All he could do was whine about his sneakers getting all wet."

"Wet and muddy," Peter clarified as if in his own defense. "And she didn't mention that they were brand new, too."

"Sneaker Boy?" Genny knew she was repeating herself, but it was really too perfect. It started as a smile, but it turned to a giggle. A high one that she just couldn't stop. Not until she had laughed until she cried and gotten wet spots all over Peter's lapel when she hugged him, could she finally speak.

They were all looking at her strangely. Smiles on their faces even though they didn't know why.

"Gram, you remember the one I told you about, on the computer?"

"Yes. The one who plays such good games." Her grandmother smiled as if she'd known all along. As if there was no question that the world worked this way.

"Do you want to tell my husband what our shared name means?"

"Well, if you are Sneaker Boy, of course you had to marry Kim-Ly." Then Gram poked Genny's new husband in the ribs to emphasize the joke. "Our name means Golden Lion."

Peter simply looked stunned. "All of those games we played on-line at the Scrabble site, and you are the Golden Lion?"

"It fits her does it not?" Gram suddenly glared at him and he blanched.

"It's perfect. Just as she is. Perfect."

Gram nodded as if making sure he understood that last point clearly.

———

Peter kept nuzzling Genny's neck as they danced around the State Dining Room floor. Though it was a warm day in June, it was their first dance as a couple after all, Peter had made them play a Christmas carol.

"It is the wrong carol," she told him though she didn't really care. "This is not the first one that we danced to."

"I couldn't remember what it was. I could only remember the first time I held you in my arms."

She kept her head on his shoulder and let him tease her. It had been such a perfect day. They had married where they met, out by the National Christmas Tree, now just a tall spruce awaiting next year's decorations. It was a huge affair that had drawn an astonishing crowd of well-wishers. A near-death experience had made the President even more popular. In Thailand, a right-wing faction had been stripped of all power, the left using the excuse of the trumped-up attack to perform a major housecleaning of the ranks. Maybe now there was a chance for peace at Preah Vihear.

Tomorrow, she would go to her office in the East Wing. Despite Peter's offers of a role in the Department of the Interior, she had decided to stay with UNESCO. The Director had created a position specifically for her. World Heritage Convention Ambassador to the U.N. Her mandate, to be an advocate for the Heritage Sites with the hundred-and-ninety three member nations' Ambassadors.

The First Lady's office had been converted to a tech center that would let her reach around the world, flying an hour to New York only when essential meetings occurred.

Maybe when Peter retired, they would move to New York or perhaps Paris, so that she could be near the UNESCO headquarters.

For now, she simply let herself float in the arms of the man she loved.

"I'm not sure how much longer I can stand it, until I get you out of that incredible dress."

She knew exactly how he felt. Peter looked so glorious in his tux.

"Well, Mr. President husband, there is only one way that is going to happen."

"What? If I deport everyone in the room?"

"No." She looked up into those dreamy eyes and kissed him as they danced. She could hear the cameras snapping away and simply didn't care. She was too happy.

"No. The only way the President of the United States will get the First Lady of the United States out of her dress, is if they are standing in the middle of the Oval Office."

She rested her head back on his shoulder as he groaned quietly.

Yes, a perfect day indeed.

ZACHARY'S CHRISTMAS

__Vice President Zack Taylor's__ political career thrives—his star shines brightly. The only thing missing? Someone to share it with.

__Melanie Anne Darlington's__ brother embraces the White House career he was born to do. Unfortunately, Anne's own future shines as clearly as a snow globe blizzard on a dark winter's night.

This holiday season, each day opens a new window to the vista of both their futures in Zachary's Christmas.

INTRODUCTION TO ZACHARY'S CHRISTMAS

Busy with other projects, it would be two more years before I returned to the White House.

I missed the White House. I missed the decorations at Christmas. I hadn't checked in with many of my favorite characters in what seemed to be forever.

After the long hiatus, I browsed back through the various White House stories. All of the way back in Daniel, I ran into his sister: Melanie Anne Darlington. All I really knew about her was that she came from one of the South's first families—a long-time Kentucky farm—and she had a penchant for sending her brother lewd Christmas cookies.

I saw the potential for a little brother– big sister conflict, but that wasn't really the story I wanted to tell. Despite the four years between us, my sister and I had been more likely to pull together than push apart when confronted with the craziness that was our family. So, I didn't want to play up that aspect... instead, I wanted to find her love interest.

As she didn't work at the White House, she had to fall in love with someone there. I didn't see Anne as a political figure, so that limited her options.

Then one day I was out poking around in the back forty—looking up some weird fact in The Night Is Mine *for another project—and I stumbled on a character that I had rather liked, but had completely forgotten about. In* The Night Is Mine, *Vice President Zachary Thomas of Colorado puts in an appearance so brief that it can only be called a cameo. As a matter of fact, we only see him on TV and he never speaks a line—even if he is, supposedly, near the center of a conspiracy.*

He then languished in office for a number of years—as Vice Presidents of the United States are prone to doing. Now, I had rediscovered what little there was written of him.

To discover who he was, I actually had to turn back at his pending love interest.

Anne's brother, Daniel, had originally come to Washington, DC to seek national attention to the Slow Food movement and his farm's role in promoting it in America. Slow food is the opposite of fast food, focusing on local cuisine and products.

I tried that on for size. And while the Slow Food movement originated in Italy, it wasn't enough for me to hang a major crisis on, especially not one that would engage the attention of the Vice President.

However, the crisis of global warming certainly was significant enough. The impending disaster that awaits us in the melting icecaps is sufficient to cause alarm. Of course the naysayers are almost as vehement in their denial as the doomsday predictors. That, I felt, was sufficiently contentious ground for my Vice President. And being champion of the cause would definitely be attractive to Anne Darlington.

Anne's disaffected attitude at the opening of this book was also something I was familiar with. There have been times in my life where I have felt so helpless that I don't even know where to begin. Perhaps the worst of those was after the series of personal and career events that eventually launched me on my bicycle trip around the world. Options kept opening up for me, but they were too foreign to my way of thinking at that time to be comprehensible. I gave Anne that moment, sitting in her brother's White House Chief-of-staff chair.

The higher cause that would eventually break her from that frozen place where every action feels simultaneously pointless and hazardous, I didn't discover until I was very near the end of the book.

I have tried writing from massive outlines, white boards covered in connected-circle mind maps, and stacks of shuffled index cards. I've tried redrafting over and over to discover a story—once going through nine complete drafts that utterly destroyed the spontaneity of the story hidden beneath it.

Now I write more slowly, my thoughts rarely slipping more than a scene ahead to test the waters along with my characters as I go.

In that state of utter dismay, leading a North Polar expedition can make as much sense as being a White House Chief of Staff. (Um, you'll see what I mean when you get into the first scene of the story.)

However, to Zack's and Anne's good fortunes, I have also learned that every now and then, if you listen and look carefully enough, the answer is self-evident. Especially when that answer is finding the right person to be with.

CHAPTER ONE

Brother, *is it ever* tricky to break into this place," Melanie Anne Darlington plummeted into her sibling's office chair. Then she had to scrape her hair out of her face; long hair and a thick parka complete with a furred collar and hood kept trapping her behind a blond curtain. She'd never been good at being a woman of mystery.

Daniel would know of course, that his big sister was dropping in for an unannounced visit since the moment she'd hit the outermost layer of White House security. Not quite like the old days when she could drop unexpectedly out of the hayloft and scare the daylights out of him—a joke that simply never grew old—but there was still satisfaction to be had. And she'd come accompanied by her own personal White House guard—looking very spiffy in his blue uniform and white hat—just in case he didn't welcome the "surprise."

"Hey, Sister. Where's your rifle, Anne? I assume you're hunting polar bear in that outfit." His lazy Tennessee accent was more diluted by Washington DC every time she saw him and it made her feel even more alone than she already did, which at the moment was saying more than a thing or two. But his smile was warm as always and that helped some.

"You will *not* be insulting my parka. It's never seventeen degrees on

December first! Don't you gentlemen pass laws and sign bills against precisely this kind of travesty?" The city was cloaked in ice and a recent snow.

It had looked magical from the airplane and the cab, with all the landmark buildings popping up out of the vast whiteness as if they themselves were formed of snow. And signs of Christmas had been everywhere, from a tiny wreath above baggage claim to giant fake candy canes on street lamps to the massive National Christmas Tree on The Ellipse.

Once afoot though, the cold had cut right to the bone. But if Daniel thought he'd be getting away with insulting her attire, he had another think coming.

Of course Mister Cover-of-*GQ*—the blond boy-genius turned White House Chief of Staff by the age of thirty—would never think of wearing a parka. His corner office glowed a warm orange with the setting sun. Her own little brother had a southwest-facing corner office in the West Wing—that was completely crazy. The only sign of Christmas from here was a massive wreath on the Eisenhower Executive Office Building across the street. The White House hadn't been decorated yet.

"I'll have them draft special legislation just for you. Would you prefer a military escort with portable heaters?"

"Now that be sweet of you," the Tennesseans' way of calling someone a jerk in public, "though maybe if you selected a few particularly hunky ones, that would have some nice possibilities." She slapped her hand against her coat's thick padding, "If the apocalypse hits tomorrow, this is going to be far more practical than one of your three-piece suits and designer-Ralph wool coats, City Boy. Besides, how am I supposed to hunt a decent bear, even a stuffed one for Christmas, when they've confiscated my popgun at the front gate." She waved a hand at the guard who had escorted her through the last leg of her journey. "Do you think the spiffy soldier will lend me his sword if I bat my eyelashes?"

"He's not a soldier, he's a Marine, and I think he'd be crazy if he did." Daniel looked up at the man in question. "We're fine here, Jeffrey; you'll want to escape while you still can. She's a man eater."

The Marine saluted and, in a flash of humor that she suspected was rare for a White House honor guardsman said, "Thank you for the warning, sir." He did a neat turn on his heel and marched back out into the hall to his post outside the Oval Office, his boot heels sounding smartly against the hardwood flooring.

"Am not a man eater."

"Are too."

"Am not," she looked up over his shoulder, "am I Mr. President?"

Daniel startled to his feet and she belatedly rose to her own as Peter Matthews strode in through the side door of Daniel's office. The President was a tall, handsome man with dark hair and lively eyes that always made him look even kinder than he already was.

"Hello, Anne. You been out moose hunting?" He came around to offer her a friendly handshake. He earned additional points for recalling that she went by her middle name.

"Sir, between you and my brother you are two of the handsomest ex-bachelors around, but you share the same lousy sense of humor. I'll talk to your wife about fixing that for you."

"Trust me, Genny has tried," the President dropped into the other chair and she and Daniel resumed their own. It still startled her every time he did something like that; Peter Matthews always had time to be pleasant.

"If you two have something to talk about, I can go upstairs and see you later." But the President was patting his hand in the air for her to stay in place.

"Nothing that won't keep. How's the farm?"

"It's..." She was finally warm enough to unzip her coat. Toying with the zip gave her a moment to steel herself before confronting Daniel. It was what she'd come to DC to talk to him about. Gently. After testing the waters very carefully. Daniel had always been crazy about the family farm. By some strange chance, that was what had led him to DC and the White House. Even here in the Chief of Staff's office— when the historical decorators offered him a selection from the greatest works of art—he'd put up four big panoramas of their family farm, one in each season.

The rest of the furniture was ornate, classic, probably from some period of history they'd tried to teach her about in high school when she couldn't care less. Memorize the facts, spit them out, get the A, forget them. The only incongruous part of her brother's office was his desk. The piece itself was a majestic piece of cherrywood, but a battle raged upon what little showed of its surface with no victor yet proclaimed. File folders in a rainbow of coded colors teetered against other stacks of plain manila. Thick-bound volumes bore official looking report titles that were gleefully driving the lone computer monitor inch by grudging inch toward its doom off the edge of the desk.

The only reason that she could tell it was cherrywood rather than battered old plywood was a small, carefully walled off corner that contained only two objects. A beautiful Advent calendar with only its first door opened stood stout guard over the wedding picture of her brother and Alice now-Darlington III—the coolest sister-in-law on the planet. A top CIA analyst, she was even smarter than Anne's brilliant brother. Their wedding on the farm had been...

The farm.

Sighing that things never seemed to go quite the way she intended, she turned to face the President.

"The farm sucks, Mr. President." She could see Daniel jolt upright out of the corner of her eye so she turned to face the problem head on. "The farm is jes' fine, baby brother. So relax yourself some. It's only me who is going madder than a hatter. You were built for that place; I wasn't. The foreman, the manager, Ma and Pop, the streaming hordes just begging to work at the cuisine training center on the model Slow Food farm of the entire Southeastern US—none of them need me there."

"But you did all of the Thanksgiving events and it was amazing."

"Thanks. And I'd rather shoot myself with a popgun than go through it again." She'd done the grand hostess gig for the Darlington Thanksgiving—the fanciest affair on the farm's annual event calendar. Dinner for hundreds, not a Tennessee Congressman who hadn't been invited along with his family. She'd made sure that *Food and Wine* as well as the key food bloggers had not only received the recipes, but invitations to the banquet as well. It had been a grand affair and Anne had been at the center of it. That was one of the things that had driven her to escape the farm now, Ma and Pop had been pushing her to take on the estate's entire event division and she'd...run away. Real mature, but there was not a chance that she'd be telling her little brother that.

"I'm bored shitless," which was also true. She could do these big events in her sleep now, and she couldn't imagine feeling less excited about anything.

Daniel flinched at her language.

Maybe she had gone a little too far considering the company. She turned slowly to face the President. "Sorry sir. You may not know this, but I was raised on a farm. I speak that way far too often for Daniel's liking. I failed my kindergarten training to be a polite Southern lady and never recovered."

"A farm, really?" He offered in mock surprise. "I grew up in DC. I'll trash talk with you any day you want."

She knew from various visits over the last three years since Daniel rose to Chief of Staff that Peter Matthews could barely say "darn" without blushing and her brother wasn't all that much better.

"You're on, sir. Some night we'll each have a beer, which is about my limit anyway, and we'll choose a topic. Maybe you," she pointed at her brother. "We'll make him attend but won't let him speak. I'll tell you childhood horror stories, like the first time he kissed a girl—she was six and he was seven, the mad womanizer—I'm the one who caught them."

"And you haven't let me live down Becky Carpenter yet."

"Hush now. I'm not talking to you, I'm talking to the President," she kept her attention on Peter Matthews. "You can tell me Washington stories. I still don't understand how my dirt-loving brother ended up at the center of power and I ended up at the center of whole passel of dirt."

"Just lucky I guess," Daniel growled. "I'd trade this in a heartbeat, if —" He bit his tongue.

It was an interesting moment. The President had gone very still. Anne considered gunning for Daniel while he was down but decided that was too cruel despite her big-sisterly responsibilities to harass him whenever possible.

"If what, Daniel?" The President's tone had gone soft and difficult to read. "I wouldn't be the first President to run through two Chiefs of Staff. Do you want out?"

"No, sir," he immediately replied. No doubt, no equivocation. Her brother had grown a real spine while she wasn't watching—which only made her feel all the more lost. Like an elf kicked out of the Christmas workshop for painting candy canes pink and black, but who had nowhere else to go because Santa's workshop was indeed at the North Pole.

"If what, Daniel?"

"It's an honor to serve and—"

"He did grow up on a farm, didn't he?" The President turned to her, interrupting Daniel. "I'm from DC but I know when someone heaves a shovel of horse crap at me."

"*That* was horseshit, Mr. President. And yes sir, my brother is slinging it." She turned back to Daniel, "Maybe I should become Chief of Staff and you should return to the farm. Neither of us is where we want to be."

"Give it to me straight, Daniel," the President spoke in his this-bill-will-pass tone that was so effective on national TV.

Daniel dug his hands through his hair, actually mussing it up. Anne was sorry she'd trapped him enough to make him feel that way, but she didn't know how to take it back in the current situation.

"We're doing so much good here, Peter," Daniel had dropped the honorific, which she could see surprised the President more than anything that had come before. Then Daniel did finally blush. "Sorry, Mr. President. I came to DC to help jumpstart the Slow Food movement, farm-to-table. I came to promote fresh, unprocessed ingredients that are farmed rather than GMO agri-business. I had never imagined what I've ended up doing here. It's amazing and I love it!" He started picking up folders off his desk. "The next G-20 meeting. The Southeast Asia trading pact. Watershed restoration. I wouldn't want to miss a single day of it."

"But you miss the farm that," the President turned to her, "your sister hates."

"I do, Mr. President," they said in unison with exactly the same intonation.

———

Zachary Thomas typically went directly from his office to the Oval Office when visiting the White House. President Peter Matthews had made it clear that his Vice President was to be barred from no meeting and was always welcome there. VPs had so often—and occasionally notoriously—been kept out of the loop, that even after five years Zack couldn't get used to the privilege. There were VPs who had never once used their office just next door to the Chief of Staff's. The bulk of his own staff worked across the street in the Eisenhower Executive Office Building, but he was in the West Wing at least a portion of every day.

He heard the President's laugh from Daniel's office, so he turned in rather than continuing down to the Oval. Janet offered her typical teasing smile—that of a woman on the verge of retirement who had offered more than once to run off to Tangiers with him—and waved him through.

"If only I were a few decades older, and we were both unwed," he told her. Janet had aged very well, but he'd met her very attentive husband.

"We need to be finding you a wife, Mr. Vice President. Or I will leave poor James for you."

"I just might take you up on that, ma'am. Best warn him to start looking." They traded winks then Zack strode up to the threshold.

Peter Matthews was the first President since Polk in the mid-1800s who wore his dark hair casually long—LBJ's gray coif had only appeared after his retirement. It made Peter look boyish and handsome, aided by being the youngest President ever elected. The gray that came with the office was only beginning to show. Daniel, his Chief of Staff, wore his blond hair short, but he had that California surfer-boy handsomeness despite his Tennessee farm heritage. Neither had the military bearing of having served, though it was hard to fault the choices the President had made over the years.

Zack was more of a tall Colorado boy—Colorado Springs born-and-buttered. It was a distinction little understood outside the state and one used carefully inside the state. His hometown had shrugged off almost all of its early counter-culture roots except in small outlier enclaves like Manitou Springs. Now it was known for one of three things: the US Olympic Training Center, the Air Force Academy, and headquarters for over fifty Evangelical churches. When spoken in-state, Zack only had to add one word, "I'm from The Springs...Academy." That was a whole conversation had, and answered. Out-of-state, he just said "Colorado" without even mentioning the city's name. It was easier that way.

Daniel sat as respectfully as always, perhaps sitting so carefully upright in order to be seen across the prairie-sized expanse of paperwork he called a desk. The President remained in his chair, looking more relaxed than Daniel, but proper as always.

Beside him, in profile, sat a woman with a beauty as surprising as Daniel's. They were obviously related, so this must be the sister he'd heard tales of but never met. Melanie Anne Darlington. Daniel's rugged handsomeness had been translated into her fine features; his short blond hair transformed into a sun-streaked cascade that spilled down over the furred collar of her oversized parka.

The mood in the room was an odd mixture. Daniel was confused and perhaps angry. The President and Daniel's sister were both laughing, hers a bright spill on the air.

"Hello, Mr. Vice President," Daniel spotted him and rose, just as he would for the President. It was always a kind compliment that his predecessor had certainly never offered...before he'd been hauled off for treason on other matters.

The President glanced over, "Hello, Zack."

The woman turned and the full impact of her sparkling eyes, the darkest blue he'd ever seen, almost had him stepping backwards. Behind those beautiful features was clearly a very sharp mind. And her beauty while not of some fantastical portion, was all the stronger for the woman who lived behind them; she was vibrant. A massive parka hung open from her shoulders, but the bulk made it difficult to assess her figure.

"Where do I sign up?"

She looked up at him in surprise. She too had risen along with her brother but it was a fair way from his own six-two down to her five-foot-six.

"For the polar expedition that you're obviously leading," he clarified.

"Have to bring your own parka," her smile went from tentative to radiant.

"Done," he offered a hand and she shook it firmly. Fine fingers had nothing to do with this woman's obvious strength. "Zachary Thomas. But expedition leaders can call me Zack."

"Thank you, Mr. Vice President. I'll remember that. Anne Darlington, expedition leader." Then she turned back to the President. "See? At least one man in this administration has a decent sense of humor."

"Only happens around beautiful women,"—which she was and more. She had a much stronger accent than her brother, unmistakably Tennessee. Like a blond and slightly taller Holly Hunter who he'd always had a weak spot for in the movies. "You sound just like—"

"Don't you be doing that," she cut him off and shook a finger at him. "I do *not* sound like her. Not if you want to stay on my expedition. Besides, she's from Georgia. That's a whole different place," she pronounced 'whole' as if it had three or four Ls, exactly as Holly Hunter would have.

"Yes, ma'am," he saluted her sharply. Zack looked to Peter Matthews, "Should I come back later?" The tension still rippled about the room. Though no one had ever accused him of having a sense of humor before, she made him want to try. "In the meantime, if the lady would like, I can go out and rustle up a dog team with sled. That might prove difficult in Washington DC, but I'm willing to give it a go."

Again that laugh spilled forth so easily and brightened the room still further. Then she turned to her brother.

"Okay, Daniel, I'll make you a deal. One time offer, but you must decide right away. I'll go back to the farm, but only if I can take my team with me," she stepped over and hooked a hand about Zack's elbow to demonstrate their solidarity.

"I'm sorry, but you can't have him," Peter Matthews shook his head. "Zack still has a job here."

"With all due respect, Mr. President...Tough!"

Zack didn't even try to stop the laugh that come out of him as she faced down the President of the United States.

"This man here," she lifted Zack's elbow as if she needed to clarify which one, "applied, was accepted, and signed the ship's articles. He's mine now. Besides, I like his smile."

And when she smiled up at him, he couldn't help but return it.

"Hate to correct you, Ma'am. Truly I do," Zack should be backing away, this was Daniel's sister, but he was enjoying the little scene and the way her hand felt on his arm. "However, there are no ship's articles as I'm ex-Air Force, not Navy. And I regret to inform you that I did swear before the nation to uphold this Vice Presidential office as well as several other odds and ends. Like, oh, the Constitution."

"Traitor!" She let go of his arm, clasped her hands over her heart, before collapsing back into her chair as if struck down. "I've been betrayed. I suppose you may have him back, Mr. President. I wouldn't trust him though. Far too honorable. Unlike me."

The President waved Zack to a seat. The only open one was close beside Ms. Darlington, which was just fine with him.

"So, what are we debating?"

"Whether or not Daniel and I should trade jobs. What do you think?"

He could only assume she was joking, but there was something in the President's look that made him less than certain. Normally that would cause Zack to approach such a question with caution and diplomacy. But with Anne Darlington sitting beside him...

Clambering back out of his chair, he grabbed Anne's wrist, dragged her to her feet, and tugged her around the desk after him.

She giggled, which was awfully cute on her. So he went with it.

"Out, Daniel. Out!" Zack shooed him away.

Daniel remained paralyzed for a second, then, puzzled, scrambled to his feet.

Zack bowed toward the woman as if she wore an evening gown rather than a heavy parka, jeans, and craftsman-stitched custom-made cowboy boots which said just as much as a designer gown would have about who she was. The Darlingtons weren't just Tennessee farmers; they were one of the power families of the South.

"My lady leader, your chair awaits."

———

Anne curtsied, holding out the hem of her parka, before sitting regally in the seat as if on a throne.

She looked up at the three men.

Vice President Zachary Thomas utterly charming and terribly handsome in his role of momentarily playing the jester. He was tall, dark-haired, and wore one of those close beards that he kept at just a week's length. On his strong face, it looked mature and thoughtful rather than unkempt as most such beards did. She'd never much fancied a man in a beard, but the Vice President perhaps could convince her otherwise. His military background was easily seen in perfect posture, an inordinate strength for a politician, and a degree of self-assuredness that few men had.

The President still sat with an unreadable half smile on his face.

And Daniel remained on his feet, looking actively distressed.

Then she looked at the desk in front of her and began reading report titles: *Antarctic Climate Change Update. Southeast Asia—an analysis of potential armed conflict over China's latest Spratly Island militarization. Terrorist activity in...*

A bit overwhelmed, she looked up again.

The President of the United States still sat directly across the desk and was watching her with a carefully neutral expression. As if in some alternate reality he'd consider it if both she and Daniel said yes. There was an unnerving thought.

She'd never really appreciated what Daniel did before. He sorted, filtered, prioritized all this information into a form digestible by the man sitting across from her. It didn't look hard from the other side of the desk—but from here it looked impossible. And the responsibility of it was overwhelming.

Her kid brother stood there, shifting from foot to foot, a nervous habit he'd had since he was a little boy.

"When did you change so much?" It was barely a whisper, but it was all she could manage.

Daniel shrugged uneasily, as if uncertain what she meant. Maybe he didn't know how different he'd become; she almost didn't recognize him. The fine suit was the least of it. The beautiful and brilliant wife, the amazing job, finding a place he belonged in the nation's capital—in the heart of it. Taken altogether it was an alarming change.

Only that trademark shifting of feet—which she suspected only happened now in his big sister's presence—still identified him as the boy she'd known since birth. He was her very first memory. She'd been three on the day her brother had come home and squalled right in her face—the moment before burping up all over her. It was a day she had yet to let him off the hook for.

Well, she knew one thing about him in the here and now for certain. Anne rose to her feet. "*You* belong here. Right here." She swiveled the chair partly in his direction and moved away.

She shoved her hands in her pockets and pulled the parka tightly about her. A chill shivered through her and it was all she could do to hide it.

Yet another place she *didn't* belong.

"I'll just go up to the Residence. See you later, Daniel. Mr. President and Mr. Vice President."

She slipped out of the office, past Daniel's secretary, and wished she could pull up the parka's hood. Would have, if it wouldn't make every single Marine and Secret Service agent stop her as she crossed from the West Wing to the Residence.

She passed through hordes of Christmas decorators, all escorted by multitudes of Secret Service agents. The White House was transforming around her, but still she remained the same. She wished they could redecorate her so easily.

Anne plowed through and—more by luck than thought—found her way out of the West Wing and over to the Residence. For the first time in decades the Chief of Staff lived in the White House—the President had given Daniel use of the third floor. It was a holdover from the year when both Peter and Daniel had been bachelors.

Now the President, his wife Geneviève Matthews, and their little girl Adele lived on the second floor. Daniel lived on the third with his wife Alice.

And she lived...in a parka while wandering through the long halls of the White House. A few people eyed her curiously, but she made it to the elevator and up to the third floor without being stopped. At least that one thing had gone well today.

CHAPTER TWO

After *their meeting was* done, Zack Thomas swung through his office to gather his coat. He took the stairs down to the West Wing lobby. Clutters of rushing staffers dodged aside to open a passage for him. Heading up the stairs, the Communications Director passed him, in a deep debate with one of the speechwriters, offering a quick nod without breaking stride.

It was decorating day and while the West Wing didn't get the level of treatment accorded to the Residence, a stream of volunteers did what they could to remain out of the way while totting mantel swags, holly boughs, and curiously two of them carrying a child mannequin in a Victorian-era Christmas outfit.

"Please tell me that isn't headed for my office."

The young woman holding the mannequin's shoulders mumbled something about that being up to the West Wing Director of Decorations and moved on without recognizing him.

Zack seriously hoped that the Victorian motif was whimsical or even ironic rather than thematic to this year's decoration plan.

He finally reached the lobby, which the decorators had yet to reach and the congestion eased to normal levels of West Wing mayhem. With her impeccable timing, that he could only credit to her having him wired with a geo-locator when he wasn't watching, his assistant appeared from the opposite side of the lobby. She was dressed in one of her understated wool knee-length designer coats that looked so good on her tall, slender frame; the red wool a tasteful contrast to the dark brunette swing of hair that brushed her collar. She moved like an elegant VP-seeking missile through the heart of the crowd and they all stepped aside for her.

Cornelia Day held his coat's collar for him as he shrugged into it.

"What else do I have today? Anything pressing?"

She retained his entire schedule in her head, just one of her many daunting skills. "Surround yourself with people smarter than you," was the one rare piece of advice from his father-the-two-star-General. Cornelia was definitely one of those people. She'd served him since she'd interned for him as the Governor of Colorado, straight out of Claremont McKenna College—graduated at nineteen with full honors. He'd moved her to his full-time assistant four weeks later and six months after that he wondered how he'd ever survived without her.

"End of day wrap up with me. Not even a dinner meeting," she buttoned her coat as if the EEOB offices were far more than a hundred feet from the West Wing. Cornelia often complained about having to move from Southern California to Colorado to work for him. But her time there had prepared her wardrobe for the current Washington, DC cold snap. She added thin, black leather gloves and a cashmere scarf.

She indeed looked ready for a polar expedition—DC style. It would be hard to find a person more the opposite of Anne Darlington. Anne had looked storm-tossed when she'd retreated from Daniel's office wrapped deep in her massive parka. She'd frankly looked...miserable.

"Hit me with the short version."

"Seven a.m. breakfast with the present governor of Colorado. You asked me to specifically remind you not to call him an idiot."

But the man was.

"Simply because he doesn't agree with your prior policies," she read his expression easily of course, "does not necessarily reflect on his mental capacity."

"And yet he is."

She sighed and then nodded, her shoulder-length hair slid forward and back in a sharp slicing motion that emphasized her narrow face and dark eyes, "And yet he is. But your life at next month's fundraiser in Denver will be easier if you don't remind him of that."

"Got it. I'm going to make a call."

"Should I wait?" She already had her tablet out to make any notes he side-spoke to her.

"No. Go home for a change. Have some eggnog," and he briefly wondered what Cornelia Day did in her time off. Did she even have a life outside the office? "We're done for today."

She squinted at him momentarily. He could feel her attempting to peer inside his head and read his thoughts. He barely had a clear idea of them himself, so he wished her luck.

"Tomorrow morning," the slightly worried look didn't clear. "At the Hay-Adams, seven a.m."

At his nod, she moved off.

He crossed to one of the guard's desks. "Could you call the Residence for me? Third floor."

Anne wished Daniel would show up and answer his own damned phone; it had rung until she thought it might be a new and effective form of torture. She'd been on the verge of snatching it off the cradle anyway, her hand mere inches away when it had finally stopped.

She held her breath.

It didn't restart.

Counted to ten.

Still nothing.

She retreated to a seat in the Music Room at the top of the White House Residence and stared eastward. In the distance, a peek-a-boo view of the Capitol Building's dome was etched in yellow light against the darkening sky. The bronze Statue of Freedom atop the dome stood with her butt facing Anne; a fact she knew from past curiosity. Though the distance made it impossible to actually see the butt from here, she could feel it. Why wasn't this a surprise?

Tennessee. She'd just escaped Tennessee, but it was still awfully tempting to call the family plane to come right back and pick her up. Why did she think DC was going to be any better? Because it rhymed with Tennessee? Maybe she should try Gay Paree next—at least the number of syllables would match properly. All she needed was a time machine to take her back to 1920s Paris.

If she—

There was a discreet knock on the open Music Room door.

She glanced over her shoulder and then spun to her feet in surprise, almost catapulting herself to the floor. "Mr. Vice President."

"Team leaders are supposed to call me Zack. I'm fairly sure that was in the ship's articles."

"Typical Air Force, didn't read before signing. Why are you here, sir?" Not that she was complaining; she was inordinately pleased to see him. He was handsome, but not in the way of the President or her brother. There was a quietness to his face and a calmness in his bearing that the other two men lacked. He had thick hair, not long, but thick and nearly black. His light brown eyes were kind on an open face that reflected every emotion.

"Well, I tried calling, but you didn't answer the phone. Never going to get your expedition team put together if you don't pick up the phone when they call." He was leaning against the doorjamb in a comfortable slouch that not only made him look entirely pleasant, but also made her feel a little more relaxed.

"Not my phone. Though if I'd known it was you come a-calling, Mr. Vice President..." She would have...what?

"Well, it seems that we're stuck with the formality, doesn't it? Therefore I must ask myself what would cause Leader Darlington to relax?" He moseyed into the room; he really was from Colorado. Since when did a man mosey? When did it ever look so good?

Her pulse picked up a notch with each step he took toward her which was a completely ridiculous thing to happen.

He stopped a step away and looked down at her. "It seems that you have a problem, Ms. Darlington."

"I do?" Only a few thousand of them, but they were difficult to recall with him standing so close. Zachary Thomas was often listed atop those most-eligible-bachelor lists, not that she ever noticed such things. He was one of those rare men who had built a political career without being married or being eviscerated in the press when he did date.

"Yes," Zachary nodded to himself with a firm surety that didn't quite tip over into arrogance though it certainly was thinking about doing just that. "And I have the cure. Get your coat."

"I find that order a little preemptory for my taste, Assistant Expedition Leader Thomas. If you're taking me somewhere cold, you can find another victim."

"Somewhere warm, but you'll want the coat to get there. Besides, there's no point wearing such nice boots and not using them. They really are great boots."

She looked down at her cowboy boots. Classic Lucchese, understated dark-brown leather with elegant hand tooling and stitching. She used them hard, so they were a little battered, but soft as slippers on her feet. She'd mainly worn them to the White House to tease Daniel who had once lectured her for not wearing a nice dress and high heels when she visited. She hadn't worn high heels since her senior prom—when you were five-six, all heels did was make tall people think of you as a pretender. Of course tall women only wore them so that they could brag; Anne had banned them from her closet years ago.

She inspected Zack again. Maybe she'd just pretend to enjoy herself. If she did it long enough, it might catch on. But the military man needed to be taken down at least one peg.

"And the *order* to march?"

"Old captainly habits that will probably never change." At least he was honest about that.

She hooked her arm through his—a little alarmed at her own presumption, but not willing to look foolish by letting go immediately —and led him out into the Center Hall that stretched the length of the third floor.

"I'll need to fetch my coat. So, Air Force Captain?" she asked to cover her sudden nerves. "Is that good?"

———

Zack looked down at her in surprise. He always forgot how little civilians knew about the military. It almost made him regret this visit. But he remembered that lonely look as she'd left her brother's office and couldn't bear the thought of her sitting up here alone. Especially as Peter and Daniel still had a long list to cover before their day would be over.

"It's better than lieutenant, less than major."

"And nowhere near general. Too bad. I was hoping for a general."

"You wouldn't like it. Their star insignias are sharp and prickly."

"Whereas captain's bars aren't nearly as problematic? Which only matters if someone gets up close and personal," she let out a great mock sigh. "I was so hoping for a general."

He almost kept walking straight down the hall when she turned for a bedroom halfway down the north side. If she knew that a captain wore bars, she certainly knew where his former rank fell in the hierarchy of military officers. Zack made a mental note never again to underestimate Anne Darlington. And he had the sneaking suspicion that he would, many more times before he finally learned that lesson.

On the bed, an explosion had happened with only a small corner of a large knapsack protruding. She didn't travel with a fleet of suitcases and cosmetic bags and who knew what all women traveled with. By what was showing from the confused pile, she might have been heading out for the back country just as likely as visiting DC. He had the distinct impression that with Anne Darlington a man simply got what he saw without any games.

And once out of her parka, there was a great deal to like about what he saw. He'd watched her for a long moment before he'd knocked at the open Music Room door where she'd sat so still and at peace. She was neither some sleek urbanite like Cornelia nor a solid girl. Her cobalt turtleneck clung tightly to a balance of strength and femininity that he rather liked and he'd never quite seen so wonderfully melded before. When she'd spun to her feet in the Music Room and faced him, he'd been hard pressed not to do more than glance at her fine figure. Again neither sleek nor voluptuous, merely designed to rivet a man's attention if he had a single ounce of taste.

She gathered her parka and, turning, caught him staring at places he shouldn't be.

Mind out of the gutter, Zack. Daniel's sister. Yet he'd been the one to flirt with her, *prickly general's stars* indeed.

They picked up Harvey at the elevator—ex-football running back turned head of the Vice Presidential Protection Detail.

Impressively, Anne didn't flinch away. She must have become used to the tight security with her brother's escort.

As he and Harvey had ridden up to the third floor earlier, he'd warned Harvey that they might be going to the concert at the US Botanic Garden. It was perhaps the shortest notice he'd ever given to his security detail and he felt bad about that. But Zack wanted to surprise Anne Darlington. Wanted to see if he could erase that sadness. It didn't fit her well, like a bad choice in clothes. He still wasn't sure of the impulse that made him think he was the Santa who could wave his hand and suddenly she'd be cheerful once more, but he was here nonetheless.

He sighed. Actually, he knew where some of the impulse came, but getting on the wrong side of the White House Chief of Staff would not be a good idea.

"Harvey, please tell Chief of Staff Darlington that his sister has stepped out for a few hours." Which wouldn't begin to cover it if Daniel decided something inappropriate was going on, which there wasn't. He was merely taking a beautiful lady to somewhere warm, and a public concert.

And he decided to stop thinking about that either way before he was turning in circles worse than a helicopter with a shot-up tail rotor.

When the elevator reached the main lobby they picked up two more guards. Their dark suits and coats looked like dark blots on the explosion of cheer that had struck the Residence earlier in the day. Paper snowflakes the size of toboggans dangled from the ceiling. Trees almost invisible beneath storms of multi-colored ball ornaments cropped up around every corner. Any vertical feature, whether a column or archway, positively dripped with cheer. It was a very different White House than the years of Katherine Matthews or when a lonely President had lived here by himself.

They picked up another two agents plus a pair of SUVs when they reached their own vehicle. His traveling doctor and the serviceman carrying the Vice President's nuclear football—a nondescript leather satchel that contained forty pounds of the most effective communication equipment ever designed—rode in the trailing vehicle. Day or night, he was never supposed to be more than a few hundred feet from the football. One of his only two official duties: break a tie vote in the Senate and blow up the world if the President was out of commission and the US was attacked.

They climbed into their own SUV and the vehicle's heavy doors were slammed and locked. They would pick up the last of the escort at the outer gate.

"How many agents follow you around?" Anne's whisper barely reached him despite her sitting next to him in the back seat and the exceptional sound insulation provided by so many layers of armor.

"I'm afraid that's a state secret, Ms. Darlington. Strictly need-to-know."

"And I don't need to know. Don't even think I'd want to."

Her voice had become so small that he began to worry. A Secret Service escort was a daunting envelope to enter and he'd had five years practice, six if he included the run-up to the first election. "Truth be told, I don't know either. Unlike some protectees, I don't try to tell the Secret Service how to do their job."

"You were right though," her voice abruptly returned to normal as they headed out of the White House grounds and picked up a four-motorcycle escort.

"I was?"

"Shockingly, yes," and that initial teasing tone that had so captivated him at their first meeting finally returned.

"I'll alert the media. It's a first. Better yet, tell the President for me, would you? He'll be thrilled. What was I right about?"

"Getting out and about."

"I'm glad." *Yes,* he told himself, *being kind to a beautiful woman did work out sometimes.*

"So, these men and women all follow you wherever you choose to go?"

"They do."

"Excellent!" Anne slapped her gloved hands together. "We have a team now. North Pole here we come."

"That's a little farther than I planned for this evening."

"Spoilsport!" She may have stuck her tongue out at him, it was hard to tell with the little bit of streetlight that filtered through the tinted windows. "Could you at least have them turn up the heat so that it doesn't *feel* as if we're going there?"

That he could do.

———

Anne had assumed they were headed to some stuffy Washington museum or gallery that she'd already visited too many times on prior visits. She'd promised herself to present a happy face because it was a huge relief just to be out, under any circumstances, and away from her own whirling thoughts.

And it was deeply kind of Zachary Thomas. Rather daunted by the man escorting her, she'd gone right through panic and decided that her only chance at sanity now lay in the land of the ridiculous. The Darlington Polar Expedition had suddenly become the most rational part of her evening. A stuffy museum would get her back to reality soon enough.

But the first of the Smithsonian museums, then a second and a third were passed by. The National Gallery disappeared astern as well while their craft continued racing up the National Mall toward the Capitol Building. She'd thought a vehicle transporting the Vice President would be more...luxurious. Other than the surprisingly heavy doors—that she'd tried to close herself and was ultimately glad for the Secret Service agent's aid—the interior was no fancier than the Suburban they used on the farm to fetch important guests from the airport. However, the company now was stratospheric in comparison and her head was still spinning.

"Why are we going there?" She pointed up and ahead. "Lady Freedom has her butt facing me and I find that rather rude of her."

The Vice President ducked down and to the side to peer upward at the top of the Capitol dome. "How did I never notice that?"

"I thought men always paid attention to women's butts."

"Not when they're twenty stories up and made of bronze. Now, when they're as nice as y—" He bit off the words, but it was too late.

Harvey, the Secret Service agent in the front passenger seat, had a sudden coughing fit that sounded suspiciously like a laugh.

She didn't bother holding back and let her laugh loose. At least for a moment. It was cute that the Vice President had just been caught ogling her behind. It was even cuter that he was embarrassed. And then it struck her that he wasn't embarrassed because he'd been flirting; he had an obvious talent for that—one she appreciated and enjoyed returning. No, he was embarrassed because he had actually meant what he'd been about to say.

Anne started to ask the next question, but became very self-conscious of the two agents sitting in the front of the vehicle. Keeping her thoughts to herself earned her a couple of worried looks from Zack Thoma—*No!*—from the Vice President. Which thankfully was all he had time for before the agents announced their arrival.

She read the sign: United States Botanic Garden Conservatory. Large dark letters on a typical DC sandstone block building.

"Are you kidding me?" she turned back to the Vice President as the agent opened his door and he climbed out to the sidewalk. "It's night. The temperature is sub-Arctic. And you're taking me to tromp through a bunch of gardens coated in ice?" Even though she still sat on the far end of the back seat from his open door, the cold wrapped around her legs.

"The more fragile gardens are indoors," he had to lean down to continue speaking to her still in the car as she wasn't moving. "Trust me, they'll be warm enough for you to be removing your parka."

"So that you can ogle me some more?"

"I'll admit that is an advantage to the situation from my point of view. One that I assure you I hadn't thought of until this moment." His words sounded sincere, but she could see the hint of a smile exposed by the shining interior dome light that made her suspicious.

"Well at least you're owning up to it," and she didn't particularly mind that he wanted to; which was the interesting aspect of it for her. Usually men who stared irritated the crap out of her.

"Now can we move along?" He extended a hand, palm up, back into the car. "The Secret Service gets very nervous when I stand still out of doors, especially as this is an unscheduled visit."

If the Secret Service became nervous about having the Vice President exposed, then they were concerned about his safety...as in someone shooting him. She grabbed his hand and scooted out of the car. She was all set to drag him to the Conservatory's open doors. But she couldn't.

When she reached the sidewalk, she could finally see what the Suburban's roof had hidden. To her right loomed the massive dome of the Capitol Building with Lady Freedom's gowned backside on clear display. Directly in front of her, the Conservatory's massive front wall ended after a single story. Above it soared a myriad array of glass and steel greenhouses. There were angled ones, round ones, and in the front and center a gigantic tower of glass that rose a half dozen stories. Inside the glass were masses of foliage lit brightly from within like a science-fiction-in-space forest, all tucked safely beneath mighty glass domes that looked very Old World.

"If milady is quite done being a gaper..." Zack trailed off but the nudge was sufficient to get her moving. A circle of agents formed up close behind them and they hustled in.

"How do you learn to live with..." she waved a hand toward the dark night now safely on the other side of the closed doors, "...that?" Daniel's guard had always been fewer and looser on the rare occasions when they'd gone out on the town together. The size and tightness of the Vice Presidential Protection Detail emphasized the imminent threat that always surrounded him.

"You don't. At least I haven't. But we never talk about it either: the President, Daniel, or I. Odd, but there it is. Now, before us we have an adventure that requires neither sled dogs nor polar-worthy parkas," he waved toward a cloak room. "Shall we proceed?"

Anne sniffed the air tentatively. It was warm and didn't bite at the inside of her nose. It was also moist and rich with intriguing scents. The air hung thick with fresh soil, the clean scent of chlorophyll hard at work making oxygen, and foreign scents of strange plants.

While the building's facade had been nearly fortress-like, the interior was impossibly lush from the very first step. There were potted begonias dangling from the ceiling, thick with blooms despite the season. Massive variegated Algerian ivies of green-and-white reached up wrought iron lattices mounted on the walls, granite pathways led between planters thick with exotics where every step was a new adventure.

Anne had always thought she had a grip on at least the flora of the world around her. The Conservatory had been custom-designed to shatter that illusion. She knew food crops but these plants served no real purpose beyond being joyously cheerful. She would have felt sorry for them trapped in their Conservatory cage but that would lead to a dark place on her own account, so she focused on the plants instead.

Yellow iris and yellow azaleas she could pin down. The scarlet rose-mallow and the African tulip tree she only needed a quick peek at the name placards. The flowers made of bright orange vertical petals with sprays of white cups springing out of them like tiny water fountains mystified her. Lollipop flower—*Pachystachys lutea.* Nope. Not even a clue. But it was a jungle flower and she'd never been to the jungle—at least not until now.

The jungle grew inside the primary greenhouse dome and massive trees climbed upward to fill the space. Nor were there simply unfamiliar trees. Their branches also supported other growing and flowering plants, dripping orchids, perky epiphytes, and hundreds of butterflies—they were like Christmas painted by an inspired elf with a palette of a thousand colors.

As promised, the heat and moisture were lush here and she felt warm for the first time since arriving in DC. There was a pleasant crowded closeness that was lacking in the American wilderness. The only close comparison she had was on a research trip she'd done into the Louisiana swamp and that had a dense, brooding feeling. Combined with a brutal heat and humidity, the swamp was her least favorite place ever.

The other thing that had happened without her noticing was that her hand had remained looped through the Vice President's arm the entire time. A time that had passed in a surprisingly comfortable silence.

She looked up at him, "You're a very pleasant man to be around, Mr. Vice President."

"And you've become a very quiet woman."

"Sorry, but I do like plants. Each has managed to find a niche and adapt to it. Every one has its own story and I find that fascinating. That the gardeners have managed to make them all coexist under glass in Washington DC is one of the closest things to a miracle it has ever been my good fortune to see."

"I thought you were trying to get away from the farm," his voice was a tease.

"That's different," and she could feel her shoulders tightening up in self-defense as if she was about to be battered by a foul winter storm. "Can we have a subject change?"

"How do you feel about model trains?"

"About what?"

He pointed down as a small train wove beneath the leaves of a massive poinsettia before trundling across a wooden bridge and ducking into a tree trunk.

"What's a train doing here?"

"Did you also miss the buildings?"

Anne followed his finger as he pointed. DC was on display here, but hidden. Intricate copies of dozens of landmarks worked in wood were tucked here and there among the foliage, tiny windows brightly lit from within. A reproduction of the Capitol Building stood not five feet away and she hadn't even noticed it among the incredible foliage.

"It's no more than knee-high to a rose bush."

The building's great mass had been reduced down, but it was intricate and elegant in dark wood rather than its true white stone. She leaned in and squinted at the tiny Statue of Freedom. "At least this time her butt isn't facing us." A different train trundled by—the engine blue rather than red this time and a long line of boxcars—looping around the Capitol before heading back the way it had come.

Then she glanced over at the Vice President. He was watching her.

Not her body, but her face. And he was doing so with a look of surprise.

"What?"

"You really didn't notice all this? It's the best part of their yearly display. I try to never miss it."

"Played with trains a lot when you were a child?"

He faked an innocent look that didn't work at all. "Might have," then his face sobered. "The big layout in the basement was the only thing that Dad and I really did together growing up. Mostly me. He was deployed or here in DC most of the time."

"Why didn't you move here?"

"Mom's life is in the Springs. Her parents and friends are there. She's deeply involved with the Olympic Training Center as well—silver medal in freestyle swimming and a gold in team relay. It was hard on her when I followed in Dad's footsteps instead of hers, but I can only see that in retrospect. She encouraged me every step of the way. She was a good mom in a distracted sort of way; her life was at the OTC, not at home."

Anne hugged his arm briefly to her side in comfort. It felt so natural to be walking with him this way. Like the trains and model buildings, the Secret Service agents had blended into the background for her though they were only a few steps away. It helped that the agents were looking everywhere except at them. Once noticed, they were thoroughly daunting in the dark suits with their radio earpieces. That kept the other people milling down the walkways at bay as well. So it felt as if their conversation was truly private. She looked again.

"Why are there so few people here?"

"You mean other than it's a cold winter's night?"

"Yes, other than that."

"The Conservatory stays open this late only twice a week and only for the holiday concerts. Tonight it's The Congressional Hearings."

"Are they as boring as that sounds?"

Before the Vice President could answer a clear voice sounded in the distance. It was a single, high soprano note, that sounded sad and alone as it echoed down through the various habitats of the Conservatory.

The opening phrase of *Silent Night* was incongruously wrong as it reached the warm jungle greenhouse.

Almost without thinking, she followed the sound with Zachary close beside her. Zachary. Some part of her had let go of "Mr. Vice President" and she'd have to be careful that it didn't escape out into the world. That would be too disrespectful. But internally she decided that she liked Zachary Thomas very much.

Silent Night led them down corridors thick with red, green, and white poinsettias, then through a passageway beneath an arch of massively blooming purple bougainvillea. The soprano was joined by a larger group of voices as *Good King Wenceslas* accompanied them past a miniature Jefferson Memorial, the Washington Monument, and a gorgeous model of the Conservatory complete with tiny plants and bonsai trees visible through the miniature greenhouse roofs. And now that she was looking for them in their tour, the constant hum of trains was everywhere as they clattered around tree trunks and ducked out of sight under banana leaves bigger than the length of whole trains.

Zachary Thomas playing with trains in the basement. It was easy to imagine him so, despite his lofty office. Even easier to imagine him with a child or two to join him.

They reached the main Garden Court where they'd first entered, looking almost sparse now after touring through the jungle's lush growth. A small stage had been backed against the main entrance. The aisles had sprouted folding chairs in every nook and cranny. There were perhaps a hundred of them, mostly filled.

On the small stage a dozen men and women crowded close together. Three of the women wore sparkling red gowns, the other three an elegant green. The men, typically, had it easy and all wore very sharp-looking black tuxedos. At first she thought they were a choir, but spotted no violin or percussion though she could hear them clearly. Acapella. One of the men was beat-boxing a drum kit with his voice and a woman trilled like a fine set of strings to accompany the other voices. The effect was magical.

Zachary guided her to a pair of seats at the very back, close by an exit. The Secret Service agents arranged themselves in doorways and stood against the back wall, only Harvey remaining close by—clearly ready to throw himself in front of the Vice President in case there was mad caroler in the crowd.

She could see the effects of the Vice President's presence propagate slowly forward through the crowd. One head turned, then another. In moments the back half of the audience was glancing their direction, barely watching the concert.

"Zachar—Mr. Vice President?" she asked him softly. All of the attention was unnerving her.

"It's okay, Anne."

She'd almost used his name. A heat rose to her cheeks that was partly from the crowd's attention but partly from her own presumption.

"They'll get used to it in a moment."

She didn't like being looked at so much. But after a few whispered comments between companions, most turned away. Some waved. The Vice President waved back pleasantly, but quickly returned his attention to the concert. More than one of them snapped a photograph.

A photo of the Vice President.

No, of the Vice President and...

"We have to go," she whispered fiercely and started to rise.

"Why?" he kept her in place by wrapping his other hand over where hers was still tucked inside his elbow.

"They're taking pictures."

"They always do," the Vice President remained perfectly calm, keeping his voice soft enough to not disturb anyone on the other side of the two-seat buffer that the Secret Service was maintaining to all sides.

"They're taking pictures of *us*. Don't you get that?"

"My dear Ms. Darlington, they've been doing that since the moment we stepped into the Conservatory."

"They have? But the media..." How had she not noticed that? Was she so oblivious?

"You mean the *social* media—ten times faster I assure you, though curiously it is generally kinder. I am single. I have been known to escort beautiful women before, though none quite as startling as you. It will give them something to talk about."

"The only thing startling about me is how out of my depth I am."

On the farm she'd have noticed someone pulling out a camera. Visitors to the farm always wanted a photo with one of the Darlingtons, but it was done with a Southern politeness and they almost always asked first. Here there must have been a thousand surreptitious snaps with camera phones. It would be all over DC already. Picked up by the national media by tomorrow and...

"I'm so not ready for this."

———

Zack felt contrite, but not very. This sort of attention was mild compared to when he took someone to a restaurant or other public venue. He considered leaving as Anne had suggested, but he didn't want to. He was enjoying the music; the group was very good, though their current early Baroque Christmas ballad was less to his taste. And he was very much enjoying her company. She had used his name rather than his title with an easy familiarity that few women achieved and never on a first date; well, almost had.

Date?

Yes. It felt like a first date. And a good one if he was any judge. Her hand still remained lightly trapped between his own and his elbow. He liked that as well.

She wasn't one of the typical DC women he was used to—who were very focused, very goal-oriented. Over the last five years he'd briefly dated a State Department senior analyst, a Judicial Branch mediator, and a serving Air Force captain from the Pentagon's Southeast Asia division. Everyone was driven by a force that the Coloradan in him found exhausting. There was never a down moment. There was never only one thing on the table. And all of that was backed by the directness of a DC insider that left room for little else.

When Anne had concentrated on the plants, she'd looked at nothing else. She had no agenda, hidden or otherwise. Her questions when they spoke weren't about politics. In his world, he had to watch every word he said because it could be used by his date later to make a cutting point or to feed the media. Instead of speaking with infinite caution, he'd told Anne Darlington about the train set.

He'd never told anyone about that, not even childhood friends who would have gone nuts if they'd seen the elaborate setup in the Thomas' basement. It had been his and his father's alone. Zack had spent endless hours building miniature landscapes, shaping two-percent grades, and forming tunnels through tiny mountains. They'd used the smallest train gauge—the tiny Z, where a seventy-foot engine was reduced to a mere four inches long—allowing for the maximum complexity in the space they had—a twenty-story building scaled to just under a foot high in the Z-gauge world. Whenever General Thomas had come home, Zack had barely been able to contain himself until after that first night's dinner when just the two of them would go down and inspect the results of Zack's efforts.

His father might spend half an hour inspecting all the changes if he'd been away for a long time. He'd run trains over any new sections and they'd both check for performance and realism. The general's highest form of praise would be when he rolled up his sleeves and say, "Looks as if we're ready to start the next section."

Zack came to the Conservatory each year not for the concerts, or even the models of DC landmarks, but instead for the trains. They were mostly the bigger O-gauge, whose eighteen-inch long engines always felt clunky to him, but still they were very well done. It made him both nostalgic and a bit sad; which were the two emotions he most associated with Christmas.

His father was presently stationed at the Eglin Air Force Base in Florida but was often in DC. Their few dinners together were awkward, quiet, and now very infrequent. That his own son might someday be the next Commander-in-Chief had raised another wall of formality, as if there hadn't already been enough since the day Zachary Thomas had entered the academy and become a very junior officer who saluted every time his father appeared.

Yet he'd told Anne Darlington about the trains. She was smart, beautiful, and funny—the last something he definitely wasn't used to. She also offered a genuine warmth that made her stand out even more from his prior experiences.

The Congressional Hearings' rendition of *I Saw Mama Kissing Santa Claus* had him looking over at Anne. She was singing along silently, again simply in the moment. He almost leaned down to...but they were in public and he had no wish to embarrass her further. Never before had he needed to think about keeping any physicality carefully out of sight behind closed doors. Anne made him think again.

All he'd expected was a pleasant evening spent cheering her up. Instead, he was on a first date and wondering like an overeager teen if he might get a kiss at the end of the evening. The group broke into a racy rendition of *All I Want for Christmas Is You*.

She happened to glance up at him and immediately started laughing. Her merry tone loud enough to make several of the nearer concert goers turn to look.

"What?"

Anne patted his arm in a friendly fashion, "It's all over your face, Mr. Vice President."

He considered doing his best to fix that. Then he thought better of it and rubbed his hand all over his face as if trying to erase any expression. When he finished, he made a goofy face with a sloppy grin.

"Is this any better?"

"Much!" And her continued merriment verified that as true.

He did school his expression after he heard the *ka-shick* sound of several cell phones.

CHAPTER THREE

O*f course they chose* that picture." Anne was not going to give her brother the satisfaction of appearing put out by the newspaper he was waving around. His wife Alice was paying very careful attention to her bowl of fruit and yogurt.

They were sitting on stools in the Residence's third floor kitchen around the large maple cutting block island. She'd always liked this kitchen, it was elegant but cozy—dark-stained oak cabinets with brass hardware. If she ever had a house of her own, it would have a kitchen like this one. Alice wore jeans, a turtleneck, and a knit sweater in Christmas red with a complex white snowflake worked into the back. Daniel wore his inevitable three-piece suit. This President was more informal than most, often found in no more than a shirt and tie with his suit pants, but not his Chief of Staff.

"I think it's cute," Anne just couldn't leave it alone: Zachary's face distorted like a circus clown's, her own head back in the moment of the laugh she'd been unable to repress.

"*VP Fools Around With*...double-entendre intended...*Unidentified Blond*," Daniel read the headline aloud for the fifth time, each time with the same notation. Her brother always was a little predictable.

Alice didn't speak but pointed her spoon toward the small television on the counter tuned to CNN, but with the sound off. Anne's own picture, not a bad one thank god, was on the screen. Large white letters on a red background read, *White House Chief of Staff's Sister.*

"No longer unidentified. Don't I even get my own name?"

"Not in this city," Alice smiled at her. "Even if I hadn't taken Daniel's last name, it wouldn't have mattered. At the CIA I'm typically referred to as the W-H-C-o-S wife. That's pronounced whickos, like whackos. You learn to roll with it."

"Why did you take my brother's name anyway? I always meant to ask."

"I just love him that much," she smiled sweetly at Daniel.

Anne made a gagging sound.

"I also wanted to anchor firmly in his subconscious that this is permanent. I only give my heart once."

"Don't have to worry about that. My brother is more loyal than a herd of lemmings."

"He is. So are you, which is a very sweet family trait. So, when are you going to tell your brother what kind of a kisser the Vice President is?"

"Why would I tell him about tha—" And Anne knew that she'd walked right into Alice's trap. She had to remember that Alice Darlington III was a top analyst and nothing slipped by her despite the impression given by her casual attire and cheerfully unruly mop of russet-colored hair that often hid one or other eye from view.

"You...kissed...the...Vice...President?" Daniel finally slumped onto his stool, his power-smoothie still untouched before him.

"He kissed me."

"Details, Sister," Alice ignored her husband's sputtering. "I want details."

"Okay, maybe I kissed him. But he's such a gentleman that sometimes the girl has to take the initiative."

"Don't I know it," Alice sighed and spooned up some more yogurt. "Your brother has the same issue."

"I kissed you first."

"Yes!" Alice suddenly cried out. "I was exhausted. Out on my feet.

He took wholly inappropriate advantage of me. Threw me onto this very counter and ravaged me senseless."

"I did no such thing!"

"Regrettably true," Alice's voice returned to absolute normal. "And no matter how he remembers it, I had to kiss him first; though he did get with the program very quickly. Still—me, this counter, wild sex— never happened."

Anne only had to look in Alice's eyes for a moment before they both turned to Daniel and said in unison, "Why not?"

They both turned away and left Daniel to sputter pointlessly on a new topic.

To save Alice repeating her question about the kiss, because there was no question she would, Anne continued, "What skills the Vice President might lack in maintaining proper decorum in public," she tapped the newspaper Daniel had dropped onto the cutting block, "he more than compensates for in the back seat of a Secret Service SUV parked safely out of sight in the EEOB garage."

"My own sister kissed the Vice President..." Daniel's voice was soft and disbelieving.

"Drink your smoothie, dear," Alice patted his hand.

Momentarily quelled, he did just that. Alice really was impressive in how she could handle her brother. He'd always been the polite sibling, but he'd also been stubborn to the edge of monomania when- ever he was locked onto a topic.

Anne still didn't quite believe that kiss herself.

Only one of the agents had actually left the vehicle, stepping out to open her door, when she'd done it. Harvey had remained in the SUV.

Still seated, she and Zachary had both stumbled over "pleasant evening" words and then relapsed into silence. It wasn't that he'd been so kind to her that made her decide to kiss him; it was that he simply was so kind. What she wasn't going to tell her sister-in-law, or her brother for that matter, was that the goodnight kiss had been intended as only a friendly peck of thanks on the cheek. Let them think it had been little more than that.

But it hadn't happened that way. As if by some unspoken plan, he'd turned just as she leaned in and in seconds she was lost in a kiss that had her practically crawling into his lap for more. Perhaps she would have if either of them had thought to release their seat belts. Zachary Thomas' kisses didn't allow much room for thought; all she'd been able to do was feel. And the feeling had been glorious right down to her toes. Before they came up for air, Harvey also had exited the vehicle—without her even noticing.

Oh, there was something else she'd almost forgotten.

Anne winked at Alice, then she turned to face Daniel, "By the way, Brother, I have dinner plans tonight."

———

The rap on his front door was in the rhythm that Zack recognized as Harvey's.

He continued dictating instructions to Cornelia over his shoulder as he came out into the front foyer. Normally he would just shout that it was open—the ever present Secret Service a better guard than any deadbolt—but he had hopes on who he'd find there. He saw two images through the frosted glass: the tall, square-shouldered head of his Protection Detail and a shorter, lighter image that just had to be Anne. He opened the heavy door himself.

"Wow! What a beautiful house. I love the three-story circular turret." But she wasn't looking at the interior, she was looking at him, which had his body reheating rapidly with the memory of her kiss last night. Just like Anne herself, there had been nothing tentative about it. No considerations of composure or propriety. She'd apparently wanted to kiss him as much as he wanted to kiss her, so she had. It had been amazing.

"Thanks," was all he managed. Her long spill of blond hair was back in a ponytail. Not one of those high-tails that were so in fashion and looked more like a hair extension than it did like hair, but a normal tail that just gathered her hair back from her face. And though she was once again in her voluminous parka, he now knew something of what lay hidden beneath those folds. Still showing jeans and those scuffed high-end cowboy boots below; definitely his kind of girl. She looked—

"Planning to invite me in or do Harvey and I have to stay out here in the cold until you are through with your military inspection, Captain Vice President sir?" She offered a sloppy salute.

"If I let you in, I may not let you leave again."

"Forewarned is disarmed. If you let me in, I may not *want* to leave again," her smile was sassy though she spoke completely matter-of-factly. "Besides, it's cold out here."

"I'll risk it," he held the door wide. Anne walked in. Harvey began to turn away. "Come in, Harvey, get warm for a minute. Cornelia's almost through for the day. Then if you could escort her back out through the gate, I'd appreciate it."

"Yes, sir, thank you. As Ms. Darlington may have remarked in much more colorful terms on the way here, it's cold enough to freeze a sled dog's behind tonight."

Zack shared a look with him.

Harvey stepped part way in then stopped. The head of his Protection Detail looked over Zack's shoulder and whispered quietly, "Incoming, sir." Taking a step backward, he closed the front door with himself on the outside and Zack inside.

He turned to see what had made a top Secret Service agent go into full retreat.

Anne stood in the center of the foyer with one arm out of her parka, not waiting for him to assist her. But she was frozen in place facing the Living Room archway in the awkward position of shoulder and elbow still raised even though the coat had slid free on that side.

Just stepping into the far side of the hall, Cornelia came out to see who the new arrival might be. There couldn't be a greater contrast in two women.

Anne as five-six of healthy and vigorous Tennessean. From the back he could see Anne's ponytail was held by a black rubber band. And she'd opted for no more than a well-tailored black denim shirt that matched her designer jeans. She looked modern and ready to join one of Mom's Olympic swimming teams.

"Hello, I've *read* so much about you," Cornelia, of course, smoothing the way with her perfect manners.

———

Anne thought about trying out a crushing-guy-grip thing, but it would fracture the woman's perfect manicure. Cornelia's cool gaze assessed and discarded Anne as a hick from the wilderness. This was exactly the sort of woman she'd expect the Vice President to be with—long, cool, and elegant. And he was with her, clearly Anne's arrival had interrupted something. So what was she doing here if he already had—

"She's my assistant. My right hand," the Vice President stepped forward. "Anne this is Cornelia Day. This is Dr. Darlington's sister, Anne Darlington."

"A pleasure," Cornelia spoke with all the warmth of the December evening, dark and bitter on the other side of the door. Assistant or not, she was dancing along the thin edge of rude. Anne had obviously trampled on forbidden territory.

Cornelia was six-one of DC elegant—not a hair out of place and her silk blouse perfectly complemented both her complexion and the Merino wool slacks that reached down to her two-inch heels: so five-foot-eleven of Cornelia and two inches of Kate Spades. She looked ready to take on a shark—either the aquatic or the legal kind—and there would be no doubting the victor in any contest. In the elegant reception hall of the Vice Presidential residence, Cornelia looked the perfect hostess. And before her, Anne felt as if she'd been beamed down from another world onto the center of the immaculate white Persian carpet to be glared at by Kennedy and the two Roosevelts.

One Observatory Circle was an elegant 1800s mansion built on the grounds of the National Observatory. She'd been captivated by the wide verandah that wrapped around the house. She'd gathered a few facts about it from the Secret Service agent who Daniel had insisted on sending rather than letting her take a cab. She'd been in dozens of the finest homes across the South. Many had far more pretension than this home, but few had such perfection and such artifacts.

"It's Dr. Melanie Anne Darlington, actually," a fact Anne typically played down. And in these elegant surroundings, she sounded pretentious but she couldn't stop herself.

Cornelia faced her directly, her shoulders squared beneath her Armani jacket. "Dr. Darlington. Bachelors in English Literature. MBA.

Doctorate in Plant Sciences. All at University of Tennessee." She'd obviously done her homework.

"Yes," Anne acknowledged. "Valedictorian in all cases, you might add."

"I'm just a former USAF captain," Zachary chimed as if oblivious to the battle forming up in his front foyer. "That leaves me out of the running in this high-powered room."

Anne reached for a sense of humor in the situation, but had trouble finding it at first. Then she did, "Well, one of the three of us is also Vice President of the United States. I'm not sure that actually counts for much, but it must be worth something. Perhaps you can barter it for a free ice cream at the Lincoln Memorial."

Zachary nodded, "I hadn't thought of trying that. I'll give it a go next time I'm there."

But Cornelia Tight-ass scowled at Anne's light tone. Apparently even making fun of the Vice Presidential office was forbidden.

Then the Vice President changed topics as if nothing was going on. "Cornelia, in the briefing package for the climate meeting, I need a breakdown of each of the G-20's actual conservation efforts in the last decade. Hard numbers, not guesses from some analyst who doesn't give a damn."

She produced a tablet computer in an expensive red leather case that was as elegant as she was and made a notation.

"I think that's it."

"Very good, sir," she walked to the coat closet as if she was completely at home here. But Anne was secretly pleased that she did so with all the stiffness of the stick they had each just rammed up the other's butt.

Anne was glad for the thick white area rug that covered much of the hall because the way Cornelia was walking, her heels would have worked like jackhammers on the hardwood flooring that showed around the edges. Each step shook her slender frame with its intensity.

At the door she turned for what Anne feared was one last scathing attack, but all she said was, "Eight a.m. meeting with the Speaker on the Hill, Mr. Vice President. Good night, sir."

When the door closed, Anne sighed with relief. "Is she really gone?"

The Vice President didn't answer, but remained staring at the inside of the door.

Anne moved up beside him so that they could stare at it together.

"I certainly didn't see that coming," he said softly.

"I thought you didn't see it at all."

"Not blind, Dr. Darlington," then he grimaced at the door. "Well, not completely blind. Cornelia has been with me for seven years and never gave me a single signal."

Anne was on the verge of calling him blind again, but decided in favor of a far softer, "Well, you've been given a clear signal now, I'd say." She'd have gone for it with her brother, but it wasn't nice to kick a Vice President when he was down.

He nodded his agreement reluctantly.

"Are you sure you want me to stay? At some point I'm going to be gone again," or fall off the edge of the planet, "and you clearly depend on her."

He shook it off and turned from the door to face her but she could still see the concern remaining.

"No, please stay. Besides, I'm guessing..." then he smiled, abruptly at ease. "I'd lay three-to-one odds that I'm not the one in the doghouse here."

"That makes no sense at all."

He took her parka and carried it to the front closet. "I rather think it's about *you* not being good enough for *me*. I've dated before and never had this reaction from her."

Anne certainly hoped that's what it was. She wasn't even good enough for herself and she'd come to terms with that...or was trying to. At least that was a playing field she understood.

"You know what I need, Mr. Vice President?"

"What, Dr. Darlington?"

"I need a beer. Please tell me that you don't just have white wine."

"Yes!" He pumped a fist in the air. "If you tell me that you like football, I'm *not* letting you leave."

"College or pro?" It was an important question among football fans.

"College of course," his smile was electric for her knowing there was a distinction in the first place. "The Air Force Academy Falcons."

"Might have watched a game or two...in which the Tennessee Volunteers totally tromped their flyboy behinds," Anne crowed with delight and began feeling much better about how the evening was going. "Seem to recall a total choke back in 2006." The two teams were in different conferences, so the meet-ups were few and far between.

"One point. Give me break. We went for the two-point conversion—"

"And missed it! And don't even get me going on the 1971 Sugar Bowl, 34 to 13."

Zachary groaned as if it was yesterday even though neither of them had been alive back then. "We tromped the Army this year," he offered as a lame recovery. "Just like I bet we did to Stanford last night. I recorded the game but haven't watched it yet. Do *not* tell me."

"I would nev-ah," she placed an offended hand upon her chest in mock horror. "But it may or may not have been just like what the Navy did when they whupped your behinds last month," she slapped the verbal football back down in his turf.

He stopped and looked down at her, "How did you know all that?"

She offered her best smile, "It's either because I'm a Southern football genius or it's because I can use the Internet just as well as Ms. Cornelia Day." Or because she had a younger cousin on the Navy team. "The key question you should be focusing on at the moment, Mr. Vice President, is the location of my beer."

———

Once they'd crossed through the formal Dining Room into the Pantry Kitchen for a couple of tall cold ones, Zack led her on a tour of the house. As soon as the words, "It's in the Queen Anne style," were out of his mouth, he stopped using any other name for her. As with everything else, she simply took being dubbed "Queen Anne" in stride.

"I always did want to be queen for a day."

True to the form popular in the late 1800s, the first floor had few hallways and fewer doors, one room simply opened onto the next. The broad veranda curved around the cylindrical three-story turret that defined the southeast corner of the house. On the first floor, the circular room extended off the Living Room.

"The Christmas tree is usually in that nook of the Reception Hall; they move out the grand piano," he pointed with the neck of his bottle. "This year I had them put it here in the turret. I like the way the lights reflect off all of the windows."

"And I see that's the sole decorating decision you've made about the house in the five years you've been here."

"Perhaps." He looked around. The mansion was exactly as he'd received it. White area rugs with understated floral designs, stark white couches and chairs, and muted wallpaper that—now that he thought about it—made it feel more like a museum than a home. Without anyone to share it with, he hadn't been motivated him to make it a home. It wasn't something his family had much skill at.

He led her back through the Reception Hall, past the elegant staircase that climbed up through the core of the house in successive turns, and into the Library—the only room he really used other than the bedroom. His sole mark here was the half dozen shelves of thriller novels he read when he was too sick of State Department reports. He thought about the upstairs, he hadn't even changed the quilt that had been on the master bed. "Okay, more than perhaps."

"Same problem I have. Couldn't care in the least."

Again Zack was left to scratch his head in Queen Anne's wake. Each of the women he'd dated had said almost identical things on entering the house, "It's so beautiful. There's so much you could do with it." Even the ever-practical Cornelia had made a few comments about the availability of other furnishings from whatever department took care of such things. He had exchanged the JFK portrait between the bookshelves with a picture from home, but that was all he'd done.

Anne simply didn't care.

The Library was the most comfortable room in the house. There was room for a sofa and several armchairs. Arches led to the Reception

Hall and Living Room with a small doorway leading into the Garden Room. He'd never been much of a one for plants, but some Navy steward had maintained it well enough for Anne to remark, "Nice."

To the north was a broad bay window looking out over the Observatory grounds during the day. To the south stood the bookcases and a television. If he wasn't entertaining, this was where he spent most of his time at home.

On one shelf he had a half dozen pictures that Anne had stopped in front of. He moved up behind her, close behind her, and enjoyed the feeling that they were almost embracing—definitely close enough to...

Seeking distraction, he looked over her head, "The family."

"I can see them both in you. Are they close?"

"As close as they want to be, I suppose. Which means if either one fell off the edge of the world, the other might or might not notice. They're both quite driven people in their own, deeply separate fields."

"And you became Vice President by sitting around on your lazy behind."

"Absolutely! Best method there is. Also, I should warn you that I was always the black sheep of the family, caring about people as people rather than for their roles on the ever-precious team." She didn't glance up at the surprising amount of bitterness that had slipped into his tone, having instead the courtesy to let him recover his equilibrium without comment.

In an unconsciously smooth sideways move she shifted from the narrow space between himself and his family photographs, to inspect the one larger picture from home—the one that had usurped JFK's place of honor. He had to smile at himself, don't underestimate Queen Anne Darlington.

She had just given him the space to recover; as wholly conscious a movement as him sidling close behind her in the first place.

"Is this a real train yard or your model?"

Even his father had not picked up on that. Zack had spent hours making sure every detail of his miniature train yard had been perfect, hazing the photo just enough to make it art rather than a model railroader's brag piece. He was inordinately proud of that image, but it also made him a little sad as he'd never had anyone to share it with.

When he didn't answer her, she looked at him, directly at him for the first time since when she'd crossed over the front threshold. She didn't speak, but just studied him.

"What?" His throat had suddenly gone dry.

"I think Mr. Vice President that it is dangerous for two such lonely people to stand here in such silence."

Lonely? But he was almost never alone. His typical day ran from seven a.m. to seven p.m. Late evenings he often as not had dinner meetings or reports to study, phone calls to return to earlier time zones to garner favor for a key piece of legislation, or...

"Lonely?" he managed a whisper but it didn't sound like much of a question.

"I think we have two choices," Anne remained serious and, unlike usual, he couldn't detect any hidden smile waiting with a joke.

"Which are?"

"You had mentioned a Falcons' game you recorded. Option one, we can sit on that couch and watch it." This is where he usually watched games and somehow Anne had figured that out. Sitting close beside her was an attractive option. He could see them laughing together over pizza, beer, and touchdowns—could see it very easily.

"Or?"

"Or," she took a very deep breath that caused some very nice shifts down her body that he did his decent best to ignore. "Or, we can just acknowledge where this is going and you can show me where the Vice President sleeps."

Zack Thomas had received many offers of sex over the years: some coy, some blatant, some little classier than a street walker's offer. He didn't think that he'd ever in his life received a more sincere offer than Anne's forthright statement.

He knew that with her it wasn't an offer of sex, it would be so much more than that. He didn't need to answer.

She stepped up to him and slipped the beer bottle from his fingers. She set both of them on coasters on the low white coffee table, then she held out her hand. When he took it, her touch was cool with condensation from the barely touched bottle, but her clasp remained firm as he led her to the central stairs and up into his bedroom.

———

Anne had not planned on ending up here. Hadn't even thought about it. But looking at the train picture, something had shifted deep inside for her. The care it must have taken. Every car had been meticulously real despite its tiny size. The rail yard hadn't merely been a clustering of narrowly-spaced parallel tracks. Instead tiny bits of gravel little bigger than sand grains had been spread all through the yard. Switching lights, yard workers, and even a tiny lone dog sniffing a wheel of the foremost engine. She could only imagine what it took to be the boy who'd done that.

When Zack reached for the light, she stopped his hand. Outside the winter might be cold, but it was also clear and the moon was a bright slash on the thick carpeting. In the room's warmth, the cold light warmed as well. Keeping their hands joined, she turned to face him and rested her other hand on his chest.

"This would be a good time to kiss me, Mr. Vice President."

"I'm not so sure about that," he nuzzled her hair. "Isn't it a bit presumptuous of me to think of bedding the expedition leader? Sounds like a court-martial offense to me. I want to approach this cautiously."

"If it's going to be your last night on earth, I'd suggest we enjoy it."

"You may have a point. Tonight we make love, for..." His hand was stroking her hair. With only one small snag, he freed it from the rubber band. He leaned down to kiss her where neck and her shirt's collar met beneath her freed hair.

"...tomorrow we might freeze to death. Or Cornelia might have me killed." She allowed her own hands to admire the softness of his beard, his strong jaw, and trace down over his very nice chest.

"Or Daniel might convince the President to send me on an extended tour of darkest Florida to be eaten by alligators." He mumbled into her ear.

"Don't miss Disney World as you head south. It's great fun," she loosened his tie, slipped it off his head, and at an opportune moment, slid it over hers.

"I was thinking more of Wolf Creek Pass." He removed her blouse and the bra followed quickly after. His lightest touch made her want more, his caresses were intense enough to unbalance her soul.

"What's that?" Anne had the sneaking suspicion that they weren't going to make it the last few steps to the bed.

"Ski area," he'd knelt and mumbled through his first kiss, which was between her breasts. "First to open in Colorado every year. Great place for Arctic training."

"Sounds cold," it would be if the room weren't so warm because the rest of her clothes had disappeared while she was appreciating this shoulder of the former soldier now kneeling before her.

"Lodge has hot cocoa and greasy French fries in front of a big fireplace."

"I've never skied, so I'll wait for you in the lodge. Greasy fries sound good," she knelt as well and tipped her head back to give him better access as his lips explored her shoulder. She wasn't in the mood for waiting for anything. She had thought they'd have a slow, loving experience. But the only reason she didn't drag him to the floor was that he was now headed there and dragging her down with him. She leaned down over him as he finally lay exposed in a patch of moonlight, seeking the kiss they'd never quite gotten around to.

He stopped her an inch away, holding her easily aloft with a hand on each shoulder.

She again tried to close the narrow gap that separated them, but still he resisted.

"You've never skied?"

"I've also never bedded a Vice President of the United States. So let me go if you want to be the first." She leaned in again, but still he kept them easily separated.

"You have to have skied."

"I've also never flown a fighter jet or swum across an ocean. Is that going to make you cast me from your bedroom?" He was working his way toward a sharp nudge in the ribs.

"We'll have to fix that you've never skied," the moonlit expression on his face remained serious. "It's important."

"Why? To see how fast I can turn into an icicle?"

"No," he brushed one hand down from her shoulder, over her

breast and hip sending a shiver of need through her. "Because it is the only thing I can see standing between you and perfection."

With the same easy strength that he'd used to keep her at bay, he pulled her in, and she didn't fight him one tiny little bit. Perfection was about the farthest thing from Anne Darlington, but if this beautiful man wanted to believe otherwise, she'd do her best to convince him that he was right.

She also had been right the first time. Making love to Vice President Zachary Thomas for the first time was neither a hot nor fast event. It was slow, gentle, and made her feel as if maybe, just maybe, she had discovered a small corner of perfection herself.

CHAPTER FOUR

W*hy are you wearing* a tie?"

"Oh," Anne brushed her hand down the smooth silvery silk of it. "Isn't it pretty?"

Daniel looked at her strangely, blinked twice, and then his face froze and she couldn't read his expression. That was unusual; she could always read what her brother was thinking. Or rather had been able to. He rose from his desk and closed the door to his office before returning. He sat beside her rather than circling back to his own side of the paper mountain.

"Don't start, little brother. I'm feeling too good for one of your lectures."

"That's Zack Thomas' tie."

"Vice President Zachary Thomas'," she corrected and Daniel blanched at his slip into inappropriate familiarity. "He gave it to me and I find myself unwilling to return it yet."

"Melanie Anne..."

"Daniel Drake Darlington the Third..." she could match his threatening tone any day.

"I don't care if you're screwing Vice President Thomas—"

"You don't?" That stopped them both for a long moment, but he was the first one to recover.

"Okay, I do. But that's not the point. How many people have seen you while wearing that tie? I'm not the only one who would recognize it; that's one of his favorites."

She hadn't thought about that. She had worn it all through their long night together—wrestling in bed, eating ice cream and watching the football game while curled together on the Library couch at three in the morning. It had been the only clothing either of them had worn through the long night. And when they'd only made it back up to the second landing in the stairs where, with no protection close to hand, they'd had to improvise, she had found a few interesting uses for it. And this morning she'd slipped the neck loop under the fold of her denim collar and snugged it up properly. She'd never worn a man's tie before but it was far better than nylons on any day of the year.

"Maybe nobody else noticed?"

"Shall we find out, big sister?" Daniel almost sounded nasty. It wasn't really in him to succeed at such an endeavor, but he tried. He picked up a remote control and turned on one of the several televisions he had in his office.

And there was her picture. It was a long shot, through a major telephoto with all of its blurriness and foreshortening effects. But it was unmistakably her, in her big parka with the front still open because she was still near heat stroke from the thoroughness of Zachary's parting caresses. And, as the commentator was helpfully indicating with circles and arrows and a scrolling line below, there was the same tie that the Vice President had been wearing the prior day.

Next were side-by-side photos of Zack yesterday and of her coming in through White House security not twenty minutes ago. Again the same tie.

Well, the hog was in the waller now. No easy way to get it back out.

"Top item on the seven a.m. news," Daniel complained. "Ahead of Russia, ahead of the Japanese yen. Do you have any idea what trouble this is going to cause him? I don't even know where to begin to—"

She was trying to cut him off when the door to Daniel's office swung open and the President strode in already in mid-sentence, "Is that really Zack's tie on—"

He stopped. Frozen still when he spotted her.

Anne flapped the tie at him.

"Huh," the President grunted in a way that he'd never have done on national TV. "I guess it is."

He inspected her for a long moment, "How are you feeling, Anne?"

"You mean other than my little brother throwing a Southern-fried hissy fit?"

"Yes," he smiled down at her. "Other than that."

That's when she belatedly realized she was still sitting and scrambled to her feet along with Daniel. "My body is, well, Mr. President, rather pleased with the situation. My brain is as confused as—" she re-chose her words in mid-sentence, "—a chicken at a hog-calling contest."

Oddly enough that seemed to tickle him immensely as he smiled at some grand joke that only he was in on. "That's normal, then. Okay."

He considered a moment longer as he inspected her through narrowed eyes, then he clapped his hands together with some clear decision. "You all are having dinner in the Residence tonight. Daniel, would you let Zack and our wives know?" And he was gone.

Anne looked at the now empty doorway then back to her brother, "I thought I was confused before he walked in. What is he so all fired pleased about?"

"I don't know," Daniel settled slowly back into his seat. "But what it does mean, big sister, is that we're having dinner with the President and First Lady tonight. Please wear a dress."

"I didn't bring one." Had never needed one because she'd never had dinner with the President before, nor slept with the Vice President—two firsts in less than twenty-four hours. She was on a roll.

Daniel narrowed his eyes at her, then called out toward his still open office door, "Janet, I need someone to take my sister out clothes shopping. Then get a message to the Vice President and the First Lady about dinner."

Anne was going to offer to tell Zachary; it would also give her a chance to apologize for any trouble this was causing. Then she realized that she had no idea how to get in touch with the Vice President.

She headed for the door.

"Would you please take that damn tie off?"

She thought about it, then nodded toward the television. "I think that dog has already slipped the leash, don't you?"

Zack had been in meetings all day. The peremptory invitation to dine at the White House arrived in the same sixty-second break in which Cornelia filled him in on "Tie Gate." There were times he hated President Nixon and then there were times he just pitied the man. Every DC disaster for the last forty years had been tied back to his screw-ups at Watergate. Zack wondered if he himself should feel honored that his private life had been added to the legacy.

As his day progressed, he caught up with more photos of Anne Darlington as she traveled about DC. He had to give the woman points, she'd worn his tie proudly every step of the way. It looked damn good on her.

However, he was not ready for how it looked when he stepped off the elevator onto the Second Floor of the Residence. He and Harvey followed the sound of laughter from the elevator to the President's private Living Room.

As there were guests, two Secret Service agents flanked the door. Frank Adams was a massive man and the head of the President's Protection Detail. Beatrice Ann Belfour, commonly known as Beat, was a powerfully curved, much smaller, and supposedly even more dangerous version of her husband—though that was hard to imagine. It was generally agreed that the Presidential couple had the most dangerous team in or out of the military guarding them. Harvey joined them out in the Central Hall and Zack continued into the Living Room.

He nodded to the President and First Lady; nodded to Daniel and Alice as well before he caught sight of her.

Zack had expected Anne to still be wearing the silvered tie, which she was with the knot loose down to just above her breasts, but that was about all he recognized. Sometimes a man was lucky. He'd thought that many times since meeting Anne Darlington. And he'd thought it continuously as they'd romped back and forth through his hundred-and-twenty year old home. Still, it hadn't prepared him for this.

"Holy cow, Queen Anne. You're radiant."

"They did things to me," Anne flapped her hands helplessly. "I tried to stop them, but they overpowered me. Who knew that there were gangs of toughs inside dress shops and salons."

"Be quiet and just let me look," he knew she'd ignore his command. Except she did remain quiet. She also blushed and glared at him—both fiercely.

Her hair, that thick bounty of long hair he'd so enjoyed toying with last night, now shone as it spread over her shoulders. She had bought a dress, the kind that might have killed a lesser man. It wasn't sheer but it clung in amazing ways. Last night he'd seen the incredible conditioning of a life spent on a farm and riding horses. Tonight, her dress revealed it in whole new ways. He'd always thought himself unreasonably fortunate in the women he'd dated, but Anne Darlington was cut from a whole different cloth—in this case one of sky blue silk that complimented her dark blue eyes.

She'd retained her cowboy boots, though someone—he was sure it wasn't her—had thought to polish them to a brilliant mahogany shine. The skirt bloomed just above her knees, like she was ready for a country dance. A silver belt at her slim waist matched the tie, which was tucked under an over-wide starched collar that would have looked wrong on a woman with less strength of shoulder. The dress offered no cleavage, but instead was downright sinful in its accent of her shape.

"I want a picture of you in that for my shelf."

"I want a picture of your jaw hanging open," but she said it softly and offered him a smile of understanding. It was the same smile she'd offered as they stood before his photograph of the train set; one of deep sympathy and infinite understanding. Of course she'd understood the importance of his statement even if he hadn't when he'd said it. No one except his family and his trains appeared on that shelf. Yet still he wanted her there.

He moved over to hold her for just a moment. As he pulled her into his arms, Zack knew for certain that this wasn't going to be some typical DC affair, here and gone almost as fast as the news cycle. This was a woman he was going to hold onto for as long as possible.

———

Anne tried several times that evening to shoo Zack away, but wasn't having much luck with it. And the others weren't helping.

In the President's personal Living Room, she had ended up on one Chesterfield sofa with Zack while the President and First Lady Geneviève Matthews took the one opposite. Both couches were done in liquid brown leather. Daniel and Alice occupied a pair of wing-back armchairs. It was clear that the First Lady had made this room very masculine for her husband's sake. Anne wondered if he noticed quite how comfortable he was here.

The hand of the Christmas spirit had touched lightly here even though the family Christmas tree dominated one corner. Presents were already accumulating under the pine branches which were covered in homey ornaments that could only have been gathered over decades of time. The glasses they used for eggnog had a holly pattern and the appetizer plates had that same pattern painted on the white china. But little else existed to mitigate the sheer maleness of the room.

They'd chatted about world events at a level that Anne was fairly sure she wasn't cleared for. Every now and then Daniel would start to raise some objection about her clearance level, and the President simply ran right over him. Geneviève, who Anne was still having problems with calling by her first name, didn't even bat an eye. After the second time, Alice nodded as if the President's choice made perfect sense. Zack had eyed her a time or two, so it wasn't just her imagination. Eventually only she and Daniel were twitching at the frankness and details revealed on certain topics. The President was welcoming her to a whole new level. On previous visits, the few times she saw Peter Matthews, conversations had turned instantly mundane in her presence. Not pointless or dumbed down, merely of no great import. Not so tonight.

The eggnog was spiked, which had gone straight to her head, but she managed not to wobble as they had adjourned to the Dining Room. She congratulated herself on making the transition comfortably as they crossed the Central Hall. Walking beside Alice and chatting about CIA analytical methods and how Alice had applied them to understanding why in the world Daniel had fallen for her, they approached the three agents who had moved down to the West Sitting Hall.

The Christmas elves had been here as well, with a much heavier hand. Great wreaths the size of a horse blanket hung along the walls. Woven streamers of red and green velvet draped the columns. It was elegant, tasteful, and decidedly merry.

The agents looked both in and out of place in the fine hall dressed in its Christmas attire. The three of them wore good quality dark suits and sat comfortably in nice period furniture.

She waved at Harvey who waved back. The other two were inspecting her with a degree of scrutiny that at first felt invasive it was so intense. Then she realized they were probably studying her for characteristic motion, potentially dangerous actions, or who knew what went on within a top agent's mind. Having finished whatever their inspection was, the huge man waved back in a friendly enough fashion. The woman still watched her carefully.

Then all three leapt to their feet as the President came into view behind her. Suddenly they looked like some Tom Cruise *Mission Impossible* team—dressed for a party and armed to kill.

"Dinner call," the President said in a friendly fashion. "I'll make sure trays get out to you."

"Thank you, sir. Very kind of you, Mr. President."

Anne glanced back as their party entered the Dining Room. The agents remained on alert, inspecting the long and empty hallway carefully before returning to their seats.

Maybe the transition to whatever inner circle she was being welcomed wasn't quite so comfortable. They were in the most heavily guarded home in America. They even had guards inside. How far away was the officer with the nuclear football? The medic in case the President choked or had a stroke? What about...

"What in blue hills am I doing here?" She whispered to Zack as he held out her chair.

"Being the first woman I've dated who has been invited to the First Family's table."

Anne was overwhelmed by several elements of that statement and went for the least scary one, "We're dating?" Though why she thought that was the *least* scary...

"Haven't you been watching the news?"

She sat and he took the chair close beside her. She'd hoped for a little more distance from the emotional power that Zack was wielding over her. But he was right and she'd known that from the moment she'd seen the look in his eyes as he'd arrived tonight. She was in so much trouble. No, she'd known it since they'd stood together in front of that childhood train photo. It was impossible that she somehow knew so much about him so soon, and yet it also felt perfectly right that she did.

They'd had a wonderful time last night, definitely the best sex she'd ever had. And Zachary Thomas wasn't only a powerful man, he was an immensely considerate lover. Either his past as an Air Force Captain or his present life as the Vice President gave him a certain tendency toward macho, but it was well balanced by his innate kindness. Her past experiences were with men who had smoother manners and gentler personalities; not Zachary's raw force of character.

In a dress—which made her feel exposed rather than beautiful— he'd looked at her as if she was indeed a queen—which made her feel beautiful rather than exposed. But seated side by side at the circular table, with their knees bumping against each other far more often than could be blamed on their relative positions, Zack was completely overloading her senses.

He was right, they were dating. She, Anne Darlington, was dating the Vice President of— Anne really wished she was a drinking woman.

The Dining Room also reflected a woman's touch. Christmas here was knick-knacks on the mantel: candy cane candles, a line of matryoshka wooden nesting dolls but in the form of reindeer, and an old steel frame with three aged brass bells just like the ones on the four-horse team they used to pull the farm's "sleigh." In Tennessee it had wheels rather than runners, but the Darlington farm had offered children free hayrides in it since the late-1800s.

They'd seated Daniel across the table which wasn't far enough—his constant hovering was making it hard to be herself; almost as much as wearing a dress. To her right sat Zack and Alice, who were still discussing climate change and world politics—apparently the Vice President had found the analyst he was looking for in Anne's sister-in-law. Alice rattled off project names and statistics as if this was her CIA specialty rather than North Korean and Chinese politics.

To her left sat the First Lady and President Matthews. Anne was a little surprised that they hadn't ended up man-woman the whole way around as was done at almost every formal dinner she'd ever attended or given. Sitting next to the First Lady was almost as daunting as sitting beside Zachary.

Geneviève was easily the most alarming woman Anne had ever met.

Of French-Vietnamese descent, not only was she a Director for the UNESCO World Heritage Convention, she notoriously had saved the President's life, married him, and given him a daughter—presently asleep with her nanny. As if that wasn't enough, the First Lady was a renowned beauty, as tall as the President with a statuesque figure, pale skin, and a lush fall of dark hair.

Why was Zack even looking at Anne when he could easily have his choice of similar smooth, urban beauties? Well, maybe not like Geneviève, but at least like Cornelia Day. Anne was so out of her league here that—

She shut down the thought and did what she could to survive the evening. Thankfully, her family entertained frequently and she'd known how to be social at a dinner table since before she'd learned to tie her shoelaces. If only Zachary hadn't hooked his foot around hers beneath the table. It forced her entire body to hum with anticipation throughout the meal.

Over dessert of sweet wine and braised pears, the First Lady winked at her, "This problem I know," she offered in her light French accent that only added to the perfection, unlike Anne's own Holly Hunter imitation making her sound all the more rural.

"What problem?"

"Oh dear. You are so in the beginnings that you do not even see. *Mais oui?* I have forgotten what that is like. I think that makes it a very good beginning. Very good. You must be calling me Genny from now on." Anne looked to Zack for some explanation, but he was talking to the President and Daniel about the Washington Redskins football team. Alice however, was leaning around Zack and watching the First Lady.

"Really?" Alice leaned further forward and looked carefully into Anne's face.

Anne almost reached for her napkin to wipe it clean. Or maybe she'd just hide behind the linen, do a magic trick and disappear.

"Oh!" Alice blinked in surprise. "I missed that," she spoke to Genny, then she flashed a huge smile at Anne.

"What?" Anne would have hissed it at Alice, but knew from experience that the best way to avoid attracting the attention of other people at the table was to speak perfectly normally.

True to form, there were two distinct conversations going on. The three men discussing a topic she'd be much more comfortable with, and the two women in deep cahoots over some thing or other that had Anne shifting nervously in her seat.

"Men," the First Lady clapped her hands together in a peremptory fashion. "Men, you are now going away. Watch one of your games or conquer the world to make your women safe."

The President leaned over to kiss his wife, Anne noted that it was far more than a casual act, then dutifully rose to his feet. Daniel—always too reserved—merely squeezed his wife's hand. Zachary rose, then leaned down to kiss her on top of the head. It was sweet and did nothing to calm her sudden nerves.

She looked at him, hoping that he'd see her expression begging him to take her away. But Zack didn't and merely proceeded on his way out the door with the others. Or perhaps he did and ignored it because no one argued with the First Lady.

Alice moved her teacup and then herself into Zack's seat. Now Anne was truly trapped.

"Frank," the President called out to the head of his Protection Detail as the three of them entered the West Sitting Hall. "Please tell me there's a game on."

In moments Frank and Harvey had followed them back to the Living Room. Beat headed in to check on the other women. And Zack wished Anne luck.

He was having trouble hiding his smile from the others. He'd seen Anne's panicked plea; couldn't have missed it from atop a Rocky Mountain peak. But she was just going to have learn the hard way—the same as he had—that Kim-Ly Geneviève Beauchamp Matthews was not as terrifying as she looked. Well, perhaps she was, but she was so awfully nice about it. However, the First Lady was not a woman to be denied and he wasn't about to try.

The President opened an armoire and revealed a large television. Frank dropped into one of the armchairs and began inspecting a football schedule on his phone.

Harvey looked at Zack as to whether he should stay and Zack could only shrug. Watching a friendly game with "the guys," he wasn't any more sure of the protocols than Harvey was. As VP, he'd been a common enough visitor on the second floor of the White House, but mostly as a part of social functions, which were a recent innovation.

First Lady Katherine Matthews, prior to her untimely death, had entertained without the President on the third floor where Daniel and Alice now lived. She and the President were only ever seen together when in public. The top floor had been Katherine's domain and, to the best of Zack's knowledge, the President still never went up there.

The White House had become a livelier and friendlier place with the arrival of Genny Matthews. She entertained more and it was as much through her as through Zack's own daily interactions with the President that he and Peter had become friends. But the President was very reserved in many ways—DC born and bred and perhaps overly self-conscious about his role. He only truly relaxed around his childhood friend turned helicopter pilot. Anne should be glad she wasn't facing Emily Beale; she was even more daunting than the First Lady.

———

Anne half rose to follow the men anyway, but when she turned, the female agent stood in the doorway. She was powerfully curved, and terribly imposing in her dark suit. A beautiful woman, but her standout feature was her eyes—they missed nothing.

They clearly didn't miss Anne's halfhearted attempt at beating a hasty retreat. She moved into a blocking position in the doorway. The agent was only a few inches taller than Anne, but Anne gave up any hopes of retreat when she noted how completely she blocked the doorway—she filled it more effectively than a woman twice her size.

"Beatrice," the First Lady spoke up without turning, "could you make us some tea, please? I would, but I fear that Anne will still need to decide in her mind that she is where she belongs. *Oui?*" Her position effectively blocked any escape to the left.

"Yes, ma'am." Beatrice offered a glare that told Anne she wasn't going anywhere, then turned for the small family kitchen. The main kitchen was downstairs from which their dinner had arrived via a dumbwaiter, to be served by stewards who ascended in the tiny elevator and had now departed.

"No, Genny," Alice blocked Anne's options to the right. "We don't need to worry. She's from Tennessee. Anne is too polite to run, even given the chance."

"Just..." Anne had to swallow against a dry throat, she really did need some tea. "Just try me. Give me an escape route and my next stop will be—"

"One Observatory Circle," Alice offered calmly. "While the Vice President might appreciate that, it is far too soon to appease him so easily."

Anne didn't want to appease him, she wanted to burrow up against his chest and hide from the two women facing her. Beatrice returned with a tray laden with rattling china, lemon, sugar, and milk. Make that three women facing her. Make it four and then she could be hiding from herself as well...which was exactly what she couldn't do. The First Lady was right; she couldn't run.

"Besides," Genny patted Anne's hand and she felt soothed despite herself, "it is time we came to know you just as it is time for Peter and Zachary to become more properly acquainted."

Anne was about to ask why now was any different than yesterday, but then decided she wouldn't like the answer.

"I looked for cookies, ma'am," Beatrice shrugged, "but—"

"The President has eaten them all, I know it is *très problématique.* He does this always, I must fight with tooth and nail for my share."

Anne recalled the box she'd stuffed into her pack before leaving Tennessee. "I brought Christmas cookies, ma'am. For Daniel, but I forgot to give them to him. They might be a little stale, but I can run up to my room and get them."

"Too distracted by a handsome Vice President, perhaps?" Alice teased.

"It's not fair that my favorite sister-in-law gets to tease me."

"As your only sister-in-law, I find the honor of 'favorite' unimpressive in that respect, but gladly accept it in all others. However, there's not a chance I'm letting you escape that easily. They're in your room?"

"On the night stand," Anne did her best to sound grouchy, but she liked Alice too much to put any heat behind it.

Alice left in pursuit of sugar and Beatrice returned to the kitchen at the kettle's shrill whistle.

The Dining Room was suddenly very quiet.

The First Lady reached out and took her hand. "My good friend, Anne. Do not be so afraid."

"I'm not actually afraid of any of you. Merely terribly humbled and completely out of my element."

"You are not scared, you are *terrifié!* But I agree that it is not of me or Daniel's Alice."

"I don't mind if she's afraid of me," Beatrice returned carrying a large snow-white teapot with black raven silhouettes soaring across the surface.

"Oh foof," the First Lady waved a dismissive hand. "You are not scary to the people you love."

Beatrice's easy shrug of acceptance also lifted her jacket enough to reveal the large handgun in the shoulder holster that rested against the side of her breast.

"It is," the First Lady returned her attention to Anne, "the man who has so touched your heart. *Mais oui?* He is what you cannot account for."

Anne did not like being so thoroughly transparent. However her likes and dislikes appeared to be of little consequence in this case. She toyed with Zack's tie a bit and felt a sense of comfort that only reinforced her growing feelings for him. She'd barely taken it off except to shower before dinner. Now she wished she'd run while she'd still had the chance.

"Here they are," Alice returned with the large box of homemade Christmas cookies.

That's when Anne remembered just what was in there. "Perhaps we should send down to the kitchen instead..." She reached for the box, but Alice held it away out of her reach as she sat down.

While Beatrice joined them, facing the door, and the First Lady poured, Anne tried to signal Alice about just what kind of cookies were in the box.

Alice merely smiled and began slitting the tape. After three years with Daniel she knew exactly what sort Anne always made for her brother.

———

"No games happing in the Eastern Conference, Mr. President," Frank announced.

"How about some Scrabble?"

Zack opened his mouth to say it wasn't really his game, but he'd be glad to take on the President—but Daniel cut him off.

"Don't! No, Mr. Vice President," Daniel began pulling beers out of a small mini-fridge. "Don't even think it. He and the First Lady would play at international levels if they could afford the three days for the World Championship. With their pseudonyms they anonymously rule the online Scrabble world."

The President was doing an impressive job of looking innocent and shocked. He was a skilled enough politician that Zack might have bought it...if he hadn't seen Frank Adams shaking his head warningly from close behind the President.

"How about Western Conference?" Zack went for the safe play.

"San Diego State is facing down Colorado State tonight," Frank announced.

"If they win," Harvey noted, "that will knock the Air Force Falcons completely out of the running after the whupping they took from Stanford."

"Hey," Zack did his best to glare at his agent. "I thought you were supposed to defend me?"

"Only from bad guys, Mr. Vice President," Harvey answered easily. "Bad teams, I've got no help for you."

"They weren't bad. They just..." It was a losing argument anyway, because...

"...got their butts kicked," the President wasn't being helpful either.

"I could have outrun those guys," Harvey muttered, "and I'm not talking about back in the day."

To tease Zack, Anne had rooted for Stanford during the game when they'd watched it last night. Last night? Had it been so recently? He tried counting back the days, but it didn't work. He reached two and that was as far as it went. The concert at the Conservatory and last night. He'd never, well, not since his Air Force days, slept with a woman on their second date.

Last night he may not have slept much, but he'd certainly made love to Anne Darlington. As memorable as those moments had been, they were not the highlights that came first to mind. Much more strongly he remembered her lying in his arms on the Library couch wearing only his tie and one of his dress shirts unbuttoned, curled up together beneath a blanket and content to just watch the game as if they'd done it a thousand nights before.

But most of all, he remembered when she had turned from his photo to look at him. *I think Mr. Vice President that it is dangerous for two such lonely people to stand here in such silence.*

He had been raised beneath a shroud of impenetrable silence. He had escaped and filled his world with his own achievements: Air Force, state Senate, Governor, and Vice President. But Anne had seen past that so effortlessly. She'd also seen the boy he'd thought was carefully hidden—so deep that Zack himself only saw him on rare and particularly lonely nights.

A bright laugh sounded from across the hall just as Frank turned up the volume on the television.

"Tonight," one of the announcers spoke snidely as if he knew the Vice President had just tuned in, "San Diego is expected to trounce Colorado State with a projected sixteen point spread and secure their place in the playoffs."

Bad news all around.

———

When they opened the cookie box, sharp ginger and sweet sugar overwhelmed the scent of the chamomile tea until it was thick in the Dining Room. Anne wanted to hide her head in shame as the other three women howled with laughter over the cookies. Even Beatrice's serious demeanor had cracked as the first of "Anne's Specials"—as her Christmas cutout cookies were known in the family—were revealed.

Alice picked up a decidedly sneaky looking elf spiking Santa's eggnog. That wasn't too bad.

Beatrice's selection was a pair of gingerbread reindeer lying together as if exhausted by sex. A little too reminiscent of Anne's own position in Zack's arms last night.

Then the First Lady reached into the box and unearthed Mr. and Mrs. Claus. Santa was bent down as if peeking under his wife's red royal icing dress complete with white trim.

The three of them were laughing and comparing the cookies.

Anne resisted hanging her head, "I made them to embarrass Daniel, not me."

"And how is that working for you?" Alice bit off the sly elf's head.

"About as well as usual," Anne suddenly felt very sad. Nothing was going the way she'd planned this holiday season. She'd always enjoyed Christmas, it was a wonderful time on farm, but this time all she felt was misery.

"She needs a cookie," Beatrice nudged the box across the table.

Anne reached in without looking. For a moment she didn't even remember making this cookie, but it had her trademark style. And then she remembered the painstaking decorations she'd done. Gingerboy and gingergirl stood hip to hip with their arms around each other's waist. She'd decorated it to be Alice and Daniel; after all, the box had been intended for them. It was the one sweet cookie in a box of questionable elves and sated reindeer.

She tried to hand the cookie over to Alice, "You should save this one, I made it of the two of you."

Alice studied it, but didn't take it from her. "That doesn't look like me, that looks like you."

"No it doesn't," but even as she said it, Anne was studying the cookie. The gingergirl didn't have the curly brunette mop that always looked so cute on Alice, instead she had long blond hair like Anne's own. Why had she done that? And the gingerboy didn't look like Daniel, but instead was mostly faceless with nondescript hair.

Geneviève leaned in closely and rested a hand on Anne's shoulder. "Now that you know what your true love looks like, you can finish this cookie and make it *idéal*!"

It would take only the tiniest bit of royal icing to draw in Zack's dark hair and beard, his warm brown eyes would be hard to match for they were so alive, and of course a silver tie, for she would always think of him in it. Then it would be—

"My what?" The First Lady's words had finally sunk in like a hammer blow.

"Twelve seconds," Alice looked up from her watch. "You have an impressive reaction time, sister. Slow on the uptake, but your recovery time was far better than mine. When Emily told me that I loved Daniel, I heard her sooner, but it was at least a minute and a glass of wine about so large," she held her palms way apart, "before I was able to respond."

"My grandmother," Genny said with a happy smile and a soft sigh. "On our farm in Vietnam while the President waited in the kitchen and my sister Jacqui—who is so very shameless—flirted with him. Gram said I already knew who was inside of my heart and I simply decided she was right because Gram always is."

They all turned to Beatrice. She grimaced before biting off one of the reindeer's heads and rinsing it down with some tea, "Frank told me. I had to go and help invade Panama before I figured out he was right."

Then they all turned back to Anne.

She bit off the gingerboy's and then the gingergirl's heads, eliciting a grin from Beatrice, then replied with her mouth still full, "I still don't know squat."

They all laughed, but Genny's smile told her that she wasn't fooling anyone, not even herself.

How could she *not* love the lonely boy turned into the magnificent man?

CHAPTER FIVE

W *hat do you mean* you have to go?"

The days flew by as Anne settled into a lovely routine at One Observatory Circle. Her dinner with the First Family had been leaked by the First Lady's press office and duly noted by the gossip columns. The media's tone had shifted immediately from "Who is this tramp?" to "Is the nation's most eligible bachelor finally off the market?" An elegant move by an elegant First Lady.

As the spotlight shifted to the Darlingtons, Ma had swung into action. She'd been very pleased for Anne—other than being a little huffy about finding out through the media rather than directly from her daughter. Anne had called her as soon as the news broke, but CNN had beat her call to Tennessee. There was little the two of them hadn't shared over the years and her mother had been as enthusiastic as her new female friends had been after dinner that night.

Mary Annette Darlington also was the advertising and marketing specialist of the family. By day three of Anne's affair with the Vice President, the Darlington Estate web site had shifted in tone. Family history press packets appeared, tracing their roots back to Colonial times, as did individual profiles—Anne's cast her in an uncomfortably heroic light. She couldn't quite put her finger on it, for all of Ma

Darlington's facts were true, but they made Anne sound like so much more than she knew she was.

A week passed, and most of a second, but Cornelia Day had become no more pleasant than at their first meeting. Anne had developed some patience with her constant animosity. After all, protecting the Vice President was a concern they shared. But that one common shared goal certainly wasn't enough to warrant a peace accord.

"Thanks, Jim," Zack said to the Navy steward who was serving them breakfast. Short stack with coffee for her, tall stack with sausage, bacon, orange juice, and coffee for him.

"Thank you, James," she echoed, but her heart wasn't in it this morning.

The sunlight, for a century so carefully measured and timed by the Naval Observatory, shone down out of a clear blue sky oblivious that the USNO now supplied the nation's time markers from an atomic clock, rather than a solar sighting.

Zack had taken her to see it one evening, a short and very chilly walk across the campus. It consisted of a dozen racks of nondescript computer equipment and a sign that said "USNO Master Clock" in bright red electronic letters. Another displayed the official time out to the kazillionths of a second. They'd also walked through the largest astronomical library in the US which was impressive and almost utterly meaningless. She'd gotten to peek through a twenty-six-inch refractor telescope, which was oddly forty-feet long and showed startling objects. Clearly the technicians were used to looking at far more strange and esoteric things than a Horsehead Nebula, so she had not delayed them long.

Zack's Dining Room at One Observatory Circle had a long formal walnut table with elegant chairs. It could easily seat a dozen, instead the two of them sat across from each other at one end. One of the stewards, probably Sharelle for she had the best eye, had placed the flowers so that the table didn't look empty, but rather their part of it was simply smaller. The fire snapped warm and bright in the fireplace, a simple garland draped over the mantelpiece. The room had none of the homey touches that the First Lady had placed about the White House Residence.

Despite spending nights at the heart of American national time-keeping, Anne rarely cared what time it was more accurately than morning versus afternoon. But now their time together was growing short and she was discovering that she cared very much.

"When?"

"I fly out to Italy this evening."

"Tonight?" Anne's heart stopped along with her fork halfway from plate to mouth.

"The Climate Conference at Courmayeur. I've been working on it all week," he was looking at her in a slightly bemused way.

"Courmayeur." By sheer force of will, Anne managed to get her fork underway again and placed the first bite of pancake in her mouth. She chewed because something was there, not because she could taste it. She'd heard, she knew, but it simply hadn't impinged on her world until this moment.

"Italy. We've grown tired of the idiot rioters both for and against the environment. Rather than some major city, we're going to meet very quietly in a tiny Italian resort."

"You're leaving for Italy this evening." And what was she supposed to do? For an entire, glorious ten days, she'd done absolutely no thinking. All she'd allowed herself to do was feel.

The days had been spent touring about DC, more at the whim of the agent the Secret Service had assigned to guarding her than her own. Detra was a overtly positive, buxom blond who was immensely entertaining.

"You're my first protectee you know. Solo I mean. I've been in the Protection Detail for over a year, an agent for three years since I qualified. So you shouldn't feel worried about my being some beginner. I haven't lost anyone yet," she barely slowed down for a perky smile filled with perfect teeth. "What do you mean you've never seen the Declaration? Your file said that you were D.A.R. One of your direct relatives signed."

Her mother was from Georgia which had been one of the original states, and had brought her membership as a Daughter of the American Revolution across state lines to Johnny Darlington's farm, along with her accent. No one could ever tell whether mother or daughter had answered the phone, not even Daniel, which had led to some spectacular opportunities to give him lectures throughout the years.

"That's huge," Detra had proclaimed. "Let's go find it!" And they'd be off.

Evenings had been spent with Zack. She'd dined twice more at the White House, once with the First Family and once with just Daniel, Alice, and Zack in the upstairs kitchen. They'd attended a holiday concert of Handel's *Messiah* in the National Cathedral. It was one of the most moving things she ever heard; the space itself was beautiful enough to be a religious experience even without the music.

And there'd been a "strictly social" dinner at the Speaker's house in Georgetown. Even though Zack and the Speaker were from different parties, it was clear they were quite good friends. And the Speaker's wife had made no attempt to disguise her joy at the social coup of being the first to host Anne Darlington.

Anne had been to far too many formal dinners to disappoint and had forced herself to purchase a second dress for the occasion.

Now, whether her reputation thrived or crashed and burned, Mrs. Speaker would gain bragging rights in either direction. Ultimately, despite the circumstances, she'd found herself liking the Speaker's wife.

That had left only a few evenings at One Observatory Circle. The second night she'd worried about how to discreetly move her meager belongings from the White House to the Vice President's without imposing. Zack had solved that by simply asking if she wanted to pack her bags after the First Family's dinner.

It was the nights that were so new to her. They soon felt as if she'd never been anywhere else. Anne had never lived with a man before. Stayed with them on occasion, but there was no doubt that she and the Vice President were living together. When you were handing off the toothpaste tube while brushing your teeth together in the same bathroom, there was no avoiding the fact.

And tonight she'd be living...where?

"I was rather hoping you could come with me, unless you have somewhere else you have to be."

"Italy?" Anne knew she was being thick headed, but couldn't seem to shake it off. She'd had her morning coffee. Goodness, she'd had amazing wake-up sex and a beautiful man to scrub her back in the shower, though he'd insisted on washing her hair each morning which took forever to dry. But he enjoyed it so much, she hadn't had the heart to use a shower cap.

Still, her mind was having trouble keeping up with the new play that had just been called. "Italy," she repeated once more.

"Uh-huh," Zack was clearly enjoying the moment, grinning at her over a sip of his orange juice.

She took a deep breath and held it. Not that she was all that great at doing so for very long, but she'd always told herself that if you couldn't make a decision in the amount of time she could hold her breath, then it wasn't time to make it.

Did she want to be with Zack? More than any man in her past...or that she could imagine in her future, but she couldn't hold her breath long enough to think out the consequences of that one.

Did she want to travel to Italy? She loved Italy.

Did she want to travel to Italy with the Vice President? That answer was far less clear.

She could see in his eyes that there was more than merely the travel. It was the quiet of the man facing the boy's rail yard picture.

If she traveled with him, she would be labeled "mistress." They both knew that.

If she traveled with him, it would mean far more was happening between them than an incredibly pleasant affair. It meant they were lovers who were...

Anne was running out of air. She needed time on that last point but that quiet in his eyes worried her. She didn't want to hurt Zack's feelings either. To cover the small gasp to refill her aching lungs, she reached out with a fork and snagged one of his link sausages and bit off the end.

"Well, Mr. Vice President," even in the most intimate moments, she had yet to wholly drop the honorific, "that doesn't strike me as *much* closer to the North Pole."

"Actually, Expedition Leader, Courmayeur is well north of DC. I checked for you. It is almost four hundred miles farther north."

"So is the state of Maine. I'll have to inspect my expedition supplies and get back to you." She could see the hurt on his features and she reached across to take his hand for a moment.

He squeezed it very hard as if holding on for dear life.

She felt much the same way. "Just give me a few hours. I remember you mentioning this, but I never thought I'd go along."

He nodded and managed to dredge up an easy smile for her, but she could see that it cost him to do so. She almost said yes right then, but that was the happy mistress' answer, not the lovers'. And definitely not the—

Anne chopped off that thought hard, though it wasn't far away. If she was ever going to spend her life with a man, it would be someone like Zachary Thomas. Just like him. But she didn't want merely to be some man's wife no matter who he was.

She did her best to return his smile and could only hope that he didn't see what it cost her.

———

They rode to the White House together in silence, where Cornelia eyed her coolly as the Vice President disappeared into his first meeting. Every single agency in DC wanted input on what he was going to say at the upcoming conference.

When the US had announced that they were sending the VP, it had forced all of the other countries attending to step up their game. Second- or third-level department heads were being replaced by vice-ministers, and even undersecretaries were completely passé. Now it would be a conference of people who could actually make decisions.

Anne didn't know why she was hesitating here in Zack's outer office.

Apparently Cornelia didn't either. She slowly melted from cold to curious, without quite looking up from her desk.

Anne kept looking over her shoulder, as it felt like there was another person in the room. In a way, there was. Someone had decorated the VP's office into a full Victorian-style Christmas. It was the happy-ever-after of Scrooge; the party that Mr. Fezziwig would have thrown in Scrooge's youth. Garlands and a wreath sported bows in period fabrics. Some fine weavings—clearly museum pieces—had been hung on the walls. And a girl-mannequin in full attire stood looking out the window at the EEOB across the street. She was complete with a Christmas basket and, Anne peeked beneath the bright cloth, a—she tapped it with a fingernail—plastic figgy pudding.

Beyond the window, another light snow was falling on DC. Mid-December had not eased off from the chill and bluster that had begun the month which still made the parka her coat of choice.

"Is there something I can do for you, Ms. Darlington?" Cornelia was as polite as could be, a dangerous sound. How little would it take for her to maneuver Anne's reputation right into the mud or... But she hadn't. Instead she had kept the Vice President right on schedule and prepared him for the upcoming trip.

"Was it your idea?" Anne wasn't quite sure where the question had come from.

"The Victorian décor? No way." It was the one hint Anne had heard of her California background—an accent and speech pattern otherwise very well hidden.

"No. Sending the Vice President to the climate conference. It's brilliant actually," and it was more brilliant each time she thought about it.

"No. It was the Vice President's. Many have labeled it political as the President is already well into his second term, but he doesn't care about how it looks. He cares about the results." Cornelia's voice had once again grown haughty.

But Anne could only nod. That fit the man she knew. The Coloradan who had complained about the failing snow on the ski areas in the same breath as the raging wildfires across his home state and others. President. Somehow she hadn't thought about Zachary Thomas being the next obvious candidate. An immensely popular one even without the climate conference.

"Sorry," Cornelia offered in a contrite voice. "You bring out the nasty in me. I don't even know why."

Anne looked at her in surprise. "I thought that was obvious. Either you love him yourself or you are convinced that I'm not good enough for him. You won't find me arguing on either point."

"You are wrong. You are very good for him. *That* is the problem."

Anne decided that sitting down would be a good idea at that moment. Suddenly she was the shortest one in the room, both the mannequin and the seated Cornelia towered above her. "How is that a problem?"

Cornelia didn't fuss with her pen or straighten her notepad. Instead she simply folded her hands atop her desk and looked at Anne with a forthrightness unbecoming to a Southerner.

"Already he depends on you. I often hear him discussing ideas in meetings that are unusual for him. You make a thoughtful man think even more deeply."

Anne could only blink in surprise. She and Zack often spoke about whatever he was reading; over a meal, riding in the motorcade, or curled up together. It gave them something to talk about other than themselves. But that she was affecting his decisions was another new idea in an already busy morning.

"When I joined him, I had a terrible crush on him. I was fresh out of college at twenty—three year program; an overachiever and valedictorian like yourself. But he was already thirty. I knew I had a choice: take a chance that he would have me and perhaps ruin his career with my youth, or work for a man I respect immensely. I chose the latter."

Anne still was unable to move under the steady weight of Cornelia's gaze.

"You are much nearer his age and I can see how you are changing him for the better. He is different with you than any other woman and if you suddenly decide to go, the effect could be devastating—not only on the news cycle, but on him as well. He's never taken anyone to see the Conservatory for Christmas before. It is something that he does every year and for some reason it is very private to him. Yet he took you. I don't know whether or not to trust you, Ms. Darlington."

Anne knew the reason behind Zack's privacy and once again hurt for the lonely boy alone each Christmas, journeying to watch the model trains. She was also in awe that he had shared it with her. Had she returned the favor? Anne had shared her body and her joy with him, but she hadn't shared but a glimpse of her own inner turmoil. It had taken her a decade of chafing at the bit before she'd known that the farm was no longer for her. She had come to DC more as a declaration to herself than to Daniel that she was moving on.

But she didn't know to where.

"Would it make you feel any better, Ms. Day, that I don't trust myself either?"

She tipped her head in thought, a long elegant gesture. For the first time Anne could see the nerves behind the careful façade. Cornelia presented the DC shark to the world, but there was someone softer inside and it made Anne feel more kindly toward her.

"I'll make you a deal, Cornelia."

The woman arched a single eyebrow at her.

"I'll make sure that you're the third to know if I turn out to be trustworthy, next in line after the Vice President."

"And who before that?" her tone turned suspicious.

"Me."

Cornelia actually laughed, a wholly unexpected sound that lightened her face. For an instant a much younger girl showed through. She reached across the desk and offered a firm handclasp which Anne returned in surprise.

"I may like you yet, Ms. Darlington."

"The surprise is mutual, Ms. Day." Anne suspected they could even become friends, which was an even greater shock. Anne had plenty of friends back in Tennessee, but they were more for socializing with. Aside from her mother—who she'd discovered to be a wonderful and thoughtful woman once they'd both survived Anne's terrible teens— Anne had enjoyed more heart-to-hearts with astonishing women in the last week than in the prior decade.

"Will we be seeing you on the plane, Ms. Darlington?"

"Anne. And I don't know yet. I'd best go talk to my brother and see if he can help me decide."

"He left for the Hill an hour ago. He's not expected back until after it would be time to depart for the airport. Would you like me to try and reach him for you?"

Anne shook her head. She didn't know if he'd be of help anyway, but her options were running a tad bit thin. She certainly wasn't going to talk to the President about the implications of her sex life with his VP.

Cornelia's phone rang.

Anne waved for her to take it, "I'll go wander the halls and see what inspiration strikes."

"Good luck," Cornelia mouthed as she lifted the phone. It looked as if she meant it.

———

"The CIA analyst is here for your next meeting, Mr. Vice President."

Zack waved a hand for Cornelia to send him in without looking up from his notes. "Find out what they'd like for lunch and order two of them, would you?"

"Peasant under glass. Make it a cute one."

Zack glanced up to see Alice Darlington grinning at him. "I've been following up on the conversations we had last week, so they sent me to brief you." She plummeted into the chair across his desk in a way that he was learning was a Darlington-woman trademark—native-born or married-in. Alice wore a red cardigan with a brown moose knit in above her left breast. Knitted snow slipped down from the white collar in tiny stitches of white, some landing on the moose's back and antlers. She wore a matching knit hat that did little to control the brown curls of her hair.

"If you can't find a cute peasant, I'll take a turkey on rye and a Coke. Thanks, Cornelia."

His assistant disappeared.

Zack looked down at the thick files Alice was holding and did his best not to wince. What he wanted to do was track down Anne and talk her into going with him, hours had gone by and he still hadn't heard her decision about Italy. Instead, he'd focus on climate change and pay attention to the present. "Please tell me there's a short version to those files."

Alice had shed her hat so her cheerful nod swirled dark hair over her green eyes. "No, wait, these are the short version."

Zack gave a dutiful groan and hoped she was teasing.

"Or we can talk about my sister-in-law."

He glanced at the door, saw that Cornelia had considerately closed it, and he turned once more to face Alice. Did he dare? Was it cheating to talk to one woman about another? Or even worse, discussing Daniel's sister with his wife? He decided that he didn't care.

"I'd like that."

"Good! Eleven days you've been playing house together, if you count the first night before she moved in as well. Please tell me you have done more than had sex with her."

Zack had to blink hard to catch up with the conversation.

"Of course I have. We've eaten, slept, showered, watched football. A wide variety of other activities."

"So, playing house with the pretty lady. But what about *her?*"

"What about her?" One of his specialties was his ability to anticipate and even control the conversation. He'd crossed from the Colorado Senate into the Governorship in only three years. He'd stopped strikes, proposed and passed wildfire legislation, even managed to lead migrant workers and union leaders to the same table and hammered out accords between them. Keeping ahead of Alice Darlington was being another challenge entirely; he wasn't even sure what the conversation was.

Alice thumped the stack of files down on his desk, crossed her arms, and flipped enough hair aside to glare at him with one eye. "You do know why she came to Washington DC, don't you? And before you answer that, no, it had nothing to do with you."

Zack had lost sight of that. He thought back to that first meeting in Daniel's office. She'd been...sad. She hid it well beneath that wall of easy humor, but the sadness had been there. And lonely.

"Two such lonely people," she'd said.

Somehow, this beautiful charismatic woman thought she was alone in the world. He'd watched her laughing with Alice, the First Lady, and even the agents, Beatrice and Detra. He'd seen her tease her brother until the Chief of Staff was at a complete loss for what to do next—and Daniel *always* knew what to do next.

"Ah, the light goes on!" Alice pointed to the ceiling as if she controlled the sun itself.

Anne had come to tell Daniel she was done with the family farm, but never a word about what came next. They were practically living together and Zack suddenly understood just how little he knew about her. Her hesitation at breakfast this morning suddenly made perfect sense, as if she was finding her way in the dark—one step at a time. And he had left her alone on her journey.

"I have to go find her," he pushed to his feet just as Cornelia opened the office door carrying a lunch tray set up for two.

"She's with the First Lady, Mr. Vice President," Cornelia set the tray down and looked at him levelly. The anger and mistrust that had simmered all week and flared every time Anne was mentioned had disappeared. Instead...

Zack slowly lowered himself back into his chair as the two women watched him.

"Well, I wouldn't presume to interrupt her there." At his nod, Cornelia withdrew, but he suddenly wondered who's side she was on. He pulled over a sandwich and a bag of chips. "Let's see what's in those files, Alice."

"As you wish, Mr. Vice President," and she opened the first one.

Anne had wandered for much of the morning. Detra had caught her mood and faded into the background. Anne's badge gained her admittance to much of the complex and she let the ebb and flow of the Christmas tide carry her along. The West Wing was a hive of activity and purposefulness that rapidly drove her toward the Residence. She discovered the China Room and the Map Room, but neither held her attention.

She spent a while sitting with the main White House Christmas tree in the Blue Room. It was a peaceful corner, well out of everyone's way. The eighteen-foot blue spruce was even bigger than the farm's traditional monster. The White House had elicited ornaments from fifth-grade classes in every state capital. Tens of thousands of white balls had been sent out and the best of each school had been chosen to travel to DC. Hundreds of red-nosed reindeer, green-clad elves (who weren't spiking Santa's eggnog), and cheery Santas adorned the tree. Some bore the state fish or bird; it was a very merry tree.

"What if?" she asked the tree. It was a fairly obvious question.

What if she and Zack became a couple?

What if he was elected President at the end of Peter Matthew's second term?

Would she be sitting here some few years in the future and the grandest achievement of her year would be the theme of a White House Christmas tree? She'd rather be back on the farm if that was the case. There, at least, she knew what was needed and expected of the only Darlington daughter. The farm needed her, or could at least make good use of her, but she didn't need or want the farm.

She—

"Look!"

Anne glanced over to see a tour was entering the room. Cameras out, snapping pictures. Except they weren't looking at the tree, nor photographing it.

"It's that woman." "The Vice President's girlfriend." "Oh, she's so much prettier in real life." "Can I get your picture with us?" "Can I—"

Anne put on her best happy face, and retreated as quickly as possible without being rude. Down the Central Hall. Past the Vermeil Room and the Library. She almost ducked into the latter, but the open doors and cloth ropes indicated that tours would invade there as well.

The double doors at the end of the hall plunged her into yet another crowd forming up.

"It's the Visitor's Lobby," Detra had magically appeared at her elbow and Anne almost cried out in relief. "We need to get you out of here. Let's go see the Kennedy Garden." And with a casual looping of her arm through Anne's they were out into the freezing cold and fluttering snow even as people were calling her name. She'd never even had a chance to see the decorations.

"You're kidding me," her teeth were chattering before they'd gone five steps. Her parka was hanging in Daniel's outer office back in the West Wing.

"Sorry, best I have on short notice."

The rose bushes had been pruned back to little more than twigs rising from the soil. The grass was hidden beneath snowy paths. A dozen fake reindeer, in full harness, were standing in the central path of garden. One of the two lead reindeer was leaning forward as if to nibble a rose bush. A mighty sleigh filled with giant bags overflowing with ornaments were at the far end of the path.

"At least you're wearing boots," Detra commented.

Anne looked down at the agent's shoes, barely as high as the snow and definitely not up to making the crossing with dry feet. Anne felt bad for saying anything.

In moments, they were through the garden and an agent had a door open into the East Wing. Anne ducked inside and did her best to suppress her next shiver.

"Might I suggest a coat next time you want to visit the gardens in mid-December, ma'am."

She looked up and recognized Beatrice who was clearly amused by the situation.

Anne had to admit that it was hard not to be. "Seen a lot of protectees running scared?"

Beatrice and Detra both nodded, "From crowds of tourists? All the time."

Anne turned to her agent who was trying to be circumspect about knocking the snow out of her shoes. "Thank you, Detra."

"My pleasure, ma'am."

Then Anne figured out the implications of Beatrice's presence. The East Wing was the First Lady's domain and if the head of her Protection Detail was here, so was the First Lady.

Well, with Daniel on the Hill and Alice locked away in some cloister out at CIA headquarters in Langley, she was down to two options. She could call Ma and have a nice whine together; that would cheer her up but probably move her no closer to an answer. Or she could see if the First Lady was available. Anne remembered Geneviève's easy kindness every time they'd met, but that wasn't enough to tip the scale in favor of approaching the daunting First Lady. However, her comment to Anne the first time they were alone together came to mind. "Do not be afraid."

She was and she didn't like it.

Maybe Genny Matthews—she no longer thought of her as Geneviève nor the First Lady, but Genny—was the woman she *needed* to talk to.

"I don't suppose that..." No, she must be as busily scheduled as the President.

"She has just ordered lunch," Beatrice informed her. "She is part French and does not believe in working through lunches. Let me see if she's available. I can easily make the order for two."

Moments later, Anne was being escorted up the stairs and into the second floor of the East Wing. Down a long corridor that was little more than a blur of door signs: Calligraphers Office, The Office of the Social Secretary, Social Media Director, Event Coordinator. She was shown into the First Lady's office without even a pause to catch her breath; which was just as well as it also precluded any chance to second guess herself.

Like Daniel's, it had a southwest corner exposure. Except it over-looked the Kennedy Gardens with its plastic reindeer, the Residence, and the White House grounds rather than West Executive Avenue and the Executive Office Building.

Like Daniel's—in a crowded building where space was at a premium and size denoted importance—it was a large and comfortable space.

Unlike Daniel's it was immaculate, intensely feminine, and had a communications center that looked as if it could run a war.

CHAPTER SIX

hat in the world do you do here? Fly the space shuttle?"

"*Bonjour,* my dear Anne," Genny turned from her desk, which faced the view, and rose to greet Anne. Her dress of pale rose linen looked both practical and fashionable. Her easy hug was thoughtlessly welcoming, simply a natural extension of Genny's warmth. "*Non.* But at times I think that perhaps I could have while it still flew. Such fine technology as this still does not limit the nonsense that it can convey. The many countries of the UN must talk and talk and talk before they can make even the smallest decision."

It was easy to forget that the First Lady was also the UN "Ambassador" for the UNESCO World Heritage Convention. She was the chief peacekeeper and dealmaker for the thousand World Heritage sites and the hundreds under consideration. No wonder she needed so much conferencing equipment. There was little that couldn't be done at the Darlington's farm with a phone or a tactfully worded e-mail; this was a very different-colored horse.

Genny waved her to a small side table. Unlike the monster at the Vice President's residence, this table could seat only four, six in a pinch. However like Zachary's home it lacked...

"What happened to Christmas?" All Anne could pick out was a

two-foot tall Christmas tree standing on a low side table and a small quilt of a polar bear staring upward at a starry sky.

"The French and the Vietnamese are far more understated than Americans about the season. I decorate the Residence for Peter and for the photographers. I decorate my office for myself. For us, the season is about sharing and food."

And as lunch was delivered, Anne knew that she'd be hard-pressed to argue. A winter minestrone with thick slices of fresh-baked sourdough. A small cup of yogurt and melon drizzled with honey accompanied by small selection of cookies that were, thankfully, White House chef elegant rather than Anne Darlington outrageous.

"You have reached the problem," Genny was the first to break the silence of good food.

She had. Apparently far too obviously.

"We will ignore that while we eat. Instead, I will speak of what *I* am troubled by, so that you may stop worrying for a time." And Genny began discussing the challenges of World Heritage site selection: limited funds, uncooperative governments, rampant poaching in the nature reserves, and no actual authority to implement solutions. "Everything it is a negotiation."

"Everything everywhere," Anne agreed.

The Darlington Estate had grown to encompass dozens of different efforts. Everything from horse breeding—they specialized in the Tennessee Walkers, tall majestic animals—to a fine dining restaurant with a menu almost wholly produced on the farm. Flour was one of the few things that was brought in from outside; honey or sorghum was used for sweetenings and wine was "imported" from the next valley over. There was an educational center for Slow Food and local farming techniques. In nearby Johnson City there was even a campaign center for lobbying Congress regarding non-GMO products, hazards of mono-culture farming, and the like. A hundred projects with a thousand demands.

"Yes, it is just so," Genny waved a hand toward the communication center behind her. "I must decide if the Pacific Island nations that are likely to be submerged by global warming have a higher claim to recognition than the primeval beech forests of the Ukraine. Both will be gone without UNESCO protection. Both may be gone even if it is granted. How am I supposed to make these kinds of decisions? *Je ne sais pas.*"

A pleasant hour flew by as she and Genny discussed different ways to approach that problem and others. Over a second cup of tea and the chocolate-dipped macaroons, Genny nodded as if reaching some decision.

"Hmm?" Anne asked as she debated whether to stop or to try a chocolate sable cookie. Go for it.

"You are as good at this as I thought you would be," the First Lady abstained from another cookie.

"As good at what?" Anne bit down and, at her intentionally amplified yummy sound, Genny Matthews caved and took one as well.

"I know the site buildings and the regional history. But I know little of nature. On our farm in Vietnam we only grow coffee and what food we can for ourselves, but I never care for that just as you do not care for your farm."

"No. Wait. I—" At Genny's raised hand Anne sputtered to a stop.

"I do not say that you do not love it or do not wish it well protected, but you wish someone else to do it and not you. I know this feeling as much as you do."

"Right down to the heels of my boots."

"That is why I come to work for the UN. That is how I met your President. I try to force him to fix a problem with an ancient temple that Cambodia and Thailand fight over. I did not think he is going to marry me for seeking his aid."

"What are you saying?"

"I am saying that you care very deeply about the land, about any land. You do not care so much for the tending, but your heart has no question about the land. While you are in Italy, you must look at Mont Blanc Massif. When you return from Italy, we will talk of what you see."

"Italy?" Anne almost lost her china teacup at the sharp veer in the conversation's direction. "I still don't know if I'm going. That's actually what I wanted to talk to—"

"Piff! Of course you are going to Italy. It is so romantic a place. You will see Courmayeur. You will eat fine food in a tiny *ristorante*. You will make passionate love in an Italian villa."

"But…" Anne didn't even know where to begin. "But…I don't want to hurt Zachary's—the Vice President's reputation. The media will look at me and—"

"I am a French-Vietnamese woman. I fall in love with your President after his very popular first wife is dead—though the stories I hear about her…" Genny shivered as if all of her office windows were suddenly open to the December storm wrapping its fist around DC. "You are American woman in love with an American man; your states are as close together as two pea vines compared to my country and Peter's. This makes it much less of a trouble. Go! Enjoy Italy."

And once again, events swept out of Anne's control.

The UNESCO World Heritage Ambassador to the UN assembly turned back to her work. Detra gathered her up in the East Wing hall and handed over her parka. In moments she was down through the tunnel underneath East Executive Avenue and into the garage beneath the Treasury Building. The black SUV slid out into DC traffic and a thick snowfall.

"Where are we going?" Anne gathered some thread of common sense as they passed the Jefferson Memorial and turned east. "Isn't the Vice President's house that way?"

Detra nodded affably. "It is. Nothing wrong your sense of direction."

"But—"

"Andrews Field is this way. Air Force Two is just warming up on the tarmac. The Vice President is running behind."

"But—" Anne tried again.

"One of the Navy stewards packed your clothes and other belongings. They're right behind you."

Anne twisted around to see her knapsack and the clothes bag with her two dresses. Not a single piece of it was appropriate for where she was going; Italian women always dressed well and she'd come to DC with little more than jeans and turtlenecks. Of course, there was nowhere to buy fashionable clothes quite like Italy.

The last "but" she could think of, which was also the first, had been answered by Genny Matthews, the woman who loved the President.

Was Anne herself *in love?* Genny had pointed it out at that first dinner as if it had been a neon sign blazing on Anne's forehead. Cornelia Day seemed to think so as well. It was getting hard to deny, so she supposed she was. That sounded like a lame revelation.

"In love" was supposed to have lightning bolts, choirs of angels, and hard-bodied men. Okay, perhaps it did have the first and last of those, but where was the heavenly choir? It was the right season after all. She'd never imagined that love would arrive like a favorite pair of slippers, but it did fit ever so fine.

So, no longer a question, she was in love. In love with Zachary Thomas. She tested it as they zipped onto the field. The thought had a warm, cozy, fireside feel to it and was as natural as their lovemaking.

The next question: what was she going to do about it? Not thinking had gotten her this far and she considered sticking with that plan of action.

No.

It was time to stop drifting, she checked her mental calendar. The Thanksgiving banquet had been twenty days ago. She'd been living at One Observation Circle for the last eleven; living with someone—which should not be a first at her age, but it was.

Definitely time to take some control of...

The SUV slid to a halt. Detra jumped out and opened Anne's door before she could. Seeing what was outside waiting for her, they might need the jaws of life to extract her from the vehicle. Splashed like a poster across the windshield, a Boeing 757—looking terribly long and sleek and painted in the blue-and-white livery of the United States of America executive aircraft—dominated her view.

But worse yet, the press corps was ranged behind a rope line and a phalanx of Secret Service agents, awaiting the Vice President's arrival and departure.

Except he wasn't here yet and every single one of those cameras were pointing at her vehicle.

Definitely time to return to not thinking about what was happening.

Then she heard a cry of police sirens and the cameras swung away... most of them.

———

Zack climbed out of the first SUV. The Secret Service had put him in the decoy vehicle and placed agents and the officer with the nuclear football in the limo behind. He never argued, Harvey said "go that way" and he went.

He headed for the rope line, Harvey had assured him that everyone there had been cleared and checked, so that he could approach without worry. That's when he spotted the lone SUV parked off to the right, yet on this side of the rope line.

Agent Detra Willand stood by an open door, looking into the vehicle with a puzzled expression on her face. He didn't know if he'd ever been happier to see a particular Secret Service agent in his six year association with them. If Detra was here, that meant—

Zack veered over to see what the problem was. As he peeked over Detra's shoulder he spotted Anne, rooted to the seat.

"Any problem, Agent Willand?"

She started. The first time he'd managed to surprise an agent. "Hello, Mr. Vice President. Sorry, sir. We appear to have hit someone's panic level."

"Mind if I try?"

Detra stepped out of the way, shifting into the protective circle that included Harvey and several others. He leaned in.

"Hi, Anne. Comfy? My, doesn't this feel familiar."

"That's a very big plane, Mr. Vice President," she didn't respond to his light tone.

He was so happy to see her here that he'd dance if that's what was needed and to hell with the press.

He gazed out the front windshield with her for a moment, "It is a big plane, isn't it? I believe that the President's is quite a bit bigger." He pushed for the double-entendre, but apparently it didn't catch.

"And that's a terrible number of reporters and cameras, sir."

"It is."

She didn't turn to him as she spoke, "I'm going home."

"I have two pieces of comfort for you to convince you otherwise."

"Which are?"

"Second, they're here to talk to me, not to you."

"What's first then?"

"I won't be the one flying that big beast. The largest fixed-wing plane I ever flew regularly is a glider, a sailplane. They're quite wonderful, you know. No engine, just you and the sound of wind. Really amazing."

She finally looked toward him, he could practically hear the snapping of the cords that had connected her to the aircraft and reporters. "You flew sailplanes?"

"Uh-huh."

"For the Air Force?"

"I was damned good at it too. Still have my license. Want to go up in one?"

She eyed him cautiously, "With you as the pilot?"

"Only room for two. Is that a problem?"

"Maybe."

Zack wondered what it would take to get Anne moving. He was sorely tempted to toss her over his shoulder and carry her to the plane. She awoke some primitive part of him that thought cavemen just might have had the right idea. He also thought that Anne would understand the joke...in the privacy of his own home. However, he'd been a politician long enough to know exactly how poorly that might be perceived by the press. He knew that while the Secret Service was circled close behind him, not far beyond them several dozen news service people would be assuming that he was busy necking with his girlfriend before he left on the flight.

He'd had worse ideas.

So he did.

After a muffled "mmfph" of protest, she gave as she always did: easily and completely. Anne Darlington played no games, held nothing in reserve. It was something that he both had no experience with and couldn't get enough of.

Then something shifted. He was no longer merely kissing a beautiful and willing woman. He couldn't identify the change, but was now kissing Melanie Anne Darlington. Whatever Alice had warned him of, Anne had made some decision and he was helpless before her.

Harvey cleared his throat behind him, once, then twice, then quite loudly.

Zack wanted to tell the man just how high a cliff he could go and jump off.

Someone bumped into him hard enough to jar apart his kiss with Anne.

Harvey mumbled a soft, "Sorry, Mr. Vice President."

Zack shifted back a few inches still under Anne's magic spell.

"You okay?" He whispered her.

"Not even a little," but she took his hand when he offered it. "North Pole would be simpler."

"But half the fun."

At the Press line he did manage to keep the questions directed to him, partly because Anne refused to speak. But there was no question about the photos on tonight's news, the Vice President holding hands with his girlfriend as they ascended the long steel stairway into Air Force Two.

———

When the big hatchway door closed behind them, Anne felt a surge of relief as visceral as diving into the swimming pond on hot day. In moments, she could hear the metal stairway rattling away and the engines began clawing to life.

"Oh my god. Please tell me that I never have to be doing that ever again in all my natural born days. Or any others."

"Depends. Are you planning to keep hanging out with me?"

She looked up at him. Zack was looking down at her...affectionately. The best kiss that any woman ever gave a man, and he was...still a man. She wanted to grab his shoulders and shake him, but the two Secret Service agents who had been last aboard the plane might tackle her to the carpet if she tried.

"Well? Are you?" This time she noted that though his voice was a tease, the eyes still hid the little boy.

"Get over it, sailplane boy. You're stuck with me. Even with that madness," she hooked a thumb out toward the scattering Press pool. Then she looked about for a distraction. "Can I get a tour? Our family jet would fit into this plane's overhead stowage bins."

There were four sections. First class had been replaced by a state-of-the-art communication system that completely humbled the First Lady's. You could run a war from here. Then she swallowed hard, that was *exactly* what you could do.

To the right, a narrow passageway slipped around the side of a blocked-off room. The door bore the Seal of the Vice President, the same as the President's except for a black outer ring and a white background on the center making it starker than the President's. That and the word "Vice," which Anne tapped lightly with a fingertip.

"You are like a drug, Anne," he understood her gesture. "A dangerous vice."

Okay, perhaps he'd been as affected by their latest kiss as she had. Maybe he was simply better at hiding it.

Zack swung open the stateroom door, and tossed his bag on one of the seats. Anne shrugged her shoulder and her knapsack plopped into the other executive brown-leather chair. His thick garment bag and her painfully thin one had somehow made it to the tiny closet ahead of them. There was a small desk between the two chairs, a tiny lavatory, and a three-seat couch that was long enough it might convert to a bed.

"How do you feel about joining the mile-high club?"

She took one look at the thickness of the walls on the stateroom— not very. "Dream on, Mr. Vice President."

He tried to pout, that was not going to work on her, before leading her out a second door and into the third section of the plane. Either side of the aisle had four business class seats facing small tables. Cornelia Day was already hard at work on whatever file came next. Other advisors and aides filled the additional seats.

Cornelia looked up at Anne and offered a genuine smile.

Anne returned it, "I don't have an answer for you yet, but I am working on it."

She acknowledged Anne's report with a sympathetic nod and returned to the paperwork laid out before her.

They both ignored Zack's puzzled, "What?"

The back of the plane had eight more rows of four seats each. A quick peek showed that most were filled with Secret Service agents. Detra and Harvey were in the front two seats. Beyond that, there was nothing more to see so they turned and headed back forward.

"What did you do to her?" Zack asked after they reentered his stateroom.

"To who?" Anne looked around and did her best to play stupid.

"Be glad I don't carry around a lie detector. Cornelia, that's who."

"What about her?"

Zack rolled his eyes.

"It's a girl thing, Mr. Vice President. I could tell you—"

"But you'd have to neuter me first. I get it. Forget that I asked."

"Anything you say, Mr. Vice President."

"Anything?"

Anne should have seen it coming, but Zack had been sneaky. Whether it was the Air Force Captain or the politician who'd set the trap, she wasn't sure. That didn't make it any less effective. He had locked both fore and aft stateroom doors without her noticing. He sat on the divan and scooped her against him as the plane's first motion unsettled her balance.

"You'd better take your time, Mr. Vice President, or we'll never make it to a mile-high," she whispered against his neck. "And if you aren't very quiet, I will kill you, treason or not."

Their clothes didn't even make it to the end of the taxiway. By the time they were powering down the runway, the plane wasn't the only one headed aloft.

Zack slipped from the bed so as not to wake Anne. Out the window fluffy clouds revealed a blue stretch of the Atlantic far below. They might have started while still on the ground, but making love to Anne

Darlington had occupied him all the way to cruising altitude and then some.

As he was dressing, Zack watched her sleeping. Her hair spread over her face and down onto the blanket tucked up about her chin. He could see it many ways. Now blond, someday going to gray. Maybe one year short and the next longer again. He could imagine what he never had before, finding the same woman in his bed for all the days to come. To make love to a whole series of Anne Darlingtons separated from each other only by time.

Making love to Anne Darlington.

He'd had the thought before, but this day had been a repeated lesson in new perspectives. Anne had been defended by her sister-in-law Alice and had converted Cornelia to a staunch champion—something Zack knew was very difficult to achieve.

And then there'd been the President.

Zack had just been gathering up his papers when the President strode into his office and Zack knew that his chances of tracking down Anne before the flight had just dropped to zero. Peter Matthews hadn't moved like that when they'd campaigned together. He'd always walked with confidence, but now he moved with an inner surety. He strode forward and Zack knew it was his wife's doing. With a woman like Kim-Ly Geneviève Beauchamp Matthews behind him, a man couldn't help but be incredible.

He looked again at Anne asleep on his couch and knew the feeling exactly as he recalled the conversation.

"Hey, Zack."

"Mr. President."

But Peter Matthews didn't continue. He'd simply stood in Zack's office doorway and looked at him.

"Mr. President?"

He rubbed at his chin before speaking, another old habit. He'd seen the man redraft whole sections of speeches on the fly while making that simple gesture.

Didn't bode well.

"I'm not one to be telling you how to live your life, Zack..."

"But?" This could only be about one thing. "How does she gain such champions so easily?"

Peter smiled, "You'd have to ask my wife about that one. You're running in two years?"

No question on that topic either. "Someone has to fill your shoes when you're done with them, Mr. President."

"Thought so. Genny has her own ideas about you and Ms. Darlington; must say I agree with them—you two seem to fit well. But you also need to look to the future. You're never going to find a better woman to stand beside you."

"Christ, Peter," this conversation had just blown far past any honorifics. "We've been together less than two weeks. Give me a break."

"Nope," Peter just smiled at him. "Not when I've seen what I've seen. About time you began seeing it too. Safe trip, Zack. Bring us back a climate accord that has some real teeth in it and we'll find a way to get it passed." Then the President shook his hand and was gone.

Zack brushed back Queen Anne's long hair so that he could see her face as she slept on in Air Force Two's stateroom. They hadn't paused to convert Air Force Two's stateroom couch into a bed, his need for her too great after a day of dreading that she wouldn't travel with him at all and that she'd somehow slip away while he was in Italy.

He didn't know what President Peter Matthews had seen, but he agreed with him on one point, he'd never find a better woman to stand beside him. Now he had a new task, convincing her that he was worth standing beside.

He slipped out and closed the door behind him. He sat down opposite Cornelia in the conference area. She had slowly annexed the entire table until the other three occupants had moved elsewhere seeking a work surface. The paperwork was organized by country, environmental zone—air, water, soil, substrata—and market sector.

It took a moment to find his enthusiasm for the task; his mind was still with the woman asleep in the stateroom.

"When are you going to tell her?" Cornelia whispered without looking up.

"Tell her what?" Cornelia never whispered when she had something to say, though with four cabinet assistant secretaries sitting across the aisle, he appreciated it. He wasn't exactly comfortable discussing Anne Darlington even with those closest to him; he really didn't want the opinions of the Departments of Energy, Transportation, Interior, and Commerce as well.

"That you love her, you dolt."

Maybe he wasn't comfortable *at all* discussing Anne with those close to him. Not once had Cornelia Day ever addressed him by less than his proper title; not even when it had been the decidedly awkward Mr. Vice President-elect.

"What is it with you women?"

She didn't answer, but he could see her smile though she remained bent over her paperwork.

Zack decided to keep his mouth shut and focus on global climate change and ways to fix it. At least that he had a chance of understanding.

CHAPTER SEVEN

I f *Anne had needed* proof that she was in love, she found it on the ski slopes of Courmayeur. Because only a woman in love would be crazy enough to learn this ridiculous sport. Boots, bindings, skis, poles, thermal underwear, thermal waterproof pants, hats, goggles, inner gloves and outer mittens...she'd have needed less equipment to visit the International Space Station. She'd refused to give up her bulky parka and denied that ten degrees Celsius below freezing was merely nippy.

"Next time I lead an expedition, we're going to Tahiti. At least it has the right number of syllables."

"It what?" Zack slid to a neat stop and helped her once again rise from where she'd landed in a heap.

"Never mind."

"Though you in a bikini I think is an excellent idea."

"Not a chance, Mr. Vice President. I'm never taking off my parka, ever again. I'm going to be permanently chilled to the bone by this. And no, don't even think about making any jokes about helping me into a hot shower."

She could see by the smile showing below his sunglasses that was precisely what he'd been thinking.

After her fourth face plant into the snow, she'd was ready to jab Zack with a ski pole. She must not have been serious about it though or Harvey would have noticed and moved in closer to protect him. Secret Service agents swarmed the hill—some on skis, others on snowmobiles. And there was a large, treaded snow beast of a machine that rumbled suspiciously close by.

"Okay, it's beautiful. I'll admit that." They were high in the Italian Alps. The gondola ride from Courmayeur up the mountain had been spectacular, the town nestled in the heart of the valley below. The ski area was over the ridge and filled a bowl in the mountains. It felt as if the world was suddenly very far away. The air was biting, but it was also crystal clear in a way that Tennessee was on a cool autumn morning when the cut hay fields were still thick on the air and the first geese from the north passed by the farm's lake honking in dark Vs against the blue sky.

And it was her first fall in almost an hour. She'd graduated from the insultingly designated *bunny* slopes up to *facile*—even if "easy" was trying to kill her. Zack was proving to be a very tolerant teacher. Though she was sure that he'd be much happier zipping down those impossible cliff-like trails she'd caught glimpses of from the gondola, he hadn't given even the least hint of it.

A gondola ride into the Italian Alps with the best lover she'd ever imagined did make it difficult to complain. But she made the effort on his behalf.

"So this is what you do for fun?" They were quite close together, but because he was on the downhill side they were nearly eye to eye in height.

"Absolutely."

"Do you ride horses?"

"About as comfortably as you ski. I'm guessing you're good?"

"Remind me to show you my collection of blue ribbons. They cover a whole wall."

"Of your bedroom, Ms. Darlington? Is that an invitation?"

She couldn't let him have the victory that easily. "If you make a formal application for an entry visa, I'll take it under consideration." Then, before he could reply, she pushed off with her poles, aimed her ski tips downhill, and managed a turn without turning into a human snowball—a definite victory.

As she worked her way down the trail, down the *piste,* the mountains changed and shifted in every direction, except to the northwest. There, the Mont Blanc Massif soared above all the others, its many-fingered white peaks as distinctive as a fist raised against the sky.

Genny had said to look at the Massif and the country around it... she couldn't stop. The Great Smoky Mountains of Tennessee were soft, rolling hills worn with age. These mountains were tall, vibrant, filled with life. A tourist brochure that Anne had found on the villa's desk had pointed out that Mont Blanc was the third most heavily touristed natural wonder in the world, after the Grand Canyon and Niagara Falls. The tallest mountain in Europe, it dominated the skyline.

"That was amazing!"

"What was?"

Zack shoved against her shoulder and she tumbled into a snow bank...a snow bank at the foot of the lift. She turned and looked back up the slope, she'd skied the whole way down without another fall. She hooked a pole behind the Vice President's knees and yanked sharply forcing him to land beside her with a grunt.

"I *am* amazing!" She told him as she leaned in to kiss him.

"And don't you forget it." His admonishment made her hesitate.

She wasn't amazing. She was just Anne the-Vice-President's-girl-friend Darlington. Anne didn't turn aside from the kiss, but neither did it feel as incredible as it usually did.

She was rapidly becoming an adjunct to a spectacular man and that was a good thing, but it was far from being sufficient.

Zack pulled back to look at her, "Tell me what's wrong. How can I help?"

He couldn't. That was the real problem. No one could; it was something inside of her that was lacking. There was a desire, a focus, *an ambition* that others had but she'd never found. And that thought made her head hurt.

He'd risen to his knees—the Secret Service was moving in from the protective circle they'd formed to help him the rest of the way up. Anne grabbed the front of his ski jacket and yanked him back down into the snow, then kissed him hard.

Not thinking had worked well for her original plan. For now, she was going to stick with that.

CHAPTER EIGHT

The conference wiped out Zack's days and the dinner meetings took most of Zack's evenings. Other than that first afternoon on the slopes, his only time for Anne had been when she accompanied him to the dinners with other countries' representatives or when he curled up against her in utter exhaustion. Not exactly an opportune moment for pursuing his plan of discovering more about her.

Instead, she had listened while he raged against changes proposed and rejected—sometimes by his own "advisors" staunchly guarding their hidebound American thinking. She had made quiet suggestions that often worked to convince Japan or Iran to shift on one key point and Indonesia on another. And most of all she'd become an anchor that he couldn't imagine not finding in his bed every night. There were times when all he wanted to do was to lie quiet for even a minute with her curled up against him and her head on his shoulder.

She had known he needed a distraction and had told him of her own explorations while he'd been locked away discussing carbon credits and "clean" coal. Along with Detra, they had hiked some of the lower slopes of the massif.

"The wildlife here is incredible. We saw a mountain goat and a whole family of chamois—they're sort of half goat and half antelope.

And we hiked up into whole fields of rhododendron that must be incredible when they're in bloom. There's a stark beauty here. I tracked down the local botanist and she said there are twenty-five hundred species and sub-species of flora, and that's just above the tree line. It's an incredibly rich environment. I was hoping to see a marmot, but they hibernate for up to ten months of the year, just as any sensible creature would in this frigid snowy place you have led me to."

The tease sounded and felt normal, but there was a sliver of reserve there since that kiss in the snowbank. Not that she gave less, but that she'd taken to deflecting even the subtlest of his inquiries about herself more than usual.

"Now's not the time," she'd whisper softly and sometimes they'd make love. Other times they would simply sleep still clinging to each other.

Well, for better or worse, the meetings were on hiatus for the day.

"A whole day together," he teased her in the shower. "Think that you can put up with me for that long?"

"It will be a burden, Mr. Vice President, but," she'd been scrubbing his back with a soapy washcloth, then she slid it down and forward between his legs, stealing his breath away. "Somehow I'll manage."

He turned on her and they both managed just fine.

A day off, he thought as he made a study of lathering her breasts, they could ski again. No, she worked down his chest and stomach until once more her hands were on the verge of killing him with pleasure, he wanted something different.

Ice skating? He pushed her back against the dark tile wall. No, still in the cold category.

Going into Milan or Turin for the day? His mind still worked as she wrapped her legs about his hips and her arms about his neck and he pressed her back against the shower's wall. Without warning the Secret Service ahead of time, that could cause problems.

If it was just him, what would he do? Anne clung to him as if she'd never let him go and Zack knew what the old saying "two bodies as one" truly felt like. He knew exactly what he'd do.

But first he had something to do here, and now he concentrated on it with all of his ability to give pleasure to another.

"Mr. Vice President, have I mentioned how stupid I think this is?"

"Several times," he replied from his sailplane seat close behind her. They both wore headsets so that she didn't even have to raise her voice to speak.

"Well, I'm saying it again. They dragged us up here, they can drag us right back down." At least she wasn't cold. She'd been freezing, until they closed the Plexiglas canopy and the tiny cockpit had warmed in the bright sun.

"See the red handle on the floor between your knees? Give it a good sharp yank."

Anne took one last look at the world she knew and wished it goodbye. The sky was Italian azure. The very tops of Mont Blanc's snowy peaks ranged at eye-level along the northern horizon. Far below, deep in the shadowed valley, lay the picture postcard town of Courmayeur.

Straight ahead flew a tiny tow plane attached to a long cable that once again bucked and jerked them about the sky. She heard that plane's engine grinding along ahead of them, and also felt the engine vibration transmitted to them down the cable. All about them the wind roared as if in a foul temper.

"We could be walking the Viale Monte Bianco. Green garlands over the street with wooden chicken ornaments dangling from them."

"Chickens? Really?"

"Really. And I discovered a charming little *trattoria,* just as Genny said I would, on the Via Roma. We could go in for a *caffe.* Because you're from Colorado, you can get a gelato even though it's the middle of winter. By evening, the every tree and bush will be lit with tiny white lights. And the crèche here is not a simple little tableau of statues; it has real people, donkeys, a manger, everything."

"Sounds wonderful. Let's go."

Anne waved her hand at the sky. "We can't because you have us ten thousand feet up in the air."

"Closer to fifteen thousand. Though Courmayeur is at four thousand, so we're close enough to ten thousand feet above the ground."

"Well get us down!" If she dared, she'd unbuckle, turn around, and throttle the man.

"So pull the red handle."

"But we don't have an engine."

"Soaring team captain my last two years at the Academy. We placed first nationally both years. Pull the release."

"Couldn't you have been a jet pilot instead like a normal Air Force captain?" Before she could think again, she gave the handle a yank.

The world changed as if they'd stumbled, or rather come off a stumble to find themselves at last walking gracefully. The cable dropped away in slow motion. The tow plane rocked its wings as if it was waving goodbye before it rolled on its side and plummeted down and away. With the cable detached, the flight of their sailplane smoothed out and she felt as if she was floating. The only sound now was the roar of the wind—which didn't seem nearly as malevolent as a moment ago—and the pounding of her heart.

Zack flew them along as smoothly as if they were on a rail, a rail across the sky.

Her feet were in the fiberglass nosecone, perhaps a quarter of an inch from the sky. There were four instruments: speed, compass, a miniature airplane floating along a horizon, and the last one ominously pointed at zero with the numbers one through five both above the zero and below it.

From the waist up she was surrounded by glass and sky. If she didn't turn enough to see the impossibly long and slender wings, she could be sitting alone in a chair ten thousand feet into the sky.

"Ready?"

"For this? No way. This is incredible."

"No, for this," the tone in his voice should have warned her as the nose tipped forward. That last traitorous instrument stopped pointing at zero and was soon pointing down at two, then three, then she was looking straight down at Courmayeur and the Dora Baltea River that flowed at the bottom of the Aosta Valley.

The moment before she could scream, the joystick between her knees—that must be attached to Zack's control—pulled right back into her lap. The sailplane's nose swung upward in a graceful effortless arc until she was looking straight up into the sky. They kept going, tipping on their back until she hung upside down and she now understood the reason for the four-point harness attaching her so solidly to her seat. And still she floated off it. Then with a lazy roll, the earth went from being over her head, to off the left side, and finally back to sensibly lying flat far below.

The rush of blood to her head eased back into her body, the floating freedom of it forced out a cry of delight that echoed in the tiny cabin. "That's better than sex, Zack."

"You're right, this was a bad idea. The first time you actually use my name, and it's to tell me that there's something better than sex with me."

She wanted to giggle as he swooped the plane downward in a lazy spiral. "It's the risk you take, Mr. Vice President."

"My ego is very bruised," he said lightly. As they spiraled, she could see the Secret Service's escort helicopter hovering to the south.

Harvey had thrown a fit, but Zack had convinced him that there was no mad saboteur lurking at the sailplane rental counter. Though they'd left an agent posted there to make sure that the clerk told no one about just who had taken one of their sailplanes aloft until they were safely returned.

Zack came out of the spiral into a wing-over-wing that rolled them all the way over sideways until they were right side up again with the same gentleness as them trading positions in bed.

"Your ego shouldn't be bruised. What's between us, that isn't sex."

"It isn't? Then what is it?"

"If I have to explain it, Mr. Vice President, it rather defeats the point."

———

Zack nosed the sailplane down again, just so that he could watch Anne's hair float up in the negative gravity. He kept pushing it over to do an outside loop, an entire loop in the sky, but with the cockpit turned to the outside instead of the inside of the circle. It was a tricky maneuver but he could still feel the proper control changes drilled deep into his muscle memory. The Schleicher ASK 21 sailplane was a solid performer and took them under effortlessly: nose aimed down, upside down at the bottom of the loop with the g-force dragging hard against them, finally nose straight up. Rather than going over the top and back to level flight to close the loop, he continued to drive the plane upward, bleeding off the speed until they hung suspended for a moment pointing straight up but going nowhere.

Then they began falling backward and he kicked the rudder pedal to twist them back into a nose-down dive. The thermal air currents coming up off the deep valley were sufficient that by the time he once again leveled out he had lost only five-hundred feet since releasing the tow; it was going to be a magnificent flight.

Flying *was* better than sex.

But it wasn't sex between them?

Then it was making love. And she was right, there was no need to explain.

Love is what passed between them. Love is what dug down warm and safe beneath the covers with them. It was the rich taste of that one special, private dinner they'd shared last night of Tagliatelle with Chestnut Flour in a Venison Sauce and a Controfiletto of Piedmontese Beef at the Pierre Alexis 1877 with the G-8 ministers. The massive brickwork arches, the winter flavors, and having Anne at his side all combined to make it one of the best meals of his life.

"This is slow food, Mr. Vice President," she had said. "That is why it is so good. It is never hurried along, and it is all locally sourced."

He couldn't agree more as he flew them high above the mountaintops of the Italian Alps. A sailplane was not about speed, it was about the joy of flight. A joy the woman seated before him provided at every moment in its purest form.

"I love you, Anne."

"I love you too, Mr. Vice President."

"And still she calls me by my title," he sliced a sharp bank toward the Massif, placing Mont Blanc itself dead center in the windscreen; a blinding snowfield glaring in the morning sunlight.

"Yes, sir."

"And what will you say when I ask you to marry me?"

"I will say no, Mr. Vice President."

The joystick slipped out of his fingers and he slammed against his harness as the sailplane stalled and twisted into a dive.

———

Anne barely had time to catch her breath before he recovered, but even she knew that the plane wasn't supposed to do what it had done.

"I'm sorry, Zack. Really I am. There could be no better man than you. But the answer will be no."

When he didn't respond, she wished she could turn to see him, but the harness made that impossible in little more than peripheral vision. Besides, she didn't know if she could stand to look at him.

How many sleepless hours had she spent on that very question?

She would be a good wife for a Vice President, perhaps even a good First Lady if he was elected.

...and she would become a wretched and bitter person. How much would he love her then?

Unable to tolerate the continuing silence, she finally removed the headset and simply let the roar of the wind fill her mind with white noise. She had taken all the joy out of the flight, but she hadn't expected the question, and so had answered it too bluntly. She could have been gentler about it but, now that it was out, she didn't know how to fix it.

No more exhilarating loops or flips. No stomach-dropping dives or stalls.

Zack simply flew them over some of the most beautiful landscape she'd ever seen and she did her best to not let him see her wipe at her eyes even though he sat directly behind her. The romance, the sensual play was gone as if it had never been.

He swirled them down the Aosta Valley, carved an effortlessly graceful turn, and brought them back toward Courmayeur.

They were lower now. They crested the brow of the ski area. The slopes were peppered with multitudes of skiers in colorful ski jackets against the white. Even though they were little more than dots from this elevation, she could now pick out the better skiers. They moved as smoothly as the Vice President flew his sailplane.

She tried not to think about the fact that she'd probably just lost any chance at "Zack" privileges and would soon be sent packing homeward on the next commercial flight out of Italy.

He swooped down over Courmayeur, caught in the throat of the narrow, steep-walled valley. Individual buildings were easy to see, despite their snow-covered roofs. The small villa where their nights had been so cozy. The tiny *trattoria* where she'd hoped to lead him tonight for penne with wild boar sauce and chocolate gelato. The large conference center that Zack would once again be immersed tomorrow, but now with her knife of refusal stabbed into his back.

"If I could take it back, I would," she whispered. But it did no good as her headset was clenched in her lap.

Instead, all she could do was look out at the near-vertical cliffs and—

"What's that?"

Zack barely heard. He'd been flying numb, which was a good way to kill them both. Even something as simple and forgiving as a sailplane called for constant attention to detail. He'd brought them too low and if they didn't find a good uplift, he'd never make it back to the airport.

Her answer would be *no?* That couldn't be right. Sure, it was far too soon to ask, but she already knew for certain that it was a no? Nothing had ever felt so right in his life, not his Air Force service or the two election nights where he'd been chosen as Vice President.

Anne was gesticulating off to the left. He glanced over and couldn't tell where she was pointing. He needed to figure out how to turn the plane in the narrow valley without catching a cliff wall, and get back out into the Aosta Valley.

He could see that she was yelling as she thumped her forefinger against the cockpit glass.

"Put on your damned headset if you have something to say, woman."

His growl of irritation must have been louder than he intended.

Anne scrabbled on her headset, still speaking as she did so.

"...d you see the explosion?" Again her fingertip pounding against the glass. "Look, there's another. Though the first one was way brighter."

He caught a small thermal at that moment and milked it for two-hundred feet of lift. As he did, he glanced left and caught a glimpse of what looked like a flash of sunlight off the snow cap atop the peak. Except the sun was at the wrong angle and the flash was instantly lost in a cloud of snow.

He found another couple hundred feet and saw a half-dozen dark figures standing back on a craggy limestone outcropping and throwing something out onto the snowfield. It was a motion he recognized, the same way you'd throw a...

Zack clicked on the radio that linked him to the Marine's Black Hawk helicopter following close behind, "Harvey." Anne went silent the moment Zack spoke. "Atop the ridge, ten o'clock from my position. Six, seven figures, tossing grenades. Do you have them?"

"Grenades?" Anne squeaked from the front seat.

"Hold, we're climbing for a better angle."

He started sliding in for a better view himself, when one of the distant figures made a different motion.

Zack slammed the joystick forward and right. There was a sharp slapping sound close behind him. A sound he knew too well. Though it had been a long time, it was impossible to forget.

"What was that?" Anne was twisting about looking for the source of the sound.

"We've been shot at, but all they hit was the plane," he tried to keep it light so that she wouldn't panic. No room for that up here.

"Are we going to crash? Are you hurt?"

"Interesting priorities there, I *feel* hurt. But *I'm* fine and so is the plane; I wonder if the insurance waiver will cover this. We have no engines, no fuel, and no hydraulics for them to damage. We're as safe as we can be without armor." And whatever bastard had just tried to hurt Anne was going to go down and go down hard. He keyed the radio again, "Harvey. People atop the ridge are armed and shooting. We took a couple hits, but we and our craft are five-by-five."

"Roger, Sidekick. Remain clear. Coordinating with Italian authorities."

"Sidekick?" Anne asked, impressively level-headed for someone who'd just been shot at, probably for the first time in her life.

"My whole family's Secret Service codenames were designated with to start with S. I'm Sidekick, naturally. Mom was Swimmer the one time she visited."

"And your dad is Sir."

Zack laughed. Even after ripping out his heart, she could still make him laugh. "Sidewinder, but yes, he is. He used to fly the F-14 Tomcats which packed the sidewinder missiles."

"That's..." Anne trailed off, twisting in her seat to look back toward the ridge. "Is that what I think it is?"

"I don't know, what do you..." But he didn't finish as he too turned and looked. His evasion had taken them farther up the valley and cost him some altitude, but they could still see the cliff face above the town.

What had changed was that a cornice of ice and rock had let go at the top of the mountain. Far more than would have happened naturally. It unfolded in slow motion, the first snow slip, an ice tumble, a rocky jut of the cliff. The first explosion that Anne had spotted must have been a more substantial device, followed up with grenades after the first one had broken the mountainside loose, but hadn't quite knocked it off. It certainly had now, the entire cliff face was in motion.

The slide began losing form and mutated into a seething curtain of boiling rock and ice.

"They started an avalanche. We have to warn the town," Anne cried out.

"No time." And there wasn't.

They could only watch in horror as it picked up speed. Within seconds, the jumble of ice and rock reached the tree line. Twenty-foot conifers were swept up like matchsticks. Farther down the slope, sixty-foot larch and spruce fell just as easily. The shattered trees only made it easier to see how broad and fast-moving the avalanche was.

Small chalets which perched on the lower slopes disappeared. Below them lay the town.

The valley was so narrow at this point, practically choking Courmayeur into two pieces, that there was little for the avalanche to hit. But what was there was hit and hit hard.

The river and the road were buried. And the biggest building in the whole town, the conference center—where they were supposed to be meeting today but had taken a day off to allow tempers to cool—disappeared beneath a blizzard of snow and a crushing load of ice, rock, and trees.

There are people down there," Anne looked down at the wreckage. This couldn't be real. Moments before there had been an idyllic stretch of a beautiful mountain town climbing through a narrow pass up into the main village. Now the entire width of the pass was nothing but chaos.

"Harvey," was Zack's answer. "Patch me through to Aviano Air Force Base, encrypted."

When Harvey responded, she could hear gunfire in the background over her headphones. Zack turned the plane and glided back over the wreckage. Even as she looked down, she saw someone crawl out from under the snow and flop to the ground. "Survivors, Zack."

"I know," his voice was a growl.

That more than anything helped Anne return to the moment. She had to work the last sixty seconds backwards to make any sense of it.

Conference center that was hosting the International Climate Change and Control Conference destroyed.

Avalanche.

Explosives.

Men throwing explosives.

That first massive flash she'd seen.

The first big explosion hadn't unleashed the avalanche as someone had hoped. But they'd thrown enough grenades afterward to finally break it loose.

Terrorists. Some terror group who didn't like the I4C conference. Never in her life had Tennessee felt so far away as this instant. The farm was safe, familiar…this was horrific.

"This is Aviano tower, go ahead," she heard over the headset.

"I need to speak with your commanding officer."

"And who is placing this request?"

"This is Captain Zachary Thomas, former USAF and the Vice President of the United States. Get a move on!"

It took only seconds and Zack was describing the situation to a colonel. Then he began issuing rapid-fire orders, "I need you to scramble every helo pararescue team you've got on-base and tell them to bring their dogs. We need Search and Rescue as well as medical elements. The flights are not to enter the valley directly, we don't want to trigger a secondary avalanche. Have them land in the town or in fields to the far side. And not to pull rank that I don't have, Colonel, but move it."

It would have taken a stronger man than the colonel or a stronger woman than herself to argue when Vice President Zachary Thomas used that tone.

"Pararescue?" She didn't know the term.

"You might have heard of them as PJs, parajumpers. The Air Force PJs are the toughest warriors out there. Ever wonder who Delta or SEALs reach when *they* dial 911 from the center of a battlefield? It's the PJs. I flew with them as pilot for most of my career."

"I thought you only flew…sailplanes," she suddenly felt deeply foolish. She should have known that someone like Zack had done so much more than fly a sailplane and fix someone else's jet. That's what she'd guessed, because he was so competent about everything he did. The train engineer turned jet engineer, but she'd been so wrong. He flew into the center of battles to rescue people.

"Fixed wing, this is the biggest plane I've flown. Put me in a Sikorsky Black Hawk and that would feel like home far more than One Observatory Circle. How did you not know that about me?"

He circled them down lower.

"I didn't want to use the Internet to get to know you. It seemed like an unfair advantage going into the relationship. I remember 'military service' from your campaign, but that's all."

His voice was a low growl that she could barely hear over the wind's roar as they circled downward, "Yet another reason to appreciate the goddamn woman who won't have me."

Anne decided that it was best to pretend she hadn't heard or else she'd start crying. Maybe even beg to take back her own words, though she knew they were the right ones.

"There," with a hard bank they swooped down toward the beginner's ski slope that had caused her so much trouble just a few days ago.

"Sir, what are you doing?" Harvey sounded livid. "Return to Corrado Gex Airport immediately. That's an order, sir." Gunfire still echoed in Anne's headset. She finally spotted the helicopter still high above the valley. It was in a hard bank, a line of tracer fire arced from its side across the blue sky like a golden laser beam. Even as she watched, it twisted hard in the other direction, but the line of gunfire merely changed angle to remain on target.

"Out of range," the Vice President spoke in that tone again. "We're landing here, Harvey. You just make sure none of those bastards gets away. Sidekick out."

For the next sixty seconds Anne alternated between holding her breath and fighting a scream that kept trying to emerge from her chest. She didn't know if it was the near misses with the tops of towering spruce, the low cables of the chair lift, or the occasional skier rushing right in front of them as they raced toward the calamity. Perhaps it was her own rage at what had just been done to the innocent people of this town.

"Who, Zack? Who would do this?"

"Insane environmentalists. Even more insane jihadists. Sick psychopaths. Doesn't matter. Not our concern right now."

"Right," she looked at the fast approaching snow field. "Our concern is surviving the landing."

"Oh ye of little faith. *Our* concern is helping those people." Even as he spoke, he landed on the snow field. They skidded along for a heart-stopping few hundred feet—missed two skiers by inches, eased to a stop, and then in an incredible anticlimax, tipped gently to the side until one wingtip rested delicately on the snow. Within seconds, they were both out of the aircraft and racing toward the disaster.

———

For Zack, the next hours passed in a blur.

Zack and Anne had joined the other villagers converging on the area of the slide. The few who had managed to rescue themselves were tended to or carried off. Then began the arduous task of calling out and digging.

Anne had a natural flair for organizing panicked people into useful work parties and they soon had clear markers up defining areas which had been searched. The ski patrol came down off the mountain and offered their skills and manpower, but Anne remained in charge of whole sections of the effort.

Zack hadn't done this level of brute force labor since the Air Force and was soon solely focused on the task in front of him. Call, listen, step. Call, listen, step. Dig down into rock, ice, or rubble if there was even a hint of a sound.

Eventually Harvey had landed and tried to extract him, and almost earned a fist in the face for his troubles. Zack's anger needed a direction. His anger at the senseless violence and death that six years in war zones had not inured him to. His anger at the attackers. And underneath, his pain at Anne's unexplained refusal.

Ultimately Harvey and the other Secret Service agents had collected around him and they'd all worked together as a team. The Marines had the only helicopter in the area, which was rapidly converted from security to medevac.

Then pararescue jumpers and a half dozen combat-search-and-rescue dogs had parachuted down out of the sky like angels from heaven. The search began moving much faster with the CSAR dogs' keen senses and the PJs' incredibly advanced skills. The fatalities were light, but the casualties were soon overwhelming hospitals as far away as Milan. Helicopters, both American and Italian, were soon dotting every open field, rushing out the injured, rushing in with aid.

Night fell, lights came on, and the work continued. The work turned deeply grim when they reached the conference center. The representatives who had decided to work through the day had been caught. They uncovered people he knew, had talked to, fought with, and respected. They were now battered, freezing to death, or worse. The fatality count which had remained in the teens for some hours rose sharply and passed fifty before the night was through with no signs of abating soon.

It was late afternoon of the next day before he was dragged away, no longer able to do much more than stumble about. The American delegation had been missing four. Two they'd found in a shattered corridor, the other two were found hours later around four a.m.—very much alive and happily sharing body warmth beneath the conference table that had saved their lives.

Ready to drop in his tracks, Zack knew that he was becoming more of a hindrance to the operation than an asset. Time to pull back, regroup. Most of the other delegates had returned home. There would be another conference at another time. Many had sought him out among the wreckage to shake his hand and promise that they too would return to finish what had been begun. Others had worked beside him for a time until one by one it became clear that political delegates were not up to professional rescue standards and were escorted away by their security teams.

Harvey had let him fight on until he was one of the last, but between the increased size of his Protection Detail—under threat of renewed terrorist activity—and the news coverage that had discovered him laboring in the midst of the disaster, he was causing more problems than he was solving.

The retreat didn't stop at the hotel room. He was soon swept aboard the same Marine Two helicopter that had wiped out the terrorist cell—with their still-unknown affiliation. They had fought to the last man and died just that way. No one had stepped forward yet to claim the deed.

Marine Two whistled due to the many holes that the terrorists' bullets had punched, but it reached Milan safely. Air Force Two was in the air before his brain clicked into place and he missed Anne—an oversight he might never forgive himself.

He took one look at Cornelia and didn't have the heart to wake her, rather doubted if he could. Her unerring radar had found him within minutes of landing despite the chaos and she hadn't left his side since. He'd had to carry her to the plane and belt her in himself.

He moved on to the back of Air Force Two where his Secret Service team and aides were seated.

"Where is she?"

Harvey didn't answer, he was passed out in his seat. Of the few still awake, no one knew.

Zack grabbed Harvey's shoulder, finally had to shake him hard to rouse him. Harvey came to with a fist headed for Zack's jaw. Despite starting from a dead sleep, it connected hard enough to send Zack tumbling backward to land in the laps of the two agents across the aisle. One grunted in his sleep, one didn't even do that.

"Oh my god. I'm so sorry, Mr. Vice President," Harvey struggled up out of his seat. "Are you okay, sir?"

With Harvey's help, Zack clambered out of the two sleeping agents' laps. He rubbed at his jaw. It wasn't broken. He checked his aching teeth with his tongue and detected no chips. But oh brother, it was going to hurt for a while.

"Is that how you wake up? When you find a wife, she's in trouble, Harvey."

"Uh. Are you sure you're all right, Mr. Vice President?"

Zack patted the agent's shoulder, reminding himself to never do that again with a sleeping Secret Service agent. "Nothing that time won't heal, Harvey. Sorry to wake you," he worked his jaw again and a jolt of pain was his reward, "more sorry than I'd expected. Where's Anne?"

Harvey blinked at him stupidly for a moment.

"We need to turn back and get her. She's—" Zack started to turn for the cockpit.

"She's already gone, Mr. Vice President." Harvey rested a

restraining hand on Zack's elbow. "Sorry, I assumed you knew. She flew out this morning. Commercial flight. Destination Tennessee."

Zack eyed Harvey and was just tired enough to consider returning the favor of fist to jaw.

"Gave me a note," he found it and handed it over.

Zack read the single line. "You were wonderful."

Were!

Past tense.

Harvey must have spotted the rage that swept over Zack.

He held up both hands as if in surrender, perhaps in retreat. "Through Agent Detra Willand. I never saw Ms. Darlington, Mr. Vice President, or I would have made sure that you saw her. Detra said she worked like a demon until the PJs got a command-and-control team in place. Only then she collapsed. After the medic cleared her, she caught a ride to the Milan airport with the British minister."

"Where's Detra?"

"Escorting Ms. Darlington home."

Zack wished there was a chair handy for him to collapse into, but they were all occupied by sleeping agents. Some of their clothes were still wet, many torn, only two still had ties. They had scrapes and bruises, one had his arm in a sling. He probably didn't look any better; they'd battered themselves against the disaster right alongside him.

"Harvey, when these guys wake up, tell them that I'm giving each of them a thousand dollars out of my own pocket to spend on their families this Christmas. Christ knows they deserve something better than that, but it's a good start."

Harvey hesitated.

"You too. I know you have no one special for Christmas, though you damn well should."

"I'm not the only one who should, sir."

Zack grimaced. He'd barely had time to absorb the idea that he'd found the only woman for him, before Anne had slapped that down hard. "Just don't spend it all at the horse races," he dodged Harvey's sympathy.

"Yes, sir," and then he smiled. "Awfully sorry about the chin, Mr. Vice President."

Zack offered his best nonchalant shrug and ignored the pain in his jaw; Harvey had really caught him. He went back to the 757's VIP stateroom. He almost crashed face-down onto the couch, but he was just exhausted enough that he could still see Anne lying there, curled up asleep after they'd had sex.

No, damn it! They'd made love. He knew the damned difference.

Then he dropped into his chair.

He just didn't know what to do about it.

CHAPTER TEN

A*nne arrived at the* Darlington Estates Farm in far worse shape than she'd left it, which was really saying something. She'd left in a fit of pique, wishing there was some way, any way out of her own life.

An idyllic affair with a powerful and wonderful man.

An Italian getaway.

And she'd been the one to find the remains of the Thai Minister of the Environment, whom she'd recognized by the Old World cufflinks that he'd worn to one of the dinners…there'd been little else to identify him by, though she was doing her best to block out that particular memory.

He'd been the first of many. Though there had been the miracle moments as well. She'd seen fewer and fewer of either as the relief effort took some shape and her role shifted away from the front line itself. Her ability to organize dinner and entertainment for five hundred guests had translated surprisingly well. "Winery Tour" in her mind became the search through the bar and night club that had also been demolished by the avalanche. The "Main Meal" was naturally the conference center hall and meeting rooms. The "Kitchen Tour," an ever-popular viewing before a Darlington dinner, was all of the staff and help areas. The "Crops Tour" started working the open field and roadways. "The Stables" were all of the little chalets.

Thankfully, it had been mid-morning and there was a day's hiatus of the meetings, so most of the people had been out of the building. Had the attack been planned as a demonstration with minimal casualties? Or had they not known about the hiatus and intended to kill both government officials and townspeople alike? None of the answers reached her. Detra also claimed no further knowledge.

Three Caucasian, three Arabic. No IDs. Mercenaries for some industrial super-conglomerate? A personal vendetta against some single member at the conference?

The Vice President's decision to attend had indeed escalated the rank of politician that every country had sent and thus increased the value of the target.

For the hundredth time she wished she'd never left home. Had merely watched the disaster as some obscure news piece on television. She'd never confronted death in any form more violent than a clean hospital bed or under hospice's gentle care.

Zack had been magnificent. She'd kept receiving reports about some group who wouldn't identify themselves, but were proving very effective. They covered twice the ground of anyone other than the PJs. She'd finally gone to see who they were for herself and had spotted Zack and his phalanx of Secret Service agents lifting sections of a collapsed roof. Mother, child, dog, and a form wrapped in a sheet had emerged. They were handed off to the medical teams and Zack had moved on to the next structure.

She had retreated back to her temporary headquarters in a single-car garage that had been untouched by the devastation. There she had continued until she could barely see the three-man military team that came to take over from her.

Anne had thought about going to Zack, but what more was there to say? He hadn't seriously proposed, but she'd ended the relationship just as thoroughly as if he had when she turned him down.

When the British Minister of the Department of Energy and Climate Change had offered her a lift to wherever she wanted to go, she took it. Sitting in the car morphed into gathering her belongings at the untouched hotel where she couldn't bear to imagine Zack finding her. The first step toward home had become a second, then a third. By the time she'd reached Milan, she was on a conveyor belt back to the farm; every choice turned toward Tennessee right down to two open seats on a one-stop flight to Charlotte, North Carolina leaving in an hour.

Her mother had taken one look at Detra and herself and sent them both off to bed without questions.

Anne didn't remember undressing, but must have because she'd woken to find her clothes in a heap on the carpet.

Now she sat on her bed, showered and dressed in fresh clothes, but with no energy to do more despite a dozen hours of near catatonic sleep. The broad queen size four-poster bed that had rarely seen a man let alone a husband. The flowered curtains and matching bedspread: ivy twined improbably with buttercups and field daisies. Oaken bookshelves with dressage trophies from high school and steeplechase from college. She barely recognized it as her own room after the last two weeks.

With the changes that she had gone through, that her heart had gone through, it was impossible that she was still the same person. She held up a hand and twisted it back and forth. It was definitely hers and it was attached solidly enough to her arm, so she must be herself. Even if she didn't feel it.

A soft knock and her mother slipped into the room. She looked completely the Tennessee matriarch. Leather, knee-high riding boots. Snug black slacks. A white, pleated-front blouse exquisitely tailored to advertise both figure and wealth without ostentation. Her gold-blond hair a perfect coif. Minimal makeup on her clear skin. Mary Annette Darlington fit her looks well, thoughtful and kind with a spine of steel when needed. Except now she looked very worried.

"Can you talk about it yet, dear?"

Anne could only shake her head no.

Her mother came in, closed the door quietly, and then simply gathered Anne against her bosom. She smelled of talcum powder and ever so slightly of horse. She'd already had her morning ride. It was the smell of home.

"Agent Willand caught me up over breakfast. Italy sounds awful."

"Parts of it."

"You're not in the news."

Anne flinched.

"And no, I'm not telling anyone about how wonderful you were. There's marketing, and there's my baby girl. Guess which one wins."

It was an old routine going back as far as she could remember. "Baby girl always wins," they said together, but Anne was unable to join in the laugh.

"They'll figure it out at some point, but Zachary Thomas has made such a big splash I just may have to vote for him myself when the time comes." Which was quite a concession because her mother had always voted straight line for the other party. "Is he really as wonderful as he appears to be?"

"He's better."

Her mother let her go and rose from the bed, then sat in another chair and scooted it up until their knees were practically touching. In front of them, a grand arched window looked out across the fallow winter fields, the big horse barn of natural wood with a green roof. Beyond it ranged the misty Smokies of the Cherokee National Forest, as familiar as the feel of her own hands and as foreign now as remote wilderness.

"Now, child. I know that face. That's a face I've watched since the day you were born to light up the world. But it's not being very lit at the moment."

"Vice President Zachary Thomas proposed." Anne hadn't meant it to slip out like that, hadn't meant to tell that to anyone, anywhere, ever.

"Might quick by my reckoning, but he's a wise man. Knows when he's met the best woman he ever will. Other than myself of course, but I'm taken after all and old enough to be his mother no matter how hard I do try to not look it."

She wanted to snap at her mother. There was nothing special about Anne Darlington. But Anne had made the mistake of saying that before and her number one fan, her mother, had stepped up to the plate. From there she'd line-driven the initial pitch right back down her throat, in front of Jeffrey L. Walters and his family. Jeffrey, the only even marginally decent candidate before Zachary, wisely had run for the hills.

Her mother couldn't seem to see the truth. There was nothing special about her. Pretty, wealthy, polite, and from a socially powerful family. None of that sounded like it had anything to do with her.

"What did you tell him?" Her mother asked it like a foregone conclusion.

———

"She turned you down?"

Zack could only stare into his whiskey and nod. He was slouched on the couch in the Oval Office.

He'd come straight from the plane, a flight for which only he and the pilot had been awake. The President had taken one look at him, pointed toward a couch, and poured three fingers of whiskey. He was down by two with one finger to go. The problem was that, if it was football and not whiskey, the fourth down was over before he'd even had a chance to call the play.

"Said it almost without my asking. 'If you ask me, I will say no, Mr. Vice President.' She even calls me that during sex—I'm mean when we're making lo—" He rubbed the glass against his forehead, but the President had poured it neat rather than over ice so it did nothing to cool his brow. "Sorry, too much information."

Peter shrugged that it was okay. "I'm so sorry, Zack. I really thought she was the one for you."

"Thank you, Mr. President. I was starting to think that myself."

The last finger of whiskey had gone somewhere and the President refilled his glass. Reset the ball, three fingers to go. Maybe by then he'd be down.

"You earned a lot of good will in Italy. The rescues. Calling in your old pararescue unit. It will stand you in good stead next year."

"Let's just make sure the next conference is somewhere flat, like Nebraska."

"Deal. I think you can make any plan you want after your performance over there, both before and after the attack. You saved the lives of dozens of countries' top politicians. I know it was awful, but it was still well executed."

"That's not why I did it," Zack stared down into the whiskey. Anne would know why, knew why. There had been no question as they landed the sailplane and sprinted to help, helping was just what people did. Or should do. So few did, but Anne, with no military training, had raced to help.

"I know that's not what motivated you," the President said patiently. "Of course I know that. But I'm trying to find you some light from the situation, buddy."

"And why is he in need of light?" Genny Matthews came striding in, looking like her normal million dollars in a soft green dress that complemented the room's Christmas ornaments. "*Merde!* Zachary you look awful."

"Perfect. Goes exactly with how I feel."

"Anne turned him down." Zack was glad that the President was there to explain, he didn't think he could say it again without his heart dying.

"You ask her already?" Genny spun on him. So much for someone else taking the front-line defense.

"No! Yes. Not really. She said, 'I love you, Mr. Vice President.' I asked what she was going to call me when I asked her to marry me and she said, 'I will say no, Mr. Vice President.' I don't exactly call that encouraging."

Then the irate First Lady turned on her husband and Zack once again hoped for relief. "And what do you say to him when he tell you that his heart is broken?"

"He said no such thing," Peter Matthews held up his hands in self defense. "I told him I was sorry. What else was I supposed to do?"

The First Lady made a noise deep in her throat like a Black Hawk engine that was grinding to life but had no fuel. Zack wondered if the President would be sleeping on the couch tonight. Then he wished he hadn't thought that because it reminded him of Anne sleeping on the couch on Air Force Two and that led him back to...

Whiskey.

His second glass was only a finger down.

Two to go.

Would six fingers of whiskey get him a new down? Ten earn him a first down plus yardage? No. It would get him a blinding headache and solve nothing. Regretfully he set aside the remaining two fingers.

"What are you going to do about it?"

"About what?" He looked up at the First Lady who was still storming back and forth in front of his couch. "I think I lost the thread of the conversation."

"About Anne?"

Zack shrugged, "She said no."

Genny Matthews stared at him in disbelief for a long moment, then smacked her palm against her forehead.

CHAPTER ELEVEN

This is Anne," she almost hadn't answered her cell phone. She didn't trust unlisted numbers. She hadn't even known there was cell reception out here at Beau Ridge.

"Hold please." And some thin thread of Southern politeness had her agreeing and in moments she was listening to Christmas carol hold music. She was sitting on top of her favorite horse, looking at the most beautiful vista in the entire Smokies: the forests behind her, the rolling foothills and the farm below, and in the distance the sun glinting off Boone Lake.

Christmas was only days away and she knew she was going to be a crashing bore on the family. She was past being able to help herself and her mother had merely patted her hand and promised, as she always did, that things just had a way of naturally turning out for the best. Ma was even right on occasion, but not this one.

To shake off her depression, for her family's sake if not her own, Anne had saddled up Mephista. Her blood bay mare was part sweetheart and part she-devil. She was also a true dark red with a charcoal black mane and tail that reached down to her hocks which only made her more dramatic—and didn't the mare just know it.

Anne had ridden across the farm fields and up into the Cherokee

National Forest before Detra awoke. The Secret Service had been on the verge of recalling Detra, and Anne had worried about the loss of the agent's cheery take on the world—it was all that had kept her sane these last few days. Then the news of Anne's own participation in the Italian disaster recovery had broken.

For days Anne had been obsessed with the ongoing news coverage of the event. Perhaps by the intense media focus on Zack as well, but she wasn't going to admit that to her mother or herself.

Then yesterday her own face had appeared on the screen.

VP's Girlfriend Saves The Day!

Anne Is Disaster's Darling!

Where is Anne D.?

Some PJ, answering questions before his unit pulled out at the close of the search-and-rescue effort, had offhandedly referred to the exceptional initial coordination by "a Ms. Darlington" that could be credited with directly saving dozens of lives if not more. He then quietly disappeared back behind his anonymous Special Operations smoke screen and received no more attention than a horse gave a kitten—one or two sniffs from the media and then a careful step around.

The Tennessee farm, on the other hand, had been stormed by reporters and the Secret Service had left her protection in place, even added a few more agents. She only felt a little guilty for escaping and leaving it for Detra and her mother to handle today.

Out here she was alone. Beau Ridge was where she'd always come as a girl, riding Jolie before she'd learned the skills to ride Mephista. Jolie was now a dozen seasons gone and Mephista was showing signs of gray on her muzzle, though she showed no hints of easing down some. More than the house, out here was Anne's home. The quiet place where there was no one but her and her horse. She couldn't even see the house from here, though most of the farm was visible. Tall trees and rolling hills masked the buildings.

The air was chill enough that she could see her breath, but there'd been no frost on the ground. Here was her place and she was alone at last.

Except for the stupid Christmas carols.

It was all Darlington land for miles around, one of the grand old southern plantations saved by generations of hard labor. Beyond the eastern side of the property the Smoky Mountains were wrapped in the cool fog that gave them their name. She'd always liked the ride up to Beau Ridge through the cove hardwood forest. It was the most diverse biome anywhere in the country; yellow birch, basswood, sugar maple, and magnolia dominated this section of it. The trail circled low around the back of the ridge, with the sweeping vista as a surprise exit from the woods.

The Christmas carol on the phone changed to one she really didn't want to hear. It had been sung by the Congressional Hearings acapella group and they'd done a much better job. She should get Zack to pass a law against Muzak; not that she still had any link to him.

Anne was on the verge of hanging up when the operator finally returned to say, "I'll connect you now."

A sudden chill shook her enough for Mephista to look up from the grass she'd been cropping. If this was Zack, she'd—

"*Bon chance,* Anne. We have reached you. That is so very good. I'm sorry, I could not make the New Zealand Ambassador hang up sooner without being rude."

"Uh. Hello Ms. Matthews."

"None of that, Anne. It is Genny. You know this. Tell me about the Mont Blanc Massif."

"I don't want to—" But Genny hadn't asked about Courmayeur, or the disaster, or the disaster that she'd made of things with Zack. She should have said goodbye to him, but hadn't been able to face him to do so. It was her greatest regret, because it had been cruel and cowardly.

"The Massif?"

"*Oui!* Did you know that just twenty percent of World Heritage sites are natural? The rest we call cultural, man-made. We have so very many applications for more to be named and protected, but I do not understand them well. So, when I work with the UN, I can not do the natural ones justice as they need. Tell me of the Massif, the flora and fauna, whatever you know. I visited Chamonix on the other side of the Mont Blanc Massif, but all I see were skiers and *le charmant village.*"

"First, if you are in Italy, you must call it the Massiccio del Monte Bianco or they will not speak to you." Anne found herself sliding easily into the topic. Genny was a very willing audience and they were soon discussing details Anne was only peripherally aware of having learned on her days while Zack was in meetings, as she and Detra had hiked or chatted with the Italians of Courmayeur. Once she'd learned to name it properly, the locals had been only too happy to talk about their region of the Alps.

Anne dismounted and tied Mephista's reins to a handy tulip tree. Jolie had always grazed placidly wherever you left her, Mephista would wander off just for spite.

"Oh, that is all so very helpful. It will be perfect when you come to Washington."

"When I—"

"You will teach me and I will teach you. I never knew so much about how the wilderness is affected by the cultural pressures. Well, I know this, but I am not so good as you at putting it into words. And working with the UN ambassadors we have need to put it into words scientifically, but not in a way they won't understand. You have the knowledge, the family name, and—I am ashamed to say it so bluntly— the class that is necessary to work with them."

"But—"

Genny's smooth voice and soothing accent were backing Anne into a corner until it felt as if an avalanche of words was landing upon her.

An avalanche.

One of those in a lifetime was enough.

"I'm sorry, Genny," Anne broke in. "But I'm not coming back to Washington, DC. Nor to the UN in New York."

"Oh but of course you are," Genny didn't sound the least bit unsure. What would it be like to be a woman without doubts? Anne couldn't even imagine.

She leaned her forehead against Mephista's neck. The horse's fur was coarse and familiar. The horse turned enough to snort at her hair, the mare's breath a warm wind across the back of Anne's neck.

"I..." She thought back over their talk, then checked her watch. Most of an hour had gone by and it had happened in an eye blink. "I loved talking to you about this project. It's fulfilling to use what I studied in school and on the farm to good end. Perhaps I could work with you on something again..." Anne steeled her resolve, "...remotely. Like this. From here. Not in—" She clamped down on her tongue before she sounded completely infantile.

Genny's laugh was utterly delighted. "I told you that you and I would become such good friends. I can not wait to see you again soon."

"Didn't you hear me?" Didn't anyone hear her? Her mother had told her everything would be fine. Genny was convinced that she would... "I'm not returning to DC. Not while," she swallowed hard but couldn't manage his name, "he's there."

"But Zachary is not here."

"Then where is he?" And Anne cursed herself for falling into the trap of wanting to know.

"Why he is there," Genny said with absolute confidence. "You must look around, my good friend Anne. There is a whole world waiting for you."

"What do you mean he's *here?*"

Then she raised her head and peeked over Mephista's dark withers. "Oh shit!" Then she clamped a hand over her mouth to block any other foul language.

Somewhere in a distant corner of her mind, Genny's laugh was a merry ringing of bells.

In the foreground, not even a hundred yards away, Zack Thomas was riding up the trail with Harvey and two other agents in tow. Zack rode as naturally as he did everything else. Harvey managed; the other two would be lost at the first low tree branch.

If she were mounted, she'd run. No one could catch her in these hills if she rode Mephista.

Except maybe Zack, who rode his saddle far more magnificently than she skied, even though he did hold the English bridle western style. No hat or gloves, he wore a sheepskin jacket that he hadn't bothered to button over his sweater. The man was part polar bear. He should go to the North Pole with Santa and the elves and leave her alone. But he was here.

He was *here!*

No one knew about this place, not her mother, not anyone.

Oh.

They'd traced her phone while she spoke to the First Lady about the Mont Blanc Massif and UNESCO World Heritage, the first intriguing idea for Anne's future that she'd ever come across.

She ducked her head back down behind Mephista's neck and spoke into the phone.

"Friend or not, I'll get you for setting me up like this, Genny."

"Good. I am looking forward to it, because you must come to Washington to do this to me. *Au revoir!*" And the phone went dead.

She peeked back over Mephista's neck. Zack was still there, looking even better than he had a moment before.

———

Zack knew he shouldn't be grinning; he was facing the woman who had told him no. But after he dismounted and walked up to the other side of the beautiful red mare and looked at Anne across the horse's withers, he couldn't help himself.

"God, but it's good to see you, Anne."

She ducked her face out of sight again so that all he could see was the top of her head as her face rested against the bay's black mane.

He moved in so that he'd be right there when she popped back up again, but Anne's horse had other ideas. He saw the horse try to swing her hindquarters into position for a kick, but he knew the motion and shifted toward her head. The mare was smart enough to anticipate, perhaps even have planned on that, as she swung her head to nip at him. Only good reflexes saved him from the sharp click of her teeth inches from his arm. Then she gave a snorting horse laugh. Yes, she'd known exactly what she was doing.

"I don't think your horse likes me very much."

Anne looked over the withers again, only her eyes and the top of her head showing. "Mephista is a very smart horse."

Mephista. Devil horse. Of course Anne Darlington would ride such an animal. "Is there any chance of us speaking without an ornery horse between us?"

"No!" She said it sharply enough that the horse turned a worried look in Anne's direction. "And she's not ornery, she's...lost." The last word was a bare whisper.

Zack tied his own horse's reins to the same tree as Anne's, then circled around the tree until he was on the same side of the red mare as Anne. The agents all dismounted with a look of relief and moved off to set up a perimeter, which wasn't necessary, and to give him and Anne a little space, which he didn't know what to do with.

He rested his hands on her shoulders and slowly turned her to face him. He didn't expect what he saw when he did; he'd never seen Anne cry before and it undid him. At a loss for what else to do, he pulled her into his arms and she didn't fight him. She lay her head against his shoulder for a long while, not sobbing but merely sniffling from time to time.

When he stroked her hair she moved back and then another step until she bumped into her horse. She wiped at her eyes with gloved fingers, then looked up at him. It was clear that she wasn't going to speak first and this was up to him. He wished Genny was here—she'd rounded on both him and her husband about what idiots they were. Maybe that was the place to start.

"Genny says that I'm an idiot."

Anne didn't leap to his defense as some part of him had hoped, instead she eyed him as speculatively as her horse had.

"She did a good job of making her point."

Anne nodded, "She does that. Why are you an idiot?"

Okay. Definitely not leaping to his defense. "It's not completely clear. She had many, many points. I think the main one is that I'm a crappy listener."

Anne squinted at him in thought. By the tip of her head he'd say that she didn't agree, but wasn't sure enough to argue the point either.

"You came to Washington looking for what *you* wanted to do."

"I did," her surprise told him that that fact had been lost for her as well.

"You swept me off my feet from the first moment I saw you, Anne, and I let that be enough for me," he was feeling his way along here.

Her insatiable joy and humor had overshadowed every memory, but there had also been her expression as she'd sat behind her brother's desk: an expedition leader overwhelmed by the vast wilderness in every direction. That brief glimpse of sadness as she'd sat alone in the Music Room before he invited her out to the Conservatory concert.

"But that wasn't enough for you. I can see that now, but I didn't before. Or maybe I did but chose to ignore it. So, talk to me, Anne Darlington, and I promise to listen."

"I—" she looked away and brushed her hand on Mephista's muzzle. "I don't know what to talk about. It's...I don't even know what *it* is."

Zack didn't either. But he knew a question that must lay near the core of the matter and it had an answer he definitely wanted to change. It was a Hail Mary play. When the quarterback had no hope of saving the game and no time, he risked everything. Heave the ball high and long, let it loft through the air forever in a clean spiral that seemed to defy gravity, and pray that there was someone able to catch it far down in the end zone.

He took her hand and tugged her gently away from her horse. He led her to the edge of the ridge and guided them to a fallen log overlooking the rolling mountains bathed in the morning sun. Hoping to keep the connection, he didn't release her hand but went for the grand play, the Hail Mary of them all.

"Tell me why you said no."

And as the morning passed and the sun warmed the day, she did. They spoke of her not wanting to be merely Mrs. Zachary Thomas, not Mrs. Second Lady, not even Mrs. First. For the first time, they spoke of her dreams and his. Of the brilliant, vivacious woman unable to find what she wanted and the lonely boy who, in seeking approval of others might one day lead the nation.

"I'm supposed to give you this," he fished into his pocket. Genny had said he would know when to hand it to Anne and though she'd refused to say how he'd know, she'd been right. He did.

"It's a job offer," Anne read it. "Genny is the UNESCO World Heritage Centre's 'Ambassador' to the General Assembly. She is offering me a job as her special assistant in charge of all natural-site applications."

"What do you think?" It sounded like Anne Darlington, and he liked that.

His answer came when she cradled the letter to her chest beneath clasped hands.

This time he was the one to brush the hot tears from her cool cheeks.

"What?"

"I would love to do this. I don't think I knew how much until she and I talked about it for so long...while you were busy tracing my phone call location." She glared up at him, but it worried him less than it might have a few hours ago.

"*I* would never do such a thing to the woman I love," he hooked a thumb toward Harvey. "*He* did it for me."

"The woman you love," she didn't make it a question which he also found deeply encouraging.

"Yes, Anne Darlington. And I seem to recall that you said the same thing about me."

"I remember that too," she read the letter in her hands again, then cradled it back against her chest. She looked out at the horizon for a long time and he let her be.

He too looked out, more than a glance which was all he'd spared the view since they'd arrived. He could see why she loved this spot, had come here seeking answers. Her mother had said that was what Anne did, rode off into the wilds of the estate and always came back so much surer of herself. He could see why.

She belonged here.

He'd like to show her the mountains of Colorado, but he could see them ending up here. His home was no more than a set of trains sprawled across a large basement and memories of a father who was rarely home. Here a family could grow. Here there might be a place for the both of them in some distant future.

"Zachary?" It was the first time she'd used his full name except by accident.

"Yes, Anne?" She still looked out at the land, but he knew that she too was looking far into the future rather than at the rolling forests of the Smoky Mountains.

"When it's time for you to ask your question again, I'll have a different answer for you."

And she was right, it wasn't time yet to ask. Like Genny Matthews' job offer, Zack knew that he'd know when the time was right to do so.

They sat hip to hip on the log, his arm around her waist, and watched the sun chase the shadows over the hills.

CHAPTER TWELVE

ack's second trip to the Darlington Farm was as unlike the first as could be. The first time he'd come with fear in his heart and the First Lady's diatribe on idiot men still ringing in his ears.

This time it was the Darlingtons who had extended the invitation and they all had come. Not just he and Daniel with his Alice, but the First Family as well. The Secret Service had done their usual job of securing the property, made easier because the party had remained small.

"We agreed years ago," Mary Annette Darlington had informed him, "that each family who works the estate would have their own Christmas and be with their own families. For Thanksgiving, the Fourth of July and so on, we are all together, but for all of us the Darlington Estate is closed and private for Christmas."

That didn't mean they lacked the capacity to set out a grand spread when the occasion arose. They not only fed the Secret Service agents who had to work the Protection Details in two separate shifts of Christmas dinner. Zack and Anne had also made sure that the families of the men and women who had fought the Italian avalanche with him were invited as well.

The main estate itself was a grand set of buildings. Much like the

White House, the lower stories of the old plantation house had been converted into the offices, kitchens, and tourist areas. The family ranged very comfortably throughout the top floor. They filled four of the five bedrooms. Any fantasies he'd had picturing Anne skiing were more than allayed by the magnificent series of photos of her with her horses and their trophies that adorned her room. The age progression of a beautiful girl growing into a stunning woman each in high boots, jodhpurs, helmet, and form-fitting black wool blazer was enough to undo him.

Downstairs, the period furniture had been preserved and the simpler period Christmas decorations had been hung. Not so upstairs. Great swags of holly and spruce were draped about the central sky-lit hall. In the very center stood a tree as grand as the White House's Blue Room Christmas tree. It was decorated with two hundred years of handmade ornaments; some were simple children's work, others were utterly elegant.

"These were Anne's work when she was younger," Mary Annette whispered with obvious pride as she toured him about the tree. Her gesture picked out a cluster of six eggshells. They'd been poked at either end to be emptied and allow a ribbon to be threaded through the middle. The white surfaces had been pen-and-inked with fine geometric patterns in a wide variety of colors. "It's in the Hungarian tradition, not that we can boast anything so exotic in our heritage. The Darlington's are very boringly Anglo-Saxon I fear."

Johnny Darlington, Anne and Daniel's father, had taken him on a tour of the estate. He was gruff at first but slowly warmed up to him as the evening chilled. Zack could soon see just where Anne had inherited her wry sense of the ridiculous from; not from her studiously perfect mother, but from the taciturn farmer who loved the land as much as his daughter did.

The highlight of Christmas Eve was definitely the meal. Actually, it was cooking the meal that was the most fun.

Being a family that had practically founded the American branch of the Italian Slow Food movement, they had a magnificent kitchen in the residence. Much of the day was spent in and out of the expansive room with its long counters of polished granite and multitude of burners and ovens. Beveled glass fronted the cupboards filled with china and crystal. A large pantry extended off one side. The dark hardwood shone with the high polish not from wax but rather from generations of feet crossing and recrossing the surface. The windows looked out over the estate's lands where the food had come from.

The preparations began with Johnny carrying in a large ham clearly stamped "Darlington Farms." But Anne and her mother were definitely the women in charge and the First Lady was soon in the midst of the fray. The three women were wearing aprons and laughing as they worked.

"I can barely barbecue," Zack had confessed when asked.

"I'm shocked," Anne pressed her fingers against her breast. "How did they ever let you into Colorado, never mind make you their governor?"

"I cheated, I was born there. And I never told. It's my dirty little secret."

"Well, it's out now," Anne had dragged him to a counter and pointed at a pile of carrots. "You know how to use a peeler, don't you?"

He had to confess that he did and was soon put to work washing and peeling.

"Sucker," Alice mouthed at him. She was in the kitchen, but had managed to stay on the sidelines as she played with the First Child. Adele Gloria Sebiya Matthews was a year old and about the cutest thing he'd ever seen. It was easy to imagine Alice playing with her own child someday.

Then he glanced at Anne as she and Genny leaned down to consult a recipe that looked as if it had been scribed generations before. Anne with a child, with their child...that too was easy to imagine. Very easy.

Anne's mother must have read his expression and winked at him.

He leaned over to the President who had been relegated to cutting up fresh pumpkin for pumpkin pies, "What is it with Darlington women that they always know what we're thinking?"

"Trust me, Zack, it's not just the Darlington women. I dare you to try and slip something past Genny. I need to warn you, as President to hopefully next President, forget the Russians or the Chinese. The truly inscrutable ones are our women."

"Love them like mad—"

"Absolutely!" Peter agreed.

"—but never understand them."

"Not a chance."

And then Anne looked at him as if she'd just overheard the entire conversation, which was impossible as Daniel was making a walnut flour in the food processor at that moment. Her smile said yes to so many things.

———

"Here, this one is for you, Pop," Anne had been chosen as the Darlington's Santa, which included a silly red hat and the duty of parsing out gifts from beneath the tree.

Last night's feast had gone long into the night but Anne had little to contribute. Her awareness of Zack had grown until she'd lost her capacity for words and was content to just listen and enjoy as Genny and her mother had compared notes on handling men. The President and her father had done their best to pretend they couldn't hear the stories that were being laughed about around the whole table.

The two women had also discussed the birth and initial year of the First Daughter, asleep in the cradle beside the First Lady's chair, in such graphic detail that Anne had finally spoken up to forbid that topic.

Her mother, the premier social tactician, had already forbidden politics and farming from the table which had initially left the two men adrift, but they had eventually joined in on other matters.

Zack had been as quiet as she was.

Last night, when she'd finally taken him to her bed, neither of them had found any words. They'd been gentle and loving and it told her that she was only at the very beginning of learning what the future held for them both. When he'd rested his hand upon her bare belly for a long moment, she'd only been able to tuck her head against his chest and nod. Someday. Someday soon. And then their child was going to grow up in a very unique house.

This morning she'd found her voice again, "I have to warn you,

Pop," she pointed at the package's label, "this is from my brother, so it must be a tie." Something her father had never worn except at formal dinners.

Instead it was a fine-knit scarf of gold leaves, blue sky, and running horses—hooves raised high in the trademark Tennessee Walker stride. It had been double-knit so that both sides were finished. Alice's handiwork.

"Oh my god, I want one. I'm going to steal yours, Pop. Watch out."

"Not a chance, Melanie Anne Darlington." He wrapped it around his neck and flipped it in a loose knot to make his point.

"No you aren't," Alice said sternly. She plucked another box from under the tree, "You're going to open this instead."

It was a perfect match, except for her initials worked into the sky at one end. She put hers on, kissed Alice, reminded her that she was Anne's number one favorite sister-in-law, and went to hug her father.

He pulled her into his lap, something he hadn't done in years, and pulled her head down to kiss her soundly on the top of it. She snuggled in for just a moment, before sitting up and holding out both of their scarves.

"We match."

"You always were my Johnny's little girl," her mother sighed. "Daniel took after me but like your father, you're happiest when you're out on the land. I kept trying to convince you that running the estate was in your blood, but it isn't."

"No, it's in Daniel's," the President noted. "I promise, I'll give him back in just a few more years. Anne was right, this is where he's supposed to be, but I still need him for a while."

"How didn't I know that?" Anne slid onto the footstool and turned to face her father, resting her elbows on his knees. Her build and coloring, even her accent was from her mother. She'd always thought she was destined to be just like her. "How did I miss that?"

Her father, always a man of few words, reached out to brush a hand down her cheek and tap a finger on her nose as he always used to, "Weren't paying attention, were you? You were always bigger than this place, always thinking outside the box."

"Your cookies," her mother groaned. "I'll never forgive you, Johnny, for getting her started on those cookies."

And Anne realized that's where she'd gotten it from. She'd never thought about it, but could remember her father teaching her how to make cookie boxes with "airholes" in them and a reindeer antler sticking out through one. And it wasn't just the cookies; it was the whispered wry comments, the off-kilter observations, that had only been between them.

Her mother was regaling the room with the trials and tribulations she'd suffered when Anne and her Johnny were collaborating on any number of projects. She and her father were left in a small moment of space. She looked up into his deep blue eyes, the only physical thing she'd inherited from him.

"Love you, Pop."

"You're glowing, honey. All I ever asked for."

"I'm happy. Maybe for the first time since I last rode Mephista to the steeplechase."

"About to get better, honey. Turn around."

And there was Zack. Somehow he'd absconded with her official Santa hat and now sat on the floor at the foot of the tree.

"There are two presents for Queen Anne, one big and one small," he intoned as if announcing something to a royal court. "Which would she like first?"

"Big one, duh, Mr. Vice President!"

"A wise choice, my queen," he winked at her before calling out. "Bring in the big present."

And Alice came in carrying what Anne first thought was a stuffed toy dog—until it squirmed in her arms, released an ear-shattering yip of excitement, and licked Alice's face.

"Eww! No fair. You're not mine, you little terror. Here, sister-in-law, I think this troublemaker must be yours."

Anne held up her hands, "Oh, gimme! Gimme! Gimme!" The puppy had no qualms about transferring to her arms. It nestled happily in her lap and licked Anne's nose. Her—Anne lifted the dog's front legs to check—her fur was one of the softest things Anne had ever felt.

"She's a Sheltie," Zack reached out to scratch the dog's head and received a nipped finger for his troubles. "Big enough to be a real dog and keep up on hikes, small enough travel with you or even to be trained to ride in a saddlebag when you go horsing about the countryside."

Anne poked her nose against the dog's cool one and got a happy tongue loll as a reward. "She's perfect. I'm going to name her Zackie, because she's probably going to be just as much trouble as the man who gave her to me."

"And if you call her Zackie, what are you going to call me?"

"I think that should be obvious, Mr. Vice President." At his groan she waved a hand at the big box she'd tucked around the side of the tree. "That is your *big* present."

"He's going to love this," she whispered into the dog's fur and hugged it tight on her lap. They'd never spoken of it, but he'd known she was a dog person. Maybe he knew about farms. On a working farm a cat wasn't a pet, it was a furry form of rodent control that occasionally condescended to scratch a little girl for petting it. Dogs were what kept a person company. And the White House did have a long tradition of canine residents.

Zack sat cross-legged before the tree. He began methodically unpeeling one of the back flaps of his gift and she sighed.

She scooted down to sit on the living room carpet in front of him, keeping Zackie in her lap. Anne reached out, grabbed a corner of the paper and yanked at it, creating a massive rip.

Everyone leaned forward to see what it was. But she didn't care about them. She just watched the man she'd come to love so easily as her gift registered. It was with almost reverent hands that he peeled back the rest of the paper.

When he looked up at her, it wasn't the man's eyes that looked at her, it was the boy's. But this time they were filled with hope.

"A fresh start. For the whole family. For you, for me, for our children. Maybe not for this scamp," she waved one of the puppy's paws at him.

He looked back down at the train set.

"The train shop—who knew there was such a thing—said it was the very best starter kit. I bought it in N-gauge, one size bigger than the one you had as a child so there could be no borrowing. A true fresh start."

Again he looked at her with his soul bared before her. He pulled her in and kissed her. The puppy barked loudly then licked the bottom of both of their chins from where it was confined between them.

"Okay, maybe I need to rethink the dog gift," Zack muttered as they parted.

"Don't you dare," she hugged the puppy close which made it wriggle with delight.

"You make my small present almost irrelevant, my dear Anne."

"Gimme! Gimme! Gimme!" She repeated her earlier call earning her a laugh from her family and the First Family except for Adele who was happily asleep on the belly of a stuffed bear that was larger than she was.

He reached into his jeans pocket and extracted a square blue-velvet box and opened it. Inside was a simple, yet elegant ring. It had a single emerald the color of the forest set in a twisted band of silver and gold. No chill diamond of ice or frozen hearts. Two precious metals combined to grow together, becoming a luminously green future larger than either of them could imagine.

"I think you've struck her speechless," Alice called from some-where behind her.

"Yes, there are times that a man can do just that," Genny whis-pered softly.

Anne heard a sniffle from her mother, but couldn't look away.

Zack remained sitting before her, complete Santa hat in front of the family Christmas tree, holding aloft the incredible gift of his heart.

"You said your answer might be different if I asked again?"

Anne could only nod. It was all so fast, but it wasn't, because it was also so perfect.

"Well?" he whispered to her.

"You have to ask if you want an answer," she whispered back.

"Oh, right." Zack rose to kneeling on one knee and spoke up. "Melanie Anne Darlington, before these good friends and family, will you make me whole for the rest of our days? For everyone knows I am incomplete without you. Please marry me."

"Oh god yes, Mr. Vice President." No need to hold her breath for even an instant to be sure of that. He understood that she couldn't say yes while she'd only been half a person, but neither could she be whole without him.

Once he'd slipped the ring onto her finger, she threw herself at him, knocking him flat on his back among the piles of torn up wrapping paper.

She kissed him under the Christmas tree while everyone else cheered and clapped, and a puppy chased a small blue velvet box across the rug beside them.

ROY'S INDEPENDENCE DAY

When **Sienna Arnson** *joins President Peter Matthews' senior staff as his National Security Advisor, she feels supercharged by the challenge. If she could fly, she would. Succeeding as the best NSA ever strikes her as a good goal...to start with.*

    Secret Service Counter Sniper Roy Beaumont *views D.C. from his station atop the White House roof and has never looked further. When Senior Agent Frank Adams drags him from his high perch to protect the new NSA, he discovers a new target centered in his sights.*

    Together they discover the true meaning of Roy's Independence Day.

INTRODUCTION TO ROY'S INDEPENDENCE DAY

I've always been curious about the sniper mentality, it is very different from the average soldier as research into Kee Smith for I Own the Dawn had taught me. So, I was reading a lot about snipers as I was looking for another Independence Day romance to complement Frank's Independence Day.

And frankly (pun intended), I missed Frank.

Frank Adams is one of those characters that good scenes always seem to happen around. From his conflicts with Mark Henderson and Emily Beale in The Night Is Mine *to his own July 4th love story, interesting events follow him everywhere.*

From Zachary's Christmas *I knew that I had Cornelia Day, Zachary's assistant, waiting in the wings for true love, but she struck me as a woman looking for a Christmas love story. I don't know why, she just did.*

I often start a book knowing very little about my characters. Roy's Independence Day *is perhaps the one I knew the very least about before beginning. The few bits I had were that Roy was inspired by a combination of Alvin York and my sole job ever that was directly related to my college major of geology.*

Sergeant Alvin York was one of the top snipers in World War I. Yet he was not a complex man. He was a pacifist who came to believe that it was as more his duty to protect his fellow soldiers than it was to not kill the enemy. From the moment of that decision forward, he became one of the most lethal snipers in history. I liked that purity of thought: To protect. Got it! Good.

But in both Gary Cooper's movie portrayal of him in Sergeant York *and his own writings, he sounds like the good old boy from the Tennessee backcountry that he was. Today's modern snipers are still often "born with a gun in their hands." A bone-deep familiarity with shooting is a very common element among successful snipers. But the modern sniper is typically well educated and successful in a wide variety of skills in order to integrate into modern special forces.*

So I went looking for a combination of "good old boy" (whatever that cliché might mean) and a modern, educated man (whatever that cliché might mean).

That's where my job in geology came into play. I spent a summer between my junior and senior year of college working on a project in southern Quebec and northern Vermont mapping three-hundred-million-year-old rocks that no one in their right mind could ever care about, other than the professor who had gotten a grant for the project. (It was the job that convinced me to never work in geology again.)

On the weekends, our southern Quebec team would drive down to meet with the northern Vermont team, but never the other way around. This is because their summer base camp was in the corner of a ski lodge. It had a shower —a luxury beyond imagining after a week in the field—and a bar, which was even better.

A combined afternoon and evening, with a two-hour drive either way, was our total time off each week.

The bar was run by a good old boy, Vermont-style. He wasn't much older than us college types, perhaps thirty, but he'd been born and raised in the Great Northern Kingdom that is the top corner of Vermont. He served up humor, stories, and stump jumpers in equal quantities. A stump jumper is a near lethal mix of alcohol that "will make you wanta go out and jump stumps after just two of them." That was always an excuse to tell the story of how he'd done just that with his pickup, ripping the rear axle completely off his truck when he failed to clear a too-tall stump.

He's also where I got the definition of a Yankee that Roy espouses on his first date with Sienna. Decades and many retellings late, I have yet to find a flaw in the logic of it.

That was all that I knew about Roy. A Yankee sniper who worked for Frank Adams and whose job it was to lie on the roof of the White House. A team of snipers is there day and night, in any weather, whenever the President is in DC. When he is in transit in or out of the White House, they are joined by a full SWAT team.

This strikes me as one of the most boring yet high tension duty stations possible. Even among snipers, known for their patience to take a day to slip into a position where they may wait days more for their target, this has got to be a true test of patience.

It was thinking about that, and what they might do with that time to remain vigilant, that sent me searching for something for the snipers to talk about among themselves. What more do guys enjoy talking about than pretty women. Pretty women, and a job that is an excuse to check out every single one passing by, sounded like a great solution. Though I'd bet even that gets old after a while.

That's why Sienna was gifted with long red hair as she walked up for her first day of work at the White House (it had to be her first day or they would have noticed her before). That would be enough to snag the attention of even the most bored male.

How to have a meet-cute when they're a hundred yards and five stories apart? Have her be so observant, that she notices his attention. But who would be like that and why would she be coming to work at the White House?

It was answering that question that gave me Sienna's background as the new National Security Advisor. But being military trained wasn't enough. Being military born and bred, just as Roy was as a sniper—that idea charmed me. On top of that, I had just been poking around The Night Is Mine *and I liked Marine Corps General Edward Arnson, the man in charge of the Marine One helicopters. Wanting to see more of him gave me the idea that Sienna was his daughter, but I didn't know that until I wrote the museum scene.*

The reception for the French president is what led my hero and heroine to France. I didn't know what they would be doing there until they tried to get on that dinner boat.

That's how this story grew organically, as so many of my stories do.

This book evolved more organically than almost any other. The parts I love about it as a writer are those moments, the spontaneous ones that I didn't see coming any more than my characters did. Frank standing over Roy as he's watching Sienna, the museum, Dilya and Sienna, discovering Frank and Beat's choices during the reception in The Residence...each of those moments were precious to me.

It wasn't quite the swan song to the series, I knew that. But there was a feel to it that told me the end of the series was coming. Roy's Independence Day made for five books in the series. And the story was wrapping up many of the threads, but not all of them.

That would be the next Christmas story which was yet to come.

CHAPTER ONE

C *heck out this. Southwest* Gate."

By the tone over his radio headset, there was no question what Roy was being asked to check out. Not some depressed loon looking for "suicide by cop" achieved by jumping the fence. Nor some a-hole who thought he could actually cover the seventy yards between the fence and the White House without tripping a dozen alarms and alerting the ground teams.

Secret Service officer Roy Beaumont swung his sniper rifle around until he could see the Southwest Gate. He had the broadest field-of-view of the grounds from his perch on the roof of the Residence. Hank lay on the East Wing roof and wouldn't see squat, which would totally bum him out. Fernando's post on the West Wing roof had prime sight-lines to the Southwest Gate. Mike was on the other side of the roof facing Pennsylvania Avenue and Lafayette Square and couldn't see this direction at all. Mike's was the most boring post because idiots always came across the wide South Lawn, rather than bolting for the short crossing to the North Portico, probably because of the attraction of the Oval Office overlooking the South Lawn.

As Secret Service counter snipers, they were set up for overlapping fields of surveillance and fire. They provided overwatch protection for the ground security teams, but their primary duty was to monitor the distant stretches of D.C. in search of threats. Any decent sniper could attack from a half mile away, a good one from a full mile or more. The shot could be taken from a hotel window or a parked van. It was the counter sniper's job to find them before they found the White House.

And on the incredibly long, boring watches, they also had overlapping views of any distraction. Sometimes it was a cute kid with a balloon out on The Ellipse (and it never hurt that cute kids often had cute moms in tow). Or a gaggle of dumb-ass protestors whining about something the Secret Service snipers couldn't even figure out from their signs—they really needed better PIOs, Public Information Officers. It could even be a cool car, though after a while it took a lot to be cool. By the fortieth or fiftieth Ferrari to swing past the White House even that sweet ride began to pale. Only one thing didn't.

Roy spotted her through his open left eye and let instinct guide the rifle scope to her face so that he could see her with his right eye. No question who Fernando was on about, just the way the woman walked was something special.

Monday morning on the last day of June had dawned beneath a brilliantly blue sky which left Washington D.C. sparkling. By midday it would be cooking his brains lying out on the roof on overwatch, but for the moment the day felt fresh and alive.

And the woman walking up from the Southwest security gate embodied life. There was a spring in her step. She wore professional clothes, which at the White House seemed to be synonymous with damned dull, but even they couldn't hide this woman. A shock of dark red hair, which gathered fire-gold highlights from the summer sunlight, framed her fair complexion. Her shape was very nice indeed and even professional clothes couldn't hide her overall fitness. He scanned down. Good legs wrapped in sheer hose, runner's or cycler's legs. Despite the youth of her face, hers wasn't the wild energy of some teen or twenty; this was a woman grown and powerful, and she absolutely knew it.

"Damn!"

"Told ya," Fernando sounded very pleased, as he should. This woman was prime material.

"Shit, man. Can't see a thing from here." Hank was definitely missing out.

Suddenly the woman was gone from the scope. She'd jinked sideways out of his view fast enough to mistrack even his sniper instincts.

Roy scanned the sidewalk, but he saw no cause such as someone else in her way or an unexpected mountain lion on the South Lawn. He re-centered on her face.

This time she was looking right at him with brown eyes beneath strong brows and she looked eight kinds of pissed. She gave him the finger, then disappeared out of sight into the West Executive Avenue entrance to the West Wing.

He laughed. Not one in a thousand noticed the snipers lying on the White House roof—though they were always there if the President or First Lady was in residence. If either of them came out, whether to walk the gardens or to cross to Marine One, a full SWAT team would be up here as well. No planned movement today, so it was just the snipers and the sky. The few people who picked out the counter snipers typically cowered down and scuttled a bit. Not this one.

Attitude. A hot redhead with attitude. A seriously fine start to a long summer watch.

"Enjoying something about the view, Agent Beaumont?"

Any warmth of the morning drained out of Roy as he rolled over to look up at the speaker. How six-two of barrel-chested, bad-ass senior agent moved so quietly was a constant mystery to all of the counter snipers. Dressed in a charcoal gray three-piece, the head of the Presidential Protection Detail looked completely out of place on the White House roof and yet there was no question that he absolutely ruled the roost.

"It's," Roy cleared his throat and tried again. "It's a beautiful day to be sitting overwatch, sir."

"Uh-huh."

The guy must be getting way too old if a hot woman didn't do it for him. Though Roy had seen his wife, Agent Beatrice Anne Belfour, and she was a seriously fine piece of agent.

"It's not nice to be pointing your weapon at civilians." Rumor was the President wouldn't even make the crossing to the Marine One helicopter if Frank Adams wasn't at his side. It would take a better man than Roy to argue with the leader of the PPD. Or maybe a dumber one —as he could feel himself about to do just that.

"How else are we supposed to assess civilians on the grounds without pointing our weapons at them?" He did his best to sound completely innocent. He had binoculars close to hand, but the Nightforce rifle scope on his heavily modified Remington 700—called a JAR by the Secret Service for "Just Another Rifle"—was much stronger and offered a superior view. And why in all creation was he teasing his boss? Maybe he really enjoyed getting in trouble as so many of his ex-girlfriends had told him. Crossing Frank Adams was a sure way to pull guard detail on a Congressional aide—a truly meaningless assignment.

Frank Adams' eyes scanned the distance over Roy's head as if reprimanding Roy from turning away from his post. How were you supposed to please a guy who wanted everything perfect all the time and wouldn't even respond to a bit of banter? Roy sighed and rolled back onto his stomach. The guy was a typical, senior-level square with no sense of humor...or hot women.

The silence was so long Roy almost turned to see if Adams still loomed behind him or had slipped away as silently as he'd appeared.

"Yep. I never solved that problem," Adams finally broke the morning stillness. "Beware pretty women; they can be hell on ya."

Roy did glance over his shoulder to see a bemused smile on Adams' face—the guys would never believe him because it was a known fact Frank Adams didn't smile. He decided silence was his best option and turned back to his sweep of the grounds.

"Met my wife at the wrong end of a gun, Roy," Adams sounded pretty damned pleased about it. "Just be careful of what you're looking at."

"Yes, sir." Hard to imagine someone pulling a weapon on Adams and expecting to live through it. Though Roy had met his wife—the head of the First Lady's Protection Detail—and maybe Adams had been the one lucky to survive.

It was only after Adams silently departed that Roy realized that the head of the PPD had actually used his first name. Roy hadn't known he even knew it.

———

Sienna Arnson made it from the White House entrance to the Oval Office without taking a single breath. Ten minutes in security, another fifteen to sign and countersign the receipt of her permanent badge, and seven more waiting in the outer office with the President's three secretaries for company. New breath-holding world record! And if she didn't remember how to breathe very soon...

"Maybe I'll be the first ever person to faint on the Oval Office rug."

"No. You wouldn't be the first," an amused voice said from close by her elbow.

She'd thought she was alone except for the secretaries diligently focused on whatever mayhem lay on their desks this morning.

"Good morning, Daniel," She'd met White House Chief of Staff Daniel Darlington III several times before, enough that she felt more at ease for his presence. She risked a small breath that did nothing to ease all of the tension of her first day serving in the White House. He was the sort of person who everyone called by his first name. Daniel did that to people, even angry senators demanding Presidential access and being told "no." At the moment she appreciated it. He was desperately handsome, surfer blond, intensely brilliant, and invariably kind.

"Who before me?"

"Well, me for one," he bowed as if fainting in front of the President would be an honor. "My first time in the Oval was the interview that jumped me from being the ex-assistant to the President's recently deceased first wife to being the new Chief of Staff. In fact, maybe I'm still locked away in a rubber room and dreaming all of this. Oh, I do like the sound of that. Is this Walter Reed Hospital by any chance?"

Sienna laughed with him, but knew the feeling. She'd worked her ass off to get here, but it still didn't seem real. To make it to—

"You can go in now," one of the secretaries waved her forward.

She took the first step, but Daniel didn't accompany her. "Aren't you coming?"

"In a minute. You go ahead," he waved her on.

"Bravery is taking action when you're scared spitless," she whispered to herself as there was no way she could spit right now even if her life depended on it. Just one of a hundred lessons her father had drilled into her over the years; drilled being the operative word. He'd been a Marine Corps captain by the time she was born. Now he was a brigadier general. Being a grownup in her mid-thirties hadn't slowed down his need to provide advice for every single occasion. The wonder was that this piece actually had relevance at the moment.

Squaring her shoulders—and ignoring Daniel's friendly chuckle as if he had read her mind—she proceeded through the door. And made it two steps before stumbling to a halt.

You've been here before! The internal shout did nothing to unglue her feet from where they'd become rooted on the glossy hardwood floor. Five years ago she had accompanied her father here when he became the commander of HMX-1—the group responsible for the Marine One fleet of helicopters. Kathleen Matthews had still been alive then. Oddly, the first First Lady of President Peter Matthews had left the Oval Office décor untouched. It had looked as plain as day on Sienna's first visit.

The President's second wife had clearly taken a hand. The bulk of the Oval Office lay to her right. The two couches and circle of armchairs that had been in blah-beige were now a rich, chocolate-brown leather. Their sharp contrast to the light walls and bright parquet floor felt much more powerful, as if to say "serious work is done here." The prior administration's selection of soothing pastel paintings had once again been replaced by the portraits of George, Abe, and J.F.K. who all looked down at her from their perches high on the wall as if to ascertain she wasn't about to royally screw up.

First day on the job, boys. No promises.

There was no fire in the grand fireplace, but the broad mantel had two stunning bouquets of peonies that somehow only emphasized that this was the seat of Presidential power.

Geneviève Beauchamp Matthew's hand had clearly been at work here. Sienna wanted to grow up to be just like the First Lady. But as she was neither a tall, curvaceous French-Vietnamese nor a senior level director of UNESCO World Heritage Centre, that wasn't going to happen.

The view to her left was even more daunting. Backed by the

morning sunlight sweeping in through the curved windows, President Peter Matthews was standing by his desk, leaning down to make some quick notes. It was alarming how much he'd aged. Elected as one of the youngest Presidents in history, barely past the legal age of thirty-five. The seven long years since had definitely taken their toll, but there was still an intensity and a liveliness to him. With just six more months until the elections, he'd be retired in eight. When he was, she'd be out of a job, but she didn't care.

Sienna felt a gentle shove against her back and stumbled forward as Daniel gave her a push. She turned to tell him to cut it out and she had just a moment to see his smile before he closed the door on her heels. She wished she'd thought to flip him the finger before it closed, just as she had to that sniper on the White House roof. Her father had taught her situational awareness, making the sniper easy to spot. But when he had aimed his weapon at her, it had been completely infuriating. Who did the swine think she was?

It was also her first day on the job and being treated as a threat had just pissed her off all the more. When he'd quickly recentered his aim on her, she somehow knew he wasn't looking at her as a threat but rather as something to leer at. It had tipped her over the edge. If he thought for a second that—

"Hello, Sienna," the President tossed his pen down as if the Roosevelt Desk was just...his desk.

"Hello, Mr. President." She'd get a handle on this in a minute.

"I don't suppose you'd be willing to call me by my given name?" He made it sound sad and plaintive. "My wife will barely use it because I was already President when we met. Please?" He tried a pout which didn't work at all on his strong face.

"Not a chance, Mr. President." Maybe she'd never get a handle on this.

"I was afraid of that. Well, I do apologize for bringing you in so late in the administration, but your predecessor as my National Security Advisor seemed to think a shot at being the next senator from North Carolina was more important. Can't imagine why."

It was something of a surprise that the home of the nation's largest fort, Fort Bragg, actually liked the former NSA. While the National

Security Advisor wasn't actually a part of any intelligence agency—rather an appointee of the President—the military still generally despised NSAs on principal. The fact that he had been a retired two-star Army general before becoming the NSA probably hadn't hurt, but it would also put her at a distinct disadvantage having no direct military service herself.

The President was clearly awaiting some sort of a response. It was definitely her turn to speak.

"It will be…is an honor, sir."

"I'm just very glad to have you aboard. I really do appreciate the skillset you bring and not just as an interim fill-in. I can't afford anything less than the best in your position."

"Thank you, Mr. President." Sienna felt about six feet tall with the compliment, but her nerves downgraded that to her normal five-six within seconds. Then they once again threatened to make her feel seven years old and four feet tall.

"The nerves go away eventually," he remarked with disarming empathy. "Just ask this man," the door opened behind her.

Daniel, at last. Thank the lor—

"He's lying," Vice President Zachary Thomas said as he walked into the Oval. "I didn't hear a word, but I wouldn't trust him if I were you." His flat Coloradan accent gave no hint as to whether he was joking.

"Why not?" Sienna was feeling too disoriented to make sense of anything at the moment.

"Eight years ago he chose me as a running mate. It puts me in a prime seat for this election. Care to tell me how that makes the least little bit of sense? You tell me how and I'll take it back."

"I can't imagine how it would, Mr. Vice President." Which the moment she said it, she knew it had come out all wrong. "I meant—"

"No. No." The Vice President laughed aloud and held out his hands to stop her. "That was perfect, don't mess it up by trying to straighten it out." He dropped into one of the two armchairs at the head of the room, the other clearly for the President by its somewhat more dominant position.

Sienna studied the two men. Both were tall, dark-haired, and dressed in immaculate suits, but you would never mix them up.

All of the President's Washington, D.C. upbringing showed in a formality that defined him despite his attempt to put her at ease.

Zachary Thomas looked as if he was ready to slouch his way onto a horse, though she knew he'd barely ridden prior to meeting Daniel's sister just last winter. They had been married in May at a small ceremony on her family's farm. The fact that the Darlingtons were one of the first families of Tennessee and the Vice President was rapidly becoming the presumptive nominee of his party, had of course made the event headline news around the world.

There had been a great deal of scuttlebutt about the wedding being motivated by the upcoming election, but her father had put the kibosh on that. "Never seen a pair like the two of them. They both get so mushy together a man has to look the other way. The President's no less in love with his wife, but they are two very driven, very serious people. The Vice President and Anne Darlington-Thomas are..." he searched for a word he was comfortable with, "...gentler. No less impressive, just gentler."

Sure enough, while waiting for the meeting to begin, the two men were talking about their wives.

"Anne and the First Lady are plotting something for the Fourth, but they aren't letting me in on it. How about you, Peter?" So, the Vice President was on a first name basis with the President. Braver man than she was.

"Not a word, Zack. Of course with our luck, it will all be for the World Heritage Centre and not a thing for us. Maybe we need a plan of our own."

"I'll bring the beer if you bring the dogs...but I'll wager they'll surprise the hell out of us just like always."

The two men shared a smile of happy complacency, so sure of their spouses.

The President and the Vice President had an almost Laurel and Hardy smoothness to them as they continued bantering with the other people arriving for the meeting. The two men had grown very close ever since the Italian avalanche that had rocketed the already popular Vice President into the stratosphere for his rescue efforts. Again, something had changed behind the scenes that she'd only been able to observe externally.

Well, now she was a step closer to the inside for all the good it did her.

And her father had been right, the Vice President was completely mushy about his wife. Why couldn't she ever attract mushy? She attracted either the ones so driven that their career meant far more to them than she did. Of course, she was the same way, so the driven types made for a bad combination both ways. The other kind she fell for were the total dogs, like that damned sniper. Worse, she fell for them every time. Well, not this one, mostly because she wouldn't have time.

She was now the new National Security Advisor to the President of these United States of America and by god she was going to be the best one ever, even if it only lasted seven months. Six months and twenty-one days. A lot could happen in so much time.

With only a slight hint from Daniel—once he finally arrived—she took the position on the couch closest to the President's chair as the others settled in their familiar places. Secretaries of State, Defense, and Homeland Security. Treasury, economics advisor, and the Directors of National Intelligence and Drug Policy. Even the White House Chief of Counsel and the U.N. Ambassador were in attendance. Last in was General Brett Rogers, the Chairman of the Joint Chiefs of Staff, arriving precisely one minute early. His preferred place was standing between the Vice President and Daniel. Everyone had come to the first meeting with the new NSA. The entire National Security Council was in attendance, the statutory attendees and the regulars, as well as the advisors and the additional participants who were typically present only when needed.

But no pressure.

It was probably too late now to get out of the meeting by fainting.

There would be no nice smooth handoff from the former advisor to her. He was spending the start of his new senatorial campaign at home with a late spring flu. She was on her own.

Greetings of different qualities vibrated through the air and she did her best to calibrate and quantify them. Director of Homeland Security and National Intelligence were old college frat buddies who could barely stand each other. General Brett Rogers didn't smile at anyone and kept strictly to himself. She knew from prior meetings with him over the years at her father's house that he was taciturn by nature, not temperament. He would speak when he had something to say but not a moment before or after.

For the thousandth time Sienna wondered at the tack she herself should take. There were many here ready to discount her. She was the youngest NSA of the four female NSAs there had ever been and the only woman in the room this morning. She also knew from a lifetime of experience that the only female types discounted more thoroughly than blondes were redheads. She'd considered dying her hair to brown, but for better or worse had stuck with natural, dark red, and it was too late to change it now.

She would be...

She glanced at the gorgeous grandfather clock that stood guard by the door closest to the President's desk and would have overwhelmed any lesser room than the Oval Office. It was straight up eight a.m., the scheduled start of the meeting.

She would be...herself, just as her father always described her: a natural-born hard-ass.

"Good morning, gentleman. Mr. Vice President and Mr. President." She raised her voice to cut through the conversations. The room quieted as she flipped open the cover on her tablet computer and tapped it awake.

General Rogers gave her a terse nod of approval for the timely start —an unexpected show of support.

"Item One on today's agenda: the South China Sea and what the Chinese are doing there *this* time." A hard-ass with a sense of humor. That worked for her.

Daniel snorted with a suppressed laugh.

That was a better start than she'd expected. Then she started in on the reports she'd spent most of last night and this morning assembling into a coherent presentation.

It only took a few minutes before she and the rest of the group were fully engaged by the information she had assembled. Input and suggestions sounded in rapid-fire succession and she fielded each one, able to answer most and flagging the strays for further research. Thoughts of anything else faded away: May morning, Oval Office, new job, and jerk Secret Service snipers.

Sienna had many lovers who had accused her of "being the job." It had never been more true than her first moments as the National Security Advisor sitting in the Oval Office.

And she was fine with that.

Ninety minutes on. Ninety minutes off.

Roy's sniper detail rotated down into the Secret Service room in the basement of the West Wing every hour and a half. Not that time off was actually "off." Lunch hour was the only true break they ever came close to having, and even that rarely happened.

There was always paperwork, studying new threats, or helping the prep team for the next Presidential outing. It would be so much easier if the country's leaders just locked themselves in on Inauguration Day and didn't come out until their replacement trundled their belongings in the door four or eight years later. It didn't work that way so the preparation tasks were endless.

By his final watch on the roof that day, he was sure he'd missed her —best looking woman he'd seen in a long while. A bummer, but that was the job. Wouldn't have minded another look no matter what Frank Adams thought about it.

The city was emptying. Rush hour madness had set in.

Roy didn't exactly relax his vigilance, but for some reason, crazies tended to stage their attacks early in the day. Maybe by the time they had their cappuccino or overdose of McGrease, the little aliens in their heads would leave off with their "special" instructions for a while. Now it was just the steady drone of distant traffic. The White House and the wide grounds made it a relatively quiet haven among the commuter madness.

This bubble of silence always made him think of hunting back home in Hardwick, Vermont. He and his father had spent endless hours tracking through the forests around the backside of Lake Elligo. Sometimes with rifles, sometimes bow and arrow, but most often simply armed with fishing poles. His father rarely spoke, except to instruct, and Roy had come to love the peace of those times.

Lying here atop the White House roof, much of his view was of the big white oaks on the White House lawn. A manicured reminder of the oak, maple, and Norway pine forests of home. As evening settled over the city, he tried to imagine himself setting up camp under a lean-to alongside a fast rushing stream thick with dinner still swimming in the cool water.

Fernando's double click over the microphone had his attention swinging before he even wholly returned to D.C. A little more circumspect, he kept his rifle close to hand and slipped out his binoculars.

Again, there was no mistaking her. She'd been inside the bubble of the White House for a full day, which he knew to be exhausting, but she was still going a mile a second.

Halfway to the gate, she glanced back over her shoulder and slammed to a halt as if she'd hit a glass wall.

For a long moment, she was looking at the White House itself, her grin as wide as a little girl's given a brand new toy. Then her eyes tracked upward.

Her smile shifted. No less radiant, but now she looked...dangerous.

She very deliberately scratched at the side of her nose with her extended middle finger, then whirled on her heel and was gone.

He could hear Fernando's laugh on the murmuring D.C. air though he was stationed over a hundred feet away.

———

Sienna lay on her Georgetown bed, her body vibrating with exhaustion. The National Security Council meeting had been scheduled at a full hour, and she closed it at exactly fifty-nine minutes. It was an act that seemed to take everyone by surprise, except for Daniel who nodded in thanks—clearly very protective of his boss' schedule.

The President had welcomed her once more and they'd all filed out as his next meeting filed in. General Rogers fell in beside her as they moved through the outer office.

"If you have a moment?"

She'd hoped to try and find her office. She had met with the former NSA a number of times there. It was also where Daniel, the President, and others had interviewed her, but now it was finally hers and she wanted to see it. Instead, she followed the general.

That "moment" had led to two hours in the Situation Room. She'd been too busy trying to keep up with his sharp mind to be shocked by the plainness of the room. So many movies and television shows portrayed the darkly mysterious room with hand scanners, mahogany tables, leather armchairs, and massive screens covered in situational analyses. Beyond the pair of Marine guards standing at attention outside the door, it was about as undramatic as could be.

In truth, it looked like any standard white conference room with a few too many phones and a few too many television screens against one wall.

The general, who must have had a detailed awareness of her resume, had proceeded to grill her as if for a job interview. Dartmouth, Yale, Oxford. Rand Corp think tank. Some time in Stratfor studying geopolitical influences to forecast military hotspots. Through her father's connections and her own, she'd arranged for a three-year study on normalizing the six US Commands. She'd spent six months each at: USNORTHCOM and USSOUTHCOM which covered North and South America, USAFRICOM, USEUCOM which included all of Russia, USCENTCOM which was the hell of southwest Asia, and USPACOM from the West Coast to Japan, China, and Australia with Antarctica tossed in for good measure.

At some point she couldn't identify, her interview with the Chairman of the Joint Chiefs of Staff had shifted from interrogation to consultation. Having proven her understanding of the big picture to General Roger's satisfaction, he was soon testing his own understanding of power centers and friction motives against her own observations.

Unlike any other conference room anywhere, each time the general called out to the apparently empty room, "We need to see a map of the distribution of Chinese forces from Hong Kong to Australia," or "What is the current estimated stability of the ruling regime in the Congo?" hidden Marine Corps intelligence officers would leap into action. Within moments the information would be on the main screen. At her own request, a key tabulation of activities of NATO versus EU alliances was pushed down from the big screen onto her tablet computer. She could get used to this.

When the general departed with no more than a solemn nod of approval, she suspected she'd passed a test more stringent than Daniel's and the President's original interviews.

She'd spent a quiet hour in the Situation Room—in the Situation Room!—working on better answers to some of the general's unresolved questions. Or at least unearthing better questions of her own.

Her next foray to reach her office passed close by the Vice President's. His assistant, the rather daunting Cornelia Day, had flagged her down and asked if she had plans for lunch.

She didn't have plans to eat...ever, especially not with the way her head was already whirling. She'd only met the Vice President a few times and had never sat with him one-on-one. Cornelia took advantage of Sienna's brief hesitation to conduct her into Zachary Thomas' White House office, decorated in what she finally decided might best be called, early tongue-in-cheek style.

The very first thing she noticed was an HO-gauge train set on a lovely 1700s table of Quaker simplicity and craftsmanship. It resided in a place of honor close by the big window facing the Eisenhower Executive Office Building and she suspected that if she asked about it, they might never find another topic. So she glanced at the rest of the office.

There were stunning photos of the Colorado Rockies and also the softer hills that she could only assume were near his wife's family residence in Tennessee. There were photos of skiers and the two of them on horseback. If she'd seen a full set of horse tack or a pair of downhill skis tucked behind the door—she checked and there weren't—she wouldn't have been surprised. There was one picture of the former Captain Zachary Thomas, looking very official and handsome in his dress whites with an alarming number of service ribbons. It had cropped up in the news a lot after the Italian disaster. But it was another photo, hung close beside the trainset, that caught her attention and finally gave her the ability to speak.

"Why haven't I ever seen this one?" Not the most gracious of openings. To cover her gaffe, Sienna pointed to the image of a very handsome and somewhat younger Zachary Thomas with three other men all clowning around. They wore flight suits and were clearly enjoying each others' company too much to pose seriously in front of the massive Air Force rescue helicopter that must be theirs.

"Always struck me as a bit disrespectful. Our job was hauling out a lot of very hurt people. But my Anne"—again with the mushy tone —"insisted I put that one up."

Obviously she'd done all of the decorating, but Sienna wasn't going to tease the Vice President about that. "No. It makes what you did more human. You should definitely release it."

"Well, that makes two votes to my one. The President always said not to argue with women who we don't have two shakes of a rattler's tail chance of understanding anyway. I'll give it to my people." And Sienna learned that the Vice President gave full respect to his President when outside of Peter Matthews' presence.

His smile was easy to return. They spent most of lunch discussing favorite D.C. restaurants. In his own way, that too was an interview only a little less demanding than General Rogers'. In the hour she gained a real sense of the man and learned that he probably deserved all of the respect he received in the press.

Daniel had snagged her as she once more entered the hallway a mere twenty feet from her own office. He led her back to his office, thanked her for keeping the meeting on time (apparently the first National Security Advisor to do so in this administration—and perhaps any other), then introduced her to...she'd have to check her notes.

All afternoon she'd felt as if she'd been targeted by that sniper. This advisor...Wham! That superintendent...Bang! The Secretary of Defense (who clearly felt her age, gender, and having a pulse completely disqualified her for the job, though having a chest at least gave him something to look at)...Kaboom!

There were only three large offices on the west side of the West

Wing's first floor: White House Chief of Staff, Vice President, and her own. She didn't make it there until six o'clock in the evening.

And yet as she'd walked out of the White House, with little more brain activity than one of her brother's zombie movies, she couldn't help but look back and smile.

Day One as the National Security Advisor.

Check!

And if she could avoid screwing up, there were still two-hundred and three more days to go until the next President's inauguration.

That's when she'd remembered the sniper and glanced up. Was it the same one? She had no idea as he was little more than a silhouette far above. At least there was no sniper rifle aimed at her this time, but his binoculars weren't exactly cruising back and forth across the lawn seeking trespassers. Flipping him off this morning in full view of the White House had been perhaps a little rash. So, she was more subtle about it this time.

She'd heard a second counter sniper on the West Wing's roof laugh, but for some reason it was the one stationed on the Residence who had caught her attention. She supposed it proved that the girl still had it if she kept him riveted so.

It had put a bounce in her step, which was all that sustained her until she had made it home.

She shouldn't have laid down in her suit; it would be too wrinkled to wear to the White House again without a trip to the dry cleaners if she lay here much longer. However, the thought of moving was even worse. Maybe if she just lay very still then it wouldn't crease. Not a problem; she wasn't sure if she'd ever move again.

She didn't have time to worry about suit wrinkles in the morning as she awoke with barely time to change out of her crumpled clothes before rushing out to the CIA for a round robin of briefings and meetings there. Next time she'd set an alarm *before* she lay down.

CHAPTER TWO

R *oy kept an eye* out for the babe all week. No joy. The sniper's call of no clear sighting didn't begin to describe his pain.

Frank Adams had decided that riding Roy Beaumont's ass was his new duty assignment. Pretending to hate it was one of the requirements of such an assignment, but Roy was actually fascinated by the challenges.

Route planning was supposed to be a sniper's version of peeling potatoes or scrubbing toilets. It took a lot of time and infinite attention to detail. When moving the President around, he could never be moved by a predictable route. That meant before each trip, multiple routes had to be scouted. Then decisions were made about where to station blockades, agents, police, dogs, and overwatch counter snipers. The final decisions on that last point were made by CS technicians like himself, mostly staring at maps, photos, and 3D mapping software that would make an online map user wet their pants. He was suddenly Adams' sniper whipping boy for route reviews. Adams even flogged him through "lessons learned" reviews of previous route selections and how they could have been improved.

There was only one major drawback to the change in duties. Sometimes on break Fernando or even, god help him, Hank would tell him about sightings of Roy's "girlfriend."

His big mistake was denying any such thing.

Ever since, the guys rubbed it in every chance they had. All locker room shit. "He *lo-oves* her, but he don't even know her name!" "He so hot for her that he's humping his rifle at night." And on. And on. With no more imagination than a tree squirrel trying to hide a winter's worth of acorns from another tree squirrel.

It *was* aggravating to know she was one of the seventeen hundred people who worked at the White House and all he could do was sit in the Secret Service's basement office and wonder where. Not a chef, they would enter through the Main Residence. Nor one of the First Lady's staff, as they'd head for the East Wing. She was West Wing which narrowed it down to a thousand and change. Not in the Secret Service office—because otherwise he'd have seen her while poring over route maps until his eyes were redder than a winterberry—down to an even thousand.

If he was so poor at narrowing target selection as a sniper, he'd never have been allowed in the service at all, but he couldn't find a way to focus it down any more. So he fell back on his father's training as a hunter—sit still and wait. By the end of the week, he had run that option dry as well.

Fernando was right, he really needed to get a life. But even if Roy did, he should never have listened to his friend.

"Come on, man. You got to meet my cousin. She will love you." Uh-huh. Uh-huh. Fernando was one of those crazy Latino guys for whom every woman was somehow his "cousin."

"It's the Fourth, man." Anyone who could, pulled duty on the White House roof for the Fourth of July. From there, snipers had prime seats for the nation's Number One fireworks show above the Reflecting Pool and the Washington Monument.

"So? We gotta go out and make some fireworks. You wanta watch or do you wanta do?" Fernando's tone left no question about his choice.

Having too little common sense left by Friday night, he agreed to meet "Fernando's cousin." After the last watch, he showered and changed. Fernando just shook his head sadly. "You don't know how to dress up for the ladies, man. This girl, she is hot."

Jeans and black tennies along with a flannel shirt against the cool evening seemed fine to him, but apparently it was too country hick for Fernando who'd grown up in Philly. So Roy dug around in his locker and fished out a moderately fresh t-shirt that said USSS in bold letters across the back: United States Secret Service.

"Shit man. Kind of place we going, they see that, they all going to leave!"

Roy had worked damn hard to earn the right to wear that shirt, but could take Fernando's point. The last clean shirt he had said, "Snipers do it with precision."

"Now we're talking man," which told Roy exactly what sort of night it was going to be.

So he shrugged on his USSS jacket just for spite and Fernando groaned, but gave up protesting.

They hit a couple bars and knocked back a couple beers. As they worked their way down the food chain from bistro to bar to dive, he was pleased to see that his jacket did indeed clear out some of the chaff. More than once it opened up space at a crowded bar and Fernando admitted he might be onto something.

"How far down we going?" A back alley would be a step up from their present locale.

"Just warming you up, man. Don't any of you Vermont boys know how to party?"

Sure he did. You sat back somewhere quiet, which was most of Vermont, and you watched the stars with a six of beer and a friend to share it with. Or during the ski season you headed into the bars of Stowe and hit on snow bunnies there to ski the mountain and slide into a quick fling.

Fernando led him into a dance bar named Jake's Hole nowhere near the nice end of town, and D.C. had a whole lot of not nice. "Hole" was a compliment the place didn't deserve; it rated about a four for habitability, on a scale of a hundred. He, Fernando, and Hank grabbed a chunk of the bar to observe the local talent.

"I didn't believe you, hombre," he slapped Fernando on the back feeling all the camaraderie that happened after three beers. "The women here are all two Budweisers and above."

"Say what?"

"Old joke. How many Budweiser Clydesdales would it take to haul me away from the woman? They're tough horses; two is a pretty high number."

Fernando's smile was brilliant on his dark face, "I told you so, man. These are my cousins."

Some were indeed Latino, but others were Chinese slender or African dark. There were women who were more curve than woman, their bodies teasing with all there was to explore. There were long and lean ones who it was easy to imagine would wrap around your body where they'd cling until a man had nothing left to give. About the only type missing was an average white women. And there was absolutely no sign of a spirited, perfectly proportioned redhead.

He danced some, drank more, and wondered if the redhead was a better dancer than he was. He hoped so for her sake. Around beer six, the three-beer buzz was wearing thin and he decided that maybe the women here weren't as hot as he'd first thought. Or maybe they decided he wasn't. A couple took a run at him but didn't seem very committed to the effort. Or maybe he was the one who wasn't— couldn't tell and didn't care. They drifted away quickly. He ended up in a corner booth with Hank trading war stories and drinking depth bombs: a beer with a shot of whiskey dropped into the glass. Chug it down to get your shot back.

Fernando disappeared with some long-legged Latina about the time Hank lost all ability to form coherent words. Roy poured Hank into a taxi, prepaid the driver, and walked home in order to clear his head.

In less than four hours they'd completely trashed what might have been a lazy Friday night hanging out with the other snipers on rooftop watch and viewing the fireworks. The sun was gone and he heard the first boom of The National Mall's fireworks show when he was still several miles out. The only part of it he could see from here was the occasional red or blue glow on the horizon. Every once in a while there was a lull in the traffic and he could hear the distant rumble of an explosion. Around here he was just glad it wasn't gunfire.

He thought of tonight's White House counter sniper team with some envy. Even more envy for those who'd set up picnics in the town park of Hardwick. His hometown's fireworks shows were only everyone's reservation-bought roman candles and crackers, but it always made for a good picnic excuse by the lake as the fireworks sparkled over the water with sharp snaps and pops. He'd kissed his share of willing girls by the light of those homegrown firework shows.

Fernando was right about one thing: it was time for Roy to let go of his White House redhead fantasy.

Crap!

"Happy Independence Day, Roy," he told the dark city before beginning the long walk home.

Five long miles and the only thing that was clear by the end of it was that he was in for a doozy of a hangover in the morning.

It was the one thing he got right.

———

Sienna spent the Fourth buried in her office. With most of the staff on holiday, she closed her door against the other senior staff who—like her—didn't have a life and worked.

The heavy boom of the first firework and the sudden glare of light through her windows brought her back to reality. Stepping out into the hallway she was rapidly swept up in the tide headed out to the South Lawn. Many who'd had the day off had used their clearance to the grounds to bring their families to one of the prime viewpoints for the show. A large and merry crowd had gathered on the lawn.

The stars only barely showed above the city, but the South Lawn fountain backed by the Washington Monument and the distant Thomas Jefferson Memorial was one of the best night views in a city that truly shone at night.

Sienna had wound up near the First Family who had come out for the display. She sipped a beer that the Vice President gave her, judiciously for she'd barely eaten all day, and was thrilled when Daniel's wife stuffed a paper plate into her hand with a grilled burger and chips despite the late hour. There wasn't a bit of fancy, it was pure picnic comfort food—definitely the First and Second Ladies' doing—and a quick glance showed that they absolutely knew their men who were standing side by side enjoying their own burgers and brews. As the fireworks lit the sky with explosions like flowers, rings, and glowing horsetails, her thoughts had inevitably tracked to the roof.

She moved farther down the lawn to give the First Families some space...or so she told herself. It was only when she caught herself watching not the fireworks, but rather the briefly illuminated snipers on the roof, that she knew she was doing one of her fixation things. Somehow he'd become a symbol to her.

The world will be watching you, Sienna.

Thanks, Dad. Just the confidence builder I needed.

And that stupid sniper only served to reinforce her father's comments. It wasn't as if most people knew what a National Security Advisor was or did—hell, she hadn't until she'd been dropped into the role. After her first full week, she had to admit she still wasn't sure, but the Powers That Be had seemed pleased.

"Never argue with the Powers That Be," she told the distant sniper.

Earlier today Sienna's mom replied to her "Week One down. Doing fine!" text with a "You go, hon!" and a triple smiley emoticon that let Sienna feel every bit of her mom's joy. But Sienna knew that wouldn't hold Dad. General Edward Arnson was a man who liked to assess the status of any situation personally. She really didn't have time for it, but she caved after only a token resistance, knowing that she'd earned her Arnson persistence straight down the paternal line and there was no escaping the inevitable.

They'd agreed on a time to meet Saturday morning.

Mom was wise enough to leave the two of them to it.

Saturday morning they hit one of their regular spots, the Smithsonian National Air and Space Museum on the Mall. It was close by the Capitol Building—which always made her father grumble about "a waste of space." The museum was nearing the end of the renovation of the Boeing Milestones of Flight hall, but it was still roped off. So instead of meeting beneath the Apollo 11 Command Module, they met at the rope line in the hallway and looked in. The additions of the LEM lunar lander and the original Starship *Enterprise* shooting model made them both smile for different reasons.

"Most incredible thing I ever did as a young Marine," her father said gruffly. "I flew the secondary helo for two different Apollo recoveries, including that one right there," as if she didn't know he'd flown for that splashdown. Why else did they always meet here? "Got to watch the whole show from two hundred feet. Would have liked to have shaken their hands, but it was back when we still tucked them straight into isolation trailers for fear of them bringing back some space disease. Of course they had to get their camera moment crossing from the helo to the trailer, so it was a darned useless to-do but it played well on the media. Don't ever let the media control your decisions, Sienna. You hear me?"

"Sure, Pop. I know that."

As to her reason for smiling—her own crush on Jean Luc Picard—she kept to herself. Especially as this *Enterprise* was the wrong model—the NCC-1701 classic versus *The Next Generation's* NCC-1701-D.

While they stood and watched at the rope line, a pair of the exhibit handlers were lining up the *Enterprise* in an x-ray machine, imaging its interior structure section by section. They looked silly in their heavy lead aprons using machinery so archaic that it would never have been allowed on the show. She kept waiting for one of the technicians to just whip out a tricorder and get it done with.

She talked through with her dad what she felt she was free to discuss as they wandered out of the hall and into the "America by Air" exhibit. The early passenger liners, and nose cones for the 747 and some Airbus, weren't really of much interest to either of them. The second floor with its rovers and the more recent "Military Unmanned Vehicles" exhibit were more their speed. She really needed to get back to the White House to catch up. Or at least try. Her first week had buried her and even working the holiday had barely dented the backlog.

As they walked and talked, she found it odd to have the shoe on the other foot. She'd always been able to tell when her father had reached the limit of what he was allowed to tell her. It was just an understood part of being a general's daughter.

But now she was the one having to be careful about what she said. It wasn't a question of clearance, her father's went as high as hers, it was a matter of compartmentalization—which had its own logistical problems in running a command that she wasn't going to think about right now. So she told him more about the people than what they said, which was a mistake of a different color.

"Damn the man," her father growled. "Doesn't Hayward have any respect? I'll—"

"Do absolutely nothing, Pop!" Sienna stopped him in front of a bank of flight simulator rides with lines of children jostling for a chance to be next. "I know how to handle dirty old men, even when they are the misogynistic Secretary of Defense. I've run into enough of them over the years. If he hates me now, he'd really hate me after one of your 'talks'."

"Could be. Could be," her father admitted, though he sounded grumpy about it. "What about that young whipper-snapper over there?"

Sienna could feel the tease, her father was always pointing out likely men—especially when it served to change the subject from somewhere uncomfortable such as his daughter no longer being twelve. It wasn't that he wanted her to be someone's wife—she'd confronted him on that. "Just want you to be as happy as your ma and I are, that's all."

She'd had a heart to heart with Mom as a backcheck. "Love the man to death, but don't marry a military man lest you have a penchant for being alone. But your father is a sweet man behind all his busyness being a general."

Sienna turned to follow her father's line of sight.

He *had* picked out a likely one. Sandy blond hair and six feet of solid, he was strong in a rough-hewn way. Which described his face as well. He would never be called handsome, if it wasn't for the smile he was aiming at the eight year old girl he was lifting off one of the simpler simulator rides—lifting her like she was made of helium not human despite her stoutness. He wore a badge, so he was helper, not parent.

His smile, Sienna decided, was lethal. As if to prove Sienna's observation, the young girl was completely smitten and did her level best to engage the man even as he helped an eager young boy aboard. He must be a docent—one of the thousand volunteers who helped keep the museums of the nation's capital running. As soon as the boy was settled, he didn't brush off the little girl, but instead knelt until they were eye level. It was awfully sweet.

Once the girl was gone off with her mother (with several backward glances, and not just from the little girl), he rose to his feet, though it looked like it cost him. A hard wince and a moment weaving with tightly closed eyes.

"Think he had a rough night last night," her father whispered, which with him meant that only the closest dozen or so people could hear him. Thankfully, this was D.C. and no one cared.

There was no question that he was hungover...but still taking time to be kind to the little girl. She liked that.

The docent checked on the boy then scanned the busy hall. His eyes didn't skim; they tracked steadily about the room, assessing everyone. She'd seen it often enough in her consultations with the US Commands to know that meant soldier or some other form of military training. Even police didn't move that way, or look so good doing it. Military yet still volunteering in another way—more points in his favor.

Her mother's admonition about military men slipped into her thoughts and slid away just as quickly. Advice was everywhere, decent guys were few and far between, especially ones who looked the way he did. He was definitely the sort of man who should always wear tight black t-shirts.

When his inspection reached her and her father, his gaze didn't slide by. Instead his blue eyes focused on her with a positive target lock. His eyes popped wide and his jaw dropped. Just like in a cartoon.

It forced a laugh out of her.

"You definitely have his attention," Pop grumbled in her ear.

She had. It happened to her on occasion, but never quite so

dramatically. He took a half step in her direction, stopped, turned back to the boy he was obviously supposed to be watching, then back to her. Trapped.

"Are you going to put the poor man out of his misery?" Leave it to her father to take pity on a fellow soldier. Except her father wasn't a soldier, he was a Marine—a distinction she'd had clear in her head before she hit pre-school.

"I don't know, Pop. What has he done to deserve it? Hungover means he was drunk last night while I was working. Not the best recommendation." She made her decision and turned for the stairs up to the second story. As she moved past her dad, she whispered to him, "Is he dying yet?"

"Near to a coronary," he chuckled and moved up beside her.

She continued leading her father away.

"Have you got a good reason why we're moving so slow?"

"I'm not moving slow. I'm just taking my time to admire the exhibits."

"That's my gal," her father sounded quite pleased. "Hard-ass to the core." It was one of her father's highest compliments. She used to wonder how different her life might be if she wasn't; if she hadn't spent her entire childhood trying to live up to his "hard-ass" standard. It didn't mean she was nasty. It meant she demanded the absolute best of herself and everyone around her. And some hungover docent, no matter how nice he was to a little girl, wasn't going to come close.

She was just about to pick up the pace, when a hand touched lightly upon her arm.

"Excuse me, ma'am."

At the instant of contact she knew who it was.

Even that simple gesture riveted her attention on him. And it was a very nice view, other than his bloodshot eyes. His shoulders weren't particularly broad, but they were very strong. And the plain black t-shirt followed the taper of his waist down. His eyes, blue with distance, were a powerful statement in a strong face up close. Again she was struck by the strength of his rugged face, but she wasn't about to give ground just because he was so good-looking. Not handsome exactly, just extremely...male.

"Aren't you supposed to be watching the little children?"

"The museum is used to me being unreliable." He said it as if he was bragging.

"Oh, like that's a good thi—"

Her father nodded back toward the simulators. Another docent was there helping the children. She wasn't letting him off that easily.

"Won't the little girls miss you?"

"It's not the *little* girls who I'm interested in."

He was either forthright, brash, or a jerk and Sienna couldn't tell which.

"I'm sorry for intruding, ma'am...sir," he nodded to her and her father in turn.

At least he had manners, and a soft New England accent. It wasn't Massachusetts or Maine but might have been New Hampshire or Vermont.

"But I just have to know who you are." And he aimed his powerful smile at her as if it would melt her knees. Well, Sienna was made of stronger metal than that.

"The Goddess Aphrodite," she snapped at him.

"No arguments from me. Then you, sir, must be the Lord God Zeus to have such a daughter."

"Been called worse in my day." Her father's smile was not helping. Wasn't he supposed to be on her side?

Sienna glanced about the main hall. Though it was early, the museum was getting busier by the minute, yet they appeared to be in their own little bubble despite their proximity to a main staircase. It was as if the chattering families somehow sensed they shouldn't interfere with their small group. Above them hung the *Gossamer Condor*, the first human-powered airplane to fly a mile-long figure-eight course and to eventually cross the English Channel. It looked so frail, yet had achieved so much.

Frail had never been one of her choices.

"Sienna—" She turned and scowled at her father who stopped talking with a half cough-half harrumph before trying again. "My daughter finds your condition less than...impressive."

Roy smiled back at the man. Ramrod straight and clearly a soldier, Roy could feel him watching the crowd behind Roy out of habit just as Roy was watching the other direction. It made him feel a little safer. He also saw Julie was growing impatient with having to cover his simulator when she'd been headed on break—specifically a bathroom break.

"Well, sir, I find my condition less than impressive as well. It was a lesson hard learned about one of my..." he almost said 'fellow snipers,' but something told him that would open a whole different discussion than the one he wanted to have with the lovely Sienna. "Work buddies who I've already sworn on a bottle of aspirin that I will never listen to again."

Even her attempt at a sneer of disbelief looked amazing on her face. Her every thought was painted there, clear as day. And Sienna Whoever in a light blouse tucked into her pleasantly tight jeans had a body even more serious close up. Her combination of slender and curve was perfect in the way Jennifer Aniston's was—a bit of knowledge he could only blame on his big sister's crush on Chandler while they were growing up.

"I'm sorry, but I'll have to get back to my station. I simply wanted to ask if you," he turned fully to face her. He could smell her soap and shampoo and the gentlest hint of honey—too light to be a perfume so must be her. She was a hundred times more powerful up close than through his rifle scope.

She arched her eyebrows, naturally strong rather than studiously plucked, which he liked.

"If you would please have lunch with me today?"

Out of the corner of his eye, he could see her father—for there was no mistaking their having the same eyes and even the same manner of movement—watching his daughter. So, he too didn't know how to predict her next action. Independent thinker. Another plus. So many women didn't stand their own ground and left it to him to make decisions for both of them—which could get irritating as hell every time he made the wrong choice as if he had misread some secret code book.

The lovely Sienna would speak her own mind when she was good and ready.

"Fine!" Then her smile turned wicked. She tucked a hand in her father's arm and started off. "Fourteen hundred hours in the White House commissary," she called back over her shoulder, assuming that would shut him down.

He waited the beat so that she would think him stymied by White House security. Then he called after her, "I work here until then. Fourteen-thirty?"

She actually stumbled in surprise and barely resisted looking back toward him.

Her father's laugh told him he'd won that round.

Without a further glance at her fine walk—which he'd observed was very fine when she'd first walked away from him—he returned to Julie who was now mincing foot to foot.

"You owe me, Beaumont."

"I do, name your price."

"Lunch!"

"Sorry, I've got a date."

"Might have known," then she rushed off, leaving him surrounded by a milling hoard of happy, eager, short people bouncing up and down as they awaited their turn on the ride.

He and Julie had had some fun, but it had never gone much past some heavy flirting except for one night that had never been regretted, but also hadn't been repeated. Fun, but no spark.

He took a moment to watch Sienna the redhead and her powerfully built gray-haired father as they faded back into the crowd. Any fears he'd had about his abilities at target acquisition were gone. He'd be able to track her through New York streets at night if he could see a single lock of her lush, thick hair that must feel like—

A sharp tug on his jeans had him reaching down to lift the next boy aloft. His hangover was no longer as brain-piercing as it had been; the aspirin was finally kicking in.

Progress on many fronts.

———

Fourteen hundred hours slipped by as she delved into the implications of the latest reports on North Korean missile production.

Fourteen-thirty should have slipped quietly by while considering the completely different views of the Joint Chiefs and the Secretary of Defense regarding US force requirements in South Korea. The Chiefs wanted to push some of those forces into the South China Sea's piracy situation, also sending a message to the Chinese military buildup in the region. Defense, as far as Sienna could tell, wanted to take the fight to North Korea and turn the DMZ into the next Afghanistan.

But by fourteen-thirty-five she gave up all hope of concentrating. There was no way she was going to go out and see if there was some bleary-eyed docent hanging out at the White House gate. Besides, he was probably off having a three-beer lunch at his favorite watering hole. But her blood sugar had crashed a good hour ago and she wouldn't be getting any more work done until she'd eaten.

The commissary was quiet on a Saturday afternoon. The normal mayhem of weekday staff crowding the halls was gone; only a hundred or so hard-cores were scattered about the building. A cluster of Secret Service agents identifiable by their dark suits and coiled earpieces sat at a corner table to the back.

Several secretaries, looking no less harried than on weekdays but at least more comfortable in slacks and sneakers rather than dresses and heels, had gathered at a table in the middle of the room and were chatting happily.

She could envy them that simple circle of women. Her world had always been defined by men. Among her father's cronies—the pilots she'd hung out with at the HMX hangars where the Marine One helicraft were kept, and within the military she had come to know so intimately—women at high command levels were still the very rare exception.

She needed comfort food today and selected lasagna, a big hunk of bread with butter, a tiny plate of salad, and a bottle of juice.

It was only when she turned that she spotted him. Impossibly, the docent from the museum was sitting in the front of the room, close by the entry door but not where he'd be noticed if you weren't looking for him. His back was to the corner, setting him up to survey the entire room, but all he was watching was her.

His gaze was so steady that it drew her toward him until she ground to a stop just feet from the table. So steady that…

"Oh no! It's you."

He nodded happily, "It is. Nothing wrong with your powers of observation."

"The sniper on the roof," she wasn't in the habit of restating the obvious, but it just came out of her.

Again, his pleasant nod as if it was the most normal thing in the world for him to be here. His dark eyes were now clear and sharp, he'd shaken off the results of whatever excesses he'd imbibed last night.

"How…" No, that was a dumb question: sniper, who'd recognized her at the museum.

"Who…" Almost as meaningless: he was a Secret Service counter sniper. One of the most elite gunmen in or out of the USSS.

"Why?"

He kicked out a seat across from him with his foot. "Why don't you sit down before your knees let go and I'll tell you."

"Not the most courteous of men."

He shrugged, "Vermont born and bred. Don't see much point in doing the standing and bowing thing when it isn't called for. As Ma always said, I never was long on formal."

Somehow trapped by his unflinching gaze—if he'd looked aside for even a second she might have broken whatever spell he had cast over her, but he didn't—she settled into the chair and placed her lunch on the table.

"The way you walk, Ms.—huh, still don't have a last name for you— Ms. Sienna Aphrodite Goddess-of-Beauty, is an amazing thing."

If the next thing he said was what a fine ass she had, she was out of here. And as the NSA, she'd make sure he was reassigned somewhere far away and never came near her again.

"You walk as if you were more alive than any dozen other people put together."

"That's…not what I was expecting."

"Oh, I could remark on any number of other aspects to your walk that I expect would give you an excuse to ship me out—"

She definitely did not like being read so easily.

"But I rather like this posting, even before I saw how you could light up a day." And with no more ceremony than that, he bit into a monstrous ham sandwich that had been untouched as he awaited her, despite her late arrival. No matter how casual he wished to appear, he'd been sitting and waiting, too wound up to eat. Or perhaps too polite, despite his protests to the contrary, to start without her. Either way it was an unexpected and nicely flattering compliment.

"Vermont?" Sienna prompted him and took a bite of her lasagna making it clear she wasn't going to be the one talking.

"The Northeast Kingdom."

"Vermont is the size of half a postage stamp, how can it have something called the Northeast Kingdom?" She spoke with her mouth still mostly full, a habit she'd learned while standing too many watches beside the military she'd been studying.

"Clearly the lady doesn't know the true definition of a Yankee. Air Force brat?" he asked her.

"Marine Corps," she admitted. And all of the moving around that implied.

"Huh. Don't get a lot of Marines at the Air and Space Museum."

"Dad flew recovery helos on Apollo 11 and others," and she was giving out more information than he was. She didn't like it.

"So, you grew up mostly south of the Mason-Dixon Line, I suppose." He made it sound as if he pitied her poor lost soul for such a burden.

She took a bite of salad so that she had an excuse to restrict herself to a nod or she'd tell him a thing or two about Southern women.

"Well," and he settled back as if he had all the time in the world to tell a story and she didn't have a mound of reports already deep enough to hide most of her desk. "To anyone outside the US, a Yankee is someone inside. Inside our country, a Yankee would stake his claim north of the Mason-Dixon Line. North of there New England and in New England, a Yankee means Vermont. Oh, Maine might try, but they'd be wrong as could be."

"And inside Vermont?" He was obviously waiting for the prompt.

"Why someone from The Northeast Kingdom, of course." He said it as if it was a complete given.

"And inside the TNK?"

He snorted a laugh at her acronym. "Someone who eats Ma's apple pie."

"Which you do."

"Best in the world," he sounded ready to defend it to the death.

"That still doesn't tell me what the TNK is except a bunch of arrogant boys who can't cook for themselves."

Rather than protesting, he leaned back in. "It is the most beautiful place on earth. Green hills that roll all the way from sunrise to sunset. Trout in the streams just begging to be roasted over the fire. The woods smell of oak and pine and are deep enough that nothing but the birds or the deer will ever find a man."

"A poet," she teased him, but could picture it so easily.

"Spoken like a city girl," he teased her right back.

And he was right. Marine bases were big, busy places. And Marine Corps generals were not posted far afield. Suddenly she wished she could see his great Northeast Kingdom. Instead, she could picture the pile of work on her desk. It was—

"Do you shoot?"

The question was such a non sequitur that she could only blink at him in surprise.

"I see you drifting back to work and I see it worrying at you. Daughter of a Marine. Do you shoot?"

"Daughter of a Marine Corps *general*. Yes, I shoot."

"Christ. Your father is a Marine general? Surprised he didn't have me shot for hitting on his daughter."

"He..." No. She wasn't going to tell him that her father was the one who'd pointed this man out. "He knew I could take care of myself if I wanted to."

"Excellent. Let's go."

She looked down at her lunch, which she'd finished without noticing, and then back up at him. Whimsically, despite the fact that she was never ever motivated by whim, Sienna decided it really had been a crazy week and she could do with a break.

"There's no way I'm going to outshoot a sniper."

"I didn't say a competition. I was thinking more about unleashing some of those nerves hunching up your shoulders. They're awfully nice shoulders—one of those things I'm probably not supposed to be commenting on," and his tone told her there were many other implied compliments waiting their turns.

She wondered if they'd all be delivered so nicely. He'd skipped over the typical "nice ass" comment, only occasionally disguised as "you've got a great walk, babe." And if he'd looked at her chest, she hadn't caught him at it.

"You've got to relax if you want to shoot well," he slipped effortlessly back into the earlier conversation.

"I know that."

"Then let's go. We have a range just down the street a piece." He shoved back his chair and stood. When he turned to reach for his jacket was when she saw the big USSS across the back of his t-shirt, and the Glock tucked in a holster at the small of his back. Only the most trusted were allowed to carry a firearm inside the White House. Initially hungover or not, it said a great deal about this man and his integrity.

———

Roy spent the four block walk to the Secret Service building trying to figure out if this was real or not. Out in the July sunshine, she was even prettier than when sitting across from him. It was like she was powered by the open air even though they were walking through the heart of the city. It was so easy to picture her walking through the deep woods. Tipping her head back to breathe in the pine sap-scented air brushed as clean as could be by a fresh running stream nearby.

The more they talked, the less certain of himself he became.

Her White House security badge had annoyingly small print of her name. It wouldn't have been any problem pinned on a guy, but he didn't want to be accused of staring at her breasts while he was just trying to read her tag. And the woman never looked away to give him a chance to peek down at those nice curves, or the badge. While they'd been talking, he'd had a hundred percent of her attention which was so unusual that he could instantly tell when her attention had drifted back to work.

He'd blurted out the first thing he could think of to keep her attention, "Do you shoot?" How lame was he? Yet it seemed to have worked when he followed it through, making it up as he went.

The one thing he could tell about her badge was that it was the same as his: the rare "all pass." It gave her permission to enter both wings and the Residence of the White House. They were very rare outside the Secret Service and meant she was probably very high-level staff. Even cabinet members had to have a Secret Service escort when moving beyond the West Wing.

It irked him to know that if he'd been assigned to internal security, he'd have known who she was a week sooner, but he'd been on overwatch rotation and not included in briefings about staff changes inside the building. Then he'd been dumped into route planning with Frank Adams or some other high-end agent constantly hovering beside him. He learned more about route planning this week than in the entire year prior. He'd torn apart prior plans and reviewed future ones until he could see at a glance where the gaps were and how best to fill them.

But he still hadn't been briefed on senior level knock-out redheads.

She'd remained coy about her name and he didn't feel comfortable using her first name without permission, so he was stuck with the Goddess Aphrodite. He couldn't remember if she was love or beauty or something else. The longer it lasted, the more certain he became that he'd gotten it wrong and never should have crawled out of bed this morning. But he did enjoy working with the kids and it was a nice change from sniper duty. Then Sienna Aphrodite had slipped into his sights with her knowing smile and lively eyes.

Down the street, through the mirrored doors, and up to the front desk they'd talked mostly of the weather: the seasons of D.C., Vermont, and where she'd done most of her growing up near Marine Corps Air Station New River in Jacksonville, North Carolina. She was the first city girl he'd ever met who had thoughts beyond shops and parties and the status of this person versus that one.

At the security desk, he moved in to vouch for her as a visitor. She slid her badge across the desk and it was as if he'd ceased to exist.

"Greetings, Ms. Arnson," Marlene, who usually greeted him with the sharp edge of her tongue, was all smoothness and silk to—

"Wait! Arnson? That—" he pointed a hand helplessly toward the Air and Space Museum. "That was Brigadier General Edward Arnson?"

"Yes," she replied, deeply amused by some internal joke. "My father and I share that name."

"Shit!" He wiped at his forehead. "He's—" Then he clamped down on his tongue. Both Marlene and Sienna were looking at him with amused expressions. "Notorious." Notoriously strict and intolerant of anything that wasn't absolutely perfect about the President's protection. He and Frank Adams were two of a kind. Rumor had it that Arnson had turned down two promotions in order to remain in charge of the Marines at HMX-1.

And Arnson didn't limit his opinions to his helicopters or the Marines stationed aboard them. He'd never faced the man himself, but he'd heard stories and seen the shredded remains of USSS agents not living up to his standards.

Sienna was still smiling at him, as if waiting for the other shoe to drop. Sienna...Arnson.

"Oh shit!"

She laughed in his face.

He *had* been briefed on her, he'd just never seen the photo of the new National Security Advisor. "You're..." He stopped himself, but it was far too late.

Marlene was going to be spreading this story far and wide. If he thought the ration of shit Fernando and Hank had unleashed on his head was too much, he was in for a blood bath now.

He took a deep breath and looked down at her. National Security Advisor Sienna Arnson was awaiting his final reaction. But so was another woman, one he guessed was used to hiding deep in those liquid brown eyes.

"I believe," he drew it out just a little and saw the most tentative of smiles from the inner woman rather than the NSA. "I believe I promised my Lady Aphrodite a bit of shooting."

Her smile shifted. There was a distinct pause. Then, rather than going radiantly dangerous as it had on the first day when she was leaving the White House, it went soft and warm. That's how he knew he'd made the right choice.

In his peripheral vision he could see Marlene giving him a nod as if she didn't quite believe what she was seeing—Roy Beaumont actually doing something right.

He took Sienna's arm and guided her down the marble and granite hall toward the basement range. Once she was a half step ahead of him, he turned casually and stuck his tongue out at Marlene.

A dozen paces down the hall, Sienna asked quietly, "Did you enjoy doing that?"

"I did," he admitted. And would never again forget that the NSA missed absolutely nothing.

Roy led her down a long flight of stairs and through two sets of double doors, where they collected ear muffs and goggles before going through a third. The range had shooting bays separated by sound-muffled panels that also stopped ejected casings from pinging the next shooter along the line. Down a long, concrete tunnel there were ten targets hanging from wires. Some of them were a long way away.

Saturday afternoon was apparently a quiet time on the Secret Service basement shooting range. There were only three other shooters in the ten lanes.

The distance didn't bother her, but she was less certain about the man. Her position as the National Security Advisor had only knocked him off track for a moment. And he might be the first person other than her parents to see her as herself rather than the NSA or "some woman." She'd never, not until that moment in the Secret Service lobby, realized the difference herself. Yet when he had set aside her position and continued to treat her as the woman she'd been at lunch, her world had shifted just a little bit.

They visited the armorer.

"What do you shoot?"

"A...handgun?" How was she *supposed* to answer?

Roy sighed and took her hand. She couldn't ignore the easy strength of his big hands as he assessed her own. And it wasn't merely size he was interested in. He poked at muscles, flexed her fingers, even ordered her to make a fist around his two forefingers and squeeze hard before he turned back to the armorer.

"Let's try her on a Glock 43 slimline subcompact. I may be back for the 19 compact but I don't think so. Five magazines until we see how she does."

"What? Think I can't handle the big, bad gun?" What was she even doing here with him?

"No, I think it will fit your hand better and give you better control. You have medium hands but very fine fingers. It will actually kick a little harder because it's the same 9mm round, just less gun. I think you have the strength to handle that."

Okay, she was going to shut up now. He hadn't taken offense at her sarcasm. He heard her mistaken assumption and had simply corrected it. Why now, when her life was crazier than it had ever been, had she finally met a decent guy? These were stolen minutes. For the next seven months, she didn't have time for a guy, much less a decent one—jerks took less time to deal with even in a relationship. She was too busy, just like she'd been for the last—Sienna was not going to count the years.

He led her over to one of the shooting desks between a pair of the sound panels.

"Besides..."

And she already knew that smile. Here came the next compliment wrapped up in a tease. Oddly, she was intrigued to know how he'd pull it off this time. Then, for the first time, he very deliberately looked down at her chest.

"With your build, this is the weapon you'd want for a concealed shoulder holster carry."

"Are you saying my breasts are too small?" And then she knew that her unconsidered reaction was exactly the one he'd been counting on her having.

"Nope. I'm saying they're just about damn perfect and this is the gun to go with them."

Sienna didn't want to be charmed. He was talking about her chest like...like...like no one else ever had. She couldn't pin down what was up with Roy Beaumont. Then she could see him shift back into sniper mode. Almost like a cuckoo clock, this complete and total "guy" would stick his head out, tease her, and then duck away.

"This is a Glock 43. There's no safety as such. You—"

"I've fired a Glock before."

"Okay," and he backed right off. Even her father didn't do that. Roy took her at her word. Maybe she was the one he was driving cuckoo.

She checked the weapon was clear, loaded a magazine, and pulled the slide to chamber the first round. She could feel him watching her every move intently, but he made no comment.

The target looked to be fifty feet out, a third of the way down the deep range. The outline of a man with two sets of bullseyes on him: one on the face, the other centered on the chest.

The lane was clear.

She raised her weapon and sighted down the iron sights through her dominant left eye and—

"Hold it." Roy stopped her before she could move her finger alongside the barrel onto the trigger. "Keep your finger off the trigger."

Which was exactly where she had it placed, alongside the barrel rather than through the trigger guard. *Don't touch the trigger until you're ready to fire,* one of her father's lessons. *And don't draw the damn thing unless you intend to fire it.* Another one.

Roy then began to handle her. He kicked one foot to set her stance a little wider. Hands on hips to twist her slightly more to the side. He worked his way up her body and then out her arms making tiny adjustments. Sometimes he'd move something, like her elbow, back and forth until he was sure she could feel the difference.

Last was her head. Without taking the least advantage, his fingers slid into her hair and shifted the angle of her head tilt ever so slightly. It was a gentle, intimate gesture. One she could easily imagine leading to other places that she hadn't gone in far too long. Three years working the US Commands had elicited a lot of offers—very few of which had been even interesting enough to consider as she'd had so little time for extracurricular activities.

"No, leave your shoulders where I put them. You're raising them up again."

He left her to slowly find the position he'd set her in rather than laying his hands back on her and making the adjustments himself. She considered not returning to the initial position just so he'd have to put his hands back on her, which was too lame for words.

Besides, she could feel when everything settled into the "right" position. There was a cleanness to it—at least it was the best word she could find.

"Now, don't hold your breath when you fire, just pause for a moment before each squeeze on the trigger. Go when you're ready."

She liked the feel of the smaller Glock 43, the way the butt nestled neatly against her palm—once Roy was done adjusting her grip. She could feel the straight line of wrist, elbow, arm, and the solid support of her other hand cupped beneath the gun and her hand.

Sienna considered showing off, firing a fast series of shots like those she heard battering away in other lanes, but something about Roy's presence...she wanted to do her best. She squeezed off the first round.

No comment.

Another.

A whispered, "Don't adjust left, but *think* left. That will be enough correction."

She thought left and sent the rest of the magazine after the first two without eliciting any other comment—one per breath. There was a peace inside her as she made sure the weapon was clear and set it on the shooting desk.

Roy pressed a button and the chart flapped backward as the overhead wire pulleyed it to them.

"Nice shooting. Your father trained you well."

She did her best to ignore the two shots out in the five ring to the right. An eight, two nines with one just catching the edge of the bullseye, and one fully in the black of the ten. Ignoring the first two, it was one of the best groups she'd ever shot in her life.

"He never taught me the sort of things you did," she tipped her head and shifted her elbow to demonstrate.

"Different weapon. He probably ran you mostly on his Sig Sauer P226. And the Corps teaches differently. I gave you the base position we start recruits in. You build stance variations from there." And he lifted her empty gun, which looked silly in his big strong hands, and demonstrated a slow turn. The muzzle of the weapon never wavered that she could see, but his shoulders, hands, and head position shifted as he rotated from chin over his left shoulder to chin over his right. He then dropped to a squat and did the same thing, but the shifts were more dramatic.

It was easy to forget that something so apparently simple as firing a sidearm was also so complex. He made it look easy. This was Roy's specialty and he would be far more skilled in this arena than she was— or her father, which was hard to admit.

"Besides, the P226 is a lot of gun with a heavy round and would require a slightly different stance. I'd wager you hurt here after shooting it," he poked a finger into a shoulder muscle she knew all too well from past experience, "and the slide sometimes caught you here." His fingertip drew a line of fire across the webbing between her thumb and forefinger.

"Okay, Mr. Smarty Sniper. Show me your stuff." She needed a moment to recover from the unexpected intimacy of him knowing things about her body that only she should know.

She hit the "Out" button and sent the target flying back down-range. She didn't stop at the fifty-foot mark.

"Hey!"

Sienna kept her thumb down on the travel control.

"C'mon! I don't have my rifle here," he whined as it passed the hundred foot mark. She ran it right to the back wall at fifty yards.

"Head shots only. And your grouping had better be at least as good as mine."

"Blindfolded with my back turned and no mirror?"

"Maybe next time. This time I'll let you off easy."

He set down her empty Glock 43 and pulled its much bigger brother out of his back holster—a Glock 21 that fired .45 cal rounds.

There was a weapon that looked proper in his hands. The fearsome warrior now stood before her in all his lethal might. Damn, but it looked good on him.

She stepped aside to give Roy room. He'd taken a minute or two to get her positioned.

It took him less than five seconds. He just went...quiet. Not frozen, but so still she suspected a deer could walk right by him in his precious Vermont woods without being disturbed.

The shots came impossibly close together. No, she caught the rhythm of the last few. She had fired once per breath, he was firing once per heartbeat.

He stopped at six, which came all within the same caught breath for her. Then he punched the "In" button before dropping the magazine and clearing the chamber.

"Same number of rounds to be fair."

The target arrived. Every shot was in or touching the much smaller black bullseye of the headshot except one.

"What was that?" She asked before she could stop herself. One shot had hit two inches high in the center of the target's forehead. The rest of his grouping would have fit easily inside the chest bullseye that she'd only managed to really hit once, and his was at three times the distance.

"Number three," he sounded ticked. "I typically drop the first two in the center of the chest and then shift for the head for the next two. I remembered a moment too late that I was already at the head and you had specified only head shots. So it went high. That high on the forehead, it might easily glance aside of the bone without penetrating the skull."

"That's amaz—"

Somewhere down the lane a series of shots rang out so fast she could barely separate them. It wasn't machine gun fire, but it was impossibly fast. Either two per heartbeat or someone with the pulse rate of a hummingbird.

There was a soft but heartfelt, "Damn it!" from the same direction.

A few seconds later there was another impossibly fast barrage, this time without the curse.

Two targets that had been against the back wall at the far end of the shooting gallery as Roy's had, started winging their way forward.

Roy leaned back to look down the gallery and then gathered up both of their weapons and the small pile of magazines. "C'mon. This should be good."

They arrived at the same time the targets did.

Sienna focused on the targets first. One had a lot of holes in the black at the center of the chest, one through the neck, and the rest inside or touching the black of the head bullseye. The other had near perfect groupings in the two blacks without any strays.

"Getting sloppy in your old age, Beat." The speaker was looking over at the target with the neck shot. She was a short but very shapely woman with Eurasian features and a streak of bleached blond in her dark, chin-length hair.

"Still a spine cutter, Kee." The first shooter—who had apparently been the one to curse after her round—was an equally powerfully-curved woman with dark, dark skin and just the first hint of gray in her black hair. She tapped her stray shot with the tip of her handgun.

Sienna had to swallow hard at the thought. These two women were shooting to make sure that the person wasn't just stopped, but stopped dead. Just like Roy shooting chest then head. They were talking about cutting the spine to stop an assailant. She knew *of* this world, but not about it. No matter how much she'd studied, she'd never been in a war zone, never had to shoot a live person.

Then a big, deep voice back down the gallery boomed out, "Who the hell shot this piece of crap?"

Sienna winced just knowing someone had found her target.

Roy groaned. It shouldn't be possible. It was Saturday afternoon for crying out loud.

But when Roy looked, there he was as real as life. Frank Adams came striding up the line with his and Sienna's chart flapping from one of his big hands.

"That's mine, I'm afraid, Mr. Adams," Sienna admitted freely, showing not the least flinch of mortal terror. How did she do that?

"I'm not talking about the chest. It's obviously civilian and nice enough shooting for one. Wouldn't take much to make you a decent shot if you can already do this, Ms. Arnson."

Of course Adams had known who the hot redhead was, even the first day on the roof. It ticked Roy off that the answer to the mystery woman's identity had been glaring over his shoulder all week; not that Roy would ever have considered asking him.

"I'm talking about this piece of crap," Adams aimed a finger right at Roy's high number three.

"Was shifting for a head shot, forgetting I was already there." It was an awful admission, because it meant he'd made a shot without thinking about it. But it was the truth, so he said it.

Frank tipped his head down enough to look at Roy over the tops of his shooting glasses.

Roy wasn't sure what prompted him, maybe hoping for a laugh from Sienna. But for the second time in the same week, he talked back to the head of the Presidential Protection Detail. First he raised his right hand.

"I do hereby solemnly swear that I'll never screw up again as long as I shall live. So help me god."

"So help us all," Frank boomed out with the solemnity of a Southern preacher with absolutely no faith in his flock. He turned to his wife. "Beat, send down a fresh pair of targets. Send them all the way down."

Beatrice Anne Belfour was the head of the First Lady's detail and Frank's wife. She was also rumored to be even more lethal than her husband. Roy was just glad he'd never had a chance to find out.

The other woman he hadn't seen before, but there weren't too many top shooters named Kee. This had to be Kee Stevenson, one of the top snipers in the country. He'd heard she was working with the FBI's Hostage Rescue Team on loan from the Army's 160th Night Stalkers helicopter regiment. He'd hoped to shoot against her someday in a competition, but he'd never expected to meet her in the presence of his boss.

"Beaumont," Frank Adams voice snapped him back to attention.

"Sir."

Adams set down his massive Sig Sauer P226. Then pointed for him to reload both Sienna's lean Glock 43 and his personal 21. Then he waved to Roy's ankle.

Roy lifted his pant leg and pulled out the Walther PPK he kept there and set it last in the row. It was a weapon of last resort, rarely used beyond twenty-five feet. But Roy knew it intimately and could use it very effectively; it had been the concealed carry piece his dad had given him for his sixteenth birthday—James Bond's gun, though in a smaller .22 caliber—and he'd worn it ever since.

Adams snorted derisively but made him lay it down alongside the others. He probably wore a howitzer alongside one of his massive legs.

"Shoot the two targets heart left, head right, heart right, head left. Eight rounds from your and my gun. Four each from the 43 and that wimp-ass excuse you call a backup piece."

Roy wanted to protest.

Wanted to just walk away.

He'd brought Sienna here for a little shooting and mostly some flirting, never suspecting how good she already was. And how quickly she learned. She remembered the body-feel of each positional correction perfectly.

And the feel of her body.

It had almost killed him to take his hands off the soft curve of her hips once he'd touched them. The warmth of her shoulders, the lean strength in her arms, and with his hands full of her hair it had required more self-control than he knew he had to merely adjust her head then back away.

And now Adams was being a total bastard—just as he'd been all week correcting every little thing Roy did—and was trying to make him into some kind of a goddamn fool in front of her.

Well, it wasn't going to happen.

Roy braced himself.

He'd never tried such a challenge. .45, .357, 9mm, and .22. Four very different weapons from three different manufacturers. And it would be easier to shoot until empty, but Adams wasn't even going to give him that. He rocked up on the balls of his feet and then resettled his heels solidly.

He could feel the background fading. Adams glowering behind him. Beat Belfour's impenetrably dark eyes observing every detail and Kee Stevenson's almond eyes so narrow he couldn't tell what she was watching. Off to his right, Sienna Arnson, the general's daughter.

To his left.

Four weapons.

Two targets.

They were all that matter—

"Double time it!" Adams' harsh bark didn't penetrate Roy's focus beyond the content of the added challenge. "Fire NOW!"

At his shout, instinct took over. Roy grabbed the first piece. Adjusted for the Sig's weight and hard kick, then unleashed it downrange. Chest, cross to head, down to chest, cross back to first head. Repeat. Drop the weapon. Next. Repeat. Next.

With his final weapon, the lightweight Walther PPK, he intentionally fired a fifth round.

He didn't watch the approaching targets as he cleared all four weapons.

Beat didn't pull them down, she just let them hang there. He forced himself to look up. The holes were slightly different sizes in the paper. The heavy rounds of Adams' Sig rose slightly from one to the next—it was hard to recover the feel when firing so quickly—the last barely touching the top of the black. The heavier .45s from his own weapon held steady. The other groupings were more consistent as well.

Nothing was wholly off the black.

Except that final one that had gone precisely where he'd sent it.

He gathered up his weapons and headed back toward the armorer to turn in the borrowed Glock 43 and the unspent rounds. He signed for number of rounds fired and reloaded his own weapons.

The last round, the fifth from his .22, was dead center of the target's forehead. Exactly where he'd placed his third shot when shooting for Sienna. Right where he'd like to put a round in Frank Adams for making him do that in front of her.

He was a half block down the street outside the Secret Service building with no idea of how he got there or where he was heading, when a hand took his.

It jolted him back to reality. He'd know her hand anywhere—since the very moment he'd first touched it while assessing what weapon would be best for her grip.

"I'm…" Roy didn't know what to say.

…sorry my boss enjoys jerking my chain?

…sorry it was such a crappy first date?

Sorry for…he didn't know what.

"Roy. Just stop a moment. Easy. Just stop."

He stopped, but didn't know what to do next.

———

No matter what those two amazing women did, Sienna had never seen anything like what Roy had just done. And by the long silence with which the other three had looked at the two targets after Roy had finished shooting, she'd guess they hadn't either.

She guided him over to a concrete bench along the sidewalk and made him sit down. Sienna let him just sit for a moment. The afternoon sun on his face. The lazy Saturday afternoon traffic rolling by. They were a couple blocks back from the tourist mania, so the sidewalk was relatively quiet. A couple of pigeons came over to see if there were any breadcrumbs for the begging, but soon waddled off in search of more promising subjects.

"What was that?" She asked only when she felt him come back enough that he might answer.

He scrubbed at his face with his free hand, she hadn't let go of the other yet. Still he held his silence.

"Roy?"

"Adams hates me. Wanted to humiliate me in front of you. I'd say he did a pretty thorough job of it."

Sienna's specialty was assessing situations as they developed. And her gift? She was far more consistently right than those around her. She tried to keep it based on an immense body of research, but occasionally, she just knew. Her consistency had eventually earned her the respect of four of the six US Commands' generals. The other two had been hard cases like the Secretary of Defense so she'd learned what she could from them (some of it how *not* to command) and moved on.

The problem was Roy had the situation completely backwards, but there was no way to tell him that. Say it head on and he'd just deny it. Call her a fool.

It had been a test. Performance under pressure. Three top shooters observing Roy, and Adams must know it was her and Roy's first "date"—for she couldn't deny that's what it had become. She didn't have any misconceptions about privacy inside the security bubble that was the White House—there wasn't any. There was discretion, but there was no privacy.

Adams had seen an opportunity and grabbed it—to test Roy.

Knowing that discussing it head on wasn't going to get her anywhere, she came at him sideways.

"What do you know about the two women?"

Roy eyed her strangely for a long moment, but soon began giving her chapter and verse. He was careful to let her know what was fact and what was rumor. It was crazy how the pieces fit together in unexpected ways.

Kee had served under the Two Majors, as they were now called inside military circles. Majors Mark Henderson and Emily Beale had formed the most responsive and mission successful helicopter company ever within the already impressive 160th Night Stalkers. Roy didn't know about them, but Sienna had met Beale during the major's last days at USCENTCOM and never been so impressed by anyone, man or woman. Her replacement, Warrant Officer Lola LaRue Maloney was almost as amazing in her own way and the 4th Battalion D Company was still one of the go-to teams in President Matthews' black ops arsenal.

Beat Belfour, even though she was in the same service as Roy, he knew even less about.

"Woman is just so damned serious. Makes her scary as hell because you never know what she's thinking. She makes Frank Adams look like a teddy bear."

"A teddy bear who you metaphorically shot in the head." Now she could approach the sore spot.

"Yeah," Roy bowed his head down to stare at the sidewalk. "Only shot I've taken in anger since putting a BB into my big sister's backside when she was ten and teasing the crap out of me. Adams will never forgive me that last shot any more than my sister did. You don't suppose he won't notice?"

She couldn't help herself. It just caught her funny side. This big strong man, a one-man complete personal defense team, worried about shooting a paper target in anger, and doing it perfectly.

"I think," she managed between giggles, "he might...have noticed."

"I suppose," he finally smiled for the first time since they'd sat down, "that it was better than if I'd shot the target in the balls."

"Imagine the look on his face if you had."

And soon they were both laughing.

It was a good moment. Sienna's good moments were always on the professional side, but this was a good moment on the personal side—such a rarity that she wanted to wrap it up and cherish it carefully. The warmth of his smile. The laughter in his eyes—

Then he kissed her.

Everything else fell away in that moment: her need to console him, the nagging background worry of the unfinished work on her desk, how inappropriate it was for the newly-minted National Security Advisor to be kissing a near stranger on the D.C. streets. All gone.

Roy's kiss didn't allow thoughts of anything else to intrude. It was about a confused man and a woman who was wondering if she'd ever met such an honorable person before. It was about a woman who had only ever seen herself "as the job" and a man who somehow looked past that.

When she finally broke off the kiss, it was for none of those reasons, but rather because she felt so...full. Like she wanted to dance and laugh and sing and weep all at once and if the kiss lasted one second longer she might try to do all four simultaneously and simply collapse from the internal chaos of it.

Roy didn't pull away or apologize or do any of those typically male things. Instead he looked at her steadily and brushed a callused thumb along her cheek.

"Clear in your sights, Mr. Sniper Man?" Because his eyes somehow really saw her in a way she'd never known was possible.

"Clearest ever, Ms. Sienna Aphrodite. Say, maybe that explains it. Did you put one of those goddess-type spells on me?"

"No. Explains what?"

"Why I suddenly specialize in being an idiot in front of Frank Adams, of course."

She almost bought into it. Was almost angry that he was back to worrying about Frank instead of focusing on the best kiss ever created.

But then she saw that hint of a tease in his eyes.

"Frank Adams, huh? Okay. You want to think about him, go ahead. But I have news for you, Mr. Sniper Man."

"This should be good," he sat back and crossed his arms. Gods but he was so gloriously male and she couldn't resist poking at him.

"You don't get another kiss until you can come back and tell me something personal about Frank Adams and Beatrice Belfour." Besides, she absolutely needed a little mental distance here to understand what had just happened. Because the female in her, who she knew so little about, was ready to jump him here and now on the city street and the woman who she was needed to slow the other one down.

He just gaped at her.

"And it had better be something nice."

CHAPTER THREE

ienna, Roy was sorry to discover, was a woman of her word. He managed to talk her into going out for pizza on Sunday night— very relieved that she was a woman happier to dine on a sniper's budget than a senator's. But he wasn't allowed even a good night kiss before she slipped away in a taxi.

His plans to pump Adams for some detail, any detail, were foiled when Kee Stevenson was waiting for him in the Secret Service ready room Monday morning.

"You're with me," clearly this was going to be her idea of a hardship assignment. She looked as happy as a losing candidate giving a concession speech.

"No, I have roof duty."

Kee handed him a sheet of paper. "Do what she says. Don't screw up. Adams."

He handed it back and wondered if he should go wash his hands, just as he would after handling some dangerous viper. Kee didn't give him a chance.

"Bring your two favorite rifles. Let's go."

He grabbed the case for his JAR—after all, the Just Another Rifle was the bread and butter of a Secret Service counter sniper—and after a moment's thought selected the HK PSG1A1—a rifle he'd always liked. Kee eyed him as if now Roy Beaumont was the dangerous viper. Or perhaps as if for the first time, he was actually of interest. Unlike Sienna, Kee Stevenson was wholly inscrutable and he'd bet neither of his guesses was accurate.

They went.

He considered pumping Kee for information about Frank and Beat, but her silence was just as daunting as Beatrice Belfour's and he reconsidered his plan. He couldn't even find a gap in her silence to ask where they were going; he was just a piece of meat along for the ride.

They headed south out of the city in a standard black SUV. He wondered if it wouldn't be safer to move the President around in an unmarked five-year old Chevy rather than the massively escorted motorcade made up of distinctively black-and-tinted armored vehicles, but no one was asking him.

Instead, all he could do was look out the window and watch D.C. roll by. They headed south. If Kee Stevenson was working the Hostage Rescue Team, maybe they were headed to Quantico. Was he being transferred there?

That gave him a jolt. He wouldn't put it past Adams to shuffle him out of the White House for even speaking with the NSA. Normally it wouldn't bother him. Especially after only two dates and one kiss. Such a change of logistics wouldn't rate more than a phone call or maybe a text: "See you, honey. It was good to be with you, but just transferred out of state on no notice. Thanks. Bye." In other words good, but not that good. Actually, with a lot of his past relationships he'd have welcomed the excuse. But for some reason, being jerked away from Sienna Arnson did not sit at all comfortably with him.

He nudged and prodded at that puzzle as Kee drove south out of D.C. Abe kept his eye on the city from his high stone perch, not caring crap about Roy. And if there was any Jeffersonian wisdom waiting for him, it wasn't coming from the domed monument. Despite driving through the land of such greats, he ended up no wiser.

Sienna had gotten under his skin. And not just the way she looked or had abandoned herself to one of the gentlest and sweetest kisses he'd ever had. It had always seemed to him that he and women knew what they wanted from each other and just took it—hard heat fired by lust and not much else. Sienna, the woman behind her NSA shield, was soft and gentle at heart and had somehow burned herself into his system.

When he thought of her, it wasn't the kiss. It wasn't *just* the kiss. He remembered her laughing with merry abandon over pizza at his account of his Friday night lack of exploits with Fernando and Hank. Her insightful questions into his childhood had explained his path to being a sniper in ways he'd never thought about. And he could still feel her soft hand clasped against his own rough palm as she led him to sit on that concrete bench.

The problem came when he asked her about herself. If you needed an example of a conscious career path driven by sharp intellect, you got Sienna Arnson of Washington, D.C. It was as if the woman didn't exist separate from her career.

On the opposite end of the spectrum, Roy knew he wasn't a driven man. If you needed an example of someone who just happened to be able to handle the heavy math of advanced ballistics and was tough enough to survive every form of training they could throw at him, you got Roy Beaumont of northern Vermont. He figured his best attribute was being too thickheaded to know when to quit.

"Huh, what?"

Stevenson had made an unexpected turn. Quantico was still a dozen miles away when she pulled up to a security booth alongside a big hangar. A hangar surrounded by helicopters not airplanes.

"You got a one-track mind, Beaumont. Give me your ID."

"I'm a sniper. We're supposed to have one-track minds." He handed over his badge.

"Uh-huh. And that's why you're wearing a stupid-ass dreamy expression rather than even saying 'Good Morning'?" She rolled down her window and handed both of their badges to the gate guard. The Marine Corps gate guard.

"Always dreamed of being a sniper."

"You keep thinking that and I might as well turn this car around and dump you back in Adams' lap. Don't think either of you would enjoy that much."

"What do you mean?"

She took back the IDs and handed his over as they rolled through the gate. "I mean, if your goal is to be a sniper, you're already there. What's next?"

"Huh." He'd never thought about it, but now that she'd mentioned it, he had kind of been in cruise mode for the last year. He'd made White House sniper. Didn't get much better than that.

"You're never going to be Chris Kyle with a record number of kills, neither am I for that matter, even though I'm probably as good a shot."

Roy leaned back to think about it, but didn't have a chance as Kee parked and they carried their rifles—she toted an unmarked case, battered and scuffed with hard use—through the back door of the hangar. There were a dozen helos parked in here.

As his eyes adjusted from the bright light outside, he could start to see details. Like the fact that every one of them was painted in the distinct green and white of the President's aircraft. These were the Marine One aircraft and their cohort of flying guard ships. That meant—

"Well, looky what the cat dragged in," General Edward Arnson strode up in Marine Corps fatigues and a dark blue t-shirt with USMC emblazoned across his broad chest. He nodded to the rifle cases, "Mr. Docent showing his true colors."

"Um, yes sir." Roy didn't know what else to say. He'd kissed this man's daughter and had been hoping to do so again. Looking at General Arnson, he wondered if he'd still be alive by the end of the day, never mind achieve the impossible and find out something "nice" about Adams and Belfour.

"Show some pluck, son," Arnson slammed a sidefist into Roy's arm hard enough to rock him sideways. "Gonna need it if you're going after my girl. Ain't me you need to be worrying about."

And Roy would believe that after hell froze over and cactus trees grew in Vermont.

"What can we do for you today, Kee?" The general's rough affability softened when he addressed the hard-edged Stevenson.

"I called in. Frank Adams wants me to take Beaumont here aloft. Do some target work."

Which was news to Roy despite half an hour in her presence. He'd done some shooting from helicopters...and been lousy at it. Anything beyond a few hundred yards was impossible to nail because of the vibrations and air currents. As a sniper he thought about breath, pulse, wind, temperature, and could even account for the Earth's spin on long shots. But with no stable platform, it was almost impossible to make a clean shot. From a helicopter, it was a challenge just to keep the target anywhere in the scope.

"Beaumont, huh," Arnson was inspecting him again.

"Yes, sir, Secret Service Agent Roy Beaumont." So Sienna hadn't told her father anything about him yet. Was that a good sign or a bad one? At the museum it had been easy to see how close they were. Maybe they didn't discuss personal matters? Or—

"Seems a hole just opened up in my schedule. What do you want to start him in?"

And Roy knew he was screwed.

"Let's start him in a Hawk, General. Don't know if I can trust him yet to not drop his gear off a Little Bird."

"Hey!" But they both ignored him and turned to the Hawk and began chatting about a "young scamp" named Dilya, who was apparently the First Child's part-time nanny. Roy was struck by how little thought he'd given to all that went on inside the building he'd spent so many hours lying on top of. It was just...the White House.

"Jeezum Crow!"

Both Arnson and Stevenson turned to look at him.

He just shook his head and they turned back to their conversation. Here he was as shallow as a mud puddle on a D.C. summer day and he was interested in the National Security Advisor, one of the most highly connected power players in the entire D.C. scene? She was responsible for wrangling the Joint Chiefs, intelligence, and cabinet secretaries into some form of agreement and he was responsible for...peeking through a rifle scope.

Roy tuned back into Kee Stevenson's conversation to escape quite how small he suddenly felt.

"...I tell you that Beat and Frank understand my kid way better than I do. I'm half tempted to put a bow on Dilya and stuff her under their Christmas tree this December."

Roy nearly tripped on the flat concrete trying to catch up with the conversation.

"Too bad you love her so much," General Arnson commented dryly.

"Yep. Too bad," Kee Stevenson may have actually smiled, but if she did, it disappeared as fast as it had arrived.

"Take me about ten minutes to get the bird prepped," the general peeled off toward the cockpit.

"Take me about the same with this cargo," Kee led him to the big open door in the side of the helicopter.

Roy couldn't believe he'd just missed exactly what Sienna had asked him for. He might be way down the ladder from the NSA, but it didn't mean he didn't want to try for her.

He'd never met anyone like her.

———

Sienna knew it wasn't Roy on the roof the moment she arrived at the White House. The one atop the West Wing tracked her briefly and then swept away to look elsewhere. The one on the Residence barely hesitated as his sightlines swept by her.

She had learned the rhythm of the overwatch changeovers and just happened to be passing by the Secret Service room in the West Wing basement when the relief snipers headed aloft. No sign of Roy.

It was a stupid, schoolgirl thing to do—one that she'd never done as a schoolgirl—but she found an excuse to catch the next shift change as well. She spotted a Latino sniper headed out—one who she could easily imagine being the infamous Fernando, introducing Roy to his "cousins" all over D.C.'s worst bars.

Before she could move in to ask about Roy, the Secretary of Defense stepped up to spread more of his officious misogyny all over her. It took a couple of hours to prove that, just perhaps, she knew more about how USAFRICOM mishandled black ops force requests than he did.

It was an example of asymmetric warfare with him; she couldn't bring the big hammer to such a small battle and expect to win. While it would be far easier to simply slap the facts upside his head, that would lose all of the future battles. Instead she did the whole pretend-that-he-knew-more thing until she could finally transform her idea into his. It almost made her nauseous. Thankfully, she'd already briefed the President on precisely this problem, so at least he would know the true source of the solution.

Lunch wasn't an option, as she and the Assistant NSA had to tackle Egypt's most recent problems with the falling revenue at the Second Suez Canal. The plunging price of oil had made it cheaper for cargo and oil vessels to travel around the Cape of Good Hope rather than pay the high tariffs at the canal. The Catch-22 was that Egypt needed to pay off their canal building bonds. If they defaulted on those loans, then there was an even bigger headache coming to an already unstable government.

By the time she next managed to look at a clock, Roy was already a couple hours off shift.

And he hadn't thought to come by her office to at least say good evening or offer to get her some dinner.

He had all the consideration of...of...the Secretary of Defense!

Well wasn't that a disappointment! She rested her elbows on her desk and massaged her forehead.

A knock on her door had her jerking her head up so quickly that her neck almost seized up.

"You—" But it wasn't Roy who she was going to set straight about the right way to treat a woman you had kissed as if you had invented the concept personally.

Instead the head of the PPD, Frank Adams, was standing in her doorway.

"Evening, ma'am."

"Good evening, Frank."

"Are you okay, ma'am?"

She slumped back in her chair, "I look that bad, huh?"

Frank offered a puzzled smile, "Someday some woman will explain to me how to step around that question without getting slaughtered."

"Not a chance. I did a pinkie swear at birth to never reveal trade secrets."

"Should have known. You just look like it's been a hard day and I'm guessing that your blood sugar floored out a while back."

"Good guess."

"Go home, ma'am. Get some sleep or you'll never make it past the first month."

Sienna eyed the piles on her desk, the long list of unread e-mails, several bearing unread attachments which would lead to unread...

"Maybe you're right."

"Trust me," Frank offered a friendly smile and she did her best to return it.

"I just wish—" And there was no way she was going to mention Roy to his boss.

"Ma'am?"

"Nothing, Frank. And it's Sienna to you?"

"Not going to happen, ma'am. But I will tell you as a matter of, shall we say, general interest, Agent Beaumont is out for special training. He's not on the grounds today or tomorrow."

"Oh," and that popped the balloon of her blood-sugar fueled anger at him.

"Matter of fact, I expect he's hurting worse than you are. If that makes you feel any better, ma'am."

Sienna returned Frank Adams smile, "It might, Agent Adams. It just might."

———

In the first five minutes, Roy had gone through a dozen stages of frustration until he became sure that he truly didn't know anything. Not one single little...

It had started when Kee Stevenson had told him to pull out his first-choice weapon. They were sitting side by side on the 60's cargo deck, their feet dangling just inches off the immaculate concrete floor of the HMX hangar.

The Black Hawk UH-60, when upgraded and painted with the President's green-and-white livery, was dubbed a White Hawk. Even the escort craft that never carried the President, like the bird they sat in now, was armor and weapon heavy. They also carried flares to distract incoming missiles and enough spotting and surveillance equipment to pin down the enemy from much farther away than most craft.

But it was still the same sized craft as any 60. As soon as he swung the forty-six inches of his JAR up out of the case, he snagged the tip of the barrel on the fifty-two inch high ceiling of the cargo deck.

"Lesson one about helos," Kee spoke in a drill sergeant monotone. "Never have a weapon too long to swing inside your available space. Pack that beast away. Pull out your second choice."

He pulled out the Heckler & Koch PSG1A1.

"The HK is a better choice for helicopter work because it's eight inches shorter with the stock folded so you snag it less until you're ready." Kee flipped open her own battered rifle case and slipped out her own weapon.

He hadn't known that's what she shot with. And that explained the odd look she'd given him when he'd selected it as his second choice. It had been a consideration that maybe, just maybe, this fool of a White House counter sniper was worth her time if he selected the same weapon she used.

"Bought this myself."

Roy was having a serious case of rifle envy. It was the exact same model as his own, and yet it was a wholly different weapon. She had the Schmidt & Bender 3-27, seven thousand dollars worth of scope he'd been dying to try out, but that wasn't it either.

Kee's rifle was well used; it had seen a lot of very hard miles and it showed. The polymer stock was worn smooth just where her cheek would rest. Every single finger position was outlined by wear-use. How many shots did that take to happen?

There was a shine to a weapon that was perfectly maintained but had run through so much service. And it had a new barrel. That meant she'd run about ten thousand rounds through the last one and had to replace it recently. How many barrels had Kee Stevenson worn out?

Roy shot a lot to keep up his skills, but it was all range work. Kee's rifle was a weapon of war.

"To successfully snipe from a helo, you have to add several factors to your shot. First let's talk about isolating yourself from rotor vibration."

Roy was too well trained to need to fire prone. He constantly worked his way through the positions from lying flat to standing without even a tree on which to rest the rifle in order to retain his shooter's flexibility. Kee started him through variations of sitting firing positions that he'd never considered.

"If your tailbones are on the metal deck, you may feel more stable and connected, but what you're actually doing is transmitting the cargo deck vibrations into your skeleton. Roll back on your ass just a little more."

He did, and didn't like the unfamiliarity of the position.

"That's it. If it feels all wrong, then you're getting it right. Keep working that until it feels normal. Any time you sit anywhere for the next few weeks, I want you off your tailbones."

"Now, let's start talking about pilot factors. You'll never get to fly with the best pilot ever, Major Emily Beale."

"Why not?"

"Bitch retired to fight wildfires and have children. Go figure. When she flew it was like you were sitting on bedrock. She could hold a helo so still it might have been built right there in the sky. Fly with Lola Maloney and she'll fish you across the entire sky—she flies like she's dancing."

"She any good?"

"Chief pilot of 5th Battalion D Company."

"I meant as a dancer," he said it because the 5D wasn't the stuff of myth, they were the stuff of legend. If this Lola was chief pilot for them, she was one of the best pilots alive, anywhere. And that Kee flew with the 5D...no wonder she was one of the best snipers going.

Their standards were stratospheric.

Kee eyed him closely. It was hard to tell with her narrow eyes, but she probably rolled them at him before she sighed. "Lola's a damn sight better than you, white boy. And you want a hot lady like the NSA, you better start taking lessons."

Roy decided that in the future, he'd keep his mouth shut.

General Arnson announced he was ready—Roy had been peripherally aware of the general preflighting the White Hawk. In moments they were aloft and Roy decided Arnson flew like he hated Roy. He aimed for the air pockets and slid sideways almost as often as he flew straight ahead.

Or maybe he was just messing with Roy.

Which with the way his day was going wouldn't surprise him one bit more than a dairy cow on the front stoop.

Kee clearly enjoyed proving he didn't know shit about his own specialty as a sniper. Frank Adams was the bastard who'd sent him to this punishment in the first place. A punishment General Arnson clearly enjoying handing out.

And Sienna Arnson was so far out of his reach that—

Well, this had better be the day his life bottomed out, because if it went lower, he didn't want to know about it. Then just as they were flying into the shooting range, General Arnson called out evasive maneuvers and twisted the helicopter through a complete sideways roll.

Roy almost lost himself and his weapons right out the open cargo bay door; might have if not for the monkey line attached to his flight vest and the helicopter's door frame.

The general's laugh attested that Roy had a lot more to worry about than just Sienna's opinion.

CHAPTER FOUR

T*hey spent Day One* busting me down."

It was Tuesday night and Roy had showed up with a bouquet of dahlias, take-out Chinese, and a pint of Ben & Jerry's Cherry Garcia —announcing "Authentic Vermont ice cream" as he'd pulled it out— just on the chance of her being in the building and having a free moment. Sienna forgave him every one of her evil thoughts from the prior night, told her secretary to shuffle her schedule for an hour, and closed her office door against the outside world.

The Chinese food had cooled off halfway, and tasted fantastic. The ice cream had warmed just enough that it didn't break the plastic spoon as she kept dipping into it. The flowers kept drawing her eyes almost as often as Roy's strong face. It was so expressive. And somehow it had been transformed over the last two days.

"I should have seen it as it was—classic training tactics. Break down all assumptions and habits so that they can then build up new techniques without tripping over the old. But being just a dumb jerk from the woods, I didn't see it until just this afternoon."

"What happened this afternoon?" Sienna didn't even bother correcting the dumb jerk comment. He struck her as naïve only about himself. Now he was more sure of himself and also seemed more certain that he was living who he wanted to be more than any man other than her father. He had a real need to protect and serve that he'd found a way to express as a sniper. A sniper who had impressed Frank, Beatrice, and Kee in addition to herself.

"Shot eight of ten in the black at five hundred meters from a hovering helo. Five of ten moving at fifty knots at three hundred meters."

The way he said it told her that was pretty spectacular. "What did Kee Stevenson have to say?"

"She stated I: 'had promise'."

"She what! Why that stingy, cheapskate—"

Roy held up his chopsticks to stop her. "No, seriously, it's okay. Kee is so incredibly good that it may have been the highest praise I've received since the day Frank Adams allowed me on the White House team. She taught me to do things I'd been taught were impossible. But she found a way around them, I think she developed half of the techniques herself. It was just incredible."

And there was the change. It was like when a soldier achieved a hard-won promotion. There was a new confidence. And since his easy surety of himself had been what first attracted her to him in the museum, the impact was now doubly strong.

"However," Roy continued as he fished out another piece of massively over-breaded, deep-fried, and sauced piece of General Tso's chicken—did he normally eat such things?

She could feel herself gaining weight just watching him. Sienna had stuck mostly with the twice-cooked beef in snow peas and the Cherry Garcia which sort of defeated her own argument.

"I appear to have failed miserably on another front," his sad expression looked like only partly a put-on.

"What was that?"

"My personal quest," he was watching her intently.

"Your quest?" Something in his look was making her throat go dry.

"I almost found something nice about Frank Adams and Beatrice Belfour..."

"But," she had to prompt him.

"...but I wasn't paying close enough attention and I missed it. Something to do with Kee's kid."

"Dilya." Sienna hadn't met her yet, but had been warned that no warning would prepare her for the meeting.

"Dilya. Something about how Frank and Beat understand the kid better than her mom does. But I didn't catch what."

"Surely that's got to be good enough to—"

"Nope," Roy cut her off. "I got the ground rules straight from the National Security Advisor herself. Don't see going back on my word any more than she would."

Well, the NSA was regretting her challenge at the moment. At first she'd needed to keep Roy at a distance. Her attraction to him was so powerful that she'd needed to blockade it and buy some thinking time. Now she'd had some thinking time—in between the minutes of mayhem that was her life—she was no wiser on the subject of Roy Beaumont.

However, the way she was feeling about him had shifted in that time, shifted to an even stronger draw than she'd first felt. She poked at another too sweet saucy glob of General Tso's to distract herself, but with Roy Beaumont sitting just across the table, it wasn't working. Somehow he had gained confidence without gaining arrogance.

"Well," she glanced at the clock and winced. She had a long night ahead of her no matter what advice Frank Adams had given her. But the clock gave her another idea.

"The way I see it, you have another twenty-five hours to complete your research."

Roy glanced at his watch, and she was amused to see him spin the outer dial to mark the deadline before glancing back at her. He didn't ask, he just waited.

She wasn't going to be that easy, and bit down on her General Tso's. Life would be so much better if fat and sugar didn't taste so good.

"Okay, I give. What happens in twenty-five hours?"

"In twenty-five hours I'm attending a reception for the new French ambassador in the Residence."

"Which means?" She was relieved when he took the last piece of chicken from the white take-out container, because then it would no longer be tempting her. She waited until he'd almost bit down on it.

"Because I'm allowed one guest. And if you want to get lucky, Mr. Sniper Man, you'd better have your answer lined up by the time you escort me to the reception."

He froze with the ball of chicken just inches from his mouth.

"You want me to be your date at a Residence reception?"

"No. You're going to do that anyway. You need an answer if you want a chance to get lucky *after* the reception."

He continued to stare at her completely goggle-eyed.

He didn't even flinch when the last piece of General Tso's slipped out of his chopsticks and landed in his lap.

Sienna didn't even try to hide her smile as she dropped her final question.

"You do own a suit, don't you?"

His nod wasn't all that different from one a bobble-head doll might have made.

———

Roy tried to delay getting dressed at the end of the shift. After a day back on the White House roof, he began to understand just how much Kee had taught him. He saw the city through different eyes, even though all she'd taught him was how to shoot better from a moving platform. The city now looked so still and...simple.

Which is exactly what tonight wasn't going to be. He'd wanted Fernando and Hank to be long gone before he pulled out his suit, but even that one wish wasn't going to happen. They got into some stupid game of hoop with a balled pair of socks and a small wire garbage bin.

Finally out of time, Roy pulled out the dry cleaning bag he'd smuggled in this morning.

He had their full attention in under three seconds.

"Yo, buddy! What's up?" Fernando three-pointed his socks into the top shelf of Roy's locker. "You disappear for two days with your rifles and now you be suiting up. Did you defect to a Protection Detail?" Any sniper worth his salt looked down on the guys in the close protection details. Those guys wore suits and fought with handguns and their bodies. A sniper belonged up in the sky making sure the guys on the ground stayed safe.

"Not a chance," Roy denied. "I've just got a dinner tonight."

"You sure ain't going back to Jake's Hole in that rig," Fernando plucked at his coat sleeve. Roy smacked his hand away and brushed at the dusty thumbprint on the charcoal gray of his only suit.

"I'm not going back to the Hole this side of ever." Even if Sienna walked away from him tonight, she'd given him another standard of woman to think about. One he'd never imagined before. Somewhere in the night he'd decided that if a woman the caliber of Sienna Arnson wanted to be seen with him, he sure as hell wasn't going to be the one to turn away. "It's just a dinner."

Hank grabbed the duty roster and scanned down it. "Only event tonight is some fancy over at the Residence. Don't see your name on the list. What gives, Roy?" Another drawback to having friends who were also in the Secret Service, they'd all been trained to hate unanswered questions. It had been drilled in so deep that it was in their DNA like an unstoppable itch until it was answered.

Roy finished changing and struggled with his tie, ignoring Fernando's telling him he should have bought a clip-on.

Still, there was no way he was going to besmirch Sienna's reputation with these jokers and if he had to suffer their questions, fine. But it didn't mean he was going to answer—

"Wait a darn minute!" Hank was staring too intently at the guest list.

Fernando had retrieved his socks ball and was once again going for the long shot into Roy's locker.

"The redhead. What was her name?"

"Which redhead?" Fernando wasn't really paying attention. He'd moved on to going for a bank shot off Roy's temple.

"Roy's redhead."

Maybe Roy would have been better off protecting Sienna's reputation if he'd just walked out of the locker room straight from his shower and attended the reception naked.

"Roy's redhead?" Fernando stopped and looked at Hank with a puzzled expression.

"Yeah. You know—"

Roy could see that Fernando didn't know, but the light of dawning comprehension on his face told Roy that making it two for two was too much to hope for.

"Roy's redhead?" Fernando said one last time looking at Roy aghast. "The new National Security Advisor?"

Hank looked down at the roster he still held in his hands, "Yep, she's on the list, as a plus one guest. Wait! You met the redhead?"

Fernando beaned Hank in the face with his socks. "No, doofus. How did you ever make the Service, huh? He didn't *meet* the redhead; he is her date. This dog is the 'plus one' of the National Security Advisor."

"Huh," Hank grunted as he processed the fact.

Question answered. Check. Next. Roy cringed and waited for it.

"Is she as hot in person as she is through the scope?"

Roy could barely remember the "hot redhead" walking up to begin her first day as the NSA, because she was so much more than that. But he had to rub it in the guys' face a little.

"Way, way, wa-ay hotter."

Fernando groaned as if he'd been stabbed in the gut.

Hank held up a hand to deliver a high five.

Roy raised his hand to receive his triumphant slap.

Someone at the end of the row of lockers cleared his throat.

Roy glanced over to see Frank Adams watching him with a look that said he'd better not be celebrating what he looked to be celebrating.

Shit!

He just couldn't catch a break in this outfit.

———

Sienna had fussed and worried about her dress. First she'd worried about overdressing, then about underdressing for the occasion. It was her first official White House reception for a foreign dignitary. Not being a head of state, the French Ambassador didn't rate a state dinner, but ambassadors did deserve formality.

If she'd been able to go in one of her business suits, she'd have been fine. But she'd invited a date. And that had started her down the path of dressing up for the occasion. Then a call to the First Lady's social secretary for any guiding tips—which Sienna had thought to be an utterly humiliating act to do, but had been very graciously answered. She told Sienna that dressing up would be *very* appropriate in no uncertain terms.

But she hadn't help clarify *how* dressed up.

Right before she melted down, a young voice said from the door of her office, "That's nice."

Sienna spun to look at who had spoken. And then looked again. The girl standing in the doorway deserved a second look. She was in her mid-teens. She had dark skin and an elegant face. She had jet black hair that cascaded past her shoulders in a smooth ripple.

There was a friendly openness to her face, but the captivating feature was her eyes, they were the oldest eyes Sienna had ever seen. They were hazel and appeared to leap out of her face. She was defined by those eyes. They changed a very pretty teen into a gorgeous young woman. She was dressed in a simple black dress that left her long in the leg down to her black, ankle-high boots.

"You," Sienna smoothed her own dress for the hundredth time, "don't think it's too much?" It was discreet at the neck with an asymmetric draped collar, short-sleeved, and high at the knee. But she hadn't anticipated quite how well the forest green jersey clung.

"Are you bringing a date?"

"I am," Sienna said cautiously.

"Two thumbs up. You'll cook his brain but still be elegant. It's a win-win."

"Thanks." Now that Sienna had taken fashion advice from her, it seemed awkward to ask the girl's name, as if they were already past that.

"Kee said you might be melting down right about now."

"Kee sent you?"

The girl's shrug explained it wasn't that simple.

And that told Sienna exactly who this was. Kee's adoptive daughter, Dilya Stevenson, the First Child's nanny.

"You need this," Dilya came into the room, undoing a small silver brooch she had pinned by her left shoulder. Without even asking permission, she came up and added it to Sienna's dress.

"What is it?" A four-footed animal with a big snout of some sort.

"A honey badger."

Dilya waited for a reaction, but Sienna didn't know what it was supposed to be.

"It's a symbol of strength—small but fierce. Just remember, 'Honey badger don't care.' If the nerves get you, just remember that. You can look it up on the internet later, but you're out of time right now." And she headed for the door just as Sienna heard approaching steps.

"Dilya?" Sienna called out and the girl turned. "Thanks," she rested her hand over the tiny pin.

"Sure thing," then Dilya whispered across the room. "Remember, 'Honey badger don't care.' Got it?"

Sienna shot her a thumbs up just the moment before Roy strode into her office as if he was out walking his grand Northeast Kingdom. He was...astonishing. Some men looked better in a suit, some worse. Some suits wore the man, so that the man disappeared behind the impression of fine tailoring. Not this one. Roy Beaumont absolutely wore the suit. His ruggedness wasn't transformed, rather it was counterpointed, making him look twice the man she'd thought him.

He strode right past Dilya as if he didn't even see her. He stopped only inches away from her.

"You," Roy spoke barely above a whisper, "are absolutely, knock-me-down gorgeous in that dress, Sienna."

Sienna could see Dilya's smile and two-thumbs-up gesture before she slipped out of the room.

She wasn't sure how he could judge her dress, because his eyes had been riveted on her face the whole way across her office. Now he stood so close that his face filled almost her entire field of vision. She wondered if she was about to have the crap kissed out of her, which would totally screw up what little makeup she'd applied.

His look said it was a very close thing and she figured it would be worth the price and then some.

Then he glanced down every so briefly and burst out laughing.

"Can't even compliment a girl and keep a straight face?" Her pride came prickling to life like—

"First, you left *girl* way behind. Hell, you look so amazing that you left woman behind too, except then I don't know what you are. I do know you're scaring the crap out of me, that's why the pin is so damned funny. 'Honey badger don't give a shit!' Indeed."

"I," Sienna swallowed hard trying to process the compliments, "I heard it differently."

"There's this video—"

"So, I've been told."

"Watch it and you'll get even more why you scare the crap out of me."

Sienna rather liked the idea of scaring the crap out of a man like Roy. "Are you planning to kiss me?"

"Haven't found the answer to your question yet or you bet your ass I would be. Sorry," Roy glanced aside for the first time. "I'm not really drawing room material."

"Are you trying to bow out?"

"Not if you're going to be wearing that dress the rest of the evening. I want a chance to look at you in it some more."

"How about if I offered you one-time, special dispensation on that kiss?"

"Nope. Lady set a challenge. Besides, the way I figure it, the night is still young. Give me something to do while all of you head cases are doing whatever it is you do at these things."

As if she knew. Again Sienna fought against being charmed and barely managed to hold ground. "Maybe you should have just asked Dilya yourself."

"Kee's kid?"

Sienna nodded.

"All I know is her name and that she was some starving orphan from Uzbekistan who now has full clearance all the way to the Oval."

"Really?" That pretty teen could just walk into the Oval Office?

"Buddies with the Main Man himself, according to the briefing docs."

"She was just here."

"She was?" And Roy looked about the room in bewilderment. He'd been so focused on Sienna that he hadn't even seen someone else was in the room when he arrived. That tipped Sienna right over the mush line.

"It's time for us to go," or she was going to kiss the crap out of him no matter what he said. As she turned for the door, he rested his hand ever so lightly on her arm.

"Just one thing first." He reached into a pocket and pulled out a small plastic container. "I figured a corsage might be excessive, but I hope you like this."

It was a single, miniature, yellow rosebud, on the verge of opening.

"Do you always give flowers to your dates?"

Roy harrumphed in thought. "Can't say as I do. Guess you're a special occasion."

"Well, free tip for you: Don't stop," she couldn't remember the last man to bring her flowers.

He reached out to pin it to her dress, hesitated, cursed, and then tried again.

She left him to be totally flummoxed by how to pin it in place.

He finally slipped the fingers of one hand inside the neckline of her blouse. His knuckles brushing along her collarbone stole her breath with the power of the simple contact. He quickly pinned the rose close beside the honey badger, then slid his hand free as if it had been burned.

"Best I can do," he said roughly.

She looked down to see that he'd pinned the rose so that the honey badger appeared to be sniffing it. Or maybe it was about to eat it.

"It's perfect, Roy. Thank you."

Then he offered his arm. She slid her fingers around his elbow, felt the strength there of a man who trained hard. She felt safer than she expected, than she'd ever thought possible for her first visit to the Residence.

She didn't need a honey badger or a rose, she had Roy Beaumont at her side.

———

Roy had done the math.

He'd been with the White House Counter Sniper Team for just over a year. Call it fifty weeks because of the two weeks he'd taken off to join his dad for the opening of hunting season and several weeks for periodic refresher training. He'd spent approximately half of that time on the roof and the other half on the unending daily crap work of being in the Secret Service (or trying to get warm between the winter watches). Roy had laid atop the Residence for roughly a thousand hours.

For the first time he was standing precisely twenty-seven feet below his normal post. And that twenty-seven foot decrease in altitude was one of the most terrifying things he'd ever done.

He knew most of the people in the room, either because he'd been briefed on them and watched them from his perch as they transited the White House grounds or he'd seen them on television just like the rest of America. He knew a total of three people in the room: Frank Adams, Beat Belfour, and his date. He'd been introduced to the White House Chief of Staff once, but that didn't count because the man wouldn't remember—

"Hello, Roy. Glad to see you again." Daniel Drake Darlington III held out a hand and Roy shook it out of pure relief. The Chief of Staff's hand was strong. He sported weightlifter calluses which was more than most of these soft, political men. It definitely counted toward Daniel's credit.

"Very kind of you to remember, sir." It was stiff and awkward, but it was all he could muster.

"A bit of a change from overwatch."

Roy looked for any hint of an insult, as if Roy was an unwelcome intruder from some lower class, but everything about Daniel appeared genuine. Rumor stated that he was a genius and one of the kindest people in D.C. Maybe both were true. "Takes my breath away, a bit, sir."

"Daniel," the Chief of Staff insisted.

"That will take some getting used to as well, sir."

"Doesn't it though."

And for that Roy swore he would try to loosen up around the man.

Daniel turned to Sienna, "Welcome to the Residence, Sienna."

"Thanks, Daniel." There was an easy familiarity, though Roy noticed that her voice was little more than a hoarse whisper even if the Chief of Staff didn't.

Daniel was pulled away as Roy glanced down at her. Her pale white skin, which made her brown eyes such a visceral shock, was tinging blue. He leaned over until his mouth was close by her ear and his nose was practically buried in her hair, "Breathe!"

"You first," Sienna joked, but managed to start breathing again.

He was momentarily mesmerized by the movement of her chest as she breathed deeply several times, but managed to shake it off before she noticed.

That dress had been messing with his mind since he'd pulled his own suit out of the back corner of his closet. Imagining Sienna out of her Washington-dulls and dressed up had been hard to formulate into an image, until the very moment he'd stepped in at her office door. The breath had been knocked right out of him. Snipers were trained to capture an entire image and then process it while ducked back in safe hiding.

That first, full-length glance of Sienna Arnson dressed to dazzle had done just that and it still was. Though she stood close beside him, he could still visualize every single detail of how she'd looked as he'd entered. Smiling, happy, and drop-dead gorgeous. She made him feel as if he'd been smacked upside the head like...like a squirrel that had jumped off a high branch and missed the next tree only to thud down onto the pine needle-strewn ground. He needed to go lie in a field somewhere until his head stopped spinning.

Sienna out of her Washington-dulls and in a cocktail dress—at least he suspected that's what it was called—was revelatory. If he'd been gobsmacked by the National Security Advisor, he was blown out of the water by the woman revealed. And the neckline that exposed just the very first rise of her exceptional breasts was giving him a great deal of trouble—they weren't over- or under-sized, they were just exquisite. The dress teased and enticed, invited a man to look and imagine. And those thoughts led down to a trim waist defined by curvy hips. Her legs, he really wasn't going to think about those legs, because they were—

He tore his attention away and back to the room before he forgot how to breathe.

"The room may be daunting, but the fantastic way you look isn't helping matters," he muttered softly to her.

"Really? Cool!" She sounded far too pleased and he vowed to never speak again.

They were both still rooted in place at the entrance to the main hall of the second floor of the Residence. They had ascended the Grand Staircase together rather than taking the elevator and been just fine as they crossed the intricate parquet floor to stand in the archway that opened onto the Central Hall.

The hall was a dozen feet high, twenty wide, and stretched for about a dozen miles down the entire length of the Residence. The last colors of sunset filled the giant half moon window at the very far end with bold oranges, deepening to red even as he remained riveted in place.

The room's carpet was white, the furniture rich green leather with dark wood, and the walls the palest yellow. There was a grand piano, potted trees, and a half dozen of his fellow agents posted discreetly along the walls. The doors to either side led to the Yellow Oval Room and the First Family's private apartments. This President didn't live on the third floor. Rumor said he wouldn't even set foot there since his first wife's death—for they had been her private apartments. Hearsay stated that he hadn't been up there while she was alive either, but Roy hadn't joined the White House detail until after Geneviève Matthews was already the second First Lady. Now Daniel and his wife lived upstairs, the first Chief of Staff to do so in many decades.

But all of that wasn't what defined the room. It was the half a hundred people circulating in the massive space who made this not just another overly fancy gathering. The power elite of Washington, D.C. filled the room. Daniel, the Vice President, and the President, all accompanied by their knock-out wives. The Chairman of the Joint Chiefs of Staff in full uniform—and General Brett Rogers who had been a Special Ops soldier for decades and had the battle ribbons to prove it. Cabinet members, congressional leaders...it was a daunting array for a mere sniper to be caught in.

There was conversation and laughter, serious circles of discussion and casual ones, men in expensive suits and a stunning array of women in amazing dresses—some of whom really shouldn't be, but some of whom absolutely deserved to wear such attire.

He'd seen Sienna checking her dress in the occasional mirror as he'd escorted her to the Residence. She didn't have a single thing to worry about.

And still both of them remained riveted under the stairway landing's arch.

"Sienna?"

She looked up at him wide eyed, her chest still moving a little too fast.

"Don't hyperventilate on me."

"Why?" She actually gasped a bit. "You think fainting would be bad form at my first White House party?"

"Screw that. You faint and I'm stuck here with these people by myself."

"What? You wouldn't just sweep me into your arms and take me away from all this?" Her breathing sounded a little more normal.

"Hmm," Roy considered the scenario. "I can work with that. Go ahead. Faint away and I'll get us both out of here pronto."

"Remember what honey badger says," someone whispered from close behind him. Then, before he could turn to fully see who it was, he felt a sharp push in the center of his back. A long slip of a dark girl faded sideways into the crowd.

"Who was that?"

"That," Sienna managed as they now moved slowly toward a nearby knot in the crowd, "was Dilya Stevenson. She gave me the pin."

Roy looked around, but she'd disappeared somewhere. When he

focused front, there were the President, the First Lady (who was at least as beautiful in real life as the magazines made her), and a couple he didn't recognize. He'd guess they were Mr. and Mrs. French Ambassador—correction, Mrs. and Mr. French Ambassador as the title was hers, not his. Roy felt a slight rearward tug on his arm of Sienna slowing.

"You've got no worries, lady," he told her when they were still a few steps away from the group. "You're the most stunning woman in the room."

She shot him a quick look of surprise and then he could see the NSA shield start to drop over her.

"Don't do that. Just be you."

It had been one of his dad's rare lessons from back when he was trying to figure out how to impress girls.

"Besides, Sienna Arnson is amazing enough to scare the crap out of me even without the honey badger pin. Bet she scares everyone one else too."

He didn't have time to see her reaction, because they'd arrived.

Sienna didn't have time to sort out her feelings about Roy's last several comments. Combined, they made her feel a little taller and a little stronger. Even so (she dug her fingers hard into his arm to make sure he didn't get away), Siena wasn't letting go of Roy's bulwark of strength and support.

"Good evening, Mr. and Mrs. President, Mr. and Mrs. Ambassador. May I introduce Roy Beaumont?" He did the nod and handshake thing, being effortlessly polite.

He thought she was beautiful, she'd heard that enough to know it was true. But that Roy thought her beautiful while they were walking up to the exquisite First Lady dressed in a long sheath dress of gold with an Asian flower design flowing up the front in soft lavender was utterly ridiculous. She'd have attributed it to his trying to flatter her, except Roy hadn't done that...ever. If he really was as straight-ahead a guy as his occupation implied then—

She flipped to her college French and did her best to ask if this was the ambassador's first visit to D.C.

No for her, yes for him. *Shoe is on the other foot, Mr. Husband to the Ambassador.* Of course the French were more open to powerful women. Then why had Roy told her to check her NSA persona at the door? It hadn't felt as if he was trying to put her down or box her in. Maybe he was just... Now was not the time to ask.

First Lady Geneviève Matthews joined in easily, her French fluid though with an unusual lilt that must be her Vietnamese upbringing. It quickly became obvious that Roy and the President barely spoke a word of it and were soon left out in the cold. But Roy didn't appear abashed and took it in stride as he did everything else.

She half listened as Roy made some joke about locking the First Family away in Fort Knox or with NORAD down under Cheyenne Mountain for the entire term of office. Rather than being offended, Peter Matthews was soon chatting about Roy's job with what sounded like genuine interest.

Sienna lost the thread of the French conversation at the President's amused comment to something of Roy's that she'd missed.

"You had Kee Stevenson drag you aloft? Now that is one tough woman."

"Noticed that myself, Mr. President." Roy didn't look at all surprised that the President knew Kee. As if it was so normal for the Commander in Chief to be hanging out with military snipers.

"You met her kid yet? She takes after her adoptive mother with a vengeance."

Roy glanced in her direction, as if to make sure she heard what he was about to say next.

"Is that why Kee wants to give her away to Frank Adams and Beatrice Belfour as a Christmas present?"

The President laughed easily, "Two hardcore agents who never had kids didn't stand a chance around Dilya. I mean that girl has us *all* wrapped around her little finger, but Frank and Beat dote on her as if they were her grandparents even if they aren't old enough to be."

Sienna could see the look of smug victory on Roy's face. He'd found out something nice about Frank and Beat and obtained it from the most unimpeachable of sources.

"I knew it," Dilya's voice sliced right into Roy's smug expression. She'd come up behind them, carrying a two-year old who was the spitting image of her First Lady mother. The toddler's dress was a luminous gold to match her mother. It also served to accent how nice Dilya looked in her elegant black.

"Knew what?" the President asked.

"These two," Dilya nodded at Sienna and Roy. "Something about Frank and Beat. Like they've been scheming on it."

Sienna could see that somehow Dilya knew exactly what was going on, no matter how impossible that was. In fact, she was clearly enjoying outing their little conspiracy to the President.

"No," Roy stumbled out. "We just..." But he had nowhere better to take it than Sienna did because they had indeed been scheming. Scheming on how he was going to get a second kiss tonight. And at the rate he was going, a whole lot mo—

"Let's get to the bottom of this." The President barely had to raise his hand for Frank to materialize at his side. If Roy's height and strength had made her feel safe, Frank's breadth of shoulder overshadowed even the personal power of the President. He became the dominant force of the group, probably of any group he was in.

Oddly, Roy didn't fade.

Sienna was used to judging and working with power dynamics in a group, and it was a close thing between Roy and Frank as to who was the more impressive.

The President glanced around and also caught Beat's attention. In a moment, she joined her husband.

"Mr. Beaumont here wants to know why you two never had children of your own that makes you so dote on Dilya?"

"No, I—" Roy tried to protest, but the President's broad wink shut him down.

Dilya squawked as well and only looked a little quelled by the President's, "Hush, you." Clearly her little plot had spun out of her control in a way she hadn't anticipated. Sienna suspected that few things did that to Dilya.

Frank Adams cast a baleful look at Roy that Sienna figured would have melted any lesser man right where he was standing.

It was Beatrice who laughed. "Because we love the kid so much."

"I do not think your answer," the First Lady stepped up, "is such enough to answer my husband's question even though he would hide it as Mr. Beaumont's." The First Lady took her daughter from Dilya's arms and hugged her close. The little girl started to play with her mother's hair. Sienna was charmed that Geneviève Matthews did nothing to stop the damage to her perfect coif, instead she turned enough to kiss her daughter on the nose.

Frank looked sad and Sienna wondered how she could rewind this so that the question had never been asked. Somehow go back to before she'd set the challenge to Roy. But it was too late.

"It was both of our faults, Mr. President," Beatrice answered soberly, resting a hand on her husband's arm. "I was out in the field, specializing in assignee protection in hazardous situations, as you may recall, sir. I loved it and didn't want to back away. But by the time I eased off—"

"I was the head of your detail by then, sir," Frank Adams cut off his wife who was having some trouble speaking. "I refused to be some absent father—as heading your detail is not a part-time job—who might have to step in front of a gun and cost my kid having a father. I was going to resign, but Beat wouldn't let me. She said this was too important and she was right, sir. Then she stepped in as the First Lady's head of detail and I didn't want her to give that up. It has been an honor."

Sienna's breath caught in her throat. Their impossible sacrifice was deeply humbling.

The President didn't even hesitate. He reached out and shook Frank's hand solemnly in both of his. Frank nodded and they were done.

Sienna heard the First Lady curse lightly under her breath, "Mens!" She shifted her daughter into one arm and wrapped the other around Beat and hugged her tightly.

"This one," the First Lady joggled her daughter, "is just starting on her terrible twos. Any time you wish to steal her, please do." Then she shifted from joking to intimately sincere. "I know of no one she would be safer with."

"Aw crap," Dilya's sniffle summed it up.

Beat shifted back into her serious, head of the First Lady's protection detail mode, which no longer looked as daunting as it had only moments ago, then turned to Dilya. "Kee loves you too much to do it, but if she ever cuts you loose, Little One, you know where you're always welcome."

"Yeah," Dilya sniffled again, hugged Beat, and then grabbed the First Child and practically bolted from the room.

Frank and Beat faded back into their discreet, watchful mode along the walls. The President and First Lady were swept up into fresh conversations and suddenly she and Roy were left alone in a momentary vacuum in the middle of the crowded hall. It had been as if an air space had been formed around them with the President, a space that no one else had dared to cross and the effect still persisted for a few moments.

"Do me a favor, beautiful," Roy laid his hand over hers where it was still tucked around his arm.

"Sure. What?" She wasn't surprised by the rough tightness of her own voice.

"No more quests. I'm not so sure that I like the answers."

Sienna could only nod in response.

———

The rest of the evening was a blur to Roy. He shook the hands of more people in the next two hours than he typically did in a year. He unearthed stories of the Vermont woods that had made others laugh... without knowing quite what they had said to make him tell each particular story.

He was only really conscious of two things.

First, the incredible safety of the situation. All of the back-stabbing knives in the room were sheathed in polite words, and he was fine ignoring those. Though some cabinet secretary, who made Sienna clench unexpectedly hard on his arm, was saved a quick thrashing by the sudden arrival of the Vice President. Even on his best behavior the secretary's manners weren't all *that* impressive. However, Roy decided it would be a poor tactical move to punch the man for his tendency to speak to Sienna's breasts, so instead he maneuvered himself to block obvious sightlines and avoided the whole situation.

Other than verbal forays, this was one of the most secure rooms at the moment, anywhere. And because the gathering was in the central hall, it would take a missile strike to have a chance of reaching them. A sniper never was on the front lines like the ground details, but somehow the twenty-seven vertical feet from his rooftop had moved him through some strange zone between "outside" and "inside" the Secret Service's protection.

The second thing that dominated Roy's attention through the evening was his infinite awareness of the woman who never let go of his arm. At first he was relieved because he didn't want to be caught alone in a place he so little belonged. When he realized that her attachment in turn was part of an unstated mutual protection pact, he didn't complain. Sienna wanted to be next to him so that she wasn't cornered by some jerk? Fine with him.

Her skill on the social battlefield was utterly daunting. People of all calibers had sought a few moments of Sienna's time. He didn't recognize what was happening at first, but it soon became clear. She had a view of such clarity about global situations, that they were coming to her for interpretation.

Roy often had trouble following their questions. After a while he realized that was because the inquirer didn't have a clear grasp of what they really wanted to know either.

Sienna's answers however, were crystalline. By the time she was done, both the inquirer and himself understood not only the intended question but also the situation in a new light.

The tension between the nuclear powers of India and Pakistan as seen through the lens of current Indian military purchases and at-home manufacturing efforts of military products. The delicate alliance balances among the vastly different countries in ASEAN, the Association of Southeast Asian Nations who had been enemies for thousands of years and were now discovering how to be trade partners. The...

Sienna's knowledge was encyclopedic and her insights laser sharp. She delivered them not as he would have, with a get-a-clue tone, but instead with a gentleness that he was rapidly learning was her trademark. A gentleness backed by an intellect too powerful to ignore.

But as the evening progressed, he found his favorite moments to be when it was just the two of them. That's when she relaxed and was able to tease him about not having worn a suit in over a year, and he learned more about what it had been like growing up as a girl with a military father. When he caught himself keeping a mental list of things he would and wouldn't do when he became a father, he practically choked on the beer he'd managed to scrounge up from somewhere amid all of the champagne and cocktails.

———

Sienna had managed to make her first glass of white wine last most of the evening. She'd also survived the evening, which she certainly wouldn't have without Roy's stalwart support. She'd worked a dozen years toward this goal without realizing quite what she was doing.

Her father's fascination with the strengths and shortcomings of the American military complex had become his daughter's. She'd double majored in military history and political science. And that was before her graduate work in socioeconomics and geopolitics.

She'd been too busy during her first week of being the National Security Advisor to realize she actually *was* the NSA. This evening had brought that home with a vengeance and Roy had been the only anchor that kept her from sitting down and whimpering in a corner. With each successive little "chat" she'd become more and more who she already was. It was a more powerful transition than her valedictorian speech at Yale's Jackson Institute graduation ceremony with her Masters in International Relations clutched tightly in her hand.

Sienna had started the evening deciding that survival was going to be ninety percent "Honey badger don't give a shit!" and ten percent Roy Beaumont. But there was something about the way Roy kept looking at her, and adding one of his straightforward, practical world explanations that illuminated particularly complex scenarios, that had her shifting that assessment. By the end of the evening she decided it was about forty percent Roy, twenty percent honey badger, and just maybe forty percent her as well. Their "cooperative dynamic" was both encouraging and intimate. But beyond that it was familiar and easy, as if she and Roy had been doing this sort of thing since forever rather than having met just a week ago.

A few people had left. As with any party, the first wave mostly included those who had grown bored through their own lack of popularity. She judged that she could perhaps slip away with the next tier of departures, which would include those with unfinished work or other plans for the evening.

Roy hadn't given her a single smug look about finding out a piece of Frank and Beatrice's story. Not one hint that by their "deal" there was a potential for something more happening between them this evening. Perhaps she understood. Roy was the perfect gentleman and what they'd found out about the heads of the First Family's two protection details was not grounds for any hint of smugness.

"*Excusez-moi.*" French Ambassador Magda Armand came up to them. She was one of those effortlessly elegant women. Several inches taller than Sienna, with a fall of silver-white hair. Her husband appeared a mismatch, ever so slightly round and frumpy despite his immaculate suit. He was now snoozing quietly in one of the armchairs with a book in his lap and an unfinished glass of port on a nearby table. For an instant she wondered how much Roy would pay to be allowed to do the same, though he'd shown no signs of wishing to be anywhere other than at her side.

"*Bonsoir, Madame Ambassador.*" Sienna's burgeoning thoughts of escape momentarily quashed, she became intensely aware of the fact that her feet were killing her. For any future parties she would wear flats, no matter what others said, especially if they were as elegant as the Madame Ambassador's.

"As your friend does not speak French, we will converse in English."

Roy bowed his head in mute acknowledgement, thoughtfully deferring to the fact that the ambassador had sought out Sienna. After so many years associating with the military and the commensurate male assumption that the man was of course the center of attention, Roy was still a constant surprise.

"You know of our security challenges."

Sienna did. "Generally open borders combined with being one of the most active allies in combating terrorist organizations. It has made your country a prime target."

"Yes. Precisely. My country would be very interested in hearing the insights of America's National Security Advisor on improvement of our borders' strengths. You very much impressed General Dumont while *vous étiez présent* at USEUCOM."

"I would be glad to speak with him at his convenience." And watch her jammed schedule force her personal life to disappear even further than it already had. Not that she'd ever really had one. Actually, with Roy, she'd glimpsed a sliver of hope for a personal life.

"The challenge, if I may Madame Ambassador," Roy spoke up, "is that your problem runs far deeper. Your government is seeking to create control in a chaotic world. In the Secret Service we create narrow slices of security, just wide enough for our heads of state to move safely through. Most state security that I've studied had been border-based and yet we are a global economy. I have sat for hours at airports watching the number of flights in transit through that one terminal at that one airport. Comprehensive border control is no longer a viable approach."

"You are with the Secret Service, *non?* Does your National Security Advisor need protection even in this environment?" The Ambassador made it a soft joke but there was interest behind it as well.

Sienna would have to say yes. Maybe especially in this environment —at least for moral support if not for any physical danger.

"It is my honor to escort Ms. Arnson this evening, ma'am."

The ambassador looked at Sienna for an uncomfortably long moment. "If I may be the advisor for a moment: do not let this one slip through your grasp."

"I'll try, Madame Ambassador," because how was she supposed to explain this was only their third date. Fourth if she counted Chinese food and ice cream.

"So, Agent Beaumont, what advice do you have for my little country?"

"I'm just a sniper, ma'am. You have people in your Ministry of Defence far more skilled than I am at these matters."

The ambassador continued to watch him and Sienna kept her mouth shut. Through the evening she'd learned that if there was enough silence, Roy would often step into it with an insight from an unexpected angle. Apparently Magda Armand had made a similar assessment during the times their discussion circles had overlapped this evening.

"Well," Roy rubbed at his chin. "I'm from Vermont and we hunt deer there. There was a particularly pretty doe that kept slipping away from me time after time. In the end I stopped doing what I'd always done: setting up blinds in trees to watch on high, tracking along fresh trails used by others, and the like."

"I see the analogy," the ambassador nodded. "How, if ask I may, did you finally capture your doe?"

"Oh, I didn't."

"What?" Sienna burst out. "Then what's the point of that story?"

And finally she could see that she, at least, had walked right into his trap. His smug, knowing smile that she'd been waiting for all evening was finally on show. There was a warmth to it as he turned to gaze at her with his soft blue eyes.

"I sat and waited for her to come to me of her own accord."

And Sienna realized that was precisely what Roy had been doing all evening. The perfect gentleman. The thoughtful date. The man who didn't push or assume. He had indeed watched her from "on high" atop the White House roof and tracked her from museum to White House to a Chinese dinner in her office. But tonight, after he'd won his victory, he had merely bided his time.

"As I say before..." the ambassador trailed off.

Sienna knew. "Don't let him slip away." She tightened her grasp on the crook of his elbow. After how little she knew him, it should feel abrupt. But by some odd series of events that eluded her, they had skipped past so many of the typically cordial and careful steps of early dating. She knew intimate things about Roy and he of her. They could be months into their relationship, if it had contained more than that one kiss.

"As to your problem, Madame Ambassador," Roy turned back to the evening's guest of honor, knowing full well that he'd left Sienna at least momentarily overwhelmed. "You must stop doing what you've always been doing. You are correct, your borders are open. Some of your politicians and popular press talk of trying to close them again, but you touch eight other countries by land alone."

"Do not be forgetting the English and their Chunnel."

"Nine then, plus sea or air. Your borders are past closing. Your nation and others are still grounded in symmetric thinking in an asymmetric world. Don't waste time or effort on borders, instead spend all of your energies directly on the problem. To move the President, we don't lock down a city, instead we secure a path. Sorry I can't be more specific, ma'am. As I said, I'm just a sniper."

"And yet you know our borders enough to remember even Andorra, Monaco, and Luxembourg." The ambassador watched him for a long time, long enough for Roy to shuffle his feet. Sienna could see him preparing to apologize when the ambassador turned back to Sienna. She rested a warm hand on Sienna's arm and squeezed it gently.

"You must come to talk to our people. And you must bring this one with you. Oh, to be young in Paris once again." She squeezed Sienna's arm again with a totally different meaning, the first of confidence, then second in a woman-to-woman intimacy that Sienna had little experience with. Then Magda was gone.

"Wait!" But it was too late. "I don't have time to go to France," she told Roy for lack of anyone else to address.

Before he could respond, Frank Adams stepped up to them.

"Agent Beaumont. My office. Eight a.m. tomorrow."

"Yes, sir. May I ask why?"

"The President tells me the NSA is going to France."

Roy didn't even show surprise.

Sienna considered and decided that she wasn't surprised either. Magda Armand was not the French Ambassador by chance and must have already spoken with the President. And apparently, what the President knew, Frank Adams knew as well.

"Which means what to me?" Roy clenched his elbow against his side, as if to squeeze her fingers for reassurance.

She'd only be gone for a few days, far more than she could afford, but she'd be back.

Then Frank's smile turned positively evil as he faced Roy, perhaps finally finding a target for retribution after the forced revelation of his own story.

"Which means you're going to need to own more than one suit."

CHAPTER FIVE

Their walk back to Sienna's office passed in silence. Roy was puzzling at Frank's comment, but becoming no smarter for all his thinking. Maybe Dilya had somehow found out he only owned the one suit and told Adams. But what did it mean? Needing a second suit meant he'd be off the roof more. The White House roof was one of the few places in all of D.C., as far as he could tell, where a man could feel the wind and weather and have some degree of privacy.

It wasn't until they reached Sienna's office that his thoughts turned back to the present.

He leaned against the door jamb and watched her transformation. As she crossed the threshold her entire demeanor changed. She shifted like a sniper blending into the landscape. In the Residence she had been elegant and patient, thoughtful and unconsciously feminine. No hair flips, hip-swinging sashays, or any of the other wiles he typically observed; instead she was simply a beautiful woman operating in an arena dominated by men.

In her office she accelerated until she was almost a blur like The Flash: checking phone messages, tapping the space bar for a quick glance at the computer screen—followed by a grimace, probably at the number of new messages as she didn't pause to actually read any of them.

In seconds she'd also fetched her coat and changed from heels, that had done some wonderful things to the shape of her calves, into sneakers. It was another thing to like about her. She didn't retain the heels or change into designer flats. She now wore a tired pair of black converse with a complex white design drawn all over them. They were wholly inappropriate with the fancy dress and somehow wholly appropriate on Sienna Arnson.

With a startling efficiency, she was soon standing just a step away looking up at him. Looking farther up than he'd grown used to through the evening. Heeled, her five-six had became five-eight. Flat-footed she was made more female. He'd dated women both tall and short, but Sienna kept changing on him.

And still she merely watched him.

"What?"

"You're blocking the door," yet she was making no effort to get by him.

He was. "I am. Must say you have a comfortable door frame."

She rolled her eyes at him, but it earned him the laugh he'd been after. Her humor, like everything else, came from all of the way inside. Every one of her emotions was so clear and pure.

"How did you ever survive what you've been through and still be who you are?"

"Who *I* am?" As if she didn't understand the question. She wasn't playing coy, she really didn't know what she'd been doing to him all evening.

Of its own volition, one of his hands reached out to brush down her hair. Between one breath and the next, the NSA was again gone, and Sienna leaned her cheek into his palm.

He could find no words to express what she was doing to him.

Unable to resist her, he used that light pressure of cheek to palm to draw her toward him. She could have slipped away by merely straightening her head, but she eased forward as effortlessly and gracefully as any doe walking through the woods.

He didn't kiss her first. Or hold her first. Or...they simply came together in a single, body-long sensation from thighs to hands to lips.

Their first kiss had been a surprising accident of a whirlwind of emotions. Their second was of shared wonder. Roy had never been so aware of so many things at once. Her scent really was honey sweet, like the taste of a distant hive on a summer breeze, full of flowers and life. Her kiss was rich with depth. And her body—he was a goner. Her waist fit his hands as if custom formed for the purpose. When he dared to slide them down the least little bit, the rising curve of her hips brushed the inside of his palms.

She groaned as he pulled her in tighter, a ripple felt as much chest to chest as mouth to mouth. He couldn't get enough of her. Couldn't get her close enough. Had to—

"Whoa!" Sienna's protest came out on a half moan.

He pulled her in tighter and she gave against him for a long moment, before pulling back.

"Seriously, Roy. Whoa."

How was he supposed to stop when—

But the lady said stop. Unable to actually let go, he simply held her against him and nestled his face in her hair.

Her arms didn't withdraw from around his neck, she too continued to hold him as tightly as he did her.

Even in the heat of sex he'd never felt a woman the way he felt Sienna against him though they were both still fully clothed.

They remained unmoving for an impossibly long moment—one that he never wanted to end.

Then she eased a step back out of his arms and he, god help him, let her go. A gap of air formed between them, their final contact was his palm against her cheek that she trapped momentarily against her shoulder before he let his hand drop.

"Whoa!" She repeated one more time, though he'd already stopped.

―――――

"Whoa!" Sienna really needed to stop saying that. Her nerve endings were very, very happy, but her nerves had neared panic mode.

As her mental faculties slowly reengaged, she became aware again of their surroundings.

"This is my office."

Roy grunted an agreement sort of sound.

"We nearly did...something in my office."

Again the grunt of agreement.

She looked up at Roy and squinted her eyes at him trying to see the truth of his next answer. "This wasn't some male marking the female's territory was it?"

"I'm not a golden retriever."

"No," she had to agree with that. "More like a German shepherd, warm and cuddly but incredibly dangerous when aroused."

His smile told her that hadn't come out right.

"Maybe 'riled' would have been a better choice of words."

"Well, I admit that you're an arousing kind of lady. But I don't get riled up much." His gaze drifted up over her head and scanned the room. "As to pissing on your personal fire hydrant, can't say as it ever crossed my mind. Frankly your office scares the hell out of me, my Lady Sienna Aphrodite. Every time you stand here, I remember just what the hell you do for a living."

She turned and tried to see it through his eyes. It was one of the three largest private offices in the West Wing, other than the Oval of course. Right in a row along the west wall: the Chief of Staff, the Vice President, and the NSA. She had room for her disaster of a desk, a small circle of meeting chairs and a sofa by the window, and a table that could seat ten for a meal or a planning session. Every bit of furnishing and decoration was historic.

"Must say it scares the daylights out of me as well."

Roy slid his hands around her waist from behind.

It took only the slightest shift in weight to be leaning back against his chest.

"Somehow, Sienna, that doesn't make me feel much better. We snipers want our National Security Advisors to be supremely confident. You know, in addition to already being brilliant and stunningly beautiful."

"I'll file your request in a suggestion box. In the meantime I'll do my best to not show that I'm freaking out."

"Maybe this will help." He removed one hand from around her waist, and hit the light switch. The room was plunged into semi-darkness, only the lights of D.C. filtering through the sheer curtains she'd closed against an earlier sunset, and the open door behind them. Then he swung the door shut and he turned the lock with a click that seemed to echo through the room.

"What are you playing at, Roy?"

"Not playing, Sienna. 'Less you say stop, I mean to have my way with you."

The NSA was horrified at taking such a liberty in this pristine office. But he hadn't called her Ms. National Security Advisor. Not once in the whole evening, perhaps not once since she'd met him.

He always called her Sienna.

And it made all the difference in the world.

She was ready to be turned and pinned against the door. She was even ready to have her beautiful dress damaged as he tore it in a frantic need to get skin to skin. Neither thought upset her particularly.

What she wasn't ready for her was for him to wrap his arms back around her. He simply buried his face in her hair and held her tightly against him. She could feel his arousal pressing against her from behind, but he didn't make any moves.

Instead, he held her tighter and tighter until she could barely breathe. Then his hands began to roam. His rough calluses caught slightly on the jersey fabric and offered teasing glimpses of how his hands would feel on her skin.

"Having his way with her" was apparently a slow study. A hand brushing over the curve of her hip. The other sliding upward between her breasts, and a single finger tracing the line where her collarbone was revealed by the dress' scooped neckline. When his finger traced just the slightest rise of her revealed breasts, she wanted to shout at him to get on with it. But she discovered that this time she actually was far too close to hyperventilating to speak.

At quite which juncture his hands went from being outside the dress to the soft material being a puddle about her ankles and his hands on her skin, she couldn't quite trace back to the point of occurrence.

Though she absolutely remembered the moment he removed his own jacket and shirt. The flash of heat when he finally let them connect skin to skin took her knees right out from under her.

He let her momentum take them to the thick carpet.

"I don't—"

"I do," his whisper cut her off.

"You've had protection with you all night?" She actually giggled at the image of him shaking the President's hand with a pocketful of condoms. "At the reception?"

"Protection is part of my job." He actually said it with a matter-of-fact voice rather than a wry tone which had her giggle escalating.

"Did you bring more than one?"

"I didn't bring a whole box...but I came close. Do you always ask so many questions when a man is about to ravage you?"

Sienna figured she probably did. So she stopped and concentrated on giving as good as she received.

And Roy was absolutely incredible at making sure she truly received.

CHAPTER SIX

R *oy felt as if* he'd slept a dozen hours, though he knew for a fact it was less than two. A man didn't get his chance with Sienna Arnson and waste a moment of it on sleep. Somewhere after they'd transitioned to his apartment, but before she'd demonstrated what she could do to him with a bar of soap in his shower, they had collapsed into his bed.

Not once had they performed the frantic-coupling-and-done that defined so many of his experiences. Not that all of their lovemaking had been slow or gentle, but it had been very mutual.

He'd learned many things about Sienna. She liked to snuggle. Most women clung, Sienna snuggled. She was easily enough embarrassed to appear shy or inexperienced, but like she did everything else, she made love with a complete commitment to the task at hand. She gave of herself more than any woman he'd ever had.

And whether it was due to imagination or prior experience—which he promised himself he'd never ask—she was a very creative woman. A couple of things he asked her to remember just what she'd done, because he'd been in such throes that his memory was faulty.

Like the shape and feel of her. She wasn't a workout queen, but he could feel the contours of the muscles that lay beneath that ever-so perfect skin. She must rule a stair stepper or some similar machine. Her glutes, when he cupped her exquisite behind with both hands to drag her more tightly against him, were astonishing.

So, he was on the bounce when he entered Frank Adams' cubbyhole office at one minute to eight the next morning.

And one look at Frank Adams' desk was enough to make him feel as if he hadn't slept in a week. Adams was one of those neat-freak managers, so his desk rarely held more than the day's duty roster and the all-important Action Sheet that was every known movement of all of the White House protectees. On the wall hung only two small photos: his and Beat's wedding photo and an autographed picture of the President shaking Frank's hand.

This morning there was a stack of four two-inch black training binders and Roy had the nasty feeling all of that reading was for him.

"Good morning, sir." He tried to make it as cheerful as he'd felt the moment before he stepped into the room, but Adams was back to being the Head of the PPD—one hundred percent hard-ass.

"Roy Beaumont," Frank flipped open a file, but didn't bother to look at it.

Roy could see it was his personnel file.

"You master every task I assign you more rapidly than any other man on my team, yet you make no effort of your own to improve your position."

"Kee Stevenson may have pointed that out to me earlier this week, sir." He'd meant to give it more thought, but spare time had been a little sparse on the ground these last few days.

"Sit, but don't speak again."

Roy sat and barely managed to bite back the "Yes, sir."

"You are one of the best technical shooters we have. Your teams consistently have better attention to task, even when you are merely a team member rather than a leader. The thorough analyses you made of route protection plans last week were both insightful and better than the double-blind originating marksman."

The first Roy had heard of it.

"And Ms. Stevenson remarked on your exceptional ability to

acquire and integrate new skills rapidly." Adams closed the personnel file, still without looking down at it.

Then he slid the stack of training notebooks across the table. "You have forty-eight hours to digest these."

Roy had worked through these types of manuals before; it was technically possible to plow through one of them in a week if he did nothing else.

"Four—"

"I did not give you permission to speak yet, Beaumont."

Roy bit hard on his tongue, but kept his anger to himself.

Adams spun the pile so that Roy could see the bindings.

Head of Protection Detail Procedures

Protection Detail Management: Domestic

Protection Detail Management: Abroad, France

National Security Advisor: Protection Requirements and Methodology

Adams was turning him into the head of Sienna's Protection Detail.

"Now you can speak."

Roy didn't know what he'd say if he could. But it didn't matter, he couldn't manage a word.

"Yeah, bro," Frank's voice slid into a funky uptown Manhattan, way uptown, that Roy had never heard from him. "Dat exactly how I be feelin' when dis shit come down on top o' *my* head." It was a level of accent that couldn't be faked. Frank Adams was from the streets of upper Manhattan, maybe even the projects by the sound of it, and that was a bad place to climb out of. What's more, he was revealing his past to Roy who had never even heard it whispered about.

"But I'll be responsible for..." Roy gestured helplessly toward Sienna's office, "...her life."

Frank dropped his accent and said kindly, "Welcome to the club, Beaumont. Now get to work."

Roy took his manuals and got.

———

Sienna tried not to be piqued when Roy didn't respond to her message asking if he could join her for a quick lunch.

It was harder when he ignored the dinner request.

If this was his idea of morning-after treatment she was going to murder him. The man didn't get to wholly redefine "great sex"—which he absolutely had—and also lead her to discover an inner passion that she hadn't known she possessed, and then get all...*guy* on her.

Knowing that Roy's life wasn't necessarily in his control, she tried to take it easy, but every time she looked about her office, she couldn't.

She believed that he had no intention of "marking" her territory, yet he absolutely had.

This morning she'd taken two steps through the door and been standing on exactly the first place they had made love. It would always be that spot of carpet, right there by the door, their first time ever together. And the couch he'd eased her onto afterward and given her a splendid naked massage while his body had recovered enough for her to take him by straddling his lap while he sat in the chair she usually occupied at the head of the conference table. They'd flirted and petted against the side of her desk when she had to turn on the desk lamp to locate her underwear, which for reasons unknown had been in the exact middle of the conference table.

It was by the soft glow of that lamp that they had stood back and inspected each other. Roy's sturdy power wasn't only in his face and his strength went far beyond his hands. He was beautiful in the way a Navy destroyer was—his looks so perfectly suited to what he was: incredibly male. And his long soft whistle as he inspected her had left her blushing and foolishly pleased. It wasn't a wolf whistle, but rather one of simple astonishment. And all of that had been only a prelude to the romp at his apartment. Completely unlike her, wholly unbeliev-able, and absolutely glorious.

Then today Roy Beaumont had gone silent though they worked only one floor apart in the same building.

She didn't have time for dinner anyway, so by nine o'clock she was exhausted, hungry, and the woman in her needed some slight reassur-ance that the best night of her sexual life had *not* been a one-night stand. She dropped down the stairs by the Cabinet Room that landed close by the door into the Secret Service ready room. If Roy wasn't there, maybe she could still find Frank Adams.

She spotted Roy right away, it wasn't difficult as he was the only person in the land of low cubicles and conference tables. He was at the far back of the room studying something on his desk.

"Hey there."

He didn't respond.

She wove her way in between the tables. One had maps of Boston and a binder labeled "Presidential travel: July 12." A whole set of tables had an Africa tour laid out on them country by country even though she knew that wasn't scheduled until September.

She tried another "Hey!" when she was nearly to Roy.

Nothing.

That's when she realized he was asleep sitting up. His head was propped up on his fist. A black notebook was opened before him. She read the page title: *Acceptable vehicle selection for protectee transport post-attack (categorized by medical condition)*. A list of vehicles followed with advantages and disadvantages listed.

No wonder the man was asleep.

His desk included the remains of a couple of sandwiches. There were also several cans of Coke. If she drank that many in a day she'd be vibrating with manic energy for a week, yet Roy slept. His phone lay on the desk, shoved to the side. She tapped it awake and could see her text messages.

When she touched his shoulder, he jolted awake as fast as his phone screen. It wasn't some smooth, clean rousing of a lover. One moment Roy was completely out, the next moment he had a hand clamped around her wrist and his other hand resting on the butt of his sidearm.

"Oh. Sorry." He let her go immediately and looked at her with those clear blue eyes that were wide awake. They were the eyes of a wide awake *agent* triggered into full alert mode.

She waited as his gaze slowly softened. When he finally smiled, she figured the *man* was now awake as well.

"Hey beautiful," he murmured after glancing about the room to make sure they were alone. Definitely awake.

"Hey yourself. You didn't answer my messages."

He scrabbled for his phone, checked them, and cursed. "Sorry, I set the damn thing on silent so that I could concentrate."

"Yeah, I see you concentrating," she made a deeply nasal snoring sound.

"Didn't realize I'd nodded off. It's a bit dry," he slapped at the notebook in disgust.

"What are you reading?" She flipped it closed to read the title.

He grabbed it to block her, but the open notebook had been propped against three others.

Her attention jumped straight to: *National Security Advisor: Protection Requirements and Methodology* then *Head of Protection Detail Procedures.*

"Adams made you..." she couldn't even say it. She could process information quickly, but this was too much. Too big.

"The head of your protection detail? Yes. At least through France."

"You would..." How in the hell was it possible? "Take a bullet for me?"

"Lady," he reached out and took her chilled hand in his big, warm one. "I'd have done that since the first time I met you."

It was too big for Sienna to comprehend. But she did know one thing for certain, there was going to be at least one more morning-after.

She tugged on their joined hands.

"Lady, I need my sleep tonight."

"So do I," she agreed and managed to get him moving. "So we won't try to finish the rest of your protection supply just tonight...maybe only half of it."

They barely managed to use one before passing out in each others' arms.

CHAPTER SEVEN

*I*t *was Adams himself* who drilled Roy the morning before the flight.

And Roy totally blew it. He had the reporting structure correct, but the timing of "all safe" updates wrong. He kept allotting more duties to himself than he should have as head of detail.

"Trust your people to do their part of the job," Adams admonished him again and again. Then completely destroyed the lesson by saying, "But if anything goes wrong it lands a hundred percent on you, not on them."

Adams kept at him for two hours and Roy would swear that half of it wasn't anywhere in the manuals. Throughout the interview Adams didn't refer to the manuals or any testing sheet. Everything must be engraved in his memory. That's when Roy realized that a lot of those procedures had probably been written or at least heavily updated by Adams personally. It made him both more and less daunting. Those books represented every practical lesson learned by prior protection details since the 1901 assassination of President McKinley. Adams had had to flog his way through them once upon a time and then enhance them from his own experience.

The idea that Roy might be adding to those one day wandered into his sights and he liked the way that thought felt. He would have to study them more on the flight.

Adams slipped a plastic-coated card across his desk to Roy. Rather than being some sort of a failing grade, it was a list of contacts. Secret Service overseas, USEUCOM search and rescue, French Ministry of Defence, the French COS (their version of the US Special Operational Command), Paris police... It was an amazing compendium of phone numbers and radio frequencies.

"Now forget the damn manuals," Adams waved a dismissive hand. "Trust your instincts. We've spent a lot of money training those over the years. Remember! Nothing is more important than the survival of your protectee, nothing. You come under friendly fire from a Paris SWAT team, you find a way to take out that SWAT team and clean up the political fallout later. If there's a bomb blast, there had better be a Beaumont-shaped shadow covering your protectee. We clear?"

"Clear, sir." Despite his desperate need for sleep, he'd lain awake for hours the last two nights with Sienna snuggled hard against him. Whether it was his Yankee upbringing, his father's taciturn training, or something inside himself, he'd always felt the need to protect. The Secret Service had been a clean fit to his way of thinking.

But with Sienna curled back against him, his arm tucked around her, and her fingers laced into his even in sleep, he'd found an entirely new meaning to the need to protect. He'd been trained endlessly that his life was less important than that of the person he was protecting until it came to him naturally. He'd thankfully never had that training tested in a real-life situation, but he didn't anticipate any of the common problems like freezing under fire or second thoughts.

He hadn't been exaggerating when he'd told Sienna he'd have taken a bullet for her from the first time they'd met. There was something precious about her. The world would be a lesser place without her in it. And his own world was infinitely expanded by having her in it. He'd finally slept with his nose in her hair and woken with her in his arms. Nothing was more important than preserving that.

"Roy," Adams eased back in his chair and sounded almost friendly, the way a black bear appeared friendly the moment before it tore you into tiny pieces. "Your instincts are among the best I've ever seen.

Trust them. Because, believe me, nothing prepares you for when it goes wrong. If it makes you feel any better, when it does go south and you feel like you're just making it up as you go, we've all done the same."

"You?"

"There was a carefully underreported incident where it came down to Beat and I, the President and the future First Lady under heavy fire in a foreign country. You'll be too busy to be terrified or worry; that's when your instincts will kick into gear." Then he offered a wry smile, "The shakes will come later though, that I can promise." Then he straightened up. "Now get the hell out of my office. I've got work to do."

Roy stood at his own desk out in the main area and decided Adams was right, to hell with the books. Now it was time to start thinking about his own detail.

He considered for a long minute, then messaged the Paris office. He'd pick up two stringers and a pair of vehicles from the office there for his team. Then he prepped a pair of flight cases. In the first one he packed his sidearm, his backup, and a Glock 43 for Sienna if there was an emergency. He signed out five extra magazines for each, because if that didn't do it, they'd be done for anyway.

In the second case he put the new CSASS rifle. It wasn't even in distribution yet, but he'd been part of the team to test the Compact Semi-Automatic Sniper System and he completely agreed with the selection of Heckler & Kock's modified G28 as the new weapon of choice. And at the moment he appreciated it all the more because it folded down neatly to two-and-a-half feet long rather than the typical four to five feet for a top sniper rifle. He made sure that he had the clearance paperwork for all four weapons. He almost tossed in the *National Security Advisor: Protection Requirements and Methodology* manual as well, but decided that Adams probably knew what he was talking about.

Then he laughed. Of course Adams knew. He'd asked Roy plenty of questions this morning that weren't in the manuals. As much as he'd been testing Roy, he'd also been teaching, making sure Roy knew what he needed most. He dumped the damn manual back on the desk, tapped the laminated contacts card tucked in his shirt pocket, and strode out of the office, giving Adams a cocky wave.

Then he'd slunk back in for his own suitcase and jacket.

———

"I'm sorry, Roy," Sienna greeted him as soon as they met out at Andrews Field. She lugged one of those square black cases that lawyers and airline pilots always carried. He took it from her and almost dropped it.

"Thing weighs a ton."

"All of the prep materials I need for France but haven't had time to look at. I'm going to have to work the whole flight. I'd sort of hoped—"

"Not much privacy," he pointed at the plane waiting for them on the tarmac. The National Security Advisor was rated as a mid-level protectee. The high-levels included: the First and Second Families, Presidential candidates who'd won a few primaries, visiting world leaders, and occasional high-risk individuals.

Mid-levels like the White House Chief of Staff, the NSA, and the majority and minority leaders of the Congress almost always had an agent driver and someone watching their home. Roy had been aware of the agent who had discreetly followed them back to his house the three nights that he and Sienna had managed together. If Sienna had noticed, she gave no sign.

Low-levels were on the lists and watched, but not constantly monitored. Dilya was a low-level when she was at school, but a high-level when she was traveling with the First Daughter.

When a mid-level picked up an overseas assignment, their team size increased two-to ten-fold depending on a wide variety of factors. One thing it earned them was a private jet. In the NSA's case, it was a ten-seater Gulfstream G450—a small, sleek aircraft that would punch across the Atlantic in just six hours.

But a G450 offered no privacy for what he wouldn't have minded spending the ocean crossing concentrating on.

"I," Sienna sounded a bit indignant, "do not have a one-track gutter mind."

"But you make it such a nice one-track gutter to contemplate."

"Hey."

"What?"

"Look at me."

He hadn't realized that he wasn't. He'd been busy inspecting the security. Outer layer guards. An immaculate cleanliness to the hangar and the base that made it much harder to hide things that didn't belong. The behemoths of this part of the airfield, the four jets of the Air Force One and Air Force Two fleet had a standing honor guard. The Gulfstream 450 presently boasted a guard herself in addition to two pilots and a mechanic going over their preflight checks.

"Sorry. Habit. I'm just checking security."

"Now I'm the one who is sorry. Go back to doing that."

"But pay attention to you while I'm doing it?"

"Of course."

"The problem with looking at you, Goddess Sienna Aphrodite, it makes it hard for me to concentrate on anything else." He offered her a leer which earned him a laugh, then he turned to inspect where he would set up if he was a sniper aiming at the NSA or her plane. He was pleased to see that the most likely hides were all inside the base's security perimeter.

"What I was saying before some rude, crude gentleman interrupted me—"

"Never have been accused of being a gentleman before." They headed across the tarmac between the hangar and the airplane which opened up new ranges of fire that were *not* inside the Joint Base Andrews' perimeter. A peek-a-boo view of a low office building to the east would be his first choice. Even though it would be a lousy and difficult shot, he slowed a half step to keep between it and Sienna.

"I had been hoping that we could talk a bit during the flight, as I was *fully aware* that we wouldn't have the privacy for what I really want to do. See, women sometimes have one-track minds as well."

"I admit to liking the one-track. The talking I'm less sure about."

She was quiet as they handed off the luggage to the pilot. He handed the paperwork for the two weapons cases to him as well. The pilot read them very carefully, inspected the contents, countersigned that he was aware they were aboard, and stowed them with the baggage. Roy went aboard carrying only a small notebook, his phone, and Sienna's massive briefcase.

They settled in their seats.

"Soda, beer, and wine in the fridge at the rear," the copilot pointed as he boarded. "Some snacks too. This morning's inflight movie is Tom Hanks in *Castaway* and then—"

"Then," the pilot came up behind him, "Your choice of Harrison Ford crashing into the ocean in *Air Force One* or *White House Down*. Yeah, yeah." He nudged the copilot forward. "You folks need anything, just let us know, otherwise you can self-serve." He closed and latched the outside door, then entered the cockpit himself, sliding a privacy curtain half closed. A clear message of: 'We'll leave you alone, but you're welcome to duck your head in.'

"So, you're not much of a one for talking?" Sienna teased him.

Not one for talking? He'd talked more to her than all of the rest of the women in his life...combined. And she made it so damn fun. She didn't judge him for having less education or worldly experience. Instead she listened to what he said, gave him the space to develop his thoughts.

It had been a joy to offer her the same. Sienna's conversations ranged far and wide. She joined together scattered bits and pieces into logical, sensible structures. Then she turned around and tried to tear them back apart. It had become one of his favorite games with her, watching her build those clear towers of thought and then help her poke holes and dig out crevices while she struggled to patch them back together with new ideas.

"Nope," he teased back. "Never was much of a talker."

"Liar."

"Well, not before you. You make me feel..." He wasn't sure how to finish that sentence and thankfully the plane's engines winding to life gave him an excuse to leave off.

Sienna Arnson made him feel so...alive. As if he'd been asleep on his feet for years and was finally coming awake.

He looked across the table at her. They'd sat in a pair of comfortable seats that had more in common with armchairs than his usual coach-class airplane seats. He'd taken a backward facing seat, letting her fly forward. There was a matching setup across the aisle and a sofa to the stern, facing across the cabin to a large-screen television.

Her attention was already drifting down into the first of the thick briefing folders she'd extracted from the case by her feet. Any strands of hair that had slipped loose from the roll at the back of her head, she slipped between her lips. She didn't chew on it, but simply trapped it between clamped lips as she concentrated.

They taxied away from the hangar and the pilot announced they were first in line for takeoff so they should "hang onto their stirrups."

He'd come to know every curve of her features, even how they changed, like the shape of her cheek when she smiled. The angle of her shoulders when she was exhausted or fresh off a workout. The way her eyes narrowed when she was concentrating, yet her brow remained clear and unfurrowed. He wondered how time would change her. He was a little surprised to realize that he'd like to be around to find out. It was easier to imagine waking beside her every day than not doing so.

Every day for how long, Beaumont?

He wasn't used to such a question. Thinking about his future hadn't preoccupied him much over the years, as both Kee and Adams had pointed out. They were smart people who he respected immensely, so maybe it was time he started.

The engines roared to life and the plane bolted down the runway.

So: *every day for how long, Beaumont?*

He couldn't imagine ever not wanting to be beside her when she woke.

He could imagine her with...

"Do you want children?"

"Do I what?" Sienna shouted back over the takeoff roar, but her look of shock showed that hearing him wasn't the problem. The folder she'd opened fell to the floor and she didn't even notice.

Now that he'd asked the question, he did want to know the answer. He shrugged, at something of a loss to identify where the question came from. Partly Frank and Beat's choice, partly the mischievous Dilya, and partly the gorgeous First Lady with the cutest kid ever.

The plane lifted and took to the sky.

Sienna watched him without speaking until they were well aloft.

"Do you?" She asked softly once the engine noise had dropped enough to speak normally.

He wanted to shrug, as if it wasn't any real difference to him one way or another. But the images from the White House reception were too clear. He'd never really thought about kids, no more than he'd thought about his long-term career. He was a shooter, that's what he did—until he suddenly became the head of the NSA's protection detail.

Kids were part of being a normal family, at least for others—until he imagined Sienna's children. He could see her with them so easily.

But not if they were another man's.

"Yes," he finally answered. "Yes, I do want kids. If they're with you."

———

That shot went straight to Sienna's heart, slamming her back into the plane seat. She tried to see into Roy and discover where the question had come from.

Well, parts of that were easy. Frank, Beat, Dilya, the First Kid: they all added up to make a man think about children.

But that wasn't what he'd said.

He'd said, *If they're with you.*

She wanted to parse and analyze the words. Break them down for inner meaning and nuance.

But Roy was too forthright a speaker. When he meant something, he said it in as many words. Any other man, any decent man who wasn't trying to make her crazy, would have said, "I don't know where that question came from. But I'm just kinda curious if you were one of those women who wanted a family or are you some kind of careerist?" Complete with insulting tone as if the two were so mutually exclusive.

And Roy had said, *If they're with you.*

"But we've only known each other for—" She had no idea. She knew him so well, but did she know him at all?

"Seven days as of 10:17 a.m. tomorrow morning. That's East Coast time. 15:17 Paris time."

"Seven days?"

"Six days and eleven minutes as of right now," he tipped his watch in her direction as if to prove his point.

"Six days and eleven minutes?" She wasn't making any headway with the concept. She'd once lived with a man for six months, even been talking about becoming engaged, and didn't begin to know him as well as she knew Roy.

"Twelve now," he smiled. "Not that I'm counting."

"And you want to know if I want to have children?"

"Uh-huh."

"With you?"

"Uh-huh."

"Did you just propose to me?" Even if he didn't connect the two, Sienna knew that he wasn't the sort of man to talk about having children out of wedlock.

Roy blinked hard. But he didn't have the decency to look abashed for more than a few moments. "Huh."

"Huh?" It had been a very noncommittal sound.

"Can't say as that's what I was asking. Six days and twelve minutes seems a might bit quick for that."

"Thank god."

"So let's table that part of it."

Sienna sagged, but it wasn't only with relief. She had to admit that there was just a little disappointment there as well which, as Roy might say, was surprising as all hell.

"For now, anyway," as if he was reading her thoughts. "But I would like to know your answer to the first question."

"Children? With you?"

"Just askin'."

Never having had a conversation like this one (Ever! Anywhere!), Sienna didn't have much to go on.

There would be no synthesizing a well-researched set of options into an actionable scenario. There was no National Security Advisor report or think-tank modeling she could fall back on.

Children? With Roy?

The second part was easier to answer. She'd seen him with the children at the museum. And she'd listened to the lessons of the forest taught by his reticent father, but inhaled by the child right down to his core. Even his treating Dilya as an intelligent grownup rather than dismissing her as some teenaged girl.

With Roy? No question. It was hard to imagine a man who'd be a better father.

Actual children? Little Siennas running about the house? That was far trickier.

She watched out the window as shore gave way to bay, then after a brief splash of green that was Delaware, true ocean. To hold a child who reached up and mussed her hair at a glittering party. To watch her turn into whatever version of Dilya the girl might become. Or a boy cut from the same cloth as Roy Beaumont. There was a truly breathtaking image.

She looked back at him, waiting patiently. All of his attention focused on her as he waited for her answer. A man who thought her answers were as important as his own. Who had proved time and again that he thought her pleasure was as essential as his own. A man of such integrity that he wouldn't even steal a kiss when it was offered because of some whimsical challenge.

"Yes," the word slipped out on its own, but she felt no desire to take it back. Children with Roy only had one answer, though she repeated it just to try its flavor, "With you? Yes."

He nodded carefully, "Good to know." Then his smile lit up and erased any doubt she might have.

The insanity of the moment set her to giggling. She wasn't ready to marry Roy but would have his children without a moment's further doubt. It was too crazy. Her giggle escalated, she couldn't tamp it back down.

Roy finally caught the ludicrous edge of the situation and added his own low laugh to hers.

"Just be damned glad there's no privacy, Roy Beaumont. Or I might let you start trying right on that couch back there."

He glanced over his shoulder at the half-closed curtain, then back at her with an eager grin she'd long since learned to recognize.

"No, Beaumont. Just...no!"

"Spoilsport," he muttered though she could tell he wasn't really serious.

An eager grin she'd long since learned to recognize.

Long since.

Six days and twenty-whatever minutes ago he'd been a total stranger. They had been together for a grand total of three nights. But it didn't feel like infatuation. It felt like nothing that had come before. There was no thought necessary to know how she felt.

It was a damn good thing he'd taken back his second, unintended question.

For now, he'd said. Not really taking it away.

Three nights together that felt like three months they were so familiar and comfortable. Always at his place for obvious reasons. Her abrupt return to Washington, D.C. at the President's request had caught her unprepared. Since stepping in as the new NSA, she was living in her parents' home this past week. She'd meant to find a place of her own, but hadn't had a moment to think about that yet.

She retrieved the folder that had slipped out of her fingers at Roy's question and opened it on the table between them. Then she leaned forward.

"Roy?"

"Uh-huh."

"When we get back..."

"Yes?"

"Let's have dinner and stay at my place."

"Sure thing."

He knew where she was living, but he wasn't making the connection quite yet.

"I think it's time I brought my boyfriend home to share a meal with my parents."

"Uh—Uuuh!" The wind came out of him as if he'd just been punched in the gut.

Which seemed only fair after what he'd done to her. Now Paris was approaching far too quickly, so she turned back to her work.

She was pleased to notice that it took Roy a fair amount of time before he started breathing normally again.

CHAPTER EIGHT

R oy *looked out the* window at the hangar and grimaced.

He'd specifically set up their landing at a remote hangar at Paris-Orly. It was supposed to have a grand total of two agents and two unremarkable cars.

"Wow!" Sienna was looking at him. "Who just got on your bad side? I'm guessing their life expectancy has plummeted in the last five seconds."

"Good guess," he gestured out the window and she looked. A line of five black Citroën DS5 sedans were waiting for them, looking like a school of sleek racing machines ready to eat alive anyone who got in their way. A cloud of motorcycle police were waiting as well.

By the time the plane halted, he wouldn't have been surprised if a marching band trooped in. At least there weren't any reporters.

"Stay!" He pointed to Sienna in her seat and clambered out of the plane as soon as the steps were down. A line of very formally dressed Frenchmen and women organized themselves by the cars.

"This is for me?" Of course Sienna hadn't stayed put. They were going to have to talk about that.

"No. It's for some other National Security Advisor."

"Oh. Right. New to the job, I keep forgetting. I guess this is my show. So, *you* stay." She made it funny, then trooped forward with her two-ton briefcase in tow.

A man dressed in recognizable protection department suit came up and handed over his ID. "Jankowski. This is Chen." Per standard, because they were overseas, the two were Diplomatic Security Service people—close enough to being the foreign version of the Secret Service to work just fine.

Kristian Jankowski, the DSS three-year man was a sturdy Pole, just like his name, with a Brooklyn accent mostly erased. Sandy blond hair kept reasonably short.

Mabel Chen, he'd stick with her last name, was a tiny Chinese woman who was too slender to be wearing a shoulder holster. But her small purse swung heavy so he'd trust to her six years in the DSS that she knew how to get to her weapon when necessary. He handed back their IDs.

"You two aren't exactly low profile."

"What did you expect?" Chen asked with a distinctly Midwestern accent, "a couple of suave Frenchmen in natty suits? This is Paris in the 21st century, we fit in just fine. At least I do. Jankowski has a wife; she's like some crazy mix Italian-Jewish-mother from Scotland. It makes him certifiable. Which now that I've said it, makes him fit in just fine as well."

"And I'm loving it," Jankowski put in. "Gotta find a man for you, Chen."

"Like that'll solve my problems."

"Or a woman," Jankowski was perfectly amenable.

Chen ignored him. "How about you, Yankee Boy? You on the loose? What are you doing after we deliver your package to somewhere safe?"

Roy chose to follow Chen's lead and ignore her comment as the best course of action. But he liked the easy back and forth between her and Jankowski. It told him that they had been together a while and worked well as a team.

"Couldn't you have been even more visible?" He changed the subject.

"Sure," Chen nodded, her long dark ponytail fluttering in the light breeze. "We're in France. We could have hired some mimes or something. Why? You gonna be an asshole about it?"

"No," Roy looked down at her, way down. If she broke five feet it would be a miracle. "I'm gonna be an asshole about this goddamn parade instead of my requested two vehicles."

Sienna was busy doing a glad hand with all sorts: some in military uniforms, others in a slightly more elegant version of Washington-dulls to mark them as governmental uniforms.

Chen pointed. Behind the cavalcade sat a pair of sedans: a newish blue BMW X5 SUV and an older gray Mercedes C-Class that no one would ever mistake for an executive vehicle. About as nondescript as a man could desire.

"Shit!"

"Tell me about it," Chen groaned. "We had the site pretty well checked out—hangar secure, scouting the area—then *they* rolled in sirens and all."

"Okay, not your bad. Let me grab our bags. I have a couple cases Customs is going to take their time with."

"I got it for ya," Jankowski went and collected the bags that the pilot had unloaded.

"We sure aren't doing crap else with all this going on," Chen finished for him.

Normally Roy could fit a week of gear into a small knapsack. He hated that now he had suits, shirts, and dress shoes. At least Sienna traveled about as lightly as he did, except for the briefcase she had consumed during the flight. He had watched in fascination as she went through it all—literally all.

She made few notes, mostly she read, but then she'd suddenly jump back three folders and double-check some fact, often without having to hunt for it. Her memory must be photographic. No, or she wouldn't have to look back. Pattern recognition. He'd wager that she remembered which folder, roughly where in the stack, and the general look of the page she wanted.

With different training, how good a sniper would she have been? Very, was his guess.

With different training could he be the NSA? There was a complete laugh.

He moved up to the group at the same moment that a customs officer put in an appearance.

"Passports please?" He asked in lightly accented English.

Once Sienna's had been barely glanced at and stamped, Roy handed over his along with his Secret Service ID, and the list of weapons and ammunition he was transporting into the country. The official glanced at the list, inspected Roy for a moment, then signed the customs release with a flourish and stamped his passport.

"I will ask that you try to refrain from shooting anyone while in France, the paperwork is enormous," he winked.

Roy winked back, though he didn't feel like it.

"We're in this car," Sienna sounded a little breathless from all of the attention.

"Hold on a moment." Roy doubled back to his DSS team. "What's your frequency?"

Chen told him.

He turned on his radio, set the frequency, and shoved in his earpiece. "Got me?"

"Five by five, Yankee Boy."

"Okay," he took the handgun case from Jankowski. He holstered his own Glock 21 at the shoulder, dropped his backup into his ankle holster, and slid the Glock 43 for Sienna into his back holster. He took two magazines for each and dropped them into his pockets.

"You expecting that kind of trouble?" Chen had sobered.

"Nope. Just like to be ready for it when it shows up." He also took the rifle broken down in its soft case so that it looked like little more than a tourist knapsack. He stuffed the other three magazines for each sidearm into the pack's side pockets and gave them back the empty handgun case. "Don't follow. Take some other route."

"Why?"

"I don't want our two vehicles identified with these," he waved at the line of black Citroëns. "But be close enough that I can call you."

They nodded and he went to sit beside Sienna in the deep leather of the Citroën DS5. The whole way into the center of the city with

Sienna and whoever else it was in the car—he hadn't bothered to pay any attention to introductions yet—he felt like a bug on the road. Any moment a big-ass windshield could come along and they'd be flattened.

The police drove like maniacs, performing maneuvers he wouldn't have risked on a closed training circuit, never mind in Paris traffic. The steady, "Bee-boop! Bee-boop!" of their sirens was really getting on his nerves. When they roared up to the roundabout encircling the Arc de Triomphe they actually closed the busiest road he'd ever seen for the flashing instant it took the motorcade to surge through the intersection.

He kept his silence through security into the governmental center where they'd be holding the meetings.

They had a metal detector, but on flashing his Secret Service ID, he was waved through the detector which offered a shrill burp of complaint but was ignored.

He made it up to the fifth floor conference room. It had those crazy high French ceilings with curlicues and ornamentation that probably went back to some dead emperor. It would clearly be the working space for their meetings, but for now it was a reception complete with liveried waiters bearing trays of alcohol and hors d'oeuvres.

When one of the ministers asked him how the flight was, he couldn't hold it in any longer.

———

"What the hell is *wrong* with you people?"

Roy's shout almost made Sienna flip the flute of champagne she'd just been handed into the French President's face.

There was a sudden stunned silence.

Sienna had never seen Roy mad and it was a terrifying sight. He'd said that he didn't get riled much and she now knew that was a good thing. She wanted to cower, and his ire wasn't even aimed at her. He had grown until he was more imposing than Frank and Beatrice combined. How could she have considered life with this man when she didn't even know he was capable of such raw...fury.

It was clear by the pin-drop silence that everyone was as shocked as she was.

That meant that it was up to her to tame the unexpected beast in their midst.

She sidled up to his side, almost reached out, but on second thought pulled her hand back, remembering how hard he had grabbed her when roused from a sound sleep.

"Roy?" She tried to make her voice soft and soothing. Instead it acted like a trigger.

"You!" It was clear he was addressing the entire room and wasn't going to be soothed until he'd had his say.

Protocol would suggest a shrug of apology to the President, but Roy had never struck her as being irrational. She would give him the benefit of the doubt and just pray he didn't destroy US-French relations in the meantime.

"You ask the National Security Advisor to come to Paris because you are tired of being targets. Good! She's glad to help. France has been a good ally. Then you make that show at the airport—not to mention the drive here—as if to tell every single terrorist that an exceptionally high-value target has just arrived in Paris. A protection detail I could have been managed with three agents will now require twenty or more."

Sienna hadn't even thought of that. And he was absolutely right. His words to Madame Ambassador at the White House Residence had stuck with her as she'd reviewed all of the briefing reports on the flight over. They'd colored her thinking, forcing her to dig deeper...but not deep enough.

"Sir," Roy turned to General Dumont dressed in his full military dress uniform complete with gold braids dangling from shoulder to chest and the red band around his billed cap. "I'm sure that you, like the United States, train your soldiers not to salute when in the field because it draws a sniper's target on the officer's chest."

Dumont nodded carefully.

"So why did you draw one on the American National Security Advisor? If there had been a single photographer there, I would have put her on the plane and sent her right back home. We move the President in public because we have no other choice; his profile is too high. But with all of your pleasant show you are sending flyers to every terrorist: 'Here are my most valuable assets. Hit them, please.' "

Again the shocked silence,

Roy scrubbed at his face. "My apologies for the tone of my outburst," then he looked about the room before continuing more calmly. "But no apologies for my words. You have made my job here harder, that's fine. It's my job and I'll do it. You have endangered an honored guest. I'm sure that she was briefed on the dangers before she accepted the President's request to act as his NSA."

Sienna nodded confirmation. But all of the Secret Service's briefings on varying attack scenarios, including issuing her a pass to the White House bunker in case of attack—a particularly rare item—hadn't brought the message home as clearly as Roy's tirade.

"But I ask you to consider, is this clusterf— Is this *fiasco* typical in your protection plans for your own people and your own country? If they are, it's time to wake up and start thinking. If you need another example: I'm a complete unknown to you. I stepped off a plane and waved a badge any decent forger could have made in a few hours."

Then he unholstered his sidearm and thumped it down on the fine wooden table, that probably dated back to the seventeenth century, hard enough to make everyone wince. Then he pulled a second one from his back waistband and thudded it down beside the other.

Five magazines followed, including one for his ankle piece though he didn't reach for that. He noticed the fifth magazine of .22s and slipped that one back into his pocket without comment. He didn't touch his knapsack that she hadn't seen him wearing before, which made her wonder what it contained.

"Enough rounds to shoot everyone in this room twice. Five of you would get shot three times if I don't miss. Any takers? You trusted me with no more reason than you wanted to believe that friends of your country were getting off an unmarked plane. This time you got lucky. Next time maybe you won't. Wake up people."

———

"Way to start my meeting off with a bang, Roy."

"Glad to help," he still sounded gruffly angry as he led her down a corridor she hadn't recalled traversing on the way to the conference room six hours earlier.

Their entire arrival had been overwhelming and elegantly French from the shining motorcade to the ornate décor including statues, murals, and paintings they'd passed enroute to this room. It had been thrilling...until Roy unloaded both verbal barrels on them.

The reception had collapsed before it started. When talk resumed, it was already focused on the topic of her visit. Soon they had cleared the waiters out of the room and were discussing existing security strategies over empty champagne glasses and trays of abandoned canapés.

Now, Roy was leading her into some nether region of the building that still had carpeting, but it was thin and there was little else going for the decorations.

"Where are we going?"

"Not where they expect," and she heard the smile in his voice.

"Which is?"

"There are a dozen agents waiting in the garage: four vehicles, black Ford Explorers with tinted glass, very hard to miss."

"But you said—"

"There is a police escort up on the street waiting to guide them to your hotel room at the Hotel Raphael Paris." He yanked open a door, cursed soundly at the occupant when he discovered it was an office. Sienna only had a moment to see her wide-eyed alarm before Roy slammed the door shut again.

She pointed to the next door down the hall clearly marked *Sortie*.

"But—"

"Where, my apologies to both you and the Raphael, you won't be staying." He entered the stairwell as if it was a room-clearing target rather than deep inside a highly secure governmental center.

"I won't?" She had to scramble to keep up with him as he descended the five flights of steel stairs. At a small door, a lone security guard sat at a metal detector waiting for anyone to actually use this entrance at eight at night. He looked bored to death with his obscure outpost in the labyrinthine building.

Roy merely waved at him as they exited without even turning so that his face would be seen. It seemed rude, but she did the same. Two people exit quietly. Wholly unmemorable.

"You won't. The caravan will arrive at the hotel and I wish I could see how long it takes whoever is watching to determine that no one is getting out except for Service agents."

There were two cars parked at the curb—neither one a black-and-tinted SUV. Roy escorted her into the backseat of the first one then slid in beside her.

"Beaumont! Where are you taking me?"

"Mabel here," he hooked a thumb toward the Chinese driver who couldn't possibly be named that, but kept his attention outside the car, "highly recommends a small hotel in the fifth district."

Sienna turned to look at the second car. It was following them, but not too closely.

"No," Roy admonished her. "Don't do that. It draws attention to the other vehicle."

"Oh? And you trying to look out every window at once isn't just as obvious?"

"She's got you there, Yankee Boy," the driver said in alarmingly familiar American. Perhaps she *could* be named Mabel.

Roy leaned back with a sigh. His only other concession to her being right was a soft curse of, "Crap!"

R oy, *Sienna decided, was* a very tricky man.

She'd been afraid that after his tirade he was going to turn her into some kind of prisoner. She'd never been to Paris with a beau and had looked forward to seeing some of the world's most romantic city together.

But he didn't lock her up. Quite the opposite.

"They're expecting a redheaded beauty with a phalanx of guards hitting the high end of Paris' offerings. So put on a blouse and nice slacks then tuck your pretty hair under a scarf. The four of us are going out to dinner as two cheerful couples."

And they had. Sienna would bet that her dinner in a classic French street-café with three Secret Service agents had been far more enjoyable than a meal with the ministers she'd spent the afternoon and evening with. The only oddity to the meal had been when Roy seated her, he set her with her back to the Place de la Sorbonne where the sidewalk café was half tucked under the trees and his own back to a wall.

"Wouldn't I be safer if it was my back to the wall?"

He'd eyed her in a way that said she just might end up that way later—they did have connecting rooms. "Field of view. Yes, your back is to most of the crowds. However, that means I have a broad view of anyone who may be coming at you. Chen is watching east and Jankowski west. We've got you covered."

And indeed, he did put her back up against the hotel room's wall on that late Friday night and she'd enjoyed every single moment of it. And for all of the hotel's lack of multiple stars of acclaim held by the Raphael—where she was *not* staying—the bed was very comfortable for two, though the shower was a little small.

On Friday's flight over she'd identified gaps in her briefing reports, and spent that first afternoon's meeting filling them in, with data from the people who lived and breathed French security.

Sienna had spent Saturday's meetings walking the dicey line of telling someone else how she would run their country if it was hers. If not receptive, at least they'd been very thoughtful by the time the long session was over.

And Saturday night she'd won her bet with herself.

The French President had rejoined them for the wrap-up of the meetings that night and the whole team had sat down to a very formal spread from some of the best chefs in Paris. But it hadn't been half as much fun as that late Friday dinner with the three agents swapping stories around a table so small that their knees kept knocking together. It hadn't even raised a speculative eyebrow from the Parisian agents when she'd moved her chair to sit beside Roy for coffee and dessert as they watched the people of Paris flow by—something she'd never dare try here.

At that ending-night dinner—in tune with her thoughts as ever, or perhaps as concerned with protecting her reputation as her life—Roy had been careful to place himself down the table from her.

And she'd missed him.

It was ridiculous. They'd been within ten feet of each other for days, and she'd missed being able to lean over and drop a line to make him laugh. She'd been able to hear him telling his stories but could only catch enough to know that they were ones she hadn't heard before.

As if to make up for it, Sunday started warm and glorious.

Roy was a generally gentle lover, but he set new standards in the pre-dawn darkness. By the time he was done, she didn't feel sated, she felt worshipped.

She awoke again as dawn was finally breaking. Just like it was supposed to in Paris, the drapes to the microscopic balcony fluttered gently in the breeze as the rose pink light of morning washed across the city and Roy's splendid body.

Sienna watched him for a long while. The July weather was warm enough that he had thrown back even the thin sheet and lay exposed like some Greek statue in repose.

A week and a day.

In a week and a day her life had been altered. Perhaps irrevocably.

Somewhere in yesterday's meetings she had noticed the first shift. She had spent Friday being the investigator and Saturday morning being the coach. But by the afternoon she had indeed been the National Security Advisor for the United States of America. She'd been able to help the French piece together new strategies to address the worst of their problems. Nothing had been solved, but there was a lot of promise for a more secure future.

And what of her own future? NSA for six more months. She'd been approached by several strategy consultants before the President's offer had preempted all others. She knew those offers would be renewed when she left the White House. If she didn't screw it up in the next six months, her future was sound.

Then what?

Children with Roy?

Marriage to a man willing to rage against the ministers of France in her defense?

That had been the true test. Not how he made her body feel. Not his obvious honor and integrity. Oddly it was his fury that had proved his true feelings to her. The depth of it, the complete outrage on her behalf. No agent merely concerned with his protectee's safety would have ranted so. If that was all it had been, he'd have lodged a complaint with their Secret Service and run it through channels.

Roy Beaumont. Always careful. Always steady. He was a forthright man who always spoke his mind. What had it cost him to peel back that layer on his emotions?

She smiled down at him still sleeping beside her.

Did he know that he loved her?

Did *she* know that she loved him? She nearly laughed aloud. Sienna Arnson loved a man. Loved *this* man sprawled naked in the light of a Paris dawn.

She tried to judge the future against this newfound present. Was he a man she could love all her days and he the same of her? "There's a dumb-ass question," she could practically hear Roy say, he'd said it more than once during the meetings. "You can plan for the future, but you can't predict it," his follow-up rarely softened the blow. More than once he'd cut through the chaff and political backloops with his forthright...Yankeeness.

Could she picture starting a life with Roy?

More than any man she'd ever met.

She brushed her fingers ever so lightly along his cheek. He woke as he always did, one instant out, the next totally present. But this time it wasn't the agent who woke beside her, but the man.

Sienna then set about proving to the man just how she felt about that change in who he was with her. When she'd driven him past speech, past control until her merest gesture made him quiver, then she'd straddled him and finally let him send them both to a place she'd never been with any other man.

CHAPTER TEN

I t's *July 14th," Sienna* said as she wandered naked out of the tiny shower. "Which means what?" Some remote part of Roy asked the question.

The rest of him was too busy admiring the naked woman before him. Not merely her body, which was impossibly firing off some thoughts that they had only just finished exhausting. But also the thoughtless ease with which she moved as she dried and buffed herself with a towel. The wet look was exceptional on her. Her dark red hair had slid into the deepest auburn, its wet tangle emphasizing the strong lines of her face. And her fair skin had reddened to a warm luster from the blazingly hot water she preferred.

But it was the internal contrast that was distracting him the most at the moment. She was soft, welcoming, eager, and sweet. He knew her expressions when enjoying a meal among friends, the look a half instant before she laughed, and at the moment of a cascading release shuddering down her frame.

He also knew her looks when thoughtful, diplomatic, or completely frustrated. The last was revealed by an absolute calm and a solid bastion of silence that was wholly formidable. He'd watched her teasing Mabel Chen and standing up to the Presidents of both the US and France.

The many moods of Sienna Arnson. He could imagine spending a long time learning them, though he doubted he'd ever understand them all. He wondered how she'd look lazing beside a Vermont waterfall after a long fall hike through the oaks. How her face might age with wisdom and joy.

And a part of him desperately wanted to know how soon he could entice her back into bed so that he could again brush his fingers over those amazing curves.

"Roy!"

"What?" She stood facing him, hands on hips, and stark naked except for the towel clenched in one fist. How was a man supposed to think with such a view.

"Speaking here, Beaumont."

"Lusting after your incredible body, Arnson." Which was when he realized Sienna never stood like that herself. She was merely imitating his own stance when she was frustrating him.

She threw the towel at his face then turned for her suitcase.

He admired the view from behind until she was dressed.

When she finished—as if her sleek capris, open sandals, and blouse just thin enough to hint at the black bra beneath wasn't equally distracting—she once again faced him and planted her feet, again mocking his style.

"Listening to me now, Beaumont?"

"Nope!" He made a point of looking her up and down, another image he'd store away for a long time and savor.

"Bastille Day. *La Fête Nationale. Le quatorze juillet.*"

"Is that like Romeo and Juliet?"

"Not in any way, except that this Romeo might soon end up as dead as week-old toast."

"It seems unfair."

"What does?" A light flush of irritation colored her cheeks. Gods but she was fun to tease.

"The peasants overthrew the Bastille prison in 1789 and beheaded poor Louis the Sixteenth and dear Marie let-them-eat-cake Antoinette in '92. And you think that's an excuse to go party?"

She stuck her tongue out at him.

He keyed his radio, "You two awake and ready for breakfast yet? We have a parade to go watch."

Jankowski mumbled something that might have been, "About goddamn time."

"How?" Sienna demanded.

"Downstairs in five," he keyed off and shrugged negligently. "I know shit. It's my job."

"Should I thank Chen or Jankowski for educating your dumb Yankee ass?"

"I'm hurt," Roy slapped a hand to his chest. "You said you liked my ass."

She rolled her eyes and he used her momentary inattention to cross the two steps that separated them and crush her against him. She practically purred as he held her hard.

"How the hell did you become so important to me?"

"It's your job," she mumbled into his chest.

It wasn't funny. It wasn't that he wanted her. It was that he could *not* imagine living without her. Not today, not tomorrow, not in ten years.

For a day and a half he'd sat in meetings and watched her heart. Her commitment to helping. Her gentle hand with ministers and military men who needed a good smack. The only one in the room with a whole clue other than Sienna had been General Dumont. As old as Sienna's father and sharp as hell. He had been the one to clue Roy in on Sunday's importance to France. He had planned to stay until Monday "because even National Security Advisors get the occasional day off," as Sienna had informed him, but this was even better.

The general had told him of the day's events and where to be for the best experience.

And it started with the largest and oldest military parade in all of Europe. Down the Champs Élysées from the Arc de Triomphe to the Place de la Concorde. The President had invited her to stand beside him at the end of the route, along with ambassadors of many countries.

It had only taken the slightest glance from Sienna for her security detail to respectfully decline.

"Thank you, Roy," she'd told him as soon as they were alone. "It would be quite an honor, but I'd rather go play. Besides, they'd probably turn it into another meeting and I'm tapped dry."

He let his smile tell her that he had no complaints about her decision. "You gave them a lot. They now need to take ownership of your suggestions or they will remain as solely your skills rather than them making them their own."

"And when did you get so smart?" He remembered the warmth of that moment. Sienna was brilliant and for her not to think him a burden was a gift.

"Sniper, remember?" It was surprising how often that was the answer to her questions. He'd learned about the difference between training and deeply integrated skills with thousands of hours of practice. But he had never realized how ingrained his role had become in his life.

Yet Frank Adams had seen more than just "sniper" in him. No one jumped from counter sniper to head of detail. And now that he thought about it, neither had he. He'd always picked up the scut work of planning and analysis. Only now in retrospect did he understand that Adams had sent that type of work his way far more than he did to others. He'd also been team leader of his sniper squad for the last year which had involved management skills as well as ensuring a deep integration into other teams: ground prep, close protection, SWAT, and air.

"Roy? Where did you go this time?"

"A, uh, far off land filled with naked dancing women."

"Give me a break."

"They're all redheads, and they elect you their queen."

"And I make you the court jester."

"Works for me."

"Any chance of getting a straight answer from you today?"

"Apparently not," but he could see she wasn't as amused as he'd hoped. "I'm finding my world is a little out of its familiar balance since the moment you walked across my scope sight."

"Is that a good thing or a bad?"

He kissed her quickly and shooed her toward the door. "It's neither one. It's the best thing."

And she was, the best thing that had ever happened to him.

———

Sienna liked being someone's "best thing." Even more, she liked being Roy's "best thing."

They bought small strong coffees and large croissants from a tiny shop that fronted the parade route. They applauded the marching troops. Who could resist cheering a cavalry that still rode horses rather than tank-based armored cav or an air cav who flew helicopters. An entire phalanx of marching K-9 unit earned roars of approval from the packed crowds and squeals of delight from the numerous children. A goose-stepping squadron of visiting Mexican falconers in nineteenth-century uniforms complete with hawks and eagles perched on their padded sleeves was a stunning sight. And there was no emotion possible except awe as tanks and mobile missiles rolled down the Champs Élysées.

They climbed the steeples of the Notre Dame cathedral where she snapped a photo of Roy posed with a gargoyle; and Mabel shot a photo of her and Roy with the entire city of Paris laid out behind them.

Roy led them to a quiet lunch in the back garden of the Musée Rodin. It had been the sculptor's home: an open, airy structure filled with magnificent light. If it were a dozen sizes smaller, she could move right in and happily never leave. The ground floor was dominated by a large marble of an intimately kissing couple. *The Kiss* which sounded even more luscious in French, *Le Baiser.* The garden itself was dominated by a greened-over bronze of *The Thinker* and dozens of his other works.

Chen punched him in the ribs for making some crude conjectures on what the three meter high statue was thinking up there atop his stone pedestal. She'd taken to doing that after she determined that their height difference was too great to smack him on the back of the head. It looked as if she threw good punches, not that they fazed Roy in the slightest.

Beneath the shade trees—on a lawn anonymously populated by dozens of other French couples and families on holiday and so green it might have come from an artist's palette—they ate Brie, thin slices of salami, and marinated artichokes on torn-off sections of fresh baguette. Because the three agents were on duty, they all four had soft cider rather than red wine. It was easy to forget she was actually the center of a very safe sphere of protection except when she noticed how rarely they looked at her and how thoroughly they watched the crowds.

She was reminded of Roy in the Smithsonian National Museum of Air and Space. He hadn't spotted her by glancing at the crowd, his gaze had tracked through the hall in a careful sweep until it had alighted on her.

That evening, no one complained about the long wait for a boat cruise along the Seine.

"Teach me to do what you do."

"Guard people?" Jankowski sounded skeptical.

"No, shoot people," Mabel stated.

"Neither," Roy said, of course reading her intent along with her question. He must have noted her watching them watch. "Okay, Sienna. We're standing in a queue of people, what do you see?"

She began listing them, "A bridge, some buildings…" she was able to name more than a half dozen of them, "…the Seine, a queue of people, a departing boat, a—"

"That's enough. Now point to the places you just named in the order you named them."

As she swung her arm back and forth, up and down, she began to feel foolish. She was like a wind-up clock on steroids pointing high, low, back and forth. Roy let her continue until she reached the end of her list—she had to guess at the order of a couple of them—and she could feel the heat in her cheeks.

"Now let's try this. Turn in a slow circle, only looking at what is exactly in front of you as you turn. Try not to look too obvious about what you're doing."

She did a slow casual turn.

"Now what did you see?" He asked when she once again faced him.

It was far easier to list them in order. Also, she would be able to turn back to just the right angle to locate any one of the things she'd seen. Again, he let her run down all that she could recall.

At the very end, while he was busy nodding in a job-well-done fashion, she whispered to herself, "And the man I love." There was no hesitation this time. No second thought. No clench in the stomach.

Her world rocked as if they were already on the boat instead of still standing on the stone quay that had remained unchanged for perhaps a thousand years. In a desperate grab for equilibrium, she shot out a question to buy herself a moment.

"Okay, wise-ass Beaumont. Tell me what *you* see."

He didn't look away from her for even an instant. He also hadn't scanned the crowd when she did. For all she knew he hadn't even glanced around in the last five minutes.

"At one-thirty I see a woman who is either from the central Sahara or is about to collapse from heatstroke. Either way, she's far too warmly dressed for a July day in Paris, so I'm keeping an eye on her. At four o'clock," Roy waved a hand negligently off to his right without turning, "is a man who has been standing at the exact center of the bridge for over ten minutes. He is alone yet doesn't appear to be waiting for someone as he isn't looking around. He is just watching the boats load and unload. A company agent keeping an eye on his investment? A writer busy thinking about his next novel? Or perhaps a shooter watching for a target? Or maybe he just likes boats? At six-thirty, behind me, someone has Chen's attention, so I'm keeping my eye on her to see if her 'person of interest' acts in a suspicious manner."

"Actually," Chen spoke up, "it's just a really cute guy. I don't see squat."

Sienna couldn't tell if she was joking or not and decided she'd be more comfortable if she assumed Chen *was* just ogling a cute guy.

"At nine o'clock, Jankowski—"

"Damn, but French babes slay me," he grinned at her and went back to chatting with Chen, but looking elsewhere as if idly enjoying the day.

"Okay, okay," Sienna held up her hands to stop Roy before he could continue. "You made your point."

"With multiple agents, especially undercover as we are today, we can observe a wide field for potential threats without attracting any attention."

Sienna glanced around and they were indeed being ignored. The attention she'd temporarily attracted as she'd turned her circle pointing at all the sights of Paris like a hick from Reims had drifted away. Not a single person had marked their conversation among the general hubbub of tourists eager for a "French" experience on the Seine. She wondered if French people ever rode these dinner boats and somehow doubted it, except perhaps when escorting foreign guests. Roy and his team had attracted no attention because they didn't act in any way out of the ordinary. Even their tone was lightly conversational, blending easily into the background.

"You missed one," she didn't know if she hoped Roy would pick up on the tease or not.

"You didn't let me finish."

"I'll bet you'd still miss this one. Go ahead, tell me about everyone you're watching. But you're missing one, really obvious person." She wasn't going to give him the hint that it was someone who couldn't stop watching him for even a moment. No man had ever made her feel so safe. She was safe in his arms and under his protection.

He didn't fall for it and look about. Instead he squinted at her and used his brain. She could hear Chen snort and cover a laugh when she got it.

Roy's head quirked in Chen's direction, but he still didn't figure out Sienna's riddle.

Jankowski actually found an excuse to turn a slow and careful circle, but he too missed it. Which had Chen snorting again.

Then it clicked in for Roy and he offered that slow smile of his. His lips curved up until she could imagine how his smile would taste. That was the other real gift he gave her. Against all odds she'd found a man who actually *saw* her. Not just the National Security Advisor, but also the woman who Sienna herself had barely known about before Roy.

"Perhaps I did. Won't happen again," he whispered for her ears alone.

Or tried to.

Chen punched him solidly in the ribs, again, and he grunted at the blow.

Then he leaned down and kissed her.

Was it any wonder that she loved this man.

CHAPTER ELEVEN

R*oy helped Sienna down* the stone steps onto the river boat. Not that she needed the help, she was an incredibly capable woman. But he liked the feeling of taking care of her—a way to pay her even a little of the respect she deserved.

He'd been watching the long boats slide quietly by for several hours, disgorging and reloading their passengers. There were tour boats that probably carried several hundred in closely packed quarters as tour operators called out the sights over too-loud sound systems. The dinner boats were filled instead with comfortable tables, each set for one or two couples. Fine linen tablecloths, cloth napkins, shining silverware—it was fine dining for a hundred. Thirty feet wide, over a hundred long, deep enough for a galley below yet still low enough to slip beneath all of Paris' bridges. When they approached, the dockhand had taken a surprising amount of money to pay for the four tickets, but the *maître d'* escorted them like guests of honor to the very bow. They'd been waiting for a no-show on the dinner reservations— another suggestion from General Dumont. Roy made a mental note to ship the man a couple quarts of Vermont maple syrup in thanks.

Sienna had been following his inspection as he noticed exits, the height of railings if jumping overboard was the best option, and so on.

He could see her learning what he did minute-by-minute. He could only imagine how his 101-level lesson in observation was now being integrated into national security methodologies and strategy shifts. Sienna's mind worked like that. It scooped up little facts and used them in strange ways.

He'd had his tirade at the start of the Paris meetings and after that managed to mostly keep his mouth shut. Of course—because Roy's luck was running so consistently terrible lately—it turned out that the US Ambassador to France had been in the room. He'd reported the tirade to his boss in horror, who in turn had told the Director of the Secret Service to tromp one Roy Beaumont. It had then come full circle as a seventeen-word e-mail from Adams.

Hear you kicked their asses. They must have needed it bad. But, Brother, you do *like living dangerously.*

No judgment. No correction. No signature. But he'd left the e-mail thread all of the way back to the US Ambassador to France for him to read. And because Adams did nothing by accident, the message had been clear, "You're on the front line, it's your call. But next time you may want to think a bit first."

That more than anything else demonstrated what had happened to him this last week. He was now head of a protection detail, a politically sensitive one. It wasn't the first time he'd asked himself why the hell he'd ever come down off the roof.

But if he hadn't, then he wouldn't be the man escorting Sienna Arnson to her dinner table in the very bow of a boat on the Seine.

"Totally worth the price of admission."

"What are you talking about?" She sat as he held her chair for her.

"You."

"What price?"

"The hundred changes you've already caused in my life."

"And the thousand to come, Beaumont," Jankowski dropped down beside him without any ceremony, leaving his "date" Chen to take care of her own chair beside Sienna. "Trust me, voice of experience here. Spend five or ten years with a woman and you won't recognize yourself ever again. Hell, one year."

"Yeah, your socks match now. Why else do you think I introduced you two?"

"You're a Philistine, Chen."

"You were a slob, Jankowski."

"I was," he spoke to Sienna. "But it wasn't my wife who cleaned me up."

Roy exchanged glances with Sienna. She was being amused by the fact that they were taking his and Sienna having a lasting relationship as a given. He slid his foot forward until their ankles brushed. She continued watching their dinner companions, but returned the pressure. Her smile was lit by the soft candlelight. He liked it for several reasons.

First, she looked incredible in the warm glow, maybe he should get some candles for his bedroom. He was fairly sure women liked that sort of thing, though he'd be damned if he was buying any of those stinky, scented ones.

Second, he liked it strategically. The light was low, little shades on the candle lanterns kept the light aimed down at the table. It made for better nighttime viewing of the Paris buildings and monuments along the Seine. It also made one individual versus another indistinguishable more than a few tables away.

"So, if your wife didn't clean you up, who did?" Sienna inquired nicely enough that she might even have been sincere.

"I did. First time I saw her I knew I had to do something if I wanted to catch her."

"What about you, Yankee Boy?" Chen rocked her chair back on two legs. "What are you going to change to win this lady?"

"He already did it," Sienna answered for him.

"I did?"

"You did," she looked at him with those deep eyes of hers. "You came out of your precious sky to walk by my side."

"Don't know as I'd have done it for anyone else." Couldn't imagine how she understood the scale of that change, but she did. His Sienna understood even that.

"I know," she mouthed silently across the table.

As least that's what he thought at first. Then he thought back. There had been an extra syllable on the end.

You.

I know you. It didn't fit. Her mouth shape wasn't right for "know."

Then it clicked and he stared hard at her.

She'd said, *I love you.*

Oh crap! It was one of those moments where if you didn't know what to say, you were totally screwed.

But...he *did* know what to say. Much to his own surprise.

Sienna was watching him carefully, awaiting his response to her throwing her heart out on the table.

He sipped at the glass of ice tea the waiter had barely deigned to serve him when there was perfectly good French wine available.

He did love her, but he couldn't let her have all the fun.

She'd started changing him the moment she walked up the White House path fifteen days ago. Not even knowing her, she'd made him think there was more to life, more to *him* than he'd found so far. By the time they met, he was already smitten. And now—god help him—he knew he'd never find another woman like Sienna. He'd never told a woman he loved her. He was afraid it would somehow come out wrong, or choke him or something.

So he made a different choice.

"About time," he whispered back to her.

Her laugh of delight lit up the evening. And for once Chen was seated too far away to give him one of her "Atta Boy" thwacks.

"Yow!" a sharp pain lanced up from his shin where it had just been kicked.

Chen's grin was appropriately evil.

And for once, Jankowski hadn't missed a thing.

CHAPTER TWELVE

S *ienna had obviously entered* some sort of a dream state.

Four weeks ago, she'd been in a Fort Bragg think tank, analyzing the communication architecture of worldwide political information by the US Commands. Then with no explanation as to why, she'd been flown to D.C. and interviewed for three straight days by the outgoing NSA, the White House Chief of Staff, the President, and a laundry list of others. One week spent with the outgoing NSA and she'd landed in the chair.

Now, at the end of her second week as National Security Advisor, she'd consulted with the powers of France and been listened to most attentively. Even without Roy's "icebreaker" they had been open to suggestion; after it they had been truly respectful. By the end they were asking her if she'd like to come work for the French government instead—and she didn't think they were merely being polite.

Best of all—also absolutely the most surprising—she was sailing through Paris with the man she loved. And he loved her back.

They had nibbled on crostini with Brie and slivered fresh basil while opposite Notre-Dame. Eaten an exquisite French onion soup as they floated by the Passerelle des Arts. Dined on steak au poivre as they passed between the Musée du Louvre and the Musée d'Orsay. A strawberry crème brûlée was soon to be served along the packed tables of holiday merrymakers. They were a very happy and content crowd.

The evening was so warm that she'd have been fine, even without the gray-and-gold woven shawl Roy had insisted on buying her. It was beautiful work though, and she wrapped it as tightly around her as a hug.

"Sienna on the Seine. They should make a movie about me."

"You've got the best damn luck I've ever seen, Yankee Boy," Chen shook her head in obvious disgust. "Or perhaps Ms. Arnson does—with the exception of being stuck with yourself."

"Why?"

"We get to watch the Eiffel Tower blow up from a boat on the Seine!" Jankowski practically crowed.

"Damn good show," Chen offered in her Midwest declarative style.

"They're blowing it up?" Roy blinked in surprise and all three of them burst out laughing. Roy took it well, as he did everything except challenges to her safety.

"Fireworks show, Yankee Boy," Chen was the first to recover enough to explain. "Bastille Day, it's the best show of the year and Ms. Arnson lucked into a spot on one the boats that will be floating by the tower for the show."

"Remind me not to make reservations in the future," was Roy's only comment. The wait in line had been a long one—those willing to wait to take the spots of no-show reservations. And he'd done it for her without knowing how huge the payoff was.

"There are days I love this job," Jankowski said, then grimaced. "But the wife will kill me when she hears."

"So, don't tell her. You can trust me to keep your secrets," Chen's tone implied absolutely not.

Sienna looked at Roy. Still he scanned the distance, ever reliable, ever vigilant. What secrets would he keep for her? Anything. And what would he tell her? Anything she asked. He might not think to volunteer something, but he'd answer any question truthfully.

"Roy?"

"Uh-huh." But she knew she didn't have his attention.

"Roy?" She tried it a little louder.

It wasn't until Chen glanced at Roy and then twisted around to see where he was looking, that she felt the first prickle of chill. She pulled her shawl closer and turned as well.

Over her shoulder, the Eiffel Tower soared above the river bank. It was still well ahead of them, but they were crawling slowly toward it along with the clutter of boats jamming the waterway. She glanced at her watch—11:20. The show should start in just a few minutes. Parisians dined late and celebrated even later.

"What is it?" Chen whispered.

"It's called the Eiffel Tower, Mabel."

But she didn't smile or even respond. That's when Sienna identified the look on Roy's face. He was no longer scanning. It was that moment of recognition in the Air and Space Museum, the moment before his eyes had bugged out in surprise.

Target acquisition.

He pulled out the pack that he'd shoved under his chair and dug out a pair of binoculars. They weren't little tourist binoculars; he'd been carrying high-powered sniper binocs with him all through Paris. He always had the backpack, and she'd never given it a second thought.

"Jankowski. Is the Tower opened or closed for a fireworks show?"

"Closed. They clear the people off early for safety during the show."

"The riggers should be long since done."

"Mid-afternoon," Chen confirmed.

Sienna looked at the angle of Roy's inspection, then tried to follow the line up to the Eiffel Tower. At first she thought they were spots in her eyes from staring so hard. Then she remembered what Roy had said about exactly that. "You see more with a relaxed open eye."

She tried relaxing and the spots didn't go away. "Those are moving lights on the—"

"Keep your voice down. Steady and conversational." And in just that tone, he asked, "Which of you is a better spotter?"

"Jank," Chen said. "And don't think that doesn't piss me off."

Roy passed the glasses to Jankowski.

Then Roy rose from his seat, taking his pack with him, and moved around to the narrow space between her and Chen's backs and the ship's bow. The tour company hadn't left a lot of space there, but somehow Roy fit in despite being a big man. It also was an unlit space and made him nearly invisible to the other passengers.

Out of the corner of her eye, she could see Roy pull out something else.

A rifle scope. What else did he have in that bag?

She decided she'd rather not know.

Using only the scope, he began to inspect the tower.

"Damn it," his curse was soft. "I make four, no, five."

"Five," Jankowski confirmed. "Range in the dark? Four hundred meters. First-level restaurant is at fifty meters up. I place them at almost a hundred meters."

"Last minute check of the fireworks?" Chen offered.

"Too last minute," Roy countered.

"Daredevil climbers. Like extreme base jumpers or something. Want the thrill?"

"Nope, next."

Sienna saw what they were doing. Trying to find some rational explanation for five guys up on the Eiffel Tower just minutes before the fireworks show. "Reporters?" she offered. "They're always doing the stupidest things."

"Security at the base is pretty serious," Chen decided. "At least enough to keep stupid tourists and reporters at bay. They had to plan to make it inside."

"Sienna," Roy slipped a laminated card into her hand. It had a list of phone numbers. "Start with Paris SWAT. If they don't respond the way you want, call your buddy Dumont."

Sienna pulled out her phone, "What am I telling them?"

"Two things. Chen, I need all the napkins."

She started collecting them.

"First, don't shoot at the guy in the boat on the Seine."

Chen had collected the four napkins. He folded them in half, laid them together, and wrapped them around something she couldn't quite see. There was the distinct tearing sound of duct tape that had several other table's guests turning. As there was nothing to see, they soon went back to their own conversations.

Then Roy shifted position enough for a lick of candlelight to shine on the barrel of a rifle. He'd taped the napkins around the tip of the barrel. Poor man's silencer. No, a sniper rifle probably already had that. It was a flash suppressor so that he didn't draw any attention.

"Second, tell them they've got at least five suicide bombers up on the Tower."

She heard the soft click as the rifle was assembled and a snap that she was fairly sure was a magazine locking into place.

Sienna had no room for doubt. This was Roy.

She started dialing.

CHAPTER THIRTEEN

R*oy watched them through* the scope.

He needed proof that he was right. He knew he was, but that wasn't enough.

He huddled in the shadow with the rifle resting on the railing as he squatted. But it was useless, the boat was rocking too much.

Order the boat to shore?

They were mid-channel with heavy traffic to both sides. He'd already seen that the dinner boat didn't maneuver quickly. It was designed to mosey along a slow-running river, not deliver troops.

Their actions were wrong for a fireworks team. They were sticking to a single level horizontally rather than moving up or down a vertical line of wiring that might have been tested due to having a last minute problem.

Extreme base jumpers—seeking a showy stunt—would have gone straight to the top.

Reporters would have stayed on the stairs.

These guys were way out on the structure, all lined up along one side.

Demolition work. They were going to cut all of the struts down that one side.

But still, he didn't have proof.

He could hear Sienna getting heated up on the phone and then hanging up with a soft, "*Merde!*"

Even if she reached Paris SWAT, it wouldn't be in time.

"Far left," Jankowski called softly.

He swung the scope. A man stood on the corner strut. He was fumbling inside a pack.

Sienna got through to Dumont and began speaking in rapid French.

The fumbler pulled out a square block of something, and slapped it against the metal.

C4. No firework in the world would have been placed like that. He passed along the sighting and heard Sienna echo it to Dumont.

"Winds aloft?" He couldn't feel crap down in the boat between the river banks.

"I see a flag," Chen replied. "It's not doing much but its moving. Call it ten K from the north-northeast."

"Is that kilometers or knots?" He hissed it out.

"Sorry, kilometers per hour. Told you Jank was better at this. Five knots, give or take."

Roy clicked the scope's adjustment one notch for the effect the light wind would have on his bullet during its long flight. He also rotated the vertical adjustment to compensate for the fact that he was aiming upward at a target, not down. The bullet would have to arc up higher than the target, and then fall to strike home.

"I need something soft," he was on one knee, but he could feel the boat's motion moving him at its whim from his contact with the wooden deck.

Chen handed him a bread roll.

He'd have laughed if he had time. He slipped it under his knee and it squashed flat and useless.

Then, before he had time to ask, Sienna handed him her folded-up shawl. It almost broke his focus. He didn't want this memory attached to his gift to her.

But it was exactly what he needed so he dropped it on the deck without comment.

He loosened his hips the way Kee had taught him until his leg could move separately from his torso. He would hinge at the hip and keep his torso and hands steady.

Roy flipped off the safety.

He sighted, let a small correction from some deep-honed instinct shift the crosshairs slightly left of the target.

Then—for better or worse—he rested his finger on the trigger and began to apply the two-point-seven pounds of pressure he had it set for.

*S*ienna *would never forget* how surreal the event was. She and Chen sat as if casually chatting while they provided a shadow for Roy.

In reality, she was on the phone with Dumont who was working multiple phone lines in the background.

Chen was relaying information from Jankowski as spotter.

Everything conversational. Nothing happening here, folks.

Except Roy was...

She was turned just enough to see the napkins he'd taped in a tube around the barrel flop about. There was no flash, no bang. The shot itself was no louder than the small crackers and other noisemakers that were in use along the shore. More noisemakers on the boat were adding additional cover. Chen was spinning a wooden toy that gave out a sharp "Clack! Clack! Clack!" as she quietly relayed instructions.

"Don't waste time, buddy," Jankowski had said right before Roy shot. "If one of them figures out what's happening, they might throw some manual trigger."

Roy didn't shoot every heartbeat, but perhaps it had been every other.

It was about every twenty of hers—she was surprised her heart could even beat that fast.

"That's five," Jankowski announced. "All look to be clean hits."

"Dumont," Sienna echoed the reports over her phone, "says that a SWAT sniper got two more around the other side."

"Must be strapped in. None of them fell, But I don't see any movement," Jankowski reported.

The first firework went off. It made her jump, but there was no unwarranted explosion along with it.

"We didn't have a chance to warn the firework display controller before that first one," Dumont continued speaking over her cell phone. "But we're having him not set off anything on the level the bombers were working. We have a special squad headed up there right now to clear the bodies and explosives. The fewer people who know about this, the better."

Silently Roy packed away his weapon. There was a smell of scorched cloth from the improvised napkin silencer. But that soon faded.

He settled back in his chair as they were serving the crème brûlée.

"I believe that we'll need fresh napkins," Chen said.

Sienna didn't know whether to laugh or to weep.

All of her discussions with the Parisian authorities. All of their preparations. All of the hatred of a bunch of crazies. And it had ultimately come down to one observant man sitting in the right place with the right hardware—and it had all lasted under five minutes.

In a world of asymmetric warfare, that's what it came down to.

The strategies of her predecessor were going to have to be completely rethought. She'd known of the existence of small, unreported events that were resolved without the public's knowledge. The former NSA had told her how the future First Lady had saved the President's life, unreported. Delta Force took down drug lords and warlords with near perfect invisibility. Drone strikes were public, but when it was a two-man strike team on the ground, what the drone saw was never reported.

The world had changed irrevocably. Since the American revolutionaries had hidden behind trees rather than marching in the open to face the British, the balance had shifted. The recent wars in Iraq and Afghanistan had brought the lesson home.

And as she'd just seen, the trend was continuing. Rather than giving her a chill, it made her eager to get back to work. There had to be methods to achieve what Roy had just done on a consistent basis.

Fresh napkins were brought.

She missed her shawl. Glancing behind her chair where Roy had knelt, she didn't see it in the shadows.

"Where is it, Roy?" Sienna patted her shoulders.

"In my pack. I'll replace it for you."

"No, you won't."

"But—"

"I know what you're thinking, but you're wrong. It will serve to always remind me how safe you can make me feel."

He actually stood and brought it around the table to drape it about her. His grip was strong on her shoulders and she wasn't sure who was comforting who.

Tomorrow there would be a post-mortem and multiple security meetings before they flew back to D.C. But for now it was just the four of them. It might have been a somber table, but it wasn't. But neither was it a joyous one. Instead it was soft-spoken and they all treated each other very gently.

That night when she and Roy curled up in the same bed, they didn't make love. Instead he simply held her so tightly that she could barely breathe.

He held her a long time before he spoke. It was a lesson for her life, giving Roy the space to find his words.

"No amount of training prepares you."

All of those hours on watch, he'd never had to shoot anyone before.

"They were bad people, Roy, bent on doing unreasonable harm. You probably saved hundreds of lives in addition to a national landmark."

"Probably," he admitted at length.

"Head of detail doesn't mean you aren't still one of the top shooters. It also doesn't mean that you don't have feelings."

She could feel his nod against her hair.

He rubbed his hand along her back for a while.

"Hell of an Independence Day," his voice was thick with chagrin.

She laughed and patted his chest. "I need to start teaching you French."

"Why?"

"Because July 14th is not their Independence Day. On the first anniversary of the storming of the Bastille prison, they held a *Fête de la Fédération* to celebrate the unity of the French people even though it was the middle of the French Revolution."

"Unity, huh?"

"Uh huh," she did her best to imitate one of his grunts.

"How do you feel about unity, Sienna Aphrodite?" It was ridiculous, but she was utterly charmed by his nickname for her. She knew she was up on no pedestal, for Roy truly saw her, but still it tickled her.

"We're lying about as close together as can be." Was he actually talking about their unity? As a couple? If he was, he was going to have to say it himself.

"I think we could manage to get a little closer," he rolled until they were lying nose to nose wrapped in each other's arms and she'd hooked a leg over his hips to hold him close.

"We could, if you think you're going to get lucky tonight."

"Oh, I think I have an inside track on that," Roy tone was far too self-assured even if he was absolutely right.

"What makes you so sure?" Sienna brushed her lips over his.

"Unity Day," he kissed the tip of her nose.

"July fourteenth."

"*Le quatorze juillet.*"

"That's what they call it," Sienna agreed.

"Say you'll marry me, Sienna." His voice turned suddenly harsh and thick with emotion. "Say you'll be my wife through thick and thin, good and bad, because I don't know how I could ever live a day without you."

Sienna couldn't imagine how she'd live a day without Roy.

But his speech—rough and all mixed up in need and the evening's events—wasn't what she wanted between them. There would always be love and truth, this she knew. And safety, because nobody delivered that like Roy Beaumont.

But she also wanted a lightness in their unity. She wanted Sienna Aphrodite as well.

"Marry you?" She did her best to sound a little puzzled by the idea. She hadn't quite forgiven him for saying "About time" when she'd said that she loved him. She leaned back just enough to see the truth in his eyes revealed by the Paris lights which glowed through the soft curtains.

He nodded tightly.

"Sure," she kept it light as if the most important change in her life was of little consequence.

Then she stole one of Chen's lines.

"Yankee Boy."

*After ten years, **Damien Feinman's** duties as Sit Room watch officer let him see it all: the good, the bad, and the disastrous. But nothing prepared him for the beauty and power of the new Chief of Staff.*

* **Cornelia Day's** new role as White House Chief of Staff leads her to the Situation Room where every crisis comes home to roost. A dozen years of assisting the now-President-elect never prepared her heart for what awaits her there.*

* Only together can they save Christmas in the nation's capital. Only together can they survive Damien's Christmas.*

This time I knew quite a bit about my heroine. In Zachary's Christmas Cornelia Day was an important character with multiple scenes, a modest amount of dialog, and several detailed descriptions. She came to her own story with a past, a political history, and most importantly a political future.

President Peter Matthews has been in office since before my first book in The Night Stalkers series, The Night Is Mine. He has led a country with hope and determination, with a strong ethical air. With his retirement, it seemed appropriate that the series closes with him. (Yes, it is intentional that I never mention his political party. He represents the kind of person I would like to vote for, independent of partisanship.)

What I wanted to pass forward was the hope. We live in a great nation. It is one rife with challenges, as are all nations, but I like to think that we stand as a beacon of what is possible. During my travels around the world, I was often told that the United States is just that.

The most articulate example is when I was bicycling through Macedonia—one of the friendliest and loveliest countries I visited in my eighteen-month tour. At that time I was there, 1993, the land-locked nation was in terrible straits.

Greece to the south wanted to annex them, pointing back thousands of years to stake their claim and blocking all southern borders until Macedonia caved in. They had only recently seceded from war-torn Yugoslavia to the north—

achieving a uniquely peaceful secession. They knew that war would be coming soon however—it held off until 1999 when a third of a million Albanian refugees piled into this small country of barely two million. I watched the trickle of news in daily horror as the countryside I had ridden through so happily was shredded over and over for the next several years.

In the midst of this, I sat talking with a circle of people my age over a meal. One of them explained that in the quiet moments, when they were thinking about who they were and what they hoped to do, they would sit back, cross their feet comfortably, interlace their fingers behind their head, and say, "Ahh, America."

I often think of these kind and hopeful people and can only wonder what became of them.

I was born into a land of hope and possibility and fully understand how lucky I was to be so. The more I research and write stories, the more I understand this. That is why I write the stories I do, always holding up that bit of light.

But back to this story and its change of fictional leadership for the United States.

To replace President Matthews I had Vice President, now President-elect Zachary Thomas. To replace the lovely Genny Matthews, I had Anne Darlington-Thomas. To replace Zachary, Daniel steps up from White House Chief of Staff.

Not only was this a natural progression for Daniel, but it was also an homage to John Spencer who played Leo McGarry in the television series The West Wing. Leo went from Chief of Staff to Vice Presidential candidate at the end of the series. However, the actor, John Spencer, died of a heart attack just an episode or two before the election that was to be the series closer. I wanted to give Leo the promotion he deserved—so I gave it to Daniel.

The obvious choice for Zachary's new Chief of Staff was Cornelia Day. She had made it clear in Zachary's Christmas that she knew how to manage the barrage of information and people who would want the President's time.

But who was waiting for Cornelia? How was this woman who I had made so sharp and so daunting going to fine true love?

That's when I found an account that said several chiefs of staff over the years had made the White House Situation Room into their second office. So, I began researching the Sit Room and discovered that the staff of duty watch officers only ever serve a two-year tour.

There was my answer: who would be so good, so skilled, that he would stay in that role long term. Enter Damien Feinman.

And to contrast him with Cornelia, I gave him a part of myself. I have always reveled in finding the humor in any situation. I have learned to keep much of that amusement to myself over the years, but I didn't used to. I was as likely to break into an appropriate (or better yet inappropriate) snatch of a Broadway song as I was to speak. Poking fun at myself was a major priority in my life, until I realized that some of it was putting myself down, and I stopped doing that.

However, I once had a girlfriend who had an almost complete lack of a sense of humor. She was very different from Cornelia Day, but she took herself and everything around her very seriously—I gave that to my heroine. (How she put up with me for as long as she did I'll never know.)

It was a stark enough contrast that my friends would comment on it— frequently. And that contrast is what gave me Damien Feinman whenever he was around Cornelia. (I heard from a mutual acquaintance years later, that my ex-girlfriend had eventually developed a great sense of humor of her own. I like to think I had some part in that.)

The last piece to developing Damien was a realization that I've written so little about libraries and librarians. I love the former and really love the latter —I even married one. She tells me I would have made a great librarian and I often wish that I'd had the idea to pursue that as a career, but I didn't. So, Damien was a chance to bring a librarian into the story, which ultimately gave me the excuse to use the greatest library of them all for my story's climax.

Why is this the final book in The Night Stalkers White House romance series? There is a lifecycle to a series. It is born in a moment of hope and possibility. That start is followed by book upon book of discovery: characters barging in with stories to tell, a lifecycle to the plot moving on. And ultimately, with the final book, there comes a moment of completeness.

This became the last book in the series because it completed the stories that I wanted to tell about this place, this time, and these people. There may be some future time when I revisit them, but for now, I have told all of the stories that I found there.

I know from past experience that I will have a period where I mourn their loss. They were companions as I traveled through the cycle of the seasons that occur out in the world.

But I also find great joy in them. It is a cycle of story well told and greatly enjoyed, by me. That is why I write. To spend time with characters I find fascinating and to tell their stories.

It isn't to chase publishing markets or to make a dollar more in one place than I might have elsewhere. It is to tell story...no, to discover story. And to reach that place where my cycle is complete and that story is told in all of its completeness.

I know that tomorrow I will be starting on another book in another series. That I will hope-discover-complete those stories and series as well.

But for now, there is this moment between the completion a series, but before it launches out into the world and becomes an object for sale.

In this now, I sit here with a strange smile on my face and a feeling beyond peace...perhaps it is serenity.

I could wish you no greater gift than to find that end of story, end of series moment of happiness and contentment.

...full well knowing the joy that awaits you around the corner of tomorrow.

CHAPTER ONE

Standing on the threshold of the White House Situation Room shouldn't be this strange, but Cornelia could not remember a single moment of greater change in her life. Taking the next step seemed beyond her capabilities. And it wasn't merely the Situation Room—which was actually a large complex of rooms in the basement of the West Wing. This was the entry to the President's Briefing Room, the keystone conference room. This is where the nation's hardest decisions were made and she absolutely didn't belong here.

"Well, here's a day I never thought I'd see," President-elect Zachary Thomas chuckled from close behind her. "The day anything would slow down Ms. Cornelia Day."

Fighting to keep her reactions to herself, she took the step, and the next five, her heels echoing as she crossed the pale gold marble and then onto the dark blue of the carpet surrounding the conference table. In her eight years as Vice President Thomas' assistant, she had never entered this room. *Didn't he know that?*

The dark walnut table had six armchairs down either side. At the near end was the lone chair that must be the President's and at the far end there was a wall of video screens. More chairs lined either sidewall as well as more large screens.

The room felt wrong, too simple for what it was. The governor's conference room in Colorado was several times larger and much more nicely appointed. Of course the Roosevelt Room and Cabinet Room upstairs were just opposite the Oval Office, but the Situation Room should look like more than an afterthought. It was so small for what happened here. If all the chairs were filled it would be more cramped than the coach section on an airplane.

Then she looked at the clock. Local time and—she barely managed a breath against the tightness building in her chest—President time. He had his own clock. Nothing so succinctly stated the purpose of this room as him having his own clock.

She *really* didn't belong here. She didn't even know which chair would be hers, or more troubling, why it would be hers.

"This," Zachary Thomas came up beside her and rested his hand on the head chair, "will typically be mine starting on Inauguration Day."

It was the Monday after Thanksgiving. They had barely seven weeks to form their new administration. Cornelia's head hurt just thinking about how much there was to do.

"And if you don't think that's scaring the daylights out of me, you've got another think coming. That one," he pointed to his immediate left, the chair she'd stopped close behind, "is where my White House Chief of Staff will be sitting."

Cornelia rested her hand on the seat back and tried not to be physically ill. At the President of the United States' left hand. "How did this happen?"

"Cornelia."

She managed to look up at his dark eyes.

"It happened because I need someone to keep me from screwing the pooch...too often. You've been with me since before I was the Governor of Colorado, almost a dozen years. You know me better than anyone, even Anne."

Cornelia doubted that. First Lady-elect Anne Darlington-Thomas had shown a heartfelt understanding of her future husband since the day they'd met last Christmas—an affinity that neither Cornelia, nor Anne had expected. But Cornelia wasn't comfortable correcting the President-elect on her first-ever visit to the Situation Room.

"There hasn't been a policy decision in all those years that you didn't offer something on."

"Even when I disagreed with you," she managed a smile.

"Especially when you disagreed with me. You know how many people were willing to speak truth to the Governor, never mind the President? I need someone who will."

"I can't believe you did this to me, Mr. President-elect!" Daniel Darlington strode into the Situation Room.

His hearty greeting echoed Cornelia's sentiments exactly.

"Hey!" He aimed a finger at the chair her hand rested on. "That's my chair!"

Cornelia snatched her hand back.

"Nope," Zachary pointed to his right. "*That's* going to be yours very soon, Daniel."

"I still can't believe you did this to me," Daniel repeated but he moved to the designated chair and dropped into it as if there was nothing unusual. It fit him. With his immaculate suit, surfer blond hair, and charming smile, Daniel was one of the most politically savvy people, and well-liked ones, in DC. He had proven he was an exceptional White House Chief of Staff and she had no doubt that he'd make an amazing Vice President. "I'm supposed to be back on the family farm in two months. Remind me again how you convinced me to run with you?"

"I asked and you said yes. You didn't even whine much," Zachary sat in his own future chair at the head of the table. Cornelia wished he'd at least squirm a little as he did, so that she wasn't the only one so obviously out of place.

"And I expect to regret it for the rest of my days. But my wife said she'd vote for me, so I caved. Sorry Mr. President-elect, but you're not the one Alice voted for on our ticket."

"Likely story."

The two men shared smiles that told Cornelia this was going to be her life for the next four to eight years. They were both simply too pleased with themselves and each other. It didn't help that, through Anne, they were also now brothers-in-law.

Cornelia was halfway into her seat when Daniel aimed that charming smile at her.

"Careful. If this all goes wrong, you'll be the one in the Vice President's chair eight years from now. Four if I have the good sense to quit while I'm ahead."

She collapsed into her seat with far less dignity than she'd intended. She straightened both her spine and the line of her best Ann Taylor suit to regain her composure before replying.

"I will change my citizenship tomorrow," she said with all of the dignity she could muster.

"Aruba's a good choice," Daniel suggested with a casual ease that unraveled her attempts to set a tone befitting the White House Situation Room.

"I'd go with Australia," Zachary riposted. "Better beer."

Cornelia sighed. They were here for their first Sit Room briefing as the incoming administration. And if this was any indicator for how their schedule was going to go over the next four years (never mind if there were *two* terms) she would go insane managing it. Except that wouldn't be her job anymore. Zachary Thomas would have a body man and a fleet of secretaries. Her job would be about managing his information flow, not his hour-to-hour schedule. *Definitely time to up your game, Cornelia.*

"Personally," a new voice sounded from behind her, "I prefer German beer. There is a beer called Rieder Dunkle Weisse—dark white—in Bavaria. Very traditional, very local. It does not ship well and should only be drunk in Munich and only in the fall. However, considering the next five-year projection for regional stability, I would not recommend an actual citizenship change to Germany at this time, Ms. Day, nor Aruba. However, I must say that I think that chair fits you very well."

Cornelia could only look at the man aghast. Everything they'd said in one of the most secure rooms in the world and—none of it was private. She wouldn't forget that lesson soon. Which was the point of the newcomer's lesson.

The tall, dark-haired man looked vaguely professorial in a slightly rumpled suit. But in contrast his bearing and broad shoulders said military. His New York accent went well with the slightly pompous tone of his thinking he was the smartest one in the room.

———

Damien Feinman always enjoyed this moment, though he knew it was no surprise to the Misters Elect. He considered this to be one of the perks of being head of the Situation Room duty watch.

Every word said in the Briefing Room was overheard by the room's National Security Council watch officers. This allowed the occupants to simply ask for any data and his watch would provide—one of their many duties. He'd always felt that a direct demonstration was the most effective on that point, which was very evident by Ms. Day's chagrined expression.

Damien had studied her file and was still scratching his head over it. Valedictorian at Claremont McKenna in three years, unheard of at that college. The debate team had won at the national level and been top three internationally for all three years she was on it—the last year as president. Straight to the Colorado Governor's office. Everyone in Washington had assumed that Governor and then Vice President Zachary Thomas was dallying with her on the side. However, shortly before he began his run for President, Zachary Thomas had married Anne Darlington—and Cornelia Day had stood as maid-of-honor. If she wasn't with the President-elect on the sly, then the intelligence indicated that she had even less of a life than he himself did.

However, Ms. Day in person was a very different woman than the one in her file. One look at her upright bearing made it impossible to imagine her doing a single improper thing. She sat like a dancer—her posture Audrey Hepburn perfect.

She stood to greet him. No, she *rose* to greet him; she even moved like a dancer. He'd had the hots for a girl in high school, for what little good it had done him, who went on to dance for the American Ballet Theatre. Ms. Day's simple rising from her chair was more graceful than Jara's dancing had been. Her merest movement made his breath catch in his throat.

The Elects offered him friendly smiles and handshakes which was kind of them. Ms. Day followed suit. She stood six-one in her two-inch heels. Her long fingers were as slender and fine as she was. There was an elegance to her that had nothing to do with her finely tailored suit. Unadorned right down to her unpainted nails except for a simple gold necklace chain. Her face was as slender as her body. Her straight fall of deep brunette hair was immaculately sliced at shoulder length and swung back and forth with the neat precision of a knife at her cautious nod of greeting.

"I'm Marine Corps Captain Damien Feinman. Situation Room, senior duty watch officer."

"Cornelia Day," her tone polite, but cautious. By using only her own name she managed to accuse him of intruding and his listening in to be unwelcome.

It was easy to see why she'd picked up the nickname "The Shark". Insanely intelligent, lean, and apparently lethal to anyone getting in the Vice President's way. Damien had heard rumors that congressmen would rather face Zachary Thomas than his assistant on any day of the week. Dangerous and, the one thing that the file communicated least of all, beautiful. She was the killer combo. *And ten gets you twenty, Damien, she's as chilly on the inside as her reputation on the outside.*

"I'm one of the National Security Council duty watch officers in charge of the Situation Room," he moved to the chair beside Daniel so that he could look at her across the table for the briefing. No normal human had a file of her caliber and he wanted to unravel the puzzle of what data was missing. He liked puzzles and the woman across from him presented a fine one. He hoped the mystery wasn't too simple to solve—so many people had only a few layers to their truth. Even the President-elect and the Vice-President-elect were not complicated men. Skilled, absolutely. Complicated? Both were moderately predictable, straightforward alpha males mitigated by a solid layer of decency and good upbringing.

"So, your job is to listen," Cornelia still sounded a bit indignant about that, but was covering it well.

"To listen and to provide. This room is manned..." he paused a beat to tease the two women currently on the watch desk, "...or perhaps I should say peopled twenty-four hours a day by a minimum staff of five personnel. Three duty officers, a communications specialist, and an intelligence analyst."

"And which are you?" Cornelia's tone said she wasn't going to cut him a single inch of slack this side of Christmas.

"He," Zachary said, "is our friendly, neighborhood anomaly."

"We keep trying to straighten him out, but it doesn't do any good," Daniel agreed.

"Details on Ms. Day," he spoke loudly into the room and watched her for a reaction, then cursed under his breath. He should have changed the order of the presentation. If she was already offended, this was just going to make things worse, but it was too late.

The screens just beyond the end of the table flashed to life. Pictures from kindergarten through the recent election day rotating on one screen and an extensive bio on the other. He didn't bother to turn to read it, having memorized the key points. Instead he watched her, but her expression revealed nothing.

"Parents divorced. Mother a senior-level Raytheon engineer and father a high-school math teacher, the latter recently incarcerated because he did that thing with a female under-age student that you aren't supposed to do." Crap! Now he was sounding like an asshole starting on the most personal point. But he'd wanted to poke at that chilly facade; couldn't resist doing so.

"Does your precious file also indicate that I have neither seen nor heard from him since I was three? Not child support, not a birthday card or Christmas present?"

It hadn't.

Her tone was absolutely flat, impossible to read hurt or pride into —*Just the facts, ma'am.* No wonder she scared the crap out of congressmen and senators alike; the woman was unreadable.

He typically started with the most personal information as a test. Most were shocked, dismayed, put off, even angered at the volume of information he had at his fingertips. Cornelia was calm and made it sound as if she was questioning his own intelligence for choosing such a starting point. There was more shock from Zachary Thomas, who had employed her for over a decade, than there was from her. That degree of composure was unique in his experience. More rather than less intriguing on his puzzle scale.

"Merely an example of the types of information we can supply." He dismissed the rest of her file with a spoken word and spent the next twenty minutes giving the room's three occupants a rundown of the capabilities of the Situation Room and its staff.

With the Misters Elect both in the top tier of the current administration, there was no need to compartmentalize information during this briefing. He'd been given authorization by the President that Ms. Day was also to be brought fully up to speed rather than awaiting Inauguration Day and her shift into the role of Chief of Staff.

For the Misters Elect this was old news. And it seemed no matter how fast he fed the information to her, Cornelia Day absorbed and cataloged it all. He wondered if it was a facade or if somehow her mind really was so quick and orderly that she could indeed remember the NSC staff's capabilities when she would have need of it.

He finished and waited, watching her.

Her smile was infinitesimal.

The cordovan-red leather portfolio—as slim as she was—that she had set on the table when she'd sat down had remained untouched, unopened. Now she reached out with her slender fingers, but merely turned it slightly so that its edge aligned more precisely with the table's.

Damien was fascinated. He'd seen plenty of men and a few women sit about this table over the years. A person, of either gender, that he couldn't read rated as either a cyborg or zombie—at least on the inside. That tiny smile gave her away as being neither.

Completely intrigued, he waited for what came next.

"You, Mr. Feinman," she inspected him with those dark brown eyes of hers. Was there a hidden laugh behind that thin smile? "Never answered my question."

Damien puzzled at that as her smile grew. What question?

He burst out laughing and slapped the table. *What was he indeed!*

The Misters Elect were looking at him as if he'd lost his mind.

He supposed that it was rude to laugh in the face of the next Commander-in-Chief, but was unable to help himself.

Both Zachary and Daniel chuckled along with him, but it was tentative. They didn't get it.

Only the woman across the table truly understood the joke and, while she didn't laugh, her smile went completely radiant—doubly so for how unexpected it was on her serious face.

Damien, still fighting for composure, rose to his feet and bowed deeply. It felt more like the curtain call at the end of *No, No, Nanette* in high school—in which he had played Jimmy the cheerful philanderer and, ironically for a Brooklyn Jew, wealthy bible salesman.

"As to what I am, my good Ms. Day," he had to fight down the laugh. "I am the *intelligent* officer..."

Which almost earned him her laugh but not quite.

"But mostly—"

———

"He's the librarian."

Cornelia twisted about to see National Security Advisor Sienna Arnson stride into the room, her long red hair fiery bright and her shapely figure looking great in a Diane von Furstenberg dress. A woman who wore bright summer colors at the beginning of the DC winter and could somehow make it work. Her own charcoal slacks and jacket seemed dowdy beside the NSA.

Sienna sat in the chair beside Cornelia and directly across from Damien. But Sienna's answer did little to explain the man.

"You're...what?" Librarian was about the last title Cornelia would have expected.

Damien sighed for his stolen thunder and dropped back into his seat.

"You lack," she resisted the urge to ask if he bought his suits at Sears, "the military snap and precision I would expect from a handsome Marine Corps Captain. Now I understand why." And she should *not* have said handsome even if it was undeniable.

"Story of my life," Damien agreed and scowled at Sienna. Then he turned to Cornelia but raised his voice. "Story of my life, please."

In moments the briefing screens were filled with an array of images: high school photo, looking sharp in Marine blues complete with gold buttons, white hat, and sword. Damien Feinman looked good in his present suit whatever its origin, but he was remarkable in his dress uniform.

She scanned the biographic feed. High school drama department. Library school and Naval ROTC—odd combination. He was two months younger than she was—selfless Pisces to her own overly determined Capricorn. Marine Corps intelligence at Quantico for two years. Ten years at—

"I thought National Security Council assignments to the White House Situation Room were only for two-year tours."

"That's why he's our anomaly," Zachary repeated his earlier statement.

But Damien wasn't looking at Zachary or at her. He was looking at the screens.

Cornelia followed the direction of his gaze and sighed. She didn't have an eidetic memory; no photograph of the information existed in her head—there was far too much of it. But she was *very* good at picking out what didn't fit in an array of information. Many people, especially those subjected to her occasional in-vain attempts at relationships, found her ability disconcerting. She could see him wondering how she had zeroed in on that so quickly.

She read more during his puzzled silence. He too had been valedictorian and his climb through the ranks had been at a pace even combat officers rarely achieved. Clearly he too rose to a challenge.

"Now that you know how this place works," Sienna spoke up, "let's get into our first current affairs briefing. Until now, your intel briefings have been background material and longer term issues. As the others are already up to speed on world affairs, please let me know if I'm going too fast for you, Ms. Day. Starting with Africa."

The screens shifted again, but Cornelia wasn't watching them.

She was watching Damien Feinman as he slowly turned from the summary of his life to look at her. He was inspecting her carefully as if she was of sudden interest. They each had their skills, was it now a "contest" to see whose were more useful?

Cornelia arched a single eyebrow to voice the challenge and he offered a nod reminiscent of his mock bow to accept it. *Game on.*

CHAPTER TWO

Cornelia didn't know why she was always felt a jolt of surprise whenever she saw the President in the White House, and yet she did every single time. Over the last two terms, she'd had very little to do with President Matthews. Her primary contacts were with his three executive secretaries and Daniel; the President himself she never interacted with. He probably didn't know who she was.

At the end of the Sienna's hour-long briefing on the world at large, but before the meeting could break up, President Peter Matthews swept into the room.

"All rise," Damien called out like a court bailiff. He sent her a saucy wink. Then he snapped a Marine-smart salute to the President. "Good morning O Commander-in-Chief, my Commander."

"Sit down before you fall down, Feinman," was the President's easy greeting.

Damien remained standing respectfully despite his outrageous welcome.

Cornelia was fascinated by the various reactions as everyone rose to their feet. Zachary and Daniel became noticeably more casual in their speech—also offering cheery, even teasing greetings to the Commander-in-Chief—yet much more formal in their manner. Ties were surreptitiously straightened, jackets that had been over the backs of chairs were hurriedly donned. Sienna Arnson smoothed her dress carefully. She herself had neither shed her jacket nor fussed with the kerchief in her breast pocket that matched her blouse. She simply rose quietly and waited.

Damien, who had seemed unable to sit still during the course of the meeting, had slowly discombobulated himself. His tie had been eased, off center. He'd run his hands deep into his hair while trying to make a point, leaving it thoroughly mussed. His jacket had been left back at the watch stations from when he'd gone off to assist with items that were challenging the rest of the staff. His shirt sleeves were rolled up unevenly.

"Did I miss the surprise part yet?" President Matthews was immaculate in his three-piece pinstripe.

Zachary and Daniel exchanged looks, not of complicity but rather of confusion.

"The surprise part?" Sienna asked uncertainly.

Damien was keeping his thoughts to himself and Cornelia chose to emulate his example.

"Oh, did I forget to tell *anyone?*" President Matthews looked very pleased with himself as he sat in the chair that Zachary had occupied during the meeting. "Not yet, Cowboy. Move down one."

"That would be Flyboy. I'm from the Air Force Academy, not the flatlands of Colorado and you know it." Zachary moved to Daniel's chair and Daniel to Damien's.

Damien, rather than taking the next chair, circled around the other end of the table.

"What?" the President asked him.

"Boys on one side, girls on the other. Seems rather trite." Cornelia was amused as Damien scooted Sienna down one seat and sat between them.

"Ms. Day," the President said courteously, proving that he did indeed know who she was.

Realizing that she was the lone person still standing, she too returned to her seat.

"First," he turned to his right, "how far are you two into your transition team?"

Zachary and Daniel exchanged worried looks.

"They," Cornelia used the term loosely, "have filled just under three hundred of one-thousand-forty-two open positions," and Cornelia had made most of those decisions herself because her boss had been too busy catching up with his Vice Presidential job since the election.

"When did that happen?" The President-elect did a poor job of covering for himself, as usual.

Cornelia kept her sigh to herself, but could hear Damien chuckle.

"That explains the steady stream of intelligence and personnel-clearance requests we've been processing lately."

She turned, a little startled at how close he suddenly was, seated in the next chair beside her.

"I've only told you part of what we do here. Those requests cross our desks as well. Never dull here, I can promise you."

She'd remember that.

"You two geniuses," the President addressed the Misters Elect, "do have the good sense to keep Sienna as National Security Advisor, don't you?"

Again Zachary and Daniel exchanged quick glances.

Cornelia read the look and made a mental note. "I'll get that taken care of. Congratulations, Ms. Arnson."

Sienna looked slightly dazed for a moment. "When they hadn't approached me, I'd just assumed—"

"That they were still too dazzled about winning the election to think clearly, even though four weeks have passed by since?" Cornelia finished the sentence for her.

"Yes, that's it exactly. The answer is yes, by the way, once they get around to asking me. I'll cancel the feelers I put out to other agencies."

"Good," the President thumped a hand on the table, cutting off Zachary the moment he opened his mouth to actually ask.

Cornelia was starting to enjoy this. The President- and Vice-President-elect were both so confident; she'd have to remember the advantages of keeping them slightly off balance.

"You two," the President continued, not giving them a chance to speak, "have an administration to prepare. You need to stop thinking about my lame duck operation and get moving."

"But—" Daniel didn't get past the first word of his protest before the President turned to her.

"You, Ms. Cornelia Day, are as of this moment, my White House Chief of Staff. Sorry Daniel, but that means I'll need your formal resignation by end of day unless you want me to fire your butt."

"I serve at the pleasure of the President," Daniel said it formally.

She could see him swallow hard. By his bewildered expression, it was going to take him a while to come to terms with the change. For herself, she simply filed the fact for later consideration. No, there wasn't even the need for that. It made absolutely logical sense. It would smooth the often rough and occasionally acrimonious transition from one administration to the next. By naming her his White House Chief of Staff, President Matthews was showing a great deal of consideration for the incoming leadership.

"I'll leave it to the two of you when to switch offices but, Daniel and Zachary, make it soon—as in today. You two need to focus on the next administration. Cornelia, go to Daniel when you get stuck, but with your reputation I don't expect that to happen very often."

Again, more than she expected, but she had sufficient self-awareness to think that she had at least some skills at her job. If not, she never would have agreed to it when Zachary had swung by her office on Election Day and said, "Of course, if I win, you're my Chief of Staff. You know that, right?" Not waiting for her answer before rushing off to his next media event.

"Ms. Day, you should be able to get much more done now that you have the power of your future job. That's effective immediately, Damien." The President pulled a folded piece of paper out of his jacket's inner pocket and handed it over to him.

Cornelia took the liberty of reading the letter over Damien's shoulder to see that the President had already formalized her transition to his Chief of Staff.

Damien nodded his assent. When he attempted to return the letter, the President indicated that it should go to her.

Right. It would now be her responsibility to make sure it was properly filed. Whatever that meant.

The President rose and they all scrambled to do the same.

He shook her hand, actually taking hers between both of his as if to solemnize the moment.

"Best of luck! You're going to need it to survive these two." He nodded at Zachary and Daniel then departed without shaking their partially extended hands, but wearing a big smile. They were all such men.

The meeting ended. Mr. President- and Mr. Vice-President-elect were already deep in consultation regarding next steps on setting up their administration as they left the room.

Sienna still looked a little dazed as she followed in their wake.

Cornelia finally managed to unlock her knees and sit back down.

"I serve at the pleasure of the President," she whispered it to herself.

"That was a hell of a kicker, wasn't it, Ms. Day?" Damien asked from so close beside her that she jolted. "Sorry, guess you forgot that I was still here. A lot happening I know. No problem, we duty officers are used to being invisible."

When he started to rise, she rested a hand on his arm to keep him in place.

He waited her out while she sorted out her jumbled thoughts. She knew exactly who she wanted to keep and not keep from the current administration. The list formed rapidly in her head. And now she could take immediate action on building her own team: speechwriters, assistant chief of staff, press relations... The list wasn't endless, and thankfully it no longer felt that way. She also had a long list of appointments that she expected Zachary Thomas would sign off on with few changes, as soon as she double checked a few of them with—

She turned to Damien who was still eyeing her hand resting on his arm.

The new White House Chief of Staff caught him studying her hand.

Her file had said no attachments, other than the now dismissed possibility of one with the President-elect, and her ringless fingers were only a confirmation of that. It was ridiculous, but he liked the look of her hands. Fine but not delicate. He was—clearly losing his mind.

"Many Chiefs of Staff," Damien told her so that he'd have something to fill the sudden silence, "make the Situation Room into their second office." Was he being overly forward in hoping that this one would as well? She was just another White House Chief of Staff, after all, and he'd seen six of those in his ten years here. She would only be Number Seven, nothing more. Yet it wasn't that simple. Was he such a cad that her gender was leading him to inappropriate preferences?

Cornelia finally withdrew her hand as if freeing him to rise and go.

If they had wild horses in DC, they weren't going to drag him away. But he couldn't think of any reason to stay beside her either. Thankfully, she spoke before good manners would make him attempt to stand once more.

"Perhaps," the surprise was gone from her voice at her sudden promotion. Over the last few minutes, somewhere in that amazing mind of hers, she had either set aside or fully integrated her changed role into her identity—and he'd bet on the latter. "You could take a moment to explain the implications of my new role from your perspective."

It was a very smart question. He had learned during the course of the briefing that it was the only kind she asked.

As he did explain, she began to relax. Not her breathtaking posture, but now removed from the powerhouse personalities of the country's leaders she began asking more questions. It had been hard to calibrate her silences during the earlier meetings. Her rare questions hadn't provided sufficient reference.

He finally pieced together what was missing: Cornelia Day was shy. He'd never have expected that of her, but the more they spoke, the more true it seemed. But shyness had nothing to do with intelligence.

Whenever Damien had to instruct new staff, he always worked to find their level of knowledge first and then teach them starting at that level. Once it was only the two of them, he found Cornelia Day's level easily enough—higher than he'd thought despite reading her file then sitting across from her these last two hours. But the more he described the NSC's capabilities, the more insightful her questions became until she was nearly speaking on Daniel's level—and he'd been Chief of Staff for five years.

"Well, that's the gist of it," he finally ground to a halt. Still she hadn't taken a single note.

She nodded, and glanced at the wall clock as if she'd been in the room enough times for it to become habit. Not at her wrist—she didn't wear a watch. No instinctive reaching for her phone—which had been confiscated at the Sit Room's entrance to avoid unauthorized calls, photos, or recordings.

"Past one," he noted. "How do you feel about lunch?"

"It depends," she looked at him without blinking as if she was going to hypnotize him.

"On?"

"On whether or not you're going to answer my question."

It wasn't enough for her that he was head of the duty watch. She was now asking the next level question of who he was that he had retained a position for ten years that none held for more than two.

He could get to really like this woman.

———

"I rarely eat here," Cornelia told Damien while the waiter eased in her blue leather chair as she sat down. The wood-paneled walls of the Navy Mess in the basement of the White House were adorned with large paintings of the Navy's ships dating from when the national fleet moved only by sea and wind.

"Where do you usually eat? *Do* you usually eat?" Damien's nod to her slender body was frank and easy-going.

She'd heard that one often enough. Her metabolism burned calories at an alarming rate. Missing a meal could set her into a lightheaded tailspin if she wasn't careful.

He'd recovered his jacket, but his tie was still in disarray and she resisted the urge to straighten it. He dropped into his chair and hopped it toward the table, pinching his hand between chair arm and the underside of the table with a silverware-rattling bang.

"I typically opt for a sandwich at my desk or a takeout salad from a nearby coffee shop when I'm working at the Vice President's office in the Eisenhower Executive Office Building." The VP's only staff space in the White House was an office with an assistant's outer office —which until an hour ago had been her exclusive domain for eight years.

Damien looked around critically, "I actually can't remember the last time I ate here. My shift allows little time for breaks."

"And yet today, here you are."

He turned his attention fully back upon her. His gaze locked on with such a force as to be palpable. "And yet today, here I am."

She almost asked after the occasion, hoping for a different answer than she suddenly expected, and then decided against it. It was one of those moments that was either to curry her favor because she had easy access to President-elect Zachary Thomas, or it was because...she sighed to herself. Why did men always treat her like a woman rather than a person?

"A chance to dine with..." he offered a friendly smile, warning her all too well that his next words would be *such a beautiful*—"...the new Chief of Staff."

Not quite what she expected, making her glad she'd internalized her sigh.

Very glad actually. Having spent most of the morning with Damien, she was rather enjoying his company. He lacked the hard DC edge that so many people acquired here. At times she was afraid that she had acquired that edge as well, and past all recovery.

"You have an unanswered question," he showed enough wisdom to change the topic. "I'm a fourth generation librarian on one side and a third generation Marine on the other."

He waited, but she didn't know for what. For her to step into the middle of some assumption? Instead, she ordered the chicken fajita salad and a glass of caffeine-free Diet Coke—she needed neither high, chemical nor sugar—and kept her silence. That appeared to amuse him as he ordered a burger and a root beer.

"My great-great-grandfather on my father's side was one of Carnegie's first librarians right here in DC."

"That would be five generations."

"My grandfather was a black sheep and made his living as an insurance salesman. No one can account for him, least of all my grandmother."

"That makes you a Marine on your mother's side?"

"It does. Grandma was in the Marine Corps during Vietnam through Desert Storm—clerical work. Mom served in a somewhat more enlightened age and is still an MV-22 Osprey pilot—though just a stateside trainer now."

"Which explains what about you?" Actually it told her a great deal —high intelligence, deep motivation, and an unusual view of the world. But she wanted to know what conclusions it had given him.

"As the first one to combine the two professions, it has given me an immense respect for strong women." This time his nod to her communicated just that.

Cornelia wasn't quite sure what to do with the sudden warmth inside her. People always saw her as a political player without being a woman at all, or as a woman who could only possibly be interested in marrying well in Washington no matter how often she proved otherwise. Each election cycle she had to deal with all of the freshman senators and congressmen coming to meet the Vice President and thinking they were God's gift to his "lonely" assistant. The offers had redoubled with his marriage this spring when it became clear that the rumors about them having a romantic connection were untrue. She'd tried wearing a ring for a while, but that had only served to increase the seediness of the propositions.

She wondered if Damien was the first person to see her as both woman and political player at once. Her mother certainly didn't. All she saw was a daughter she loved but didn't begin to understand.

The setting of the Navy Mess in the White House basement was beautiful, the food excellent, and the company...exceptional. The conversation ranged widely across literature, politics, and his mother's service experience as a female Marine.

It was only after she was climbing the stairs back to the first floor that she realized that Damien had still managed to avoid answering her question of why he was the long-serving "anomaly," though she no longer thought it was intentional. Or perhaps he had. His intelligence and clear insights placed him sufficiently above any norm that his position made sense.

Cornelia swung by her office, but Daniel was at her desk and on her phone, deep in conversation. She continued down the hall and stepped into the Chief of Staff's secretary's office.

"Good afternoon, Ms. Day. May I help you?"

"Good afternoon, Janet." Daniel's secretary was an institution, guiding the secretarial pool like a steady helmswoman on a storm-tossed sea. An apt metaphor after staring at the nautical wall paintings in the Navy Mess over lunch. Though Janet looked more ready for a spot of tea than to sail a ship.

In addition to her computer, Janet's desk had a notepad, a framed picture of her husband and family, and a small Christmas tree made of copper wire curled up like branches each dangling a cheerily colored ornamental ball. The day after Thanksgiving weekend, it was the first sign she'd seen of Christmas in the White House.

Cornelia handed over the President's letter, "I suppose you can make sure this goes wherever it needs to go."

Janet read it quickly, nodded once, and set it in the center of her desk. "I'll take care of it, Ms. Day."

"No reaction?" Cornelia couldn't resist asking.

"Perhaps *About damned time!* would suffice," she raised her voice for only a moment. "That is, if you're asking for my personal thoughts." Janet smiled pleasantly. "You're enough to make me rethink retiring. I like Daniel immensely, but I rather expect you will be more fun to work for. Don't fear, ma'am—"

"Cornelia."

"Yes, ma'am. I'll stick around at least through the transition. Let's go look at your new office." She rose from her desk. Janet was trim, neatly gray-haired, and dressed in better than average Nordstrom. A single strand of pearls and matching earrings spoke of a woman from some era prior to the one she actually belonged in.

Cornelia stepped over the threshold casually this time—concentrating so that Janet would have no cause to tease her—and came to a stop in the middle of the room as naturally as possible.

To her right was a grand fireplace. The Chief of Staff, *she!*, had one of the two corner offices on the same floor as the Oval Office—National Security Advisor Sienna Arnson had the other—which gave her two walls of windows. The last wall had large panoramic photos that she assumed were the Darlington's Tennessee farm.

For herself...perhaps she would see if the White House collection or the National Archives had any renderings of the Lincoln-Douglas debates. She had studied those debates very carefully and it had become the key structure for her own successes. The most prized volume in her library was the first edition of Lincoln's collection of those debates that Mom had given her as a college graduation present.

The office's general motif was cream and white. A couch and a couple of armchairs formed a group by the fireplace. A long white-washed-oak conference table dominated the corner window space. The open curtains gave her a view of her old office in the EEOB and to the south: the pergola and masking trees of the Oval Office patio, as well as the back of the pool's cabana. She'd never sat out on the stone-flagged patio and now she had her own private door to it.

The last corner of her office was filled with a large, wrap-around desk with several guest chairs...and a pile of folders so deep that there was little chance of seeing any guests from the big desk chair beyond.

"I swear that man does his filing by tornado," Janet huffed out. "I've never seen him hesitate to find a file, but the Lord alone knows how it's done."

Cornelia circled around enough to see that there were even a few piles on the floor under the desk. She didn't want to disparage her predecessor, especially as he was going to be her Vice President, but this would never do.

"I think you need a garbage can," Janet voiced the thought for her. "Several."

"I'll get you a stack of burn bags," Janet agreed heartily. "The extra large kind."

If only it could be so simple. What she really needed was a librarian. But she wasn't about to call the one who…she looked down at the wall-to-wall carpet in some surprise.

"What is it, dear?"

Her office was exactly on top of the Situation Room. Damien's watch desk would be directly under the patio outside her window—perhaps she wouldn't be going out there. She took a deep breath and waved Janet over.

She sat in the chair Cornelia indicated.

"Okay. Let's sort through this and see what we have."

Cornelia might need a librarian, but she definitely wasn't calling Damien.

....

CHAPTER THREE

....

Damien glared at his phone.

It had rung a hundred times over the last week, but not once had it been a call to warn him that the Chief of Staff was on her way down to the Sit Room. She'd been here any number of times, slipping along in the wake of the President or the President-elect each time, and then hurrying out as if avoiding him.

Had he been too pushy? He knew he was bad about that. Every time he met an attractive woman, his mind immediately painted all of the possible scenarios. And with Cornelia Day his imagination had been working overtime. He could see her laughing easily whenever he dug deep enough to find that funny bone she struggled so hard to keep hidden. He could picture quiet dinners together. And, just as easily as he could imagine how she might look morning-tousled, he could picture her growing old and how stunning an—

"Shit!"

"What's wrong?" both Bettani and Gerardo startled from their duty watch officer positions to either side of his central seat.

"Nothing!" He was just being his normal idiot self.

"I know that look," Bettani accused him.

"No, you don't!" He glared at her. The three of them sat on the upper tier of workstations, each with triple computer screens. Marko, the communications specialist, and Felice, the intelligence analyst, sat in the row directly in front of them, just low enough to not block anyone's sightlines to the big screens on the walls.

Marko and Felice were now turning around to look up at him.

"I absolutely know that look," Marko crowed.

"Shit!" No way this was going to get any better. Pulling on his "Marine Corps" wasn't going to save him any grief either.

"Who is she?" His coworkers exchanged looks, but no one had caught on. That was some relief.

"No way!" He informed them. A warble tone and he dove for the phone. *Saved by the bell.* He spotted the display the moment before he spoke. "Good morning, Ms. Day. How may I be of assistance?"

He could see Bettani exchanging a startled glance with Marko. They mouthed whispers at each other.

"Day?"

"The new Chief of Staff."

Their stereo "Ohs" and knowing nods had him turning away to glare at Gerardo who had the decency to find sudden interest in the data on his screens.

"Do you ever make house calls?" Cornelia's voice didn't have the businesslike brusqueness that he'd overheard during meetings in the Sit Room. Instead it was...gentler. Still business, but less fiercely so.

Then her question registered and that stopped Damien for a second. "House calls?"

"I have—"

Bettani made a small whoop of delight close behind him that stopped Cornelia cold.

"I have," she had to clear her throat to start again, "some issues here and, frankly, would appreciate the assistance of a trained librarian."

He glanced at the queue on his screen—seriously ugly at the moment. White House Chief of Staff Cornelia Day had not been neglecting her massive duties to the new administration, despite being immersed in the old one, and had inundated his team with background checks and information requests. Then Damien turned further and caught sight of Bettani's knowing smirk. That's when he decided that she could just double up on her workload for a while.

"I'll be there in a minute," he hung up. Anger wasn't in his usual repertoire, but he could feel it coursing through him. It built as he rose, straightened his tie, and donned his jacket.

"Gotta be all purty for your date," Bettani drew out the words in an obnoxious singsong.

He slammed his palm on the back of her chair forcing her to turn and fully face him.

Damien got right up in her face.

"You do *not*, I repeat, *not ever* talk about the White House Chief of Staff or any other senior staff with anything but the utmost respect. Not in my Sit Room. We clear?"

Bettani was wide-eyed in shock. He could see Marko out of the corner of his eye also in shock.

He slammed her chair back to facing her console, "Now get some goddamn work done. I want that queue caught up before I return."

Damien stormed out of the room. It had never been so silent.

———

"Perhaps this wasn't a good time," she greeted him as Damien arrived in her office. Cornelia could almost see curls of steam coming off his collar.

"No, it's fine," he paced from the holly-bedecked fireplace mantel to the twinkle-light framed windows and back. She and Janet had selected carefully from the decorator's offerings and she thought that their choices had made the office cheery yet tasteful. Wishing to be non-denominational, she had vetoed the crèche for the center of her conference table in favor of a Victorian porcelain Santa's sleigh with reindeer. The effect was warm and pleasant, but Damien didn't appear to notice as he steamrollered up and down her carpet. Maybe he didn't like Christmas.

Finally he plummeted into the chair across her now immaculate desk—which bore only her portfolio and a small wire-form tree to match Janet's—practically snarling as he did so.

She merely raised an eyebrow and waited him out.

"I just made a complete jackass of myself," he sighed and continued to study something in the vicinity of his feet. "Not unusual, but I really did it spectacularly this time."

"About what?"

His eyes flickered to hers for a moment, then back to his feet.

"Okay," Cornelia did what she could to catch her breath. She wished she'd left a few of Daniel's files on her desk so that she had something to occupy her hands for a moment. She could think of several possible scenarios. First woman in the job. Or merely the first person to follow in Daniel's immensely popular footsteps. Or was it...personal?

"Let's just say," his smile grew and shifted wryly sideways as if he was finally starting to see some humor in the situation, "that I became a little defensive."

"I wouldn't know anything about that."

He laughed aloud; she'd never met someone who laughed so easily. "Do tell."

"During my first trip to the Hill as Chief of Staff, I met a wide range of aides and congressman who did not consider me to be worthy of my predecessor."

"To hell with them."

"That is not really an option. I have to—"

"No! Seriously, Ms. Day, to hell with them. If they want access to the President, this one or the next, they're going to have to go through you. They damn well better get used to it."

She'd never thought of it that way. "For Zachary Thomas as first Governor then Vice President, my responsibilities were...defensive."

"Guarding the gates like a good Marine," he nodded a solid confirmation.

"Now, it is less clear. I am discovering that I am an extension of the President's voice, or I'm trying to be."

"Do. Or do not. There is no try."

"And now you're quoting Yoda at me?"

Damien shrugged and slipped a little lower in his chair.

"Are you sure you're a Marine?"

"You asked for a librarian's help, so that's who I brought. I left the Marine downstairs," then he grimaced. "Oh brother did I."

Cornelia almost asked for details, then thought better of it. Straightening her jacket, she turned to the matters at hand.

———

Damien loved the gesture. It was like Captain Picard straightening his uniform just before he gave an order. Cornelia Day in command of a starship wearing a form-clinging Star Trek outfit. *Wow!* Way better than Janeway. Even better than Dr. Beverly Crusher who he'd had a weak spot for from the very first episode.

"The quantity of information flowing toward the President," Cornelia folded her hands neatly on her desk as she spoke, "is staggering. At the moment I'm trying to manage two administrations and it is completely overwhelming."

"Despite the evidence of your immaculate desk."

"Twelve burn bags and three new filing cabinets."

He could easily believe it; he'd seen Daniel's desk before.

"I'm seeking suggestions on the proper filtering and organization of information."

Now *that* was his kind of problem.

As they discussed the options he couldn't help watching her stillness. It was strictly external—her mind was moving at an incredibly rapid pace. It was as if her thought processes consumed all of her attention until there was nothing left over for her physicality. Even her eyeblinks were alarmingly wide-spaced; he could feel his own eyes going dry from unconsciously matching her steady gaze.

"One page," he finally suggested. They'd discussed a dozen different techniques: priority tagging, electronic queuing, and others.

"One page?" She tilted her head to the side, the tips of her hair now draping across her shoulder rather than brushing her collarbone. Her long neck elegantly on display. She made him want to see things that he definitely shouldn't be thinking about the Chief of Staff... though he had to admit that he had been thinking them all week.

"Mom had a colonel who used to say that if someone couldn't distill their idea down into a single page, then they hadn't finished thinking it through enough. I've never forgotten that. What's the average length of a memo delivered to your desk?"

For the first time since he'd first seen her, she opened her tablet computer. She tapped a few keys, stroked her finger down a spreadsheet column, and studied the result.

No guesses for Cornelia Day and an indexing system that included number of pages. This woman was making his inner librarian swoon with delight.

"Average is eleven pages with a first standard deviation of only three."

"Don't these people know how to communicate a thought?"

"Oddly," more taps on the screen, "other than the head speechwriter, not a one. His average memos are typically two pages and his speeches trend six minutes shorter than any prior writer's."

"Hire that man!"

"I already did," she didn't even look up from her screen. "His assistant averages fourteen pages and eleven minutes longer than the last decade's average."

"Fire his ass!" Damien felt like he was becoming a swashbuckling captain on an old cutter. "Keelhaul the blaggard!"

Cornelia raised a single eyebrow at him, à la Mr. Spock.

"Seriously. A speechwriter who—" And then Damien snapped his mouth shut. He was talking to the White House Chief of Staff about one of her key staff members, one who'd been with the administration for over three years. That was seven kinds of inappropriate. "Sorry."

"Interesting," Cornelia mulled the thought.

"Are you channeling Mr. Spock intentionally?"

"Who? Oh, the Star Wars character? No."

Damien groaned and slapped his hands over his heart.

"What?"

"Star Trek! Not Star Wars!"

Her thin smile was unreadable. Tolerant perhaps? It goaded him on.

"You were doing great as my fantasy woman right up until that moment." Then he heard his own words and bolted upright in his chair. Unable to contain his embarrassment, he jolted to his feet. "I'm sorry, ma'am. I have deeply overstepped the bounds of propriety. Please allow me to formally apologize. If you wish to file a complaint, I will make no argument." He held parade rest, looking straight ahead at the wall.

Cornelia was a long time answering. "I've never been anyone's fantasy woman before."

"Then, if you don't mind my saying so, ma'am, every man you've met is an idiot." He sighed. "Definitely including this one."

"Sit down please, Mr. Feinman."

After checking to see that she actually meant it, he settled slowly back into the chair.

"First, let us dispose of the question regarding the assistant speechwriter."

That snapped his attention back to her, but he didn't trust himself to speak. He'd just embarrassed himself in front of his team and now in front of her and she was pretending as if nothing happened.

"I suspect," she still studied her tablet, "that the head speechwriter doesn't approve of him much. I observe here that his speeches are relegated to the less critical staff and occasions."

———

And I observe over there a handsome man who has just called me his fantasy woman.

No one had ever called her that. Her lack of allure was something she'd come to accept about herself. Her skills were in the workplace, not the bedroom. Her lovers never stuck. They arrived as often as she let them, but they consistently departed fast enough that there was no question who was the problem in the relationship—six-week average with a two-week first standard deviation. The outliers were a one-night mistake and a four-month data point that never should have occurred. She'd have cast out the latter except she hadn't had that many relationships and without him her averages slid downward badly.

By staying focused on the White House speechwriters, she managed to control her reactions. Not only did the compliment move her, but also Damien's instant and complete retraction. No, not retraction. He hadn't unsaid his words, he'd merely apologized for them in a remarkably sincere way.

She really didn't have time for "charming" at this moment in her life, but Damien Feinman absolutely was.

"Perhaps," he tested her silence—which was a blessing as she had no idea what to say. "Perhaps you should find a better speechwriter."

"Perhaps..." With the thought planted, it only took her a moment to recall a couple of speeches she had heard that indicated a great writer behind them. It only took her a few moments to think of who. When she did, it made her sigh.

"What's wrong?"

"He's a writer for the other party."

"So? Does he want to be writing for the President of the United States? That's the real question."

"I'll have to ask. Thank you, Damien." It was a very good idea. And it was out of the box of too-easily accepted partisanship. She'd definitely have to remember that. *Get out of the box.*

"My pleasure, ma'am." So, he was going to remain safe behind his formality. It wasn't mere politeness. She could hear the Marine ingrained deep in him by both the Corps and his mother.

"Stepping back to the one-page concept," she wasn't yet ready to confront the main topic that still lay untouched upon her desk.

"Yes," Damien cleared his throat and relaxed slightly. "The entire idea must be presentable in a single sheet. There can be and typically should be supporting documentation, but the core of it must be pared down to the essentials. Two pages at the very most, but push for one."

"Perhaps I should require it to be double-spaced as well."

Damien's burst of laughter had her looking up from the tablet, which had long since blanked to save its battery.

She raised the Spock eyebrow at him again. Did Damien actually believe that she didn't know about Spock? She'd had a crush on the half-Vulcan ever since her mom had introduced her to the classic Trek as a pre-teen. She'd felt like a traitor switching her allegiance from Nimoy to Quinto as an adult, but at least he was within a decade of her own age. Teasing a man was not in her standard repertoire, but

Damien was so sure of himself that she was finding it difficult to resist.

"I like the evil way that you think," Damien was slowly relaxing back into his chair. "I'd give them the single-spaced permission, but you'd best specify a minimum font size or you'll go blind in short order."

"Definitely," she agreed. It was easy to share his smile on that. "As to the final point..."

Cornelia took a deep breath. She couldn't think of the right way to confront it. The early December darkness had fallen even before they'd started and now it was well past time to leave. Janet had signaled from the door an hour ago that the President had returned to the Residence for the night and she was going home.

For her entire first week as the Chief of Staff she'd been avoiding Damien because...

Because she was attracted to him? He was a very attractive man, she'd have to be dead to not notice.

Perhaps she should go out of the box, the one she kept drawn so carefully about herself. She took a deep breath and decided to be brave.

"Damien. Do you have any plans for dinner?"

His face displayed a brief battle between surprise and delight.

When the latter won, she decided that perhaps she didn't mind being someone's fantasy woman. For as long as it lasted anyway.

CHAPTER FOUR

D*amien had to struggle* against being dazzled.

"Take me to your favorite place to eat."

Had she said "restaurant" he'd have struggled to think of somewhere nice, but "to eat" had only one answer.

"It isn't upscale or Californian or—"

"That's fine."

So, he'd taken her at her word.

Ten minutes on the Metro and a couple minutes of chilly walking at either end didn't seem to affect her in the slightest. Donning only a stylish but understated blue wool coat and thin black gloves, she appeared untouched by the freezing evening. Her scarf was a cheery knit in Christmas reds and greens; it gave her color and made her eyes and chill-reddened cheeks appear brighter.

He second-guessed himself all of the way to Molly Malone's. The big oak tree out front had long since lost its leaves for the year, but it was so thickly strung with multi-colored Christmas lights that there seemed to be as many bulbs as there had been leaves. It lit the while stretch of sidewalk as if the tree were the shining Star of Bethlehem.

The moment Cornelia stepped through the door, she shouted out, "It's perfect!"

"Glad you approve!" A gorgeous, urbanite, DC insider who thought a cozy pub was perfect place for dinner. What wasn't to like.

Molly's was the best Irish pub outside of Ireland. The brick walls dated back nearly as far as the Marine Barracks across the street—the oldest in the country. "Irish" decorated the walls—there was no other good word for it. Old cruise line posters, paintings of ships, photos of rambling greensward and rocky coasts, all capped by a massive picture of the mythical warrior-hero Finn MacCool. All of the trimwork was in rich woods that really did hearken back to the mother land—even for a third-generation Brooklynite like himself.

For the season, tiny live Christmas trees in pots had appeared on every available ledge and surface. Wreaths adorned the few open spaces on the brick walls, and painfully bright stars shaped from white neon lights only enhanced the normally gaudy atmosphere of the place.

However, he'd forgotten it was Friday night. The downstairs booths and bar were packed solid.

"You brought me to a Marine bar?" Cornelia leaned in close enough for him to hear her, smell her, practically feel the heat from her body despite her coat.

"I did." He had. And once again he was second-guessing himself. The place was filled with them. "The Marine Barracks is directly across the street. Sorry, I wasn't thinking."

"You dare to bring a woman to a bar filled with Marines at their prime? You really are a brave man. Do you think I can find a handsome flute player to take me home?"

"I'll snap his damned pipe if he tries," Damien growled out, earning him a smile and a gloved hand tucked about his elbow. Of course she'd know that the Marine Band was housed at the oldest Marine barracks in the country. The location selected by Thomas Jefferson himself when they were laying out the city. "Let's try upstairs."

And then he laughed aloud.

She looked at him quizzically but he just shook his head.

She had elicited exactly the response from him that she'd intended—a Marine-like snap and growl. The thing she probably didn't understand, was that he meant it. *Really* meant it. He wasn't merely feeling protective about Cornelia; he was feeling possessive. It wasn't his place, but if another man tried to touch her, he'd have to be careful not to punch him. And wasn't that the biggest joke of all. *Damien Feinman, totally gone on a woman.*

A table vacated just as they finished battling their way up the big staircase to the second floor. A quick dive and grab and they got it before anyone else.

He was just about to take her coat when a slap on his back knocked him into her. Only a quick hand against the brick wall and another around her waist kept them from both going to the floor.

"Look who crawled out from under his big white rock!" Mick was waving over a group of Marine Intelligence guys who must have arrived close behind them.

"What the hell are you doing here?" Damien tried to snarl it out but he was too busy focusing on letting go of Cornelia. His hand didn't want to leave her waist. She might be impossibly lean, but he felt her strength as well. And so warm though her thin silk blouse. His hand had slipped inside both her coat and her unfastened designer jacket when he'd grabbed her.

"Training a bunch of plebes. Intel 101—Marine style—for Career Day. *Here's what we do. Come join us!* Same old, same old. You know the drill."

He did; it had worked well enough on him—eighteen and trying to figure out how to afford University of North Carolina at Chapel Hill's stellar library program. Naval ROTC had paved the way. Doubling down on political science had been his golden ticket.

In moments his quiet dinner with Cornelia Day had turned into a free-for-all with the two of them trapped against the back wall as more and more people showed up. Soon there were seven of them at a table for four.

"Christ, Lady," Brion looked at Cornelia. "What the hell is a looker like you doing with a loser like Damien? Please tell me you have more of a sense of humor than his usual pickups."

Before Damien could leap to her defense, Cornelia planted an elbow on the table and her chin on her palm. He didn't even know her spine unbent enough to be able to do that. It did leave him sitting just a little behind her and able to follow her shoulders' lines. Very nice indeed.

"Maybe I should take the Fifth on that until I know more," she faced them as smoothly as she did everything. "His usual lot?"

"Analysts," Vaccaro joined in. "He's got this wicked weak spot for analysts. Some are cute enough, but frankly boring as hell."

"Tell us you're not boring as hell."

"Yeah. Or we'll have to go find another table."

Please! Damien thought loudly but was unable to get a word in edgewise around his friends. He checked on Cornelia, but she was giving no sign that any of this was bothering her.

"Naw, mate," Caron leaned in. "Not an open table in the lot. 'Sides, you see any others as fine-looking as her to spend an evening with? No offense, ma'am. But you are a real pleasure to be sitting near."

"You sure you're with him?" Mick tipped his head toward Damien in disgust. "Any of us would be glad to show you what a real Marine is like."

"A real Marine?"

She was answered by a chorus of, "Aye!" and "You betcha!"

"I don't think so," she sat up once again, ever so primly perfect. "I didn't hear a single 'ooh-rah' in the bunch. So apparently, not a Marine in sight. What is a damsel to do?"

The guys all looked properly chagrined.

Damien burst out laughing and before he could stop himself, gave her a brief hug around the shoulders. She was amazing. And felt amazing.

"You're incredible," he whispered in the moment that she let herself tip into him.

"Didn't get an ooh-rah from you either," she whispered back.

"Librarian first. Marine second. But I'll ooh-rah for you anytime you want."

"So do it."

"Ooh-rah!" He managed a good one before the laughter overtook him. It was echoed up and down the restaurant by any number of patrons. The call echoed from downstairs as well.

More importantly, she leaned into him a moment longer, before sitting upright once more. No woman, dressed or not, had ever felt so good in his arms.

"That sounds like my call!" A deep voice spoke from the head of the table.

Damien looked up then scrambled to his feet as did the other Marines. They all snapped sharp salutes even though none of them were in uniform. General Arnson returned it smartly.

"Crap! When a bunch of intel geeks salute me like it means something, makes me wonder if I'm getting old."

Vaccaro found the general a chair and they all squeezed in tighter. It left Cornelia constantly bumping him from shoulder to hip. The turn of the corner on the other side kept her from nudging up against Brion.

"Ms. Day," the general nodded. "Been hearing good things about you from my daughter."

"Your daughter?"

"Sienna," Damien prompted her.

She inspected the newcomer. If his daughter was National Security Advisor Sienna Arnson, that meant this distinguished gentleman was Brigadier General Edward Arnson. He headed up HMX-1, the helicopter squadron responsible for Marine One and the thirty other VIP transport and support rotorcraft. His reputation was beyond sterling.

"A pleasure to meet you, sir. I've traveled aboard your aircraft with the Vice President."

She managed to keep her smile to herself as all of the others around the table looked at her in surprise.

"And you call yourselves Marine Intelligence," the general sounded disgusted but his eyes gave away his amusement. "Not a one of you dolts thought to ask her name?"

"They didn't," she couldn't resist rubbing it in. "Apparently I am merely 'a looker' who was picked up by a passing Marine because she couldn't help herself around him." She did her best to bat her eyelashes at Damien and had never felt so ridiculous.

He, however, looked very pleased with himself at the moment.

She rather liked that the others had sought him out and were willing to tease her. It said a great deal about Damien and the closeness he engendered in his friends. A skill she knew that she lacked but could definitely admire.

And teasing was not something she was used to. She'd taken the palm-on-chin pose from some movie, she couldn't remember which one but it had been accepted. That she'd been able to give back as good as she got rather surprised her.

Damien slid an arm across the back of her chair as if staking his territory. Cornelia would have to see about him not getting too self-assured. She considered a gentle elbow in the ribs, but couldn't think how to make it look normal rather than something from a self-defense class.

The general shook his head sadly at the state of affairs, doing only a moderate job of hiding his own smile.

"Day," Brion twisted to her in surprise. "Cornelia Day? The new White House Chief of Staff?"

"A glimmer of light at last," the general groaned.

"Holy hell, mate," Caron smacked Damien hard on the arm. "Good on ya!"

"You see, Ms Day?" The general looked at her, a friendly smile lighting his face. "This is what they give me to work with. I wish you better luck with that one." The gnarled finger that he pointed at Damien wasn't threatening. Instead it was as if he was pointing out the best of poor choices.

She looked around the table and decided that if these were the "poor choices" then the Marine Corps was in awfully good shape.

"I need a beer," the general groaned even more dramatically.

"Make it two and I'll join you," Cornelia replied with some bit of humor she hadn't known she possessed.

"That's a deal, Ms. Day. We'll just leave the rest of this lot to fend for themselves."

———

The meal had passed in a single breath.

Damien had breathed in a quick gasp anticipating total disaster when the others joined them, and breathed out several hours, a good meal, and a couple of pitchers later.

The general unwound enough, something Damien hadn't seen in a decade of knowing him, to tell war stories. From being an eighteen-year-old hothead helo pilot in the last days of the Vietnam War, up to his nephew and niece-in-law flying for the Night Stalkers—the famed Henderson and Beale.

They'd discussed the latest non-classified intel over Guinness stew and Irish bangers. Russia being ever more rabid. The disasters of Southwest Asia overshadowing the disasters of the Middle East. As the meal progressed he could see more and more how his peers took to testing their ideas on Cornelia. She might not be a trained intel officer, but her insightful questions even had the general harrumphing a few times. Damien himself wasn't surprised at all, yet more than once she forced his thinking down another layer with her questions.

Her questions.

"Do you have opinions of your own?" Damien wasn't sure quite where that came from.

"Excuse me?" She sounded affronted. Some of the others looked askance at him as well.

"What I mean is, your questions are fantastic. You really make us think about our assumptions. But I'm not sure what Cornelia Day is thinking."

"It's not my place."

"Not your place?" Caron nearly exploded. "Lady, if it's not yours, then whose is it?"

"The President and the Vice President. Policy is not part of my job. My duties are to promote the success of the President's agenda. No more. No less."

That earned her silent consideration from around the table.

"So, no thinking for yourself?" Mick teased.

Damien had slowly learned to read Cornelia's body language. Even partway into her second beer, she still sat like a dancer. Her sense of humor remained as it had started, smart and sharp when she was applying it and nonexistent when she was thinking on other matters. His question and the table's follow-up stiffened her already straight spine.

"My thoughts?"

Mick nodded amiably, unaware of the juggernaut that was about to land on his head.

Damien checked and noticed that she had the general's full attention. So he too had learned to read her. Or perhaps, because of his daughter being the National Security Advisor, he understood the true caliber implied by Cornelia being a senior-level White House staffer.

"My thought is that you Marine intel boys need to get your heads out of your asses."

The shock of silence rippled around the table.

Damien kept his smile to himself. *This* was the Cornelia Day that he'd seen in his files. He'd begun to doubt her existence, having only conversed with the thoughtful, even-tempered woman prior to this moment.

"Your mandate is to gather the information needed by your forward forces. There are 182,000 active-duty personnel who depend on your information. They are in need of *tactical* intel. Everything I've heard tonight has been *strategic* in nature—not even that. It has been top-tier political in consideration and as I'm sure Damien can tell you, not the most accurate or well thought out because you are basing your assumptions on tactical data. If you wish to work for the Defense Intelligence Agency, the NSA, and the half dozen others who operate at the strategic level, then go there and do that. You are Marine officers. Your duty is to the men and women out there on the front lines. I hope that what you've been saying tonight wasn't the speech you gave to the plebes earlier today. If you're wondering why Damien is working at the White House and not you, it's because he embodies these distinctions in his thoughts and in the service he provides."

A few of the guys actually blushed as they looked to him for his response. General Arnson was keeping his thoughts to himself.

"Cornelia," Damien spoke to get her attention, to haul her back from the sharp cliff edge she had walked out onto. "I need you"—to take a breath—"to come teach at my next class at NIU. The students at the National Intelligence University really need to hear that distinction from someone more convincing than me."

She nodded once sharply, whether acknowledging the end of her rant, or his invitation to NIU was accepted was unclear.

"My pleasure."

———

"I don't know what came over me," Cornelia hugged her coat more tightly around her. It was no colder outside, but she suddenly felt chilled to the bone.

"Whatever it was, it was utterly magnificent," Damien was practically chortling as he squeezed his left hand over where hers was tucked around his right elbow.

"But I ruined the dinner," she'd been working it so carefully. Had begun to feel that these men might actually like her for being, well, not the woman who had just told them they were full of it in front of a one-star general. God she was hopeless.

"Not for a second," Damien practically crowed with delight.

"It's fine for you to be happy. You didn't just alienate an entire department of the military."

A light snow began falling, fluttering and glittering past the streetlights. She normally loved this moment when the city turned magical. Colorado had thickened her California blood but she had never gotten over the wonder of her first major snowfall after joining the Governor's office. But it was hard to enjoy it when she was busy blowing up her career. And after only one week on the job!

"I now represent the President of the United States. I should never have spoken—"

"The truth?" Damien's voice turned unexpectedly harsh. "They were all trying to impress you. That's a male analyst's form of flirting: *Look at how smart I am*. Well, you called their bluff. Gave the general some food for thought as well."

"I couldn't even look at him," Cornelia wanted to hide her face against Damien's shoulder.

"Well, you impressed the hell out of the only two people at the table that mattered."

"Who was the other one..." she trailed off when Damien glanced at her sidelong. "I—"

She would just keep her questions to herself from now on.

The snow was staying light and calming. Apparently they were walking back to the White House. It was an hour away at a brisk clip, the only speed appropriate for this weather, and she didn't mind even though she wasn't properly dressed for it. She needed to burn off some of the nervous energy coursing through her.

The rest of Barracks Row was fully decked out for Christmas: frame shop photos of Santa Class, bicycles with red and green flashing lights, a kitchen store window filled with holiday cookie cutters. It was a three block long line of Christmas cheer and twinkle lights and she couldn't wait to get out of it. She finally felt as if she could breathe when they reached the end of the Row and turned left onto Pennsylvania Avenue.

"What were you going to say?" Damien prompted her when she slowed from mad dash to merely panicked hurry.

"I was going to ask something rude."

"Don't stop now, Cornelia. You're on a roll."

"I—" but she couldn't go any further.

"You're going to ask why I'm the other one who mattered?" He asked it with a level of perception and a degree of frankness she was truly coming to appreciate in him.

She nodded and held onto his arm so that he wouldn't just walk away in fury.

"It's not the same reason as the general."

Cornelia tried to puzzle it out. Damien could slow down her intel requests, but she expected that he had too much integrity for that. He could bad mouth her to other Sit Room staff causing the next two years to become decidedly awkward in the Situation Room...as if she wasn't doing enough of that job herself.

He still didn't answer as they walked past the bright Capitol Dome with its towering blue pinnacle of the Capitol Christmas Tree and began walking the length of the National Mall. Through the glassed-front of the Air and Space Museum she could see the great planes and spaceships of the last century. And some century yet to come—the original shooting model of the Starship *Enterprise* had been placed in the same hall as the Apollo LEM and Chuck Yeager's X-1 that had broken the sound barrier.

Face it. Head-on. Deep breath. Doesn't help. "Why then are you the other one who matters?"

"Explanation or demonstration?" Damien finally asked in a voice so soft she barely heard it.

"Demonstration?" What did he mean by that? She meant it as a question, he took it as her choice.

Using her left hand as guidance where it still tucked about his elbow, he turned her into his arms. One moment they were walking side by side beneath the snow-spattered sky. The next she was being kissed in front of the glass wall of the museum.

This was definitely a Marine-first-librarian-second kiss. She assumed that he'd let her loose...if she wanted an out. But from the first instant, the cold of the winter's night was scorched from her body. Her pulse roared to life.

Had she known that she wanted to kiss him?

Maybe.

Had she seriously considered it?

That answer blurred as she sank into it. Neither of them were demonstrating much beyond their most primal, animal intelligence. She wrapped her arms around the bulk of his Navy pea coat and held him tightly so that he wouldn't think to stop.

Wouldn't think.

Don't think.

She sagged against him, trusting the Marine to hold her upright because her own legs weren't up to it.

Her arms could barely reach around his chest and shoulders to clasp behind him. Yet his strong arms overlapped as they wrapped about her and held on.

He offered to pull back, to make this kiss as merely a moment of heat.

Cornelia wasn't ready to let go and kept him pulled in tight against her.

Some passing motorist beeped their car horn in a cheery pattern.

Only when her heart raced so fast that she couldn't catch her breath did she break the kiss. She leaned her head against his shoulder, not yet ready to let go.

"Holy hell, Cornelia. What was that about?"

"Stop being an analyst for a moment, please." She could feel his chuckle better than she could hear it despite their thick coats separating them.

"Well, if that's your standard kiss—"

It wasn't.

"—I can't wait to see what comes next."

"Analyst."

He shrugged at her accusation.

Her pulse and breathing finally slowed enough for her to be aware once more that she had legs and by some miracle they were still able to support her.

"That," she managed to stand upright and pat a hand on Damien's cheek, "wasn't my standard *anything*."

"Well, it certainly worked for me, ma'am, whatever it was."

It had worked for her as well.

"You okay to keep walking?"

Not trusting herself to speak, she nodded.

"Good, because I'm not. Okay if I lean on you?"

Slowly they joined hands and headed along the sidewalk once more. Except—

"That's the Capitol Dome," Damien stated with some surprise.

"It is," Cornelia sought her best disenchanted tourist voice. "And that is its Christmas tree on the front lawn."

"We've already been by there."

"We have," she managed to keep the surprise out of her voice.

With a ceremonial nod that might have been part bow, he turned them about and once more they were headed back toward the White House.

Cornelia never thought a giggle was a seemly utterance for a woman grown. So she fought down the desire to do so and simply said, "Thank you, kind sir."

"Kind sir, my ass. Kind sirs don't wonder how many minutes it is until we can try that without our winter coats."

"Many."

"Crap!"

"I could invite you up for a nightcap, but I live another fifteen minute walk west of the White House," Cornelia tried to parse the words as they slipped out of her mouth. If she understood them as individual words, she might be able to edit, correct, and verify prior to release. But they slipped out as a single cogent thought far beyond her control.

Damien guided them past the gauntlet of national museums and most of the way to the Washington Monument before he spoke again.

"Are you sure?"

"I'm not sure of anything." However, "except that the answer to that is *yes.*" Cornelia didn't try to analyze her response. For once in her life she would live in the moment. Just this one time she'd let go and do something not because it was right, but because she wanted to.

They walked past the National Christmas Tree on the Ellipse, fully decorated, but still dark for tomorrow's tree-lighting ceremony. The silence wrapped warm about them in the frosty air.

————

Getting to Cornelia's condo was either the longest or the shortest walk of his life. It would have seemed impossible that she'd invited him back to her place, if not for that kiss. Damien had expected her kiss to be as smooth and perfect as she was. Instead, there'd been a mind-blanking heat that had fired up his body on a cold winter's night. He couldn't try that again soon enough—he had to know if it had been real.

And yet, walking down the length of The Mall through the falling snow, passing monument after monument with her hand once again on his arm—like a couple who'd been together forever—had passed far too quickly. Again the idiot-around-women part of his brain was imagining what it would be like to make this walk together each night, each month, each—

Typical! He really needed to get control of his thoughts. *Not a chance with Cornelia beside him.*

They walked in silence through the snow. When she turned off the sidewalk in front of a beautiful old brickwork building renovated into condos, she stopped.

He didn't ask again if she was sure. He didn't want to break the peace that stood between them.

Instead he simply waited.

She didn't turn to study his face. Nor did she drag him ahead like some overeager wanton. Cornelia simply kept her hand on his arm and, after only the briefest hesitation, continued up the front walkway as if they'd done it a thousand times.

"Ms. Day. Sir," the elderly doorman welcomed them after buzzing them through the secure door.

"Thank you, Mr. Rivers."

He handed Cornelia her mail and they rode the elevator to the third floor.

Her condo was as neat as her office. A small, but cozy one bedroom with a kitchen that looked little used. Soft, indirect lighting. A full-wall bookcase that was filled with both political memoir and thriller. There was little art on the walls, just a few pictures of her with the President-elect before he was the President-elect. They spanned over a decade of time, but she looked little changed. Even in the high school graduation photo standing beside her mother, she looked like a grown woman.

The silence echoed in his ears as she hung up her coat then his in the closet.

He waited. He didn't want a nightcap. He didn't want coffee and a bit of phony chit-chat on the tastefully pale-green sofa. Her apartment, like her clothing, was a palate of neutrals or pastel shades. No strong statements here—except the woman herself, placing her shoes in the bottom of the hall closet.

Her presence shouted in the neutral room as loudly as a vermillion wall hanging or blaring music.

"God, Cornelia. You're so—" stepping close she rested a warm finger on his lips.

"I've never understood games or small talk," she whispered from mere inches away. And she replaced her finger with a brush of her lips.

"And I've never met a woman who was so forthright."

"You fascinated me from the first moment, Damien."

"Fascinated? Are you sure you aren't channeling Spock?"

"Who?" But this time her smile spoke volumes to him. And he realized that it should have the first time as well.

"Crap!" Damien growled. "And I totally fell for it that you somehow had missed a whole segment of American culture."

She ran a hand up over his chest, looking down at her fingers as she did so. He was left to look at the top of her head as she traced a line of fire upward.

"Let me guess. You're one of those girls, women, who had a total crush on Spock."

"Had?" She said it so coyly that he couldn't help laughing. "And you strike me as a Beverly Crusher type."

"No," he lied. "Troi for me. In the Season One cheerleader outfit."

"Liar." Cornelia didn't make it a question. "You always go for the brains." She leaned in to rub her nose on his neck. "Me too," she whispered.

"Guilty," he slid his hands onto her waist and up her ribcage.

It *was* fascinating: how she felt against the curve of his palm and fingers, how her lips tasted of no lipstick or balm, but rather just a hint of the espresso dark chocolate pie they'd shared and a slight spiciness that had nothing to do with their meals.

"Besides Crusher has a great body, just different." He was on the verge of saying "Like yours." But he didn't. Not because of tact, never one of his strengths, but because there was no way that anyone could feel as good as Cornelia.

His tie had disappeared when he wasn't paying attention. And his shirt was halfway unbuttoned.

"And if you're trying to spoil my fantasy woman image of you, being able to knowledgeably discuss Star Trek isn't helping you out at all."

"Do you always talk so much?"

Damien considered for a moment. "Usually, but I'll make an exception in your case." He shifted his hands to her breast and behind. Then he pulled her back into the hard kiss he wanted to try again.

They groaned in unison at how good it was.

Except for a brief foray to the bathroom for protection, they didn't make another sound as he melted onto the white living room carpet and pulled her down on top of him. The couch was too far away.

CHAPTER FIVE

Cornelia hadn't slept like that in a long time. For one thing, she was warm, an unusual event with only the sheet over her. Damien was delightfully warm to sleep next to. For another thing, her morning workout sessions might tone her body, but it didn't wring her out into limp-dishrag territory the way last night's activities had. A simpatico energy had run between them, draining her physically and energizing her...her what?

Her thoughts were as languid as her body at the moment; a very unusual state for her.

Her emotions...were as strange and distant as ever. Except they weren't the *same* as ever. They were—

"You're thinking awfully hard for seven in the morning," Damien's whispered greeting tickled her ear.

"I'm—Wait! Seven?" She scrabbled around for some covers, finally hauling the blanket around her as she crawled out of bed.

"Whoa!" Damien made a grab for her that she managed to dodge, but he snagged the blanket. He held one end as she held the other over her breasts and hips.

"But it's seven," the need to get moving coursed through her.

"It's Saturday."

"But it's seven." She always finished her stepper workout by six-thirty, shower and breakfast by seven, at the White House or the EEOB by seven-thirty.

"Cornelia. Take a breath. Today is Saturday," as if she was a child and hadn't heard him the first time.

"That doesn't matter. You wouldn't believe everything on my desk."

"Your desk is immaculate and empty."

She tried to give him a withering look, but Damien didn't seem to be the kind of man to wither. Simply because her queue was electronic didn't make it any smaller. Her inbox inherited from Daniel filled three file cabinets and what had appeared in the last week filled most of another—she was beginning to understand why Daniel had filed the way he did. Yesterday's discussion with Damien meant that she now had a plan of attack. A quiet Saturday, if there was such a thing in the White House, would be the perfect opportunity to start implementing it.

"Okay," he shrugged and offered one of his charming smiles as if that was going to work. "Come back to bed long enough to not have an awkward morning-after and I'll go in and be your assistant for the day."

"It isn't awkward. I simply have to get to work."

"But how do I know that you *sincerely* shared your stunning body and incredible sexual prowess with me if I don't have confirmation in the morning that it wasn't just an illusion."

"Because I actually did," like she'd never had with another. Damien had unlocked some strange key inside her that she hadn't known existed. She had wanted things, done things, like she never had before. And Damien had responded like a good Marine, taking the least little instruction and following it to the very limit.

Resisting his light tug on the other end of her blanket would have been easier without his smile. Sliding back into bed once she was awake was a sinful act.

But it was nothing compared to what happened for the next half hour.

———

Damien was in a daze that allowed Cornelia to slip away and head to the shower. He lay still, unable to move. Unwilling to leave the sheets that carried her subtle scent. The woman made his head spin, but her body...

"I need to find a saint to pray to," because he needed this to be real.

"An odd choice for a Jewish man," Cornelia had taken the fastest shower in the world. He'd thought to join her there, but had obviously missed his few seconds of opportunity.

He turned from burying his face in her pillow to looking at her standing at the bathroom threshold and drying herself off. Her leanness wasn't model-worthy: ribs protruding and some fear that she'd fall over in a strong breeze. Instead, she was gloriously slender. Her curves weren't blatant, they wouldn't fit her so well if they were. She was a subtle woman in both thought and form. Of course what she did between the sheets, or out on the living room rug, was anything but subtle.

He smiled as she buffed one long leg and then the other with a thick towel. He had very clear memories of how she had wrapped those long limbs about him. And even clearer memories of how she'd looked as the pleasure took her. It would have been humbling that he could please her so if not for his own memories. He'd *never* had a woman like Cornelia Day. Her transformation from elegant urbanite to passionate lover made the experience only that much more incredible.

Again, between one eyeblink and the next, she had powdered, dressed, and was standing close by, looking down at him. Perhaps in celebration of the weekend, she wore designer jeans and a simple turtleneck rather than one of her incredible silk-and-wool outfits. She even wore fur-trimmed, buckle boots that he'd bet were just the latest style—and he had to admit that they looked very cute on her. He slipped a hand out from under the warm covers to slide it up the back of her leg and over her exquisitely stair-stepped behind.

For a moment she merely looked down at him.

Had he been wrong? Had last night—

Then, without a sound, her eyes slid closed for a moment and he could see the sigh that was too soft to hear.

"God, Cornelia. You—"

And with that the White House Chief of Staff was suddenly back in the room. "Stay as long as you like. Don't bother coming in. It's your day off."

"It's yours too," he called as she stepped from his caress and strode off toward the bedroom door.

She waved a hand over her head and was gone. A moment later the front door snicked shut. Then it opened, he heard a rattle in the front closet as she grabbed a coat, and then she really was gone.

He managed not to laugh aloud until she was gone again. Her being flustered enough to forget her coat was infinitely reassuring to his male ego.

Damien rolled out of bed, then made it with military corners and wondered if that would be up to her standards. She'd left him a fresh towel, a new razor about the size of his pinkie, and no coffee. When he checked the fridge after his Navy-fast shower, he saw that no breakfast —or much of anything else—was ever served from this kitchen. He made a mental note to cook for her sometime.

The doorman was a younger man than the night before. He had the discretion to make no comment as he watched Damien leave, but his look said plenty.

The morning air had a sharp bite to it. An inch of snow slickened the sidewalks and turned the city of marble even whiter than it usually was.

He could take Cornelia at her word and enjoy his weekend. Thankfully, he wasn't that much of an idiot.

Spying out the bootprints in the bright morning sunlight that must have been hers—a snow often turned DC into a city of shut-ins—he traced her path to a coffee shop. With a large drip in one hand and a breakfast burrito in the other, he strode out to make up some time as he followed her the rest of the way to the White House. *Wherever* she wanted to lead, he was more than willing to follow.

———

Cornelia didn't know why she'd felt such a need to get out of the apartment and away from Damien. Whatever it was didn't nudge, it shoved. She wasn't running from a morning confrontation—she wouldn't mind more waking confrontations like that one. Her body felt glorious beyond any merely physical workout.

And, she took a deep breath as she passed through White House security at the Southwest Gate, she didn't mind if those future events were with Marine Corps Captain Damien Feinman. No one had ever made her feel even half as special as he had with the simplest gesture.

He didn't treat her like a woman—he treated her like a miracle.

Fantasy woman. Was that her problem? That he had her up on a pedestal for some incomprehensible reason? No more than she him. Intelligent, funny, handsome, and the things that he could do with his hands had made her want to scream with the intensity. She was—

A complete and utter basket case.

Entrance security cleared her into the empty West Wing Foyer. To her right would be the weekend watch officers in the Sit Room. The irony of that was only starting to grow on her. It was actually three large conference rooms, two smaller ones, and a massive central area which was occupied by the tiered desk of the watch. The ever-so-famous President's Situation Room was just one small briefing room off to the side. It was far more Damien's domain than the President's. Yet so much happened there.

She worked her way upstairs. The West Wing cleaning staff was long gone and only a few hardcores like herself were in this early on a snowy Saturday. Most of the light came from the understated Christmas décor that was typical for the West Wing. The Residence might get all dandified for the public tours, but here there was only the occasional wreath or the icicle lights dangling above the stairwell. For a change, it was peaceful.

So much had happened here in the last week. In the Sit Room on Monday she'd become White House Chief of Staff and met Damien. Now, six days later she was overwhelmed by the former, and the latter...was overwhelming her as well. She just needed one quiet day to get her head wrapped around what was going on, maybe two. To catch up for one single moment so that she could—

"Oh good, you're here," President-elect Zachary came up behind her with Daniel in tow just as she stepped into Janet's office. Her own desk phone was ringing.

Yes, a perfect, quiet day. Not a chance.

She waved for them to follow her through Janet's office and into her own as she rushed to catch the call.

With it being the weekend and Janet not in, someone had to really sell it to get past the White House switchboard.

She hit the speaker button then moved to hang up her coat and turn on some lights. The sun was still low to the east, leaving her office in a twilit shadow.

"We have a Mr. Pejman on the line for you. He says that you met him during the disaster in Italy. He has been calling every hour on the hour since five a.m."

She didn't recall a Mr. Pejman, but she certainly recalled the Italy disaster. A man-made avalanche had killed a number of global senior-level leaders at a climate conference. It was also where Zachary Thomas had clinched the election even before he started his campaign by how many people he had fought to save over the next two days. She had been at his side for all of it, but she recalled no Mr. Pejman.

She glanced at the President-elect, but he shrugged his shoulders as well. Cornelia was his memory for things like names. Even though, how many people had they been in contact with during that rescue.

"Send his call through."

"Ms. Day?"

"Mr. Pejman, how can I help you?"

"Are we private, Ms. Day?"

She glanced at Daniel and Zachary, just in time to see Damien walk in. He opened his mouth but she put a finger over her lips to silence him. Calling every hour on the hour early on a Saturday didn't sound like a social call. She'd been Chief of Staff for less than a week and she wasn't going to tackle this one alone.

"We are private, Mr. Pejman."

Pejman? Damien mouthed to her.

She nodded.

He ducked out of the room and she could see him bending over to use Janet's computer.

"I should very much like to meet with you in person, Ms. Day."

"May I ask what this is about?"

"I am afraid that it is not a matter to be discussed in such a way." She almost had his accent. Middle-eastern? Arabic? No, Farsi. Regrettably, Persian wasn't one of her languages—she was more of a college-French- or Italian-tourist-style linguist.

"Then I fear that I can't help you with—"

Damien rushed back into the room and handed her a slip of paper. *Pejman: Asst. to U.N. ambassador Iran.*

"It is very important that I speak with you in person, Ms. Day."

"Where are you, Mr. Pejman?"

"Katz's Deli at one o'clock."

"Katz's?"

"I will see you then, Ms. Day." And the line went dead.

"Where's Katz's?" she asked the others.

Zachary and Daniel just shook their heads.

"Oh my god!" Damien burst out. "I work with a bunch of heathens. It's the best deli there is."

"I've been in DC for eight years and I haven't heard of it."

"It's in New York. Lower East Side. Absolutely awesome!"

"New York?" Cornelia shook her head. "I am *not* going to New York."

"What," Zachary pointed, "is that slip that Damien gave you?"

She handed it over.

Zachary and Daniel studied it for a long moment, exchanged one of their mind-reading glances, then turned back to her in unison. That habit was going to get very irritating as this administration progressed.

Then she read their looks. "No. I'm *not* going to New York today."

They waited.

"I'm not a field operative. I'm barely a Chief of Staff. How can I be Chief of Staffing if I'm not even here?"

"Where are you going?" The President stepped into the room. Even on a Saturday he was well dressed, though just a blazer and no tie. More formal than his early administration. It was as if he was practicing for the role of elder statesman.

"Katz's Deli," Damien replied for her, clearly enjoying the game at her expense. Probably payback for her Mr. Spock tease.

"Oh," President Matthews smiled. "Get the pastrami. Though the corned beef is awfully good too. I tell you what, order both and bring me back whichever you don't want. Why are you going there?"

Zachary handed him the slip of paper. "He wants to meet with Cornelia at one p.m. today. Wouldn't say what was up over the phone. He seemed rather cagey about it."

The President's *bonhomie* evaporated. "Pejman?"

Cornelia glanced at the desk clock that she'd unearthed from beneath Daniel's stack of five consecutive monthly reports on the ice melt along the Arctic Northwest Passage—all of which had said the same thing.

"If I have to get to New York by one, the train will take too long. I need to see if there's a shuttle flying with room on it. Even if there is I'll be late," She cursed herself for luxuriating in bed with Damien. If she'd gotten up at her normal time, she'd have been here several call attempts earlier.

"She doesn't understand how this works," the President smiled at her. "Damien, do you have the number?"

Damien walked up to her phone and offered a saucy wink as he dialed. Then he handed the handset to the President.

"Hello, this is the President for Eddie."

Cornelia wondered who in the world Eddie might be.

"Eddie? Peter Matthews here. My Chief of Staff is headed to New York. She'll be to your location in fifteen minutes. Great. Thanks," he handed her the phone and she hung it up.

Damien picked up one of the other lines at the conference table and made a quick call.

"I take it that I'm going to New York." She didn't make it a question and no one corrected her.

"Take him with you," President Matthews pointed at Damien. "If ever there was a man who won't shut up about New York pastrami, he's it. Or maybe you should leave him behind as a form of torture."

Cornelia wanted to leave him behind so that she wouldn't be torturing herself. She needed distance, not closeness, to understand what was going on between them. Taking him to her bed had been a huge mistake...except it hadn't been and she didn't regret a second of it. But lacking time to even think about it was an increasing problem.

The President headed toward the door waving for Zachary and Daniel to join him.

They moved, leaving just her and Damien.

At the threshold, the President paused and turned to her. Any sense of humor was gone. "Remember, specifically, to ask Pejman to communicate with his father-in-law and say 'What can be done to help with this gulf between us?' Word-for-word."

Cornelia nodded indicating that she had it.

The President nodded. "That should be of some assistance. Now get moving," and he was gone.

Damien held her coat for her. "There will be a car waiting by the time we get to the West Wing entrance."

Even a car wasn't going to get them there in time.

———

"You're Eddie?"

Damien loved it when Cornelia became flustered. It was very hard to do, so he decided to enjoy the occasion.

"Only two people call me that, not even my wife." General Arnson sounded grouchy about it, but then he sounded grouchy about everything as a matter of principle. "First was my nephew's wife. Then her best friend felt all put out that he was the Commander-in-Chief but Emily was the one who got to call me Eddie. The two are so competitive about everything."

But he smiled at Cornelia. The general almost never smiled.

"My apologies, General Arnson."

"No need, Ms. Day. No need. Finding myself partial to you. Need to log a little airtime myself and we have a Bell 505 Jet Ranger X that they gave us for testing." He waved at a very sleek helicopter, the only one not painted Marine Corps green. It was done in a bright, racy orange. "Time to put it through its paces. We'll have a car waiting for you at the other end."

"Actually, I think a taxi makes for a lower profile."

He saw the general register the level of trust she had just given him. Not who she was meeting, but that it wasn't some whim that was taking her to New York either. There was a nicety to her communication.

"No car. Got it. You can sit up front with me. Leave this young whippersnapper who keeps sighing after you in the rear."

"Hey!"

"Or we can just leave him behind altogether if you'd like."

Why was everyone threatening to do that to him today? Wasn't it enough how fast Cornelia was leaving him behind? Not that she was running away, but she did always seem to be three steps ahead, leaving him to catch up. "Rangers lead the way!" and "Marines first to fight!"— neither branch had a clue. Because way out in front of them all was Chief of Staff Cornelia Day.

He did get the general aside for a moment.

"Sir, do you have a sidearm I could borrow?"

"Where's your piece?"

"In the safe at the Situation Room."

"Not doing you any damn good there, is it, Captain?"

"No sir."

"She going in alone?"

"Except for me."

"God help us," the general brushed aside the lapel of Damien's jacket and grunted his dissatisfaction at not even finding a holster there.

Damien followed him to a gun safe in the private office. The general punched in a code and pulled out two-and-a-half pounds of a monster M1911, shoulder holster, and two spare magazines.

"You let her down one little inch, Mr. Librarian, and I'll have your Marine ass on the next ship to the Arabian Sea. Clear?"

"Yes, sir." Damien knew he meant it as well. It didn't matter that Damien was on the National Security Council and in an entirely different chain of command.

"Mount up," then the general nodded toward the big .45 in Damien's hands. "But hit the can first and strap on. Don't want her seeing that you're going in heavy. And I don't want some analyst pissing the back of my new helicopter."

"No, sir." By the time he saluted he was facing the general's back.

"Yeah, yeah," he replied as he walked away sounding like nothing so much as a Jewish grandfather.

For the whole flight up, Damien sat in the back and listened over the intercom while the kick-ass general chatted with Cornelia about her service with Zachary Thomas and even gave her a lesson in flying a helicopter. He spent the entire flight staring at the cartoonish Santa Claus some wag had taped to the back of Cornelia's seat.

CHAPTER SIX

T*his is where Meg* Ryan had her fake orgasm scene in *When Harry Met Sally.*"

"Haven't seen that one," and Cornelia couldn't think of a single thing more irrelevant to the moment than a fake orgasm—there'd certainly been no need for that last night. The peaks had slammed through her so hard that she could still feel them.

The more she'd traveled on the way to Katz's, the stranger the experience had become.

Flying a helicopter for the first time had been fun and General Arnson's easy kindness had been a pleasant surprise. Starting her first ever visit to New York City by landing at the Downtown Manhattan Heliport had been a surreal element out of the movies; though the chilly wind off the East River made clear that it wasn't some glamour moment.

Somehow, in all of the years, she hadn't been a part of Zachary Thomas' trips here.

Now, after a taxi ride that had made DC drivers seem rational, she was staring at a neighborhood that made little sense. The street's four lanes were split by a median populated by struggling trees. A few construction barricades were decorated with brilliant graffiti. And several Salvation Army Santas with little steel donation buckets were ringing handbells.

"I bet only one of these is legit. The rest are just scammers," but Damien tucked a dollar or two into the bucket of each Santa they passed.

The four corners of the intersection they were dropped at had a genteel old six-story brick apartment building, a new twenty-story glass one, a park that there wasn't a chance she was going to enter without an armed guard, and a shabby-looking one-story wreck with big signs declaring it to be their destination. The neon sign spelled "Katz's Delicatessen," but only because it was broad daylight; at night it would have spelled "Kat...'s D...e...n" because most of the bulbs were burned out. There was a painted sign, that really needed repainting, and—

"Are you serious about this? We flew all this way to come here?"

"Best Jewish deli there is. Boston? Feh. Tel Aviv? They've got no idea. Katz's is the place. Can you believe that they ship salamis all over the world to overseas service men and women?" He took her hand and she let him lead her across the street.

It was the first time they'd touched since he'd caressed her behind while he'd still lay in her bed looking like a very smug demigod and she had stood stupidly over him, helpless at his merest caress. It had taken a brute-force will to leave his side. She'd had pretty lovers before, and not so pretty ones. But something about this Marine Corps captain could spoil her for life. So handsome and fit and sure of himself...that she wanted to jump him here and now.

He held the door for her and the warm air that washed over her brushed away all of her doubts and worries, at least about the meeting place. The air was so thick with smoked meats, chicken soup, and pickles that it was practically a meal unto itself.

Someone handed them each a ticket.

"Don't lose that."

Cornelia looked down at it, "Why? Are they raffling off a salami?"

"No, but they put your order on it. Fifty-dollar fee if you lose it."

She handed it to Damien. It was one too many things for her to deal with.

"What?"

"My phone is on my dresser and my tablet is on my desk at work. I'm losing too many things today." Like control of her life.

"Okay. Do you see him anywhere?"

"I don't even know what he looks like. Do you?"

"No. As soon as I saw his job, I rushed back to you. Besides this place is a zoo."

"Some help you are." But it was a zoo. Saturday afternoon the place was packed; it was actually a good place for an anonymous meeting, if they could ever find each other. A long deli counter ran down the entire length of the sidewall. The main area was jammed with dozens of beige-and-battered Formica tables with equally unworthy wooden chairs. Above the deli hung hundreds of different-sized salamis. The non-deli walls were covered floor-to-ceiling with signed photographs. Some of them were bright and new, others appeared to date from the '20s and '30s. There was so much crazy decor, signs, and photographs covering the walls and dangling from the ceiling that she couldn't even focus on the crowds of people lined up at the counter and sniffing around for an open table, their hands filled with platters of massive sandwiches.

"We'll let him find us. He clearly remembers you. Food and sit."

So they got food. She remembered the President's request and ordered a pastrami to go and a corned beef for here. When she saw the size of the sandwiches, she wondered if she could even finish a half. Probably not even that with the way her stomach was knotted.

Soon they were settled at a table with a vanilla New York egg cream, that Damien insisted was the best drink on earth, and a black-and-white cookie, oddly enough called a Black and White, that was nearly as big as her face.

"He should find us here," Damien waved upward with half of his Reuben sandwich.

She had to lean back to read the circular sign over their heads. "Where Harry met Sally...hope you had what she had! Enjoy!" with an arrow pointing directly to the top of her head.

"Nobody ever gets this table. It's a famous table. Usually people wait in line for it."

"For a table?"

"Sure. It's a superstar among furniture, the Meryl Streep of tables," he spoke around a mouthful of sandwich. "We'll watch the movie. You'll like it. Then you'll be glad that you're having what she had."

Cornelia waited until he was about to swallow. "Does that *having* include you?"

Damien coughed, choked, sputtered, then choked some more.

Cornelia took her first bite. It was good. Really good. She was half tempted to say so when she looked up and recognized a face in the crowd.

———

"Oh shit!"

"Good, isn't it? I told you it would be." Several sips of egg cream had managed to ease Damien's throat enough that an ambulance was no longer a desperate necessity. He'd have to remember to watch out for her sense of humor in the future.

Then he looked up at Cornelia's face. It had gone white as the DC snow.

He started to turn.

"No, don't!"

He faced back toward her, set down his sandwich, and eased his hand inside his jacket and around the butt of the M1911 pistol.

"Don't do that either, unless you want to get us shot."

So much for being subtle about traveling armed.

"I'm guessing that is President Javad Madani."

"The President of Iran?" Damien was suddenly very glad he wasn't eating because his mouth had gone dry way past the ability of an egg cream to fix.

"He's going to order. Shadowed by two guards. A fourth man is headed our way."

Damien managed to turn enough to see the backs of three men approaching the sandwich counter. He recognized the walk of the two who were a step behind—military, well-trained military. Their suits weren't all that different from the Secret Service dudes. And they were watching the crowd, not studying the menu posted on the wall behind the counter.

"Ms. Day?" a man asked from close beside Damien's other elbow—some bodyguard he was turning out to be. The new arrival was in his early thirties and dressed in business casual. The accent was British-English, but with more dynamics—exactly as would be typical of a Farsi speaker.

"Mr. Pejman," Cornelia didn't ask.

"I am pleased that you were able to arrive. Our—my time, it is very limited. *I* am just enroute between the UN and the airport. There is a flight that...uh, I must be on in two hours."

"Perhaps we should dispense with pretense and you should signal the rest of your party to join us." And the nervous Cornelia of this morning was gone in that instant. Now she was the smoothly cool woman who had so captivated his attention on her first visit to the Situation Room. Knowing some of what lay beneath only made her all the more dramatic and amazing.

At Pejman's signal, one of the guards did come to the table. He snapped out something in Farsi.

"Your bodyguard," Pejman translated, "may wait for us elsewhere."

"Actually," Damien had briefly considered hiding his knowledge, but then thought better of it. "This '*asshole*' has no intention of '*getting lost.*' He is very comfortable where he is." He took a bite of his sandwich and winked at Cornelia.

He could see by her sigh of relief that Farsi wasn't in her repertoire. It was almost a shock, discovering something she *couldn't* do.

"Without trust, there is no purpose," Cornelia began gathering her plate and the President's wrapped to-go sandwich. "Come, Damien."

"I agree," a man said as he came up from the side of the table opposite Pejman.

Damien spun back the other way, reaching for his holster in surprise. Thankfully he managed to stop his hand before it arrived, the other guard already had his hand beneath his jacket and was watching him closely.

Beside the tall guard stood a small, dapper man with a graying beard and a neat suit. No tie, open collar. He looked like any of the myriad of other businessmen enjoying a casual lunch, except for the two guards probably less than a second from killing Damien.

He recognized President Javad Madani from his very rare Sit Room video calls.

Damien very slowly eased his hand back to the table and the two guards relaxed only minimally.

"Yes," President Madani continued, observing the action. "Trust can be very difficult."

"Then perhaps," Cornelia remained in complete control, "you will send your guards off to get their own lunches while you join me with yours."

He studied her for a long moment, then told the guards to find some food and choose a table nearby but not too close. "And your guard?"

"He is…" and he could see that Cornelia did not know how to approach this. Marine, librarian, Situation Room intelligence officer: none of those would go well.

"I am a top advisor to Ms. Day."

"He's my most *trusted* advisor." Her smile and President Madani's nod of acceptance said that they'd cleared that hurdle.

"May Mr. Pejman join us as well?"

"As soon as you have your own lunches," again that perfect blend of courtesy and edge. *I am the one in control, but I can be kind.* It was a hell of a sexy message.

One of the guards delivered two plates and two drinks to the table and then retreated once more after giving Damien a foul look.

The other two men sat. Damien didn't like Pejman sitting next to Cornelia, but Damien had the seat across from her and the President had taken the one beside him, so whatever danger the man represented, Damien would be hard pressed to intervene quickly.

He was glad this was New York. A quick glance about the neighboring tables indicated that absolutely nothing out of the ordinary had been noticed. If something did happen, it was a city of fearless people, many armed with mace and Tasers. But the only people watching them were the two guards now carrying there own meals to an open spot three tables away where the sign above them said that Bill Clinton had eaten a whole pastrami sandwich, two hot dogs, fries, diet ginger ale, and a decaf coffee.

"Mr. Pejman," Cornelia turned to him. "I don't recall meeting you in Italy."

"My apologies, we did not. At least not directly. However, I observed that you were never far from your Vice President and I suggested that you might be an appropriate person with which to make contact. I was unaware of your promotion prior to my call. My congratulations."

"Thank you."

Damien almost laughed at the dryness of Cornelia's tone. Without it, she wouldn't be here and he wondered how much she was regretting her quick transition to power.

"Before I forget," Cornelia picked up without missing a beat. "Our President has asked me to request a message be passed on to your father-in-law."

Damien didn't miss Pejman's furtive glance across the table. Neither did Cornelia.

She turned to the President of Iran. "Mr. Pejman is married to your daughter."

"He makes her happy. And he will be a powerful man someday, if he remains smart."

Pejman tried to sit up straighter than he already was.

"Then my message must be for you: 'What can be done to help with this gulf between us?' I assume this means more than it appears to."

Damien had missed that. He had thought it was merely an overly formal phrasing that might be used between Presidents of sparring powers. He'd never have thought to repeat it word-for-word with exactly President Matthews' intonations.

President Madani truly smiled for the first time. "I was skeptical of my son-in-law's suggestion of meeting with a woman, Ms. Day. But I see now that you are strong and intelligent like my daughter. Forgive me, but our culture creates expectations that are difficult to surmount."

Damien would have asked for the hidden meaning of the phrase, now that he understood there was one, but Cornelia didn't. She knew something. No, she knew no more than he did. Therefore she had concluded...what? That President Matthews was confirming a past relationship and letting Madani know that Cornelia had the American President's stamp of approval; no other information was relevant.

"However," Madani's mood lightened, "digestion does not go well with such topics. Tell me, Ms. Day, are you married?" And he picked up his own sandwich.

———

Cornelia maintained the conversation as well as she could. Small talk was not one of her strengths, especially not with everything else that was occupying her thoughts. *The gulf between us?* Perhaps *the Gulf...* The Persian Gulf? But that wasn't *between* them.

Her role was also rather mystifying. She had thought she'd had some grasp of what her duties as White House Chief of Staff were. Those duties didn't have anything to do with a brigadier general acting as her personal pilot, currently cooling his heels at a Manhattan heliport, while she ate a corned beef sandwich with a foreign head of state —an aggressively non-allied one.

They also didn't involve having her ankles wrapped around Damien's under the table while doing so. She hadn't even been aware of it until this moment. She certainly was not going to think about him or what they had done last night; not while they sat in a New York Jewish deli discussing Javad Madani's grandchildren.

"When in the course of human events..." Madani's tone didn't change.

That wasn't what alerted her to the sudden shift in the conversation. It was Damien's ankles twitching against hers.

"...it becomes necessary for people of good will to come together over good food."

He'd opened with the first line of the Declaration of Independence, mostly. He'd paused. Waiting for...? Her answer!

"We the people..." she finally countered with the Constitution, but not *of the United States,* "...of global good will, must indeed come together."

"However carefully," President Madani countered.

"However carefully," she nodded to include that they were having a secret meeting in the middle of a busy deli.

"This time the storm enters from the Bay, not the Gulf."

Cornelia could hear the capitalized words in his soft speech. She struggled for the meaning. *The Gulf between us.* What if that was the Gulf of Mexico?

The storm.

Not Hurricane Katrina.

A different kind of storm. One involving Iran and the United States.

The storm of...an attack! There must have been plans for an attack on the United States to which Iran's president was not only privy, but perhaps essential in preventing.

And the Bay? New York? New York had Upper and Lower New York Bay, but other than the Statue of Liberty, it would be an attack on Staten Island or Brooklyn, not Manhattan proper.

"Nobody hates Brooklyn that much, though not true-blue New Yorker would miss Staten Island for a heartbeat." At Damien's whispered remark, Cornelia decided perhaps the city wasn't the target despite having two bays.

Washington, DC, however, most certainly had a very prominent one: the Chesapeake.

Did this whole conversation have to occur in code? She hoped not. But clearly the first part must be, unless it was a test of some sort. Or a precaution.

She glanced over at the two guards still watching them carefully from their table.

Damien followed her gaze then nodded. "You have well-trained men, Mr. President. Their attention to duty doesn't waver with time or a good meal," he waved genially to their own empty plates.

He was clearly saying it for her benefit. *Madani has brought his most trusted men,* Damien was telling her, *but not trusted enough to tell them who he was meeting with.* If the guards knew that she and Damien were from the White House, she suspected that they would either be more relaxed or far more suspicious rather than merely watchful.

President Madani had asked for this meeting.

President Matthews had said, *What can be done to help with this gulf between us?*

Was President Madani seeking or offering help?

"I am here," she was still struggling to connect the pieces. "Rather than...my superior, as normal channels are not...always careful enough."

The President remained silent, not correcting her. Not until she made a mistake? If she did, then what? Ballistic missiles raining down from space? Iran was one of the select nations that could launch them. No. Or they wouldn't be here.

"Does this...friendly conversation have one side or two?" She had better not be in the middle of a quid pro quo conversation with the twelfth most powerful nation in the world. And she'd wager that they held their cards even closer than North Korea and that in reality they were a few notches higher than twelfth. Perhaps no one was willing to deliver the bad news to the American allies of Canada or South Korea.

"No conversation," Madani corrected, "in our modern global economy can risk having only one side."

She was going to strangle President Matthews for putting her into this situation. Perhaps not her best idea, as that would result in a charge of treason and a life's sentence. Maybe she'd...throw away his pastrami sandwich. *You go, girl! That'll show him.*

Cornelia took a careful breath.

As if knowing her utter loss of how to continue, Madani spoke once more. "But for now, let us speak only of how I may be a friend to you."

"Bless you!"

He nodded his head at her vast relief. "We have learned, by methods I believe inappropriate for a woman to know, that there is an attack coming. It is neither chemical nor biological. I am informed that it is also not explosive or electronic. Rather, it is cultural."

"Cultural. In DC."

Damien could only offer her a shrug. Madani offered no reaction at all.

Cornelia decided her best option was to wait, especially as she didn't know how to take the next step.

"When we are teaching our young the prayers of a true believer, we often tell them: you must pray with your heart, not your words."

"You are saying I should take up prayer from my heart?"

Madani smiled tolerantly. "I can think of little better advice, but that was not my point."

"This...person," Pejman spoke with disgust, "spoke his final words as a child. Repeating them until they were past any meaning. He said: We shall cut out their heart with their own words." They were the first words Pejman had spoken since making introductions. He had seemed but a passive go-between until this moment. But his evident fury and what sounded like personal experience made him into a suddenly menacing and dangerous man who had overseen the questioning and confession of a man now dead.

"My apologies for my son-in-law. He is a very passionate man." And with those words, President Madani dropped his napkin on his plate and rose to his feet.

"You have no more for us?" Cornelia cursed herself the moment she'd said it. If he did, he'd have offered it already.

"I can only offer you my prayers during this, your Christian holiday season." Madani pressed his palms together briefly and then, after only a moment's hesitation, reached across to shake her hand.

His clasp was firm but brief.

"You are the first woman I have touched other than my wife and daughter since the day of my wedding."

"I will take that as a blessing."

"Take it as a statement that if your *most-trusted advisor* does not have the common sense that Allah gave an elephant, I shall speak to my wife about my taking a second one."

When he shook Damien's hand, without the hesitation, Damien spoke cheerfully as if to a friend. "Don't lose your food tickets."

"It is not my first trip to Katz's," the President laughed.

Damien retained the President's hand a moment longer, "And I do have more common sense than God gave a horse."

"Good. Then I shall call you friend and you shall bring your wife to meet mine when you come to visit us." He turned for the door and his guards fell into place beside him.

Pejman did not presume to shake her hand, but did shake Damien's.

"My thanks, Ms. Day." She felt that he managed his exit line without choking on it too badly.

"Pending doom. This is *really* not how I was thinking this Saturday was going to turn out," she wanted to collapse at the table and fake something. Like a belief that everything was going to be okay.

Damien held out her coat. "So, that was fun. Who are we meeting with next? The Chinese Paramount Leader at Barney's for bagels and lox about a war in the South China Sea? Then uptown to Zabar's for gefilte fish with the Russian Prime Minister to find out how soon his submarines are going to attack the East Coast? Seriously I need to hang out with you more often. I can't wait until we meet the real Santa Claus."

"You're Jewish," though she appreciated his attempts at levity.

"Technically," he gathered her to-go sandwich for the President, offered her his arm, and escorted her toward the door.

An elderly couple pounced on their table before they were two steps away.

"But I still have more common sense than God gave a horse, no matter which God he is."

"Or she."

"Or she," he agreed as he paid for their two tickets.

Cornelia had lost all ability to think. Definitely to think about President Madani's departing benediction.

But his indefinite hints at terrorist attacks was scaring the daylights out of her.

CHAPTER SEVEN

A *nd that's all he* said?"

Damien could only nod. He didn't dare look at the Sit Room clock. Who knew how many hours they'd been here. He'd intentionally sat with his back to the big digital displays that showed local and President time. They'd be in sync right now because the President was sitting at the head of the table, but Damien didn't want to know.

He'd never so appreciated his anonymous role at the duty watch officer's desk. Or so wanted to get back to it.

For the entire flight home in the back of the helicopter, they'd written down every word they could remember. After checking with him on a scribbled note, Cornelia had used General Arnson as a sounding board to force them to remember as much as possible. Then all three of them had been whisked into the Situation Room. An ever-changing array of senior staff had arrived, questioned, departed, returned...

Someone served them a late dinner he couldn't recall, but the whirlwind didn't slow—it grew. The President, the Misters Elect, the NSA, General Brett Rogers—Chairman of the Joint Chiefs of Staff, and too many others for him to keep track of were called in until there wasn't an empty seat and there were plenty more standing: Homeland Security, counter-terrorism, Secret Service...

A cultural attack.

Perhaps during *your Christian holiday season.*

We shall cut out their heart with their own words.

Though it was Saturday afternoon, substitute copies of the Declaration and Constitution had been put on display and the originals placed in the main vault at the National Archives. That President Madani had opened his conversation with the first line of the Declaration had been too much for even the skeptics to dismiss.

Beyond that, it was generally agreed that unless President Madani could offer them some further details at a later time, there was little that could be surmised or done.

Still they had talked.

And talked.

And talked.

He and Cornelia had been asked questions until they were wrung dry—every word, every nuance questioned and re-questioned. Even Cornelia's perfect posture was finally sagging.

That's what finally kicked him into action. That fact that Cornelia was less than her incredible self was so wrong that it dragged him from his own pending stupefaction.

"We're done," his voice came out as little more than a croak.

When no one paid any attention to him, he rose to his feet, and managed to find a little more volume.

"We're done."

Still no effect.

So he took Cornelia's hand in his and helped her to her feet. He could feel her shaking. Over everyone's sudden protests, he simply led her from the room.

Damien forgot to look away from the wall clock as he passed by it: oh-seven-hundred.

Twenty-four hours. They'd been on the go for twenty-four straight hours, twelve of them in this goddamn room.

Leading her by the hand, they passed by the watch desk.

Marko's low whistle of surprise was the only sound from his team, who were getting a start-of-shift briefing from the prior team. He glanced over at them.

Felice and Vaccaro both gave him a thumbs-up, and Caron whispered softly, "Bugger me! The Chief of Staff? Good on ya, mate."

Cornelia was stumbling worse than a drunk as he led her out into the White House foyer. The dawn was still lost somewhere behind freshly dark clouds.

"I have a car and driver waiting for you," the head of the President's Secret Service detail, Frank Adams, loomed up beside him. He handed them their coats. Damien had forgotten to grab them, which told him how poorly he was functioning.

"You're the best, Frank."

"No, that's my wife. But thanks for saying it. You take care of this lady."

"Already on it."

"I see that," he glanced down at their joined hands.

"Go to hell, Frank."

"Bound to, Damien. Good night, Ms. Day," he saw them all the way to the car and personally closed the door behind them.

She was asleep on Damien's shoulder by the time they reached her condo.

The morning doorman, who'd given him nothing but the evil eye at this time yesterday morning, rushed to hold the door as he carried her in. She curled up in his arms like a lover. Her head on his shoulder, her arms draped about his neck. She weighed nothing, as if her exhaustion was so deep that all substance had been dragged from her.

There was enough light through her east-facing windows, despite the glowering sky, that Damien could navigate her apartment. He lay her down atop the rose-colored comforter on the bed, he pulled off her boots, then sat down in a floral armchair for a moment to gather the energy to take off her coat and tuck her in.

It was the last thing he remembered.

CHAPTER EIGHT

*C*old.

Cornelia reached for the blanket. She wasn't under one. Still cold.

She was lying down in her coat, on her bed. The pillow smelled of... Damien! Where was—

She opened her eyes to the room, and had to squint. The heavy overcast still let too much light in the two tall windows that faced the park across the street. Once she grew accustomed to the brightness, she spotted him. He too still wore his coat, slouched in the chair by her dresser. Through the uncurtained windows, the day looked icy cold against the dark gray sky—sleeting rain slapped against the glass in hard gusts.

Damien slept as if he'd been cut down in place. His arms hanging off either side of the chair, his head tipped sideways as if some headsman had done only a mediocre job of chopping him off at the neck.

He didn't look much like a conquering hero, but he was. She remembered how strong and steady he'd been through the endless debriefing. She'd never have made it as long as she did without his constant encouragement.

And then he'd rescued her.

It was a moment that maidens in distress were supposed to recall and didn't know whether she was happy or sad that she mostly didn't. She'd never been so tired in her life. Then his hand had lifted her from her seat and she'd been whisked away in some fairy carriage that had felt like being held in his arms. And had woken up—

Cold.

Cornelia managed to regain her feet and stumbled over her leather Blondo mid-calf boots she'd chosen yesterday. They'd have been more useful if they were still on her feet. Pulling her coat more tightly about her didn't decrease the chill, neither did rubbing her feet together—two chafing icicles, not body warmth. She moved around the room, dropping the curtains into place, shutting out the too bright morning. She didn't know what time she gotten into, or at least onto her bed, but it hadn't been long enough ago.

When she passed by Damien, she jostled his arm.

"Huh?" No more than an incoherent grunt. Then a groan as he tried to straighten out his neck.

She jostled him again, "Into the bed, now."

He looked up at her, over at the bed, down at himself—at least he still wore his boots—then back up at her. "Huh?"

Cornelia decided that he was awake enough to figure out the next steps for himself. She shed her coat, and clothes over the other armchair and felt terribly bohemian for not hanging them up. Slipping on a flannel nightgown, she then crawled back under the covers and pulled them over her head.

She could hear Damien stumble to his feet. After a few miscellaneous and manly grunts, he slid naked beneath the covers. Is this what it would be like to live with a man? She'd never done that, never shared her living space except for a night here and there. Which was all she'd done with Damien. So why was she suddenly thinking what it would be like to live with the man?

He slipped a hand out in the darkness, found her breast, whispered a "sorry," then slid his hand about her waist and pulled her in as if she weighed nothing.

One thing for sure, living with a man was a much warmer option.

Ignoring propriety, she plastered herself against him: her twined arms and hands trapped between them, her legs slipping between his, her face burrowed against his shoulder.

"Well, good morning," she liked the deep rumble of his chest and pushed harder against it. How could a person be so deliciously warm? Would that be a problem in the hot summer? No, she had air conditioning. It would still be incredible.

"Go back to sleep. We need sleep," Cornelia could feel it dragging at her very bones.

"Fat chance," he pulled her in tighter until he was practically crushing her against him.

"So warm," her fingers must feel like ice against his warm chest, but he didn't complain.

"Is that all I am to you? A life-sized heating unit?"

"Absolutely."

He shifted to slide his other arm beneath her head and his powerful biceps became her pillow.

"Very warm. Very nice." And so male that she wondered what that made her prior lovers. Technically male, but they had been political and office types. Damien might work as a librarian in the Situation Room, but Marine radiated off him.

He kissed her on top of the head and she did her best not to purr.

She huddled inside his embrace and soaked up the warmth and the wonder of his embrace. The wonder of it, that was the biggest surprise. Damien didn't hold or hug her, he embraced her. He held her the same way he looked at her, as if she was more important than anything.

The sensation stilled her thoughts and quieted her soul until she was aware of only two things: Damien's warmth and his luscious smell.

———

"How in the world can you fall asleep like this?" Damien kept his question silent so that he didn't wake Cornelia.

Her flannel nightgown hid nothing, wrapping her in a second, almost plush skin. From her freezing toes pressed tight atop his own to her soft hair tucked under his chin, there wasn't a single point not in contact.

She was asleep.

His body was vibrant with need. He ached to touch, taste, feel, enter.

And she was asleep.

A power ran through him, the like of which he'd rarely felt since his six months in the Marine Corps officer training at The Basic School at Quantico. It was the course that made four years of NROTC and the three summers between look like a lazy-assed cakewalk. For six months he'd done everything from rifle platoon tactics and crew-served weapons—the Marines loved their howitzers and missile launchers—to signals intelligence and ground electronic warfare.

At the end of The Basic School you either became an officer or you became an officer—Marines never quit. But that didn't mean it was easy or that all graduates were created equal. Screw up and you didn't get a choice on where you landed—*infantry command here I come.* Graduate at the top, talk nice to the intelligence instructors, do a tour at Marine Intel, and get recommended straight into National Security Council.

He done it right: every single goddamn step of it for four years of school, a half more at Quantico, and every training course since.

The toughest instructor of them all had been the NSC's prior senior watch officer. Damien's first two-year tour at the watch desk had been pure hell and Laslow had made sure of it. Every lousy, impossible, bound-to-come-apart-at-exactly-the-wrong-moment job had somehow landed on his desk. He knew Laslow was behind it, but Damien had survived enough Marine Corps instructors that an asshole Defense Intelligence Agency liaison wasn't going to get to him.

Then, when his tour was up, he was reassigned to the Sit Room—which never happened. After two more years of Laslow hell, the man had taken him aside.

"You're it, Feinman. You're in again, but I'm out. You disappoint me and I'm going to come back from the grave to haunt you."

"You planning on dying?" The man had been at least seventy even back then—and sharp as hell.

"Wife's got family in Louisiana. I *hate* Louisiana. Dying will be a goddamn blessing."

Last Damien had heard, he was playing in the winning money of senior golf tournaments.

Damien had taken over, providing continuity to the NSC watch team for three more tours since. Any Marine up on the line who said Damien hadn't earned his captain's bars could go suck on a hot howitzer barrel. Once he'd made it, Damien had known just how strong he was.

Or thought he had.

All that had been blown away by the strength he felt holding onto the woman in his arms.

Cornelia wasn't weak, not a single ounce of her. But still he felt truly strong in this moment, protecting her from the world.

Focus on the moment! Laslow had yelled at him. Damien was always thinking about future strategy and possibilities. How to better advise the very top policy makers.

It was a variation of the tirade that Cornelia had unleashed on his Marine Intel buddies. His thinking didn't need to remain tactical, as theirs did. Instead, it needed to be focused on what was needed at the moment...and to anticipate the next. He like to think of it as: the Feinman corollary to the Laslow initiative.

That's what Damien had striven to teach the teams since he'd taken over as the leader of the duty watch. To serve the room in the very best way, it was always necessary to think about the next moment. To anticipate it. To have the information ready before they asked for it.

Sometimes the effort was wasted, when the question never came or conversation veered in another direction. But it had forced the watch team to bring a new level to their game.

And what Cornelia needed right now was sleep.

He knew that.

No matter what he needed. She—

"How much longer are you going to lie there thinking so hard?" Her voice whispered against his chest.

"You're asleep." He'd known she was asleep. She still wasn't moving a single muscle.

"Uh-huh. Clearly. And if you try to hold me any harder, our bodies will merge and become one."

"Oh, sorry," but he couldn't bring himself to ease off. All of his protective thoughts were still keeping her clasped tightly against him. "Letting you go doesn't appear to be an option."

"Good. Don't."

And she shifted ever so slowly. Sliding from huddled warmth inside the protective circle of his arms, to a lover holding him as well.

By the time he slipped the flannel nightgown off her, her breath was no longer so calm and steady.

When he finally rolled her onto her back, it was short and choppy with rough gasps.

And when the ultimate release rocked through both their bodies, he didn't feel merely strong, he felt triumphant.

CHAPTER NINE

fter another four hours of sleep and then delivery Chinese food, Damien had slid back to sleep. But that escape eluded Cornelia.

Ultimately she wasn't going to solve anything lying next to Damien while he slept. Half an hour later she sat at her desk in the West Wing. Nearing midnight on a Sunday night, there was no one to disturb her thought processes. Or her body. *Disturbing* her body? She wasn't some sacrosanct temple. Damien wasn't disturbing her body, he was messing with her emotions.

She sighed and pushed back from her computer before she even got started. It was clear that she wasn't going to find a way to compartmentalize Damien Feinman unless she assigned him some concentrated thought.

Then she pulled herself back to the computer because thinking about Damien was a one-way road. If she was going to go back to thinking about her fantasy lover—he wasn't the only one allowed to have happy fantasies—then she might as well have stayed in bed with him.

How could he even think she was asleep? She could feel his thoughts churning away almost as strongly as his arms had been embracing her. No man ever held a woman that way. She was used to...

compromising. It was a sad statement on her past, but it was true. Damien had certainly spoiled her for average men. Whenever this ended, she was going to mourn the loss, and then become a nun and take a vow of celibacy so that she could concentrate on her work once more.

First she pulled up the latest from the NSC.

Only two things in the queue, starting with the report of her own interview. She ran through it, making little more than a few proofing marks. The last lines stumped her, they were not what she had reported. Cornelia's version had included that they were invited to visit Tehran as a guest of the President.

But this version included the entire exchange about President Madani's complimentary mock proposal to her, Damien's statement about having common sense, and Madani's invitation to Damien "and his wife." She knew she hadn't said that in any of the debriefings—she'd been very careful not to even think about that, never mind say it aloud.

And it wasn't word for word, so it couldn't have been a clandestine recording arranged without her knowledge. It must have been from Damien. *Him* she could kill. Perhaps not President Matthews for getting her into this mess in the first place, but any compunction she might have had about committing bodily harm on the NSC librarian had just gone out the window.

Didn't he understand who would see this report? It was already far more obvious than she would like that they were having a relationship. Then she remembered him holding her hand as he led her from the Sit Room this morning. He'd done that in front of her current boss and her future one. She'd now flaunted it in front of the President and the President-elect—never mind the NSA, the Joint Chiefs of Staff, General Arnson, and Damien's own staff—that she was sleeping with a man she'd known barely a week. Worse, with someone who had made what now amounted to a public declaration that he could envision them married.

This was spiraling out of control and it was time to end it.

When he came in this morning, she would call him into her office and simply announce that it was over. She would miss him. The incredible sex, the charming companionship, and the way he held her—she'd especially miss that—but she had to be practical and get her life back under her own control.

No need to make a note on her to-do list, she wouldn't forget.

That aspect of her life resolved, she digitally signed the stupid memo—with its ludicrous happy-ever-after statement—as being reasonably complete and adequately accurate. She'd learned to stop fighting that battle years ago. The only way to guarantee completely cogent reporting was to write it herself and there was never enough time for her to do both that and her job.

Good enough, moving on!

The second item in the NSC queue for her attention was the action report from yesterday's meetings. There was the usual batch of naysayers, denying that an "enemy" country might ever reach out to help. Instead, it was purported, the Iranians must be instigating panic as a distraction from whatever their true purpose might be. *Follows: gross speculation and wild conjecture.* Cornelia skipped that section.

The President's response, included in the memo, had been less than kind in the words he'd used.

The catch was that those who did believe in President Madani's willingness to help hadn't been able to make any more sense of his warning than she and Damien had.

Then, there'd been a debate on how to prepare for an unknown threat at an unknown time. The NSA and CIA reported no increased chatter on suspected terrorist networks or known terrorist phones. Had they simply become wiser in their communications or were there really no communications to hear?

She went back to Madani's warning itself. Not a *gulf* this time, but *bay*. She reviewed his words carefully. He hadn't said DC, she was the one who had jumped to that conclusion. Madani hadn't denied that conclusion, but neither had he confirmed it. Was there some question? Had he shrugged uncertainly? She couldn't recall.

Damien's desk phone rang. His shift was still five hours away, but that didn't mean much when there was a crisis in the Sit Room and he'd come into work after waking alone. What was it about their schedules that kept leaving him in Cornelia's bed without Cornelia?

Maybe he should try taking her to his place. It was out in Tenleytown, but with the Metro, it wouldn't take much longer to reach the White House than walking from her Georgetown condo. Maybe he could keep her in his bed with more success than he'd kept her in her own.

"You planning on answering that?" Bettani was also in early. He'd sort of blocked out the phone. Some memory was itching at him and he hadn't found it yet.

"Damien," he didn't even look at the caller ID as he answered.

"Bay. He didn't say which bay," Cornelia's idea of a *Good morning, lover* moment—at least when she was in Chief of Staff mode.

"That's it!" Damien jolted upright in his chair. "That's what was bothering me. Thanks, you just saved me a world of heavy thinking."

"I've been doing it for hours," she sounded weary of it, but also energized. Her mind was awake, even if she must be physically exhausted.

"Come on down and we'll look at it."

There was a long pause that puzzled him. She sounded a little resigned when she said that she'd be down in a moment.

Damien shifted to the Briefing Room itself. He shut down room's microphone, so that he wouldn't disturb the duty watch—he could do his own damn searches.

Cornelia joined him soon enough, but she didn't sit. Instead she came into the room and stopped, standing still and looking at him.

"How do you look so amazing at three in the morning?" Her attire reminded him simultaneously of the woman and the lover. Her tailored suit was impeccably professional—not unisex by any means, but alone it would have made no statement beyond "feminine." However, around her collar she wore a brilliant red scarf of some flimsy material that added a flair that she didn't normally show. A flair that reminded him of the stunningly sensual woman who presented a neatly professional demeanor.

The look on her face at his compliment wasn't what he'd anticipated. No brilliant smile, not even the small quirk of one. Instead she was studying him with all the enthusiasm she might study a report on the latest requisition for a US Coast Guard ice breaker.

"There are over a hundred significant bays around the continental US." He decided that directing her attention to the screen was probably the safest choice at the moment.

She moved slowly to the first seat on the left-hand side of the table and sat across from him. But she didn't look at him, instead inspecting the map of the US that he'd put up on one screen and a USGS list of bays on another. Cornelia didn't say anything about what was on her mind.

"I think," he struggled not to ask what the hell was going on, "that President Madani meant Chesapeake Bay, but we don't know that for sure. And from what I can remember, he wasn't sure either. So let's look at major bays and how they might relate to: *We shall cut out their heart with their own words.*"

Cornelia nodded, "Also, it would have to be a significant attack, with meaning. A terrorist wants everything to be showy."

"So Seattle Public Library would be out even though it sits just five blocks above Elliot Bay."

"Why are we starting at the bottom of the alphabet—Washington State?"

"I always do that, though I'm not sure why," Damien puzzled at it for a moment. "I think that it forces me to adopt a fresh view. Looking at everything backwards."

Cornelia glanced his way for a moment at that, then nodded for him to continue.

State by state they rolled up the list.

"I've always been partial to Depoe Bay in Oregon," he told her when they got to Oregon.

"Why? It's tiny."

"It's the smallest navigable bay in the world, at least according to the locals. They have a fishing fleet, and I use the word loosely, of less than a dozen craft. That plus a couple of whale watching boats."

"Not a likely target," Cornelia pointed out.

"Didn't say it was. Just said I was partial to it."

Cornelia covered her face with her hands for a moment. He wasn't sure if she was trying to hide a smile, or was about to go looking for a gun.

When she did neither, he continued.

New York was a harbor.

Long Island was a sound.

Massachusetts Bay outside of Boston was a maybe.

The Chesapeake still ranked as a most likely.

Maine had hundreds of bays along its craggy shores, but who could possibly care unless they lived there.

Hawaii seemed too remote to feel threatening, as did Alaska.

By the time they were done they had added only San Francisco and Delaware—and the only interesting thing up the latter was Philadelphia and it wasn't technically on the bay, but rather on the river. Of course, DC wasn't on the Chesapeake either, but rather up the Potomac River from the bay.

"Are we overthinking this?" She asked when they had their list of bays down to just three. "Are we putting too much emphasis on the word *bay?*"

Damien didn't know. "It's about all we have to go on."

"All we have to go on," Cornelia sighed.

Damien had often been accused of being a little oblivious when it came to women. Bettani or Marko were always telling him that he was missing all the signals, both the *Come here, boy* and the *It's about to be over!*

Not this time.

He heard Cornelia's subject change loud and clear.

"All we have to go on?" he prompted her cautiously. Just because he heard the subject change, didn't mean he had a clue what the new topic was.

"Damien," her tone sounded dire and she was looking at her folded hands, not the screen or him.

Her hands, that he so enjoyed looking at, even when he wasn't thinking about the incredible sensations they could draw from his body, were clenched together bloodlessly white.

"We—"

"Nope!" Damien cut her off.

"What do you mean?" That forced her gaze up to study him.

"I mean that if you're thinking about what I think you're thinking about, don't think about it because you're completely wrong."

"That didn't make any sense."

"It did when I said it," he puzzled over his own words for a moment. "Just not when they came out."

"What are you saying?"

"I'm saying..." And he was about to put his foot in it, but he was afraid of what she'd say if he let her have the initiative. "I'm saying that if you're thinking about me not falling in love with you, you're already too late." Which sure as hell wasn't anything he'd meant to say.

———

Cornelia could feel the silence slide over her. That cold clear wash of Vulcanesque logic that she had cultivated as a little girl. The one that had made her the most deadly debater at Claremont McKenna—a school known for its debate-style instruction. The one that she used when faced by unfriendly congressmen or demonstrably overly-friendly congressional aides.

Cut it off! Lock it away! Be safe!

None of that garbage out there was about her. She was safe inside herself. Safe from...

Damien watched her carefully across the President's Briefing Room table. He looked as surprised by what he'd said as she felt—if she was letting herself feel.

Which she wasn't.

But she did.

Feelings that she wanted to deny as impossible, except they were his feelings.

You can never simply know *what someone else is thinking. Your job is to find out.* It was one of Zachary Thomas' favorite sayings.

"I think I just found out."

"Found out what?" Damien asked softly. His deep voice sounded as if it was being strangled somewhere deep in his chest.

"That you're feeling what—" Cornelia couldn't quite bring herself to say it. "you say your feeling."

"I seem to." He dragged a hand through his hair, mussing it completely. It was one of his more endearing habits. "It's surprising the crap out of me if that's any comfort."

"Actually, it is."

"You—"

"Nope," she cut *him* off this time. "Don't give me any clichés about my not having to respond or if the next line isn't obvious or any of that."

"Okay," he shrugged and offered one of his smiles. "I'll just wait you out then."

"It may be a long wait, Damien."

"The President of Iran didn't seem to think so."

"He is also arrogantly male. He practically proposed to me over a pastrami sandwich."

"Corned beef."

"What?"

"I had a Reuben. You and President Madani had corned beef. Pejman was the one with pastrami and he didn't propose to you."

"As I said, arrogantly male," but she was having trouble hiding her smile.

"Something one arrogant male can appreciate in another."

"And on what do you base your own arrogance other than being a Marine?"

"And a librarian. Makes me a pretty special guy." Then he leaned forward as much as the table would reasonably allow. "But do you want to know the real reason?"

"I think that the answer to that would be no." Cornelia could feel her magnetic, unthinking, purely emotional draw to him and didn't like it. Actually, she did like it and that was even more unnerving.

"I figured, but I'll tell you anyway. The real, heretofore unexpressed reason I feel so comfortable with being an arrogant male is quite simple."

"What's that?"

He reached out and rested one of his big strong hands over her clasped ones, enveloping them both with his warmth and power.

"See? I knew that you really wanted to know. But it's a secret," he whispered.

"We are in the Sit Room," and her smile did escape her control at his laugh.

"Lean closer and I'll whisper it."

Even as she told herself that wasn't going to happen, her body decided otherwise and she leaned in.

"I'm the guy who gets to tell Cornelia Day that he loves her." Then he leaned back and returned his voice to normal as if it was too much even for him. "If that isn't an excuse for unremitting arrogance, I don't know what is."

"Males," Sienna spoke from the doorway, "don't need an excuse to be arrogant. But what was yours? I couldn't quite hear it." She continued into the room and dropped her files at the chair beside Cornelia.

"I—"

"Any doubts," Sienna talked right over Cornelia's attempts to protest, "just go up to the roof and ask my Secret Service sniper fiancé. That man actually thinks I'm going to happily marry him, bear his children, and grow old together."

"You aren't?" Cornelia couldn't hold back her surprise. They were so obviously in love.

"Oh, I am. Christmas Day. You're both invited if I didn't remember to send you invitations. Not a chance am I going to let a man that good out of my sights. But I'm not going to tell him that just because I said 'yes' when he proposed, all the rest of it is true."

"But—"

"So," Sienna kept talking. "Anything new to report, other than the obvious?" She nodded toward where Damien sat with a perplexed look on his face.

Cornelia managed to control her voice. Less sure of her hands, she tucked them in her lap under the edge of the table. "Unless terrorists are going to be attacking the world's smallest fishing fleet harbor, we're still thinking that the Chesapeake is our primary candidate."

"Darn it! I didn't even think about the target not being DC. I need to get my head fixed."

"Actually," Cornelia couldn't help but feel a little envious of Sienna's clarity of thought and awareness of her own emotions, "your head seems like it's just fine to me."

Cornelia risked a glance over at Damien, but he was once again concentrating on the screen as if to verify their conclusions. It was hard not to wish that she too could talk about Damien with such heartfelt passion.

She almost laughed at that.

She hadn't just thought about being able to say such things about "someone," she'd targeted Damien. Perhaps she did need to keep her overly logical thoughts to herself and simply give her "human half" feelings time to be recognized. As she watched Damien work, she suspected that she knew what those feelings would be when they finally crystallized.

And for some reason, that wasn't worrying her nearly as much as she thought it should.

CHAPTER TEN

A *week of time hadn't* shed a single bit of light on President Javad Madani's cryptic warning.

Damien had listened to scores of theories proposed and shot down during multiple Sit Room meetings. He'd done his best to migrate back to his watch desk, and had succeeded for the most part. But he was still drawn into a much higher percentage of meetings than was usual for a man in his position. He tried not to read too much into it. He liked his role as Sit Room librarian, the one person most deeply steeped in the knowledge of not only the room's operation, but also the history of the decisions which had been made here. He pre-dated the current administration despite their double term of office, and he had some hope of post-dating the next one even if they won a double term.

But their "Christian holiday season" was now a week shorter than it had been when Madani delivered his warning. The sense of impending disaster lurked in the corners of the room while meetings were held on other topics as well. Then, the lurking shadow would crawl back into the open and knock the cheer out of any task, no matter how success-fully done.

One thing had changed though. He'd now known Cornelia Day for two weeks rather than one. He gathered his coat and headed up the stairs and along the hall to her office.

Friday night. A week ago he'd invited her to Molly Malone's Pub for dinner. A week ago they'd slept together for the first time…though it felt as if they always had.

A lot had changed between them. He was even crazier about her than he had been. Her poise ran soul deep. She was the one who always lent the calmest voice to any meeting. When the unflappable President was ready to pound his fist through the face of some conniving South American ambassador, it was Cornelia who calmed the situation. Her chill poise was often enough to convince her "opponent" that their lives would be far less challenging if they were to cooperate…fully…and right now!

Gods but she tickled him no end.

Janet waved as he entered her office, and pointed to a chair while she continued on the phone. Usually this late in the day, Janet was gone and he could just stick his head in to see if Cornelia was ready to go or if he should order in dinner. Something must be up beyond her cracked open door.

Janet, who looked like everybody's favorite grandmother, finished handing out a set of instructions on the phone. "I do care, dear. I care that the Chief of Staff has your report on her desk by six a.m. Monday morning….Yes, I understand that it is Friday night. However, the request was issued to your office on Tuesday and you know and I know that was plenty of warning. Now you must get it done or you will have to face me and then Ms. Day, and you know which will be the worse… Good!" And she hung up with more force than he expected from such a mild-mannered woman.

"Remind me never to make you mad, Janet." The threat of unleashing Cornelia's ire would be a great motivator for any man.

"That Secretary of the Interior. He is always doing everything at the last minute. Would never miss a golf game, god forbid, even in the winter, but a report on Ms. Day's desk…" She slowly reined in her righteous indignation.

"As I said," and he aimed his most winning smile at her. He liked Janet. He'd had little to do with her among the fifteen hundred people who worked in the White House, at least until these last two weeks. He'd come to appreciate her skills.

She typed a rapid note into her computer—perhaps a log entry on "that Secretary of the Interior." He knew the man, a pretentious jerk—which Damien felt described a good quarter of the cabinet and at least half of politicians.

"There's a wider world to be appreciated now that I've crawled out of my basement." He'd thought he could see everything, or at least everything important from his watch-duty desk. But up here he'd learned much more about the people who worked to keep the country running than he ever would in his Sit Room.

"Yes, there is," and suddenly Janet's full attention was focused on him.

He had a flash of insight that there just might be someone in this office more dangerous than Cornelia. Her eyes narrowed as she inspected him from head to toe. He was never very comfortable in his dress blues, but at the moment it felt as if he should be wearing them.

"If you are courting Ms. Day, you are doing a poor job of it."

"Courting? What century are you from, Janet?" Personally he thought he was doing a pretty good job of it. They were almost up to their two-week anniversary and she hadn't lost one bit of her shine—Cornelia was still the most fascinating and sexy woman he'd ever been with.

"My Harry courted me from the day we met at the march on Washington to end the Vietnam War in November, 1969. Just because we slept together that first night among the trees by the Reflecting Pool, doesn't mean he didn't still have to win my heart. So don't think you can be all *modern* and dismiss me, young man. A woman likes to be courted, and not just in bed. And if you don't get your act together, you're going to lose her. If that happens, I am going to be *very* disappointed in you." Then she offered one of her matronly smiles. "You can go in any time you'd like," Janet nodded toward Cornelia's office door before standing to gather her coat and purse.

Damien struggled to his feet and held her coat for her.

After she was gone, Damien sat back down for a moment.

Lose Cornelia? That was not an acceptable scenario.

Did he need to step up his game? That had never been an issue before. He'd also never been so smitten by a woman. No one before Cornelia had engendered thoughts of a permanent nature. Oh, he always had his fantasies of what it might be like to settle down with each woman he met, but it had never felt important before. His idle daydreams had been easy to recognize as little more than that.

He studied Janet's vacant desk.

Apparently he wasn't the only one who could imagine a long term scenario between Cornelia and himself. He smacked his forehead with the palm of his hand. He really had to stop thinking like a Marine.

"Are you beating yourself up for any particular reason?"

Cornelia leaned on the door jamb of her office. She actually leaned. Why did such a slight change make her appear so vulnerable? Again his protective, grab-and-hold instincts kicked in.

Long, elegant in a dark blue outfit that screamed power. Her blouse was a sharp white with a matching mid-waist sash that equally loudly declared feminine. The clothes flowed neatly over her, only appearing to mask the woman within. He knew what lay past the clothes and his first instinct was how much he wanted her body. But he also knew the woman who lived in that incredible body.

"Janet was right," was all he could think to say.

"She usually is," Cornelia agreed. "What about this time?"

"Are you done for the day?" Damien decided that discretion was his best option at the moment. Then he spotted her security badge. His was West Wing-only without an escort—and he'd only rarely had reason to begrudge that, he just didn't need more. Hers covered the entire White House. That gave him a great idea.

"Never," her weary smile spoke to the heavy demands of her new job. "But for today, I think so."

"Good! Come along."

"Let me just get my coat."

"You don't need it."

"I'm not going to have sex with you in some White House closet."

"While I like that image a great deal," Janet would kick his ass, and she'd be right. "I had something else in mind." He rose and held out his elbow, inviting her to take hold, just as he had on the walk to Moly Malone's.

After she studied it for a long moment, she stepped forward and did so. The sensation was no different—an essential rightness washed over him as they came in contact. Any man would be proud to escort such a woman anywhere; which didn't do his ego any harm. And maybe it was time to do a little courting.

"I'm not particularly hungry..." her protest died as he turned away from the stairs which led down to the Navy Mess.

———

Something was different about Damien, and Cornelia was too tired to make sense of it. A part of her would be glad to simply go home, let him exhaust her body with his, and hope for some sleep before Saturday morning arrived and the work resumed.

She needed to do something.

Even a quick round of sex in a White House closet didn't sound completely unreasonable at the moment. Something had to happen, because she didn't know how much longer she could hold everything in, and it was only her second week on the job.

Four years loomed impossibly large.

He led her down the hall toward the Oval Office. *No, not something more.* But he turned aside past the Roosevelt and Cabinet Rooms and along the short hallway to the Western Colonnade.

"I should have taken my coat," she clutched at her unbuttoned jacket as they stepped outside. The bitter December wind sliced around the tall columns and right through her poplin blouse.

"Sorry. I didn't want to risk the inside passage through the Press Room to the Residence. Who knows what evil lurks there."

"Reporters," she let a shudder of cold become a mock shudder of horror. "Not tonight. Please."

A Marine in a long pea coat saluted Damien sharply. Damien returned it as neatly and then the Marine, after a glance at her badge, held the Palm Room door for them and she hurried inside—stepping into wonderland.

"It's Christmas," she managed to gasp out. The entry to the Residence was aswirl with decorations. There were trees and such in the West Wing, but nothing like this.

"It is," Damien sounded very smug as he came up beside her.

"As if you are personally responsible."

"Hey! I brought you to Christmas."

"It looks to me as if it was already here."

"As if you were going to find time to make it over here on your own. See, personally responsible for taking Ms. Cornelia Day to where Christmas is. That definitely counts."

Cornelia was almost surprised he didn't leap up on a chair and beat his chest to make his point. She could feel herself relaxing. Damien's odd humor always did that to her.

Christmas in Palo Alto, California had never been white, and not even particularly cold. Her family had often traveled up to the city, and San Francisco's damp winters had a penetrating bite to them, but still not snow.

Last week's snowfall had melted away, but the lack of snow outside the window did nothing to diminish the wonder of Christmas inside the White House as Damien led her into the Central Hall. The decorators had gone mad this year. The low ceiling of the vaulted hallway hadn't made them hesitate for a second. Snowflakes the size of the Capitol Dome were held up by Washington Monument-sized candy canes—or so it seemed. It was overwhelmingly cheerful. She couldn't wait to see what was upstairs.

But Damien had other ideas and led her deeper into the bowels of the basement. At the midpoint of the long hall, he looked about uncertainly, then led her down a narrow corridor that was crowded to either side with rolled-up rugs and stacked chairs. There was barely room for them to walk side by side.

She glanced at Damien, but he was carefully not meeting her gaze.

"Let's test the power of the White House Chief of Staff," he offered cryptically. The size of his smile was impressive, and very like a little boy's about to be naughty and not caring if he got caught.

They entered another, equally cluttered hall and passed the bowling alley, several storeroom doors, and turned in at the last door down the hall. To the left was a sign for the carpentry shop—she hadn't known that the White House had one of its own. Several offices straight ahead.

To her right a small sign declared: Chocolate Shop.

Damien knocked and they were let in by a rotund man with a brown-smeared white apron and a tall white hat which had one perfect set of chocolate fingerprints near its base.

"What do ye want?" His brogue was distinctly Scottish.

The chocolatier didn't give them time to answer.

"Never mind, as if I wasn't already knowing. I'm wise to the likes of you." He somehow simultaneously scowled at Damien but winked at her.

He swung the door wider to reveal a fifteen-foot-square stainless steel kitchen packed with refrigerators, supplies, a big stove, and a prep table from which sprouted a four-foot-tall chocolate Christmas tree. The layers of branches were darkest chocolate with milk and white chocolate decorations. Lights were represented by brilliant dots of red, green, and gold fondant.

"You so much as think of touching that and I'll kill you. And if your blood smears a single bit of it, I'll kill myself right here so god help me."

It was a masterpiece and Cornelia wasn't going anywhere near it.

The chef slipped a tray out of a cooler and set it on the counter before them. "Well, don't just look, have at it, won't ye? It's why ye've come nosing about, after all."

Damien grinned at her as he leaned in to inspect the tray.

It was filled with tiny chocolate reindeer. Not flat, like cut out of a sheet of chocolate, but fully three-dimensional figurines, each less than two inches high, including antlers.

"They don't have their harnesses yet, but that's what you get for being the first ones by."

They looked charming and delicious.

"Go on, lass. You don't take one and tell me how amazing it is, me heart will be broken fair in two I can promise you."

Cornelia did take one, being very careful not to bump any others. She wasn't quite sure how to eat it.

"Just open up and pop it in."

"I feel like I'm eating Rudolph."

"Nah, I left him and his red nose in the cooler. You're safe with this lot."

Unable to deny his encouraging smile, she did just pop it in. And when she bit down it took all her willpower not to spray the Christmas tree with it. The reindeer's body broke apart in her mouth with an unexpected flood of cherry liqueur.

"Oh my god," she managed to mumble as the flavors combined and stormed her senses. "That's incredible."

The chef positively beamed.

———

By the time they escaped, they'd each had a cherry reindeer, a peanut butter inside-dark chocolate outside gnome, and a peppermint snowflake. They'd also shared a tiny glass of schnapps with Chef Andrews—just enough that Damien could feel it warming his blood. As if Cornelia wasn't already doing that.

"Okay, Damien. Top that one," she held onto his arm with both hands and leaned into him as he guided them back into the center of the Residence.

He had no idea how that might be possible. The chocolate shop had been a rumor he'd only heard about in the past.

Up the stairs to the ground floor, Damien led her through the Entrance Hall, which was more akin to a North Pole snowstorm than a hall, and into the Blue Room. This year's Christmas tree dominated the space, the topmost star nearly brushing the setting that normally held the massive gilt-and-crystal French chandelier.

By Cornelia's pleased gasp he knew he'd done well. It might not be gourmet chocolate, but it was a very pretty tree.

She was completely enamored of it. He'd thought to show it to her and move on to continue their explorations, though he wasn't sure where, but she inspected nearly every ornament.

He read the explanatory placard aloud.

"Immigrant children who came from all over the world to America were invited to paint an ornament like their country's flag. The 195 countries recognized by the United States are represented here. These include all 193 UN countries as well as the Holy See and Kosovo."

"How many of these have you been to?" Cornelia asked from somewhere farther around the tree.

"Do you see one with a red-and-white maple leaf?"

There was a long pause. "Got it. Canada. Where else?"

"Well, I've been there."

Cornelia looked at him between two branches and an ornament of Trinidad and Tobago's red flag with one black and two white stripes.

"Honest. A Marine cannot tell a lie." He held up his right hand with three fingers raised.

"That's the Girl Scout sign," she ducked out of sight as she continued her inspection of the tree.

He looked at his hand. "Actually, I'm fairly sure that's Boy Scouts."

"Girl Scout. Were you ever a Boy Scout?"

"Naw," he lowered his hand, "too busy chasing girls."

"How did that work for you?"

"Sucked. The girls all went for the guys in the cool uniforms."

"That's why you became a Marine?"

"Damn straight."

"I...don't think that I'll ask the next question," she said from somewhere opposite the blue-and-red ornament with a circled red star of North Korea. Must have been a real challenge tracking down a refugee to paint that one. He wondered if the decorators had to make some themselves.

"Well," he couldn't resist the opening, "I'll have to try on my uniform and see what you think."

"I wasn't going to ask," she wandered into sight just past the gold, black, and white that must be Brunei. "Only Canada? Really?"

"Really. I can probably name every flag here because of my time in the Sit Room, but I went from college to officer training, then straight into intel. How about you?"

"I memorized all the flags of the world as a kid. I've been to a lot of countries since Zachary Thomas became Vice President. But I've never seen much of any of them except a monument here and a meeting room there."

How could he not fall for a woman who thought that memorizing flags was something fun to do.

"I try to keep up with the new ones, like Myanmar's change in 2010, but Africa still makes my head hurt. Nothing is stable there for very long."

"Don't feel bad. They make everyone's head hurt."

She came up to him until she was so close that he had to put his hands on her waist to keep from stumbling back. "Whoever thought flags could be so sexy?"

Before he could answer, she closed the last of the gap, wrapped her arms around his neck, and kissed him. Janet would be pleased. Hell, *he* was beyond pleased. She kissed him like she meant it.

This wasn't some prelude to sex. It felt like the first time he'd fired a rifle. Handguns he could take or leave, knowledge was his real weapon, but learning to fire an M16A4 had been a voyage of discovery. He never came close to sniper skill. Most of those guys were born with a pop gun in their hands and he'd been born clutching a library card. But a rifle was a machine he'd learned to appreciate. He still tried to get range time every week or so.

Cornelia's kiss was like that. Not sex. Not an unleashing of the passionate woman she normally hid deep inside. It was soft, exploratory, and so sincere that it could take his knees out from under him.

He gave back as good as he could. He rapidly discovered that wasn't a hard task. It was like she was kissing him for the first time and it was a voyage that he wanted to be at the end of as well. The whole ride.

What she seemed to be discovering, he'd already found: exactly who he wanted to be with. And he was holding her.

She—

"I thought that was a Presidential prerogative." Sienna. National Security Advisor. Somewhere behind him.

"What is?" He meant to tell her to go the hell away, but it didn't come out right. He didn't like unanswered questions.

"Necking in the White House."

Oh! "Go away. I'm busy here."

He leaned back in. Cornelia's eyes were dreamy and warm with—

"Have you two eaten yet?"

"What part of *go away I'm busy here* was I unclear about?" But the moment had passed him by. Cornelia's eyes had refocused and were looking over his shoulder toward Sienna.

"No, we haven't eaten."

"Then I'll just blame your temporary lapse of protocol on low blood sugar. Come on. Let's go to dinner. You can bring him too if you must."

Cornelia looked at him, "Are you going to behave?"

"Not a chance," his voice was rough and he barely had control.

"I suppose," again she was speaking over his shoulder, "that I'd better bring him along or who knows what trouble he'll get into."

Then she brushed her lips ever so lightly over his.

"This will make us even."

He narrowed his eyes at her.

"Payback," she whispered, "for almost getting me to agree to do it in a White House closet." Cornelia eased away, tucked her hand in his arm, and turned him about. Sienna stood there smirking at them as if she'd heard every word. "He tried to bribe me with chocolate."

And it had damn near worked too. Crap! It had come so close to working, not that getting her naked, in or out of a closet, was his goal at the moment. He needed to get back to finding out what was behind that kiss. He fell into step beside Sienna who slid a hand around his other arm. The two women started talking about something, though he was damned if he could tell what—his ears were still ringing from the stratospheric climb of that kiss.

They headed up some stairs like the three of them were off to see the wizard together. He was in no damn mood to break into a dance step down some yellow brick road.

But maybe he should be. Janet's advice had been spot on. If this was the result of doing a little courting, he was going to try it again soon. Hell, he'd do it every damn day for the rest of his life.

Cornelia had kissed him with more than her body, she'd done it with her heart. Did she even realize that?

He'd bet not and it was going to surprise the crap out of her when she did. He couldn't wait to be the one to tell her. He almost *did* want to break into a dance as they turned along a hall.

He'd dance right down the yellow...Oval Room.

The Yellow Oval was on the floor directly above the Blue Room with its Christmas tree.

That placed the Yellow Oval on the second floor, the President's personal residence.

He swallowed hard and blinked a few times. It didn't go away. He'd stumbled to a halt. Clicking his heels three times didn't make it go away.

For the first time in a decade at the White House, he was in the President's home.

———

"Look what I found wandering the halls," Sienna called out to the assembled group.

Cornelia welcomed the abrupt change of scene.

Here the world made more sense than in the highly decorated first floor and Blue Room. Anywhere in the world made more sense than the Blue Room at the moment.

Each year at Christmas she had been invited, along with Vice President Thomas, to the President's Christmas party. And though the night of the formal party was still a week away, it was a familiar sight. The Central Hall of the Second Floor of the Residence had far more rational seasonal decorations than the floors below. There were a couple of cheerful Christmas trees glittering in the long space. Red poinsettias ringed the grand piano. Festive pine-and-citrus garlands had been draped about dour eighteenth-century paintings. And that was about the extent of it—cheery without overwhelming.

In among the décor, the President Peter Matthews, Zachary, Daniel, and a man she didn't know had gathered on a group of couches. Then Sienna wrapped an arm about the stranger's neck and leaned down to kiss him. This had to be Roy Beaumont, Sienna's Secret Service sniper fiancée. The men all looked casually comfortable together. She wondered if she was really supposed to be here, then remembered that she was the Chief of Staff now—not merely the Vice President's assistant.

She didn't normally gravitate to groups, but at the moment she welcomed them and tried to hurry the lagging Damien next to her. The kiss in the Blue Room hadn't been merely intense. Damien was the master of intense, which worked for her because so was she. But that kiss had been…languid. Not that there wasn't energy, but rather that there was a smooth perfection that had filled her body until she felt as if she was radiating light out of every pore.

Cornelia Day the Christmas ornament.

It was the only way that she could describe it. Deep and smooth, it had flowed through and out of her. Rather than leaving her breathless for more, it had grounded her with a completeness that…

That she'd never found anywhere before. Sex with Damien was great. Actually, spectacular. But it was still sex. The kiss was something different that she really wasn't ready to think about.

"Since when…" Zachary was eyeing their still-clasped hands.

When Cornelia attempted to extract hers from Damien's, he resisted. She finally accepted the inevitable and ceased her effort. It was too late to hide anyway.

"Need to pay closer attention, Mr. President-elect," Daniel teased Zachary. "They're an item. Hot gossip for days now."

"A week," President Matthews put in.

"You're all blind," Sienna stood beside her fiancée's chair with a hand on his shoulder. "They've been together since the first day in the Sit Room. Totally obvious. Though I think Cornelia was a little slow on the uptake on that."

"Never known her to be slow about anything." Zachary was studying her more closely than she was comfortable with. She had always kept her personal life separate from the office, never mentioning a boyfriend, always being careful to cancel a date out of earshot if there was a late change in work plans.

Damien nodded agreement that Sienna had it right and the other men inspected him with renewed interest. She could see that slightly smug aura of self-satisfaction coming from him. *I'm the new alpha male on the block* simply radiated in every direction. She could even feel it in the strengthening of his grip on her hand.

Before she could do anything to knock him back to reality, Sienna stepped over and extracted Cornelia's hand from Damien's.

"Come on," Sienna led her back toward the stair landing, through a grand arched passage, and into the East Sitting Room. It was tucked between the Lincoln Bedroom and the Queen's Bedroom. First Lady Kim-Ly Geneviève Matthews, Genny, had decorated the space for herself with an eclectic mix of her combined French-Vietnamese heritage. Comfortable chairs, intricately carved side tables, wall pieces in dark wood, and pots of lush plants leant a tamed-jungle feel to the room.

It was as breathtaking as the woman with a thick flow of dark brown hair who sat with the First Child asleep in her lap.

Daniel's wife and CIA analyst Alice Darlington, and First Lady-elect Anne Darlington-Thomas completed the small group.

She definitely did *not* belong here. Men she knew how to deal with, even Damien's ego, but these women were a mystery, even if she *had* become close friends with Anne.

Sienna dragged her along by the hand that she hadn't released since freeing it from Damien's clasp—as if she'd known Cornelia's reaction ahead of time. She led them to an open couch and pulled Cornelia down beside her.

"I caught her and Damien Feinman necking by the Blue Room Christmas tree. I figured I'd better drag her to safety, because it looked like one of *those* kisses."

All eyes turned on her.

"Really?" Anne's question was filled with hope as she leaned forward to pour two glasses of wine for the late arrivals. "I do so *love* those kinds of kisses."

Alice and the First Lady were nodding in agreement as Sienna sighed happily at some memory of her own.

If this was safety, Cornelia was going to go back to California and study to be a dentist.

———

"So, you and my Chief of Staff?" Zachary Thomas asked as Damien returned from the family kitchen with a beer for himself and a refresher for Roy and the President.

"Seems like," Damien tried not to sound too damn pleased, but it was hard.

"Who's first?" The President asked the others.

"Who's first what?"

Everyone else appeared to know what he was talking about.

"They're debating," Daniel explained with a sweep of his beer glass to indicate the others, "which one will get first shot at beating the stuffing out of you if you hurt her in any way."

"Oh," Damien suddenly felt much less comfortable. This circle was several leagues above his usual social set.

"The Commander-in-Chief," Daniel continued amiably, "is partial to the Night Stalkers helicopter regiment. I know from personal experience that having them on your bad side is not a good choice. Though I'm not sure having them on your good side is all that much better. They're a tough crowd."

"As a Secret Service sniper turned Protection Detail," Roy spoke up, "I'll just shoot your ass and be done with you."

"Like the President," Zachary Thomas picked up without missing a beat, "I'm partial to helicopters. But I flew combat search-and-rescue for the Air Force. So, I'll be obliged to save your ass after Roy shoots it for you. Of course, in another seven weeks I'll also have the authority to call up a flight of A-10 Warthogs or a couple B-2 stealth bombers to take you out."

"So don't screw up, because we aren't the dangerous ones," Daniel concluded.

Damien blew out a hard breath. "Well if you guys aren't, then who is?"

In unison all the guys turned to face toward the round of women's laughter sounding from down the hall where Cornelia had gone.

"Okay," he couldn't argue with that.

The President nodded, as if confirming that topic was laid to rest.

"So, where's the money on tomorrow's game?" Zachary spoke up. "My Air Force Falcons have already won Commander-in-Chief's Trophy by lambasting both the Army and the Navy."

Damien groaned, "One lousy point. The Falcons beat the Academy's Midshipmen by one lousy point."

"Still a win for the Air Force," Zachary sat back with all the arrogance of a President-elect whose school had the winning team.

"We're going to trounce the Army," Damien declared.

"You're only safe saying that because there isn't anyone from the Army here to defend their school."

"We'll trounce them anyway."

"Should I call up Majors Beale and Henderson and ask their opinion?" The President's question was an outright dare.

Damien had met the Majors. Even retired and working as aviation firefighters, he wasn't going to tangle with them.

"We're still gonna win," he tried not to be sullen about how poor their starting lineup was this year.

The others laughed in commiseration.

———

"Seriously! We need to go down and raid that chocolate shop now," Sienna was immediately on her feet at the end of Cornelia's telling the tale.

"It will spoil our appetites," Anne pointed out. "Dinner is soon."

"Nonsense. Chocolate has nothing to do with appetite spoilage," Alice rose to clasp an arm around Sienna's shoulders. "We're starting a women-in-search-of-chocolate solidarity movement. Who's on board?"

Cornelia was on the verge of caving to the inevitable when the First Lady spoke up.

"Adele is still asleep," she nodded toward the two-year old half on the couch and half in her mother's lap. "But I have a solution. Could you hand me the phone?"

Cornelia did so while the two women in solidarity looked on.

"Chef Andrews? Genny Matthews here up in East Sitting Hall. Cornelia Day has been regaling us with the wonders of your confections and we were hoping that we might send someone down to fetch a sampling... Oh. Perfect! Thank you." She hung up the phone. "He is sending it right up. Apparently he had been experimenting with the Marou chocolate that I brought him from my last trip to Vietnam and would appreciate some *biased* opinions. We should be in for a treat."

There was an effortlessness to the First Lady that Cornelia wished she possessed.

"You are inspecting me with deep thoughts?"

Somewhat abashed, Cornelia repeated her thought aloud.

"Yes, it is just so. That is how I may appear, but I did not feel this way when your President was proposing to me while a renegade faction of the Thai army was attacking us in Cambodia."

"Damien hasn't proposed to me."

"And yet," Genny said with her perfect calm, "he is the first thought when you think of proposals. The first time Peter and I played Scrabble, that is when I really knew. We played just where the men are sitting even now."

Cornelia opened her mouth and closed it again.

"There are times when you simply know," Anne reassured her. "I was done in by a photograph of a model train set."

"Daniel was outsmarted by an Advent Calendar," Alice sighed.

"When Roy aimed his rifle at me," Sienna shrugged at Cornelia's surprise. "I should say his rifle scope, but the two pieces were attached at the time. He just couldn't stop watching me. Still can't."

"He is the head of your protection detail," Anne pointed out.

"I prefer to think it is my magnetic powers. Though I have to admit, the moment I met him face to face—*phfftt!*" She flicked aside the fall of hair by her temple. "Instant brain short. Other than insulting him a few times at the Air and Space Museum, I can't remember a thing I said to him. I suppose that I should have known then, but it took me a bit longer than these others."

"Well, we had our first kiss in front of the Air and Space Museum." Cornelia could remember every moment of that kiss, so why was the one in the Blue Room little more than a hazy blur yet ten times more important?

"Yum," Sienna agreed. "Great spot."

"Except it was dark, cold, and snowing."

"All the more reason to grab a warm man."

Had that been her moment? Or was it during that first meeting across the Sit Room table where she discovered an intelligence to match her own? Perhaps his look of interest across that table when he had discovered the same? No. It was before even the first kiss.

"For our first date—I didn't even know that's what it was—he took me to Molly Malone's. It's an Irish pub across the street from the Marine Barracks. It was a Friday night and the restaurant was packed with very able-bodied men."

The others *oohed* and *aahed*.

"*Very* able bodied," Cornelia wasn't exactly sure what came over her —she'd barely noticed the other men—but her tease was met with more groans of delight. "Yet he was so sure of himself that he never for a moment second-guessed taking me there. At least not until I pointed out his potential folly." And they all laughed.

And Cornelia *knew*.

Just as the other women had known. That had been the moment that Damien swept her off her feet—almost literally when his friend had pounded him on the back. It was his confidence, yes. But most of all it was his easy willingness to laugh at himself first of anyone. Here was a man who sat in the one place in the world best suited to see mankind's worst moments—disaster had a direct feed to his desk—yet still found paths to joy.

"Aren't they just the cutest thing when they're so sure of themselves?" Sienna sighed happily.

They were, Cornelia agreed, but it wasn't without reason.

Any further discussion was interrupted by the arrival of Chef Andrews himself. He'd changed to a clean apron, though he'd missed the chocolate fingerprints on his chef's hat as he delivered a whole new range of chocolate delicacies for them to sample.

CHAPTER ELEVEN

hat is going on with you?"

Damien did his best to look innocent. It had been a week since their "Residence date" as they were calling it between them—their impromptu dinner with the First Family both present and future. Without Janet's suggestion, he'd never have thought to take Cornelia to the West Wing to see Christmas or stumbled into that wonderful dinner. He'd learned a powerful lesson from that.

So, tonight, when Cornelia was too busy to take a break, he'd gone out into the dark night and picked up some take-out Chinese. They were presently eating at the big oak conference table in her office, while eager little porcelain reindeer watched them carefully. She flipped through a thick file as she ate. Janet had declined to join them as her husband was arriving soon to take her out to dinner.

"All week you've been far more...solicitous," she used her chopsticks neatly to pick up a slice of twice-cooked beef and a snow pea as she continued flipping through the file.

"Was I that bad before?" If so, he didn't want to hear about it.

"No, you were wonderful before. Now you've tipped over into amazing." Cornelia continued doing three things at once as neatly as she always did everything. In fact, the only time he'd ever seen her do only one thing at a time was when she was in his arms—which he decided he should take as a high compliment. "So, what are you up to, Feinman?"

Janet came in with a stack of memos. Most, he was glad to see, were only one or two pages long. Out of sight of Cornelia, she sent him a broad wink.

"Well," he kept a weather eye on Janet so that he could gauge her reaction. "Being solicitous is what comes from being in love with you."

Janet's snort of laughter wasn't seemly on a woman of her age and dignity.

That dragged Cornelia's full attention out of her file, even making her chopsticks pause halfway back to her plate. She looked at Janet, who wasn't making the least attempt to appear innocent, then at him.

"You," she pointed her chopsticks at Janet, "have been messing with my dating life. What did you do to Damien?"

"Oh no, Ms. Day. I would never do that," shocked hand to ruffled blouse.

"You should have been an actress," Damien should never have said a thing to begin with. It only encouraged them.

"I might interfere with your *love life* though. Your boy needed a good nudge."

"Hey. I'm a man, not a boy. And that wasn't a nudge, it was more like a hard boot in the ass."

"Shush when your elders are speaking."

"She threatened me," he did his best to make it sound like he was a whining child. It didn't help that she was right.

"Threatened you about what?"

Damien caved, "Taking you to the West Wing to see Christmas was only partly my idea. She," Damien pointed an accusing finger, "said I should be paying more attention to you the person than you—" he almost said 'the goddess in my bed' but caught himself in time, "—as a girlfriend."

Janet's glare told him he was entering the danger zone. Maybe he *should* listen to himself and keep his mouth shut.

"Would have helped if she hadn't been so right," he grumbled out the last, ignoring his own directive.

"He's a good sort, Ms. Day, best I've seen since my Harry. Damien merely required a little hint to bring out the best in him."

Damien kept his *harrumph* to himself.

"Now what has Cornelia Day in such a twist?" Janet actually planted her fists on her hips like some over-dramatic actress.

"I'm not in a twist," she denied Janet's accusation. "Except over the latest disaster that is Egyptian politics," Cornelia tapped a finger on the thick file she'd been studying.

"But—" Then Damien bit down on his tongue remembering his own "be silent" advice.

Janet was looking at him. Waiting.

"But you are." She was. "And have been since the dinner in the Residence last week."

Janet nodded as if once again he'd done something right. "Don't stop there, young man." She set the memos on Cornelia's desk and headed back to her own.

"What's going on, Cornelia?" He kept his voice low. Not because he was trying to hide anything from Janet; that was clearly a waste of time. Rather he did it to soothe whatever was bothering her.

"What do you mean?" She stabbed her chopsticks hard into a perfectly innocent piece of shrimp egg foo young and left them there.

"Ever since that night you've been even more yourself than usual. More studiously Cornelia Day than the Cornelia Day I met in the Sit Room that first day."

"You're making as much sense as usual," she reached for her file, but he intercepted her hand and trapped it between his. He could feel nerves coursing within her that he hadn't noticed until this moment.

"You are brilliantly meticulous. You are my idol of rational thought. Just to be clear, I'm not accusing you of being Spock."

"That's good," her voice went suddenly small and he realized how many men must have said that or something similar to her. Only someone who didn't know her would call her "ice bitch" but he could practically hear the phrase echoing about her. So many times that she had come to believe it of herself. She gave a chilly first impression.

"It's not true. All those assholes were wrong. You have more warmth and passion inside you than any woman I've ever met."

"You haven't met many women then."

"Like you? I've met a grand total of one, Cornelia. You're it. That's why I can say I love you and mean it. Nobody gobsmacks me the way you do."

She looked up at him and impossibly she looked to be on the verge of tears. He wasn't sure he could handle a crying Cornelia Day. His world wasn't structured for such things.

"But all week you've been ever so careful. Last week you were slouching against a door jamb while Janet teased me and looking relaxed about the whole situation between us. I haven't seen you out of your formal best since." He indicated her buttoned blazer. "What's going on, my lady?"

"My lady? Now you're getting all knightly on me?"

"Hello, Marine and librarian. I come by noble and knightly and arcane—all three—completely naturally. What do you do completely naturally?"

"Be a stone cold bitch," it came out on a gasp of pain that totally belied the words. *Shit!* He hated that he was right.

"Well, either I'm attracted to stone cold bitches, or everyone in your past was an idiot."

"Which seems more likely?"

"That they were all idiots. Seriously, you're lucky you found me. New evidence, fresh in, shows that most of my gender are utter goons."

Cornelia sniffled and looked at him, really looked at him.

He didn't carry a handkerchief. He'd always thought it too old-fashioned but now he wished he had one. He'd buy a whole stack tomorrow. In the meantime he lightly brushed a knuckle past the corners of her eyes and it came away wet.

"You really do love me."

She didn't make it a question, but he nodded to confirm the truth—as much inside himself as for her. It really wasn't a question.

"That's what happened to me last week in the Residence, before the dinner," her voice was a gentle whisper.

"What?"

She touched the ends of her chopsticks but didn't retrieve them from the heart of the egg foo young. "I understood that I loved you."

The soft words didn't slam into him as he'd expected. Instead they were a gentle wash over him, a benediction as solid and complete as his oath of office on the day he became a Marine Corps officer.

When he leaned in to kiss her, she tasted of soy sauce and salty tears.

Then she silently rose, indicating he should stay seated. She stepped over to her office door, looked briefly into the darkened outer office, then closed and locked it. Turning off the lights, she crossed back to him.

The lights of the EEOB filtered through the curtains and the dark winter's night as she sat straddling his lap.

"It's not a closet, but I hope it will do," she whispered as she embraced him.

This time all he could taste on her lips was her smile.

Making love to Damien in her own office felt a little risqué, a little wild. Cornelia decided that maybe she needed that in her life. Maybe the cold that she thought wrapped around her came as much from the inside as the outside.

As his lips traced down her neck, she leaned her elbows back on the conference table, opening herself to him. He unbuttoned her blouse and, as he continued his journey, she ran her hands through his soft hair.

Maybe she had become the job too completely. It was necessary. Zachary Thomas was too charitable with his time. He was a good man who needed someone to control how much came to his attention how quickly.

She had become his control until she embodied it.

As Damien eased her bra aside, some part of that control slipped away. A piece of that hard shell broke off and scattered like snow onto the white carpet. And when he lay her there, naked beneath him, warm and safe in his arms, her shields shattered.

The ever-so-studiously constructed Cornelia Day that she had first formed as a precocious, over-tall preteen had become more than a persona—it had become her. Yet Damien had seen past that from the first moment. And he proved once more, evoking responses she'd never known were possible, that he would never see her any other way. Not merely desirable, which would have been a big enough surprise on its own, but as worthy in and of herself.

She'd always presented that to the world.

But as Damien made love to her, she knew all the way to her core that she truly was worthy of a man like him.

CHAPTER TWELVE

A *tuba Christmas?"*

"Tonight at the Library of Congress. Led by the Marine Corps Band tuba section."

Cornelia stared at Damien. "You do understand what's happening here?" They sat alone in the Sit Room.

He waved a hand at the massive files spread between them. "I've been reading the same things you have. What's happening is absolutely *nothing.* Every single idea here is conjecture. Whatever President Javad Madani heard, there isn't a shred of evidence that any of our intelligence agencies can scare up."

"But—" He cut her off with a raised hand.

"I'm not saying that his warning isn't valid. I'm saying that we don't have a single hypothesis or communication here that gives us the least insight into its meaning. This—" he gestured helplessly at the pile of reports perfectly mirroring his own feelings, "—mess isn't helping us with anything."

She knew that. The problem was that as their "Christian holiday season" was fast coming to a close, the number of days in which an attack was possible were decreasing. Most leaders of intelligence and Homeland Security now agreed that it was a non-event.

Even if President Madani had heard a valid rumor, they still insisted, *that doesn't mean it actually came together.*

"The naysayers' perspective isn't invalid. No chatter. No unusual activity."

"We're the last true believers," Damien sighed and looked back down at the files.

That was what had drawn them together, to double-team the files once more in the hopes of finding some overlooked connection. Six hours later all it had earned them was a frustration that almost had them sniping at each other.

We shall cut out their heart with their own words.

"No unusual activity near the inscriptions on the Lincoln Memorial," Damien shoved aside one report. "No unusual activity at the Supreme Court or the Library of Congress. Scans of surveillance footage at the Capitol record only the usual crazies. It's even been too damn cold for all but the most hard core protestors on the Mall." Report after report was shoved aside until the only thing remaining was the slim file of her initial debriefing.

Damien flipped it open and began reading Madani's words aloud:

What can be done to help the gulf between us?

When in the course of human events it becomes necessary for people of good will to come together over good food.

This time the storm enters from the Bay, not the Gulf.

President Matthews had explained that one. President Madani had helped him foil a bio-weapon of mass destruction from being smuggled in through the Gulf of Mexico. So, not the "Gulf" this time. The Chesapeake Bay still remained their most likely candidate.

An attack coming. It is neither chemical nor biological. I am informed that it is also not explosive or electronic. Rather, it is cultural.

We shall cut out their heart with their own words.

I can only offer you my prayers during this, your Christian holiday season.

Cornelia sighed. She'd read every one of those phrases a hundred times until they were ingrained in her memory.

A very discreet inquiry through the US interests section of the Swiss embassy in Tehran—technically the only diplomatic connection between the two countries—had returned two words from Pejman: "Nothing further."

"I wish we could call Javad right now and ask again."

"You wouldn't be able to reach him."

"Why not?"

Damien flicked on the microphone that would connect the watch desk and said aloud, "*Shab-e Yalda.* We'll see how long it takes them to figure that one out."

Within moments a watermelon and a pomegranate appeared on the screens.

"Not very long, I guess," Cornelia looked at them. "What do they have in common other than both being red and messy to eat?"

As if in answer, a title appeared on the other screen.

Shab-e Yalda: Winter Solstice Party (Iran)

Successive lines were typed in rapidly:

Highly popular gatherings where food, drink, and poetry (esp. by Hafez) are shared

Typically lasts past midnight

Red fruit symbolizes dawn and life

Gatherings symbolize coming together in times of darkness

"All right, already. Enough," Damien called out.

One more line appeared before they stopped:

Ancient origin: Celebrates triumph of Mithra—Sun God—over darkness

"You done good, Bettani."

"Suck my tush, Damien," a woman managed over her own laughter.

It was the first time Cornelia had ever heard any at the watch desk talk back, or talk at all to the Sit Room. She liked that they felt comfortable enough to do it, even knowing she was there as well as Damien.

"As I said, big party." Then he made a loud raspberry sound before flicking off the mic switch. "So, I have a suggestion."

"A tuba Christmas?"

"Absolutely."

Cornelia looked at the pile covering half of the big conference table and decided that maybe he was right.

———

The streets were too bitterly cold to walk. Washington often dropped below freezing, but ten degrees was frosty even by a Marine's standards. They caught the Metrorail to Capitol South and nearly froze as they hustled the two blocks through the dusk and Friday evening traffic that was always completely mad around the Capitol Building itself.

"I can't believe you've never been to the Library of Congress. How in the world can I be in love with a woman who has never been there?"

"I don't have a lot of time to read. Especially lately," Cornelia pulled her scarf tighter and hurried faster along the icy sidewalk. Damn but the woman had legs, he practically had to jog to keep up with her long stride.

He risked a laugh and nearly froze his lungs.

"If this is an outdoor concert, you're a dead man."

"It's not. Besides, the Library of Congress isn't only about books to read."

"What else then?"

"I'll show you," he decided that stopping to admire the Court of Neptune Fountain and its stunning bronze statuary would probably get him attacked.

"Right, like a tuba Christmas." He ignored her sarcasm and led her up the broad flight of stone stairs.

"I've always loved the Library of Congress; this is what a library should look like." The Thomas Jefferson Building covered an entire city block and rose three full stories. The main steps led them into the middle story. The Ground Floor was all offices and archives. The entry was at the First Story.

Not pausing at the main arches—it was really too cold to stop and point out the busts of history's great writers stationed in circular windows far above—they practically burst through the front doors into the Great Hall.

Cornelia staggered to a stop and looked about in clear shock. It was one of the grandest rooms in all of DC architecture and yet almost nobody came here. The palatial hall soared aloft for two towering stories. Grand, white marble staircases swept up either side of the hall, ornate with deeply carved balustrades. The upper story was all arches and columns making the area feel even larger because it appeared to have no bounds. And in the center stood a grand Christmas tree that looked utterly impossible in the space.

"How?" Cornelia whispered in a gasp of shock. "How did they get that tree in here? It's so perfect."

"It's a secret. I could tell you, except you're not a librarian."

In moments she'd inspected the roof, the entryways, even tapped a foot on the dark marble of the inlaid floor.

"They use a magic wand."

She rolled her eyes at him and moved closer to the tree. Over a dozen feet at the base, it towered over twenty feet high in a near perfect cone. Its branches were thick with ornaments—They were books!—and sparkling lights.

"Every librarian was asked for their two favorite books: one of historical significance, one of modern enjoyment. The top two hundred titles were painted up as ornaments: a hundred historic, a hundred modern."

"That explains the crazy collection of titles. Which were your two?" She began moving around the tree reading as she went. He followed, not wanting to be left behind again. There were perhaps fifty people already gathered for the concert, it was early yet. But several were walking about the tree, making shouting through it awkward.

"I'm not an LOC librarian so I didn't get a vote. But if I had to choose, I'd say *Beowulf* as the first work in English Literature."

"Which you've of course read in the original."

"I took it as a challenge in high school. Ended up doing my own translation, which was fairly crappy, but I did it. And I've always been a John le Carré fan. The old spy thrillers. How about you?"

"You probably tried passing girls mash notes in old English."

"Might have. And they might have been in alliterative verse as well," he admitted. "There he is," he spotted the *Beowulf* cover. "So I'm not the only arcane one in the building."

"And I'm sure those poems helped you be even more popular with the teenage girls attracted to Boy Scouts in uniform."

"Not particularly," he grimaced. Nothing quite cut to the core like a teenage girl's laugh of amused dismissal.

"I'd choose *Anne of Green Gables* or *Secret Garden* for the historical," she pointed to both of them, then tipped her head as she gazed up at the tree either thinking or reading titles. "For the modern day, I think I'd have to say *Landmarks* by Robert Macfarlane."

"I…don't know that one."

"It's about language, especially geographic language, and how it works."

He thumped a hand over his heart. He'd fallen for a woman who thought linguistics was worth reading about for the sake of itself.

"I'll get it for you for Christmas."

That one stopped him cold. Granted it was only four days away, but it was the very first time either of them had spoken of any plans further away than the next meal. It was going to be their first Christmas together.

"What?" Cornelia was inspecting him with those dark eyes he could get so completely lost in. *Could get? That ship already left the harbor, Damien.*

"Christmas. Together."

She shrugged, "I'll probably have to work."

"Doesn't matter. As long as I get to spend it with you."

She did that head-tip thing that he'd so come to enjoy. "You *are* a romantic."

"You're only just now figuring that out?"

"I'll bet you want a tree."

"Already have one at my apartment."

She turned from the huge pine to eye him carefully, "Does it already have a wrapped present under it, just in case you could 'wrangle' me there?"

"It might," he shouldn't have admitted even that. What if she was irritated? Or put off? Or—

She stepped into his arms and kissed him right there in the Library of Congress.

Life simply didn't get any better.

"What am I going to do with you? No, wait. Don't answer that.

That was the wrong question to ask a romantic so close before Christmas."

"It was," he admitted. He knew exactly what he hoped to do with her, both in short- and long-term scenarios.

———

Cornelia definitely wasn't ready for this. She had fallen in love with a romantic who was already thinking of marriage. "That gift under your tree had better not be a goddamn ring," she whispered to him.

"Not an idiot. I'm not going to propose in our first month together," Then that I'm-about-to-be-really-charming smile of his broke out. "I'm going to wait until at least New Years."

She fisted him lightly in the gut.

He spotted it in time, so her fist merely bounced off his hard abs.

"Where are the tubas you wanted to show me?" Because she certainly needed a distraction from whatever else was going on here.

"A tuba Christmas is something you hear, not see."

"You're talking about actual tubas doing what, playing Christmas carols?"

"Exactly. But they don't start for a bit. Let's take the ten-cent tour."

She had never once planned a date as thoroughly as Damien planned every little outing. He was slippery and she was going to have to watch him like a hawk over the years to come.

Years to come. *Right. Because they'd be working together in the White House together.* Though she knew that wasn't what she'd meant. They had just been discussing wedding rings.

Well, Cornelia, how far astray can a man lead you in a library?

She waved for him to begin the tour.

And he did. Either he'd studied for their date on the off chance that she'd agree to it, or he knew the building as well as any guide. Classic paintings of justice, corruption, balance, and bad legislation.

From the Visitor's Gallery on the second floor, she could look down on the Main Reading Room exactly as it had appeared in a hundred movies: three great circles of reading desks around an inner circle of the librarian's desk. What the movies never seemed to capture was the magnificent dome above.

"The eight muses in marble," Damien pointed them out high on the dome's structure where the great arches came together. "Art, Science, Religion—all women."

"As they should be," she teased him.

"But the paired bronzes below them, each pair representing the muse above them, are all men: Michelangelo and Beethoven for art, Christopher Columbus and Robert Fulton for Commerce, and so on. See? It's proof that men are good at getting things done."

"Sure, after the women think them up."

"Behind every successful man is a good woman."

"Because he needs one," but Cornelia couldn't help glancing over her shoulder. So who stood behind *her?* Who stood behind a successful woman, especially if she had missed something crucial and Javad Madani's warning *was* real? Who would stand beside her and help her be strong if hundreds or even thousands died because of something *she* had missed?

"Don't worry, babe," Damien slipped a hand around her waist. "I've got your back."

Would he if he knew what he'd signed up for? That almost made her laugh. But it would be a sad, morose sound, so she kept it inside. If anyone knew what they'd signed up for on this one, it would be the Situation Room librarian.

"Oh, there's something else you have to see," and Damien was tugging on her hand as he led her deeper into the building.

In an exhibition hall, a dozen documents were set out in formidable glass cases.

"This is the first map on which the word 'America' appears, 1507. This is our birth certificate in a way, fifteen years after Columbus." The new continents were long, thin things ranging north and south with a gap between the continents at the Isthmus of Panama, a gap that would take over four hundred more years to create. But there, just below the drawing of a parrot was the word "America".

Right next to it was...

"The rough draft of the Declaration of Independence. How cool is that?"

Cornelia would have to admit, it was pretty cool.

"When in the course of human events it becomes necessary..." she read aloud and felt a chill run up her spine.

"Okay, a little creepy under the circumstances, but look at what Franklin and Adams did to it. Talk about tough editors." The four-page manuscript had dozens of cross-outs and corrections, all done in flowing pen-and-ink script. No tracked changes on a computer document with annotations asking additional questions to accept or reject. These were strong, definitive edits that had lasted over two centuries.

Damien was like a boy in a candy store with a twenty-dollar bill. There was too much to show her, too many options. The next room was a circle in a square. It was a high, square room with all of the architectural ornamentation displayed elsewhere in the building, but set upon the intricate blue-and-white marble floor stood a circle of tall, glassed-in bookcases. At this hour they were the room's sole occupants; everyone else who arrived this late in the evening was here for the Christmas concert.

"Jefferson's personal library," Damien declared proudly as if he'd installed it himself. "He sold it to the country after the British burned the first library along with the White House and the Capitol back in 1814. He kept the books in a circle because he wanted to be at the center of knowledge."

Cornelia slowly turned to study the thousands of volumes arrayed there.

"And they weren't organized by author or size like most prior libraries. He broke them into forty-four

Chapters of knowledge grouped under three major headings: Memory, Reason, and Imagination. I would give anything to have been able to sit with him for even an hour and talk about just his classification system."

Damien's passion was overwhelming.

"Why don't you work here?"

"At the LOC? Too quiet. That's the Marine in me. Once I got hooked on intel and current affairs, I just couldn't turn back. Maybe some day, after they kick me out for slovenly behavior or some crime against protocol like hitting on the White House Chief of Staff, I'll come here. Over a hundred-and-sixty million items in the collection; it's the largest library in the world. Did you know that they have every tweet from Twitter filed right down this hallway?"

"The center of knowledge..."

"Absolutely," he tugged her arm until they were in the exact center of the rosette on the floor. "Can't you just feel it."

"When in the course of human events..."

"Wait, what?" Damien turned to her.

"*We shall cut out their heart with their own words.* That's what Pejman said their source said."

Cornelia tried not to be sick in the middle of Thomas Jefferson's library. She clutched onto his shoulder for support.

"Damien. We're standing in the center of knowledge as far as the United States of America is concerned. We're in a building bursting at the seams with our own words. And we're not a hundred feet from the first draft of the Declaration of Independence."

———

Damien's vision blurred with the shock. He'd heard the phrase before, but never given it any credence—until this moment.

Then his vision, literally, went red. Someone was setting out to destroy the Library of Congress. They were going to destroy a library. This one! Grander than the ancient Library of Alexandria.

"When? When do you think it will happen?" Cornelia's brain was still working.

All he cared about at the moment was murdering somebody with his bare hands.

He dragged himself back from the edge, forcing his own thoughts into motion.

"Before our *Christian holiday season is over.* Maybe we have some time?"

Damien looked at the beautiful collection around him. A part of him wanted to own every one of these books so that he too could someday sit at the center of knowledge as Jefferson had. No, he wanted to rush the collection out of the building right now so that they'd be safe.

And then he knew.

"No, we don't have time."

"Why not?"

"The last line of Bettani's report." He was going to have to kiss her for putting that last line up on the screen—if he lived that long.

"Shab-e Yalda. *Celebrates triumph of Mithra—Sun God—over darkness.*"

She offered him her first-ever laugh in his presence, but it was a harsh and bitter sound that echoed strangely from the glassed-in circle of bookcases. "I guess you're not the only one with an arcane sense of humor."

"Tonight. It's the solstice. This is Mithra's battle of the light of Islam extremists over the darkness of the United States of America."

Cornelia yanked out her phone, studied the contacts list for a moment, then hit dial.

Damien did the same. He had the NSA on speed dial.

"This is Damien Feinman. We've been chasing the wrong keywords on this warning from Iran. Check for chatter on Shab-e Yalda." Unlike Bettani, he had to spell it for them.

He'd have to remember to tell Bettani that too if he ever saw her again.

———

"Ms. Day. How nice of you to call at eight o'clock on a Friday night," General Arnson's tone was friendly, but dry as week-old toast.

What was it with self-confident men and their need to tease women? She didn't have time to puzzle at it right now and it was probably a simple reality that was pointless to file away for future consideration.

"What can I do for you?"

"I'm not sure who to call, but I think we have trouble."

"You solved President Madani's puzzle?" She suddenly had his full attention.

"We think so. The Library of Congress, tonight, and I didn't know who better to call."

"It just so happens that you called exactly the right person, my daughter and future son-in-law are here for dinner." Then he shouted in the background, "Sienna. Target is Library of Congress, tonight. Get to the White House and roust the President. Roy, wake up those lazy dogs you work with at the Secret Service."

"Damien is already in contact with the NSA, not your daughter the National Security Advisor, but rather the National Security Agency," Cornelia wasn't sure why she felt the sudden need to explain the obvious. Perhaps because it was the only way to make sense of what was happening at the moment.

It was her first inkling that she was afraid. She forced her voice to remain steady.

"They're checking for chatter on a new set of keywords."

Even as she said it she saw Damien close his eyes and tip his head back in frustration. "Check for frequency versus prior years. It *is* an annual holiday," he groaned into his phone.

"It looks like we have a confirmation on tonight, but he's still checking."

"Well done, Ms. Day. I'll come meet you in the Sit Room."

She had to look around to remember where she was—within the circle of Jefferson's knowledge. "I'm not there."

"Where are you?"

Her throat was too dry to answer.

"Shit! You're on site, aren't you? Goddamn it! Get out of there."

Coming from far down the hall she heart the first *blat* of a tuba. Warming up. Not music yet.

Some itch told her that it was too late. That it might be too late to safely evacuate the musicians and the public even now gathering in the Great Hall. Too late to save the library and all of its treasures.

Damien grabbed her arm. His expression said it all.

"Chatter confirms tonight," she told Arnson then hung up the phone.

"How bad?"

Damien didn't shrink under the fear, instead he seemed to grow taller. "Several hundred percent increase in messaging and social media interchanges regarding Shab-e Yalda, but only in the immediate area: DC and Alexandria, Virginia. The rest of the nation is no more active on the subject than usual. They've got four targets of interest and are pushing those out to the proper authorities. You?"

"Sienna, her father, and the Secret Service are all in motion. Sienna will be notifying the President."

"Which means—" Damien was interrupted by another deep *blat* of scales, "—that it may be up to us to solve it."

She grabbed his hand and rushed out of the circle of Jefferson's knowledge, down the exhibition hallway and slammed to a halt against the upper story balustrade that looked down on the Great Hall.

While they had wandered, the area had been transformed. The three white-marble arches at the east end of the Great Hall were now blocked by scores of tubas. A line of forward-facing sousaphones were along the back. In front of them stood dozens more players, clutching standard, bell-upward tubas to their chests. And in front of them another row was seated.

"There are the Marines," Damien pointed.

In the center section, the Marine Corps Band was dressed in brilliantly red, ornate jackets. The men wore dark blue slacks and the women floor-length skirts. Typical.

"Shouldn't they be wearing white hats?" Cornelia was searching for anything that might be out of place.

"Marines never wear their covers, our word for the white hats, indoors unless they're on duty status and wearing a side-arm in which case they want their hands free."

An array of civilian tuba players filled out the spread to either side. They were easy to separate. There were two sections in formal black and white attire—those would be the musicians from the symphony and the opera. Then there was a much less formal and larger group, who appeared to be wearing a variety of high school colors. A wide array of musicians, but nothing stood out.

The audience was a much more difficult problem. They were packed in around the base of the tree, ranging up the marble stairs, and now filtering along the mezzanine's balcony rails until they were close enough that she lowered her voice to Damien so as not to be overheard.

"Can we evacuate them?"

He shook his head. "Even if we tried, we'd be sure to create a panic that would get several people injured or killed. And we don't know when."

"Beginning or end of the concert would be my best guess."

"Beginning, that's when I'd do it." Damien's flat statement made Cornelia glad she hadn't been in the military. He'd clearly been trained to consider such matters for best tactics.

"Is there a bomber?"

"Yes and no. To actually damage the building or the collection, it would be more than a man could wear. It would have to be much bigger to do more than kill people. But I'd wager that he's here to make sure it goes off."

"Where then?"

"Well, the Christmas tree is hollow. It's built around a steel core. What you're seeing is branches stuck onto the framework."

"Magic."

He nodded in chagrin. "Yes, that's how they get it in here. But I was here when they were setting it up—I do that every year—and I saw nothing unusual. It doesn't have a door in it. They build it from the bottom up and cap it from one of those lifts. They have to take it apart the same way."

Several tubists nodded at each other and then began to run scales together. The deep notes were liquid and flowed upward. Soon the entire orchestra was warming up with scales and exercises. The hall rang with the basso cacophony.

Still Cornelia couldn't see any break in the pattern...unless the break wasn't here.

"Where would their tuba cases be?" They shouted at each other in unison.

Damien pointed. Across the hall, down the stairs, and out a side corridor. "Meeting rooms!" His shout barely reached her though their shoulders were touching due to the press of the growing crowd on either side.

She didn't need his shove to get moving. They raced around the mezzanine. Thankfully the crowds were glued to the balustrade to look down on the concert.

Getting down the stairs was a different matter. A dozen feet wide with a brass handrail up the middle, it was a solid mass of people heading toward them.

Damien took the lead and forced a path downward.

She did her best to shout an apology to the offended as they moved.

The base of the stairs turned and fanned out into the main hall. Those last ten steps were a solid mass of humanity.

She despaired of finding a way through them.

The sound was a palpable force against them. The tuning instruments were breaking into snatches of carols. The crowd was alive with excitement.

They were running out of time, and options.

———

"There!" Damien fought his way to the outside banister and glanced over the banister to where an arch opened away from the main floor. Empty. A ten foot drop.

"Climb up then give me your hands," he didn't give Cornelia a choice. Wrapping his hands about her waist, he lofted her up until her feet were over the banister and she was sitting on it. Then he shifted to grab her hands and used his hip to nudge her butt off the edge.

The yank on her arms must have hurt, but if she cried out in complaint he couldn't hear it. Wouldn't hear a scream of agony in all this racket.

He dangled her as low as he could, then let her go.

She landed clean, ten feet below.

He swung over, catching himself for a moment with his hands on the banister, then dropped down beside her.

They rushed down the side hall toward the meeting rooms.

The first room was crammed with tuba cases. At least the sound reverberating about the Great Hall was far enough away now that he could hear himself think.

He began shaking one case after another.

Empty.

Empty.

Empty.

Cornelia kicked at the first in a long row of them.

It fell and tumbled into the next. Like dominos, a whole line of them went down knocking one after another down. More importantly all of them fell as if they were empty.

He did the same to a row in front of him.

Nothing.

"Next room!" They raced back into the hallway and into the next room.

More cases, each the size of a man's torso.

He tumbled them about, knocking them over and mixing them together. There were going to be some very upset tuba players at the end of the concert. Cornelia didn't have any better luck.

In the next room were the Marine Corps Band's cases, each clearly labeled.

He hated to do it, but he kicked at the stack. They all tumbled aside.

"Maybe we were wrong."

He turned to Cornelia who was working her way down the other side of the room. The Marine Corp Band used rolling road cases for the sousaphones because they traveled so widely. Each was three feet wide, two deep, and almost four high with aluminum corners and heavy latches.

She bumped and nudged her way along them, knocking their metal corners against the walls and leaving scuffs and dings in the wood.

He was about to tell her to ease off when she practically bounced off one that barely moved.

"Check the rest of them," he instructed as he moved in.

When he nudged the case, it moved, but it was very heavy—far heavier than a sousaphone could ever be.

"The rest are empty," she called from the end of the row.

"How long to the bomb squad?"

———

"I'll find out," Cornelia pulled her phone, dialed the general and connected immediately. "We found a case, much heavier than it should be, in the meeting room off the west side of the Great Hall. Bomb, a nuke, an incendiary—we don't know."

"Roger that."

As the general told her that help was about to enter the front of the building, she turned to face back toward Damien.

He was hunched over the case, inspecting it carefully.

Close behind him, a Marine Corps band member stood frozen in the doorway.

She saw everything in a gestalt moment.

He wore the trademark blue pants, red jacket—and white hat.

Never worn indoors unless wearing a sidearm.

A glance down. No sidearm. No pistol belt.

Back to his face.

Grim. Angry. Determined.

"Imposter!" She screamed out the warning to Damien just as the man dove toward him.

"What the hell?" General Arnson shouted in her ear.

Damien turned just far enough that he dodged the worst of the assailant's blow. Still, he was slammed brutally against the case and the wall.

Dazed for a moment, he struggled to his feet.

For lack of any other weapon, the assailant grabbed a folding metal chair.

Cornelia was too far away to get there in time, so she heaved her phone right at his face.

Her aim wasn't that good, but when it struck his neck, his momentary flinch was all the opening Damien needed. His fist drove so hard into the man's face, that he let go of the chair. It was a miracle he didn't fall down dead with the force of the blow.

The chair banged off Damien's shoulder as it fell, but not hard enough to do any damage.

With a cry of rage the man managed to deliver a punch to Damien's solar plexus that sent him staggering back against the wall.

As he moved in once more, Cornelia raced toward him to intercept, having no idea what she'd do when she got there.

When she was still three steps away, there was a soft spitting sound and blood erupted from the man's shoulder, spraying a pattern on the wall before he collapsed to the carpet screaming.

Roy Beaumont stood in the doorway holding a handgun with one of those long silencers on it.

"I take it that he's your problem," Roy said as he checked the area out in the hallway and then looked back into the room.

"Not really," Damien groaned though he still leaned with his back against the wall, gasping for air. "This is," he pointed at the sousaphone case.

"Excuse me?"

"If this is all plastique," Damien knelt down with a knee in the middle of the downed man's back who cried out again. "This could hold...let's see. Half kilo per M112 demolition block? A thousand blocks easy. Call it a half ton. At least this end of the building would probably be destroyed. If it's something worse than C-4..." he shrugged.

Two more Secret Service agents rushed into the room and took charge of the prisoner.

The distant sound of the impending concert caught Cornelia's attention. She snagged her phone from the floor and looked at the time.

"Whatever it is, I think we have less than eight minutes to deal with it."

Then she thought she heard a tiny voice coming from the phone and she put it to her ear.

"Hello?"

"Ms. Day," the general called out, "are you okay?"

"We're fine, except for a bomb that will probably destroy the Library in less than ten minutes."

And then she heard it, in the background, but clear. A sound she knew because she had flown in his helicopter just three long weeks ago.

"Where are you?"

"About a minute out. I didn't know if you'd need air assets, but I went aloft in case you did."

"Damien?"

"Huh?" He looked up from where the two Secret Service agents were binding the assailant's wounds none too gently. He was refusing to speak or make any sound. He appeared ready to go to his heaven along with the bomb. She wasn't having anything to do with that.

"How do we get this out of here?"

"I'm not sure it's even safe to move."

"Well, the bomb squad is going to get here just in time to die with the rest of us. Sitting still isn't an option. Besides, we've already moved it some."

He looked around as if searching his memory with his eyes. "There's a wheelchair ramp that way, but it's right through the crowds." He scanned further. "Or... Second street, East Entrance."

He jumped up, kicked a half dozen tuba cases out of the way and began shoving against the rolling sousaphone case.

"You heard?" Cornelia shouted into the phone.

"Meet you there," the general concurred.

She stuffed the phone in her pocket and called for Roy's help. She ran to get the door and they raced down the hall.

———

Damien couldn't seem to get his wind.

The man had been a trained fighter and his massive blow had driven all the air out of Damien's lungs and maybe cracked a few ribs.

The other thing that took his breath away was Cornelia. She hadn't flinched. Not from the moment of her timely warning until she'd rushed bare-handed at an assailant five times her strength. Now she raced ahead of them opening doors as she went.

When one was locked, with a keypad code beside it, she stepped aside and waved them on.

Out of options, he and Roy used the still-rolling mass of the bomb case as a battering ram and blew the door off its lock, practically off its hinges. He'd closed his eyes at the moment of impact, but was still alive to reopen them a moment later. A good indicator that it was just C-4 wired to a timer. But with the chance of a booby trap on opening the case, going after the timer itself would be too risky.

They got the case rolling fast enough that Cornelia had to sprint to keep ahead of them. She was a whirlwind: flashing on lights, shoving aside chairs, flipping a folding table aside where it had been set up for some talk.

No time to admire the stunning architecture this time as they raced through. He didn't even dare take a moment to look at his watch. Far behind them, the concert was clearly about to begin, the fading sounds becoming more coherent.

At the northeast corner of the building, they almost ran the case into the Children's Literature Center where the hall took a ninety-degree turn. It was only with a hard scramble that they managed to make the corner and roll the case toward the East Entrance, the one away from all of the people.

They made it down the wheelchair ramp and hit the street at the same moment as the helicopter. It was a Bell helicopter, but a different one. This was a UH-1 Huey, the warhorse of the Vietnam era.

"Good choice," he shouted at the general as they rolled up to it. "I think this is too heavy for the one we took to New York."

The general yanked open a side door and they rolled the case up to it. But even with all three of them grunting against it, they couldn't tip it up into the helicopter's bay.

"Six minutes," Cornelia called out.

"Shit!" Damien looked down at the landing skid he'd been stumbling on while trying to get good footing for the lift. "How strong is that?"

General Arnson looked down at the skid, then nodded. "Strong enough."

In less than a minute they had one set of wheels hopped over the skid and a length of sturdy cable running around the case and tied off inside the cargo bay.

"That's way off center. I need counterweights if I'm going to fly this damn thing. All aboard and stay up against the far side, as far from the case as you can."

He and Roy scrambled aboard. Staying away from that damn thing wasn't a problem.

Then Cornelia started to follow them.

"Hey! You can't—"

"Don't be an idiot, Damien," she shoved past his protest and they headed aloft.

And she was right. She'd been in just as much danger all along as he had. And he'd never find a braver woman than the one now huddled beside him.

Somewhere along the way, they'd lost their coats and the wind roaring past the open cargo bay door sucked the warmth right out of them.

Cornelia had yanked on a headset and was talking to the general. He couldn't spot another headset, so he only heard her half of the conversation.

"Four minutes. Only if I'm right about the timing."

...

"Yes, it could be less, but then we'll be dead anyway."

...

"No, we don't know what kind of bomb it is."

...

"Well, if we're wrong and it doesn't go off, they can always send a team down to figure it out later."

...

"If we can get there in time, we could drop it at—"

...

"Exactly."

The general must have had the same idea she did and said it the moment before she could. This wasn't the time to ask what they were thinking.

"Two minutes. Get ready!" She shouted to him and Roy.

He nodded. Every second they got it further away from Washington, DC the better. If it was nuclear, there would be no way to save themselves no matter how fast they flew. Best to use every second to save the city.

For half a second he hoped that Cornelia hadn't figured that out, then he laughed.

"What?" she shouted at him.

He swung her boom microphone out of the way and dragged her in to kiss her and kiss her hard.

Of course she'd known that. She'd probably figured it out before he had. Probably before she'd forced her way onto the helicopter. And yet she'd come anyway. Knowing she could have been safe, she had to see it through to the end.

"I love you," he shouted at her.

She nodded. Then her eyes unfocused for a moment as she listened. She nodded her head and shouted, "Got it!" not realizing that her mic boom was still swung out of the way and the general wouldn't hear her in the cockpit.

That's one on you, Cornelia.

"Let it go!"

Damien yanked the knot loose and the case began tipping away.

Roy slid across the deck plating and planted a boot on it to hurry it on its way. It seemed to take forever to finally lean away and slowly fall off the skid. But once it did, it plummeted downward.

It was probably a stupid thing to do, but all three of them huddled in the chill of the open cargo doorway and watched the case as it tumbled down out of the sky. The general brought the aircraft to a hover well to the side and turned on a searchlight to follow it down.

Down into the Potomac. It was perfect. Between Cornelia and General Arnson, they'd decided to dump the case into the Potomac, it would at least buffer the explosion.

The splashdown sent a plume of spray aloft.

They waited and waited. It was the longest minute of his life.

"Maybe the fall destroyed the mechanism and it—"

A shaft of foaming water exploded upward. It rose well over a hundred feet high and just as wide at the center of a mile-wide stretch of the river.

It wasn't nuclear, or they'd be dead by now, but it was one damn big hole in the water.

He reached out to close the cargo bay door. As he did, he saw exactly where they were. Damien could only shake his head.

The Marine Corps at Quantico were going to have some explaining to do tomorrow about why they were detonating high explosives where a civilian river ran so close beside their own base.

CHAPTER THIRTEEN

Only by lack of a bridesmaid dress had Cornelia been able to beg off from becoming a member of Sienna's and Roy's State Dining Room wedding on the First Floor of the Residence.

"Besides," Cornelia had told her, "I'm nearly a foot taller than you are. I'd look ridiculous."

"No, you'd look lovely. Besides, are you saying that I'll look ridiculous when I'm bridesmaid at your wedding?"

That was no longer as uncomfortable a thought as it had been.

"I'll make sure there's time for all of us to get dresses," she retreated to her earlier excuse and Sienna was too happy to protest Cornelia's escape.

The three days after the explosion had been incredibly busy, even by her new standards.

Debriefing, closing the files, and sending a very back-channel thank you to President Madani and his son-in-law had occupied the first day. She'd sent them a large Katz's gift basket, with no card, delivered by Swiss Diplomatic pouch.

The second day had been the aftermath: twelve more arrests of three different bomb makers, that had then branched out into materiel providers. That was the only part of the entire operation to receive any news coverage: "arrest of suspected terrorists."

On Christmas Eve Day, an answer had come back from President Madani in the form of a beautiful, hand-illuminated copy of the love poems by the ancient Sufi poet Hafez. He had inscribed it with: "C.D., This is my favorite translation. Please share it only with a man filled with the common sense to appreciate you, J.M."

"New world meets the old world, pastrami and poetry," Damien had joked, but he'd handled the book just as reverently as she had.

Christmas Eve itself had been a very quiet, very loving night at his apartment. He'd served her a roast beef and Yorkshire pudding picnic —spread on the carpet before a small but colorful Christmas tree.

Damien had proven his ability to cook a wonderful meal and she had proven her complete inability to be of much help.

They'd laughed together through *When Harry Met Sally*, but there was nothing fake about what happened between them later that night.

She'd found a copy of *Landmarks* for him and he'd given her *The Gatekeeper*.

"Missy LeHand was called FDR's personal secretary. You may be the first woman to bear the title, but she was really the first female Chief of Staff. Hell of a legacy you've stepped into. I can't think of a woman more capable of doing it."

The way Damien saw her never ceased to amaze her.

The Christmas Day wedding party itself had grown all out of hand. According to Sienna, she still had no idea how it had happened and Cornelia had better be careful or it would happen to her.

The out-going President and First Lady had insisted that Sienna and Roy hold their wedding in the Residence. Members of the Cabinet, the entire Joint Chiefs of Staff, and a small phalanx of Roy's Secret Service friends had joined in, as well as all of the senior staff.

Cornelia's own inclusion in the immediate wedding party, if not the ceremony itself, had been a foregone conclusion. She, Anne, Alice, and Geneviève had gathered about Sienna. Wine and merriment had flowed thickly among them.

"No wine for me," Anne had declared.

Without hesitation, Genny had squealed more like a little girl than a dignified First Lady. "There will be another baby in the White House! Yes, this is perfection."

That had only wound the group up even more until everyone that passed them by looked at them as if they were more than a little bit crazy.

The fever had built right up until the ceremony, leaving Cornelia feeling positively giddy.

Or so she'd thought until the arrival of the wedding processional itself. Damien had not managed to escape being co-opted into the ceremony. Actually, he'd seemed positively delighted by the idea, though he'd declined to explain why.

The State Dining Room looked to be the center of the Christmas madness. The four corners of the room were commanded by towering white-flocked trees adorned with silvered balls that captured and reflected every single light. The walls were draped in silver and gold garlands and the ceiling had so many icicle lights that they might have been inside an ice cave. There wasn't a hint of chill, however. The great carpet of the State Dining Room had been rolled up to reveal the rich warmth of white oak herringbone parquet beneath.

Across its surface, rose petals were scattered by the two-year-old Adele—coaxed along by her tall and comely nanny, herself the daughter of a Hostage Rescue Team sniper.

Then behind the bridesmaids, who'd winked at her as they paced by, came an honor guard made up of White House Marines.

Cornelia supposed it was only fitting. The father of the bride, Marine Corps General Edward Arnson, had just been promoted from a one-star brigadier to a two-star major general for his long service—and unspecified heroism in flight.

Then, lastly before the bride and her two-star escort, came a lone Marine. At first she didn't even recognize him.

Damien always looked good to her. But in his dress uniform—complete with side-arm and Mameluke sword, and wearing his white cover—he was about the handsomest man she'd ever seen.

The man who wanted to protect her, but who hadn't shut her out either. Together they had saved the Christmas season, and the words and spirit of their country. Together they had saved *her* words.

His face was perfectly passive as he did his formal march up the aisle—sword at the ready, unsheathed and held close by his shoulder. No one would be stupid enough to challenge the couple at the altar with Damien standing guard.

And then she noticed the one tiny thing that was out of place.

Captain Damien Feinman didn't wear a captain's bars on the shoulder boards of his uniform, but rather a major's oak leaf. At her gasp, she saw the tiniest smile touch his lips before he passed her by.

And later that evening, when the ceremony was done and the cake had been eaten, after the dancing had wound down and most of the guests had left, Damien came to her. Close by his side stood General Arnson, still in his full dress uniform. And with him Zachary, Daniel, and President Matthews.

"Why doesn't this look good?" It wasn't fair that there was some crisis at a wedding on Christmas Day. She needed one day without a disaster.

Damien did one of those immaculate moves that Marines did, handing off his cover to the general who accepted it just as formally.

Damien turned back to her, and then dropped to one knee.

Cornelia forgot how to breathe in that moment.

He took her hand and looked up at her.

"Please say yes, Cornelia Day. I am a man of too many words—"

"You've got that right," the general agreed in a gruff tone that cracked a smile on Damien's upturned face.

"So I will keep this simple. I said I wouldn't propose before New Years Day, but I can't wait that long. There is no future I want without you in it every single day. Please say yes."

"He did it okay," Zachary said to Daniel.

"Better than I did."

"You did great," Alice came up beside him. "Though I wouldn't have minded if you'd been wearing a spiffy uniform like that one when you proposed."

Anne slipped beside Zachary and moved up against him. He tucked her beneath his arm and it was about the best recommendation Cornelia had ever seen for a happy couple.

"Did we miss it?" Sienna rushed up with Roy in tow. "Please tell me we didn't miss it. This is the good part."

Roy kissed the top of her head, "The good part is just starting. You'll see."

"Shush, all of you. You haven't given this poor girl a chance to speak." Nobody appeared ready to argue with the First Lady.

Cornelia tried to speak, she really did. But nothing came out.

All of these people, these wonderful couples, were hovering, waiting for her to be as happy as they were.

And kneeling at her feet, a man she loved for his wit, his wisdom, and his bravery. He wasn't just handsome, he was also beautiful.

Unable to find the words, she knelt down in front of him and simply nodded.

Reaching into his pocket, he pulled out a ring. A simple diamond in a smoothly elegant band. No deep symbolism. No scribed words. Simple truth.

As he slipped it on her finger, the joy inside was so great that she still couldn't speak.

But somewhere she found the laugh that had always been locked away deep inside her. So she wrapped her arms around him and they laughed together as their friends joined in.

CHRISTMAS AT HENDERSON'S RANCH (EXCERPT)

Henderson's Ranch #1

"This isn't right!"

Chelsea Bridges leaned forward to see what Emily Beale was looking at. Chelsea didn't see a thing wrong, but then she'd never been to central Montana before. Out the small plane's front windshield were miles and miles of rolling green prairie. Streams crisscrossed the grassland in a bewildering maze. The backdrop was the foothills of the Rockies breaking the skyline with their snowy peaks and conifer-clad sides. The westering sun silhouetted the hills, but lit their tops with gold.

"It's absolutely gorgeous!" Then she clamped her mouth closed. She was trying to reel it in. Emily was always so even-keeled and understated that Chelsea was constantly stumbling to be less...Chelsea. Emily was this perfect woman with a drop-dead handsome husband and about the cutest kid on the planet. Chelsea had only been their daughter's nanny for a few months, but she'd seen the deference and respect that everyone at Mount Hood Aviation's firefighter airbase paid Emily. In return, the woman was kind, courteous, and utterly terrifying. Chelsea wouldn't mind being all of those things.

Her husband Mark, who sat up front in the other pilot seat of the small plane, wasn't much more effusive—except around his daughter. At least he had a sense of humor, though not as much a one as he thought he did; an observation Chelsea kept carefully to herself.

Chelsea looked over at Tessa who was strapped in beside her. She had her tiny version of her mother's elegant nose pressed up against the window. "Green," she announced. Out her window was nothing but the rolling grasslands of eastern Montana.

"It's wrong," Mark agreed solemnly but turned enough to wink at Chelsea, or at least she presumed that's what his cheek twitch was indicating at the lower edge of his mirrored Ray-Bans. "Not much snow in the hills. Means another drought year next summer."

"That's not the problem," Emily responded. "Okay, drought is a problem. But that's not the real problem."

"What is, Emma?" Again the sassy wink that said he already knew what his wife was talking about. It was amazing that the man had survived this long. Chelsea would never dare tease Emily Beale; she could probably kill with a glance if she ever took off her own mirrored shades.

"It's December," Emily took one hand off the plane's wheel—if she was on board, she was the one doing the flying—and waved it helplessly at the stunning scenery before them. "We came to Montana for a white Christmas."

"I thought it was to see Mom and Dad."

"It's still supposed to be white," she grumbled and set up to land the plane. It was as much emotion Chelsea had seen in her entire two months with them. Emily Beale was never unkind, but she was cold. Or at least chilly. But that wasn't right either. The woman was frank and forthright, as much with her daughter as with her husband. Yet Tessa was often in her lap, welcome not as child to adult, but rather as a piece of Emily that was simply back in the place where it belonged. The mother and daughter weren't close; they were simply one when they were together. It was about the most incredible thing Chelsea had ever seen. It made her ache for a family of her own; not a familiar feeling.

Again Chelsea strained up against her seatbelt to look down. A herd of horses startled and looked up at them as they passed by. They didn't scatter and run, but they eyed the low-flying plane carefully.

"Horsies!" Tessa declared delightedly when Emily shifted her flight-path so that the herd was visible outside her daughter's window. Not cold at all, just...inscrutable.

"Yes," Chelsea encouraged the toddler. "Those are horses. Aren't they pretty?"

"Pretty!" Tessa burbled, and they laughed together with delight.

Chelsea had never seen a whole herd of horses before. There were at least fifty in the group of every shade imaginable: grays, browns, whites, blacks, and mixes in patchworks, dapples, and who knew what all. They were gone behind the plane too fast to distinguish more. She tucked away the trail mix snack they'd been sharing to make sure Tessa's blood sugar was up.

Even after two months, Chelsea wasn't quite sure how she'd ended up in this situation. Not that she was complaining, Emily and Mark were great parents and it showed in their total sweetheart of a daughter. And flying with Mark over forest fires was often very dramatic.

It had started with Aunt Betsy who was a cook for the Mount Hood Aviation helicopter and smoke jumping firefighters. When Chelsea's degree in psychology hadn't led to any kind of a useful job, her aunt had asked if she liked to fly. She'd shrugged a yes because she'd flown in passenger jets any number of times to visit grandparents, and a trip to Nepal for a backpacking gap year.

She'd now spent most of the last two months sitting in tiny planes of six or eight narrow seats and been paid to enjoy the scenery and play with a baby girl. Best job she'd ever had by a long way.

Tessa was a fixture in Mark Henderson's plane when he was flying as the Incident Commander high above the fire. What was surprising wasn't that they'd added a nanny, but rather how he'd done the job for so long without one. Tessa was a pretty low maintenance kid, but she was also eighteen months old and quite intelligent.

It was a late fire season, Mark had said, and MHA had still been flying fire in the Southwest. But, finally released from the summer contract, they'd come north for a vacation and brought Chelsea along with them. She sure as hell wasn't going home. They'd known that.

As they flew closer to the ranch, more and more fences became visible, cutting the prairie into smaller pastures and training rings. There were several barns, smaller residences, and cabins surrounding the main residence.

Emily flew once over the grand log-built ranch house and waggled the plane's wings in a friendly wave.

Chelsea pointed to out to Tessa, "Isn't it amazabiling?"

"'mazbling!" Tessa called out happily. Emily sighed audibly as she circled wide of the barn.

Chelsea wondered if Mark's habits were rubbing off on her, but she couldn't resist messing with Tessa's rapidly developing language set. They landed on a gravel strip that ended close beside the house and a large out-building that turned out to be a hangar.

A big man strolled out to meet them, still buttoning up his sheep-skin jacket. He was an older version of Mark; just as tall, just as broad-shouldered, his light hair going silver. But Mark's face was different. Darker, broader, and his hair was thick, straight, and almost midnight black, sharing only his father's gray eyes.

The clouds of mist puffing about with each breath of Mark Senior —Mac, she reminded herself, they'd said he liked to be called Mac— had Chelsea bundling up Tessa before the plane came to a halt in front of a hangar. The ground might be snow free, but it was far colder here than Oregon where they'd boarded the plane.

———

Doug Daniels had stuck his head out of the barn when he heard the plane come over low. The trademark gloss-black-and-red-flame paint job told him who was aboard. Some part of him had been alarmed that a client was in-bound for a ranch vacation even though they hadn't taken any Christmas reservations this year. But it was just Mark and his knock-out wife. He liked Mark fine, but he had trouble speaking around Emily Beale. It wasn't just the beauty, he knew how to talk to pretty women just fine; it was the fierce level of competence that she demonstrated at every turn.

He finished helping Logan pitch the hay into the stalls' feedboxes before heading out to greet them. The air had a sharp bite to it, wholly different from the horse-and-straw of the barn, but no moisture. As he stepped out of the barn, he noticed that there wasn't even a hint of cloud in the cobalt blue of the late afternoon sky. The temperature was already dropping though it was still an hour to sunset. It was going to get cold tonight.

Doug stuck his head back inside. "Hey, Logan. Open up the gates. If the main herd has any sense, they'll be coming this way by sunset."

"You bet, boss. Any horse that stays out there tonight needs his horse-sense meter checked."

Doug went out to help stow the plane. There was room in the hangar because he'd moved the helicopter tight to the side after the morning's flight to check the main herd and make sure there were no stray or injured. He hadn't been able to get an accurate count, but it had felt low and that was bothering him. Happened all the time. Still, it worried him.

He ducked through the hangar's side door, popped the release, and slid open the main door from the inside. It rattled and boomed in the cold air. A sharp squeal in one of the wheels had him adding "needs grease" to the infinite mental checklist that was running a working dude ranch.

Just emerging from the plane was a figure wrapped deep in a parka, with the fur-rimmed hood already raised as if it wasn't a merely brisk day, but rather a north polar night. She, for there was no chance of a guy wearing such tight jeans and making them look so good, carried an equally bundled child.

He came up and stuck his nose right into the child's hood, "Tessa, my love! Give us a kiss!"

"Kiss!" the little girl squealed and kissed him on the nose.

Then he rubbed noses with her until she was giggling before he pulled back. He'd ended up standing very close to the woman holding her. He could just see brilliant blue eyes, a freckled nose, and a bright smile in the narrow opening of the hood.

"Do you greet all the girls that way?" Her tone was light, almost musical.

"Sure." Never one to back down from a challenge, he stuck his face right into her hood until their noses rubbed and cried out, "Give us a kiss!"

———

Buy now to keep reading. Available exclusively at: www. buchmanbookworks.com

TITLES EXCLUSIVELY AVAILABLE AT BUCHMAN BOOKWORKS EMPORIUM

www.buchmanbookworks.com

(Cool tip: The author also makes more money when you buy direct.)

EXCLUSIVE DEALS AND GREAT BOXSETS INCLUDING THESE AND MORE:

Contemporary Romance

- The Complete Eagle Cove (Oregon Coast small-town)
- The Complete Henderson's Ranch (Montana Big Sky)
- The Complete Where Dreams (Seattle urban)

Romantic Suspense

- The Complete Night Stalkers 5E
- The Complete Night Stalkers White House
- The White House Protection Force Dog Trilogy
- The Complete Wildfire Smokejumpers

Go here to shop now: www.buchmanbookworks.com

USA Today and Amazon #1 Bestseller M. L. "Matt" Buchman started writing on a flight south from Japan to ride his bicycle across the Australian Outback. Just part of a solo around-the-world trip that ultimately launched his writing career.

From the very beginning, his powerful female heroines insisted on putting character first, *then* a great adventure. He's since written over 60 action-adventure thrillers and military romantic suspense novels. And just for the fun of it: 100 short stories, and a fast-growing pile of read-by-author audiobooks.

Booklist says: "3X Top 10 of the Year." PW says: "Tom Clancy fans open to a strong female lead will clamor for more." His fans say: "I want more now...of everything." That his characters are even more insistent than his fans is a hoot.

As a 30-year project manager with a geophysics degree who has designed and built houses, flown and jumped out of planes, and solo-sailed a 50' ketch, he is awed by what is possible. More at: www. mlbuchman.com.

Other works by M. L. Buchman: *(* - also in audio)*

Thrillers

Dead Chef
One Chef!
Two Chef!

Miranda Chase
*Drone**
*Thunderbolt**
*Condor**
*Ghostrider**

Romantic Suspense

Delta Force
*Target Engaged**
*Heart Strike**
*Wild Justice**
*Midnight Trust**

Firehawks
MAIN FLIGHT
Pure Heat
Full Blaze
*Hot Point**
*Flash of Fire**
Wild Fire

SMOKEJUMPERS
*Wildfire at Dawn**
*Wildfire at Larch Creek**
*Wildfire on the Skagit**

The Night Stalkers
MAIN FLIGHT
The Night Is Mine
I Own the Dawn
Wait Until Dark
Take Over at Midnight
Light Up the Night
Bring On the Dusk
By Break of Day

AND THE NAVY
Christmas at Steel Beach
Christmas at Peleliu Cove
WHITE HOUSE HOLIDAY
*Daniel's Christmas**
*Frank's Independence Day**
*Peter's Christmas**
*Zachary's Christmas**
*Roy's Independence Day**
*Damien's Christmas**
5E
Target of the Heart
Target Lock on Love
Target of Mine
Target of One's Own

Shadow Force: Psi
*At the Slightest Sound**
*At the Quietest Word**

White House Protection Force
*Off the Leash**
*On Your Mark**
*In the Weeds**

Contemporary Romance

Eagle Cove
Return to Eagle Cove
Recipe for Eagle Cove
Longing for Eagle Cove
Keepsake for Eagle Cove

Henderson's Ranch
*Nathan's Big Sky**
*Big Sky, Loyal Heart**
*Big Sky Dog Whisperer**

Love Abroad
Heart of the Cotswolds: England
Path of Love: Cinque Terre, Italy

Other works by M. L. Buchman:

Contemporary Romance (cont)

Where Dreams
Where Dreams are Born
Where Dreams Reside
Where Dreams Are of Christmas
Where Dreams Unfold
Where Dreams Are Written

Science Fiction / Fantasy

Deities Anonymous
Cookbook from Hell: Reheated
Saviors 101

Single Titles
The Nara Reaction
Monk's Maze
the Me and Elsie Chronicles

Non-Fiction

Strategies for Success
Managing Your Inner Artist/Writer
Estate Planning for Authors
Character Voice

Short Story Series by M. L. Buchman:

Romantic Suspense

Delta Force
Delta Force

Firehawks
The Firehawks Lookouts
The Firehawks Hotshots
The Firebirds

The Night Stalkers
The Night Stalkers
The Night Stalkers 5E
The Night Stalkers CSAR
The Night Stalkers Wedding Stories

US Coast Guard
US Coast Guard

White House Protection Force
White House Protection Force

Contemporary Romance

Eagle Cove
Eagle Cove

Henderson's Ranch
Henderson's Ranch

Where Dreams
Where Dreams

Thrillers

Dead Chef
Dead Chef

Science Fiction / Fantasy

Deities Anonymous
Deities Anonymous

Other
The Future Night Stalkers
Single Titles

Cover images:
Helicopter over Baghdad © U.S. Army
Declaration of Independence on White House building © izanbar
Discover more by this author at: www.mlbuchman.com

Buchman Bookworks

www.ingramcontent.com/pod-product-compliance
Lightning Source LLC
Chambersburg PA
CBHW032151180726
48284CB00001B/3